D0559634

THE BUILDINGS OF WALES
ADVISORY EDITOR: JOHN NEWMAN

CLWYD
(DENBIGHSHIRE AND FLINTSHIRE)

EDWARD HUBBARD

CLWYD
(DENBIGH AND FLINT)

Motorways ———— 'A' roads
- - - - 'B' roads and some minor roads
━━━━ Boundaries of Denbighshire and Flintshire
.... Present-day boundaries of Clwyd

0 ____ 5 miles
0 __ 5 __ 10 km

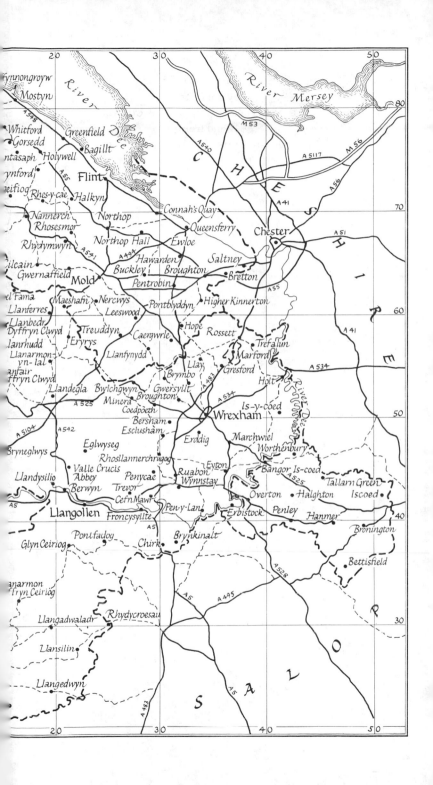

The preparation of this book has been greatly helped
by grants from
THE TRUSTEES OF THE DAVIES CHARITY
and from
THE BOARD OF CELTIC STUDIES OF
THE UNIVERSITY OF WALES

THE BUILDINGS OF WALES

Clwyd

(DENBIGHSHIRE
AND FLINTSHIRE)

BY

EDWARD HUBBARD

★

PENGUIN BOOKS

UNIVERSITY OF WALES PRESS

Penguin Books Ltd, Harmondsworth, Middlesex, England
Viking Penguin Inc., 40 West 23rd Street, New York, New York 10010, USA
Penguin Books Australia Ltd, Ringwood, Victoria, Australia
Penguin Books Canada Limited, 2801 John Street, Markham, Ontario, Canada L3R 1B4
Penguin Books (NZ) Ltd, 182–190 Wairau Road, Auckland 10, New Zealand

First published 1986

ISBN 0 14 071052 3

Copyright © Edward Hubbard, 1986
All rights reserved

Made and printed in Great Britain by
Butler & Tanner Ltd, Frome and London
Set in Monophoto Plantin

TO MY FATHER
JOHN HORTON HUBBARD
AND THE MEMORY OF MY MOTHER
ELLEN GLEN HUBBARD

CONTENTS

MAP REFERENCES

The numbers printed in italic type in the margin against the place names in the gazetteer of the book indicate the position of the place in question on the index map (pages 2–3), which is divided into sections by the 10-kilometre reference lines of the National Grid. The reference given here omits the two initial letters (formerly numbers) which in a full grid reference refer to the 100-kilometre squares into which the country is divided. The first two numbers indicate the *western* boundary, and the last two the *southern* boundary, of the 10-kilometre square in which the place in question is situated. For example, Rhuddlan (reference 0070) will be found in the 10-kilometre square bounded by grid lines 00 and 10 on the *west* and 70 and 80 on the *south*; Northop (reference 2060) in the square bounded by grid lines 20 and 30 on the *west* and 60 and 70 on the *south*.

The map contains all those places, whether towns, villages, or isolated buildings, which are the subject of separate entries in the text.

FOREWORD

This second volume of The Buildings of Wales *follows, in matters of selection and arrangement, precedents established by* The Buildings of England *and, with one exception, the pioneering volume of* Powys. *The exception is that, contrary to the original intention only the ancient historic counties (Denbighshire and Flintshire) are included and not the entire county of Clwyd as created under the 1974 local government reorganization. Because the material for it was regrettably not available to me at the time of going to press, the district of Edeirnion, which belonged to Merioneth before being transferred to Clwyd in 1974, is omitted. On the other hand, coverage is given to those Denbighshire parishes in the Conwy Valley which were transferred to Gwynedd. Similarly the Introduction embraces only the two old counties, but Edeirnion will receive treatment in Mr Richard Haslam's forthcoming* Gwynedd *volume, in which the entries for the former Denbighshire places in the Conwy Valley will be reprinted.*

I myself did all the preliminary research and extracting and have seen almost everything I describe. Where this is not the case, information obtained by means other than personal observation is placed in brackets, usually with an indication of the source from which facts or a description were derived. Information ought to be as complete as the space of the volume permits for churches prior to c.1830 and for all town houses, manor houses and country houses of more than purely local interest. Movable furnishings are not included in secular buildings, though they are in churches. Exceptions to this rule made in The Buildings of England *have not been followed in so far as mention is made of Royal Arms, sepulchral slabs, plain fonts, altar tables and post-Reformation brasses. As in the* Powys *volume, however, no attempt is made to list church plate.*

As for churches, chapels and secular structures later in date than 1830, a selection had to be made, with decisions of whether or not to include being made by significance in the light of architectural history. In cases where work of importance has been destroyed, either through demolition or mutilation, description of what no longer exists has been thought justifiable.

Many post-Reformation churches are not traditionally orientated, and the use of N, S, E *and* W *is to be understood liturgically, with the altar at the* E *end.*

As in Powys, *dimensions are given in the imperial and not the metric system. Users should thus be warned that the abbreviation 'm.' refers to miles and not metres.*

Users of the predecessor series will recognize the great debt owed to the late Sir Nikolaus Pevsner. One remains filled with admiration for the compilers and editors of the early volumes, who devised a system of presentation, description and arrangement which has withstood the test of time so well. The years in which I was associated with The Buildings of England, *working first for Sir Nikolaus and later with him, were a rare privilege and, together with the insights and encouragement I received from him, have been a constant source of inspiration. I have also greatly benefited from the help and advice of Mr John Newman and Mrs Bridget Cherry, derived from their long-standing experience of* The Buildings of England. *Mr Newman read my entire text, and his amendments (particularly to the Introduction) greatly improved the work. Professor Glanmor Williams also kindly read through what I had written, painstakingly checked proofs, and eliminated errors in connection with Welsh history and the spelling of names.*

Particular thanks are due to numerous owners and occupiers of houses, who generously permitted me to view their homes and in many instances provided hospitality. In no case was a request for access to a private house refused. It must be firmly stated that mention of a building in the text, or reference to internal features, does not in any way imply that it is open to the public. Many householders went to great trouble to provide information. I am also grateful to incumbents, priests and ministers for help in connection with churches and chapels. District Planning Officers have dealt with detailed inquiries about buildings in their areas, and architects have answered questions about their own work.

Persons whom I wish to thank in special connections are as follows. Mr Leslie Alexander (the work of Woolfall & Eccles). Mr Ian Allan (Arts and Crafts work, particularly that of H. L. North). Mr J. H. Bradbury (Prestatyn). Mr D. Leslie Davies (Wrexham and neighbourhood). Mr Richard Dean of the National Trust (Chirk Castle). Mr K. J. Denley, County Architect, his predecessor Mr R. W. Harvey, and Mr P. Eyton-Jones, Assistant County Architect (the work of their Department). Mr W. Lindsay Evans (country houses, particularly Cefn Park and Trevalyn Hall). Mr Denis Evinson (Roman Catholic buildings). Mr Edwin Green, Archivist, Midland Bank Ltd (premises of the Midland Bank and the former North & South Wales Bank). Mr Martin Harrison (Victorian stained glass). My colleague Richard Haslam for early encouragement and advice and for contributing entries including that on Voelas. Mr Robert B. Heaton of TACP (information on houses he has restored). The Rev. David Hinge (the work of R. T. Beckett). Mr Peter Howell has remained a good friend of The Buildings of Wales *and is a seldom failing source of information on Wales and its architecture, particularly Victorian buildings. Clwyd has gained much from his careful reading and correcting of the proofs. Mr Vernon Hughes supplied many facts and generously placed at my disposal his files relating to North Wales as well as his index of buildings in Wales extracted from* The Builder. *His material is identified by the letters* VH. *He also on several occasions acted as guide and mentor. Mr Philip ap*

Iorwerth of the County Planning Department and Mr Jon James, County Conservation Officer, were responsible for taking some specially needed photographs, and Mr James helped in further ways. In the early stages of work, the late Lieutenant-Colonel H. M. C. Jones-Mortimer provided facts, advice and introductions from his profound knowledge of the county. It is to be regretted that he did not live long enough to comment on my completed text. Others to whom I am grateful are Mr Paul Joyce (the work of G. E. Street) and Mr Anthony Kyrke-Smith (vernacular buildings in the Mold region).

As in the case of Powys, The Buildings of Wales has been fortunate to secure the expert services of Miss Frances Lynch (Mrs Llewellyn) for the Introduction and gazetteer entries on prehistoric and Roman remains. Because of the moorland setting of many of the sites, some are given OS grid references. In addition she has been responsible for drawing plans of hillforts.

Again as with Powys, we have not had the benefit of one of the late Mr Alec Clifton-Taylor's contributions on building materials which have enriched recent volumes of The Buildings of England. Thus I have been obliged to write this entry myself, and for introducing me to the study of geology I wish to thank Mr I. L. Norris and Mr Simon Watson. Mr Norris also saved me from error in matters of terminology. Further acknowledgements are due to Mrs Moira Ockrim (the work of Thomas Harrison), Mr R. M. Owen (Denbigh) and Mr Anthony J. Pass (the work of the Worthington family). The Rev. Canon T. W. Pritchard, author of several excellent church guidebooks, kindly permitted me to see his notes and went to much trouble in answering detailed questions. Moreover he gave of his expertise in the correcting of proofs. I must also thank Dr Anthony P. Quiney (the work of J. L. Pearson), Mr Peter D. Randall, formerly of the County Planning Department, who provided guidance at Denbigh and Ruthin and contributed from his expert knowledge of those places and of Llanfair Dyffryn Clwyd, Mr R. H. Reed, Archivist, National Westminster Bank Ltd (premises of the bank), and Mr Christopher Rowell of the National Trust.

I received a truly exceptional amount of help from Mr A. G. Veysey, County Archivist, and Mr Christopher J. Williams, Deputy County Archivist, and their staff. Mr Christopher Wakeling has permitted Mr Haslam and myself to make use of the results of his research on chapels, and these are identified by the letters CW. Mr Merlin Waterson of the National Trust helped me at Erddig and Mr E. P. Williams with Denbigh.

An invaluable guide to the identification of noteworthy buildings has been the lists of buildings of special architectural and historic importance which were compiled by the Department of the Environment and made available by courtesy of the Welsh Office. Facts obtained from them are indicated by DOE. Mention must be made of the Royal Commission on Ancient and Historical Monuments in Wales and of the help received from its Secretary, Mr Peter Smith, and his staff. Their archive at Aberystwyth now includes the photographs previously held by the National Monuments Record in

London, as well as the National Monuments Record for Wales, and information derived from their files, including descriptions taken from photographs, is marked NMR. *Mrs Judith Wardman gave invaluable assistance as copy-editor.*

At Penguin Books, Miss Susan Rose-Smith gave indispensable guidance and assistance with the illustrations. Mr Richard Andrews was responsible for the line drawings, for which lettering was executed by Mr Reg Piggott, who also drew the maps.

My largest debt of gratitude is to my father. As well as continuing his customary domestic support, he shared the arduous task of driving. Then, throughout a period of ill-health and ultimate disability on my part, he assumed increasing responsibility for ensuring that progress with the book was maintained. Without his good sense, industry, patient encouragement, carefulness and advice, I hate to think what would have become of Clwyd and of the work which had already been expended on it. With his having been involved from field work to proofreading and indexing, my father justifiably deserves the status of joint author rather than joint dedicatee.

The book is the poorer for the lack of the comments and contributions on medieval churches which the late Mr Ronald C. Williams of Chester would have made had it not been for his tragic and premature death, which occurred after he had provided only limited assistance and advice.

Despite so many helpers and well-wishers it is inevitable that errors and some serious omissions will have occurred, and they are far more likely to be due to me than to any of the persons whose names have been mentioned. It is necessary to end this Foreword with an appeal to users of the book to inform the author or publishers of any such deficiencies, so that corrections can be made in later editions.

ACKNOWLEDGEMENTS FOR THE PLATES

We are grateful to the following for permission to reproduce photographs:

Aerofilms: 9, 12

Bruce Bailey: 86

Janet and Colin Bord: 1, 3, 4, 6, 8, 10, 11, 20, 24, 82, 90, 110, 112

Bowen, Dann, Davies Partnership: 123, 124

Cadw: 13, 18

University of Cambridge, Committee for Aerial Photography: 7

J. Allan Cash: 125

Clwyd County Council (photographer Philip ap Iorwerth): 5, 14, 35, 67, 68, 83, 87, 97, 99, 115, 121, 122

Country Life: 45, 53, 56, 57, 60, 66, 71, 73, 76, 78, 85, 106, 108

Courtauld Institute, Conway Library: 84

Christopher Dalton: 30, 74, 91

Colwyn Foulkes and Partners: 116, 117, 118, 119

A. F. Kersting: 2, 16, 17, 19, 21, 23, 25, 26, 29, 33, 39, 40, 43, 49, 55, 61, 62, 65, 70, 72, 75, 79, 80, 81, 88, 92, 93, 94, 98, 100, 101, 102, 103, 104, 111, 113, 114

Courtauld Institute © Canon M. H. Ridgway: 22, 32, 41, 42, 63, 64, 77

R.I.B.A.: 120

Royal Commission on Ancient and Historical Monuments in Wales: 15, 27, 28, 36, 37, 38, 44, 46, 47, 48, 50, 51, 52, 54, 58, 59, 69, 89, 95, 96, 105, 107, 109

Ronald C. Williams (with the permission of Cheshire County Council): 31, 34

Maps and plans have been drawn or adapted by Richard Andrews and Reg Piggott.

PREHISTORIC AND ROMAN REMAINS

BY FRANCES LYNCH

The modern county of Clwyd is centred upon the broad fertile Vale of Clwyd which formerly divided its two constituent districts, Denbighshire and Flintshire. In terms of agricultural settlement this valley must always have been the centre of the region, providing rich farmland surrounded by well-drained accessible hills, and throughout prehistory there is evidence of its exploitation, though because of its attraction for later farmers many monuments have undoubtedly been destroyed. The other major valley in the region, the Dee Valley, is, in contrast, narrow and twisting, but several interesting finds are testimony of its importance as a means of access.

The upland areas to E and W of the Clwyd show marked contrasts. To the E there is a plateau of limestone, millstone grit and coal measures; in the N this is relatively low, open, fertile and well-drained, attractive to settlement in all periods and of extra economic significance in the Roman period, when its resources of copper and lead were exploited on quite a large scale. Only in the s, above Llangollen, does the eastern ridge rise to form inhospitable moorland. To the W of the Clwyd the limestone forms a steep-sided ridge bordering the Vale and to the N of the Elwy providing an attractively wooded coastal fringe which contains settlement sites of all periods. s of the Elwy the Silurian shales rise towards the central mass of rather bleak moorland known as Hiraethog, a region which seems to have been unsuitable for settlement except during the earlier Bronze Age, when many round barrows were built on its fringes.

It is difficult to characterize the broken, hilly, wooded country around the upper reaches of the Clwyd. Little modern work has been done in the area, but the concentration of finds around the narrow defile where the river enters its broad valley at Llanfair Dyffryn Clwyd suggests that more detailed studies might be rewarding. The mouth of the river, near Rhuddlan, Diserth and Prestatyn, has also been fruitful of finds, but the interpretation of settlement here is complicated by the considerable variations in coastline which have occurred, even during the last few hundred years. A large area of submerged forest was formerly exposed on the foreshore at Rhyl, and several prehistoric artefacts have come from submerged land surfaces in the district.

During the various warmer periods during the last glaciation the numerous CAVES in the limestone cliffs on either side of the Clwyd provided shelter for hunters such as the spotted hyena, the cave bear and, less frequently, man. The earliest evidence

of human occupation (*c.* 180,000 bc*) comes from Bont Newydd
Cave, Cefn Meiriadog (D), where Acheulian hand axes were
found by Professor Boyd Dawkins in the C19 and where excavations by the National Museum of Wales have found human
bones and many more implements and should help to enlarge
our picture of man's life at this time. *c.* 130,000 years later,
characteristically UPPER PALAEOLITHIC tools were left by
men occupying the cave near Ffynnon Beuno, Tremeirchion
(F), on the eastern side of the Clwyd. The adjacent Cae Gwyn
Cave also produced flint implements but of a less distinctive
kind. These Clwydian caves are particularly important in the
study of the earliest human occupation of Wales, not only
because they have produced the only *in situ* finds of the period
in North Wales but also because the environment of the cave
allows the correlation of human activity with the fluctuation of
the climate and the variation of local flora and fauna.

The population in the valley during the Palaeolithic must
always have been very small and would have belonged to hunting bands which were mobile and wide-ranging; therefore
occupation, even during the most temperate periods, can
scarcely have been permanent, and thus it cannot be claimed
that the Mesolithic occupants of the area have any connection
with these earlier men.

MESOLITHIC hunters lived in a very different environment:
the open tundra and large game were gone, replaced by deci-
duous woodland which housed much smaller prey, amongst
which the red deer was the most important meat source. To
catch these animals man devised a number of ingenious traps
and made arrows tipped with small barbs. These flint barbs –
known as microliths – are the most characteristic survivals of
the period. Several groups of these flint tools have been found
recently at Rhuddlan (F), dating from the earlier Mesolithic
(*c.* 6500 bc); and material from the later Mesolithic (*c.* 5000 bc)
has come from Prestatyn (F), at that time some distance from
the sea, though possibly the occupants of the camp exploited
the coast with its fish, shellfish and sea birds. The remains of
similar camps have also been found on the Hiraethog moorland,
in the Brenig Valley and near Llyn Aled Isaf. These upland
sites may have been the summer camps of hunters who spent
the winter in the valley, for black chert, probably brought from
Gronant near Prestatyn, was used to make microliths on the
moors.

The establishment of a farming economy in the area is poorly
documented. The NEOLITHIC material from Clwyd is rather
scrappy, and what there is of it suggests a date later rather than
earlier in the period, even though Mesolithic traditions of
flint-working would seem to survive alongside pottery and
Graig Lwyd axes. Three sites in the Prestatyn area (Gwaunysgor; Dyserth Castle, Diserth; and Field 56, Prestatyn) have pro-

* Lower-case 'bc' indicates that the date is derived from radiocarbon assay.
The actual date may be some 200–300 years earlier but exact calibration is not yet
possible, so the 'traditional' chronology has been retained.

duced finds suggestive of Neolithic occupation, but the excavation of the first two leaves much to be desired and the third
is unexcavated, though a surface collection made by the late
Gilbert Smith suggests that the occupants might have been involved in trading stone axes from the Lake District and NW
Wales and perhaps passing them down towards the S.

In view of this contact with the W – and Graig Lwyd axes
made from the rock of Penmaenmawr are particularly common
in the region – it is odd that one of the most conspicuous ingredients of the Neolithic way of life in the Irish Sea area and
several other parts of Europe, the monumental STONE TOMB,
is virtually absent. These stone tombs, surviving long after the
wooden houses and small cleared fields of the living have completely vanished, provide both an indication of the areas settled
and the cultural background of the builders, for the design of
the burial chamber and its covering cairn may vary according
to local traditions. Thus one may say that the builders of the
complex structure at Capel Garmon (D) had contacts with the
SE of Wales and the 'Severn Cotswold' tradition, and that the
much more badly damaged monument at Tyddyn Bleiddyn,
Cefn Meiriadog (D), probably belongs to the same group, for it
had at least two lateral chambers in a long cairn and contained
unburnt burials. This tradition of tomb building would seem to
have reached North Wales relatively late in the Neolithic, perhaps as a result of contacts made through the trading of stone
axes. It is all the more strange, therefore, that the Portal Dolmen tradition established in the Conwy Valley did not penetrate
to the E.

In the Clwyd area the normal form of Neolithic communal
burial was in caves, the bodies pushed into narrow crevices with
the entrances then sealed by walling. The skeletons are unburnt
and often incomplete and mixed, suggesting that they were
placed in the cave after exposure elsewhere, a system often practised in the S of England at the time. The caves at Cefn (Meiriadog; D) and the Perthi Chwarae and Rhos Ddigre caves,
Llanarmon-yn-Iâl (D), contained burials of this kind, in the last
case in association with pottery and a Graig Lwyd axe, providing much-needed dating evidence. The burials in the larger
cave at Gop, Trelawnyd (F), were in an unusual built enclosure,
but it is essentially a cave burial of the local kind. With the
bones was a sherd of Peterborough pottery, a jet 'belt slider'
and a polished flint knife, all objects of Late Neolithic date and
suggestive of southern English connections. However, a strain
of local Mesolithic tradition is still discernible in the flint-work
of the area, so it is likely that new styles coming in from the E
along the accessible limestone plateau (as they still do today)
were affecting a local population which had long been established in the area, though the quantity of material of Late Neolithic date may suggest an expansion of population at this time.

The centuries around 2000 BC saw several changes which had
a profound effect upon society. The Neolithic had been a period
without overt signs of warfare and aggression, a time when the

leaders of society were buried anonymously, mixed irretrievably with others of their kind, a time when trade flourished in specialist goods but most communities could be successfully self-sufficient in all essentials. The succeeding BRONZE AGE has a different aspect. The knowledge and growing importance of metal must have altered the economic map of Britain and of Europe, and a new individuality appears in the burial record, where individual graves reflect an interest in weapons and in personal wealth which suggests a new basis for a sharper stratification in society.

Such fundamental changes must obviously have wide-ranging and complex roots, springing perhaps from both internal and external stimuli. One external factor which looms large in the archaeological record of the period is the appearance of a new style of pottery, already widespread on the Continent. This Beaker pottery has been traditionally associated with ideas of 'invasion' – the BEAKER PEOPLE setting themselves up as new warlords, their superiority guaranteed by their knowledge of metallurgy and the weapons it could make. This single explanation for the complex developments of this obviously troubled period in Europe as a whole is undoubtedly too simple, but it is true to say that this distinctive pottery, whether brought by foreign invaders or used by local leaders adopting foreign fashions or cults, is often to be found with the new elements, copper weapons and individual burial under small round barrows or cairns.

Whatever the context of its origin the Beaker pottery style took root in Britain and may be seen developing within the country, the shape of the pot and its decoration changing over four or five centuries. For the most part the beakers in North Wales belong to the later styles and represent a spread from England rather than directly from the Continent. One from a grave in Brymbo (D) is comparatively early, but those from Henllan (D) and Bodtegir, near Llanfihangel Glyn Myfyr (D), are definitely late. Most Beakers come from burials, but these fine pots were also used domestically, as the broken sherds in occupation soil beneath a cairn in the Brenig Valley, Mynydd Hiraethog (D), demonstrate. This site also shows how Beaker pottery exists alongside other jars and urns which have an ancestry in a purely native tradition of pottery; so the foreign element in the inception of the British Bronze Age is unlikely to have been either large or exclusive.

The Bronze Age is best-known for its ROUND BARROWS, the impressively sited burial mounds of the period set on hilltops or on the spines of the moorland ridges. The limestone plateau of northern Flintshire had an unusually dense distribution of these monuments, but, because of agricultural erosion, few of them survive as impressive features, except the huge cairn at Gop, Trelawnyd (F), if it be of this date. In central Denbighshire, and particularly on the bare moorland of Mynydd Hiraethog, the barrows still stand high, dominating large stretches of the landscape. The number of barrows on the previously empty uplands must reflect an expansion of the population into new areas, perhaps as a result of the pressure of numbers or because a slight improvement in climate had made grazing on these hills, once the forest cover was reduced, a viable economic proposition. It is a pattern of settlement which is found in most areas of Britain, Dartmoor and the North Yorkshire moors being other examples.

The barrows are outwardly simple mounds of stone, earth or turves covering the human remains, which are normally cremated, though at the beginning of the period inhumations may be found. The body is often accompanied by a few personal possessions, a flint knife, a whetstone or beads of jet from the N of England or the more exotic faience, which has an Egyptian inspiration even if some unusual forms, such as that from Brynford (F), were eventually made in this country. The grave goods reflect status and a level of wealth, expressed through exotic objects from distant parts, which is fairly typical of the highland areas of Britain.

Quite untypical, however, is the famous Mold Cape found with masses of amber beads encasing the shoulders of a young man discovered in 1833 beneath a large cairn close to the River Alun at Mold (F). This seamless cape was beaten from a single nugget of gold and covered with repoussé decoration imitative of masses of bead necklaces covering the neck and shoulders. It was beaten very thin and must have been backed by leather or other strong material. This amazing piece of ceremonial wear is unique in the annals of British and W European archaeology and as such is difficult to date or to place in context. However, the association with amber beads, together with some aspects of the repoussé technique, suggests that it belongs to the later phases of the Early Bronze Age, around 1400 bc. The absence of other signs of great wealth in gold in the area makes it difficult to imagine the historical background to this perhaps priestly garment, although elsewhere in Britain the personal display of small ornaments of gold is well recorded at approximately this time.

The barrows may cover several burials, some placed there in one single ceremony (cemetery mounds which may be found, for instance, in the upland area around Moel Fama), others added successively over many years (secondary burials as found in the cairn in Ffridd y Garreg Wen, Gorsedd (F), which had been enlarged as each new burial was added). Sometimes the mound may cover only a single burial in the centre, as do the majority of the large turf mounds in the Brenig Cemetery, Mynydd Hiraethog (D). The grouping of mounds into such clusters – several of which may be seen on the Denbigh Moors (Rhos Domen and Gorsedd Bran, Mynydd Hiraethog; Mwdwl Eithin), and some, such as Bryngwyn, Tremeirchion, survive in Flintshire – may reflect a preference for single burials rather than the use of cemetery mounds. Another feature which cannot be observed without excavation is the presence of stone or stake rings playing some role in ceremonial before the mound was finally built.

Ritual features of this kind were found beneath several mounds in the Brenig Cemetery, Mynydd Hiraethog (D), which also contained some unusually designed cairns and a very fine ring cairn. Excavation here revealed that the activities inside this low stone ring were mainly connected with the burial of masses of clean charcoal, although cremated bones were also found. CIRCLES of various kinds, either banks, stone rings or circles of upright stones, are common in the Bronze Age and are normally interpreted as religious or ritual monuments, though the details of cosmology behind them must always elude us. These monuments can be found in the Hiraethog area and the hills above Llangollen, but there is only one stone circle in Flintshire, at Nannerch. In contrast, the STANDING STONES, equally enigmatic monuments of the Bronze Age, are common in Flintshire, especially in the E, and are virtually unknown in Denbighshire. Man's reasons for erecting large stones are many and various and so it is impossible to guess at the cause of this difference, for styles in pottery and tools do not suggest any sharp cultural break between the two sides of the Clwyd.

The copper and bronze tools of the first half of the second millennium bc are not especially plentiful in Clwyd, but those that have been found are of great interest. The only hoard (a hidden group, perhaps the stock-in-trade of a smith) of flat copper axes from Britain was found on the slopes of Moel Arthur, Cilcain (F). These flat axes are very primitive pieces belonging to the earliest phases of metalworking in the country; the discovery of a hoard in Flintshire suggests that already the local ores might have been recognized and exploited. Another most important hoard, the one from Moelfre Uchaf near Betws-yn-Rhos (D), contains experimental forms of flanged axes, another indication of a lively manufacturing tradition in the area. The search for an axehead which could be securely hafted resulted in the production of what is known as the 'Acton Park palstave' called after the hoard found near Wrexham. The axeheads in this hoard show links with the earlier experimental pieces from Betws-yn-Rhos and with Continental metalworking as seen in Holland. The impression gained is of a local industry with progressive ideas and great technical competence, for analysis has shown that the workers of the 'Acton Park Complex' used a distinctive high-quality metal-mix. Their products are found throughout North Wales and were occasionally exported much further. These everyday tools are not found in graves, but it is tempting to look to this successful metalworking industry when trying to explain such objects as the Mold Cape.

Unfortunately the initiative of the Early Middle Bronze Age (c. 1400–1200 bc) was not maintained and the later metalwork in Clwyd is derivative and rather dull, though the strange socketed palstave from Abergele must reflect the last flickering of an experimental tradition. The most interesting metalwork of the Late Bronze Age in the county is all imported. In the C8–7 bc there was a revival of luxury trade between Ireland and Scandinavia, and this trade passed through North Wales. Evidence of its passage is to be found in the lovely twisted gold neck ring from Bryn Sion, Ysgeifiog (F), and in the unique shale bowl from Caergwrle (F) decorated with gold leaf as the model of a small ship bobbing on a choppy sea. The great mass of bronze horse harness found at Parc y Meirch beneath the cliffs of Dinorben, St George (D), reflects the eastern arm of this trade, for much of this jangling panoply is Scandinavian in inspiration.

The hilltop of Dinorben, St George (D), now almost completely eaten away by quarrying, was protected by a complex series of banks and ditches, making it one of the best-known HILLFORTS in this region of many impressive strongholds. Hillforts are traditionally associated with the IRON AGE, a period whose new technology and intense concern for defence and protection have been attributed to waves of foreign invaders, spreading across Britain from central Europe. This simple view, which implies that British society was static until stimulated by foreign immigrants, is no longer popular. The stresses which led to the choice of hilltops for settlement and the enclosure of homesteads by palisades and later by ramparts are now believed by many to be largely internal, stemming in part from the pressure on land which results from an increase in population and a deterioration in climate, forcing a withdrawal from the moorland areas of Early Bronze Age activity. The advent of radiocarbon dating has given impetus to this reassessment of the beginning of hillfort development, for several dates in the centuries 1100–800 bc are now available, showing that palisades and even timber-framed ramparts were being built long before the new iron technology was known. It must not be forgotten, however, that throughout the Late Bronze Age there is evidence of Continental contact, some of it with military overtones, and in that period of European unrest the shores of this island cannot have been immune from small-scale invasions and incursions to add spice to the purely native tensions.

The northern March of Wales is a major area for the study of hillforts, not only because of the impressive nature of many of the sites and their defences but because of the important evidence which has come from the excavation of forts like Moel y Gaer, Rhosesmor (F), Dinorben, St George (D), and Moel Hiraddug, Cwm (F). A series of great forts may be seen overlooking the eastern side of the Vale of Clwyd running from Foel Fenlli, Llanbedr Dyffryn Clwyd (D), in the S to Moel Hiraddug in the N, and behind the coast to the W the limestone cliffs provide dominating positions from Bryn Euryn, Llandrillo-yn-Rhos (D), on the W end to Dinorben on the E. Inland there are the lesser-known forts such as Mynydd y Gaer above Llanefydd (D) and the group of small fortifications in the upper Clwyd Valley. On the Flintshire side there are several lesser sites, especially around Caergwrle, but the recent excavations of Moel y Gaer, Rhosesmor (F), have shown that relatively small, deceptively simple, sites can still provide most illuminating evidence of the social life of their builders. The route through the Dee Valley is also overlooked by fortified posts, the best-known of

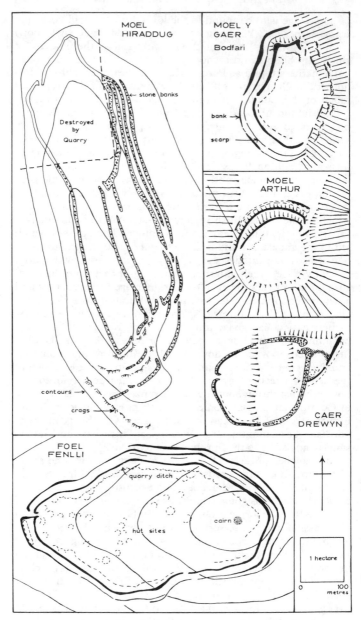

Iron Age hillforts in Clwyd
(plans by Frances Lynch after J. Forde-Johnston
and Colin A. Gresham)

which is Caer Drewyn near Corwen. The hillforts of the region are constructed in various ways according to the resources of the area; some are surrounded by ditches and earthen banks, probably incorporating a wooden framework; others by stone walls and some, such as Caer Drewyn, by a combination of stone and earth.

As its name implies, the hillfort is a defensive enclosure, built to withstand the frontal attack of a neighbouring warband. Early excavators paid great attention to these military aspects, normally confining their work to elucidating the sequence of rampart building, repair and reorganization. One of the most interesting features of the design of Clwydian hillforts, the frequent presence of paired guard chambers on either side of the entrance passage, seems to demonstrate the importance of military considerations in the minds of the builders and perhaps justifies the approach of the early investigators. However, the life of the villagers inside the fort was not simply one of war, and recent excavations have tried to restore a balanced view of the society of the time by concentrating on the houses and other structures within the enclosure. It is here that the unploughed interior of Moel y Gaer, Rhosesmor (F), has proved so important, for large-scale stripping has revealed the plans of two series of timber houses quite tightly packed within first a palisade and then a rampart. The most interesting feature of the later of these villages is that it was very much a planned settlement. The roundhouses, built with wattle walls and probably high thatched roofs, were placed in one section, all their entrances facing E, while the 'four-posters' (assumed to be storage buildings of some kind) were mostly placed together in another section. Hillforts elsewhere in Britain are beginning to reveal equally well-organized settlement plans, hinting at a strong central control of all aspects of living within these strongholds, a control which may seem at odds with our perhaps romantic picture of the swashbuckling, rather emotional Celt as he emerges from the pages of the classical authors. That picture fits more easily with the remains of fine aristocratic metalwork which is very occasionally found on these hillforts, such as the embossed bronze plaque and shield-mounting from Moel Hiraddug, Cwm (F), the important early engraved bronze hanging bowl found in one of the very rare burials of the period, at Cerrigydrudion (D), and the decorated bronze handles of buckets from Dinorben, St George (D) – no doubt the prized possessions of the leaders of these communities of rather war-like farmers.

Iron Age settlements outside the hillforts have been little studied, but there are several small banked enclosures in central Denbighshire, such as Caerau, Clocaenog, and in Flintshire which may be farmsteads of this period. One may also predict that air photography would reveal many destroyed sites on the fertile floor of the Vale of Clwyd, although without excavation their date would remain uncertain because it is probable that many would belong to the years of ROMAN rule. Apart from the discovery of Romano-British material within some of the earlier hillforts, which would seem to suggest a reoccupation of these sites, the life of the native population under the Romans is poorly documented in this region, in contrast to Gwynedd, where stone-built native farms of that date may still be seen on many hillsides.

At the time of the Roman arrival the tribal name of the inhabitants of modern Flintshire was Deceangli; their territory seems to have stretched from the Dee to the Clwyd. The western part of the county seems to have belonged to the large, widely dispersed tribe of Ordovices. These western people are known to have resisted the Roman advance very fiercely; by contrast the Deceangli, who feature little in the accounts of the conquest, appear more docile. However, the recent discovery of a huge military camp at Rhyn Park near the mouth of the Dee Valley would suggest that the Romans had to bring in a massive army before they could subdue the area and establish their legionary base at Chester. Once this base with its flourishing civil settlement was put on a permanent footing at the beginning of the C2 A.D. it naturally tended to dominate the countryside around. The Roman activity in E Flintshire and Denbighshire was mainly industrial and largely organized by the legions based in Chester. At Holt (D) there was a large works depot and tile manufactory, and at Pentre Farm near Flint recent excavations have revealed a big domestic complex which, it is thought, may have been associated with the management of the Roman lead mines in the hills around Halkyn, the exploitation of this metal being evidenced by several inscribed ingots. Prestatyn (F) has also provided evidence of quite a prosperous Roman community, but it is likely that the long-sought base, Varis, noted in the Antonine Itinerary on the road from Chester to Caerhun, lies further S, probably at St Asaph.

The Roman road which crosses the N of the county from near St Asaph to Caerhun in the Conwy Valley is the only feature of undisputed Roman origin in western Denbighshire. The area is devoid of the forts which garrisoned turbulent Gwynedd and of the busy industrial centres E of the Clwyd; prosperous farmsteads may be expected in the more hospitable parts of the county, but the evidence has yet to be recognized, perhaps because the likely building material here is wood.

The record of the Roman army in Chester begins to grow dim after the revolt of Magnus Maximus in A.D. 368, when he probably took away the legionaries to support his bid for imperial power. When the army left, its attendant industries must also have dwindled and decayed, and no doubt the population of Flintshire returned to a more agricultural way of life, perhaps in some areas harassed by the raids of Irish marauders quick to take advantage of the weakening of central control. We come now to the true dark age of North Welsh history, only fitfully illuminated in the W by the few gravestones of men who could still write Latin.

INTRODUCTION

With an area of 599,588 acres Clwyd is the fourth largest county in Wales, and in 1981 its population of 385,581 was third in size. In architectural terms it is one of the richest and most rewarding counties in the principality.

Much of the LANDSCAPE is of great beauty, especially the gently undulating Berwyn and Clwydian mountains and the fertile river valleys, such as those of the Dee, Elwy and Tanat. The heart of the county is the Vale of Clwyd, bounded by the Clwydian range on the E, and separated on the W from the Conwy Valley by the wild uplands of Mynydd Hiraethog (the Denbigh Moors).

Camden, in the time of James I, wrote that 'The Vale itself with its green meadows, yellow cornfields and fair houses, standing thick, and many beautiful churches, giveth wonderful great contentment to such as behold it from above.' Subsequent writers have been equally enthusiastic about the lusciousness and charm of the Vale, and Iorwerth C. Peate in *The Welsh House* likened it to a portion of the Cheshire Plain let down into Wales. As elsewhere in Wales, the landscape is characterized by isolated farmsteads rather than nucleated settlements. Medieval churches were associated only with small habitation groups, and not until the C19 did villages or even hamlets develop. Urban history dates from Norman times, the borough foundations of Edward I and the rise of mills, markets and trade.

As explained in the Foreword, this is an Introduction not to the whole of Clwyd but to the counties of Denbighshire and Flintshire, which comprise the gazetteer and are here respectively distinguished as 'D' and 'F'.

The Maelor or Maelor Saesneg (i.e. English Maelor) was until 1974 a detached enclave of Flintshire separated from the main part of the county by that part of Denbighshire known as Maelor Gymraeg or Welsh Maelor. It is English in character, with pastoral landscape and half-timbered buildings like those of the adjoining counties of Cheshire and Shropshire, with which, historically, it shares a similar farming economy. It is a district of great estates, though most of the country houses have vanished. As elsewhere on the marches, there are moated sites; most are English in origin and some are now deserted. Stranger than the Maelor and less easily explained is the case of Marford and Hoseley, which formed an island of Flintshire territory completely surrounded by Denbighshire.

The so-called Dark Ages saw, in the C5 to the C7, a remark-

able flowering of Celtic culture from Scotland to Ireland and
Brittany. In Wales it embraced craftsmanship, bardic poetry
and the prospering of the ancient Celtic (later called Welsh)
Church. The near extinction of Christianity which occurred in
England had no parallel, and strength lay in the institution of
the *clas*, or Celtic monastery, consisting of a body of canons
attached to a mother church. Further evidence of EARLY
CHRISTIAN ORIGINS is provided by the names of holy men to
whom most churches of early foundation are dedicated,
preceded by 'Llan' meaning 'enclosure of ...' In Denbighshire
there are thirty-eight such parishes compared with only four in
Flintshire, where, in the E, a greater degree of Saxon and Norman influence and of later Anglicization prevailed. Some enclosures are circular or oval, and though the reason for this is
unknown, it can be assumed that a churchyard approximating
to such shape indicates a church of ancient foundation.

The English kingdom of Mercia was consolidated by Offa,
who reigned from 757 to 795. It was within this period that
OFFA'S DYKE was constructed. This extraordinary earthwork
was never completed for its full intended length between the
Dee estuary and the Severn. Once considered to have been a
mere political frontier between Wales and Mercia, established
by negotiation and agreement, it is now believed to have been
of real military and defensive significance, consisting of a bank,
with a ditch on the W or Welsh side, and in places on the E side
also. It was in parts up to 60ft wide and in the main *c.*15-20ft
high from the bottom of the W ditch to the top of the bank.
Lengths survive near Bersham (D), near Chirk (D), where a
particularly impressive section extends across the border into
Shropshire, and at Treuddyn (F).

WAT'S DYKE, further E than Offa's, is a less ambitious work.
Aethelbald (King of Mercia 716–57) is likely to have been responsible for it; Sir Cyril Fox (*Offa's Dyke*, 1953) considered
that it could not have belonged to the same reign as Offa's
Dyke, and must thus have dated from *c.*700–750 or *c.*800–850.

Politically the era was turbulent, with Wales in a tribal condition during the Anglo-Saxon period. Unity was achieved only
occasionally and briefly; normally there existed three states,
princedoms or kingdoms, of which Gwynedd in the NW was
foremost. Denbighshire and Flintshire roughly correspond in
area with Powys, the middle one. A large part of Wales was
brought under single rule by Rhodri Mawr (Roderic the Great,
*c.*844–877), and unity, though not maintained after his death,
was temporarily re-established under his grandson, Hywel Dda
(Howell the Good, *c.*910–950), who is generally credited with
having revised and codified the laws of Wales. Single rule was
again restored in the time of Gruffydd ap Llywelyn before the
country once more broke up into separate kingdoms. Gruffydd
was attacked and defeated by Earl (later King) Harold, who
destroyed his palace at Rhuddlan (F) in 1063.

As in England, the Normans sought to consolidate conquest
by building castles (many strongholds were established by

Henry I); and in seeking to secure and extend the frontier of his kingdom into Wales, William I created marcher or frontier lordships along the border. His nephew, Hugh Lupus, whose earldom of Chester possessed palatine privileges, was his chief agent of conquest in the N. The crown, native princes and marcher lords were the principal figures involved in the history of early medieval Wales. Campaigns against the Normans were conducted by Gruffydd ap Cynan and his sons Cadwaladr and the chieftain Owain Gwynedd (1135–70), both of whom were in conflict with Henry II and eroded Norman dominance. Under ecclesiastical reforms the church lost its national character; Norman reorganization resulted, as in England, in a territorial system of dioceses and parishes; *clasau* (particularly disliked by the reformers) were suppressed and either disappeared or else became cathedrals, collegiate churches, houses of secular canons or monastic houses of regular orders.

In 1155 Rhys ap Gruffydd (The Lord Rhys, reigned 1155–97) brought all parts of the Kingdom of Deheubarth under his sole rule, and he was successful in campaigns against Henry II.

Llywelyn ab Iorwerth (Llywelyn Fawr or Llywelyn the Great, †1240, grandson of Owain Gwynedd) was a perceptive statesman as well as an able warrior. Early in the c13 he united Wales under one leader as no other prince had done, but in 1211 he suffered a defeat at the hands of his father-in-law, King John. Dafydd (†c. 1246), son of Llywelyn, waged war against Henry III and failed to maintain the unity achieved by his father.

Warfare was continued by Llywelyn the Last and Dafydd, sons of Gruffydd and grandsons of Llywelyn the Great. Edward I in 1276–7, three years after his return from the Crusade, led a campaign against Wales in the course of which Dafydd turned against his brother and sided with the King. Edward followed up victory with a programme of castle building. Repenting his treachery, Dafydd himself launched a revolt by taking Hawarden Castle in 1282 and thereby induced his brother Llywelyn to join in the hostilities against Edward. Llywelyn was killed near Builth in the same year, and 1283 saw the defeat, capture and execution of Dafydd. Royal response to the episode and to an insurrection by Madog ap Llywelyn in 1294 was a further set of castles, this time forming a coastal chain.

By the Statute of Rhuddlan, issued in 1284, Edward I laid down an administrative and legal system for the conquered principality and created new counties, including Flintshire, in which Maelor Saesneg was incorporated. Separate manorial or lordship grants had already divorced this from Welsh Maelor and meant that the two were no longer part of the same patrimony. The early c15 witnessed more turbulence with the rebellion of Owain Glyndŵr (c. 1354–?1416), who not only sought Welsh independence but had wider cultural aims. His campaign began in 1400 with an attack on Ruthin and enjoyed success and popular support c. 1405; but later in the decade these petered out and he died in obscurity.

'Acts of Union', 1536 and 1542–3, superseded the Statute of
Rhuddlan and created a kingdom of England and Wales sharing
broadly the same kind of administrative and legal system; the
power of marcher lords as independent rulers was abolished,
and more counties, including Denbighshire, were divided off.
Welsh Maelor was given not to Flintshire, as logic demanded,
but to Denbighshire, thus resulting in the isolation of English
Maelor, already part of Flintshire. No further major boundary
changes took place until the local government reorganization of
1974.

It is with crosses and sculptured slabs that CELTIC ART is
seen at its best. Only part of the circular shaft remains of the
Pillar of Eliseg near Valle Crucis Abbey (D). It was of the Mercian 'staff rood' type, probably of the first half of the C9.

At Llanrhaeadr-ym-Mochnant (D) is a C9 or C10 sepulchral
slab displaying a Celtic wheel cross and characteristic plait and
fret patterns. The finest sculpture is C9–11, and to this period
8 belongs Maen Achwyfan near Whitford (F). It is a free-standing,
ring-headed cross, Anglo-Viking in type. Its decorative motifs,
with much interlacement, include knotwork and plait and fret,
and there is some figurative carving. The *clasau* (Celtic monasteries) were centres of learning and are further evidence of the
culture which flowered between the end of the Roman occupation and the coming of the Normans. In Denbighshire they
existed at Abergele, Llanrhaeadr-ym-Mochnant, Llansilin and
Llanynys. Those in Flintshire were at Bangor Is-coed and St
Asaph. For *clasau* the cruciform church plan was modified to
one of T-shape with transepts across the E end, the communities
not being large enough to require a choir or eastern arm. A late
example of sculpture is a churchyard cross at Diserth (F), marking a decline from previous high standards; its cusped wheel
head and poor decoration suggest the C12 or C13.

There is no NORMAN ecclesiastical building in the county,
with the possible exception of the tower arch at Nercwys (F).
Neither is there anything which can be considered as TRAN-
SITIONAL from Norman to Gothic. The reason for this is simple:
the Celtic tradition remained unchallenged until the arrival of
the Cistercians, who brought the style which may justifiably be
called EARLY ENGLISH.

Of Cistercian MONASTIC HOUSES, Basingwerk Abbey at
Greenfield (F) was originally founded probably in 1131 as a
house of the French Savigniac order, and Valle Crucis Abbey
(D) was founded in 1201 as a colony of Strata Marcella. Both
abbeys display the characteristic cruciform plan with pairs of
chapels E of each transept, and the initial building phases of
both provide the best examples of E.E. in the county. Much at
Valle Crucis, however, dates from later in the C13, apparently
after a fire. Arcading on the interior W wall of the refectory at
13 Basingwerk incorporates a reader's pulpit and is particularly
good E.E. work, as is the enriched and heavily moulded W
18 doorway of Valle Crucis. An individual school of stone carving
may be discerned in enriched E.E. detail, particularly stiff-leaf

capitals at Valle Crucis Abbey and in a C13 doorway in the church at Llangollen (D). Late in the C13 a Carmelite friary was founded at Denbigh (D). The only other monastic foundation in the county was a house of Augustinian Bonhommes at Ruthin (D), where the church was made collegiate in 1310.

The early evolution of DECORATED is illustrated by the W window of Valle Crucis Abbey (D), which belongs to the late C13 post-fire phase and has tentative bar tracery. Fully Dec is a curvilinear W window in the S aisle at Gresford (D). Nave arcades at Holt and Wrexham (both D) are C14 but altered later. Dec also is the chapter house at Valle Crucis, which, though incorporating wave moulding, is late in date, possibly even C15.

Wave moulding forms a feature of a Dec period of rebuilding c.1310-20* at St Asaph Cathedral (F). This took place after the building had been burnt by Edward I's troops in 1282. The addition of the tower by *Robert Fagan* in 1391-2 marked the completion of the reconstruction, but in 1402 the cathedral was again burnt, this time by Owain Glyndŵr. The subsequent restoration was completed in the time of Bishop Redman (1471-95). It is likely to have been confined to reroofing and fitting up; the canopied choir stalls are likely to date from this phase. It is with the C14 masonry at St Asaph that transition from Dec to PERPENDICULAR may be observed, especially in reticulated tracery, e.g. E windows in the transepts as well as the N and S transept windows, the latter with unusual patterns of intersecting ogees. Similar transitional reticulation occurs in the E window at Caerwys (F), in the E window of the N nave at Rhuddlan (F), and in the chapter house at Valle Crucis Abbey (D), even though that is possibly C15.

Virtually all the best medieval churches are Perpendicular; a great outburst of building activity came in the latter half of the C15, and so extensive were C15 and early C16 rebuildings and remodellings that Dec survivals, e.g. in the S aisle window at Gresford and a simple one of two lights at Efenechdyd (both D), are exceptional. Bryncglwys (D), which has no pre-Perp features, must have been typical of those rebuilt as a rectangular single chamber, following the Celtic tradition of a through church without structural division between chancel and nave and having neither apse nor aisles. The parts at Bryneglwys were originally separated not by a chancel arch but by a rood screen and were demarcated by different roofs, that of the nave being arched-braced whereas the E end has a panelled wagon ceiling which in section follows the curve of the arched braces. It bears bosses, and many such ceilings are more heavily enriched. Display is also sometimes found with the cusping of diagonal struts above the collar beams of trusses, as in the Elizabethan chapel added to Bryneglwys.

Characteristic of the Perp period and exclusive to it are the DOUBLE-NAVE CHURCHES. Particularly common in the Vale of Clwyd, these have occasionally been called twin-naved, but in-

*Dr John Maddison's dating.

correctly so, as the two vessels are never identical. Double-aisled is an equally inappropriate term. It seems that in the first instance a single chamber would be extended E or W before being doubled in size by adding a second nave with an arcade between the two parts. Arched-braced roofs and wagon ceilings are common; hammerbeam roofs are less extensively used; decorative woodwork is found as cornices or panelling at wall-plate level and in the rood screens which extend across both naves. Unmatching E windows are a consistent feature, with the two differing in outline, in the number of lights or in the detailed design of sub-arches and panel tracery. Addition of the second nave might be accompanied by the building of a tower, which, plain and unbuttressed, might have a deceptively primitive appearance. Of several theories advanced to account for the double-naved type, the most likely is that it was a convenient and economical method of enlargement when additional accommodation was needed and that the idea, once introduced, gained favour and became a fashion in the region. It is possible that the form was suggested by Ruthin parish church (D), where an early C14 single chamber had a second nave added later in the century. Most such churches are in Denbighshire, but those in Flintshire include the parish church at St Asaph, and there are others at Caerwys, Cilcain, Hope, Llanasa and Rhuddlan. Among the best Denbighshire examples are Llanfair Dyffryn Clwyd, Llanfarchell (Whitchurch) near Denbigh, Llanefydd, Llanrhaeadr-yng-Nghinmeirch and Llanynys, where the N nave is the earlier of the two and has E.E. features. The largest is at Abergele, and others are at Chirk, Llanarmon-yn-Iâl, which was altered in the C18 and C19, Llanddoged, where work of 1838–9 predominates, Llandrillo-yn-Rhos, Llandyrnog, which underwent a noteworthy Victorian restoration, Llanelian-yn-Rhos and Llansilin. Llangollen was double-naved before its Victorian enlargement. St John's, Leeds, is a C17 English example of the form.

Another special category of Perp, and one to which some of the most splendid buildings belong, is the so-called STANLEY CHURCHES. They form a group near the English border associated with the great Lancashire family, Kings of Man and Earls of Derby and possessors of power and influence in C15 Flintshire. A patroness of architecture and learning was Margaret Beaufort, Countess of Richmond and Derby, and mother of the Tudor King Henry VII, who married Lord Stanley as her third husband. Sir William Stanley began the remodelling of Holt (D) some time between acquiring the lordship of Bromfield in 1483 and his execution in 1495. The aisles and E end were rebuilt, a new aisled chancel being undivided from the nave on the lines of a through church and having unusual inverted arch transoms in the E windows; a C14 W tower (Cheshire-like in its simplicity of outline and detail) was kept, as were Dec nave arcades.

The most important of several successive Perp schemes at Wrexham (D) was a mid- or late C15 remodelling, and this too involved the retention of C14 arcades, the rebuilding of aisles

and the creation of a through church with no chancel arch. As
the parish was within Sir William Stanley's lordship of Bromfield, it is likely that he was responsible for this project, especially as the Legs of Man and other Stanley allusions are
present. Nevertheless, the work differed from that at Holt in
that there is a clerestory. In later Perp schemes a chancel arch
was inserted, a three-sided apse was added at the E end and the
magnificent W tower was erected. This is one of the progeny of 24
Gloucester Cathedral's tower, with prominent pinnacles and
overall panelling, ornamentation and sculpture. It is of the first
half of the C16 and attributed to *William Hort*. Lively and
amusing animals occupy the string course in one bay of the
aisles at Wrexham, and similar beasts appear at the church at
Mold (F), where there is a profusion of Stanley heraldry, em- 22
blems and insignia, and where Margaret Beaufort initiated a
late C15 or early C16 rebuilding. Thomas, Lord Stanley, was
lord of Mold at the time. The arcades demonstrate the neatness
and regularity of Perpendicular, but the work remained incomplete, with no clerestory and little or nothing of an intended
chancel.

It is believed that Margaret Beaufort was responsible for St
Winefride's Well, Holywell (F), the supposed site of the saint's
martyrdom and miraculous resurrection and thus a place of
pilgrimage. The early C16 structure consists of a well chamber, 20
open to a bath in front, and a chapel above. Here too are Stanley 21
emblems as well as animal string courses as at Wrexham and
Mold. Mouldings and other details have counterparts at Mold.
The classical quality of the Mold arcades appears also in the
geometrical precision of the vaulted well chamber and its basin
of stellar plan, though the loss of traceried screenwork has compromised what must have been an effect of gem-like perfection.
The chapel has a polygonal apse recalling Wrexham, a single
aisle and, instead of the arched-braced trusses of the region,
there is a camberbeam roof like those of Cheshire, but with
mouldings and ornament typical of local carpentry.

Because of her association with Holywell, it has been suggested that Margaret Beaufort may also have been responsible
for Ffynnon Fair, Cefn Meiriadog (D), a Perp well chapel built
in more than one stage and now ruinous; it is of T-plan and
may once have been cruciform. As at Holywell, the well basin
is of stellar plan and has a bath adjoining, but the architectural
quality is inferior to that at Holywell and Mold, and there
are neither similarities of detail nor Stanley allusions. Stanley
insignia do appear on the font from Hope, now at Llanfynydd
(both F).

Evidence of the family's patronage does, however, exist in the
double-naved church at Ruthin (D), where the N nave dates
from the original build of 1310 but both naves have panelled
camberbeam roofs of the Perpendicular period. That on the N
is rich and ornate, being heavily carved, with tracery and circles
in the panels; the Stanleys are among the families represented
by inscriptions, badges and heraldry. To Gresford (D) Thomas 25-6

Stanley, Earl of Derby, gave stained glass in 1500, indicating an approximate completion date for what is not only the best Perp church of Clwyd but the finest medieval parish church in Wales. In the absence of evidence of further patronage on the part of the Earl, it may be assumed that visiting pilgrims provided the source of wealth for the rebuilding, as the church possessed an image which was an object of veneration. The rebuilding is to a uniform and fully completed design, but C13 and C14 work survived. This is 'the perfect Cheshire church in Wales', being superior in quality to any Perp work on the English side of the border and having the classic form of aisled and clerestoried nave, no structurally separate chancel, a W tower, panelled camberbeam roofs with carved enrichment, and a screen of English workmanship, i.e. with the standards rather than the middle rail continuous. The E end had a processional way, formed as a route for pilgrims behind the altar, but this has been obscured by alterations. The tower is later than the rest of the structure, being C16, and is not so indiscriminately rich as that at Wrexham, the ornament being concentrated at the crown, i.e. the bell stage, parapet and pinnacles. This glorious building is enhanced by worthy contents, having outstanding monuments, glass, and woodwork including stalls, misericords and a set of parcloses as well as the rood screen.

Hanmer (F) belongs to no special group or category but was a good, uncomplicated Perp church with strong English affinities, especially in the simplicity of its W tower. Nevertheless there is no clerestory; a structurally divided chancel was added in 1720, and screens and panelled roofs were destroyed when the church was burnt in 1889. Northop (F) has a nave with camberbeam roof and a single aisle and may always have been thus; but the body of the church underwent considerable C19 reconstruction and many features are neo-Tudor of 1839-40. The nave arcade, however, is genuine. So too, and probably completed in the C16, is the pinnacled W tower, which, among Clwyd towers, ranks next in quality to those of Wrexham and Gresford. Like them, its Perp surface ornament includes friezes of quatrefoils. The Gwydir Chapel, added in 1633-4 to the church at Llanrwst (D), can appropriately end this survey of Perp. Despite the date it is in medieval tradition, with panel tracery, battlemented parapets, panelled camberbeam roof and the neatness and regularity of form found in late Perp. Only a round-headed opening among elliptical ones and the absence of four-centred arches, together with details and ornament, show this attractive structure to be Stuart Gothic survival. Typical of the C17 is the woodwork, which includes panelling, desks and screenwork.

As a postscript to Perp, a little more should be said about
37 TIMBER ROOFS. The camberbeam type with panelled ceiling, as at Gresford (D), indicates English influence or linkage. Typically Clwydian are arched-bracing and arched and panelled wagon ceilings with, in some cases, hammerbeams alternating with the arched-braced trusses. Late Gothic moulding is seen

in purlins, rafters, the members of trusses and the ribs of panelling. The best roof is in the nave at Llangollen (D). Hammerbeam trusses alternate with principals which have collars
but no arched-bracing. There is heavy moulding and much
carved enrichment, especially a splendid ceiling at collar level, 38
its intricacy harking back, one feels, to Celtic patterning. The
best of all hammerbeam roofs is that at Cilcain (F), where, as 29
was usual, the hammerbeam trusses alternate with plain
arched-braced ones and where the moulding is typical of the
period and particularly good. There is no reason to suppose that
it came from Basingwerk Abbey, as has been asserted, but this
is a case where the tradition of a roof having been brought from
elsewhere seems to have some foundation.

PERPENDICULAR CHURCH FURNISHINGS are so numerous
and important that they are here listed before earlier fittings.
Among some forty late medieval brass lecterns in Britain is one
at Wrexham (D), believed to be of East Anglian origin. It was
given to the church in 1524. Greater rarities are the brass chandeliers at Llanarmon-yn-Iâl and Llandegla (both D), each with 34
a central figure of the Virgin. Their curving branches and leaf
ornament are typically Perp, as are the traceried panels below
crocketed ogees of the pulpit at Nercwys (F).   33

The only remaining medieval canopied stalls in Wales are
those at St Asaph Cathedral (F), dating from the late C15 and 35
belonging to Bishop Redman's restoration after the building
had been burnt by Owain Glyndŵr. Mr Harvey attributes them
to *William Frankelyn*. Stalls are found amongst the wealth of
furnishings at Gresford (D); they back on to parcloses, return
against a chancel (originally rood) screen and retain lively and
entertaining misericords. Chapel screens are one bay E of the
rood screen and are simpler versions of it. More rare and remarkable survivals are at Derwen and Llanrwst (both D), where 36
screens still have their rood lofts and parapets.

Typically Welsh screens are squat in proportion and rectangular in construction, with a flat soffit or coved panelling
below the loft, except for those which, as at Gresford (D), have
arched openings and vaulting. The middle rail is continuous
between end standards, with the spacing of intermediate mullions not necessarily corresponding with that of the wainscot
panels below. English practice, on the other hand, was to use
continuous upright standards, as in the Gresford screen, which,
it may be surmised, came from an English workshop. Intertwined, varied and virile stem and foliate patterns, such as vine
trail and acorn and oakleaf, Celtic in their complexity, are
found, together with tracery, ornamenting roof cornices, screens
and other furnishings. The Welsh type of screen appears at
Clocaenog (D) and at Abergele (D), where the screen extends
across both parts of the double-nave church.

Among surviving pre-Perp church furnishings, FONTS include the curiously shaped timber one at Efenechdyd (D), hol- 31
lowed out of a single block of oak, and of indeterminate date.
Early C13 and with typical E.E. moulding is the font at Gwau-

nysgor (F). Equally characteristic of the C13 is the nailhead ornament which enriches the font at Llandrillo-yn-Rhos (D). The bowl of that at Meliden (F) is also C13, or possibly earlier.

Among MEDIEVAL WALL PAINTINGS is a Last Judgement above the chancel arch at Wrexham (D). Llanynys (D) has a St Christopher in traditional position opposite the S door; it has been dated to the first third of the C15. Somewhat later in the same century is a painting at Ruabon (D) of the Works of Mercy, each deed inspired by an angel.

The county is particularly rich in MEDIEVAL STAINED
40-1 GLASS. The splendid set of 1498 at Gresford (D) depicts scenes from the lives of St Anne and the Virgin. One window, now largely of 1867, probably included a Jesse Tree from the first. A Jesse Tree also forms the subject of a magnificent window at
39 Llanrhaeadr-yng-Nghinmeirch (D), dated 1533; the late date is consistent with the Renaissance spirit which permeates the curves of the foliage and flowers from which some of the figures emerge. At Worthenbury (F) are fragments of a further Jesse, which was of 1393, but these came from Winchester College in 1822-3. Yet another Jesse, this one of the 1530s, is at Diserth (F); as often happened with this subject, the same cartoon was used for more than one light, here, however, not reversed. Tracery lights in the same window have glass of 1450 showing the twelve Apostles, each bearing a clause of the Creed. Fragments of c.1500 at Hope (F) belonged to a Te Deum window and scenes from the life of the Virgin. Consistent with the importance of Perpendicular within the medieval architecture of the county, most surviving glass is C15 or C16. Amongst the latest is that at Cilcain (F), including a Crucifixion, said to have been dated 1546.

Among MEDIEVAL MONUMENTS are products of a local school of carving, dating from the mid-C13 to the end of the C14 and including effigies (some in relief as well as in the round) and sepulchral slabs. Valle Crucis Abbey (D) has good examples of slabs. Before the C13 the quality of carved work (even that of Celtic crosses) had been limited by the intractable stone available.* Originally at the Dominican Friary at Rhuddlan (F) but now in the parish church and belonging to the E.E. period is an incised effigy with French inscription to William de Freney, Archbishop of Rages (Edessa), †1290. He was a nephew of Gilbert de Freney, who had been largely instrumental in establishing the Dominican order in England. If, as is thought, the effigy of a bishop at St Asaph Cathedral (F) represents Bishop Anian II, it is also C13, for he died in 1293. Of unusually high quality and workmanship, it is alien to the local school and traditions. Late C14 in date and thoroughly Dec in style is the monument to Dafydd ap Hywel ap Madog (Dafydd Ddu Hiraddug) at Tremeirchion (F). A priestly effigy lies on a tomb-

---

*The Welsh school of sculpture is dealt with by C. A. Ralegh-Radford in *Culture and Environment*, edited by I. Ll. Foster and L. Alcock (1963), and, with special and fully illustrated reference to funerary monuments, in *Medieval Stone Carving in North Wales* by Colin A. Gresham (1968).

chest (*see* pp. 448–9), each division of which contains a separate
compartment with shield and crocketed gable. Above, the canopy is cinquefoil and sub-cusped; equally typical of the style
are the floral motifs with which the whole is liberally sprinkled.
At Llanynys (D) and Dec in date but not in style is a sepulchral 42
cross, originally in the churchyard; a vertical hexagonal slab,
carried on a short stem, it has figurative relief carving on both
sides. Mention must be made of fragments of a rare C12 Romanesque shrine at Llanrhaeadr-ym-Mochnant (D).

Late Gothic may be traced in terms of memorial sculpture
with the monument at Ruabon (D) to John ab Ellis Eyton †1526
and his wife. A tomb-chest and recumbent effigies are of alabaster; he wears armour and SS collar, and the tomb is adorned
with canopied angel weepers, each with a shield. An important
group of the sepulchral slabs are those with heraldic shields.
Others show a grasped sword behind a shield, a very good one
being that at Valle Crucis Abbey (D; *see* p. 296) to Madog ap
Gruffydd, †1306, great-grandson of the abbey's founder. C14
slabs with floriated crosses (of a type closer in style to English
Dec work than contemporary architectural carving in Wales
ever came) are at Cilcain and Diserth (both F).

MONUMENTAL BRASSES may be mentioned here, though all
are post-medieval. The best have emphasis on line rather than
on areas of brass; especially notable is a series of portrait busts,
1626–69, in the Gwydir Chapel at Llanrwst (D) and these have
baroque character and are of filigree delicacy. They include one
of 1653 signed by *Silvanus Crue*, whose work is seen also at
Holt and Wrexham (both D). The earliest brass in the county is
at Llanfarchell (Whitchurch), near Denbigh (*see* p. 153); it also
has emphasis on line and is to Richard Myddelton †1575 and
his wife, who are depicted kneeling, with their sons and daughters. At Ysbyty Ifan (D) a plate to Robert Gethin and his wife,
both †1598, has above it a later brass to their grandson, also
Robert Gethin, its inscription completed by that of the earlier
one. At Gresford (D) a rare and excellent Gothic Revival brass
of ecclesiological correctness by *J. G and L. A. B. Waller* commemorates the Rev. Christopher Parkins †1843 and his wife.

The first Norman CASTLES were, as in England, earthworks
with timber structures, later rebuilt in stone. Of the motte-
and-bailey Basingwerk Castle at Coleshill, Bagillt (F), refortified
in 1157 by Henry II, nothing remains. A surviving Norman
motte and bailey are at Bailey Hill, Mold (F); and a motte and
bailey at Erddig (D) survive from Wrexham Castle, which was
existing in 1161. Randle III, Earl of Chester, was in 1210 responsible for Bryn-y-Castell, Holywell (F), of which a motte
and ditch remain.

Far more significant is Rhuddlan (F). Here stood the palace
of Gruffydd ap Llywelyn, which Harold destroyed in 1063. Ten
years later a castle was built by the Norman Robert of Rhuddlan, deputy of Hugh Lupus, to whom he was related. Together
they founded a borough, and the bank and ditch defences of
their town remain, as does the motte of the castle, formed from

a natural eminence and known as Twt Hill. Rhuddlan was taken
by Edward I in the war of 1277, and it was in that year that the
building of a castle on a new site began. Work continued well
into the 1280s, damage having been inflicted in the uprising of
1282. Thus we arrive at EDWARD I'S CASTLE BUILDING. At
Rhuddlan the programme was entrusted to Master *James of St
George* (fl. 1278–1307; †*c.* 1308), who had previously worked for
the Counts of Savoy and may himself have been a Savoyard. As
Master of the King's Works he may be credited with the ingenuity, skill and architectural quality of the Edwardian castles in
Wales. Master *Richard of Chester* was probably his right-hand
9 man. For Rhuddlan, Master James devised an axial and regular
concentric plan, with curtain walls enclosing inner and outer
wards. The inner ward is lozenge-shaped, and at opposite
corners are respectively round towers and double-towered gatehouses. Domestic buildings backed on to the inner curtain. A
moat on three sides (partly dry) and the River Clwyd on the
fourth provided outer defences. Some alterations and rebuilding
were carried out in 1301–4 by *Richard of Chester*.

Also begun in 1277 were castles at Aberystwyth, Builth and
Flint. At the latter, construction similarly continued into the
mid-1280s under *James of St George*, and, also as at Rhuddlan,
Richard of Chester carried out early C14 work. Of two wards,
the inner is approximately square and was separated from the
outer by a moat, drawbridge and gateway. The tidal River Dee
protected its three other sides. Circular towers occur at all four
corners, though one, the Great Tower or Donjon, is free-standing and larger than the rest. The King was probably inspired
by C13 continental keeps and may in particular have wished to
emulate the Tour de Constance at the great bastide of Aigues
Mortes. At Flint, the internal arrangement, with mural passages
and a central chamber on two storeys, is complicated in both
plan and section. A further storey was intended and may have
existed.

Also in 1277, Edward granted Hope Castle at Caergwrle (F)
to his then ally Dafydd, who had turned against his brother
Llywelyn. After he had revolted in 1282 Dafydd himself
slighted the castle, which the King made over to Queen Eleanor
following repairs begun by *Richard of Chester* and continued by
James of St George, but it may not have again been repaired
after being damaged by fire in 1283. The present ruins are
probably of building work carried out by Dafydd, between 1277
and 1282. The site is a steeply sloping hilltop providing natural
defence; the layout is of irregular plan, and at the junction of
two of the curtain walls which enclose the inner ward is a tower
rather like the D-towers found in native Welsh castles, but with
a segmental, not semicircular, outer face. Outer defences are in
the form of earthworks. The castles of the 1280s and 90s,
marked by increasing sophistication of plan, form the western
coastal chain, prompted by the risings of 1282 and the mid-
1290s. None in Clwyd belongs to that phase.

Though not part of the royal building programme itself,

'lordship' castles were instruments of the same policy of conquest and subjugation and were material expressions of the continuing existence and power of marcher lordships. Built as they were under the auspices of Edward I, it is likely that the services of Master *James of St George* were made available for the works, and the presence of at least his guiding hand may be discerned in some of them.

The old castle at Hawarden (F) was one such, and in the 1280s it was held by the family of Mohaut or Montalt. It has a complicated history, a settlement having preceded the establishing of a fortified site by Hugh Lupus, Earl of Chester and nephew of William the Conqueror. Later a lordship castle of Edward I, it holds a noted place in Welsh history; it was destroyed by Llywelyn the Last in 1265, and in 1282 Llywelyn's brother Dafydd began his ill-fated revolt against the King by attacking it, perhaps while it was under reconstruction. The layout is of motte-and-bailey type, with a circular keep crowning the mound. A curtain wall enclosed a ward in which stood the great hall. Earlier earthworks seem to have dictated the adoption of what had become an outmoded form, which would otherwise be difficult to reconcile with the probability that so expert a castle designer as Master *James of St George* was involved in the works. Unusual and ingenious, but difficult to understand, is an axially planned route which extended from a barbican to the ward by way of staircases and, it seems, a drawbridge. Edward's other lordship castles were those at Chirk, Denbigh and Holt (all D). Chirk was begun after the King had granted the lordship of Chirkland to Roger Mortimer in 1282; building continued into the c14, possibly beyond the traditional completion date of 1310. Indeed, the structure may never have been finished as intended. The plan was for a rectangular ward, 12 enclosed by curtain walls, with a circular tower at each corner and, it seems, a semicircular one in the middle of three of the curtains. On the fourth (s) side there would presumably have been the gatehouse, but a c15 range now encloses this side of the court and, as well as the s curtain itself, the s ends of the E and w walls are missing. The regularity and axiality find parallels at Harlech Castle, likewise dating from the 1280s, and also Beaumaris, built in the following decade. However, much of Chirk's interest and importance attaches to post-medieval work, resulting from continued domestic use and family occupation over many centuries.

At Denbigh was the chief stronghold of Dafydd ap Gruffydd, brother of Llywelyn the Last, but in 1282 Henry de Lacy, Earl of Lincoln, received the newly created lordship of Denbigh or Rhufoniog. Work on the new castle was put in hand at once and continued until at least 1311, even though it was perhaps never fully completed. The hilltop site falls steeply on all sides. Curtain walls are of two dates; those belonging to the initial campaign of 1282 are part of the defences of an accompanying fortified town and are punctuated by semicircular towers. The castle itself and its irregular ward, inserted within the larger

enceinte, are defined by later walls, the towers of which are
polygonal. The Great Gatehouse consists of three polygonal
(octagonal) towers enclosing a central chamber, also an octagon,
which forces a change of direction in the access route. The hand
of Master *James* here seems evident, and he is known with
certainty to have had some share in designing part of this castle.
Externally the gatehouse belongs to the realm of architecture
rather than engineering; its well-proportioned frontage, with
the gateway between two of the towers, has early C14 Dec detail,
e.g. ballflower ornament enriching the frame of a trefoiled niche
for a statue, probably of Edward I. There is also an area of
chequer patterning.

The ingenuity and complexity of the Denbigh gatehouse, as
well as its geometrical regularity, are seen again in the plan of
Holt, built in lieu of the remote and ruinous Welsh castle of
Dinas Bran, Llangollen (D), soon after the granting in 1282 of
the lordship of Bromfield and Yale to John de Warenne, Earl of
Surrey. Built on and around a rock, its enclosure was penta-
gonal, with towers at all five corners. The nearby River Dee
was diverted to form a moat, from which rose another tower.

Ruthin Castle was begun in 1277 at the same time as Flint
and Rhuddlan. It was at that time held by Dafydd, then in
alliance with the King, but in 1282 it was granted, as the centre
of the new lordship of Dyffryn Clwyd, to Reginald de Grey,
under whom building was resumed. A hilly site results in
changes of level within and around the layout and between the
rectangular lower ward and the upper ward, which is an irregular pentagon. A gatehouse to the latter may have been
begun in Dafydd's time, for it had Welsh D-towers on either
side of the gateway. Within the enclosure are the two C19 blocks
which constitute the present Ruthin Castle.

The earthworks of Tomen-y-Rhodwydd, Llandegla (D), include a motte and bailey and probably represent the castle
known to have been built by Owain Gwynedd in 1149. Other
native Welsh strongholds are Castell Dinas Bran, on a high and
prominent hill at Llangollen (D), and Ewloe Castle (F). Dinas
Bran is C13, may have been built by Gruffydd ap Madog
(†1270), son of the founder of Valle Crucis Abbey (D), and was
burnt by the Welsh in the war of 1277. Though it was included
in the lordship of Bromfield and Yale, John de Warenne, as has
been seen, left it abandoned and built Holt Castle (D) in its
stead. The curtain at Dinas Bran encloses an approximately
rectangular ward; ditches provide outer fortifications, except
where the steep hillside gives natural protection. The gatehouse
is double-towered; a D-tower cuts across one curtain, and a
free-standing rectangular tower or keep, with its own protective
ditch, had an external staircase to an upper doorway. Certain of
these features also occur at Ewloe Castle (F), which is believed
to have been the work of Llywelyn the Last, *c.* 1257. Ground
falling steeply away to two streams affords some natural defence; the site is secluded and there are ditches as outer fortifications. Within them curtain walls enclose two wards (upper

and lower). A circular tower stands in the lower ward, and in the upper is a free-standing D-tower (the Welsh Tower), with an external staircase along one of its straight sides. This tower, though C13, may be earlier than the rest of the structure and is ascribed to Llywelyn the Great. In their quiet tree-lined site, the charming ruins are now a moving reminder of the aspirations and achievements of the C13 Welsh princes.

The major coastal castles and certain of the inland lordship castles of the 1280s were built with integrated fortified towns, as were Flint and Rhuddlan (F). Therefore the subject of TOWN PLANNING should now be introduced. Edward I's new towns were places of English settlement and dominance and became centres of trade. Most were laid out as rectangular gridiron patterns on bastide lines, thus, like the Donjon Tower of Flint, embodying ideas to which the King had been introduced on his travels. Like its castle, the town of Flint (see pp. 347–8) was begun in 1277; a market was established in 1278 and a charter granted in 1284. The original rectangular layout may be traced in the present street pattern, as may the siting of the ditch and bank which, in the absence of town walls, constituted the defences. The borough grew less quickly than did many of the C13 foundations; little building or settlement had taken place by the early C17, and only with industrial development in the C18 did it become viable.

Rhuddlan (F) received a charter in 1278 and, like the castle itself, the dependent town was built on a site different from that of its Norman predecessor. As at Flint, the street layout has largely survived, and, also as at Flint, the defences were ditch and bank only. With these occurring on three sides, they supplemented the Clwyd, which enclosed the fourth. The success of many of Edward's castles depended on their being accessible from the sea; this was achieved at Rhuddlan by the enormous undertaking of canalizing the river to make it navigable. So highly did the King rate his town that he attempted to have the see of St Asaph transferred to it, but without success.

Holt (D) had no town defences, but there is vestigial evidence of a simple rectangular street layout extending between the bridge (an important crossing of the Dee) and the market place, where stands a medieval cross.

A Norman castle existed c. 1138 at Overton (F), which is still a village rather than a town and was never fortified, though it received a charter from Edward I in 1292 and its layout is rectangular. Caerwys (F), which had neither castle nor defences, is similarly of village scale and bastide-like plan. It received a royal charter in 1290 but, as at Flint, the layout remained for some centuries without being fully built up.

Denbigh, on the other hand, was planned with a fully walled town to accompany its castle, but a charter of 1290 was granted not by the King but by Henry de Lacy, holder of the lordship. As has been explained, town walls of 1282 were utilized in making a smaller enclosure for the castle. Of two town gate-

11 houses, one is destroyed, but the late C13 or C14 Burgess Gate
is well preserved, with, on its outer face, two round towers and
a battered base. Like the Great Gatehouse of the castle, it has
chequer ornament. The town proved unsuccessful, owing either
to the lack of water supply or to an exceedingly steep site, which
was in itself inconvenient as well as affording no room for expansion. Thus by the C16 a new settlement had been established
further down the hill, and the walled site has ever since remained abandoned, though it contains fragments of the chapel
which had been built to serve both town and castle. The modern
town of Denbigh is thus without a medieval church, and its
centre is the market place (High Street); streets adjoining it
came into being when blocks of buildings were erected within
the open market space itself.

We may now leave the medieval period and move on to the
mid-C16, when fortification was no longer a serious consideration in domestic architecture. But the changed atmosphere once
the Welsh Tudors were settled on the English throne can also
be sensed in another way, in the fundamental artistic change
which may be summed up as the COMING OF THE RENAISS-
ANCE. The Renaissance in Clwyd did not evolve in the gradual
way familiar in England; it came suddenly both to the county
and to Wales as a whole with the work of Sir Richard Clough,
who was agent in Antwerp to Sir Thomas Gresham. Clough's
building activities included being associated with the construction of the Royal Exchange in the City of London, founded by
Gresham in 1566 and opened in 1571. The work was supervised
by *Hendrik van Passe* of Antwerp, who may also have designed
Bach-y-graig, Tremeirchion (F). This remarkable house, which
was dated 1567-9, and which seems originally to have been
intended for commercial as well as residential purposes, was,
like the Royal Exchange, Early Flemish Renaissance in style
and built of brick. It stood round three sides of a court, but
only part of one range still remains. Plas Clough near Denbigh
was also built by Sir Richard, probably in 1567, and together
with Bach-y-graig, is likely to have been the first use of brick
anywhere in Wales, as well as introducing from the Low Coun-
54 tries the stepped gables which became widely used in the northern counties.

ELIZABETHAN CHURCHES are rare enough to give outstand-
62 ing interest to so large an undertaking as Leicester's Church at
Denbigh. Begun in 1578 under the auspices of Robert Dudley,
Earl of Leicester, who was then in possession of the lordship of
Denbigh, the church was dedicated in 1579, according to an
inscription which is known to have existed; but it remained
unfinished when building work ceased in 1584, and only outer
walls of the nave still stand. Of ten bays and 170ft long, it
would have been on the scale of a cathedral, and it is likely that
Dudley hoped that the see of the diocese would be transferred
from St Asaph. Leicester was the chief protector of Puritans at
the court of Elizabeth I, and the plan and character reflect his
ideals. Of hall church type, it would seemingly have had

round-arched Tuscan arcades. The nave windows, however, though looking semicircular, are in fact four-centred, so late did Gothic tradition survive in church building.

In the counties of England, the coming of the Renaissance can frequently be traced in ELIZABETHAN MONUMENTS AND FITTINGS, and such a monument in Clwyd is that to Humphrey Llwyd †1568 at Llanfarchell (Whitchurch), near Denbigh. Its 64 Corinthian aedicule, with ornamented frieze and further classical detail, have all the purity of Elizabethan High Renaissance architecture. In contrast, and in the same church, is the monument by *Donbins* to Sir John Salusbury, erected by his wife in 63 1588. Of alabaster, with recumbent effigies on a tomb-chest, and with sons and daughters, it is still fully in the medieval tradition.

Mention has already been made of Renaissance tendencies in glass of 1533 at Llanrhaeadr-yng-Nghinmeirch (D), and similar Renaissance development may be seen in balusters and garlands in a window at Mold (F). In the same church, but less markedly classical, are four canopied niches whose free luxuriance signals the demise of Gothic. Similarly free and flowing is an early C16 bench end at Hawarden (F). Among post-medieval glass are also two early C17 portrait panels at Tremeirchion (F). At Gresford 43 (D) there is a curious Elizabethan monument to John Trevor †1589, and at Llanarmon-yn-Iâl (D) is a similar, but later, one to Efan Llwyd, 1639. Both have three arches with, it seems, a 44 reclining effigy behind, but in fact these are only the legs and bust visible in the end arches; the middle one contains a solid panel. Classical and of Corinthian order is the monument at Llanrhudd (D) to John Thelwall †1586 and his wife †1585; columns flank a recess in which kneeling effigies face each other at a desk, and children are depicted on a frieze below.

There is no C17 ecclesiastical architecture which calls for mention, but account must be taken of JACOBEAN AND LATER CHURCH FITTINGS. At Bodfari (F) the pulpit of 1635 still has rich carving, including strapwork and figurative panels. In contrast is the pulpit at Hope (F), still recognizably Jacobean in 61 style, but more classically correct, with Ionic pilasters and with strapwork abandoned in favour of freer leaf patterns.

The Welsh hooded tombs, with open arches above a table tomb or tomb-chest and with ornamental soffits, may be included here. The first was that of Robert Wynn, †1598, at Conwy, which was followed by that of Sir Peter Mostyn †1605 at Llanasa (F); the most elaborate was at Cwm (F), commemorating Grace Williams †1642. A late example at Trelawnyd (F) has the arch filled in as a solid tympanum. Also C17 is the pulpit at Abergele (D), with foliated and floriated patterns of post-Jacobean character. As was usual in the C17 and C18, figures of Moses and Aaron accompany the Creed and Decalogue as painted on canvas at Berse Drelincourt, Broughton (D), and on a former reredos at Llansilin (D), where there is also a painted benefaction board of 1740 and a C17 altar table. This latter is of liturgical interest, having been aligned E–W against the E wall, as shown by an uncarved end. This may be associated with John Williams, Archbishop of York, who spent the latter part of his life in Wales. There is a similar altar at Nercwys (F).

Robert Jones signed boards of 1809, carrying the Creed and Lord's Prayer in Welsh, at Cilcain (F). In 1800 *Francis Eginton* provided stained glass for the E window of St Asaph Cathedral (F); its pictorial lights, of transparency style in the C18 tradition, were transferred to Llandegla (D) in 1864.

The Gwydir Chapel at Llanrwst (D) has panelling, desks, monuments, screenwork and, besides the *Crue* brasses already mentioned, a tablet by *Nicholas Stone*. This is of 1636 and commemorates Sir Richard Wynn and his building of the chapel. Consisting only of an inscription, it fails to display Stone's sculptural talents.

The departure from classical purity in JACOBEAN MONU-MENTS, with heaviness, over-ornamentation, incorrect use of the orders and naïve sculpture, reflects the architecture of the period and its dependence upon German and Flemish pattern books. Typical is that at Hope (F), with strapwork and kneeling effigies of Sir John Trevor of Plas Teg †1629 and his wife. At Whitford (F) are heraldic tablets to Ellis Wyn †1619 and Richard Coytmore †1683. The strapwork of the Trevor monument at Hope has a tendency to curving scrolliness, marking a departure from full Jacobean heaviness. Mention has already been made of the strange monument to Efan Llwyd at Llanarmon-yn-Iâl (D), 1639, and its counterpart at Gresford (D) to John Trevor †1589. Also at Gresford, and most characteristically Jacobean of all, with Corinthian columns and kneeling effigies below arches, is the monument to Sir Richard Trevor and his wife, erected during his lifetime in 1638.

Post-medieval domestic architecture has been left at the freakish buildings of Sir Richard Clough. Before seeing how symmetry became a feature of ELIZABETHAN HOUSES it is necessary to say a word about the development of post-medieval domestic planning. Essentially this involves use of the H-plan, with the hall in the centre between cross wings, the service wing being that at the lower or entrance end of the hall, permitting the latter to be entered in traditional medieval way. Such a plan automatically allows for symmetry of massing but not of detail, with the doorway off-centre in the internal angle of the service wing; much ingenuity was exercised in reconciling this essentially irregular concept with Renaissance ideals of order and balance.

A group of charming Flintshire houses, all with mullioned and transomed windows and coped and finialed gables, illustrates the asymmetrical version of the H-plan. Of these the largest is Gwysaney, Mold (F), dated 1603. Not only is the entrance in the angle of one of the wings, but the wings themselves differ. The range between the wings is virtually a double pile, and the house is very tall; thus, although it has been partly reduced and remodelled, it was of unusual size. Pentrehobyn, also at Mold, is of approximately the same date as Gwysaney, of which it is a smaller version with the more usual single range in the centre. Smaller again is Fferm, Hope (F), which is also early C17 or possibly late C16, but here the H-plan no longer remains intact, for the upper-end cross wing, if it ever existed, has been demolished, and moreover the hall has been partitioned. Every one of these houses has a fireplace on the long lateral wall of the hall, for, as will be explained more fully, by the late C16 the medieval hall with open hearth and roof timbers was being superseded by storeyed houses with chimneys and enclosed hearths. Chimneys on outside walls might be placed at a gable end as well as laterally, though the latter was common practice in Denbighshire and Flintshire, combined with an inside cross passage linking opposite doorways in the outer walls at the lower end of the hall. Chimneystacks might be of elaborate and ornate design, especially when built of brick, as at Fferm. Though extensively remodelled in 1846–7 and again later in the C19, Mostyn Hall, Mostyn (F), has to be considered as one of the group of C17 Flintshire houses on account of additions of 1631–2. The medieval great hall survived both transformations with its form and plan intact. Belonging stylistically to the set of C17 Flintshire houses, though not of H-plan, is Henblas, Llanasa, of 1645.

Pre-dating all efforts towards achieving symmetry in the Flintshire houses of the early C17, at Trevalyn Hall, Trefalun 53 (D), an H-plan had already in 1576 been squeezed into symmetrical regularity, and the house may be considered as a mature example of Elizabethan domestic architecture. Pediments above the mullioned and transomed windows provide further evidence of classical aspiration as well as giving an East Anglian flavour. The brickwork has been rendered, and internal rearrangement has obscured the original layout and led to misunderstanding of the plan and its significance. Symmetrical also, of H-plan and with stepped gables, Faenol Fawr, Bodelwyddan 54 (F), was built in 1597. It was burnt in 1984.

The evolution of symmetrical H-plan was continued in JAC-OBEAN HOUSES and an interesting variation is Nerquis Hall, 55 Nercwys (F), by *Evan Jones*, 1638. The hall occupies the full length between the cross wings, and there are lower-end porch and upper-end bay in the form of extruded corners, thus combining symmetry of massing with the traditional placing of the entrance at the lower end of the hall. As the doorway is on the return side of the porch, there is also symmetry of elevation, though the effect is lost in perspective. The plan approximates to a double pile, with accommodation occupying the space behind the hall and between the cross wings. Rhual, Mold (F), of 57 1634, is a more consistently conceived double pile, but, although the notional H-plan was discarded, the two principal rooms remained the hall and great chamber above; and traditional also (recalling a cross passage) is the route across the hall from the entrance to the staircase in the back range. The stair- 56 case itself is original, with flat, shaped balusters and square finialed newels.

The most spectacular instance of symmetry and regularity
applied to a C17 house is Plas Teg, Hope (F), probably of
1610. Its square plan has a transverse hall and great chamber,
recalling Hardwick, and a tower at each corner, recalling Wollaton; but although the whole thus suggests Robert Smythson
there is no proof that he was involved. It is, however, likely that
the owner, Sir John Trevor, obtained the plan from within the
court circles in which he was a powerful figure, with the main
elevation coming from the same source. This (the entrance
front) is of ashlar, while the other, less sophisticated façades
have rubble walling, their vernacular character suggesting that
execution was left to local craftsmen. Here also is a Jacobean
well staircase with square finialed newels, but with turned,
rather than flat, balusters.

The N range of Chirk Castle (D), though altered in the course
of C18 and C19 remodelling, may be considered as Jacobean
domestic architecture, having been built early in the C17 by Sir
Thomas Myddelton and containing great hall (now Cromwell
Hall) and great chamber (now saloon). In addition to the staircases already mentioned, the best C17 interior features are at
Plas Tirion, Llanrwst (D), where plasterwork in an overmantel
of 1626 includes heraldry and strapwork, which also occur in a
chimneypiece dated 1628. There are two good interiors in the
work of 1631–2 at Mostyn Hall, Mostyn (F), intended as parlour
with great chamber above. Both rooms are panelled, and the
lower has a pedimented doorcase as well as a heraldic plaster
overmantel. Pentrehobyn, Mold (F), has an early C17 carved
overmantel. Foxhall Newydd, Henllan (D), 1608, remained incomplete, with only the outer walls now existing; they are extremely high, and if, as is probable, the present structure is
merely the cross wing of a projected H-plan, the house would
have been enormous. Brynkinalt (D) has had a complicated
building history; nothing remains of the original plan, and it is
thus all the more gratifying that the fine E-plan entrance front,
built in 1612, and of brick with shaped gables, should survive
unspoilt, making it the most characteristic Jacobean frontage in
the county.

The Welsh border has no equivalent of Scottish and Nor-
thumbrian pele towers, and indeed TOWER HOUSES were rare
in Wales, where, as in England, castles gave way direct to
medieval hall houses. There is but one true fortified dwelling
house in Clwyd (the type is not to be confused with the first-
floor-hall houses of the S and W): The Tower (Brancoed), Mold
(F), mid-C15 and of two storeys, with an upper-level hall which
has been sub-divided; the ground floor is segment-vaulted and
there is a shallow basement also with a tunnel vault. Northop-
hall Farm (Llyseurgain), Northop Hall (F), is not a true instance
of the type, having had no battlemented walkway, but is a
first-floor-hall house (unusual for the region) with vaulted
ground storey and a well chamber below it.

VERNACULAR HOUSES are a prominent and attractive feature
in the Welsh rural scene, and understanding of them depends

upon knowledge of building materials (see pp. 89–94) and the evolution of plan types. The basic plan forms derive from the single living space, i.e. the house place or the medieval great hall, and the simple one-room cottage type developed into many variants, initially with separate rooms partitioned off as service or sleeping areas. The long house, with family and animals under one roof, and the residential portion entered through the byre, was rare in North Wales, and no example survives in Denbighshire. Further stages of sub-division were for the sleeping area to be partitioned off into additional service units, such as dairy or pantry, and horizontal division would involve the insertion of a floor to make use of the roof space and thus create the *bwthyn croglofft* or cock loft cottage, its upper stage reached by a movable ladder, maybe with an open triangular space at the entrance end, and, after open hearths had been abandoned, a chimney would be built in a gable end.

It was from about the mid-c15 that open hearths began to be replaced by fireplaces with chimneys, either inserted into existing houses or built into new ones. Initially they were used only in greater houses; they appeared in small ones after a lapse of about a century. Their introduction into earlier buildings was usually accompanied by the horizontal sub-division of the hall by inserting an intermediate floor, necessitating windows to light the new storey; this requirement was appropriately met by dormers. They had first been used to light the second floors of large houses, as in 1583 at Plas Newydd, Cefn Meiriadog (D). 49 The same house is a fine example of a three-unit type with cross passage and lateral chimney. The three bays consist of hall, lower-end kitchen and upper-end parlour. Between hall and parlour was one of the best of several framed and enriched timber partitions, with guilloche and dated 1583, like one of the dormers. It has been moved to the Welsh Folk Museum at St Fagan's near Cardiff. One, also with guilloche, is *in situ* at another Plas Newydd, that at Llanfair Talhaearn (D). It is dated 50 1585 and has an *anno mundi* inscription, as has that of 1571 at Faenol Bach, Bodelwyddan (F), though here there is but one doorway of an original pair. That part of the house in which it stands is, with the 1571 inscription, the earliest known dated example in Wales of a storeyed house with lateral chimney; Pant Idda, Abergele (D), of 1722, is the latest.

By the mid-c16 hall houses with open roofs had become obsolete, and the storeyed house with chimney and masonry fireplace was the norm. The long lateral wall of the hall was the position of the earliest fireplaces, but c16 and c17 ones, including those introduced into cruck halls, were usually internal rather than lateral, backing on to or blocking an entrance passage and often greatly reducing the size of the hall. A lobby entrance plan resulted when a chimney was built opposite the doorway, enabling two rooms to share the same stack. Llaethwryd, Cerrigydrudion (D), has a lateral chimney of 1668 and 52 another backing on to the entrance passage. Plas Uchaf, Llanelidan (D), is a late medieval hall house adapted in the c17 but 47

with the lateral chimney in the front wall rather than at the
back, as was more usual. Chimneys and entrances may alterna-
tively occur at gable ends, as originally at Trellyniau Fawr,
Cilcain (F), but gable-end chimneys are uncommon in the N,
and in Clwyd lateral chimneys and entrances and internal cross
passages predominate.

The medieval arrangement can be most completely seen at
Brithdir Mawr, Cilcain (F). Not only does it have a cross passage
with screens partition, but there are even traces of an open
hearth, which was superseded by a lateral chimney. Presumably
this took place in 1637, as this date appears upon a dormer
window which came to be required only when the hall was
divided up by the introduction of a floor. Adaptations had previously been made in 1589, the year inscribed on the upper-end
post-and-panel partition, a date too late to be that of the original
build. Among other early features are timber mullions and the
arched-braced central truss of the hall. Tŷ Isaf, also at Cilcain,
illustrates a further stage of domestic development in which the
hall was still open to the roof, but a lateral chimney was built
in from the first; nevertheless the room has undergone horizontal sub-division; its central truss and some timber-framed partitioning still exist, together with screens partition and cross
passage. Two lower-end service rooms are now combined as a
single room, and there is an upper-end parlour.

The latest phase of hall development is of significance not so
much in terms of planning but of structure, involving as it did
the use of cruck construction and the spere-truss; the latter
could be taken to its logical conclusion in the form of an aisled
hall. Such a C15 house was Althrey Hall, Bangor Is-coed (F),
where C17 alterations resulted in the emergence of an H-plan,
in an internal angle of which a storeyed porch forms an extruded
corner; such a plan was in itself forward-looking and anticipated
C17 developments.

Leeswood Green Farm, Leeswood (F), provides the best opportunity for studying a cruck hall house. It was of four bays;
the open hall occupied the two middle ones, whose three trusses
remain, though a floor has been inserted horizontally, dividing
the hall, and a chimney was built against the arched-braced
central truss. The outer walls have been rebuilt in stone; on the
other hand, a post-and-panel partition with two doorways survives within the upper-end cruck truss; also to be seen are the
doorways of two lower-end service rooms.

Another classic of its kind, and one which has been expertly
restored, is the C15 Pen-y-Bryn, Llansilin (D; *see* p. 245), whose
structure is of aisle-truss type with posts lining in with those of
a spere-truss and with arcade plates springing from them; a
fully aisled hall is thus implied, and the pattern is reflected in
the upper- and lower-end partitions. Though the structure
remains largely intact, it has been obscured by the inevitable
C17 alterations. Bryn Iorcyn, Caergwrle (F), was similar in plan
and construction to Leeswood Green Farm, and although it still
has its three central cruck trusses, together with fragments of a

spere-truss, the outer walls have been so extensively rebuilt in stone as to appear entirely Jacobean. Lower Berse, Broughton (D), had a spere-truss. The C17 saw a change of alignment, with houses built parallel with the slope of the ground, rather than at right angles to or into it.

Though regional variation in date marked the 'great rebuilding', in which numerous houses were built anew and hall houses were adapted, in general it took place in Wales between Elizabethan times and the Civil War, c.1550–1650. Adapting hall houses called not only for windows but for staircases, which were sometimes constructed within the hall area, but were also accommodated in added wings. Some C17 ones perpetuated Jacobean style and detail, e.g. at Pen-y-Bryn, Llansilin (D). Another C17 staircase is at Esclusham Hall, Esclusham (D), a hall house converted probably in 1677, but where there are still a central base cruck and two partition trusses.

Also at Esclusham was Plas Cadwgan, whose hall remained undivided; with its central arched-braced cruck and its spere-trusses, it may well have been C14, but, together with its fine C17 staircase, it has disgracefully been demolished. Humbler instances of cruck hall houses are White Cottage, Pentrobin, and Plas-y-Brain, Treuddyn (both F). Alterations to the hall of the latter included the building of a lateral chimney, and unusually for domestic as distinct from the ecclesiastical carpentry of the region, there is cusping above the collar of the arched-braced central truss. Smaller still in scale but nevertheless a cruck hall of four bays, with its outer walls rebuilt in stone, is Llan Farm, Llanelian-yn-Rhos (D). Parts of all five trusses remain, as does some external framing in a gable end; additions include a later wing as well as lateral chimneys. Tŷ-draw, Llanarmon Mynydd Mawr (D), is now reduced to the status of a ruinous barn, but is still recognizable as a late C14 or C15 four-bay cruck hall, with cusping above the collars of its arched-braced central truss; neither of the upper-end trusses remains, but a lower-end partition truss with its doorway may still be seen. A number of cruck houses survive in fragmentary form in the neighbourhood of Bryneglwys (D), e.g. at Tŷ Gwyn and Pentre Isaf, the latter with its central truss and upper-end cruck partition.

The timber framing which once abounded in Ruthin (D) still includes two cruck town houses; of these Nantclwyd House has its hall divided, not by a floor but by a chimney forming a lobby entrance, and a plaster ceiling hides the roof timbers. C17 and C18 innovations also comprise panelling and decorative plasterwork. Sir Richard Clough is traditionally associated with the Myddelton Arms, but possibly only on account of the tiers of dormer windows which articulate the roof and, like Clough's authenticated building work, are reminiscent of the Low Countries. Structurally the building is a cruck hall with spere-truss.

Lesser gentry, gentlemen farmers or what in England were 'yeomen', were numerous in North Wales; many houses are fully vernacular and regional in style, uninfluenced by fashion,

but possessing gentry status by reason of accommodation, of
C16 or C17 date inscriptions and heraldry, or of ornate woodwork of the Perpendicular period in the form of a coved dais
canopy at the upper end of the hall, or an open roof with emphasis on the hall's central truss. Storeyed houses permitted
ceilings to be used as vehicles of display with patterns of
counterchanged joists between beams framed in two or even
three stages, as impressively seen at Plas-yn-Glyn, Llanarmon
Mynydd Mawr, and Henblas, Llangedwyn (both D). Plaster
ceilings with their greater scope for decoration were an Elizabethan innovation.

Two conflicting trends are seen in storeyed houses of the
mid-C16 onwards with, on the one hand, the continuation of
regional character and traditions, medieval in origin, and, on
the other, Renaissance movement for regularity and uniformity
fused with classical discipline and detail. Renaissance influence
led to the double-pile plan, and to symmetry. The latter tended
to be about the short axis, resulting in a central entrance and
increasing the importance of the front elevation. There are symmetrical fronts at Penbedw Uchaf, Nannerch (F); Walgoch,
Nannerch; and Isglan, Whitford (F), but all still with mullioned
windows; and a central doorcase, dated 1633, at Isglan is in
Gothic tradition and has a clumsily steep pediment. Coed-y-
Cra Uchaf, Northop (F), as remodelled in 1636, has a central
chimney and lobby entry, a symmetrical three-bay front and
crude classical detail inside. It seems previously to have been
one of a series of Flintshire houses having upper-level chambers
or halls with open roofs, others being Caerwys Hall, Caerwys;
Maes-y-Groes and Trellyniau Fawr, both at Cilcain; Walgoch,
Nannerch; and probably Gellilyfdy at Babell, Ysgeifiog. Special
to the region are the C16 or C17 'cyclopean doorways', which,
consisting of massive unwrought stones, are misleadingly
primitive and ancient-looking. The only dated example,
Galltfaenan Isaf or Brynwgan, Henllan (D), is of 1601. They
were used in churches, e.g. Abergele (D), as well as houses.
Renaissance planning culminated with the incorporation, in a
double pile, of central entrance, passageway and staircase,
leading to the familiar Georgian house-plan. Right through the
C18 this progressive plan could be combined with traditional
features such as broadly proportioned timber casement windows
rather than sashes. Instructive combinations of fashion and vernacular character may be seen at the following, all in Denbighshire, mostly of brick and not necessarily double piles: Sirior
Goch, Betws-yn-Rhos, with one-bay pediment; the former rectory at Cerrigydrudion (1790) with three-bay pediment; Croes
Foel, Esclusham (1781), with pedimented doorcase; Ddol,
Eyton (1789); Tŷ-Nant, Llangedwyn, C18 though still having
timber mullions and transoms; and Bryn House, Pen-y-Lan, of
1749. Flintshire examples include Plas is-Llan, Cwm (1765),
which is one of the most bizarre fusions, with pediment, lunette
and stone mullions and transoms; West View, Halghton; Croxton, Hanmer (1793); and Rhydyddauddwr, Rhuddlan.

In the earliest symmetrical houses the staircase might be in an axial turret at the rear; in the C17 it became usual to have a separate kitchen as distinct from the hall or general living space, instead of small service rooms. One of the latter was sometimes converted to a parlour when a kitchen was added to an existing house. A cruciform plan (favoured in the C17) resulted if a kitchen was placed with the staircase in the back projection and if there was also a front porch. The cruciform plan of the brick-nogged Eyton Manor Farmhouse, Eyton (D), is due to 51 there being a porch and a rear kitchen. The house has a central chimney and was probably built in 1633.

Trimley Hall, Llanfynydd (F), 1653, is a more unusual essay in centralized planning, being a square with porch, pyramid roof and central chimney, but vernacular in certain features, e.g. stone mullioned windows. Aspiring to classicism in more than plan and the incorrect use of the orders is Halghton Hall, Halghton (F); this house of 1662 has not only stone mullions, transoms and Jacobean ornament but also elaborate and strongly Baroque side volutes to windows. Yet more unusually, even uniquely, the square C18 Bryn-y-Pin, Cefn Meiriadog (D), has a centralized plan arranged around a spiral newel staircase rather than a chimney, though there are four corner rooms, each with a diagonal corner fireplace, the flues from which are gathered into a stack above the staircase.

The UNIT SYSTEM involved the existence of two or more separate dwellings which might touch, e.g. at a corner, but which had no internal communication. Such layouts resulted either from straightforward provision of additional residential accommodation or else from the form of inheritance known as *cyfran* or gavelkind, i.e. equal inheritance by all the sons of a father. In many instances the original arrangement has been obscured by later alterations, which may take the form of enlargements linking the separate dwellings, and as a result it is sometimes difficult for this type of planning to be recognized. Some are known to exist in England, but this C17 system is usually associated with western Wales; it has been a surprise that the half-dozen following possible examples have been observed in Flintshire: Pen Isa'r Glascoed, Bodelwyddan; Trellyniau Fawr, Cilcain; Pwllhalog, Cwm; The Bryn, Halghton; Golden Grove, Llanasa; Walgoch, Nannerch; and Gledlom, Ysgeifiog. The following were noted in Denbighshire: Llaethwryd, Cerrigydrudion; New Hall, Chirk; Derwen Hall, Derwen; Plas Chambres, Henllan; Plas Heaton Farm, Henllan; Berain, Plas Harri and Plas Uchaf at Llanefydd; Bryngwylan, Llangernyw; Hafod, Llansilin; Giler, Pentrefoelas; Cae'rafallen, Ruthin; and Perthewig, Trefnant – but there may well be more; there can be no certainty that these lists are comprehensive or complete.

Groups of FARM BUILDINGS and dwelling houses comprise the farmsteads which dot the countryside; in the early stages of development, expansion took place laterally from a gable end, and if a byre was built abutting against a house with end entry a long house resulted, though the addition might just as likely be a barn or a stable, and ranges of building round three or four sides of a yard did not become usual until the late C18. Some C16 barns exist, and a number of roof trusses of queen-post type, e.g. in a barn at Llaethwryd, Cerrigydrudion (D), may be of this date. Beautifully cut inscriptions occur on roof timbers, as in a barn at Gellilyfdy, Babell, near Ysgeifiog (F), where the date 1586 can be seen. The magnificent six-bay cruck barn at Rhual, Mold (F), may possibly have been intended for domestic rather than agricultural use.

Only in the C18 did stylish and fashionable agricultural architecture appear, at first largely confined to stables, though cart sheds with sets of segmented or elliptical arches, as at Melai, Llanfair Talhaearn (D), frequently look well, especially if they carry a granary as a second storey, as at Bodtegir, Llanfihangel Glyn Myfyr (D). Faenol Bach, Bodelwyddan (F), has late C19 hammels of impressive architectural dignity. The group of buildings at Melai is of 1804; it consists of four ranges enclosing a courtyard and has a pediment and cupola. Georgian brick combines with timber framing in buildings at Cefn Coch, Llanfair Dyffryn Clwyd (D).

Among important CAROLEAN HOUSES in Clwyd there is little that can be considered typical of the period. Indeed the Old Rectory at Llanbedr Dyffryn Clwyd (D) is the only brick hipped-roof double-pile box of the latter part of the C17. It is, though, a good example, with modillion cornice, timber cross windows, bolection panelling, and a bolection-moulded chimneypiece. The staircase shows the next stage of development from the Jacobean type, with an open well and turned balusters, though still having a string and square newels, the latter flat-capped. Croesnewydd, Broughton (D), of 1696, has similar internal features and also sash windows, which if original (and they may not be) would be unusually early. C17 staircases with flat-topped newels are sometimes found with twisted or barley-sugar balusters. A wing of 1716 at Rhydonnen Uchaf, Llandysilio (D), has turned bobbin balusters and the balustrade repeated against the wall as a dado. A very good staircase, perhaps of 1725, at Faenol Fawr, Bodelwyddan (F), was damaged in the fire of 1984.

65-6 It is unexpected for a long gallery to be formed as late as the time of Charles II, but that at Chirk Castle (D) is of c. 1667–78. It is attributable to *Lady Wilbraham*, and has bolection-moulded panelling and fine woodcarving by *Thomas Dugdale*. Bachymbyd Fawr, Llanynys (D), is of 1666, built of brick with stone dressings, the latter still displaying Jacobean motifs, though the house is otherwise typically Restoration, with hipped roof and clearly intended to be of U-plan, with a wing projecting forward at either end of the main front, though only one of these now exists; there are stone cross windows.

67-8 A transition from Carolean to BAROQUE is formed by the early part of Erddig (D) by *Thomas Webb*, c.1687, for this, like the Old Rectory at Llanbedr Dyffryn Clwyd, is a double pile and of brick and originally had stone cross windows, though sashes were later substituted; here too are bolection panelling and staircases similar in their elements to that at Llanbedr Dyffryn Clwyd. Externally, however, a solid parapet, originally punctuated by more balustrading than at present, and the absence of any projecting cornice foreshadow early C18 rectangular simplicity.

Such rectangularity marks the English school of provincial Baroque with which the names of *Francis Smith* and *Richard Trubshaw* are linked. Clwyd's most thoroughly Baroque piece was the early C18 wing of the L-shaped Brymbo Hall, Brymbo (D), with a giant order of fluted pilasters and shaped gables. Sadly the past tense is applicable, for the house was demolished in 1973. *Smith* himself was responsible for the rebuilding and remodelling, 1736–8, of Wynnstay (D), which was previously timber-framed, but the C18 work has itself now been obscured by later alterations and reconstruction. Leeswood Hall, Leeswood (F), built *c.*1724–6, and attributable to Smith, had a three-storey centre including Smith's favourite device of the top storey perched above the main cornice, which was itself above a giant order of Corinthian pilasters. The block was of eleven bays, on either side of which was a thirteen-bay wing. Needless to say this prodigious house has been remodelled and greatly reduced in size.

Several early or mid-C18 brick houses with stone dressings, occasionally rusticated, repeat the massing of Bachymbyd Fawr, being of U-plan with a broad wing breaking forward at either end of the main front, though only in a few cases do the wings project far enough for the enclosed space to be considered a true courtyard. One such was Emral Hall, Worthenbury (F), remodelled by *Trubshaw* and *Joseph Evans* in 1724–7, retaining important C17 parts. Its demolition was one of the most serious losses which the domestic architecture of the county has suffered. Also of this type was the predecessor to the present Llantysilio Hall, Llandysilio (D), dated 1723, with the wings extending far enough to enclose a deep forecourt. Trevor Hall, Trevor (D), is a remodelling, carried out in 1742–3, of an earlier structure, probably a C17 H-plan house with lateral chimney, the cross wings being retained but truncated at the rear. Trevalyn House, Trefalun (D), is of 1754 and here also the wings are far projecting, giving a deeply recessed centre. Refronting in the 1720s of Pickhill Hall, Marchwiel (D), is attributed to *Trubshaw*; this produced a straight façade with balustraded parapet and a giant order of fluted pilasters, and a central first-floor window with side volutes.

One of the most remarkable, and certainly the most mysterious, of early C18 houses was Soughton Hall, Northop (F), which is believed to have been built in 1714 or 1727, though some work may have been carried out after 1732; no accurate record exists of the highly complicated Corinthian frontage, done away with in the course of C19 remodellings which were themselves remarkable. Complicated also was the evolution of Llangedwyn

Hall, Llangedwyn (D), where a C16 or C17 house was remodelled, the work extending from about the late C17 to the mid-
C18; this has itself been partly lost as a result of mid-C20 alterations and demolition, but there remains a fine staircase with
string and turned balusters. Finally, the Old Vicarage at Berse
Drelincourt, Broughton (D), built in 1715, a gable-ended
double-pile, demands to be included with Baroque examples on
account of its quoins, keystones, Gibbs surrounds, and pedimented doorcase.

The name of the Davies family means that no adequate history of C18 IRONWORK can be written without reference to
Clwyd. These great smiths had their forge at Croes Foel, Esclusham (D). In the business were *Hugh Davies* (†1702), his
eldest son *Robert Davies* (1675–1748) and third son *John Davies*
(1682–1755). A fourth son, Thomas, was apprenticed to Robert,
but it is not known if he became active as a smith. Their work
has frequently been referred to as that of 'the Davies brothers',
but this is misleading; Robert was responsible for the most
brilliant work, the technical mastery of which has never been
questioned, though designs of gates have, perhaps unfairly, been
criticized on aesthetic grounds. The most celebrated Davies
achievement is the set of gates at Chirk Castle (D), commissioned in 1712 and enlarged and resited as a forecourt screen in
1718–20; it was again resited 1770 as a result of landscaping in
the park and set up on the present site at the entrance to the
park in 1888. The three-dimensional openwork piers and their
enrichment are partly of cast (rather than wrought) iron. The
whole is elaborately decorated with scrollwork, naturalistic foliage, and other motifs.

Little work by Davies is reliably documented, and attributions have been made on the evidence of decorative devices.
The magnificent gates of *c*.1726 at Leeswood Hall, Leeswood
(F), are convincingly attributed to *Robert Davies*, though the
name of *Robert Bakewell* has also been suggested for them. The
Black Gates originally sited at the forecourt of the house consist
of overthrow, side screens, and two-dimensional openwork piers
with decorative devices, including scrollwork, tassels and diamond patterns. The piers of the White Gates are three-dimensional but have similar devices, and their truly spectacular expanse is the finest of all the Clwyd ironwork. The lodges which
accompanied them have been moved to the Black Gates, but
there remain massive stone piers. Gates with overthrow and an
unusual concentration of scrollwork, attributed to *Robert Davies*, were in 1908 transferred from Stansty Park, Gwersyllt (D),
to the East or Forest Lodge at Erddig (D). In the course of the
1970s restoration at Erddig they were moved by the National
Trust to their present site, where they splendidly close the vista
at the end of the canal E of the house.

Churchyard gates documented as being by *Robert Davies* are
at Ruthin and Wrexham (both D), respectively of 1727 and 1720;
both incorporate overthrows, two-dimensional iron piers, and
much scrollwork. Also at Wrexham is a chancel screen with

gates, scrollwork, foliage and other naturalistic motifs; this has been attributed to *Hugh Davies*, though it is more probable that *Robert Davies* was responsible, especially if, as is likely, the work was done in 1707 or later. Robert Davies probably made the screenwork and gates for the N aisle of the chancel at Mold (F) *c.*1726; a matching set in the S aisle of the chancel was made by *Thomas Cheswise* in 1732. These are no longer *in situ*, but parts have been used elsewhere in Mold and at Gwysaney, and also at the churches at Cilcain and Gwernaffield (both F).

Richard Trubshaw was also connected with two of the C18 CHURCHES which need to be mentioned here. The church at Bangor Is-coed (F) was extensively altered by him in 1726–7, and the tower is to his design; with round-headed bell openings and urns as finials, it is typical of its period. Worthenbury (F) 77 church of 1736–9 by him is also typical of its period stylistically, as well as being the best and most complete Georgian church in Wales. The building is of brick with stone dressings, which include pilaster strips and urn finials to the tower, balustrading, and keystones; openings are round-headed and there are also circular windows. The church is less typical of its time in terms of plan and liturgical arrangement, having a deep apsidal chancel, with internally a coved ceiling, pilasters and decorative plasterwork. There is a set of box pews, even though not arranged to an auditory plan, and two of those in the chancel have fireplaces. However, the pews may be contemporary with the W gallery, which dates only from 1830.

Berse Drelincourt Church, Broughton (D), was built in 1742 as a chapel for a nearby charity school; it has been altered and enlarged and has suffered the fate of so many C18 churches in having had mullions inserted into round-headed windows, but its plaster ceiling with central tunnel-vault remains. The plan was no doubt originally of auditory type. Still with early or mid-C18 stylistic affinities is the parish church at Holywell (F) as rebuilt in 1769–70, but retaining medieval fragments in the tower. Galleries are carried on piers above which rises an order of Doric columns; this two-storey arrangement is expressed in the elevations, which have round-headed windows at upper level, while the lower storey has segmental windows and an aedicular S doorway. To mention the church at Marchwiel (D) is to anticipate later C18 stylistic development, for as rebuilt in 1778 it is of clean and precisely detailed ashlar of a Wyattish neo-classical nature, with pedimented E end. Indeed the tower, added in 1789, its W doorway with large consoles and with round-headed bell openings, balustrading and urn finials, is by *James Wyatt* himself. Doubtless the plan was originally an auditory rectangle, but a chancel with polygonal apse was later added.

More impressive, however, than the Stuart and Georgian churches of Clwyd are STUART AND GEORGIAN CHURCH MONUMENTS, for many sculptors of national repute are represented by works of fine quality. The roll-call may start with the celebrated *Grinling Gibbons*, whose monument to Charlotte

82-3 Mostyn † 1694 at Nannerch (F) was probably executed by his own hand. It is a composition of sarcophagus and flaming urn with such typical Baroque enrichments as gadrooning, heraldry and cherubs; cherub heads are among details in recognizable Gibbons style. Another C17 master, *John Bushnell*, has two monuments at Chirk (D), both of 1676: Sir Thomas and Lady Myddelton depicted in busts and Elizabeth Myddelton reclining. Both have the Baroque enrichments seen at Nannerch as well as draped awnings, but the quality of arrested movement associated with this sculpture is absent. By either *Edward Stanton* or *William Stanton* is the Bold tablet at Wrexham (D), with Corinthian surround and commemoration dates of 1703 and 1705.

In the early C18 Denbighshire had its own statuary, *Robert Wynne* (*c.* 1655–1731) of Ruthin, though on the strength of his Henry Wynn monument of 1719 at Ruabon (D), he cannot be rated highly. Its three life-size figures are stiff and awkward, and the proportions of a Corinthian surround with arched canopy are no happier. A very different proposition is the monument
81 at Llanrhaeadr-yng-Nghinmeirch (D) to Maurice Jones † 1702, attributable to Wynne. Far more exuberant and confident than the Ruabon work, this too has a curving canopy, Corinthian columns and Baroque enrichments. Above a reclining effigy are simulated curtains. Another good and sumptuous piece which may be by Wynne commemorates Roger Mostyn † 1712 at Ruthin (D); and a Myddelton monument by him of *c.*1718–22
85 at Chirk (D) has three effigies and is also of high quality. Wrexham (D) boasts two works by *Roubiliac*. He dramatically repre-
84 sented movement in his striking Mary Myddelton monument of 1751–2, the falling pyramid subject of which was repeated with his later Hargrave monument in Westminster Abbey. The same artist's Rev. and Mrs Thomas Myddelton monument at Wrexham (later commemoration date 1756) has portrait medallions serene in comparison. Transition from Baroque to rococo in sculpture is exemplified by *Sir Henry Cheere* and his figure of Robert Davies † 1728 in its aedicular setting at Mold (F). To complete the list of great names, *Rysbrack* has a large and grandiose work at Ruabon (D), 1751–4, commemorating Sir Watkin William Wynn, third Baronet.

Neo-Classicism appears at Ruabon (D) with an elegant Adamish tablet to William Watkin W. Wynn † 1763. So closely do the style and detail resemble those of *Robert Adam*, who received patronage from the Wynns, that it may perhaps be to his design. Also at Ruabon and neo-classical, and with superbly refined detail, is a life-size figure of Hope (1773) by *Nollekens*, commemorating Lady Henrietta Williams Wynn. At Gresford (D) are two good early works of *Sir Richard Westmacott*, working
86 under strict Greek Revival influence. His John Parry † 1797 has a small mourner at the foot of a pedestal; the monument to the
87 Rev. Henry Newcome † 1803 has a disproportionately small standing figure. Also at Gresford and of more purely Grecian design (especially in its pedestal) is *Chantrey*'s William Egerton

†1827. By *Westmacott*, 1805, with emblems of mortality, is the Philip Yorke monument at Marchwiel (D). Late work by *West-* 88 *macott* more notable for sentimentality than for classicism is the Williams monument in St Asaph Cathedral (F); its later commemoration date is 1835, and it is one of the versions of the sculptor's symmetrical design of embracing angels. His Pennant monuments at Whitford (F) include one which, despite overheavy symbolism, is a worthy memorial to the scholarly Thomas Pennant †1798.

More C19 neo-classical examples occur within the output of the Liverpool firm of *S. & F. Franceys* and their partner *William Spence*. A C19 innovation is the polychromy achieved with the different marbles used by *A. W. Edwards* for the tablet to Susan Price †1813 at Overton (F). The Jones monument of 1779 at Gresford (D) is similar in effect.

Architecture had first been purified of Baroque excesses by a renewed inspiration from antiquity promoted by the PALLA-DIANS led by Campbell, Burlington and Kent. In Clwyd this movement produced no major examples but rested in the hands of local architects, in particular the Turners of Whitchurch. Broadlane Hall, Hawarden (F), of 1750–7, was probably by *Samuel Turner*, perhaps in conjunction with his nephew *Joseph Turner* (c.1729–1807). Of brick and stone, it was thoroughly Palladian in its conception, having a central block of seven bays and three storeys, with a three-bay pediment. Side pavilions were designed but never built. Later remodelled as Hawarden Castle, the house still retains fine interiors, which in their way represent mid-C18 taste equally well, with rococo plasterwork 70 executed by *Oliver* and enriched doorcases carved by *Phillips*. Other buildings by *Joseph Turner*, all in a competent late Georgian Palladian tradition, are the County Gaol (1775) and County Hall (1785–90) at Ruthin (D), and the County Gaol at Flint (1784–5), demolished in 1969. The heightening of the centre block of the early C18 Garthewin, Llanfair Talhaearn (D), with a three-bay pediment, 1767–72, is attributed to him. Another thoroughly Palladian composition was Pengwern, Rhuddlan (F), of two and a half storeys and five bays, with a three-bay pediment and two side pavilions, both with cupolas. One pavilion is dated 1770, but the remainder of the house is likely to have been later, possibly 1778; it survives now only in fragmentary form following a fire in 1864.

The main block at Pengwern was significantly lighter and more delicate than the earlier pavilions both in general character and in detail; upper storeys of the three middle bays had a giant order of Ionic pilasters, the slenderness of which suggested the elegant late C18 NEO-CLASSICISM introduced by *Robert Adam*. The county has no buildings by Adam himself, though he designed an unexecuted scheme for the rebuilding of Llanrhaeadr Hall, Llanrhaeadr-yng-Nghinmeirch (D); his grandiose design for rebuilding Wynnstay (D) was similarly never carried out. The Adam vocabulary of ornament is to be seen, somewhat Gothicized, in the font which he designed for Ruabon church 78

(D), 1772, and also by him is an organ case at Wynnstay (D), designed in 1775 for the Williams-Wynn London house in St James's Square.

The neo-classicism of *James Wyatt* was practised in rivalry to that promoted by Adam. His first commission in Clwyd seems to have been designs in the 1770s for alterations at Erddig (D). The resultant work, refacing the W front in ashlar and refitting interiors, is unremarkable. The Wyatt manner was marked by smooth and crisply detailed ashlar and by minimal use of window surrounds and other mouldings; a frequently appearing element was a curved bow carrying a dome above cornice level. All these features were present at Gresford Lodge, Gresford (D), a superbly elegant villa of *c.*1790 designed either by *James Wyatt* or by *Sir Jeffry Wyatville*, now demolished. 72 Plas yr Esgob (the former Bishop's Palace) at St Asaph (F) has similar features and has been attributed to *Samuel Wyatt*, who seems to have made a speciality of domed central bows. Gresford Lodge had a Doric order which in its austerity anticipated Greek Revivalism.

Among architects producing scholarly Neo-Grec in the region the greatest was *Thomas Harrison* of Chester, who was probably responsible for Glan-yr-Afon, Llanferres (D), *c.*1810, a Regency-style villa with unfluted Doric porch. Harrison's major neo-classical mansion in the county, Gredington, Hanmer (F), 1808–11, has been demolished. Also by him was the dramatic Jubilee Tower, *c.*1810–12, built to commemorate George III's fifty years on the throne, and sited on the summit of Moel Fama, the highest point of the Clwydian range and on the boundary of Denbighshire and Flintshire. *Joseph Turner* must be credited with an exceptionally early neo-classical piece, his smooth and crisp New Hall Lodge at Chirk Castle (D), 1770, consisting of a pair of aedicular pavilions with unfluted Greek Doric order; moreover his remodelling of the state rooms at 71 Chirk, 1766–73 and 1777–8, was in a Wyatt rather than a Palladian style, with mahogany doors, neat and simple doorcases, and marble chimneypieces.

Bettisfield Park, Bettisfield (F), has an extension of unknown authorship and unknown date, but probably of the 1820s; semicircular bows carry domes, and the fine interiors display Wyatt influence combined with correct and scholarly Greek Revivalism. Excellent plasterwork includes a ceiling with scallop patterns – one of the Adam features which were paraphrased by James and Samuel Wyatt. A noteworthy alteration to Erddig 73 (D) was the formation of a new dining room in serious classical style, with coffered ceiling and Doric screens, by *Thomas Hopper*, 1826–7. Classical interiors more remarkable for their heaviness than for the correct use of the Greek elements which they incorporate were formed at Brynkinalt (D) as part of alterations and remodelling *c.*1808–12, which may have been by Charlotte, *Lady Dungannon*.

The most beautiful Late Georgian house in the county is 74 Brynbella, Tremeirchion (F), of 1792–5, by *C. Mead* for Dr

Johnson's friend Mrs Thrale and her second husband, *Gabriel Piozzi*, who may have influenced the designs. Complemented by stables and entrance lodges, the whole is endowed with elegance and grace, but is difficult to categorize stylistically; the interiors, with fine fittings and plasterwork, display neither Adam nor Wyatt influence, but rather a degree of originality in their detail and decoration, as well as overall high quality of design and craftsmanship. Another fine Late Georgian villa is Coed Coch (now Heronwater School), Betws-yn-Rhos (D), of 1804, possibly by *Henry Hakewill*; this too is of considerable originality, but in terms of plan rather than of detail and decoration. Initially, and most unusually, the entrance was through a pedimented Greek Doric portico placed diagonally across the outer corner of the block, and with the main axis of the plan running diagonally through the house. The rooms and corridors are grouped round a top-lit circular staircase well which is em- 69 bellished with columns, and in which the staircase itself is not circular but branching, with its straight first flight on the diagonal axis. Sadly, the portico has been done away with, the canted corner filled in, and the internal arrangement extensively altered. Of Wyatt-like country houses the grandest is Glan-y-Wern, Llandyrnog (D), *c.*1813–14; this too is of ashlar and consists of a large main block, now minus its service wing, planned round a top-lit staircase hall. The stone staircase has iron balustrading. The main rooms have the usual mahogany doors, marble chimneypieces and plaster cornices, combined with Greek Revivalism, which here takes the form of an Ionic screen in the entrance hall. Arguably the greatest of all British neoclassical architects was *C. R. Cockerell*, by reason of his inventiveness, combined with deep scholarly learning; and the excellent Newbridge Lodge, Wynnstay (D), of 1827–8, bears ample 76 testimony to his genius and the essentially Mannerist nature of his inspiration.

Finally there is a group of early C19 houses, humbler in status, but nevertheless marked by dignity and classical discipline. All are of clear crisp ashlar, except for the brick-built farmhouse of Croes Yokin at Holt (D). Its three-bay front has double-storey arched recesses, a lunette window within a pediment, and seems to show the influence of Sir John Soane. Higher Berse, Broughton (D), is another three-bay farmhouse; it has a single central arched recess, and the doorcase is pedimented. Priddbwll Ganol, Llansilin (D), is unusually competent vernacular classicism. The vicarage at Llanrhaeadr-yng-Nghinmeirch (D), built in 1820, was excellently restored in 1960–1; it has a three-bay front, central chimney and a typically Regency low-pitched hipped roof, though the side elevations are asymmetrical, both having an off-centre pediment-like gable. Being a parsonage it partakes of the character of a gentleman's residence and has a good curving staircase and a cupola on the stable. The tendencies inherent in this vicarage reached their logical conclusion in the one at Cwm (F), built in 1847. It too has low-pitched pediment-like gables but at right angles to each other; a picturesque feature is made of their intersecting axes, and as the building has an arched entrance and chimneystacks pierced by miniature arches, it is an example of an Early Victorian Italianate villa as popularized by the designs and pattern books of J. C. Loudon.

The picturesque movement as the distinctive British contribution to romanticism had its origin in LANDSCAPE GARDENING. The formal layouts against which this was a reaction were unusually well represented in Clwyd. Most famous was the immense set of multi-level terraces and parterres formed in the 1660s at Llannerch Hall, Trefnant (D), which, like the others of its kind, succumbed to C18 fashion for naturalistic parkland. Hence the rarity and interest of what survives at Erddig (D), where the house built *c*.1687 was accompanied by a formal parterre on the E; this, like the building itself, was enlarged in 1718 or later, and has recently been restored and replanted as part of the National Trust's renovations. The late C17 or early C18 terraced garden at Llangedwyn Hall, Llangedwyn (D), survives only in fragmentary form.

Stephen Switzer, though not widely remembered, was of significant influence in the early development of landscape gardening. He was employed in 1739 at Rhual, Mold (F), and is believed to have laid out the grounds of Leeswood Hall, Leeswood (F), which was built *c*.1724–6; groves, glades and yew walks are comprised in his informal planting; a large motte-like mound forms part of the scheme, which is related to the White Gates and the vista between them and the house. Mid-C18 landscape gardening, which provided the classic setting for Palladian mansions, was dominated by *Capability Brown*. He laid out pleasure grounds at Wynnstay (D), *c*.1777, though no planting can be recognized as his; at about the same time, strangely enough, and contrary to the usual pattern, a formal avenue was made. Who it was who planned this is unknown, but after Brown's death in 1783 landscaping was continued at Wynnstay till 1785 by *John Evans*. Several jobs in the county were done by the little-known *William Emes*; in the 1770s he laid out the grounds of the rectory (now Old Rectory) at Hawarden (F); a scheme which he prepared, 1771, for landscaping at Llanrhaeadr Hall, Llanrhaeadr-yng-Nghinmeirch (D), may not have been fully carried out, but he was responsible for the fine park at Chirk Castle (D), working there from 1764 till at least 1775, and the C18 transformation at Erddig was by him (1768–9).

Landscape gardening and romanticism lead on to GARDEN BUILDINGS AND FOLLIES. *Switzer*'s scheme at Leeswood (F) incorporated an Ionic column carrying a sundial, as well as, on top of the mound, a set of monumental stone seats and a table. The park at Wynnstay (D) is a happy hunting ground for garden buildings. A Doric column commemorates Sir Watkin Williams-Wynn, fourth Baronet, †1789; *James Wyatt* gave it Roman base and capital but Greek Doric fluting. More classically correct in its Palladianism is the bathhouse, existing by

1784 and possibly by *Harrison*,* with Roman Doric portico flanked by niches and with a bath-tank in front. By *Capability Brown* is a model dairy, 1782–3, in the form of a Doric temple, 75 and originally with *Wedgwood* tiles internally. Also Doric and temple-like, but with unfluted Greek order, is Park Eyton Lodge; *Cockerell*'s fine Newbridge Lodge has already been mentioned. The main entrance to the park was by the Ruabon Gateway, an arch of *c.*1783, where a cottage belonging to a set of Early Victorian estate houses in Ruabon itself served as a lodge. Of the Wynnstay buildings the nearest to a true folly was *Wyatville*'s Nant-y-Belan Tower, existing by 1812. Derived from the Tomb of Caecilia Metella at Rome, it is a memorial to members of a regiment raised by Sir Watkin Williams-Wynn, fifth Baronet. Also to be considered as a folly is the castellated Waterloo Tower commemorating the battle.

A castellated tower being a true folly, in fulfilling no function other than serving as an ornament in the park, was built in 1810 in the Pennant domain at Downing, Whitford (F). On a hilltop site, and doubtless intended for ornament and as a landscape feature, is the circular and crenellated Trevor Tower, Trevor (D), dated 1827. At Brynkinalt (D) the River Ceiriog is spanned by a castellated bridge, next to which is a rustically picturesque cottage built of tree trunks and river stones; these may be part of the embellishment of the grounds *c.*1808–14, for which Charlotte, *Lady Dungannon*, is recorded as having been responsible. Her work at Brynkinalt may have included a now demolished china room and dairy built in 1813–14, as well as a castellated entrance lodge of the same date. By way of a postscript to this paragraph one may mention the battlemented tower by *John Taylor* of *Chapman Taylor & Partners*, Castell Gyrn, Llanbedr Dyffryn Clwyd (D), intended as a residence from the first and built, anachronistically enough, in 1977 and enlarged in 1982–3.

The landscaping of Brown was of a gentle undulating nature, but the late C18 and early C19 witnessed a fashion for something wilder and more 'horrid'. This phase of ROMANTICISM AND THE PICTURESQUE was affected by the theorizing and controversies of Uvedale Price and Richard Payne Knight, and it was at this period that the landscape of North Wales came to be appreciated, admired, and recorded in prints and engravings for the benefit of travellers and tourists. *Telford*'s Pont Cysyllte, Froncysyllte (D), carrying the Ellesmere Canal across the River Dee, added, as did Dinas Bran, to the natural drama and attraction of the Vale of Llangollen (D); doubtless it was the fame which the vale and town had already acquired that induced *Lady Eleanor Butler* and *Miss Sarah Ponsonby*, after leaving their native Ireland in 1778, to make a sojourn and ultimately settle there, and to build up their reputation as the Ladies of Llangollen. In 1780 they took up residence at Plas Newydd, which in their lifetime remained of whitewashed stone and of cottage scale with fields immediately in front, and this despite

* Mrs Ockrim considers he may have refaced it.

a transformation of both house and grounds, carried out in an exceedingly romantic spirit, over a period of some forty years. Windows were Gothicized and a Gothic library was added, but the greatest change of character resulted from the installation in every room of the stained glass and carved oak for the collecting of which the Ladies had a passion; but it was not until after the house had changed hands in 1876 that the external half-timbered treatment was applied. Yet more remarkable than the alterations to the building was the refashioning of the grounds; the garden proper was planted behind the house, and elsewhere there came into being an early instance of the picturesque at its most extreme. The process was helped by the existence of the Glen, a deep wooded dell with a stream, and by c. 1800 its character had been exploited and intensified by cascades, rustic bridges and random planting. The only C18, i.e. original, feature to survive is a Gothic niche enshrining a medieval font.

In similar spirit to the Glen at Plas Newydd is the cottage which Sir Watkin Williams-Wynn, fifth Baronet, built beside the waterfall of Pistyll Rhaeadr, Llanrhaeadr-ym-Mochnant (D), with rubble walling and a portico of tree trunks carrying a pediment faced with bark. It is almost certainly early C19. The celebrated gardens at Bodnant (D) are more notable horticulturally and botanically than for significance in the history of taste, and the house rebuilt c. 1875-6 by *W. J. Green* is unworthy of the magnificent setting they provide. Landscaping of conventional Victorian informality was begun by *Edward Milner*, presumably also in the mid-1870s, but the present character is due to the hanging gardens, which, in the form of five planted terraces, were planned by H. D. McLaren, second *Lord Aberconway*, 1905-14.

With Plas Newydd and castellated follies some aspects of the EARLY GOTHIC REVIVAL have been touched upon. There are few examples of the thin and papery Strawberry Hill variety, but to this category belongs the early C19 Siambr Wen, Llangollen (D), with battlemented parapet, corner turrets, and Gothic windows. Similar in flavour and dated 1828 is the frontage of Pentref Welsh Methodist Chapel, Mold (F). The most notable piece of C18 Gothic is the W tower of Mold church; it does great credit to *Joseph Turner*, who rebuilt it in 1768-73. Some of the detail is starved and incorrect, but ornament was copied from the body of the church, and the form and proportions are such that, at a distance, it can readily be mistaken for true Perp work of the border country.

If John Nash's Blaise Hamlet is a Regency *cottage orné* pattern book come to life, the same is to an even greater extent true of Marford (F), a charming Trevalyn estate village whose buildings unite Gothic and the picturesque. Several materials are used, and at least some of the cottages were originally thatched; Marford elements include ogee, cruciform and slit windows, cast-iron window frames, Gothic glazing patterns, brick dentil courses and gentle curves on both plan and elevation. The features mark not only housing in the village itself and the village inn and its stables, but also cottages and farms elsewhere in the neighbourhood. The more attractive and sophisticated combine bulging curves and symmetry of elevation, as in Yew Tree Cottage. Buildings outside the village include the delect- 90 able Ivy Cottage, Rossett (D). Sophistication and a measure of symmetry may be discerned in the layout and in the relationship of buildings one to another, and as a classic case of early C19 aquatints translated into reality, Marford is almost too good to be true. Disappointingly little is known about this fascinating place, but it seems likely that much building was done c.1813–15, but work may have started as early as 1803. The architect is unknown, but *John Boydell*, agent to the Trevalyn estate, may have had a hand in the design.

Manning's Green at Iscoyd Park, Iscoed (F), is a semi-detached but asymmetrical pair of estate cottages, mid-C19 in date; in contrast to the lightness and delicacy of Marford it is of predominantly Tudor style, with a diversity of materials and a heaviness reminiscent of Blaise Hamlet, and, like the most famous of the cottages there, it has elaborately decorated brick chimneys. Iscoed church was rebuilt in brick in 1830, replacing a timber-framed structure, and is of rustic simplicity, with Y-tracery betraying the early date. The church at Llanddoged (D), as remodelled in 1838–9 by the *Rev. Thomas Davies* and the *Rev. David Owen*, with *cottage orné* features, also belongs to the early Gothic Revival. Inside, they provided a three-decker pulpit against the side wall with box pews focused on it. Though there are no Commandment boards the church has interesting paintings with Welsh inscriptions. It is an entertainingly naïve pre-Camdenian ensemble.

SHAM CASTLES were another product of early C19 Romanticism. Bodelwyddan Castle, Bodelwyddan (F), was remodelled by *Hansom & Welch* c.1830–42, incorporating portions of an earlier C19 classical remodelling; there is a crenellated chimney-piece and, in the same room, plaster vaulting typical of early C19 Gothic. Externally the transformation into a castellated and irregularly massed mansion was carried out on a lavish scale. A more noteworthy remodelling of a classical house was that of Turner's Broadlane Hall, Hawarden (F), by *Thomas Cundy* in 1809–10; on the strength of the new turrets, castellations and generally asymmetrical elevations the romantically-minded Sir Stephen Richard Glynne renamed his house Hawarden Castle. 89 At the same time some classical rooms were designed by Cundy, Wyatt-like in style, especially the new library and remodelled dining room, both with screens of Ionic columns.

As residences in the form of sham castles both Bodelwyddan and Hawarden are outshone by Gwrych Castle (D), one of the most astonishing of its kind anywhere; but consisting as it does largely of screen walls and fake towers against the hillside, it must be regarded more as a vast and magnificent folly or piece of scenery. Though hitherto ascribed to 1814 and to *C.A. Busby*, it is now known that the owner, *Lloyd Bamford Hesketh*, acted largely as his own architect, at the same time availing himself of professional assistance and advice. Construction began in 1819 and may have continued into the 1850s. Contributions were made by *Thomas Rickman*, who designed Gothic detail and traceried cast-iron windows (the latter mass-produced by *John Cragg* of the Mersey Iron Foundry). Others involved were *Henry Kennedy*, who enlarged the castle in 1845-6 and 1852, and *C. E. Elcock*, who made alterations and enlargements in 1914. Internally the outstanding feature is a huge marble staircase; its date and authorship are unknown.

The years following the Napoleonic Wars saw public funds made available for building churches, mostly in the densely populated industrial areas of northern England. The motivation was not entirely altruistic or disinterested; the aim was to keep the urban masses tranquil by means of religion. Economy of construction was a prime consideration on the part of the Parliamentary Commissioners, who were appointed in 1818 and administered the two successive grants made in 1819 and 1825. 'Commissioners' Gothic' is synonymous with thin, meagrely detailed work, conjuring a vision of a pre-archaeological, i.e. historically incorrect, church, with lancets, a w tower, and of auditory plan, originally with galleries (which frequently were removed in a later reordering). Possibly also there might be transepts, but no aisles. Wales has few COMMISSIONERS' CHURCHES, and the only one which received aid from the First Parliamentary Grant is that at Buckley (F) by *John Oates*, 1821-2 (later remodelled). Also in receipt of a Commissioners' grant were Bagillt (F), 1837-9 by *John Welch*, Bistre at Buckley (F), 1841-2 by *John Lloyd*, and Gwersyllt (D), by the younger *Thomas Penson*, built in 1850-1. Though with lancets, its architecture is more solid and serious, as one would expect at this later date. On the other hand there are churches which by reason of their thinness and ineptitude could readily be mistaken for the products of the Parliamentary Grants. This applies particularly to others by *John Welch* – Ysgeifiog (F), 1836-7, though this may be by *Edward Welch*; Llansanffraid Glan Conwy, 1839, Betws-yn-Rhos, 1838-9 (both D) – and also one by *Edward Welch*, Rhosymedre at Cefn Mawr (D), 1836-7. The nadir of Flintshire architecture was reached in the work of *John Lloyd*, many of whose churches were not only awkward in appearance and ignorant in design and detail, but faulty in construction. In addition to Bistre, those remaining include Connah's Quay, 1836-7, and Pontblyddyn, 1836, both of which have been enlarged and altered. Lancet in style and thin is Pentrobin church (F) by *John Buckler*, 1843; it is redeemed by some rich and solid features, since it was built at the expense of Sir Stephen Glynne of Hawarden Castle, and there are fittings and decorations carried out by the *Rev. J. E. Troughton*, curate-in-charge.

'Middle Pointed' or C14 Decorated being the style of the Gothic Revival's orthodox development, the potential of Perpendicular for C19 requirements was little exploited. Exceptions to this rule can be found in the work of local architects; *Thomas*

Jones of Chester (*c.*1794–1859) indeed specialized in Perp for ecclesiastical buildings. His detail is neat, crisp, and knowledgeable, and it is significant that Sir Nikolaus Pevsner, while unfamiliar with his work in general, referred to his church at Pensax, Worcestershire, 1832–3, as 'an amazing job ... the degree of exactitude in the Perp detailing is far beyond what one would expect from anyone in 1832 except Rickman'. Perp ecclesiastical works by Jones include Holy Trinity, Rhyl (F), 1835 (later enlarged); a mausoleum in the churchyard at St George (D), 1836; and alterations to the churches at Llanferres (D), 1843, and (both F) Nercwys, 1847, and Northop, 1839–40. In 1832 he designed furnishings for St Asaph Cathedral (F).

As a domestic architect Jones favoured the secular form of Perp, i.e. NEO-TUDOR, with battlementing, four-centred arches, labels, cusping and rich ornament. He favoured symmetry of more than one elevation, though he never attempted to draw upon historical precedent in planning. Talacre, now Talacre Abbey (F), built in 1824–9, is Jones's best remaining house and is fully typical of his work; the stable court, consistently Tudor in style, and with a cupola, is especially attractive. His best domestic work, now demolished, was the mansion of Oteley, *c.*1829–30, near Ellesmere, Shropshire. Ashlar was used for both Talacre and Oteley, but some houses were stuccoed with mullions and transoms of timber, as at Llwynegryn, 1830, now part of the County Civic Centre at Mold (F), the Deanery (now Old Deanery) and Bryn Asaph, both probably *c.*1830 and both at St Asaph (F). Built 1843–4 and also Tudor in style, but lacking the cupola which Jones designed for it, is the County Hall (now Old County Hall) at Mold. Gresford Vicarage (D), built in 1850, was designed by Jones in collaboration with his nephew *Edward Hodkinson*, and with some characteristically Victorian features is a departure from his usual style. He must be credited with tactful alterations to the Elizabethan Trevalyn Hall, Trefalun (D), 1836–8, and the Jacobean Pentrehobyn, Mold (F). Comparable with Jones's stuccoed Tudor is the frontage of Garthmeilio, Llangwm (D), with heavy finials and ornamented bargeboards all of timber; this refacing looks *c.*1830–40 but is probably earlier. Of 1852 Pentre Celyn Hall, Pentre Celyn, at Llanfair Dyffryn Clwyd (D) is later in date but earlier in style. With labels, but still symmetrical and with vertically proportioned sash windows, it illustrates transition from Late Georgian classicism to Neo-Tudor. Halkyn Castle (F) by *John Buckler*, 1824–*c.*1827 for the second Earl Grosvenor, was designed with symmetrical elevations, classical in conception, and with a high concentration of Jonesian Tudor Gothic ornament; but as executed the details and decoration were greatly simplified and the symmetry destroyed by the introduction of a turreted polygonal tower and the incorporation of the stables into the main composition. Unusually pleasing are the diminutively scaled single-storeyed ashlar and Tudor Gothic almshouses of 1848 at Overton (F).

Though *John Buckler* and his son J. C. Buckler are best-remembered as antiquarian and topographical draughtsmen, the former as an architect was also responsible for Pool Park (D), built in 1826–9, an unusual essay in Neo-Tudor, being an early instance of half-timber revivalism. Stone was used for dressings and for the ground storey; the first floor was given densely patterned black-and-white facing, since obliterated. The plan is strictly, almost forcedly, axial and symmetrical, with E-plan front, elaborate branching staircase, and the service rooms all fitted into the one main block. Tudor Gothic lacking the refinement found in Thomas Jones's work and the Overton almshouses is the style of Flint Town Hall by *John Welch*, 1840, with his original design simplified in execution.

NEO-ELIZABETHAN can be considered as an aspect of Neo-Tudor. The domestic work of *Edward Blore* belongs to this category; by him is an addition made in 1830–1 to the former Bishop's Palace (Plas yr Esgob) at St Asaph (F). Unusually enough for an Elizabethan-style country house, Plas Newydd, Trefnant (D), as rebuilt in 1840–1, is totally asymmetrical. It is believed that the owner, *E. H. Griffith*, acted as his own architect. Small and simple Elizabethan, and picturesquely lacking in complete symmetry, is the former parsonage at Pentrobin church (F). Built in 1846, it may, like the church itself, be by *Buckler*. Tudor Gothic work, both external and internal, at Pentre Mawr, Abergele (D), is likely to be of *c.* 1830. Llantysilio Hall, Llandysilio (D), as rebuilt in 1872–4 by *S. Pountney Smith* of Shrewsbury, is notable as a classic and little-altered example of mid-Victorian country-house planning. Symmetry is deliberately disrupted by a tower; the elevations, which are of the highest quality ashlar, suffer from absence of modelling and lack much of the carved enrichment which was originally intended, just as internally the fittings and decoration are less elaborate than initially designed.

On account of its greater potential for ornament and enrichment, NEO-JACOBEAN had a greater attraction for the Victorians than did Elizabethan, though both styles were frequently drawn upon for use in the same building, resulting in a hybrid which may conveniently be called Jacobethan. In Neo-Jacobean a distinctive contribution was again made by a local architect, this time the younger Thomas Penson. The elder *Thomas Penson* (*c.* 1760–1824) was founder of a prolific dynasty of architects; he practised in Wrexham and held the post of County Surveyor of Flintshire. His son, *Thomas Penson* the younger (1790–1859), studied under Thomas Harrison; he practised in Wrexham and Oswestry, and was County Surveyor of Denbighshire and Montgomeryshire. He evolved his own version of Jacobean, characterized by fancifully shaped gables, pedimented windows and the use of ashlar. In this style he was responsible for the Butchers' Market, 1848, and former British School, 1844, 105 both at Wrexham; the remodelling of Llanrhaeadr Hall, Llanrhaeadr-yng-Nghinmeirch, 1841–2; and the remodelling of his own house, Gwersyllt Hill, Gwersyllt, 1841 (all D). Of his two sons, the elder, *Richard Kyrke Penson* (1815–86), worked in

Wales and later in Oswestry, and also held county surveyor-ships; he was an exponent of serious and competent Gothic. The younger son, *Thomas Mainwaring Penson* (1817–64), became one of the leading architects in Chester, where he was instru-mental in launching the half-timber revival. The North Wales Mental Hospital, Denbigh, 1842–8, by *Fulljames & Waller* 110 of Gloucester, an enormous building of ashlar in monumental Jacobethan style, illustrates the demands which new building types made in the C19 upon historically-minded architects.

The Gummows, numbering architects, builders and sur-veyors, were, like the Penson dynasty, Wrexham-based; *Benja-min Gummow* (†1844), known for work at Eaton Hall, Cheshire, seems to have been in regular employment on the Wynnstay (D) estate; his nephew, *Michael Gummow* (1802–76), was Wrex-ham's first Borough Surveyor and was father of *James Reynolds Gummow* (fl. 1857–74), who illustrated villas he had himself de-signed in his *Hints on House Building*, 1874. *Michael John Gum-mow*, his son, was articled to William Turner of Wrexham.

To complete the account of early Victorian domestic work there is one rather different scheme to mention. This is the restoration and interior decoration carried out by *A. W. N. Pugin* at Chirk Castle (D) in 1845–8. Here, as at his *chef d'œuvre* in this idiom, the interiors of the Palace of Westminster, Pugin used his favourite team of craftsmen and executants – the builder *George Myers*, the decorator and furniture-maker *John Gregory Crace*, *Herbert Minton*, who made encaustic tiles, and *John Hardman*, who supplied metalwork and stained glass and whose firm became *Hardman & Co*. Unlike his other compar-able jobs, Chirk involved the treatment of existing classical in-teriors, and the new colour scheme which he and Crace de-signed for the ceiling of Turner's saloon may still be seen. Even though much by Pugin has been done away with in the C20, there also remains the Cromwell Hall as remodelled by him, but 106 in a style more heavy and massive than his usual Houses of Parliament manner.

The name of Pugin fittingly introduces VICTORIAN CHURCHES. By his attacks in books and pamphlets against the meanness, both spiritual and architectural, epitomized by Com-missioners' Gothic, and by the examples he gave in his own churches and their fittings of a Gothic style revitalized by a deep understanding of medieval constructional methods and forms of enrichment, Pugin inspired a new generation of archi-tects and patrons, and not only among his Roman Catholic co-religionists. Comparatively little of Pugin's industry was directed to Clwyd, but he designed fittings and furnishings for the church of the Franciscan Friary at Pantasaph (F), including a rood screen, pulpit, baptistry screen, font and statues. These were made in 1850–1 and were shown in the Medieval Court at the Great Exhibition. In common with all too many of Pugin's church furnishings, those at Pantasaph have not been properly valued and appreciated by later generations, and little now remains *in situ* and unmutilated.

In the Church of England, the Oxford Movement, which provoked a spiritual revival in the 1840s, was accompanied by the rise of the phenomenally influential Cambridge Camden Society (later Ecclesiological Society), which, through its journal *The Ecclesiologist*, propagated Puginian doctrines and, like Pugin, advocated C14 'Middle-Pointed' as the proper style for emulation and adoption. Indeed Pugin's teachings were more readily received by Anglicans than within the Church of Rome.

Of the architects particularly favoured by the Ecclesiologists, *Butterfield* is represented here only by his rebuilding of the chancel E wall at Northop (F), 1850, with a hard and severe Geometrical E window. *Street*, by contrast, executed several excellent and characteristic works in Clwyd, many of them at the expense of Robert Bamford Hesketh of Gwrych, who employed him to build first the church at Llanddulas (D), 1868–9, then the school at Abergele (D), 1869–70. Street's most important work for Hesketh is the dramatically and subtly arranged par-
94-6 ochial group of church, parsonage and school at Towyn (D), 1871–3. The church at Towyn has Geometrical tracery, cusped lancets and other elements in the style of *c.*1300, and like all this architect's best churches is of great sensitivity, with the massing and the arrangement of the windows marked by studied simplicity and with a deeply reposeful interior. The buildings demarcate three enclosures, and are focused around a prominent saddle-backed central tower. In the masonry skilful use is made of textures and unobtrusive polychromy. Similarly possessing a sense of repose, and profoundly satisfying, is Street's Bettisfield church (F), 1872–4. Again the massing, proportions, surfaces and internal spaces are most successful.

Since Clwyd has so much excellent work by *Street*, it is striking that it should also contain his very last church, a curious and puzzling one. Built in 1881–2 at Ffynnongroyw (F), it is thin, poverty-stricken and chapel-like in external appearance. The hand of the master is nevertheless discernible in the careful relationship of nave and aisles and their massing; and the arcades, with rock-faced masonry and heavily chamfered caps, could be by no one else. Yet what a strange end to the career of a truly great church architect!

The county possesses a further complete parochial group by
91 a great Victorian architect, in the church (1853–5), school (1860) and rectory at Trefnant (D) by *Sir Gilbert Scott*, who, to his puzzlement and distress, failed to find favour with the Ecclesiological Society. The church, another Geometrical specimen, has some effective individual features, but is chiefly notable for its internal stonecarving by *J. Blinstone*, which, with foliated caps all differing, foreshadows Mid-Victorian practice. Being copied direct from nature it is an early instance of the application of Ruskin's doctrines. If Ruskin influenced the ornament and detail of the church, the irregular and informal massing of the rectory, derived from its plan, owes much to Pugin. Scott's church of St Thomas, Rhyl (F), *c.*1860–9, is also Dec and is notable for its spire, furnishings, stalls, reredos, encaustic tiles

and an elaborate and impressive pulpit. Scott included St Asaph among the many cathedrals taken under his wing. In his major operation of 1867–75, he gave back an E.E. appearance to the choir, but he claimed that a more authentic job would have been done had he been permitted to carry out fuller initial investigation. Also by him and on less evidence are the timber vaulting of the nave, the clerestory windows and a timber wagon ceiling in the choir. Good furnishings were also contributed; as well as restoring and rearranging the fine canopied choir stalls, Scott designed desk fronts, choir benches and a canopied bishop's throne. (A third generation of his family was involved at St Asaph, with a restoration by *C. M. Oldrid Scott*, 1929–32.) More modest was *Sir Gilbert Scott*'s parochial restoration, 1873–5, at Diserth (F), which he left Early Dec, with a new w front, a porch, a chancel aisle and a transept. Scott worked also at the church at Hawarden (F), which had been restored by *James Harrison*, *c.* 1855–6, only to be burnt in 1857. Repair by Scott was completed in 1859.

One other leading Victorian church architect, *J. L. Pearson*, erected in the county a typical example of one phase of his work, the church of 1860–3 at Rhydymwyn (F). It is big-boned 93 and boldly scaled and fully Mid-Victorian in its restrained polychromy, while having continental features foreshadowing the French c 13 manner of his late style.

T. H. Wyatt was responsible for all too many heavy and dull Clwyd churches. That at Treuddyn (F), 1874–5, may in addition be described as pretentious, and it is deplorable that to make way for it a small whitewashed double-naved church was demolished. Wyatt also did a church, 1863, at Prestatyn (F) with a clumsy spire. More satisfactory is the Franciscan Friary church at Pantasaph (F), built 1849–52, with *Pugin*'s furnishings of 1850–1 (*see* above). *Wyatt* here handled the Dec vocabulary with greater conviction than elsewhere; a stone spire in the form of a stepped pyramid is effective, and there is interesting and enterprising anticipation of High Victorianism in the handling of a heavy vice turret and in the spiky cusping of bar tracery and roof timbers. Noteworthy also is the fact that a chapel below the tower is vaulted. A further early indication of Mid-Victorian tendencies occurs with a bulging baptistry on the w front of Wyatt's Gorsedd church (F) of 1852–3.

The most celebrated among the Victorian churches of the county is that at Bodelwyddan (F). It is in correct and conventional Dec and has become popular and famous as 'The Marble Church'; but it is more notable for costly ostentation than for architectural quality, though it contains good stained glass. Its architect, *John Gibson*, was more successful in designing classical branches for the National Provincial Bank, of which there is an Italianate one of 1876 in Wrexham (D). A good church of his is that at Bersham (D), 1873; like Bodelwyddan it is an estate 97 church on which no expense was spared, but here money was spent with greater discrimination; it is entirely rib-vaulted. The treatment is High Victorian, with polychromy and foliated stonecarving, but the style is Romanesque, at a later date than would be expected for *Rundbogenstil*. Earlier essays in Romanesque were the younger *Thomas Penson*'s church at Rhosllannerchrugog (D), 1852–3, where the unpromising stylistic material and a pre-archaeological plan form are handled resourcefully, and the effect is not poverty-stricken. Round-arched also, with noteworthy stonecarving and once with polychromy and painted decoration, was the R.C. Church of Our Lady of the Assumption at Rhyl (F) by *Hungerford Pollen*, 1863–4, now demolished.

Among local architects building in Clwyd in the Victorian period, one, John Douglas, deserves a section all to himself (*see* below). That leaves two others whose work qualifies them for mention in this section on Victorian churches. *John Wilkes Poundley* (1807–72) studied under the younger Thomas Penson and in 1861 became County Surveyor of Montgomeryshire. His best buildings were designed in partnership with *David Walker* of Liverpool. Llanbedr Dyffryn Clwyd New Church (D) by *Poundley & Walker*, 1863, has a lively High Victorian exterior of considerable character and distinction, with polygonal apse, spired and crocketed bell turret and polychromatic masonry. Another local Gothic practitioner was *Richard Lloyd Williams* (†1908*), who studied under Thomas Fulljames of Gloucester and J. P. St Aubyn, who had himself been a pupil of Fulljames.‡ R. Lloyd Williams became Denbighshire County Surveyor and was in partnership in Denbigh with *Martin Underwood* (a pupil of St Aubyn) as *Lloyd Williams & Underwood*. A volume of sketches and measured drawings by them was published in 1872 as *The Architectural Antiquities and Village Churches of Denbighshire*. The partnership was dissolved *c*.1874. By *Lloyd Williams & Underwood* is St Mary's, Denbigh, 1871–4. Though with Geometrical tracery and cusped lancets, the church is difficult to describe in conventional stylistic terms; much of its undeniable and consistent character results from flat surfaces, and mouldings contribute little in the way of modelling. Internally there are carved capitals. The architects' average level of attainment was less interesting, the dull but competent Gwytherin (D) of 1867–9 being typical. As late as *c*.1894–5 *Lloyd Williams* was responsible for Holywell Town Hall (F), thoroughly behind the times in being in sculpturesque High Victorian, suggesting that artistically he remained rooted in the 1860s.

At this point it will be convenient to survey VICTORIAN STAINED GLASS. The strong colours and geometrical patterns of the early Victorian period are seen in the chancel windows at Mold (F) of 1857 by *Wailes*. Of the same date is a lively and colourful figure of St Michael at Abergele (D); L. B. Hesketh of Gwrych, who seems to have taken a special interest in glass, was the donor. More ecclesiologically medieval in style is an

---

* Information kindly supplied by his grand-daughter, the Dowager Viscountess Hill.

‡ There must have been some connection with Fulljames's work at Denbigh.

1860 *O'Connor* window at Bodelwyddan (F), and also the glass of *Clayton & Bell*, who were responsible for windows of the 1870s and 80s at Gresford (D), where *Heaton, Butler & Bayne* also worked in the 1870s. By them too is a complete set of windows in Douglas's church of 1877–8 at Halkyn (F). Like the building itself, they belong early within the Arts and Crafts Movement and partake of Late Victorian Aestheticism. Fully belonging to that phase is the 1880s work of *Ward & Hughes* at Bodelwyddan, together with one window there by *T. F. Curtis* of that firm, 1896. Of other late C19 artists, *Kempe* worked at Gresford (D), c. 1895–1905, and *Burlison & Grylls* at Mold (F), 1889. An important work by *Burne-Jones* and *Morris* is at Hawarden (F), where the W window, 1898, is the last stained 101 glass which Burne-Jones ever designed. It admirably displays the mastery and understanding of the medium which he and the Morris firm achieved. Later work by *Morris & Co.* occurs in other windows in the same church.

Pugin believed that Gothic was not just an ecclesiastical style, but that it embodied principles on which the design of buildings of all kinds should be based. Ruskin developed this idea, emphasizing the inherent characteristics of different building materials and the value of craftsmanship. These were the dominant influences on HIGH VICTORIAN SECULAR ARCHITECTURE. In his highly convincing and persuasive *Remarks on Secular and Domestic Architecture* (1857), *Sir Gilbert Scott* provided a rationalization and summary of the theories of Pugin and Ruskin and explained the basis on which he evolved that style of his own which is familiar from St Pancras Station and of which the best and best-known domestic example is Kelham Hall, Nottinghamshire. Second in importance only to Kelham among Scott's houses is Hafodunos, Llangernyw (D), built in 107 1861–6, bold and varied in its massing, C14 Venetian in its stylistic ancestry, and built of brick with touches of polychromy and with foliated carving enriching stone dressing. Typical of Scott also are internal fittings including Puginian doorcases, and an interesting aspect of the house is provided by associations with Liverpool and the sculptor *John Gibson*. As at Kelham, however, planning and arrangement leave something to be desired. This criticism cannot be made of Nantlys, Tremeirchion (F), where, in 1872–5, *T. H. Wyatt* created a clever and convenient layout, skilful in section as well as in plan. Stylistically the house is neither Neo-Elizabethan nor High Victorian Gothic, but contains elements of both, and is of brick and stone. In 1863–5 *Poundley & Walker* showed themselves capable of adapting their lively Gothic style to secular use with the Town Hall at Ruthin (D). An early foreshadowing of the heaviness and sculpturesque quality of High Victorianism occurs at Ruthin Castle, the main block of which has carefully calculated elements of symmetry and large areas of blank wall, Late Perp in inspiration. This part is by *Henry Clutton*, 1848–53, being largely a rebuilding of a castellated house which had in 1826 been erected amid the ruins of the C13 castle.

High Victorianism was not confined to Gothic, and the qualities of massiveness and elaboration and the inspiration from
continental sources could find expression in French Renaissance
style, as at Wynnstay (D), rebuilt by *Benjamin Ferrey*, 1858–
*c.*1865. Wynnstay is not the only instance of non-Gothic Mid-
Victorian display. Classical C17 work at Nantclwyd Hall, Llanelidan (D), was copied when the house was enlarged by *J.K.
Colling*, 1857, and by *David Walker*, 1875–6. The latter addition
was particularly large and elaborate and is now demolished. One
of the most curious instances of High Victorian display is
Soughton Hall, Northop (F), as remodelled in 1867–9. An earlier C19 recasting had oriental overtones and was possibly by
Barry. The later work is attributable to *Douglas*, but is more
florid and forbidding than was usual for him.

LATE VICTORIAN SECULAR ARCHITECTURE had its own
distinctive character, emphasizing qualities of refinement and
sensitivity. It was the era of Aestheticism and of Pre-Raphaelite
influence on decorative art and was a golden age of English
domestic architecture, dominated by Richard Norman Shaw.
He designed houses which were sufficiently aesthetic for artists
and were both impressive and homely enough to suit the wishes
of commercial magnates. Shaw and W. Eden Nesfield, with
whom he shared an office and was for a short time in partnership, developed two domestic styles: 'Old English', taking inspiration from the rural buildings of Kent and Sussex, the
features of which were irregular and varied grouping and the
use of differing materials, with half-timber, pargetting, and
tile-hanging; and secondly 'Queen Anne', with classical
elements, but owing more to the C17 than the early C18; this
too, with its gables, red brick and white-painted woodwork, was
derived from vernacular sources. 'Queen Anne' made its
appearance with *Nesfield*'s Temperate House Lodge at Kew of
1867, but its first major monument was his remodelling of
108 Kinmel Park, St George (D), *c.*1868–74. This produced one
of the grandest and most palatial of Victorian country houses,
owing as much to the Wren of Hampton Court as to vernacular sources; and its steep roofs, harking back to Mid-
Victorian fashion, are French in inspiration. Nesfield introduced
asymmetry into the elevations and retained and exploited
asymmetrical and non-axial features of the plan. The house is
of interest on account of its detailing, which includes fine external stonecarving by *James Forsyth*, as well as decorative use
of the sunflowers, lilies and other potted plants especially
associated with the Aesthetic Movement. Equally associated
with the Movement, and with Nesfield in particular, are
patterned roundels which he termed 'pies' and which, reflecting the fashion for Japanese porcelain, he frequently applied
in random arrangements.

The stables at Kinmel, *c.*1855, provide a grand Mid-Victorian Baroque display and are probably by *Burn*, but *Nesfield* was
responsible for other buildings in the grounds and some estate
109 work. Most notable is his Golden Lodge of 1868 which, square

with truncated pyramid roof and a dormer, recalls his slightly earlier lodge at Kew. It is, however, far more profuse in its decorative features, drawn liberally from the Aesthetic Movement vocabulary. For 'Old English' Nesfield abandoned the brick and tile of the Home Counties, substituting stone and slate, which are so very much more at home in Wales. At the same time half-timber and pargetting continued to be employed, brick being restricted to chimneys. This combination of materials, the ingredients of elevations of sensitive and subtle asymmetry, occurs at Talrych Smithy, c.1865-7, and Morfa Lodge, 1868; but Terfyn Cottages, grouped round their well, are much simpler, their assertive massing providing a reminder of the High Victorian Butterfieldian roots of Old English. Plas Kinmel, built in 1866 as a model dairy and home farm, is exceptionally charming, set within its own garden and conceived as an ornamental structure and place of resort in the grounds of the mansion. In its subtle composition and in many elements it is 'Old English', but it is entirely stone-built, and Gothic and Elizabethan features supplement the Old English vocabulary.

Less famous and influential than Nesfield's work at Kinmel, but no less significant and attractive, are his remodelling and enlargement, c.1872-5, of Bodrhyddan (F). The house seems previously to have been late C17, with parts of a much earlier structure incorporated. Competent replanning led to a more convenient and satisfactory domestic layout, and moving the position of the main entrance provided opportunity for a refacing to produce a symmetrical brick entrance front which is one of the most lively, resourceful and cheerful elevations of the entire Queen Anne Movement. Internally Nesfield's 'Old English' predominates, with mellow woodwork, rich and heavy mouldings and a couple of inglenooks.

The Nesfield restoration of 1876-8 at Llandyrnog (D) is unremarkable structurally, showing all too little respect for the historical integrity of this typical Vale of Clwyd double-nave church. Some windows were faithfully reproduced, but in view of the close association between Morris and Aestheticism it is surprising that the architect perpetrated such enormities as the introduction of other windows and of a bellcote, all to new designs. Also without adequate precedent is a half-timbered porch importing a touch of vernacular revivalism, and detail and ornament throughout are infused with the same engaging spirit as prevails at Kinmel. Pies abound, and especially notable are the furnishings, mostly of 1877; there are sunflower pies in the poppyheads of stalls and a bench has incised Jacobean-style patterns in its panels.

Tile-hanging used in a way which recalls Norman Shaw occurs at Bryn Eithin, Colwyn Bay (D). This remarkable house, built 1889, is an early independent work of *Gerald Horsley*, one of Shaw's most noted pupils.

It is now high time to introduce the most important and active local architect of the period, in the person of the highly talented JOHN DOUGLAS (1830-1911). Born at Sandiway near

Northwich, the son of a builder, he studied under E. G. Paley of Lancaster and practised in Chester from *c*.1860 until his death. He was in partnership as *Douglas & Fordham* from *c*.1884 and as *Douglas & Minshull* from *c*.1897. One of the leading provincial architects of his generation, he received national and a degree of international recognition, and his 500 or so buildings range from Scotland to Surrey, though most are concentrated in Cheshire and North Wales. They are mainly ecclesiastical and domestic; much work was done on the Eaton estate for the first Duke of Westminster. Douglas was influenced by the timber framing of Cheshire and the Welsh border and by the late medieval brick architecture of Germany and the Low Countries, but his buildings are anything but copyist and bear a highly individual and nearly always recognizable stamp. They are marked by sure proportions, picturesque effects of massing and outline, careful detailing, and a superb sense of craftsmanship and feeling for materials. This is particularly true of Douglas's woodwork: a hallmark of his joinery, seen not only in the fittings of houses but in church furnishings, and which expresses their construction, is the use of incised and unmitred grooves and channels, clearly indicating individual framing members. It is a detail derived from Jacobean furniture and C17 vernacular panelling. Douglas made particular contributions on the vernacular and aesthetic fronts, and Chester had its special version of vernacular revivalism in its own half-timber revival. This dates from the mid-1850s with work by *T. M. Penson*, and it received impetus and encouragement from the antiquarian and conservationist concerns of the local historic and archaeological society, alarmed by the continuing destruction and mutilation of ancient timber-framed houses in the unique Rows.

At this early stage of the revival, timberwork retained a hard and Gothic Mid-Victorian spikiness, as at Tyndwr, Llangollen (D), *c*.1866–70, and Glynne Cottage, Hawarden (F), probably also of the 1860s; only later did mellowness, sensitivity and a feeling for texture and craftsmanship appear. *Douglas* used a splash of half-timber at Bangor Is-coed Rectory (F) in 1868, but not until the 1870s, coincidentally with the evolution of his own maturity, did his carpentry acquire that same sense of enthusiasm and dedication which characterized his joinery; nor till then did he find satisfactory means of expression in vernacular, and then it was more probably under the influence of Nesfield than as part of the Cestrian half-timber movement. Nesfieldian detail was readily taken up by Douglas, whose joinery, with its C17 elements, happily absorbed 'pies' and the incised lozenge and diaper patterns which were themselves derived from Jacobean furniture. The church furnishings at Halkyn and Northop (both F) are enhanced by features such as these. Douglas's attractive Lower Lodge, 1868, at Soughton Hall, Northop (F), is strongly Nesfieldian but has hints of his own later maturity. His best vernacular house is at Penley (F), originally called Llannerch Panna, 1878–9. This, alone among his houses, owes something to historical precedent in plan, being of H-form with a great hall which has a lateral chimney. External walls are all of half-timber, handled convincingly, and the interior is endowed with an indefinable and haunting atmosphere of timelessness. On the other hand, hard and red Ruabon brick is used for chimneys, while the roof is of similar tiles which combine unsympathetically with the black-and-white. Similar materials, sometimes with stone also used and with diapering introduced into the brick, occur in the immaculate cottages and model farms which Douglas designed for the Duke of Westminster's Eaton Estate. The estate, its management and its enormous building programme hold an important place in agricultural and social history. Most of the buildings are across the border (*see The Buildings of England: Cheshire*), but some are at Bretton (F). Bretton Hall Farm, 1891–3, by *Douglas & Fordham*, with house and buildings grouping together, is a highly typical Eaton farmstead. The Gelli, Tallarn Green (F), a *Douglas* house of 1877, is built of brick and half-timber; its staggered plan makes for picturesque grouping and varied roofscape. In addition Tallarn Green has a Douglas parsonage (now vicarage), 1882, with half-timbering, and the brick-nogged Kenyon Cottages, by *Douglas & Fordham*, 1892, like Llannerch Panna, a half-timbered work with an air of authenticity.

Authentic-looking also, but in a different version of vernacular, is Llety Dryw, Colwyn Bay (D), by *Douglas & Fordham*, 1893. This is entirely stone-built and is in the manner of C17 H-plan houses of northern England. Elevations and external detail but not internal planning follow Pennine precedent. Similar in style, and memorable for its thrillingly high moorland site, is the shooting lodge of Gwylfa Hiraethog, Mynydd Hiraethog (D), which in its present form is by *Sir Edwin Cooper*, 1913, one of his several commissions linked with Lord Devonport and the Port of London Authority. As an addendum to the vernacular revival, it may be said that the half-timbered clerestory constituted, with the rest of the nave, the last stage, 1904–5, of the *Douglas & Minshull* rebuilding of St Matthew's church, Buckley (F). Also by *Douglas & Minshull*, and Douglas's only public building, is St Deiniol's Library, Hawarden 111 (F), built in two stages, 1899–1902 and 1904–6, as part of the National Gladstone Memorial. The style is Tudor Gothic but distinguished from Thomas Jones's Perp by Late Victorian smooth freshness and refinement, and by the use of red sandstone and the introduction of Elizabethan elements. The interior of the main library has fine structural woodwork.

Among Neo-Jacobean houses by *Douglas* are Wigfair, Cefn Meiriadog (D), 1882–4, and the rebuilding of Cornist Hall, Flint, *c.*1884, though this was not completed in accordance with his original scheme. Both are of brick with stone dressings and have C15 and C16 features, though neither possesses the usual symmetry or exuberance of Neo-Jacobean. Both are irregular in grouping and have a pyramid-roofed tower, and Wigfair, which is L-shaped, does not conform to any usual plan type of the period; not all the original fittings remain, but there is some

joinery with Douglas's favourite unmitred moulding. It is also
characteristic that there is a good staircase, with, at the landing,
an arcade on turned posts.

Douglas's churches are as interesting as his houses. The series
starts with Sealand church, Queensferry (F), with an ashlar interior and already exhibiting a good understanding of materials.
Built in 1867, it is an early work, pre-dating the more readily
recognizable churches of his maturity, but while its Geometrical
style and the heavy massing of the tower and vice turret are
High Victorian, the pyramid roof which caps the tower antici-
pates the later, more varied and dramatic Douglas skylines. In
addition to displaying the familiar and admirable qualities found
in all his buildings, Douglas's later churches tend to the sensitive Neo-Perp of the late C19, and his is the dominant contribution to this phase of church architecture in Clwyd. One of his
100 best is that rebuilt in 1877-8 at Halkyn (F). It is an estate
church, commissioned by the Duke of Westminster, and nothing was stinted; it is of ashlar outside and in. Perp styling is
mainly confined to a sturdy NW tower, the unconventional
placing of which shows that Douglas sought to be original; its
pyramid roof demonstrates that he already had a liking for
interesting skylines, and the placing of minute windows is
attractively piquant. For the rest, the style is Early Dec. Here
there is particularly good joinery and a splendid set of furnishings.

Conventional but excellent Neo-Perp Douglas churches are
at Rossett (D; *Douglas & Fordham*, 1886-92), Old Colwyn (D;
Douglas & Minshull, 1899-1903), and Bryn-y-Maen (D; *Douglas
& Fordham*, 1897-9), where a group comprises the church, a
house (Bryn Eglwys), which the donor of the church built for
herself, and the vicarage (1898), for which she also paid. Another Douglas group occurs at Colwyn Bay (D). St Paul's church
(Geometrical in style and large, with its first stage, 1887-8, by
Douglas & Fordham, continued 1894-5) has a magnificent and
massive tower completed in 1911 after the architect's death;
nearby is the Douglas & Fordham church hall, 1895, and the
vicarage, of the same authorship and date; St David's Welsh
Church is by *Douglas & Minshull*, 1902-3. Of ashlar throughout, and with all the freshness, smoothness and refinement associated with turn-of-the-century Perp, is the Douglas & Minshull church, 1898-1902, at Shotton, Queensferry (F). It is a
surprising and surprisingly successful translation not of Perp
but of E.E.

As a church restorer, *Douglas* was not always as tactful or
self-effacing as he might have been. At Llanferres (D) in 1891-
2 he continued a transformation begun by *Thomas Jones*, removing plaster and introducing furnishings in his own distinctive style. Yet the end result has an effect of mellowness and a
sense of craftsmanship. A similar approach to restoration was
taken by *Arthur Baker*, cousin of Sir Herbert, who interfered
with many churches in Clwyd. A typical example is at Meliden
(F), where in 1884-5 he transformed a Perp single-chamber

church, inserting lancets, destroying painted texts along with internal plaster, and making half-timbered additions. Box pews and a three-decker pulpit were sacrificed, but Baker supplied attractive new fittings, so that the church, particularly inside, is undeniably pleasing, with a rich, warm and mellow Late Victorian character and stained glass in accord.

Characteristic *Douglas* features were widely copied and were taken up by one-time pupils and assistants. Douglas-like buildings not actually by him occur at Wrexham (D), especially the former Talbot Hotel, which, with its pointed roof and twisted chimneys of purpose-made Ruabon brick, could easily be misattributed. Built 1904–5, it is in fact by *John H. Davies & Son* of Chester. Douglas's most famous and able pupil was E. A. Ould (1852–1909), who himself practised in Chester before being taken into partnership by G. E. Grayson of Liverpool. By *Grayson & Ould*, 1885, is the rectory (now Old Rectory) at Halkyn (F). The client was the Duke of Westminster, and Douglas may well have been instrumental in obtaining the commission for the partners. The house is informal and asymmetrical with tile-hanging and white-painted casements.

Thomas Meakin Lockwood (1830–1900), the only late C19 Chester architect other than Douglas with a national reputation, was born in London and grew up in East Anglia; in Chester he entered T. M. Penson's office and set up on his own *c.* 1860. His output consisted mainly of domestic, public and commercial jobs in Cheshire, Shropshire and North Wales, and, like Douglas, to whose buildings his own mature work sometimes had a superficial similarity, he received many commissions from the Duke of Westminster. In 1892 he took into partnership his sons W. T. and P. H. Lockwood, practising as T. M. Lockwood & Sons, and after his death they carried on the practice. Lockwood frequently worked in half-timber and in a brick and stone version of Tudor or Jacobean; individual features included Renaissance touches in the detailing of stonework, and windows with arched central lights, derived from Ipswich via Norman Shaw. By *Lockwood* is the stone-built former Police Station, 1881, at Mold (F), in an informal domestic Elizabethan style. The Red House, Hawarden (F), 1883, now demolished, was entirely of brick and belonged to the 'Queen Anne Movement'.

With the work of Douglas and Nesfield most of the best and most interesting VICTORIAN CHURCH FURNISHINGS belonging late in the period have already been covered. In addition to those mentioned, good examples occur at the 1897–9 *Douglas & Fordham* church at Bryn-y-Maen (D), where there is an especially thorough and complete set, and at Northop (F) of *c.* 1876–7; also noteworthy are the pulpit which *Douglas* designed for Bangor Is-coed (F) when he restored the church in 1877, and the stalls in the 1894–5 *Douglas & Fordham* chancel at St Paul's, Colwyn Bay (D). *Arthur Baker*'s furnishings with their own version of Neo-Jacobean aestheticism occur not only at Meliden (F) but at Llanrhaeadr-yng-Nghinmeirch (D), where he did a restoration in 1879–80. Not furnishings but ecclesiastical, and a fine piece of Late Victorian woodwork, is the interior of the chapel at the Royal Alexandra Hospital, Rhyl (F). Originally by *Douglas*, post-1873, and with traceried timber arcades on shaped posts (another Nesfield motif which he had taken up), it was dismantled for reuse in the new hospital building, begun 1898 and by *Waterhouse*. *J. D. Sedding*, a Late Victorian church architect of national reputation, restored Llanfwrog (D) in 1869–70, and although not all the tracery he reinstated was done reliably, good work of its own time appeared here also, his remodelling of the porch showing awareness of the vernacular revival and of Norman Shaw and Eden Nesfield. The restoration, 1870–2, of Llanfair Dyffryn Clwyd (D) was also entrusted to Sedding, who, for this double-nave church, designed furnishings with Perp affinities but of distinctive character, expressing the nature of joinery by their simplicity and areas of plain surface rather than by Douglas's more sophisticated system.

A completely different ecclesiastical tradition is represented by the nonconformist CHAPELS which are such a common building type in the Welsh scene, both rural and urban. Following the Toleration Act of 1689, itinerant worship gave way to licensed meeting houses; and from the mid-c18 these were superseded by purpose-built chapels as nonconformity took a strong hold in the country and received impetus from the c18 religious revival and throughout the c19. It must be admitted that more chapels are notable for historical interest than for architectural beauty; needless to say, rectangular chambers prevail, with seating focused on the pulpit, and the plans and arrangements devised were also ideal for singing, according with the Welsh choral tradition. Architects specializing in chapel design showed skill in accommodating the maximum of congregational seating within a given area. Among the most appealing chapels are those of early date, domestic scale and unsophisticated design, which may be termed vernacular. Such is Salem, Llansilin (D), 1831, one of the few chapels set within a graveyard. It also has a couple of cottages under the same roof as the chapel proper; single cottages rather than pairs are more commonly incorporated, and from them developed the chapel houses and schoolrooms which were integral elements in later plans. Early chapels had the pulpit not at one end but in the middle of one of the long walls, opposite a single door in small buildings, opposite or between twin doors in larger. The former arrangement permitted longitudinal elevations of three bays as at Bethel, Rhydymwyn (F), 1825, Capel Carmel, Llanrhaeadr-ym-Mochnant (D), 1836, and Ebenezer, Brynford (F), 1841, which has its own cottage. Internal rearrangement, if it included moving the pulpit, might lead to the abandoning of one of the two doors of a longitudinal elevation, and blocked doorways show this to have taken place at Sion, 1839, Pentre Halkyn at Halkyn (F), and Jerusalem, Rhosesmor (F), 1841, where also there is a cottage incorporated. Of three-bay fronts an unusual one is that of Bronington Chequer, Iscoed (F), 1822, which aspires to a Late Georgian domestic elevation but is only partly symmetrical owing to the integration of the two-storey residence alongside the chapel itself. In citing these examples no mention is made of denomination, for other than the provision of baptismal tanks for Baptist chapels, no differences are apparent in planning or fittings; but analysis of stylistic tendencies on the part of separate denominations would be of interest. In general, classical and Italianate seem to have been favoured in preference to Gothic, especially by Welsh-speaking congregations.

Conditions imposed by town as distinct from rural sites were a factor in prompting the evolution of the type with the entrance in the gable end, and this led to the placing of the pulpit on the inner end wall instead of against the long side. With galleries round three sides, usually on cast-iron columns, the fully matured chapel plan approximated to the auditory Wren type which served the needs of C17 Anglicanism so well, but with the focal point not the altar but the *sêt-fawr* and pulpit, often with a monumental organ behind. Gable-ended buildings provided opportunity for architectural display and a convenient place to mount the plaques which, with Welsh inscriptions, provide invaluable information on the dates of building, rebuilding or alteration. Jerusalem, Treuddyn (F), 1820, altered in 1867, illustrates an intermediate phase in the development of the realigned plan, being still with two doors, but having them set in a pedimented end elevation. A similar arrangement occurs in a building of 1822, altered in 1862, at Waen, Aberwheeler (D). Also demonstrated at Treuddyn are successive stages of chapel status, with the simple longitudinal Ebenezer of 1823 being superseded in 1873 by a more pretentious gable-ended Gothic building.

Architects specializing in chapel work included *Richard Davies* of Bangor (1841–1906), who worked for the Wesleyan Methodists, and *Richard Owens* of Liverpool (1831–91), who was employed by the Welsh Presbyterians (Calvinistic Methodists). Owens's chief patrons were the Roberts family (Barons Clwyd), for whom he did much at and near Abergele (D). The belief that chapels were designed by amateurs, including the ministers, is without foundation, but denominations usually favoured architects who were their own members, and there is the unique instance of the *Rev. Thomas Thomas* of Landore, who was both a Congregational minister and a prolific chapel architect; an example of his work is at Buckley (F), 1872–4.

Pride of place among impressive urban exteriors is held by Bethesda, Mold (F), with a pedimented Corinthian portico. It was rebuilt in 1863 by *W. W. Gwyther*, who handled the classical style seriously and well, and the building has a good and characteristic interior. Pre-eminent among impressive interiors is that of Seion, Llanrwst (D), rebuilt in 1881–3, with the school and chapel house cleverly planned to be included in the main block. The Italianate exterior of ashlar is almost worthy of the exceptionally grand interior, which, together with the *sêt-fawr* and other fittings, is enriched with fretwork, balusters and other

Late Victorian decorative devices. A simpler classicism is seen
112 at Pendref, Ruthin (D), 1827, altered in 1875, which boasts a
chaste segmental end elevation.

The late c18 and the c19 saw the spread not only of chapels
but also of INDUSTRY, and this changed the face of Wales as
much as of any part of Britain. From lead mining, dating from
Roman times, there sprang smelting and related industries at
Bagillt (F) and elsewhere on the Dee coast, which in their turn
led to the establishing of collieries and of port facilities. The
London Lead Company's smelting house at Bagillt (demolished) was built in 1703–4. Later in the c18 lead-associated
manufacture and industry at Flint resulted in the development
of chemical works, and these led to the making of artificial
textiles and thus to the building of the numerous big factories
of Courtaulds Ltd. At Greenfield and Holywell (both F) the
metallurgical industries were related to copper as well as lead,
and further development was stimulated by a copious supply of
water from St Winefride's Well; textile manufacture was introduced in 1777 and within thirteen years four cotton mills had
been built. They numbered impressive and distinguished
examples of Georgian industrial architecture, of the best 'functional tradition' type, but all have been demolished and there
are but fragmentary survivals to bear witness to the once flourishing industry of the Greenfield Valley. Palladian in appearance, and belonging to that tradition, was the crescent-shaped
Bleach Works at Lleweni (D), c.1785, by *Thomas Sandby*, which
must have been one of the very grandest of c18 industrial buildings.

Also in connection with lead, the Smelt, Buckley (F), now
demolished, was a notable industrial monument of c.1790, but
Buckley is more famous for the manufacture of brick; coalmining and pottery making had early been established, and in 1737
the making of firebrick began. Bersham (D), part of the empire
of the ironmaster John Wilkinson, is a celebrated shrine of industrial archaeology. Wilkinson and his brother William took
over the Bersham ironworks from their father c.1762; earlier in
the c18 the example of Abraham Darby at Coalbrookdale had
been followed when charcoal was replaced by coke for smelting.
Prosperity rested on the Napoleonic Wars and the Industrial
Revolution, since the works' chief products were armaments
and cylinders for Boulton & Watt engines. John Wilkinson died
in 1808 and production at Bersham ended in the 1820s, though
the Wilkinson enterprise at Brymbo (D) survived longer.
Remains at Bersham include those of a blast furnace and of
what was probably a boring mill – called the Corn Mill, for
such it later became. There are also several houses associated
with the works, a fettling shop, and near it the Octagonal Building which may have housed a centrally pivoted gantry crane
used for casting. Dating from 1785 was the West Ironworks, at
the site of which may be seen the weir and leet which supplied
the East Ironworks, begun in 1763. Bunker's Hill, a row of
barracks or workers' cottages, no longer survives complete.

Early C19 terraced industrial housing for colliery workers at Chirk (D) was built as Halton Low Barracks and the split-level back-to-back Halton High Barracks; the former, now Woodside Cottages, is altered beyond recognition, and the latter is derelict. Cefn Mawr (D), like Bersham, saw the establishment of ironworks, and George Borrow wrote an exciting description of the blast furnaces at night. Works at Acrefair, taken over by the British Iron Company in 1823, closed in 1888, but a blast furnace of *c.*1800 was not demolished till 1963. The Monsanto Chemical Works now dominates the industry of Cefn.

It was on Wrexham (D) and its region (which includes both Bersham and Cefn Mawr) that the impact of industry was greatest and most dramatic. With the development of coalmining and iron manufacture in the C18, and the later introduction of brewing, Wrexham itself changed from a country market town and social centre into a thriving industrial township, while surrounding countryside was swallowed up and despoiled. From *c.*1870 the brickmaking industry expanded as the red shales of the district were exploited to make the hard, and intensely red, pressed Ruabon brick and to meet the late C19 demand for terra-cotta, of which the chief source was the Penybont Works of *J. C. Edwards* at Cefn Mawr (D). The Wrexham region now presents a dreary landscape, with abandoned collieries and clay pits and traces of demolished country houses, reminiscent of the D. H. Lawrence country of Derbyshire and Nottinghamshire.

Works of ENGINEERING are in their way as impressive as contemporary works of architecture in the county. In seeking to facilitate communication between London and Dublin, Parliament in 1807 voted money for the construction of harbour works at Holyhead, and in the following year requested *Thomas Telford*, that great hero of engineering in North Wales, to report on the improvement of roads. No immediate action was taken on his recommendations, but for the Holyhead Road Commission, set up in 1815, he carried out a survey, 1815–17, of the route from London to Holyhead. Much of his rerouting and reconstruction of what is now the A5 had been completed by *c.*1830. In 1819 the Parliamentary Commission took over local turnpike trusts under the same act which authorized the Menai Bridge and a new road through Anglesey. One scheme, carried out beyond Berwyn (D), utilized the existing gradients and terrain, as Telford usually and cleverly managed; more dramatic is the section constructed at a less readily adaptable site in a gorge at Dinmael (D). Tollhouses remain at Chirk, Llangollen and Pentrefoelas (all D). Also at Chirk and deserving of mention in connection with the road is the Hand Hotel, a Late Georgian brick coaching inn, unusually well proportioned and good of its kind.

As well as working on the Holyhead Road, Telford reported on and improved the coastal route between Chester and Bangor. Not only did he bridge the river at Conwy (*see The Buildings of Wales: Gwynedd*), but in Clwyd he eased the gradient at Rhuallt (F). Other than his bridges, Telford's greatest and justly most

celebrated structure is the stupendous aqueduct of Pont Cy-
104 syllte, Froncysyllte (D), 1795–1805, with which *William Jessop*
was associated. The aqueduct was intended as part of the Ellesmere Canal, for which Jessop was engineer, but as the canal was
never completed as planned, Pont Cysyllte became only part of
a branch. A full-height structure crossing the Vale of Llangollen
127ft above the River Dee, rather than approached by locks, as
originally intended, 'the stream in the sky' consists of stone
piers carrying a cast-iron trough. The first departure from the
puddled channels hitherto used had been made with *Telford*'s
iron aqueduct at Longdon-upon-Tern, earlier in 1805. Chirk
103 Aqueduct (D), by Telford with *Jessop*, 1796–1801, and also for
the Ellesmere Canal, is not so lofty as Pont Cysyllte. Here also
are masonry piers, but they carry arches; and in this earlier
structure the trough was built up in stone, only its bed being of
iron. The Llangollen Canal was completed in 1808 as a navigable
feeder for the Ellesmere; it draws water from the Dee at *Telford*'s crescent-shaped weir of Horseshoe Falls, Llandysilio (D).

Canals as well as turnpikes and stage coaches gave way to the
wave of railway mania. Speculation, development and expansion
were at their height in the 1840s, which was also the period of
the noblest works of railway architecture and engineering. Few
railways had been built in Wales by the time the major network
of England had been completed (*c.*1852), but a notable exception was the Chester and Holyhead Railway. This was authorized by an act of 1844 and opened in stages, reaching Bangor in
1848 and Holyhead in 1850. The engineer was none other than
Robert Stephenson, and the architect was *Francis Thompson*.
Jointly they were responsible for the late-lamented Britannia
Bridge, one of the proudest monuments of the age of steam.
Thompson's stations, 1847–8, are also amongst the finest of
their kind and differ from his Derbyshire ones in being all in
the same style and similar to each other. Two-storeyed and
Italianate, and with living accommodation for the station master, they are of brick with elegant and delicately ornamented
stone dressings. Skill and variety are displayed in integrating
the iron entrance and platform canopies, though many of these
have now disappeared. Indeed a number of the buildings themselves have been demolished; the finest still standing is Holywell
(later Holywell Junction) at Greenfield (F; *see* p. 355), though
the derelict Mostyn (F) is also outstanding.

The Shrewsbury and Chester Railway likewise belonged to
the boom years. It was opened between Chester and Ruabon in
1846 and reached Shrewsbury 1848. The original stations were
by *T. M. Penson*, and the engineer was *Henry Robertson*. The
magnificent viaduct at Cefn Mawr is by Robertson and so is
103 that at Chirk (both D), the latter grouping impressively with the
canal aqueduct. Robertson, who was an ironmaster as well as a
railway engineer, was involved in promoting and constructing
the inland railway system of Wales, and was particularly associated with the Vale of Llangollen Railway and the link between
Ruabon and Dolgellau of which it formed a part.

Common in Wales, indeed perhaps all too common, is C19 and C20 engineering in the form of reservoirs. Successive stages in the styling of dams, attendant buildings and landscaping make an interesting study. For the Gothic and other fantasies of Vyrnwy, *see The Buildings of Wales: Powys*. At Mynydd Hiraethog (D) is Alwen, 1911–16, by *Sir Alexander Binnie, Son & Deacon*, for Birkenhead, with a curving dam of concrete blocks and a strongly Italianate valve tower. A later stage is represented at the same place by Llyn Brenig, 1973–6, authorized in 1972, by *Binnie & Partners*. Its draw-off tower is fully modern, and the landscaping, by *Colvin & Moggridge*, is thoroughly integrated, with earth banked up against the dam. Waterworks rather than a reservoir, the circular Legacy Water Tower at Talwrn, Esclusham (D), was built of reinforced concrete, 1933–5, classically styled.

Seaside piers, those gems of Victorian engineering, are vanishing fast. That at Rhyl (F), demolished in 1972, was of 1866–7 by *James Brunlees*. Colwyn Bay's (D) is by *Mangnall & Littlewood*, 1898–1900, but has few original features of note; the present pavilion, built in 1934, had two predecessors. Piers were one of the characteristic signs of the Victorian DEVELOPMENT 125 OF SEASIDE RESORTS in North Wales. The first resort to be established was Rhyl, the most brash and popular; like those which followed, it owed prosperity to the Chester and Holyhead Railway. The coming of the railway was not the stimulus for the founding of the town (as it was at Llandudno), for Rhyl's life as a resort had begun in the 1820s and the promenade was started in 1846. Some town planning was carried out by *Owen Williams* of Liverpool, and the axial and circus-like intersection of Queen and Sussex Streets is evidence of conscious planning, as are the promenade and the streets behind it, which are to a roughly rectangular plan instead of following the natural curve of the coastline. Stucco-faced terraces came in the 1840s, some probably inland as well as on the sea front, and much had been built by the time an Improvement Act was passed in 1852.

Rhyl has little enough to show of civic character or successful C19 planning, and even less was achieved at Prestatyn (F), despite the advantage of development taking place under a single landowner. H. D. Pochin of Bodnant (D) began acquiring land in the late 1870s and, with the intention of establishing a resort, drained and reclaimed the foreshore. Expansion was piecemeal; the former village street straggling up from the shore became the High Street and the nucleus of the town, and although in the 1920s *Sir Howard Robertson*, then of *Easton & Robertson*, designed a few buildings, no systematic town planning took place and neither a promenade nor any sea-front development ever materialized. Colwyn Bay (D) is similarly disappointing as an urban entity, though it began promisingly and has many distinguished individual buildings. The creation of Colwyn Bay was precipitated by Lady Erskine's selling of the Pwllycrochan estate in 1865. The purchaser, (Sir) John Pender, was a commercial magnate, like Pochin at Prestatyn. As architect for a new town he employed *John Douglas*, but little more than the Colwyn Bay Hotel (now demolished) and a length of promenade had been built by the time Pender was obliged to sell up in 1875. Subsequent development was controlled by the Manchester-based Colwyn Bay and Pwllycrochan Estate Company. This syndicate included the architect *Lawrence Booth*, and numerous domestic and commercial buildings were erected by the firm *Booth, Chadwick & Porter* of Manchester and Colwyn Bay, which continued to practise at the latter town well into the C20 as *J. M. Porter & Co.* It may be supposed that, as well as designing individual buildings, they guided the unremarkable layout of the town centre. The pattern is neither fully informal nor strictly rectangular, though the latter character predominates, with straight streets fitted into irregular areas generated by the coastline and the previously existing main road (the present A55). The attractive Pwllycrochan Woods rise up on a hillside, inland, behind the town centre and were exploited for late C19 villa development. Here also the layout is basically rectangular, rather than the winding roads more usually associated with spacious, sylvan suburbs. Only the steep gradients have dictated the incorporation of such curves as there are. A less likely place to find C19 planning is the modest market town of Llangollen (D), which grew up round its medieval church, the Holyhead Road and a bridge across the Dee, but a scheme of *c.*1860 shifted the centre of the town from its historic heart by prolonging the axis of the bridge as a new, straight shopping street forming part of a compact rectangular pattern. The plan may have been by *W. H. Hill* of Oswestry, though the idea is said to have come from the Llangollen builder *Morris Roberts*.

So finally we may turn to C20 ARCHITECTURE. Domestic architecture of the turn of the century is represented by Wynne's Park at Denbigh, 1905, and Maes Heulyn at Trefnant (D), 1907, both by *Sir E. Guy Dawber*, but neither shows him at his best. Cotswold at Colwyn Bay (D) by *Alfred Steinthal*, 1908, is more charmingly Edwardian, with sensitivity and feeling for texture and the nature of materials. Also at Colwyn Bay, and Arts and Crafts in spirit, is Glan-y-Don Hall (now the Civic Centre), 1909–10, by *Percy Scott Worthington*, of the Manchester dynasty. Domestic architecture overlaid with nostalgia for a vanished past is associated with Lutyens and *Baillie Scott*. Recognizably in his style is Cherry Hill, Wrexham (D), *c.* 1936, by the firm of *Baillie Scott & Beresford*, who, also in Wrexham, were responsible for No. 1 Penymaes Avenue. The Bryn, St Asaph (F), 1910–13, a splendidly sited house representing a successful confluence of Neo-Georgian and Arts and Crafts streams, is by *Gronwy Robert Griffith* of Denbigh (1881–1950), a younger son of the Griffith family of Garn, Henllan (D).

A domestic vernacular of rustic brick, roughcasting and glazing-barred casements is the style of garden cities and the best housing estates of the first half of the C20. It is represented by the Wrexham Garden Village (D), begun in 1913 under the auspices of Co-Partnership Tenants Ltd and later of the Welsh

Town Planning and Housing Trust, and includes work by *G. L. Sutcliffe* and by *T. Alwyn Lloyd*. Like most ventures of its kind it remained incomplete. Sealand Garden Suburb, Queensferry (F), dates from 1910, and was built in connection with the steelworks of John Summers & Co. Ltd.

H. L. North (1871–1941), a North Wales architect, worked in the roughcast and casement style but with specific Gothic motifs incorporated. His only work in Clwyd is a highly characteristic one, the gatehouse at Penrhyd, Eglwsybach (D), of 1927.

The late style of Norman Shaw developed into Neo-Georgian and Edwardian Baroque, and Clwyd had its own exponent of these, *Frederick Andrew Roberts* (1885–1949). He studied with James Strong of Liverpool and practised in Mold (F), where he designed public and commercial buildings which are Queen Anne in being of brick with Portland stone dressings and Baroque in their ambitiously imperial classical style. They included the Post Office (demolished), the former County Court Offices, 1910, and the Ionic Town Hall, 1911–12, with tower and cupola. Also by him, but more refinedly Neo-Georgian in detail, is the huge Miners' Institute (Plas Mwynwyr Rhos), Rhosllannerchrugog (D), 1924–6, designed in collaboration with *John Owen*. Yet more refined, with its Baroque overtones tempered by elegant Neo-Georgian features, is the Miners' Institute at Llay (D), 1929–31, by *F. A. Roberts*. Roberts was responsible for more buildings than can be included in the gazetteer.

The *Burne-Jones* and *Morris* window at Hawarden (F) exemplifies the ARTS AND CRAFTS MOVEMENT, with which Aestheticism and the vernacular revival had affinities. Founded by Morris, whose theories were inspired by those of Ruskin, the movement permeated progressive design at the turn of the century. Good glass continued to be produced in the C20 by the Whall family; St Mary's, Denbigh, has windows by *Christopher Whall*, 1918, and *Veronica M. Whall*, 1933. Fully within Arts and Crafts tradition is the craftsmanship of *Eric Gill*. The War Memorial at Chirk (D), 1919–20, is by him, and he also designed the inscription for a monument in Clocaenog Forest, Clocaenog (D). The rich and luxuriant monument to W. E. Gladstone and his wife at Hawarden (F) is by *Sir William Richmond*, 1906. Its shallow reliefs are typical of the Arts and Crafts school, and its use of differing materials typical of the so-called 'New Sculpture' of the early C20. Clwyd had an outstanding exponent of Arts and Crafts ideals in *J. H. M. Bonnor*: work of character and quality, both as designer and craftsman, is found at the church at his native Llangedwyn (D).

Thus to a movement not mentioned as such in *The Buildings of England*, for a Neo-Georgian villa and half-timbered pub found no place in the work of the author of *Pioneers of Modern Design*. It is a movement which Professor Hitchcock has conveniently termed ARCHITECTURE CALLED TRADITIONAL IN THE TWENTIETH CENTURY. With it a return is made to the work of local architects, among whom *Sir Clough Williams-Ellis* (1883–1978) may be numbered. In Clwyd he was responsible

for the first purpose-built youth hostel, 1931, at Maeshafn (D);
restoration and remodelling, 1930, at Garthewin, Llanfair Talhaearn (D); the Conwy Falls Restaurant, c.1955-6, Betws-y-
Coed (D), and, most spectacularly, the remodelling of the house
and the layout of the gardens at Nantclwyd Hall, Llanelidan
(D), from the 1950s onwards. His client *Sir Vivyan Naylor-
Leyland* contributed to the design of this opulent and theatrical
display.

Less celebrated, but more talented, and with a greater understanding of the properties and use of materials and the nature
of three-dimensional architecture, was *Sydney Colwyn Foulkes*
(1884-1971), who practised in Colwyn Bay as S. Colwyn
Foulkes and from 1968 as Colwyn Foulkes and Partners.*
Neo-Georgian houses by Colwyn Foulkes include his own,
Moryn, Cayley Promenade, Llandrillo-yn-Rhos (D), and The
Wren's Nest, 1932, Colwyn Bay (D). Though with a strong bent
to classicism, he worked in a variety of styles, as exemplified by
the following, all at Colwyn Bay: alterations and additions at
Rydal School, 1927-58 (Tudor); shops at No. 4 Station Road,
116 1933-7 (Romanesque), and at No. 7 Abergele Road, 1930
(Adamish); and the Colwyn Bay and West Denbighshire Hospital, c.1925 (Neo-Georgian). The former Williams Deacon's
Bank is Wyattish and No. 23 Ebbertson Road West,
Llandrillo-yn-Rhos (D), 1960-1, is a witty amalgam of classical
and modern elements. Yet he was by no means a slavish historicist, and his buildings all display excellent use and understanding of materials, together with careful detailing of almost
feminine delicacy. His exploitation of the properties of brick is
117 seen at St John's Church House (i.e. Church Hall), Old Colwyn
(D), 1935-7.

It is, however, as a designer of cinemas that Colwyn Foulkes
most deserves to be remembered. It is interesting to trace the
development of his style in this field. The Arcadia Theatre (later
the Wedgwood Cinema and now demolished) at Colwyn Bay
(D), 1920, was classical inside and out, with heavy internal plasterwork. There is classical plasterwork at the Plaza Cinema,
119 Rhyl (F), built 1930-1, but externally the building is more eclectic; there are Adam motifs, and the long, blank wall of the
auditorium is articulated by panels and decorative brickwork.
This elevation foreshadows the uncompromisingly emphatic
118 rectangularity of the Regal Cinema at Rhyl, with virtuoso use
of brick built up as ornament, 1935-7 (now demolished); the
Plaza, Flint, 1936-8; and the Regal, Birkenhead, 1937 (also
demolished). The Birkenhead cinema, one at Conwy (*see The
Buildings of Wales: Gwynedd*), and the Regal at Rhyl marked
the peak of his achievement as a cinema architect.

His auditoria had, freely arranged, the modernistic Art Deco
motifs which derived from the 1925 Paris Exhibition, and they
lacked the disciplined formality of the frontages. Internal effects

* The firm is continued by his son and daughter-in-law, Mr and Mrs R. Colwyn Foulkes, to whom I am indebted for much help and information concerning
the work of the practice.

were obtained in collaboration with *Holophane Ltd*, who provided silk screen curtains and schemes of constantly changing coloured lighting.

Unusually good examples of Neo-Georgian by other designers are Southsea Vicarage, Broughton (D), 1921; Colwyn Bay (D) Post Office, *c.* 1923–1926 by *C. P. Wilkinson*; and the former church hall at Mostyn (F), 1923–5, by *Grayson & Barnish*. The simple and sensitive Gothic of *Sir Charles Nicholson* appears at the church of St Francis, Sandycroft, Queensferry (F), 1912. Buildings at Howell's School, Denbigh, by *Heaton Comyn* and *Leslie Moore*, 1914, and by *Maurice Webb* 1929–30, are in resourceful collegiate Gothic. Resourceful also, but in Byzantine terms, is the church of the Holy Spirit, Ewloe (F), 1937–8, designed, interestingly enough, by *Goodhart-Rendel* – one of his many commissions associated with the Gladstone family.

The Colwyn Foulkes cinemas may be seen as EARLY MODERN ARCHITECTURE OF THE TWENTIETH CENTURY, a celebrated example of which is the Williams & Robinson factory at Queensferry (F), *c.* 1901–5, by *H. B. Creswell*. Sir Nikolaus Pevsner's assessment of it as 'Nine Swallows – No Summer' applies not only to Britain as a whole but to Clwyd. There are some flat-roofed and white-rendered houses, but none of them calls for mention in the gazetteer, let alone in the Introduction, and there is nothing of note belonging to the International Modern Style. A group of houses in Gwernaffield Road, Mold (F), *c.* 1941, has flat roofs and curving corner windows of glass bricks, but the walls are of exposed brick and not white.

As elsewhere, POST-WAR ARCHITECTURE saw the development of the Modern Movement largely in terms of public and local authority work. Excellent buildings have been designed in the department of successive County Architects, *E. Langford Lewis* (Denbighshire), *R. W. Harvey* (Flintshire) and *K. J. Denley* (Clwyd).

A blockiness inherent in the Mold houses is the chief characteristic of Kelsterton College (formerly Flintshire Technical College) at Connah's Quay (F). It is of 1952–4 by *R. W. Harvey*, with *Sir Howard Robertson* as consultant, with later additions.

In planning terms, the Queen's Park Housing Estate at Wrexham (D), begun in 1950 (first stage completed four years later), was a pioneer work by *J. M. Davies*, the Borough Engineer and Surveyor, and *Gordon Stephenson* of Liverpool. It was the first British attempt at Radburn planning, that is, a layout which ensures segregation of pedestrian and vehicular traffic, as had been achieved at Radburn, New Jersey, and elsewhere in the United States. At Wrexham the units (superblocks) comprising the system are too small to allow the principles fully to work, and the poor quality of the housing itself and of the landscaping unfortunately means that the only scheme in North Wales which holds a place in the history of post-medieval British town planning is not an aesthetic success.

Among post-war public buildings, the Guildhall at Wrexham (D), 1959–61, by *Stephenson, Young & Partners* and later enlarged, is only tentatively modern and owes much to Stockholm Town Hall. More within the rational mainstream which flowed from the International Style is Ysgol Dyffryn Conwy, Llanrwst (D), 1960–5, by *R. A. MacFarlane*, then Denbighshire County Architect, with slate-hanging and large areas of glazing. The crispness and clarity and the satisfying proportions are largely due, though, to the use of the *Vic Hallam* prefabrication system. More sophisticated in its structure, but also displaying crispness, clarity and good proportion, is *MacFarlane*'s excellent 122 Public Library at Rhosllannerchrugog (D), 1961–2. The Police Headquarters at Wrexham (D) by *E. Langford Lewis*, 1973–5, is another building of quality. *S. Colwyn Foulkes* was responsible for a number of local authority housing schemes in Wales. One of his best is the Elwy Road Estate at Llandrillo-yn-Rhos (D), 1952–6. Its circulation system is more successful than that of the Radburn layout at Queen's Park, Wrexham. Foulkesian touches include elegant glazing patterns and colourful door canopies.

The County Civic Centre at Mold (F), largely by *R. W. Harvey*, failed, through overcrowding, to make the best of a splendid site, though individual buildings are commendable. The Shire Hall, 1966–75, was classically disciplined in its initial 121 concept. In contrast, Theatr Clwyd, 1973–6, represents the 'Anti-Pioneers' phase of modernism, though admittedly its irregular massing and elevations express the complicated accommodation within. Anti-Pioneering also are the structural acrobatics of the Swimming Baths at Wrexham (D) by *F. D. Williamson & Associates*, 1965–7. A remarkable series of houses in Rhyl (F) was designed by the firm of *Garnett & Cloughley* shortly after it set up in practice there. Of 1960–6, they are of bold geometrical forms, and in this, though not in any use of historical elements, may be considered as 'post-modern'. Modern factory architecture is seen to advantage at the Wrexham Industrial Estate (D); one of the best examples is the factory of Fibreglass Ltd, with *Charles Andrews & Sons* as consulting engineers, 1970–1. The admirable Public Library at Wrexham by *James Roberts*, 1971–3, is, unusually, a public building designed by a private practice.

The best work being done in the county today is by *Bowen Dann Davies Partnership* of Colwyn Bay.* Their style, which fits happily in almost any setting, may be termed a modern vernacular and is marked by harmonious use of materials; low-pitched roofs have ridges which, in their ups and downs, reflect ins and outs of the plans. Outstanding are Maes Robert, 1973–4, a scheme of sheltered housing at Cefn Meiriadog (D); Roman 123 Catholic churches at Towyn (D), 1973–4, and Rhuddlan (F), 1975–6; Cefndy Hostel, Rhyl (F), 1973–5; and Capel-y-Groes 124 Chapel, Wrexham (D), 1981–2. The firm has also designed good private housing estates, so it is possible for this Introduction to end on a satisfactory and encouraging note.

* Mr Bill Davies and the late Mr S. Powell Bowen kindly provided help and information concerning their work.

BUILDING MATERIALS

In most of Wales, particularly the N and E (including Denbigh-shire and Flintshire), the lack of good freestone together with an abundance of oak resulted in a strong tradition of timber building, with carpenters producing more finished work of high quality than masons did. Though stone building did come to predominate in the W, timber framing extended further west-ward than present survivals suggest and was more in evidence in the towns than now. Even at Ruthin (D), where quantities remain visible, much has been lost to view beneath remodellings and refacings. Structural carpentry attained its peak of achieve-ment with roofs of the C15 or early C16, such as the outstanding hammerbeam specimen at Cilcain (F), the simpler arched-bracing and the wagon ceilings typical of churches in the Vale of Clwyd, and the intricately ornamented ceilings at Gresford, Llangollen and Ruthin (all D). Within the field of vernacular domestic building, most surviving cruck trusses are also of the Perpendicular period, together with hall houses of more sophis-ticated structure represented by spere-trusses and aisled halls. No medieval open halls remain unmutilated by subdivision, due not least to the common C17 practice of converting hall houses to storeyed ones by inserting an intermediate floor. Prevalence of storeyed structures among newly built houses led to the su-perseding of cruck construction by the box-frame, allowing greater headroom. As well as being an aisled hall, Hafod, Llan-silin (D), is a rare C15 example of box-framing, which did not become common till the late C16.

Also in the C16 the area of predominantly timber territory began to shrink, with building stone infiltrating eastwards. It scarcely reached the NE lowlands, however; in Maelor Saesneg the use of half-timber continued into the C18. The latest in-stances tended to be brick-nogged, and brick infill might replace plaster panels in the course of repairs. As in the English Mid-lands, it became customary for the brickwork to be white-washed, and in the Maelor it is exceptional to see red brick still exposed. Some patterning was given to half-timber, especially in the C17, and can be seen in Ruthin (D), but the lavish orna-mentation familiar in the border and NW counties of England seems not to have been common in Wales. Recent restorations have included the well-meaning but misguided practice of either leaving oak in its natural state or staining it unsuitably, rather than respecting the 'black-and-white' tradition.

In areas where stone replaced timber, the process began with

houses built with outer walls of stone but internal partitioning
still of wood. The post-and-panel or 'in-and-out' type was
favoured for dais partitions at the upper ends of halls; as extant
C16 examples show, it gave opportunity for decorative display.

The intractable nature of available stone resulted in random
rubble walling, and squared and coursed masonry was rarely
used before the C18. In the Middle Ages ashlar was confined
largely to Edward I's castles and to greater churches (abbeys
and St Asaph Cathedral). A tradition of whitewashing rubblework continued into the C19 in the case of churches and is still
maintained for secular buildings. A pleasing feature of the
Welsh countryside is the cottages and farmsteads with their
roughly textured and whitened walls and their slate roofs. An
earlier roof covering had been thatch (which might be of any
vegetable matter, such as fern or heather, and not necessarily
straw or reed). Some humble domestic, though no ecclesiastical,
survivals of thatching may still be seen. The available Carboniferous sandstones seem not generally to have been used for
roofing slabs as were those of NW England and the Pennines,
perhaps because they may not split readily. Major buildings
such as castles and the greater churches would have had roofs
of lead, which was mined near Halkyn and Holywell and at
Diserth (all F).

The most widespread rock suitable for building is the Carboniferous (Mountain) Limestone. This occurs as part of the
Carboniferous system E of the Clwydian Hills, as do Millstone
Grit and the shales and coal seams of the Coal Measures. It is
also found along the eastern foothills of the Denbigh Moors,
where the staggering of a number of faults forms the irregular
W boundary of the Vale of Clwyd (a rift valley during the Triassic Period). In contrast a continuous fault sharply defines the E
margin of the Vale and its junction with the Clwydians. This
hard and resistant limestone is brown when newly quarried but
weathers to grey or whitish grey on exposure. It is the main
walling material of virtually every church in the valley. The
spectacular Victorian one at Bodelwyddan (F) shows it capable
of being carved and ashlared, but, presumably unyielding to
medieval tools and techniques, it usually appears as irregular
uncoursed blocks, with stone brought from elsewhere for dressings, mouldings, tracery and ornament. Thus, even in the C19,
Prestatyn church (F) and two churches at Denbigh (St David
and St Mary) were built of Carboniferous Limestone with
dressings of yellowish sandstone of the Coal Measures. The
limestone for the two Denbigh buildings came from the Graig
Quarries near the town. In the cause of High Victorian polychromy, bands of darker Silurian sandstone were introduced
at Llanbedr Dyffryn Clwyd New Church (D), the limestone
of which is similar to that quarried at Rhewl near Llanynys
(D) – an important source for the medieval churches of the
region.

Though largely concealed by a deposit of Boulder Clay, New
Red Sandstone of the Triassic period was laid down as the floor

of the Vale of Clwyd; it was quarried at Hirwaen (D) and may
be seen either as dressings or else interspersed as walling stones
amid the older Carboniferous Limestone. The history of restorations at Chester and Lichfield Cathedrals attests to its notor-
iously poor weathering properties, and churches at Llandyrnog,
Llangwyfan and Llangynhafal (all D), where it is the principal
walling material, have received protective rendering. Some Carboniferous Limestone came from Diserth (F) and, as well as
Rhewl, an important quarry was at Henllan (D), whose own
church it supplied. Indeed, the usual practice was to employ
sources immediately to hand. Such was the case at Abergele (D)
and at Caerwys, Cwm and Gwaunysgor (all F). Even in the
mid-C19, when improved transport had broken down the traditional reliance on local materials, a quarry for a new church at
Cefn Meiriadog (D) was opened in an adjoining field.

Quarrying took place also at Llanddulas (D) on the coast, and
the light Carboniferous Limestone of buildings, landscape and
cliffscape imparts a cheerful and bright character to seaside
Wales E of and including Llandudno. Colwyn Bay (D) is almost
entirely built of it, with red sandstone used for dressings, as at
the late C19 St Paul's church, where the sandstone is from the
Triassic Keuper beds of Runcorn in Cheshire. The architect,
Douglas, drew on a similar vocabulary of materials for other
churches nearby, sensitively integrating them in their environment, i.e. at Old Colwyn (St John Baptist) and Bryn-y-Maen,
but at the latter the Cheshire Triassic sandstone (used for a
fully ashlared interior) came from Helsby.

The ubiquitous Carboniferous Limestone as used in the cathedral and parish church at St Asaph (F) is a fine-grained type
from Cefn Meiriadog; it is supplemented by sandstone, both
red of the Triassic System and yellow from the Coal Measures.
Also present is so-called 'Elwy stone', a purple Carboniferous
sandstone quarried on the River Elwy near Cefn Meiriadog.
Red rock of the Keuper Series from Hollington, Staffordshire,
is among building stones which *Sir Gilbert Scott* brought in for
his restoration of the cathedral.

The Carboniferous Limestone at Rhuddlan Castle (F) was
probably carried by water from Diserth. Being accessible by
sea, Edward I's castles were not necessarily dependent on immediate local sources as were earlier strongholds. Nevertheless
Flint Castle stands on an outcrop of yellow sandstone of the
Middle Coal Measures, and the similar stone of which the
building consists was quarried nearby; close to Denbigh Castle,
Leicester's Church and the remaining tower of St Hilary's use
stone obtained from the Graig Quarries, but Denbigh was itself
a further source of Carboniferous Limestone and that for the
castle and town walls emanated from the hill on which they
stand. Similarly a rock of Triassic Bunter sandstone forms the
site of, and provided material for, the Edwardian lordship castle
at Holt (D), and Holt church is of the same stone. The New Red
Sandstone appears at Ruthin Castle (D), both for the C13 works,
probably quarried on site, and for the mid-C19 contributions to

the castle group. Together with 'Elwy' sandstone it comprises the Red Tower of Denbigh Castle.

Superior in quality to the limestone are the fine-grained yellow Carboniferous sandstones of the Millstone Grit and the Coal Measures. The latter include Talacre stone from Gwespyr (F) and Cefn stone, which was quarried at Broughton near Wrexham and at Cefn Mawr near Ruabon (both D). Rather than being buff-coloured, as is sometimes stated, fresh Cefn stone is of a not altogether attractive sulphureous hue, and its tendency to blacken in smoky atmospheres has had a dreary effect in its industrial region of origin. Gresford and Wrexham churches (both D) are of this stone, probably from Cefn Mawr, whereas Broughton is the likely source of that used at Ruabon. Not to be confused with Cefn stone of the Coal Measures is Cefn-y-fedw Sandstone which, though belonging to the Carboniferous System, is a Millstone Grit, as are the comparable Holywell Shales of N Flintshire. Hope Castle, Caergwrle (F), and the church at Hope itself are built of Cefn-y-fedw Sandstone, as is Hawarden Old Castle (F). The stone for Hope Castle came from the hill on which it stands. Also at Caergwrle, the stone was used for encasing Bryn Iorcyn, and it seems to have had extensive application within the C17 domestic architecture of Flintshire.

Carboniferous Limestone walling frequently appears with dressings of the Carboniferous sandstones, e.g. at Denbigh Friary and Gwaunysgor church (F), where the sandstone is Talacre. Talacre stone, which formed floor paving at St Asaph Cathedral, was also found suitable for sculptural work, and a stone similar to it sufficed for St Winefride's Well, Holywell (F), with its Perpendicular elaboration. Cefn stone is durable and capable of being undercut and moulded and of taking an excellent ashlar finish. At Whitford church (F), remodelled in the mid-C19, it impressed Goodhart-Rendel, who remarked on the 'Extraordinary preservation of stone. Sharp as new ...' It is probably to the use of this stone that the Mid-Victorian Llantysilio Hall, Llandysilio (D), owes its splendid smooth walling and crisp carving.

Other buildings of Carboniferous sandstone coming from the Coal Measures are (all F) Basingwerk Abbey, Greenfield; the Welsh Ewloe Castle, Ewloe, where stone was obtained on site; and, as already noted, Flint Castle. Rhuddlan Castle (also F) is a veritable geological anthology, displaying Elwy and Talacre sandstones as well as its Carboniferous Limestone.

In contrast to the bright breeziness of Carboniferous Limestone coastline and country are the regions of the ancient Silurian rocks which underlie the Denbigh Moors and the Clwydian Hills. The fine-grained shales are frequently compacted into mudstones, and Denbigh grit from the moors has served as a building stone. Long blocks of dark Silurian stone laid as rubblework resembling Lake District masonry, either random or coursed and faced, dourly characterize the moorland and the Conwy Valley region of Denbighshire, including the town of

Llanrwst. Llanrwst church is of Silurian stone, as are, further
E, those at Derwen and Bylchau (both D). At the latter, *Sir
Gilbert Scott*'s choice of stone helps relate the building to the
neighbouring bleak expanse of Mynydd Hiraethog. Though the
well-known slates of western Wales mostly belong to the yet
older Cambrian Period, those of the NE, including those quarried near Llangollen (D) and Corwen, are Silurian. At Llangollen the native Dinas Bran is a further instance of a castle deriv-
ing material (in this case a poor Silurian mudstone) from the
hill which it crowns. Not far away, Valle Crucis Abbey has
walling of mudstone obtained from outcrops nearby, with Cefn
stone, probably from Broughton, serving for dressings and facing.

In Llanrwst (D) much rubble seems to have been covered
with pebbledash accompanied by flat and unmoulded door and
window surrounds of cement render. This practice was also
followed in Holywell (F) and Llangollen (D); and in Market
Street, Abergele (D), is a dated example of 1827.

Brick was reputedly introduced to Wales by Sir Richard
Clough when building Plas Clough, Denbigh, 1567, and
Bach-y-graig, Tremeirchion (F), *c*.1567–9. Material for the latter
may have been excavated and burnt on site or else imported
from the Low Countries, as was the brick for the contemporary
Royal Exchange, with which Clough was associated. Mention
has already been made of brick nogging in connection with
timber framing, and it was for the chimneystacks of half-
timbered houses that it found early general use, often with
the stacks ornamented with ribs forming star patterns.

Though brick was used by the late C17 for so grand a house
as Erddig (D) and in the C18 for ecclesiastical work, as at Worthenbury (F), it never gained complete ascendancy for vernacular building in Clwyd as it did from the early C18 in Cheshire.
Nevertheless it had wide application, particularly for farm
buildings and for those Georgian vernacular houses which show
Renaissance infiltration by their symmetry and attempts at
fashionable classical detail. Towns and villages also saw its extensive use: Chirk and Ruthin (both D) and Overton (F) are well
endowed with good examples, and others remain at Wrexham
(D) and Mold (F).

Dissemination of materials, first by canal and then by railway,
destroyed the hitherto prevailing British reliance on local
sources, with the accompanying demise of vernacular traditions
and regional building styles. North Wales contributed to this
revolution and to the C19 and early C20 building boom by the
export of bricks and roofing slate. Buckley (F) was a centre of
brickmaking, noted especially for firebrick, manufacture of
which began in the C18. More celebrated were the products of
the Ruabon region (D), where the red marls of the Upper Coal
Measures were exploited from the mid-C19, particularly by
J. C. Edwards. Edwards became the leading maker of the
densely hard Ruabon pressed brick, and from *c*.1870 was a
pioneer of the terra-cotta trade, sending products of his Peny-

bont Works at Cefn Mawr (D) all over the world and supplying the demand created by its increasing use in Britain. The intense fiery redness of Ruabon brick exceeds even that of its Lancashire counterpart from Accrington, as is demonstrated by the proximity of the two in Nant-y-Glyn Road, Colwyn Bay (D). Admittedly unlovely when comprising a soot-streaked colliery terrace within its native heath, this much-maligned material can show admirable qualities of strength, solidity and glowing warmth if it is used sensitively and intelligently, and particularly if it is juxtaposed with well-chosen other materials, as, e.g., at *Douglas & Fordham*'s Bretton Hall Farm, Bretton (F), where ornamental chimneys are built up of purpose-mades. *Edmund Kirby*, one-time assistant of Douglas, could also employ it imaginatively and well, though his R.C. church at Prestatyn (F) fails to show his brickwork at its most resourceful. Using the more sensitively textured brown rustics favoured in the first half of the C20, one of Clwyd's own most distinguished architectural sons showed mastery in combining structural and decorative brickwork: at St John's Church House, Old Colwyn (D), and the Plaza and the demolished Regal Cinemas, Rhyl (F), *S. Colwyn Foulkes* enriched load-bearing or cladding walls with carefully detailed ornament built up in brick.

FURTHER READING

The counties of Wales are not covered by Kelly's *Directories*, but there is the *Postal Directory of Flintshire and Denbighshire*, compiled by Frank Porter (1886) as well as the highly informative *Topographical Dictionary of Wales* by Samuel Lewis (4th ed. 1849). Then there are Slater's *Directory of North and Mid Wales* (1895) and Worrall's *Directory of North Wales* (1874). For churches the most useful source is Archdeacon D. R. Thomas's *History of the Diocese of St Asaph* (2nd ed., 3 vols., 1908–13). The Royal Commission on Ancient and Historical Monuments in Wales produced volumes on Flintshire (1912) and Denbighshire (1914); but they are not up to the standard of the Commission's later work and need to be used with caution. Though its illustrations are excellent, caution also must be exercised with Mostyn Lewis's *Stained Glass in North Wales up to 1850* (1970). More reliable as studies of specific subjects are V. E. Nash-Williams on *The Early Christian Monuments of Wales* (1950) and Colin A. Gresham on *Medieval Stone Carving in North Wales* (1968). For vernacular work the indispensable source is *Houses of the Welsh Countryside* by Peter Smith (1975). *Farmhouses and Cottages: An Introduction to Vernacular Architecture in Flintshire* by M. Bevan-Evans and W. Hugh Jones (1964) is also of value, as is *The Welsh House* by Iorwerth C. Peate (1944). Among the journals of learned societies, pre-eminent is *Archaeologia Cambrensis*, published from 1846 by the Cambrian Archaeological Association. Then there are the *Denbighshire Historical Society Transactions* and the *Flintshire Historical Society Publications*. Also of relevance is the journal of the *Chester and North Wales Architectural, Archaeological and Historic Society* (from 1849).

General topographical and travel works include those of George Borrow, Samuel and Nathaniel Buck, John Hicklin, W. Bezant Lowe, Thomas Nicholas, Thomas Pennant (illustrated by Moses Griffith), J. Poole, Thomas Roscoe and Dorothy Sylvester. Mention should also be made of *An Historical Atlas of Wales*, William Rees (2nd ed. 1972); *The History of Flintshire*, edited by C. R. Williams, vol. 1 (all that was published; 1961); *The Welsh Church from Conquest to Reformation*, Glanmor Williams (1962); *The Towns of Wales*, Harold Carter (1965); *Edward I's Castle-Building in Wales*, J. Goronwy Edwards (1944). Further studies of specific subjects are *The Early Norman Castles of the British Isles*, Ella S. Armitage (1912); *The Chester & Holyhead Railway*, P. E. Baughan (1972); *New Towns of the Middle Ages*, Maurice Beresford (1967); *Medieval Cruck-Building and its Derivatives*, F. W. B. Charles (1967); *Medieval Religious Houses*, D. Knowles and R. N. Hadcock (1971); *Medieval Castles in North Wales*, E. Neaverson (1947); *Medieval Military Architecture in England*, G. T. Clark (1884).

Studies of individual buildings, places and parishes are those of J. R. Ellis and E. W. Williams (both Abergele), G. Porter and N. Tucker (both Colwyn Bay), J. W. Williams (Denbigh), A. L. Cust (Erddig), E. A. Fishbourne (Gresford parish church), R. Willet (Hawarden), W. T. Simpson (Llangollen), Sir Cyril Fox (Offa's Dyke), J. Heywood (Rhyl), P. B. Ironside Bax (St Asaph Cathedral), A. N. Palmer (Wrexham and neighbourhood).

The volume of *The Architectural Antiquities and Village Churches of Denbighshire* (1872) compiled by Lloyd Williams & Underwood records many churches prior to restoration, as do Sir Stephen Glynne's notes on churches, printed in *Archaeologia Cambrensis*, 5th ser., vol. 1, 1884, and vol. 2, 1885. In addition to these are the items which formed the standard bibliography for *The Buildings of England*, e.g. the Goodhart-Rendel Index of C19 churches, the respective biographical dictionaries of architects and sculptors by H. M. Colvin, Rupert Gunnis and John Harvey, the volumes of *Country Life* for authoritative articles on country houses, and Charles L. Eastlake's *A History of the Gothic Revival*, etc. A list such as this cannot be comprehensive, and many other works of value were consulted in the course of research.

Of recent guidebooks there are the excellent *Shell Guide to North Wales* by Elisabeth Beazley and Lionel Brett (1971) and *The Companion Guide to North Wales* by Elisabeth Beazley and Peter Howell (1975). Both are wider in scope than *The Buildings of Wales*, but are admirable in their treatment of architectural subjects. The present writer can take some parental pride in the *Companion Guide*, having been responsible for introducing the authors to each other, appropriately enough in the great hall of Penrhyn Castle.

DENBIGHSHIRE

SIR DDINBYCH

ABENBURY *see* WREXHAM, p. 310

ABERCHWILER *see* ABERWHEELER

ABERGELE

ST MICHAEL. The largest of the county's Perp double-naved churches, and the site of a *clas* or Celtic monastery. Twin five-light E windows, two-centred, with cusping, two single-light sub-arches and panel tracery. The arched-braced roofs have cusped struts above the collars and cusped wind-braces. Brattishing at wall-plate level in the two easternmost bays. Seven-bay arcade of four-centred arches on thin octagonal piers. A similar westernmost arch is C19 in its present form and probably dates from a restoration of 1858. A w tower to the N nave has Perp features, but was raised in height and given buttresses in 1861. Miscellany of nave windows. On the N, the second from the E is not genuine; on the S, only the easternmost and the second from W are as shown in Lloyd Williams & Underwood's illustration, published in 1872. Of the new windows, some or all are of *Arthur Baker*'s restoration, 1878–9. The s nave W doorway is cyclopean, and two blocked N doorways have four-centred arches fashioned in cyclopean lintels. A blocked s doorway gave access to some form of extension, pre-dating the Perp remodelling. This may have been a chapel, though Thomas refers to a priest's lodging requiring to be built in 1304. Timber s porch of 1887. The exterior of the church continued to be whitewashed in the C19.

FURNISHINGS. The stem of the FONT is Perp. The bowl is dated 1663. – ROOD SCREEN. Extending across both naves. Its construction is of Welsh type, i.e. with continuous middle rail rather than with the standards running straight through. It has been raised in height, and none of the tracery is original. Some of the wainscot panels are, and have varyingly patterned squints. – PULPIT. C17. Leaf, flower and fruit patterns in the panels. – STAINED GLASS. N nave westernmost.

Some late medieval heads. – N nave E. A sensational, brightly
coloured window installed by Lloyd Bamford Hesketh, 1857,
to commemorate the Lloyds of Gwrych (q.v.). Grisaille, heraldry, and a central tableau of a dashing St Michael, tram-
pling a devil-headed dragon. – N nave easternmost. Also for
Hesketh, and flanked by tablets to commemorate his family,
with space left for inscriptions to countless generations. – N
nave first W from screen by *Ward & Hughes*, 1891. – S nave
E by *Shrigley & Hunt*. – S nave easternmost by *Maud Sumner*,
1958. – Dugout CHEST. – SEPULCHRAL SLAB. In the floor at
the SE corner. A late C14 floriated cross, the arms branching
into lobes. – SCULPTURAL FRAGMENTS include two early
C14 circular-headed crosses, set in the wall W of the S door,
and parts of others, loose in the S nave. – MONUMENTS.
Catherine Parry †1705. Drapery around the inscription, and
volutes, gadrooning, urns etc. – John Jones Bateman of
Pentre Mawr †1849. Large. Willow tree and weeping maiden.
– Philip Wythen Bateman †1849. Kneeling maiden with
cross and anchor. – Various C18 tablets. – Also a BRASS in
the N nave to Rev. Richard Jackson †1847 and Rev. Richard
Henry Jackson †1867. By *John Hardman & Co.*

ST TERESA OF LISIEUX (R.C.), Dundonald Avenue. 1934 by
Rinvolucri, an Italian residing at Conwy. Rock-faced rubble
limestone. Byzantine and cruciform, with dome, segmental
roofs, and an apse terminating each arm. The interior has
plain plastered surfaces, but was altered by *Bowen, Dann &
Davies*, 1971, and given a ferocious-looking TABERNACLE,
and an equally peculiar FONT, both by *Victor Neep*.

EGLWYS CRIST CONGREGATIONAL CHAPEL, Dundonald
Avenue. By *T. Roger Smith* of London (CW), 1860–1. Slated
broach spire, and a timber clerestory, thinly Gothic, like part
of a mission hut marooned above the aisles. (Timber arcades
inside.)

ST PAUL'S METHODIST CHAPEL, St George's Road. 1879–80
by *Richard Davies* of Bangor. Italianate. Two-storeyed, with
a complicated pedimented and pilastered front. Above the
entrance is a tripartite window with segmental pediment on
consoles.

MYNYDD SEION WELSH PRESBYTERIAN (CALVINISTIC
METHODIST) CHAPEL, Chapel Street. In its own graveyard.
Built 1867–8, largely at the expense of David Roberts, father
of John Roberts, M.P., and grandfather of the first Baron
Clwyd. Born at Llanrwst, Roberts set up in business as a
timber merchant in Liverpool. His firm of David Roberts,
Son & Co. also bought land, laid out roads and drains, and
resold to builders. His surveyor was the prolific chapel architect *Richard Owens*, and he it was who designed Mynydd
Seion. (VH) Gothic, with polygonal masonry, steep roofs and
plate tracery, transepts and an apse. The elaborate front has
a narthex and central gable flanked by wings which return as
two-storeyed porches. Foliated caps. In front is a granite
MONUMENT to the Roberts family. OLD CHAPEL. Dating

from 1791, but altered and enlarged. SCHOOLROOM of 1887, paid for by J. H. Roberts, later Lord Clwyd.

PRESBYTERIAN CHURCH OF WALES, Marine Road, Pensarn. Built for English-speaking congregations at the expense not of David Roberts, but of his son John. 1877–8 by *Owens*. Polygonal masonry, transepts, and the front with wheel window, narthex-like porch, and flanked by hipped wings. Foliated caps.

PENTRE MAWR, Dundonald Avenue. Now Council Offices. It seems that the house was remodelled in Tudor Gothic style, *c.*1830, damaged by fire 1850, and restored 1853. It is not clear what was done at that time. The symmetrical entrance front, with an oriel in a battlemented storeyed porch, was unchanged, and some detailing and internal features, particularly plaster vaulting, are typical of *c.*1830. Imperial staircase of good early C18 work, presumably imported and rearranged. Ornamented stair ends, twisted columnar balusters, Corinthian columnar newels.

ABERGELE HOSPITAL, 1¼ m. S. Property was bought by the South Manchester Board of Guardians, 1912, for a sanatorium. It passed to Manchester Corporation in 1914, and the City Architect, *Henry Price*, was responsible for new buildings which were opened in 1931. Extensive grounds, and buildings of ashlar-like concrete blocks, including the Neo-Georgian main block. Also a BRIDGE. There are extensions of the 1950s and 60s.

Abergele is a market town, near the coast, and although early in the C19 it became a place for bathing, it never developed as a resort. At Pensarn, ½ m. N, some building did take place close to the beach, including nondescript terraces by *Lloyd Williams & Underwood* in MARINE ROAD and SOUTH PARADE. (VH) Between here and the town centre, the MAES CANOL HOUSING ESTATE was begun by *S. Colwyn Foulkes*, 1955–60, but was not completed to his designs. In MARKET STREET, the former TOWN HALL and MARKET, 1867, is of brick, with polychromy, and a pyramid-roofed tower. Not done with confidence or conviction. On the corner of Chapel Street, the former SHIP TEMPERANCE CAFÉ AND CLUB, with half-timbered gables. By *Richard Owens & Sons*, 1906–7, under Roberts patronage (cf. Mynydd Seion Chapel, above). Further w, the NATIONAL WESTMINSTER BANK, originally National Provincial, 1924, by *F. C. R. Palmer*. Single-storeyed with heavy rustication and Gibbs surrounds.*

Further on still is a former CHURCH SCHOOL (now COMMUNITY CENTRE) by *Street*, 1869–70, at the expense of Robert Bamford Hesketh of Gwrych. Polygonal masonry and polychromatic slating patterns. U-plan, with five-light arched windows in the gable ends of the cross wings. Asymmetrical,

---

*Opposite is a dated example, 1827, of an elevation with the flat cement surrounds common in some North Wales towns.

the chief accent being an octagonal bell turret and spirelet against the inner face of the left-hand wing. A later addition in front of the central range also sensitively eschews symmetry. Behind is a separate TEACHER'S HOUSE by *Street*. In HIGH STREET, off Chapel Street, a five-storey brick MILL incorporates the stone tower of a windmill.

KINMEL MANOR, ¾m. ESE. Now a hotel. C16 in origin, but enlarged and remodelled when it became the agent's house for the Kinmel estate, *c.* 1840. (VH) Formerly called Hendre Gyda, it was renamed when Colonel H. B. L. Hughes abandoned Kinmel itself (*see* p. 280) and took up residence here. He added a large drawing room, dated 1929, and installed in it the *Nesfield* chimneypiece from the entrance hall at Kinmel. Marble fireplace surround, its frieze enriched with heraldry, putti and swags. High, pedimented overmantel, with three tiers of panelling, pilasters and heraldry, and with characteristically Nesfieldian detail. In the hall, a heavily carved Jacobean chimneypiece, also brought in by Hughes.

HENDRE FAWR, 1¼m. ESE. Mullioned windows, some, which look later, with transoms. Cyclopean doorway. A cross wing has an additional storey and, to the side, three stone dormers. Lateral chimney at the rear, with gabled breast, and, also at the rear, a window of four curved-headed lights. (An upstairs room has moulded and stopped beams in two directions. Also a stone chimneypiece dated 1633, and a plaster overmantel of 1636, with strapwork and heraldry. NMR)

HENDRE UCHAF, 1¼m. SE. Originally a two-unit plan with lateral chimney and inside cross passage. Additions have been made behind the fireplace and at either end. A datestone, and a mutilated inscription on the ingle beam, are both of 1591. The counterchanged hall ceiling, framed in three directions, has joists and two sets of beams, chamfered and stop-chamfered. Upper-end partition screen, with heavily moulded uprights, two doorways and the middle rail enriched with guilloche. A first-floor partition is also moulded and has guilloche pattern.

TOWER, Bron-y-Berllan, ¾m. SSE. An early C17 beacon watchtower, like that at Whitford (*see* p. 456).

BRYNGWENALLT, ¾m. SSW. 1867 (VH) by *Richard Owens* for John Roberts, father of the first Lord Clwyd (*see* Mynydd Seion Chapel, above). The house was large and very Gothic, with a four-storey entrance tower. Embedded in the centre was a hall with organ and open timber roof. Well over half, including the great hall, has been demolished, but the tower and a broad stone staircase remain. Gothic ENTRANCE LODGE. To the NW is TANYRALLT, once the vicarage, and later the home of David Roberts (father of John, and founder of the dynasty). Its LODGE and a nearby former FARM are doubtless by *Owens*.

PANT IDDA, 2m. SW. Whitewashed. Modillion cornice and irregularly spaced sashes. The latest known instance of a storeyed lateral chimney house. Dated 1722 (P. Smith).

(TŶ MAWR, 1½m. SSW. A converted cruck hall house, with inserted chimney backing on to the entry. Wind-braces and a lower-end post-and-panel partition. P. Smith)

CASTELL CAWR, 1m. SW (SH 936 767), is an impressively defended site, but it is difficult to appreciate because it is totally overgrown with trees. The main defence consists of a large stone rampart with internal ditch on the S and external ditch on the NW. The rampart abuts against the precipice at the N and E. The entrance is on the SW, at the centre of the approximately D-shaped enclosure. It has a single inturn on the southern side, where there is evidence to suggest the presence of one square guard chamber. The modern path runs up over the inturned rampart; the true entrance is to the l. of it. The northern rampart has a straight end, very impressive here, but getting lower further to the NW. On the S side there may be an outer line of defence, a low precipice and, on the SW corner, a low curving bank. Because of the trees and scrub it is difficult to see many of the details of this hillfort, but the main rampart on either side of the entrance is very impressive. It stands almost 32 ft above the ditch, though much of this height is due to the natural slope of the ground. In spite of the undergrowth it is easy to find the entrance since the narrow, informal path through the trees from the SW leads straight to it.

ABERWHEELER/ABERCHWILER

0060

CALVINISTIC METHODIST (WELSH PRESBYTERIAN) CHAPEL, Waen. Pedimented elevation, but preserving the tradition of two doorways with windows between. Built 1822, rebuilt 1862, according to plaques. There are two inscriptions, one in Welsh, the other an English translation.

FRON UCHAF. A roofless ruin, 600 ft up on Moel y Parc, 1½ m. NE of the chapel. An internal chimney, creating a lobby entry, is an insertion into an earlier structure. Small mullioned window with two round-headed lights.

CASTELL BACH, 1m. ESE of the chapel. Internal chimney backing on to an outside cross passage. Cyclopean doorway. (Post-and-panel partition. P. Smith)

GEINAS MILL, ¼m. NW of the chapel, beside the River Wheeler. Restored and converted by *David Brock* of *James & Bywater*, 1964.

ACTON PARK *see* WREXHAM, p. 312

ALLINGTON *see* TREFALUN

ALWEN RESERVOIR *see* MYNYDD HIRAETHOG

BACHYMBYD FAWR *see* LLANYNYS

BERAIN *see* LLANEFYDD

BERSE DRELINCOURT *see* BROUGHTON

3040   ## BERSHAM

ST MARY. A small but costly estate church, set amidst dark
   Victorian planting. It was built at the expense of Thomas
   Lloyd Fitzhugh of Plas Power as a chapel for his household
   and tenantry, and is still in the ownership of the family. By
   John Gibson. The style is Romanesque, but handled with
   High Victorian verve, for the building is of 1873, not of the
   Rundbogenstil vogue of a generation earlier. Rock-faced walling and polychromatic voussoirs. Use is made of corbel tables
   and attached shafts, and the stonecarving includes roundels
   and foliated caps. Aisleless and cruciform, with semicircular
   apse and subsidiary blocks in the angles of chancel and transepts. NW tower with porch, and with its upper stage added
   1892–3. This has pairs of tall open arches and is surmounted
97   by pinnacles and a short octagonal spire. The interior is of
   ashlar and is rib-vaulted throughout, except that there are
   tunnel-vaults in the small chambers E of the transepts. Much
   use is made of polychromy, the vaulting cells being of red
   and white stripes, and pier shafts also of red sandstone. Piers
   with scalloped caps punctuate the walls of the (three-bay)
   nave. Those in the chancel, and in clusters at the crossing,
   have foliation, and the crossing arches are heavily enriched.
   Apse windows in a two-three-two arrangement, with tiny
   oculus tubes penetrating the vaulting above the arches in each
   group. Externally these appear as roundels on the wall face,
   with additional ones making a regular rhythm. Miniature arcading in the apse, and the PULPIT and RAILS are of fairly
   pure 'Norman'. – The FONT is also in character. – CORONA
   and brass CANDLE FITTINGS.
PLAS POWER was demolished after the Second World War. A
   three-storey house of 1757 had a seven-bay front, the centre
   three recessed, and a canted bow at the left-hand end of the
   l. return. It was remodelled and enlarged by *Gibson*, 1858. He
   provided an Italianate face-lift and extended the side elevation so that the bow became central.* (Terraces, stables etc.
   remain.) Also *Gibson* ENTRANCE LODGES with wavy bargeboards and diamond glazing. They include SOUTH LODGE,
   1860 (an earlier datestone is *ex situ*), where there is also a
   BRIDGE with Gothic iron balustrading.

* Inferred from material shown to me by Mr D. Leslie Davies.

Bersham has the character of a Plas Power estate village. It has reverted to rural peace (though now intruded upon by the Wrexham by-pass) after having been a place of industrial importance as part of the empire of the ironmaster John Wilkinson. A blast furnace was first established in the later C17; in 1721 Charles Lloyd, a friend of Abraham Darby, substituted coke for charcoal in smelting, as was done at Coalbrookdale. In 1753 the works was acquired by Isaac Wilkinson, and c.1762 it was taken over by his sons John and William. (Their partnership ended acrimoniously in the 1790s.) Products included cannon and other armaments, and cylinders for Boulton & Watt engines. Unlike that at Brymbo (q.v.), the Bersham works did not long survive John Wilkinson's death in 1808, ceasing production in the 1820s.

The site offered water power as well as coal and ironstone, and in tracing something of what remains, a start may be made with CAEAU WEIR (its stepped form is not original), NW of the church. At its foot CAEAU BRIDGE, with rusticated arch and slab parapets. From its head runs the MILL RACE, a stone leet, now dry. Several houses have associations with the works. One of mid-C18 date, with hooded canopy, at the NW corner of the village, was the ACCOUNTS HOUSE or office. Next to it are two pairs of Plas Power ESTATE COTTAGES by *Gibson*, 1859. They have decorative bargeboards and diamond glazing – features which have been applied to BERSHAM BANK COTTAGES, looking down from the N. These are, though, of earlier origin, connected with the works. The most substantial survival is the so-called CORN MILL (for such it later became) opposite the Accounts House. Partly of stone (probably surviving from Charles Lloyd's ironworks), partly brick. In Wilkinson's time it may have been a boring mill. Iron windows are likely to be C19. (Iron water-wheel inside.) Beyond is the OCTAGONAL BUILDING, now a barn, built with massive brick piers. Post-1763, it seems to have housed a centrally pivoted gantry crane, used in connection with casting. The adjoining building (with iron columns) was a fettling shop. (Remains of a BLAST FURNACE on the wooded bank beyond.) FURNACE FIELD, opposite, marks the site of the WEST IRONWORKS, developed from 1785. Here is a WEIR, the LEET from which (traces behind the wall on the W side of the road) supplied the EAST IRONWORKS, begun 1763. Its site is beyond the by-pass. Above the junction of two B roads is FORGE ROW or BUNKER'S HILL, single-storey workers' barracks, built 1775. Originally thirteen cottages, complete until 1971, but now depleted.

On part of the site of the East Works a former BOARD SCHOOL by *William Turner* of Wrexham, 1874. (VH) Gothic and symmetrical. Near the by-pass viaduct BRIDGE COTTAGES, brick-nogged.

OFFA'S DYKE. A well-preserved section, $\frac{3}{8}$ m. W.

BERWYN

A fascinating spot. It has not been improved by successive additions to the CHAIN BRIDGE HOTEL (its nucleus a pub with Victorian half-timbering), and it is a pity that the opportunity to create architecture worthy of a wonderful site was not taken. The hotel stands on a narrow strip of land between the Dee and the canal which has its origin at the Horseshoe Falls nearby (*see* p. 197). The river, rushing turbulently over its rocks, is spanned by the CHAIN BRIDGE itself. A footbridge was first built *c*. 1814 for the transporting of coal from canal barges across to the Holyhead Road. A successor of 1870 was swept away in 1928, and the present little suspension bridge (the predecessors had two mid-river supports and were carried by chains below the decking) dates from the following year. On the opposite bank from the hotel, and sporting similar half-timbering, is the STATION of the Llangollen and Corwen Railway, opened 1865. Immediately upstream, the KING'S BRIDGE, *c*. 1902–6, crosses the river and canal in five arches. Moreover it abuts against, and the road which it carries snakes through, a six-arch VIADUCT of the now abandoned railway.

PLAS BERWYN, ¾ m. w. High above the river, with views of Llandysilio and the Eglwyseg Rocks. Built 1836. Three bays plus one-bay wings. Hipped roofs and a Gothic storeyed porch with tripartite doorway. A later C19 addition was demolished in the 1960s, but a pair of canted bows, clearly not original, remain.

VIVOD, ¾ m. SW. An austere-looking house, built in the 1850s or early 60s; owing little to historical precedent, but not, it would seem, in the deliberately challenging way of Butterfield or Philip Webb. Altered and much enlarged 1871, mainly following the original style. This later work was by *W. J. Green* for William Wagstaff, a solicitor who had been employed by Thomas Brassey. The house is set against a hillside, and the entrance hall, which forms part of the original build and has an open timber roof, is at first-floor level. A timber *porte cochère* is said to be of Scandinavian origin. *R. T. Beckett* made additions and several internal alterations, 1906–10, for Captain J. C. Best (Wagstaff's son-in-law) and for his son.*

w of Berwyn, *Telford* effected one of his most notable HOLYHEAD ROAD improvement schemes.

BETWS-Y-COED‡

For the village itself, in Caernarfonshire, *see The Buildings of Wales: Gwynedd*. The Conwy, forming the county boundary, is spanned by the

* Mr R. J. Best kindly helped me with information on Vivod.
‡ Transferred to Gwynedd in 1974.

WATERLOO BRIDGE* at the S end of the town. The bridge built to carry *Telford*'s Shrewsbury to Holyhead Road across the Conwy, as he recommended to the Holyhead Road Commission in 1815 and then promptly had erected. Only the seventh major cast-iron bridge ever. The 100-ft shallow segmental span and the parapets were recently altered by the Welsh Office. The chief decorative features survive: the lettering which follows the arch either side ('This bridge was constructed in the same year as the Battle of Waterloo was fought'), and the wonderful but now almost invisible spandrels with their gargantuan national plant symbols – roses, thistles etc.

COED-Y-CELYN, ½m. S of the Waterloo Bridge. A large stone-built Italianate villa. Tall belvedere tower above the entrance, with the typical arcaded fenestration in the top stage and shallow pyramid roof. Touches of granite, as well as foliated ornament above the doorway, indicate Mid rather than Early Victorian date. To the l. a service wing of simpler character; similar to it in style is a wing at the rear dated 1874. Though now containing the staircase, this wing seems to be an addition; it contains also a ballroom of double-storey height. In the main block two rooms with exuberant plasterwork, and in one of them a massive and equally sumptuous marble chimneypiece. A later owner was Owain Gethin Jones of Penmachno, Gwynedd, the historian, and the contractor for St Mary's, Betws-y-Coed, and Gethin's Bridge (*see The Buildings of Wales: Gwynedd*). There is no evidence that he designed any part of Coed-y-Celyn.

ENTRANCE LODGE. Similar in style to the main block.

Upstream from Betws-y-Coed, to the S, the Conwy takes on a dramatic, wooded character, and a number of bridges represent successive phases in overcoming the difficulties posed by the Conwy, Machno and Lledr rivers.

PONT-YR-AFANC, ¾m. S. Built *c.*1805 with a cutwater and flood arch. A level carriageway is carried over the Conwy (the old county boundary) beside the huge Beavers' Pool, on a fine semicircular arch 68 ft wide.

(PONT-AR-LEDR, 1m. S. *c.*1700. One slender elliptical arch, with a cutwater and flood arch beautifully sited among rocks.)

Even more impressive, just above Conwy Falls, is BONT NEWYDD, with the river foaming over its rocks far below.

PONT RHYDLANFAIR, the next bridge upstream, is of 1780 by *Robert Griffiths*.

CONWY FALLS RESTAURANT, 1¼m. SSW of Capel Garmon. *c.*1955–6 by *Sir Clough Williams-Ellis*. Neo-Georgian. An upper-level loggia, originally open, has been glazed in.

GLAN CONWY, 2⅜m. SSE of Capel Garmon. A stuccoed three-bay Regency villa with a segmental bow on either return. Trellised veranda.

* This entry is by Mr Haslam.

BETWS-YN-RHOS

St Michael. 1838–9 by *John Welch*, pre-Camdenian and typical of him in its lancets, low-pitched roof and shallow altar recess, balanced on plan by a w porch. More notable is the comical w front, rough (of limestone rubble) and toy-like. The porch is carried up into two octagonal turrets, capped by spirelets and linked by a screen wall pierced by an arched bellcote. w gallery. – STAINED GLASS. e window, commemoration date 1844, brightly coloured with pictorial medallions on a geometrical ground. – Painted ROYAL ARMS of Victoria.

A compact and hilly village. Near the church, but contrasting with it in their ecclesiological seriousness and functional massing, are the former VICARAGE and the SCHOOL. Both by *Lloyd Williams & Underwood*, 1861. The vicarage has hipped gables and a big staircase window.

FFARM, sw of the village. A Mid-Victorian remodelling by *Lloyd Williams & Underwood* of an earlier c19 castellated house. Their work includes the staircase and sinuous Venetian tracery. STABLES on the hill behind have lost some towers and castellations.

PLAS-YN-BETWS, ⅝m. NW. Lateral chimney and inside cross passage. (Staircase with pierced, flat, shaped balusters and square-finialed newel. NMR)

COED COCH (Heronwater School), 1⅝m. WNW. An ingeniously planned house by Hakewill, presumably *Henry Hakewill* rather than his brother James, though with a foundation stone of 1804 in the cellar, it is unlikely to be the 'Villa in North Wales' which he exhibited at the Royal Academy in 1795. Crisp and precise e and s fronts, of ashlar, with low hipped roofs and soffited eaves. Window surrounds, and a string course serves as a first-floor sill. Originally both elevations were the same, both of three bays, the ground-floor windows tall and tripartite. Placed diagonally at the corner was a tetrastyle Greek Doric portico, with pediment. This remarkable arrangement was done away with in the course of early c20 alterations,* and the splayed corner filled in. Some internal features seem also to have been removed, but the staircase is intact. Contained in a small rotunda, and lit from a circular lantern on a dome, it was approached axially from the portico, and separated from this by a small entrance hall (probably circular or oval, now destroyed) and by the corridor which serves the rooms of the two main fronts. In turning the corner the corridor follows the curve of the staircase well, from which it is divided by a screen of two Greek Doric columns with fluted antae. Steps rise between the columns, and the main flight crosses the rotunda before branching and returning in two curves. Doric columns at first-floor level, simpler than those below. The axis of the main flight is continued

* Partly by *Sir Clough Williams-Ellis*, who disclaimed responsibility for the destruction of the portico.

beyond the enclosure. In the filled-in corner of the house is now a circular entrance hall, larger than its predecessor. It has panelling, some of which may be early C18, from Plas Uchaf, Llanefydd (q.v.). A large room on the S front is a C20 addition. The house is U-shaped, enclosing a service court, and the outer side of the service wing presents an orderly W elevation.

CHAPEL. Converted from a stable building. By *Gerald R. Beech* and *J. Quentin Hughes*, 1962, for Heronwater School.

BRYNFFANIGL ISAF, ¾ m. N. A wing has been added, but as first built this was a two-unit storeyed house with lateral chimney and inside cross passage. Mullioned windows with round-headed lights, one of them dated 1585. The chimney breast is gabled and buttressed.

BRYNFFANIGL UCHAF, 1 m. NE. Lateral chimney and inside cross passage. (Staircase with flat, shaped balusters. NMR)

PENIARTH FAWR, ½ m. NNE. Lateral chimney (gabled) and inside cross passage. A pointed cyclopean doorway. Refitted 1735, and the staircase must be of this date. (Turned balusters, ball-finialed newels, and the balustrade repeated against the wall as a dado. NMR)

SIRIOR GOCH, 1⅜ m. E. A late C18 vernacular classical front, of brick. Three bays, two and a half storeys. One-bay pediment and a pilastered and pedimented doorcase with fanlight.

TŶ CELYN, ½ m. SE. (Peter Smith refers to cruck construction.)

BODNANT*   7070

Bought in 1874 by Henry Davis Pochin, a Salford chemical manufacturer and an owner of china-clay mines. The house was rebuilt, c. 1875–6 (incorporating part of a predecessor of 1792), by *W. J. Green*. Elephantine, with mullions and transoms, canted bays and half-timbered gables, like a hotel in some staid Victorian spa. At the NW corner a turret was utilized as a link when in 1898 a drawing-room wing was added, creating the third side of a N entrance court. Pochin's grandson, the second Lord Aberconway (inherited 1934), initiated de-Victorianization. (This included the importing of C18 chimneypieces. One, of c. 1720, from Arlington Street, London, was installed in the 1898 drawing room, together with panelling from Shobden Court, Herefordshire.) He also veiled much of the exterior with planting.

It is for the GARDENS, with their superb trees, shrubs and borders, and their views of the Conwy Valley and Snowdonia, that Bodnant is famed. They were given to the National Trust in 1949. Work was begun by *Edward Milner* for Pochin, whose daughter, Lady Aberconway, also did much; but the present glory is largely due to Henry Duncan McLaren, a great deal of whose work was carried out before he succeeded

* Transferred to Gwynedd in 1974.

as the second *Lord Aberconway*. He replaced Milner's sloping lawns w of the house with five planted TERRACES, 1905–14. All but the topmost are formally laid out, with their axis aligned on the S terrace of the house. The lowest, the CANAL TERRACE, has at its S end the PIN MILL, a garden house of *c*.1730 from Woodchester, Gloucestershire, re-erected here 1938–9. A tripartite loggia, rendered, with stone dressings and Cotswold stone roofs. Quoins and some Gibbs surrounds. Tower-like centre with Venetian window and a pediment with sculpture and urns. The arches of the gabled side wings date from the reconstruction.

Five-bay stone MILL, of 1837. Hipped roof, and the lower windows arched. It is in the informal area of the garden, the DELL, which extends S. The PINETUM here was planted by Pochin, and he built, and is buried in (†1895), the MAUSO-LEUM, which towers above the Dell at its far end. In thoroughly debased round-arched style, with octagonal corner turrets, three-sided apse, plate tracery, vaulting and stained glass. Internally, arcading frames tablets and busts.

Two sets of LODGE GATES of the 1870s.

OLD BODNANT (Hen Fodnant), ⅛m. SE of the house. Of lateral-chimney plan. Extensively remodelled by *Sir Howard Robertson*, 1920. Cross wing with a rear stepped gable.

BORRAS *see* WREXHAM, p. 313

BRENIG *see* MYNYDD HIRAETHOG

3050   BROUGHTON

A former colliery district. It extends from Wrexham to Brymbo as a muddle of hills, streets, chapels, housing estates and surviving countryside.

BERSE DRELINCOURT CHURCH, on the B5101, W of the Wrexham by-pass. Built 1742. It was founded and endowed by Mary Drelincourt, widow of a Dean of Armagh, as a chapel in connection with a girls' charity school. The school was founded in 1719 and endowed in 1751 by Mrs Drelincourt and her daughter, Lady Primerose. The chapel is much altered, but retains its plaster ceiling, flat at the sides and rising as a tunnel-vault down the middle. The exterior has been rendered, and the round-headed windows given mullions. Blocked S doorway, surmounted inside by a plaster shell. It was central before the building was extended W in 1828. S porch, 1930. – Seating of 1862 with older PEW PLATES. – Some original woodwork in the PULPIT. – ALTAR TABLE, from Wrexham Church. Late C17 or early C18 with spiral legs. – CHANDELIERS. One, the survivor of two dating from the 1740s, has seven branches. – The other, given to Wrexham Church in 1688, has two tiers of eight branches (incomplete) and a broad central stem besides the usual sphere. Cherub head above. Both had their iron suspensions curtailed in 1978. – COMMANDMENTS and CREED, both painted on canvas. The former has figures of Moses and Aaron (frequent C17 and C18 accompaniers of the Decalogue) and the background of the latter includes the Whole Armour of God (worn, it would appear, by Britannia) and Works of Mercy. These panels were formerly grouped at the E end with a PAINTING of the Supper at Emmaus.*

OLD VICARAGE, SW of the church. A double-pile gable-ended house of 1715. Solid parapets. Two storeys above a basement, and three bays, the middle one slightly advanced. Brick, with Baroque stone trim. Quoins of even length, keystones, Gibbs surrounds to the ground-floor windows and plain mouldings elsewhere, and a pedimented doorcase with consoles. Rusticated GATEPIERS. Mrs Drelincourt, whose house this was, in 1747 (DOE) erected a single-storey SCHOOL building on the r. of the forecourt. Lady Primerose gave the house for the use of the curate of the chapel, who had the oversight of the school. House and chapel were formerly connected by two AVENUES at right angles to each other.

ST ALBAN, St Alban's Road, Tanyfron. 1896–7 by *Howel Davies* of Wrexham. Brick exterior, with no stone dressings. Semicircular apse, round-headed windows, w bellcote.

ST PAUL, Bryn y Gaer Road, Pentre Broughton. 1888 by *Howel Davies*. Rock-faced, with lancets and a tendency to tracery at the broad, chapel-like w end. Over the chancel arch a double bellcote. Transepts sprout from the chancel.

ST PETER, Church Hill, Brynteg. A mission church of 1894. Enlarged and enriched in 1916, when it was extended w and given traceried E and W windows, some STAINED GLASS and a set of FURNISHINGS. These include a REREDOS, CHANCEL SCREEN and a TESTER over the font. They are thoroughly Bodleyesque, for the work is by *Cecil Hare*, who succeeded to Bodley's practice. Mrs Hamer was the donor (*see* below).

ALL SAINTS, Southsea. In 1884 a church by *E. B. Vaughan* was built at the expense of the Rev. Meredith Hamer and his wife Margaret. He was curate of Berse Drelincourt, but resigned the following year and became a partner in his father-in-law's business at Burton-on-Trent. The church was rebuilt, 1925–8, following subsidence. Mrs Hamer, by then a widow, met the cost and employed *Cecil Hare*,‡ with whom *A. V. Heal* was associated. Smooth and simple Neo-Perp, of ashlar externally. Cruciform, with the choir at the crossing.

---

* This was removed from the church in 1981, pending investigation of an attribution to Velasquez. This was not substantiated and the painting has been returned to the church.

‡ Perhaps indicating some link with the work by Bodley and Hare at Burton (under Bass patronage) and elsewhere in Staffordshire.

Clerestory, but an aisle on the s only. The structure is not incomplete, but the scheme underwent change and modification: e.g., as first designed, *c*.1922, narrow passage aisles were intended, with tall arcades and no clerestory. – Of the FURNISHINGS, a proposed rood screen never materialized, but there are STALLS in the Bodley tradition. – *Hare*, or perhaps even *Bodley* himself, must have had a hand in the filigree Gothic PULPIT and the *Burlison & Grylls* STAINED GLASS, which were reused from the old church.

All Saints' VICARAGE enjoys rural seclusion, ¼m. SSW of the church. Refined Neo-Georgian, of ashlar, 1921. Inventive features include the centre of the entrance front recessed between chimney stacks and carried up as a parapet. The outer bays of the garden front form shallow wings, expressed as such only by the consequent change in roof level. Central balcony.

The following three houses are described in relation to Berse Drelincourt Church.

CROESNEWYDD, ⅜m. SE. Dignified work of 1696. Brick and stone. Two storeys and a basement. Hipped roof and panelled stacks and a front of seven bays, the middle three slightly recessed. Quoins, segmental-headed windows with differing keystones, doorcase with lugs and entablature, and a moulded surround to the central window above. The front has sashes, probably early C18 insertions.* Stone mullions in the basement and timber cross windows elsewhere, with leaded glazing. The plan is not a double pile but a U, with rear wings. Two dog-leg staircases, both rising to the attics. The main one has turned balusters and a moulded string with pulvinated frieze. One room with bolection-moulded panelling and simple ribbed ceiling. Dado in the room above. An axial lime AVENUE has been mutilated. A FARM BUILDING, dated 1701, has quoins and a coped gable.

LOWER BERSE, ½m. SSW. H-plan. Remodelled 1873, with the bargeboards and diamond glazing of the Plas Power estate style (*see* Bersham). There remains part of the spere-truss of a late C14 or C15 timber-framed hall, and the lower part of a moulded post is visible. Also the arched-braced central truss, with struts above the collar, and the moulded beam of a dais canopy. (Cusped wind-bracing.) Dating from the sub-division of the hall are moulded beams and a lateral chimney with ingle beam on corbelled jambs.

HIGHER BERSE, ¾m. WNW. A good early C19 hipped-roofed farmhouse, belonging to the Plas Power estate. Three-bay ashlar front, with central arched recess and a pedimented doorcase. Square, brick DOVECOTE with pyramid roof.

---

* The shutters inside are definitely C18, but if the sashes themselves are original, they must be among the earliest in Wales.

BRYMBO   3050

Steep hills and rows of houses on ridge tops, with the BRYMBO
STEELWORKS dominating. This developed from an ironworks established in 1795 by John Wilkinson (*see* Bersham),
who had bought the Brymbo Hall estate, largely for the sake
of its coal resources. (Within the works is Wilkinson's 'Old
Number One' BLAST FURNACE, which continued in use until
1894.) BRYMBO HALL was demolished in 1973, a grievous
loss. A wing dated 1624 had an aedicular doorway and shaped
gables with fanciful finials. At right angles was a five-bay C18
range with a giant order of Doric pilasters, and highly
Baroque in its features.

ST MARY. 1871–2 by *T. H. Wyatt*. Rock-faced and cruciform,
with semicircular apse and a double bellcote over the chancel
arch. Lancets and a W rose window. Inner DOORS of the S
porch by *Waterhouse*, from Eaton Hall. A predecessor church
by *John Lloyd*, 1837–8, was on a different site.

The church is at the end of the urban sprawl. The VICARAGE,
further removed, ¼m. NE, is by *Wyatt*, c.1871–3. The former
SCHOOL, ¼m. S, is amid the hilly streets. Of 1850–1 by *R. K.
Penson*, it was, owing to subsidence, rebuilt in 1871, but possibly to the original design.

(NOS. 2–4 BRAKE ROAD. A stone-built terrace of three five-
room workers' cottages – two up, three down – erected 1815.)

PENTRE SAESON FOUNDRY, 1¼m. SW, near a crossroads on
the B5102. A mid-C19 foundry, still functioning.

BRYNEGLWYS   1040

ST TYSILIO. The unassuming exterior continued to be whitewashed into the C19. A single chamber, Perp in its early   15
features, plus the SE Yale Chapel, which is an Elizabethan
addition.* Two crudely wrought timber columns, one of them
renewed, separate the two parts. Three-light Perp E window,
arched-braced roof and, at the E end, a panelled wagon ceiling
with bosses, following the curve of the arched braces. The
chapel roof, also arched-braced, has cusped struts above the
collar. – PULPIT. C17. Panels with patterns of flowers, fruit
etc. – C17 bits, including a panel dated 1615, are worked into
the STALLS, which, in sophisticated Jacobean style, date from
Arthur Baker's restoration of 1875–6. – Also of this time the
FONT. Bowl, incorporating an earlier one, is adorned with
solemn-looking angels' heads. – SEPULCHRAL SLAB. Early
C14, commemorating Tangwystl, daughter of Ieuaf ap
Maredudd. Inscription along the base and on a centre label.
Leaf trails either side of the label.

The village lies in a broad valley behind Llandysilio Mountain.
In the buildings at BRYN TANGOR, 2¼m. WSW, is the

* Plas-yn-Yale, 2m. ENE, is a successor house to the ancestral home of Elihu
Yale's family.

arched-braced central cruck of a hall house, with cusped king-post above the collar. Traces of crucks, one with arched-bracing, at TŶ GWYN, ¾ m. w. (PENTRE ISAF, NE of Tŷ Gwyn, is a hall house, retaining its central truss and the upper-end cruck partition. The bottom part of the latter is post-and-panel, with one arched doorway surviving.)

BRYNKINALT

3030

Possession has passed by inheritance since the C10. In the C15 John ap David, descendant of Tudor Trevor, took the surname of Trevor, and Brynkinalt is today the seat of the fourth Baron Trevor. The E-plan s front, of brick with stone dressings, was built in 1612 by Sir Edward Trevor. It has shaped gables to the cross wings and storeyed porch, and small straight ones in the two recesses. Mullions and transoms (mullions alone in the gable windows) and a pointed doorway. Much was done two centuries later in the time of Arthur Hill-Trevor, second Viscount Dungannon of the second creation, and an inscription ascribes work to 1808 and to the 'Sole Design' of Charlotte, *Lady Dungannon*. Her executant architect has not been identified.* Extensive and naïve-looking stuccoed additions were made, with shaped gables and castellated parapets, turrets and chimneys. The Jacobean house was itself stuccoed over and given Gothic loggias and castellated embellishment, but was closely restored to its original appearance in 1926. Only Gothic glazing and a little castellation survive from the early C19 metamorphosis. The extensions have themselves been modified by the stripping of the stucco and the removal of many of their features, and some demolition took place *c*.1952-3. Of the additions, only single-storey wings, set back from the frontage, appear on the s. Containing drawing room on the E and dining room on the W, they are probably of 1808, but were lengthened by the respective additions of an E conservatory and the W (former) billiard room. The 1808 W front continued back as service quarters, now largely demolished, though a N screen wall is preserved. Probably of 1812, this has corner towers and a central gateway with tourelles.

The early C19 interiors are classical, with heavy detailing and much use of Doric columns. An enormous central hall has a gallery round three sides and a staircase beginning in one flight and branching into two. Ornate iron balustrading and two domed roof-lights. Doric screen either end of the dining room. In the drawing room, plasterwork of 1973 by *G. Jackson & Sons Ltd* and a caryatid marble chimneypiece. An enfilade from dining room to drawing room through two

*The drawings, which include some for variant schemes, are unsigned and undated. They have been credited to George Strutt of Chelsea on the strength of work by him being inserted in the same album, but it does not belong to the set, and may not relate to Brynkinalt.

ante-rooms, and the hall is continued by the conservatory. Also opening from the drawing room is a suite of two delightful and elegant boudoirs. The first has mirrors incorporated in the decoration, and the inner room has a saucer dome and in its plan geometrical curves. The Oak Hall in the Jacobean S front (where the original planning has been lost) has an excellent marble chimneypiece, which must be of the later C17 and of the time of Sir John Trevor, Speaker of the House of Commons and Master of the Rolls. It has lugs and a heraldic overmantel with Gibbons-like carving, side volutes and segmental head. Heraldic stained glass in this room is C17 but post-1625, and in the adjoining library is by *David Evans*, c.1840. Pictorial panels, pre-1625, in the staircase window, and over the main entrance is glass given in the 1820s by Marquess Wellesley, brother of the Duke of Wellington and cousin of Lord Dungannon.

According to the inscription, *Lady Dungannon* also 'embellished' the GROUNDS and PARK, but it is not clear if this refers to landscaping or building. Of the period is a BRIDGE across the Ceiriog, with castellated parapet. Next to it a picturesque rustic COTTAGE, with walling of river stones and tree trunks. A CHINA ROOM AND DAIRY of 1813–14 has been demolished.

In Chirk a single-storey castellated ENTRANCE LODGE, dated 1813–14, with corner tower. BRYN-Y-GWYLA LODGE (disused), 1 m. S of the house, is also castellated. Symmetrical, with corner turrets. Central arched gateway and lower side wings.*

BRYNTEG *see* BROUGHTON

BRYN-Y-MAEN

8070

CHRIST CHURCH. By *Douglas & Fordham*, and very good. Built 1897–9 in memory of Charles Frost, at the expense of his widow, Eleanor. Low, spreading proportions, combined with roofs of fair pitch, happily suit the upland site in the hills behind Colwyn Bay. Neo-Perp, with panel tracery. Broad nave, S passage aisle, and central tower above the choir. Low transepts contain vestry and organ chamber. The tower is squat and massive, with battlements stepped up at the corners, and straight-headed bell openings under labels. It has buttresses only on the E. The NW vice turret is handled with individuality, and at the top, as elsewhere around the church, are tiny windows, artfully deployed. Local limestone walling, with dressings and the ashlar interior of red Helsby. Octagonal arcade piers. The transverse tower arches, almost semicircular, have continuous chamfering. Except for the

* This lodge and the rustic cottage are across the English border.

SEDILIA there is little enrichment of masonry, most ornament being concentrated on woodwork. The nave roof, a form of hammerbeam, has tracery, and there is a set of characteristic Douglas FURNISHINGS, including not only REREDOS, ORGAN CASE, STALLS, PULPIT, LECTERN, PEWS and FONT COVER, but also the HYMN BOARD, ALMSBOX and UMBRELLA STAND. – Iron CHANCEL GATES are also original.

Mrs Frost paid for the VICARAGE and built a house for herself, BRYN EGLWYS, nearby. Both by *Douglas & Fordham* and both Neo-Elizabethan, with symmetrical three-gable fronts, and pebbledashed, with stone dressings. The vicarage, dated 1898, has bargeboarded gables, two of them corbelled out over ground-floor canted bays. Bryn Eglwys has coped gables, a gabled porch, and shaped heads to window lights.

BWLCHGWYN

2050

At the extremity of Wrexham's industrial web, with Esclusham Mountain and the Llandegla moorland beyond.

CHRIST CHURCH. Built as a school, 1867. Ten years later, *H. & A. P. Fry* of Liverpool converted it to a church, adding chancel, vestry and S porch. There is a bellcote at the E end of the nave S wall. Circular window above three lancets at the W end, and plate tracery in the E window.

PENIEL CHAPEL, ¾ m. WSW. Low pyramid roof and bracketed eaves. Two doors with round-headed windows between. Dating from 1823, though the present Italianate character belongs to work of 1861 or 1878.

A fine Bronze Age BARROW stands on an eminence just S of the A525 road (SJ 233 525). Another large mound, N of the road, at the gate to Maesmaelor, is more likely to be a natural feature. 1½ m. further W (SJ 211 518), road-widening in 1936 destroyed another barrow with several cremated burials. Fragments of only one urn were rescued. Its shape suggests an unusually late date in the Bronze Age.

BYLCHAU

9060

ST THOMAS. Built 1857. *Sir Gilbert Scott* responded to the character of the site, on the edge of the moors of Mynydd Hiraethog, for there is a strong and austere feel about this little cusped-lancet church of dark rock-faced stone. Strictly it is a single chamber, though nave and chancel are separated by a timber arch, marked externally by buttressing. Corbelled W bellcote, its lower stage arched up to make way for a window. Internally, the three-light E window has detached shafts with foliated caps. – STAINED GLASS. Contemporary E window by *Wailes*. – Iron and brass CANDLE and LAMP STANDARDS.

s of the church the former SCHOOL, 1856, and ⅛m. NE the former RECTORY, by *Lloyd Williams & Underwood*, 1862.

There was a group of three BARROWS in the pass at Bylchau, but only two can be easily seen now, and they are being gradually eroded by ploughing, when the yellow clay capping the turf mound can be clearly seen. They stand in the field just s of the church (SH 977 629).

CAPEL GARMON* 8050

A tight little village centre, with the church at one end. E of the church, against a backdrop of council houses, is the tiny former SCHOOL, dated 1854, with a diminutive bellcote over the porch. It cost only £65. Westwards, the backdrop is the awesome panorama of Snowdonia.

ST GARMON. Rebuilt by *E. G. Paley*, 1862–3, i.e. before the advent of Austin. A single chamber with plate tracery. Not enhanced by partial rendering and slate-hanging.

MAEN PEBYLL, 2m. ENE (SH 844 566), is a puzzling monument, and its correct classification is by no means certain. It has been claimed that it is the remains of a long cairn, the broken stones at the E end being the last remnants of the burial chamber. However, a sketch made in 1850 shows a single very large stone there which is known to have been subsequently blasted. Even the long cairn is doubtful, for it is only a surmise that it represents the surviving fringe of a stone mound removed for wall building. The size of the standing stone would, however, suggest a prehistoric origin.

The CAPEL GARMON LONG CAIRN, ¾m. s (SH 818 543), is the best preserved and most interesting Neolithic monument in Denbighshire. The tomb is a far-flung member of the Severn Cotswold family, a group of monuments found in Gloucestershire and Breconshire, where many features of the design may be paralleled. The presence of this northern example, together with two in Merioneth, must reflect a northward movement of people or religious ideas. This movement, which probably belongs to the later Neolithic, may have some connection with the trade in stone axes from Penmaenmawr. The monument consists of a cairn, *c.* 100 ft long and surviving to a height of almost 6 ft in places, containing a large T-shaped chamber originally entered from the side of the cairn. At the E end is a narrow forecourt fronting a 'false portal'. The cairn is surrounded by a neat drystone wall whose position is now indicated by a line of small stones, marking out its characteristic trapezoid shape. The chamber is now entered at its western end, where the walling stones have been pulled out of position, so that this almost circular chamber which still retains its large capstone could be used as a stable. The roofing stones had been pulled from the central space, the circular

* Transferred to Gwynedd in 1974.

eastern chamber and from the narrow passage and they were all choked with stone when the tomb was first excavated in 1853, though the passage had been free of debris at the end of the C17 when the monument was first entered. The monument was finally cleared and consolidated in 1924, when a few bones and sherds of Beaker pottery were found, but the chamber had been so badly disturbed that no firm conclusions could be made about the nature of the original contents. (W. J. Hemp in *Archaeologia Cambrensis*, 7th ser., vol. 7, 1927.) The chambers and passage are built with upright stones linked by neat dry walling, much of which is original. The junction of original and reconstructed walling is marked by a line of three (tiny) drill marks in the stone.

A splendid Late Iron Age fire-dog was found in a bog *c.*½ m. to the W of the tomb. This rich, almost 'Baroque' piece of wrought ironwork is the most ornate example of its class in Britain – or Europe. It would have graced the hearth of a local chieftain at a time when hospitality was one of the most important duties of a leader, and it may have been buried in the bog as a rich offering to placate the gods, perhaps at a time when Roman armies were threatening this area. The fire-dog, with its crested ox-heads and curled supports, may be seen in the National Museum of Wales in Cardiff

For PONT-YR-AFANC, BONT NEWYDD and PONT RHYD-LANFAIR, *see* Betws-y-Coed.

2040   CEFN MAWR

Industrial territory at the entrance to the Vale of Llangollen. George Borrow dramatically described blast furnaces seen at night. Works at Acrefair, taken over by the British Iron Company in 1823, closed in 1888, but a blast furnace of *c.*1800 survived until 1963. What is now the Monsanto Chemical Works had its origin in 1867, when R. F. Graesser established works for extracting oil from coal shale.

The vale is crossed not only by the great aqueduct of Pont Cysyllte (*see* p. 166) but also by a stone VIADUCT, a worthy monument of the heroic age of railway expansion. 1846–8 by *Henry Robertson*, for the Shrewsbury and Chester Railway. Rising some 150 ft above the Dee, and with nineteen arches on slender piers, it is as near to being light and graceful as so large and strong a structure can be. Abutments with pediments and arched recesses.

ST JOHN EVANGELIST, Rhosymedre. 1836–7 by *Edward Welch*, largely at the expense of the then Sir Watkin Williams-Wynn. Sprawlingly cruciform, with low-pitched roofs, corner pinnacles, Y-tracery, and a grossly heavy saddleback W bellcote. There used to be W and transept galleries. Refitted 1887 by *W. H. Spaull* of Oswestry. – ENCAUSTIC TILES. Probably by *J. C. Edwards*. – STAINED GLASS. E window by *Done & Davies* of Carlisle, 1867. (VH)

Of the dozen or so CHAPELS of Cefn and Acrefair, the oldest is
the BAPTIST, Newbridge, 1825. Half-hipped. Simple ceiling
patterning. The former INDEPENDENT, High Street, has a
front of 1857, small, three-bayed and pilastered, with a Venetian window.

By *Mervyn Edwards, Morton & Partners* of Oswestry, the PLAS
MADOC LEISURE CENTRE, its first stage (1972-4) including
a multi-purpose sports hall. Completed 1977 by the addition
of the swimming pool, faced externally in dark brick, and
with translucent plastic roofing on a steel spaceframe. The
pool, informally shaped and with palm trees and a wave
machine, was planned to complement the facilities for serious
swimming offered by the rectangular pools at Wrexham (*see*
p. 305). By the same architects the PLAS MADOC HOUSING
ESTATE, 1968-70.

Across the river, beyond Newbridge, the site of the PENYBONT
WORKS. This was one of the establishments of *J. C. Edwards*,
a pioneer of large-scale terra-cotta production, and the most
celebrated and successful of the manufacturers of the bright
red pressed brick of the Ruabon region. There remains a
LODGE with conical turret. Also a block of four COTTAGES,
employing the firm's products and built *c.*1882, for the fore-
men of the encaustic tile, terra-cotta, blue brick, and roofing
tile departments. By *George Canning Richardson*, a pupil of
Thomas Verity and head of Edwards's design department.

NEWBRIDGE LODGE. *See* Wynnstay.

CLOUD HILL. *See* Froncysyllte.

0070

CEFN MEIRIADOG

ST MARY. A small church of 1863-4, standing high up on its
own, with views of the sea and the Vale of Clwyd. Plas yn
Cefn is a Williams-Wynn house, and the church was completed at the expense of Sir Watkin, sixth Baronet, following
the death of his brother, who had initiated the work. As usual,
the family employed *Ferrey*. Lancets and plate tracery. A S
organ chamber and N vestry form transepts. Rib-vaulted
polygonal apse, the vaulting now unsuitably painted. – FONT.
Life-size angel, on one knee, holding a shell. A copy of work
by *Thorwaldsen* (in Copenhagen Cathedral) by his pupil
Theobald Stein. – REREDOS. Commemoration date 1880. Pietà
roundel, and patterns of inlaid marble. – Two late medieval
STALLS, said to be from Ruthin. Minus their misericords,
but with figurative elbow knops. – STAINED GLASS. Apse and
W windows by *Lavers & Barraud*. – A S window by *Lavers,
Barraud & Westlake*, 1878. – Brass CANDLESTANDARDS.

PLAS YN CEFN, ¼ m. S of the church. Stepped gables. Largely
C19, but with earlier date inscriptions, including an *ex situ*
one of 1600. (An Ionic chimneypiece from Wynnstay, Adamish, in contrasting marbles. NMR) FARM BUILDINGS with a
profusion of stepped gables.

MAES ROBERT. Housing for elderly people, in the hamlet ⅛ m. sw of the church. The name commemorates Robert Watkin Williams-Wynn, younger son of the tenth Baronet. 1973–4 by *Bowen, Dann, Davies* for the then Rural District Council. The layout, with two terraces of bungalows and a taller section containing four flats, is skilfully and sensitively related to the sloping and wooded terrain. Walling of grey concrete blocks, and low-pitched roofs with interlocking concrete tiles.

FFYNNON FAIR, ¾ m. ESE. The ruins of a well chapel, among the tree-lined meadows of the Elwy Valley. T-plan, with N and S transepts at the W end. Their W walls are missing, and the well basin itself encroaches upon their line. The way in which the basin was integrated with the chapel is thus not clear, and it may have been enclosed within the vanished W arm of a cruciform plan. Like that at Holywell (*see* p. 371) the basin is Late Perp, of stellar plan, with diagonal projections on three of the four sides of a square. The fourth (S) side has a later bath adjoining. There would have been canopy work on shafts. The transepts and the E arm are of different builds, the latter probably dating from a Perp enlargement and remodelling. Perp windows, with mullions and tracery missing, and two pointed doorways, their arches each of two stones. Bellcote on the N gable.

WIGFAIR, ½ m. ESE, high above the river and Ffynnon Fair. *Nesfield* made proposals for rebuilding or remodelling, 1876, but the present house is a rebuilding by *Douglas*, 1882–4, for the Rev. R. H. Howard. Jacobethan, of Ruabon brick with stone dressings, and a Ruabon tile roof. L-plan, with a W service wing, carrying a pyramid-roofed tower, and a N wing forming the main block. The staircase window projects as a canted bay in the internal angle of the two ranges. The doorway is below an oriel, off-centre, in the N gable end. The main rooms are along the E front, which is continued southwards by a wing which contained a library. This room is stripped of its fittings, but the house does retain some good Douglas woodwork, particularly the dining room and the staircase, the latter with an arcade on posts at upper level, and turned balusters.

PONT NEWYDD, ½ m. SW. Two arches spanning the Elwy, the earlier one wide and segmental. The other, with broader roadway, was intended as the first stage of a complete rebuilding. Slab parapets, partly and most regrettably replaced in concrete.

49 PLAS NEWYDD, 1½ m. NW. A fine example of a three-unit house with lateral chimney and a cross passage. Two storeys plus a pair of stone dormers, one of them dated 1583 – an early instance of their use. Mullioned windows, and two later ones with transoms. Square chimneys with moulded caps, the lateral one rising from a gable. Arched doorways to the cross passage, one now blocked, and a separate cyclopean doorway to the former lower-end kitchen. Broad fireplace arches in this room and the hall. An upper-end partition screen, with guilloche patterns, and also dated 1583, is now at St Fagan's.

Post-and-panel partition upstairs. Beams, framed in two directions, and joists are stop-chamfered, except in the hall and upper-end parlour, where the beams are moulded and stopped.

BRYN-Y-PIN, 2½m. NW. An C18 double pile, brick-built, of remarkable plan. Four rooms are grouped round a central stone spiral staircase reached by an axial corridor. Corner fireplaces in each room, their flues gathered into a central stack above the stairs. The spiral rises from the cellar to the first floor. Straight but axially planned branching flights continue to the attics.

PONT Y DDÔL, 2m. WNW. Two segmental arches, one of them wide and lofty.

BONT NEWYDD CAVE (SJ 015 710), high up on the cliff on the N side of the Elwy Valley, is not normally accessible to the public but is an important archaeological and geological site because the earliest evidence of man's occupation of Wales has been found there. The cave was first excavated in 1872, when animal bones were found, together with implements which were not recognized for what they were. A continuing programme of excavation and scientific dating has recently been undertaken by the National Museum of Wales, and many more implements have come to light. Amongst the mud and rock washed into the back of the long narrow cave some human bones have been found (with the famous Swanscombe finds, the earliest in Britain), together with a large number of Acheulian hand axes and Levallois flakes which must have come from a camp site, probably in the cave mouth. A uranium date for the stalagmite layer which covers part of the mud flow gives an estimation of at least 180,000 bc for the age of these bones and implements. There is no late occupation of this cave (except for a Second World War ammunition store) because the mouth was blocked with debris during subsequent glaciations.

In 1830, when the paths and terraces were first cut in the cliff at Cefn (SJ 021 705), human and animal bones were noticed in the soil removed from the largest CAVE, its mouth being discovered at that time. The bones were not observed *in situ*, but those collected from the spoil included pleistocene animals and also human bones of Neolithic type. The use of caves for burial was common in the Vale of Clwyd at this time. A few flint flakes were also found which have been recently identified as of Federmesser type, dating from *c.*10,000 bc and marking the return of man to this area after the last glaciation.

TYDDYN BLEIDDYN (SJ 010 721) is a now sadly overgrown long cairn standing in the middle of a sloping field above the Elwy Valley. Only one ruined chamber can be recognized lying across the NW end of the cairn. In the C19 another chamber of similar construction found to the E of it was excavated by Professor Boyd Dawkins, who found a number of inhumation burials. The cairn probably belongs to the Neolithic 'Severn Cotswold' group, since it had lateral chambers and unburnt burials, but few characteristic details survive.

DOLBELIDR. *See* Henllan.

PILKINGTON P. E. LTD. *See* St Asaph, p. 443.

CEFN PARK *see* WREXHAM, p. 310

CEFN-Y-BEDD *see* GWERSYLLT

9040

CERRIGYDRUDION

A few miles beyond Corwen, the Holyhead Road passes through bleak, mountainous country. Although the moorland is mostly under cultivation, its emptiness provides a mild foretaste of the sublimities of *Telford*'s route through Snowdonia, further on. Borrow stayed at the White Lion.

ST MARY MAGDALENE. A single chamber plus a S transept (Giler Chapel) at the E end. Double W bellcote and a big S porch. The exterior was whitewashed when seen by Glynne in 1865. He believed the transept to be C17, and Lloyd Williams & Underwood illustrated it (1872) with a round-headed E window and a gable roof parallel to that of the nave. It was presumably remodelled in a restoration of 1874, when the church's assertive lancets were introduced. Repair and enlargement in 1503 are recorded, and the date would suit arched-braced trusses in the nave, with struts and cusping above the collars.* – FONT. C18 bowl bracketed from the wall. – CHEST. Dated 1715. – MONUMENTS. Thomas Price †1668. Tablet with heraldry. – Margaret Price †1723. Corinthian surround and freely designed embellishment. Long inscription, rudely executed. – The CHURCHYARD is circular.

Former RECTORY, ¼m. NW. Ambitious stone-built vernacular work of 1790. One and a half storeys, five bays and a three-bay pediment. The doorcase has a pediment on consoles. Enlarged 1871.

(TAI FRY, 1½m. WNW. Peter Smith refers to cruck construction.)

52 LLAETHWRYD, 1m. SW. Very picturesque. Low, with stone dormers, and small in scale, except for a massive porch and cyclopean doorway. Gabled lateral chimneybreast to the l., and to the r. a room with a chimney backing on to the entry. A four-light window with timber mullions and transom. Over the lateral fireplace the date 1668. Exposed trusses with collars. An adjoining range, now farm buildings, was once a separate house, i.e. unit planning. (In it a truss, probably *ex*

*A pair of N and S slits may be considered as low side windows. They can hardly have been in connection with the rood screen, as has been suggested, for they are not in line, and that on the S is too far W.

situ, with cusping above the collar. NMR) FARM BUILDINGS including a barn with curved struts above the tie-beams (said to be dated 1661) and another with similar but lighter trusses and a (reset?) datestone of 1734. Also a cart shed with granary above.

A large round BARROW can be clearly seen from the main road (SH 956 482). It is rather unusually sited on flat land between two streams.

CAER CARADOG, 1m. ESE (SH 968 479), a univallate hillfort crowning a low hill, has been much commented upon in the past because it can be easily seen from the village. The defences consist of a single bank and ditch with its main entrance on the E side. Hints of an earlier, smaller defensive circuit inside the fort were not confirmed by small-scale excavations in the early 1960s. It is interesting to note the discovery, not far away, of an Iron Age grave with the remains of a finely decorated bowl (or helmet) which is an import from the Continent and a significant piece in the history of Iron Age art in Britain.

CHIRK / Y WAUN

3030

CHIRK CASTLE

The castle stands close to Offa's Dyke and the English border. Immediately to the S the ground drops steeply towards the Ceiriog, though the defensive strength of the site is not now fully apparent from near-to. Thus it is worth seeking out the SW view, from the road on the other side of the river, in order to see the massive building crowning the hillside. It was begun by Roger Mortimer, some time after Edward I had in 1282 granted to him the lordship of Chirkland, and Master *James of St George*, or another officer of the royal works, is likely to have been the designer. Work may not have started until the 1290s or even later, and although tradition assigns completion to 1310, the structure may have remained unfinished at the time of Mortimer's downfall in 1322. It was in 1595 that Chirk was bought by Sir Thomas Myddelton, merchant and later Lord Mayor of London. In 1801 it passed by marriage to the Biddulphs, who first took the name Myddelton-Biddulph and later that of Myddelton, and it remained with the family until 1978, when it was accepted by the Secretary of State for Wales, before being transferred to the National Trust.*

The *enceinte* was intended to be larger than now it is. The original plan was for a rectangle, on a N–S axis, with circular corner towers and a semicircular tower at the mid-point of each curtain wall – except on the S, where there would pre-

12

---

* I am greatly indebted to Mr Richard Dean, of the National Trust, who made available the results of his research on the castle, and provided answers to many detailed inquiries.

sumably have been a central gatehouse. There are thus affinities with Beaumaris Castle, of the 1290s, but with only one
gatehouse, as in the work of the 1280s at Harlech. As existing,
the structure continues s of the E and W demi-towers for only
a short distance, and it is not known if it was ever built to its
intended full extent. The fact that its towers rise no higher
than the curtains suggests that the castle may never have been
fully completed. (The towers may, though, have been truncated during or after the Civil War.) The present s range has
sometimes been ascribed to Robert Dudley, Earl of Leicester,
to whom Chirk was granted by Elizabeth I in 1563. This is
incorrect. The s curtain, and the E end of the range built
against it, containing the chapel, may be ascribed to the C15.
Also, the western section of the range, as well as some remodelling of the earlier part, is identifiable as work carried
out by officers of Henry VIII in 1529. The W curtain and its
demi-tower, known as Adam's Tower, have been little altered, and the principal domestic accommodation is on the N
and E, with the N range dating from the time of the first Sir
Thomas Myddelton. His son, also Sir Thomas, fought for
Parliament in the Civil War, and in the 1640s the castle suffered damage. More serious harm was inflicted in 1659 under
General Lambert, following the participation of Myddelton
(who had changed allegiance) in Sir George Booth's Cheshire
Rising. Reparations were put in hand in the 1660s. They were
accompanied by the building of the E range, 1667–*c*.1678,
involving the reconstruction of the E towers and the wall
between them, which had been demolished by Lambert. The
works were initiated during the minority of Sir Thomas Myddelton, fourth Sir Thomas and second Baronet. He came of
age in 1672, and the following year married Elizabeth Wilbraham, daughter of Elizabeth, *Lady Wilbraham*, of Weston
in Staffordshire. Lady Wilbraham is convincingly credited
with the designing of Weston, and she seems to have played
an influential part in the completing of the operations at
Chirk. Shortly after the marriage, an agreement was signed
with contractors from Weston, and even after the death of his
wife in 1675 Sir Thomas continued to consult Lady Wilbraham on architectural matters.

With the curtains and towers on the N and E variously
rebuilt and hollowed out, and the external form preserved,
the successive adaptations for continued habitation were remarkably conservative. Alterations by *Joseph Turner* in the
1760s and 70s involved the provision of some new windows,
and these are mullioned and transomed. In the C19 the most
notable contributions were those of *A. W. N. Pugin*, 1845–8.
Except for the Palace of Westminster, the furnishing and
decorating formed the largest, or at least the most costly, of
all the interior schemes on which he and *J. G. Crace* collaborated. Little now remains to show for it all.* From 1911 to

* Mrs Alexandra Wedgwood kindly provided help and information in connection with the Pugin work.

1946 the castle was tenanted by the eighth Lord Howard de Walden, for whom restoration and alterations were carried out in 1911–13. His architects were *Ingram & Brown* of Kilmarnock.

A miscellany of mullioned and transomed windows, ranging in date from the C16 or C17 to the early C20, dot the curtains and the five towers of the EXTERIOR. Battered bases to the towers. A turret, following the curve of the plan, rises from Adam's Tower on the W, and is probably a fragment of a former or intended upper storey. It is known as the Watchtower. A doorway near the NW tower replaced a postern on the N, blocked up in 1769. At the SW corner is the junction of the masonry of the original build with that of the C15 S curtain. A junction is also obvious on the E, where, though most of the elevation belongs to the rebuilding begun in 1667, a fragment of the original curtain meets the C15 walling of the chapel. *Sir Arthur Blomfield* restored the chapel, *c.* 1894, and the Perp E window is his. It replaced a Dec effort of 1854 by *E. W. Pugin*, who was responsible for some work at the castle after his father's death. The two S windows seem also to be of *c.* 1894. Also on the S may be discerned traces of gables which belonged to the work of 1529. The valleys were filled in during the operations of the 1660s and 70s. Two garderobe stacks may be additions of 1529. The gateway, the presumed substitute for a missing southern gatehouse, is in the N curtain, and is approached across a surviving fragment of moat. A pointed arch of two chamfered orders is deeply recessed in a much taller arch, into the rebates of which a drawbridge would have risen, and which is furnished with portcullis grooves. Attributable to *A. W. N. Pugin* is a tablet carved with the Myddelton-Biddulph arms.

So through into the COURTYARD. Here too are diverse mullioned and transomed windows. Of the S range, the right-hand part, slightly set back, is of 1529, with later windows. As on the S face, its row of gables, and those added to the earlier E end of the range, were built upon when the wall was raised to a straight roof-line during the post-Civil War reconstructions. At the same time a balustraded parapet, since removed, was provided all round the court. A doorway to the chapel, with cherub head and a segmental pediment, is of 1675. On the N is the range for which Sir Thomas Myddelton was responsible, some time between his purchase in 1595 and his death in 1631, and most probably early in the new century. By *Turner* are large windows lighting what had by his time become the state rooms. By *Pugin* the simple arched doorway of the main entrance and an inscription recording the restoration of the castle in 1846.* Sir Thomas's work did not extend as far as the E curtain, and the gap was filled when the E range was built, 1667–*c.* 1678. It is curious that, at so late a date, the principal element of accommodation in the

---

* A tablet of 1636 is probably *ex situ*, and the work which it specifies cannot be identified with certainty.

new range was a long gallery, a feature associated with Elizabethan and Jacobean rather than Restoration houses. Old-
fashioned also were the three-light mullioned and transomed
windows of the gallery (not even cross windows), which over-
look the court in a row of seven. Possibly they should be
regarded as deliberately revivalist, like Turner's of a century
later on the N, and as consistent with whatever conservative
or antiquarian motives dictated at the same time the re-crea-
tion of the E towers. The ground floor below the gallery was
built with a seven-bay arcade open to the court, and the
present façade, set forward and with porch and battlemented
parapet, is ascribed to *Pugin*. It is less austere than his doorway on the N, and a shield and riband above the entrance is
a typical decorative detail.

On the W of the court, a corbelled clock turret, with bellcote, dates originally from 1609. In its present form it is C19,
and looks as though it must be by *E. W. Pugin*. Below is an
original pointed doorway, with hoodmould, and the inner end
of the Watchtower rises flush with the parapet, for there is no
later building against the curtain. Inside as well as externally,
ADAM'S TOWER and the W CURTAIN remain largely unchanged. The tower is the only one completely to retain its
full thickness of wall, and its (later) windows give into deep
arched embrasures. Below is a dungeon, and a chamber at
intermediate level may also have been used for confinement.
Lord Howard de Walden installed a large stone chimneypiece
in an upper room. Mural passages and a staircase with Caernarfon arches. Also within the curtain, a room at the N end
known as the Magistrate's Court. It has Jacobean plasterwork,
including, above the fireplace, a figure of Justice framed in
strapwork.

The main rooms of the INTERIOR are described in the
order in which they are seen by the public. In the N range
Turner was responsible for remodellings, in a Neo-Classical
(rather than Palladian) manner, carried out 1766–78, with a
cessation of work in 1773–7. Most interestingly, *Pugin* and
Crace did a redecoration, introducing new colouring, wall-
papers, hangings etc. and possibly stained glass. It was the
only occasion on which Pugin treated existing classical interiors, and the task must have been distasteful to him. Very
little of the work survives. Different is the case of the entrance
106   hall, or Cromwell Hall, which had been the first Sir Thomas's
great hall. It was altered by Turner, but here *Pugin* effected
a complete further transformation, and the present appearance
is due to him. The stone chimneypiece, like the others which
he designed for the castle, was made by *George Myers*. Dated
1845, it has a corbelled overmantel with quatrefoil frieze.
Screens passage, panelling, and a ribbed ceiling with stop-
moulded beams. Character is bolder and more masculine than
was often the case with Pugin's domestic interiors. More typical is the detailing of the doors to the staircase hall. The
staircase itself, leading to the state rooms, is by *Turner*. Com-

pleted 1778, it replaced one for which work of 1673 is recorded. It occupies the N demi-tower, the upper stage of
which is hollowed out to form a galleried landing, and an
Ionic column stands at each corner of the stair well. Stone
stairs, simple iron balusters, and a swept rail. Mullioned and
transomed windows existed previously, but were renewed and
enlarged by Turner. Panelling by Pugin, and his colour
scheme, were done away with in the 1950s.

Though also by *Turner*, the state dining room, *c*.1770-1, is
more Adamish than his other interiors, with arabesques between the wall panels and further delicate ornament in the
coved ceiling. The present colouring replaced Pugin's darker
treatment in a restoration of 1963. Very fine late C18 marble
chimneypiece, brought in by Lord Howard de Walden. The
windows of this room and the next two are by Turner, 1771
and 1772, with leaded glazing inserted 1982.*

The saloon, which had been Sir Thomas's great chamber, 71
is heavier than the state dining room. This is mainly due to
its splendid and profusely ornamented ceiling, divided into
fifteen compartments by deep beams. The plasterwork was
executed by one *Kilmister* in 1772, and plaques of mythological subjects, painted on canvas, are by *George Mullins*,
1772-3. The colouring is that of *Pugin* and *Crace*, with blue
ground in the panels, and gilding and warmer hues for the
beams and all relief and enrichment. Corinthian chimneypiece, of white marble and red jasper, made by *Benjamin
Bromfield*, 1773. Doorcases with consoles.

Next is the drawing room. It was not completed until
c.1796, when *John Cooper* of Beaumaris seems to have been
in charge. The ceiling, however, is of 1773. Similar in style
to that of the saloon, it too was carried out by *Kilmister* under
Turner, and retains its *Pugin* colours. Doorcases are simpler
than in the saloon, and the chimneypiece is most chastely
Neo-Classical. Dog grate designed by *Pugin* and, like all his
metalwork, made by *Hardman*.

Structurally, the drawing room belongs to the E range,
which was begun in 1667 and, as already noted, contains a
long gallery. With a length of 100ft, this has bolection- 65
moulded panelling, acanthus cornice, and doorcases with
shouldered architraves and scrolled pediments. Top and side
volutes, hanging husk motif etc. to window openings and
some of the panels. It may be assumed that *Lady Wilbraham*
had a hand in the fitting up, and the excellent woodcarving,
completed 1678, was carried out by *Thomas Dugdale*, who is
believed to have worked at Weston. Carving by him in the
drawing room was lost when panelling was swept away in
Turner's alterations. The gallery chimneypieces, two at either 66

*Turner had been preceded by *William Yoxall* of Nantwich, who carried out
work 1762-4. Nothing came of Yoxall's scheme to Gothicize the state rooms, but
a rococo ceiling in a room W of the state dining room (not shown to the public)
may be the plasterwork known to have been executed at that time by *Thomas
Oliver*.

end, are mid-c18, rococo. Designed by *Pugin* are *Minton* encaustic tiles, and dog grates, with firebacks dated 1847. Also by him the pattern of ribbing applied to the ceiling. In the E demi-tower, and reached from the gallery, is the state bedroom. Apsidal. There is a reference to *Lady Wilbraham* giving directions in 1677 for its wainscot, no longer extant.

From the gallery, the chapel in the s range is entered at upper level. Its Neo-Perp roof belongs to *Blomfield*'s restoration of c.1894. No trace of the fittings which were installed in the 1670s.* Converted to a music room by Lord Howard de Walden, c.1912–13. Of that date, and presumably by *Ingram & Brown*, the gallery and chimneypiece, with overmantel incorporating c17 woodwork. An organ (since removed) was installed, with its pipes behind the timber-framed w wall, in the so-called King's Bedroom. Further w a staircase, probably of the 1670s with some earlier balusters reused. Within the 1529 build, a room which served as a great chamber. Subdivided c.1912, but now one again.

The ground floor of the E range contains the family living rooms, not open to the public. They were decorated by *Pugin* and *Crace*, with stone chimneypieces, flock papers, panelling, stencilled patterning etc. Whatever the rights and wrongs of ousting Pugin from the state rooms, it is deplorable that the work here was also eroded, with the process continuing into the 1970s. Pugin was handicapped by having to come to terms with earlier c19 vaulting. He referred to a 'ready made plaster ceiling with bad groining', probably meaning that, of radiating pattern, in the drawing room, or Bow Room, in the E demi-tower. The plaster vaulting occurs also in the dining room and ante-room, and in the corridor facing the courtyard, showing that Pugin's frontage must have been refacing of an earlier structure. Some or all of the ceilings are of the 1820s by *Thomas Harrison*, though work by *Benjamin Gummow* in 1831 is likely to have been in this part of the castle. Of *Pugin* features there survive some joinery (a doorcase is dated 1845), door furniture made by *Hardman*, stained glass by *Hardman* in the corridor, and *Myers* chimneypieces in the drawing and dining rooms, the latter especially characteristic and still with *Minton* tiles.‡ Also by Pugin a simple ribbed ceiling in the library, with its cornice and flat bosses stencilled. In this room a later c19 wallpaper and a chimneypiece seemingly made up of pieces from a c17 Welsh bed.

STABLES. 1768–9 by *Turner*, altered and partly refaced by *E. W. Pugin*. The recasting may have been begun by *A. W. N. Pugin*, for the battlemented w front, which meets the sw corner of the castle, is a simplified version of a scheme drawn up by him in 1848. By *E. W. Pugin*, 1854, a screen wall and

---

* Brought from elsewhere, a late c13 SEPULCHRAL SLAB, with foliated cross, commemorating John, son of Nicholas.

‡ The delicately carved overmantel of a small chimneypiece removed from the ante-room is preserved loose in Adam's Tower.

two conical-roofed turrets, dramatically set at the edge of the incline to the s.

Near the NE tower are GARDEN GATES made up from bits of *Davies* ironwork. The GARDENS date from the late C19 onwards. An earlier lime AVENUE marks the principal axis of an extensive formal layout of 1653. The C17 scheme gave way to landscaped pleasure grounds, 1761–74. (HAWK HOUSE, at the Lower Lawn. The first building on the site was a 'Green House' by *Joseph Turner*, 1767. *E. W. Pugin* rebuilt this as a conservatory, 1854. It was converted by Lord Howard de Walden for his falcons, *c.* 1912, being given a thatched roof, but with Pugin's bow-fronted plan retained. Restored after a fire in 1977. Beyond is what appears to be a C14 FONT. At the N end of the terrace at the foot of the gardens is a pavilion with Venetian front, i.e. with its central opening arched, and Doric columns. It is almost certainly *William Emes*'s RE-TREAT SEAT of 1767.)

The landscaping of the splendid PARK was carried out by *Emes*, beginning 1764 and continuing to at least 1775.

The GATES at the main entrance to the park are the master- 79 piece of the smith *Robert Davies* and his brother *John Davies*. Maxwell Ayrton, writing in *Country Life* in 1914, was not greatly impressed, but his comments were inappropriately harsh, and one can understand that Torrington in 1784 wrote of 'one of the most superb iron gates, ever seen'. The centre-piece consists of gates (rather out of scale with the rest), side panels and overthrow, all between a pair of iron piers. The technical mastery is great, and the flowing leafy and scroll patterns are of much complexity. Repoussé acanthus, masks, eagle heads etc. figure among the decorative devices. The top of the overthrow has a heraldic centre and much naturalistic foliage. The open, cage-like piers enclose naturalistic vines, growing from pots. Base slabs, heavy caps, and circular bal-uster stems are of cast (not wrought) iron. Lead wolves (seem-ingly supplied from London) form finials. Either side are palisade screens, less elaborately treated. Robert Davies re-ceived the commission in 1712, but at that stage probably executed only the centremost part, without the piers and side screens. Mr Ifor Edwards considers that the gates may have been intended for a site N of the castle, beside one of the roads which then crossed the park. In 1718 work on the en-larged scheme was in hand; by 1720 the full expanse had been set up as a forecourt screen in front of the castle, aligned on the gateway in the N curtain. The forecourt was abolished in the course of Emes's landscaping (which also saw the destruc-tion of Davies ironwork in the gardens), and the centrepiece and short lengths of side screen were in 1770 moved to the New Hall Lodge. An addition was made at the foot of the gates to increase headroom. The transfer to the present site took place in 1888, when the screens were reinstated, either in actuality (they are said to have been kept in store) or in facsimile. Of 1888 a half-timbered ENTRANCE LODGE.

NEW HALL LODGE. The gates spent their sojourn of more than a century between a pair of single-chamber ashlar lodges by *Turner*, 1770. Pedimented aedicular fronts, and round-headed side windows in arched recesses. The order is un-fluted Greek (i.e. baseless) Doric, a very early instance of its revival.

A lead copy of the Farnese Hercules, 1721, said (probably wrongly) to be by *Nost*, stood in the forecourt, together with a companion figure of Mars, until 1770. It has been moved from a wooded hill in the park prior to resiting.

OFFA'S DYKE. *See* p. 131.

OFFA'S DYKE. *See* p. 131.

THE VILLAGE

ST MARY. Double-naved, with the N portion, and the battle-mented W tower which encroaches into it, dating from a Late Perp remodelling. In the wall of the earlier S nave is a series of shallow recesses, and a blocked round-headed doorway, which looks C17 and is obscured by a later buttress. All windows Perp. Both E windows have cusping and panel tracery, the southern one with four lights and two two-light sub-arches, and the other, which is four-centred, with five lights and two single-light sub-arches. Two four-centred W door-ways under labels. The N nave roof has alternating arched-braced trusses and pseudo-hammerbeams, the former with fanciful carvings, mostly of animals. All members heavily moulded. W galleries and the S nave roof probably date from a remodelling of 1829. The galleries were altered 1849, and the roof may have been partly renewed after a fire in 1853, but their early C19 character, together with the plastered in-terior of the church – even the four-centred arcade is still plastered – impart a pre-ecclesiological flavour.

The FONT is dated 1662. Bowl with moulded corners and carving which includes incised roundels, a motif which appears also on the contemporary low-pitched FONT COVER, along with turned finials. – PULPIT, LITANY DESK and READING STALL have panels, with formal foliated patterns, from a C17 pulpit and reading desk. – Gothic COMMAND-MENT BOARDS, now near the W end. – CHESTS dated 1675 and 1736. – MONUMENTS. Sir Thomas and Lady Myddelton. By *John Bushnell*, 1676. Two busts on pedestals and a back-ground inscription. Folded drapery as an awning. Two large cherub heads above, and urns either side. Gadrooned base partly obscured a cartouche, 1722, to Sir Thomas Myddelton, steadied by two cherubs. – Elizabeth Myddelton. Also by *Bushnell*, 1676, and also with drapery as an awning, and two cherubs. Reclining effigy, suckling her infant son. Her por-trait was sent to London for Bushnell to work from. Added cartouche to her husband, Sir Thomas Myddelton, †1683. – On the easternmost arcade pier an inscription by *William Stanton*, 1678, to Walter Balcanqual. – Sir Richard and Lady

Myddelton. By *Robert Wynne* of Ruthin, *c.*1718–22. Three 85 life-size effigies. Sir Richard and his wife stand either side of an urn, on the pedestal of which is a relief of their chrisom infant daughter. Their son, Sir William, whose death in 1718 may have occurred after the monument was commissioned, reclines in front. Segmental canopy, with urns, garlands, heraldry etc. on Corinthian columns. Gadrooned pedestal. – Thomas Lovett †1801. By *S. & F. Franceys*. Draped urn. Poor. – ROYAL ARMS. Post-1801 Hanoverian. A painted panel. – SCULPTURE. A stone outside the church with the relief of a female figure, evidently a heart shrine.

In the churchyard the miniature Neo-Norman MAUSO-LEUM of Mary Rosamund, daughter of the second Lord Trevor, †1904, aged five. Barrel-vaulted, with a rib-vaulted internal apse. A figure of an angel, holding the child in his arms. Three successive VICARAGES, s of the churchyard. The oldest, early C18, has a rendered two-bay front. The current vicarage is Neo-Georgian, by *The Anthony Clark Partnership*, 1975. The intermediate one is Neo-Elizabethan and of 1853. Stone-built, but with timber mullions and transoms. It is asymmetrical on all sides and has a service wing. For the ENTRANCE LODGE of BRYNKINALT, further E, *see* p. 113.

From the village, as at the castle upstream, the ground falls steeply towards the river and the English border. In the garden of The Mount, sw of the church, is what is believed to be the motte of CASTELL Y WAUN, mentioned in the Pipe Rolls 1165 and 1212. THE MOUNT itself is mid- or late C18, and its façade closes the view along the main street. The WAR MEMORIAL, further N, is by *Eric Gill*, 1919–20. Commissioned by Lord Howard de Walden. Gabled obelisk of Portland stone, with bas-relief of a soldier. The street is the A5, i.e. Telford's Holyhead Road, and the brick-built HAND HOTEL is early C19. Three storeys and five bays, the middle three closely spaced and slightly projecting. All windows are tripartite, and there is a Tuscan porch. Hipped roof, and the chimneys are handled neatly. Later extension to the l. The good proportions are disfigured by gaudy awnings, and the tarted-up interior is hardly a model of how to treat a Georgian coaching inn.

N of the hotel, the former BOYS' SCHOOL, now British Legion probably of 1857 with later enlargement. Then follows HAND TERRACE, seven early C19 Chirk Castle estate cottages. Roughcast. Gothic doors and windows, and three gables, each with a ground-floor canted bow. Three further blocks of former ESTATE COTTAGES are mutilated. Next, the former GIRLS' SCHOOL, now called a discount warehouse. Stone. The original part is by *Pugin*, and was built 1843–4 at the expense of Mrs Myddelton-Biddulph, wife of his client at the castle. Small and simple, and Puginian in spirit though not Gothic in detail. Mullions and transoms, coped and finialed gables, and characteristic octagonal chimneys. Symmetrical w front with two gables, the window in the right-hand one now altered. On the s the gable end of the schoolroom (also altered) meets the mistress's house – a lovely little thing, with two-light windows either side of the door, which has a projecting stone dormer above. At the N end, an addition of 1874, with linking porch, reproduces the s gable. Further enlarged 1905, and also in connection with the present use. Last in this group, the COUNCIL OFFICES, 1902 by *Grayson & Ould*. Cheerful red-roofed Neo-Jacobean. A storeyed porch has columns, strapwork etc. Further out, on the same side of the main road, a TOLLHOUSE.

To the s, a single-arch BRIDGE (strictly just within Shropshire) spans the Ceiriog. By *Telford*, 1831. Upstream, the valley is crossed by a canal aqueduct and a railway viaduct, running parallel with each other, and presenting a spectacle of Roman grandeur. The AQUEDUCT, 1796–1801 by *Telford* and *William Jessop*, is 70ft high, and has ten masonry arches, with the piers carried up between them as pilaster strips. Like Pont Cysyllte (*see* Froncysyllte), it was for the Ellesmere Canal. Here there is no cast-iron trough, only the bed being of iron plates, with the side walls built up in stone. The VIADUCT, 1846–8 by *Henry Robertson*, and 100ft high, was built for the Shrewsbury and Chester Railway. Stone, with bold classical detail. Ten arches between pedimented abutments containing niches. Three further arches at either end are of 1858–9, replacing timber spans. Immediately N is a CANAL TUNNEL by *Telford*, ¼m. long.

METHODIST CHAPEL, s of the river, 1¾m. w. Dated 1839. Small, with a three-bay longitudinal front.

NEW HALL, 1¼m. NW. An attractive group. Stone-built house, moated, and substantially of 1757, with Victorian hipped dormers. A wing with gabled lateral chimney and some timber framing may be a survival of unit planning. Of the MOAT, with BRIDGE, one side is complete, and two survive in part. Large range of brick FARM BUILDINGS with datestone of 1788.

LEY FARM, 1m. NNE. (Crucks survive internally. DOE)

THE LODGE, 1¼m. N. Of brick, and two and a half storeys. Early or mid-C19, with two pediment-like gables bordering on Early Victorian Italianate. Ground-floor windows tripartite. Recessed centre with an unfluted Greek Doric porch and an elegant tripartite doorcase.

Built as colliery housing in the late C18 or early C19, HALTON LOW BARRACKS, ¼m. ENE of The Lodge, consisted of twelve back-to-back cottages. Now called WOODSIDE COTTAGES, after having been converted and modernized with almost total loss of character. HALTON HIGH BARRACKS, ¼m. further N, are unaltered but derelict. A shorter terrace built on a slope and comprising interlocking two- and three-storey back-to-backs.

E of the main road at Whitehurst, 1½m. N, is the site of GARDENS laid out by the second Sir Thomas Myddelton in the mid-C17, and which were stocked with deer and fishponds.

Thomas Dineley described the visit of the Duke of Beaufort on his progress through Wales in 1684: 'his Grace made an halt att an admirable *Walled* GARDEN of Trees, Plants, Flowers, and Herbs of the greatest rarity, as well forreigne as of *Great Britain*, Orrenge and Lemon Trees, the sensitive Plant, &c.; where, in a Banquetting-house, a Collation of choice Fruit and Wines was lodged by ... SIR RICHARD MIDDLETON, to entertain his Grace in this his flourishing Plantation.' Kitchen gardens for Chirk Castle were still maintained in the time of Lord Howard de Walden. The large enclosure retains an outer wall, partly of stone, partly brick, and there is terracing towards the N end. Two brick terrace walls follow an irregular plan. (One has a datestone of 1651, with Thomas Myddelton's initials, set above an arch, and an arch in the N length of the outer wall is dated 1735. DOE) QUEEN ANNE COTTAGE, a late C17 or early C18 pyramid-roofed brick gazebo, is thought to have been a boathouse. Single-storeyed on one side, with a basement on the other. The banqueting house, for which plastering in 1654 is recorded, is possibly incorporated in WHITEHURST HOUSE. This is approached between panelled stone GATEPIERS (which lack their finials) in the outer wall.

DRUMORE, on the opposite side of the road to the above. Central chimney and lobby entry. Mullioned windows.

OFFA'S DYKE crosses the park of Chirk Castle. Well-preserved stretches also exist to the N and S. Southwards it rises impressively from the valley, and for *c.*2½ m. to near Yr Orsedd Wen it forms the boundary between England and Wales, and continues beyond into Shropshire.

YR ORSEDD WEN (SJ 247 340) is a prominent and sharply defined barrow which was excavated somewhat brutally in the C19, when a central rock-cut grave was found containing the skeleton of a man laid out on his back and holding a bronze dagger. The reference to 'dark material' and charcoal suggest that he may have been in a wooden coffin. Both the extended burial and the dagger are unusual among Welsh Early Bronze Age burials, so it is particularly sad that the account of the excavation is so cursory and that the dagger has been lost, with only a rough sketch to suggest tantalizingly that it may have been of the Camerton Snowshill type. Other BARROWS formerly existed to the NW on the long ridge – Bryn Bugeilyn – now covered in forestry.

CLOCAENOG

0050

ST FODDHYD. A single chamber with W bellcote. A two-light N window is Dec. The five-light E window, recorded as having been dated 1538, has a transom at springing level, two two-light sub-arches, panel tracery and cusping. Doubtless of similar date is the arched-braced roof, with cusped struts above the collar and cusped wind-braces. Restoration by *Ken-*

nedy, 1856–7; also by *Perkin & Bulmer* of Leeds, 1882, when the s porch was added. WALL PAINTINGS were at that time discovered on the E wall but not preserved. – FONT. Stumpy, with some roll moulding, and probably C15. – ROOD SCREEN. Of usual Welsh type, with continuous middle rails between the end standards. Heavily moulded uprights and bressumer, and two stages of trail on the W and one on the E. Traceried heads to the openings, and pierced tracery in the wainscot panelling. – Pierced traceried panels in the ALTAR RAILS must be from the rood loft parapet. – PULPIT. Dated 1695. – STAINED GLASS. Fragments in the E window tracery are presumably of 1538. – Easternmost on s by *Holland* of Warwick, commemoration date 1865. – CHANDELIER. Of wood, dated 1725. – A dugout CHEST is built into the wall. – MONUMENT. Evan Lloyd ap Rice and others, latest commemoration date 1705. Painted on wood with border of skulls and cross bones. – Post-1801 Hanoverian ROYAL ARMS. A painted panel. (LYCHGATE. 1691. Square with pyramid roof.)

CLOCAENOG FOREST covers much of the upland W of the Vale of Clwyd. (A hilltop MONUMENT, 1¼m. NW of the village. Stumpy rubble obelisk of 1830, commemorating the completion of plantations by Lord Bagot. A further tablet, of 1933–4, with inscription designed by *Eric Gill*, records their having been felled during and after the 1914–18 War, and the planting of the forest having been begun, 1930, by the Forestry Commissioners.*)

A large Bronze Age BARROW, reduced and spread by ploughing, can still be recognized in the field at SJ 098 542.

On the edge of the forest near Pennant Chapel (SJ 036 547) stood a line of interesting Bronze Age CEREMONIAL MONUMENTS running across the saddle between two valleys. The eastern one in the NW corner of the crossroads was probably some form of ring cairn but has been ploughed over and is now unrecognizable. The second one (SJ 035 546) can easily be seen just s of the road. The monument now appears as a simple ring cairn, but large stones are known to have been removed from the bank and there was said to have been a small mound in the centre. The third site, just inside the forest on the W of the track to Cruglas (SJ 032 545), is a stone circle with a small central mound. Only three stones remain, but fifteen holes can still be recognized forming a circle *c*.43 ft across.

The two larger circles – CAERAU (SJ 045 522) – which stand in a clearing in the forest are puzzling sites. They are on fairly level ground, *c*.100 ft apart, and both are approximately circular enclosures with banks of earth and stones. The western one has an annexe on one side, and both are probably to be explained as settlements, though their date is unknown. Another clearing in the forest contains the remains of what has been described as the 'Ancient village of CEFN BANNOG' (SJ

---

* I am grateful to Mr Peter Randall for help with this entry.

020 509), but unfortunately very little can now be recognized there. Earlier records speak of stone hut foundations enclosed within a low bank, perhaps similar to those at Caerau. This group of enclosures in the Clocaenog area is potentially extremely important, because settlement sites are very rare in this region, whether they belong to the later prehistoric period or to the centuries of Roman rule.

Tŷ Brith. *See* Llanelidan.

Drillau. *See* Llanelidan.

Caer Ddunod. *See* Llanfihangel Glyn Myfyr.

Twr Yr Hill. *See* Mynydd Hiraethog.

CLWYD HALL *see* LLANHYCHAN

COED COCH *see* BETWS-YN-RHOS

COEDPOETH

2050

A former mining village in the hilly industrialized country which spreads from Wrexham.

St Tudfyl. 1893–5 by *Middleton, Prothero & Phillott*. An attempt at Neo-Perp, though the E window is of stepped lancets with ogee trefoils. Aisles but no clerestory. Intended SE tower not built. – Iron CHANCEL SCREEN by *H. L. North*, as a war memorial. Lightheartedly Gothic, in an Arts and Crafts manner.

Primary School, Castle Road. *c.*1972 by *Eric Langford Lewis*, Denbighshire County Architect. Round a courtyard. Much exposed steel, including the stanchions of an encircling colonnade which, because of the sloping site, becomes an upper-level balcony.

Offa's Dyke is seen to good advantage, crossing a valley ½ m. E.

At the intersection of the dyke and a B road, Llidiart Fanny has a pedimented mullioned window of 1616, and ½ m. s is Tan-y-Coed, of three bays and three storeys, dated 1758.

COLWYN BAY

8070

INTRODUCTION

When D. R. Thomas visited the site in 1857, the only buildings he saw were one cottage and a toll bar. However, the Chester and Holyhead Railway already ran alongside the coast, and development as a resort began following the sale in 1865 of Lady Erskine's Pwllycrochan estate to (Sir) John Pender, a Manchester and Glasgow merchant, and a promoter of ocean cables.

He appointed as his agent John Porter, who in 1865 himself leased Pwllycrochan, opening it as a hotel the following year. Pender's architect was *John Douglas*, with whom he made a triumphant visit in 1872. Their train was greeted with flags, cheering crowds and a military band. By then a length of promenade had been constructed, and the Colwyn Bay Hotel was nearing completion. With its steep slate roofs and turrets, this was one of the largest buildings *Douglas* ever designed; it was demolished 1974–5, and any survivals there may be of his other early buildings in the town cannot readily be identified. In 1875, following the breaking of one of his cables in mid-Atlantic, Pender sold up. Individual purchasers included Porter, who acquired the Pwllycrochan Hotel, but the bulk of the property went to a Manchester syndicate, the Colwyn Bay and Pwllycrochan Estate Company, who continued with planning and development. Members included the architect *Lawrence Booth*, later joined in practice in Manchester by *Thomas Chadwick*. After a partnership had been formed with *J. M. Porter*, son of John Porter, and himself a surveyor, a Colwyn Bay office was maintained under the style *Booth, Chadwick & Porter*, and was responsible for much work in the growing town. The firm practised as Porter & Hunter 1905–7, and, with Manchester connections severed, and with *Charles Ernest Elcock* as a partner, as *J. M. Porter & Elcock c.*1906–12. In 1912 Elcock left to enter partnership in Manchester with the better-known John Brooke. From 1912, the Colwyn Bay office continued as *J. M. Porter & Co.*

The nearby village of Colwyn, which gave its name to the new town, soon became known as Old Colwyn (q.v.). It has been swallowed up in the urban growth, and, with Llandrillo-yn-Rhos (q.v.), commonly called Rhos-on-Sea, the conurbation extends along the coast for about four miles. There are many noteworthy individual buildings, not least those by *S. Colwyn Foulkes* (*see* Introduction, pp. 86–8) in this his native place. Nevertheless the town centre has no special character; the sea front is dreary and could ill afford the loss of Douglas's hotel. The trouble is that the railway runs so close to the shore that there was, for the most part, no room for building along the promenade. The construction of a by-pass road in the 1970s did not result in visual improvement. The street plan was governed neither by strict rectangularity nor by the curve of the shore, but rather by irregular areas generated by inserting the layout between the coast and the (then) main road. Colwyn Bay developed as a residential and retirement town as well as a holiday resort, and its most attractive feature is a spacious district of sylvan suburbia, with good late C19 and early C20 domestic architecture, extending inland behind the town centre and upwards towards Pwllycrochan Woods, where curving roads ease the gradient.

CHURCHES

St Paul, Abergele Road. By *Douglas & Fordham*, the nave 1887-8, the chancel added 1894-5. Large and cruciform, with passage aisles to the broad five-bay nave. The arcades are low and the clerestory tall. Lancets, some of them cusped, and also plate tracery, turning to bar in the E window. A rose window in the s transept. Of coursed rubble limestone, with red Runcorn dressings and bands. Inside, the sandstone is used for the ashlar-lined chancel and for generous dressings elsewhere. Basic and unpedantic detailing – arches die into the rectangular arcade piers, and the treatment of corbels should be noted, as well as the chunkily quirky SEDILIA. Wagon roofs, the easternmost bay of the chancel having traceried panelling. A NW steeple was originally intended. The present noble tower is of 1910-11. It was the last work on which *Douglas* was ever engaged, and his wish to live to see it completed was not fulfilled. Bold, craggy and heavily buttressed, it has a cavernous E portal, and Somerset tracery in the lower part of the bell openings. Narthex, with a w door, added to the nave, by *W. D. Caröe*, 1920, as a war memorial. Of 1934-5 by *Caröe*, the REREDOS and RIDDEL POSTS, in his most ambitiously elaborate and filigreed Perp, with many figures, and a representation of the Supper at Emmaus. – STALLS with typical *Douglas* detail. – STAINED GLASS. w and two narthex windows by *Horace Wilkinson*, 1920-1.

By *Douglas & Fordham*, 1895, the adjoining CHURCH HALL, and also the VICARAGE, the latter gabled, and with white-painted leaded casements and a facing of polygonal limestone fragments.

St David (Welsh Church), Rhiw Road, also forms part of the group with St Paul's, and is by *Douglas & Minshull*, 1902-3. Small. Apsidal sanctuary and battered buttresses. The w window is Neo-Perp. A substantial square bellcote rises from the roof, with its own pyramid roof surmounted by an octagonal spirelet. – The SCREEN was made by *David Jones*, a local blacksmith.

St Andrew, Lansdowne Road. Begun 1908 by *J. M. Porter & Elcock*. An unexecuted design was double-naved, with an E tower to the N half. As built, the aisleless nave is in interesting Arts and Crafts Gothic. The window dressings are unmoulded, and the five-light w window is a pointed lunette, with arched-up transoms, the middle one higher than the others. Timber-framed porch. The interior does not fulfil the promise of the exterior, and the chancel and N transept (an organ chamber), added 1924, are in more conventional Perp.

St Joseph (R.C.), Conway Road. Clerestoried nave, apsidal chancel and stunted (unfinished?) NW tower. By *R. Curran* of Warrington, 1898-1900, but thoroughly retrograde, looking Mid- rather than Late Victorian. (PRESBYTERY of same date also by *Curran*. P. Howell.)

BAPTIST CHURCH, Hawarden Road. Opened 1913. Small and

seemly, with straight-headed side windows, and a Neo-Perp one in the gable.

TABERNACL BAPTIST CHAPEL, Abergele Road. Opened 1888. Gothic front.

SALEM CONGREGATIONAL CHAPEL, Abergele Road. Opened 1885. Altered or rebuilt 1903. Free and debased front, with square corner pilasters, ogee-capped.

ST JOHN'S METHODIST CHURCH, Conway Road. Begun 1882 to designs by *Robert Curwen*, but of the church itself no more than the putting in of the foundations was done at that time. The rest is of 1887-8. Polygonal masonry and a version of Dec tracery. Thoroughly churchy, with aisles, transepts, clerestory, SW broach spire and an apsidal E end. The communion table is in the apse and the pulpit off-centre. Only stalls in the transepts, W of the pulpit, distinguish the interior from a Low Church Anglican one. An attached SCHOOL-ROOM, completed earlier, has an octagonal spired turret. The arched and stone-roofed LYCHGATE, with corner pinnacles, was completed in 1882, as was the MANSE, of brick, with touches of tile-hanging and half-timber.

NANT-Y-GLYN METHODIST CHURCH, Nant-y-Glyn Road. Built 1904-5, and possibly the chapel recorded as being designed by *A. Brocklehurst*, 1903. (CW) The reddest building imaginable – brick, roofing tiles, terra-cotta tracery and all.*

WELSH PRESBYTERIAN (CALVINISTIC METHODIST) CHAPEL, Woodland Road West. Built 1879. Tall, Gothic. Central gable flanked by lower hips.

PRESBYTERIAN CHURCH OF WALES, Hawarden Road. Another very, very red building in its brick, terra-cotta and tile. Octagonal tower and spirelet, plate tracery and heavily cusped lancets.

UNITED REFORMED CHURCH (formerly Congregational), Abergele Road. By *Owen Edwards* of Rhyl (VH), 1885. Gothic. Two big gables to the street at the side.

PENRHOS COLLEGE

The earliest part is by *Lawrence Booth*, and was built in 1882 as a hydropathic. This is the tall, right-hand portion of the main front, with half-timbered upper storey. Its skyline has been altered and some original features have been lost. In 1895 it was bought by Penrhos, a girls' school, which had opened as a Wesleyan foundation in 1880. Their first extension forms the left-hand portion of the frontage, beyond an original small gable, and comprising a larger gable and a corner turret. It is of 1898 by *Booth, Chadwick & Porter*, and the same practice was responsible for numerous successive additions over the next thirty years, most notably the GREAT

---

*Mr Vernon Hughes draws attention to the difference between these fiery Ruabon products and the less intense Accrington brick of a pair of semi-detached houses above.

HALL, 1917–25 by *J. M. Porter & Co.* Mullioned and transomed windows and Neo-Perp tracery, but the interior is
classical, with a segmental barrel-vaulted ceiling. Stained
glass includes work by *Abbot & Co.* of Lancaster.

Facing Llannerch Road East is the former SANATORIUM,
a Neo-Georgian range by *S. Colwyn Foulkes*, 1936–7.

RYDAL SCHOOL

Founded in 1885, the boys' public school first occupied a house
at the junction of Pwllycrochan Avenue and Lansdowne
Road, and this forms the NW corner of the present group of
buildings. It is dated 1883, and has an octagonal corner turret. In 1890–1 it was extended E by *T. E. Lidiard James*, still
in a domestic manner. Thoroughly collegiate, though, is the
splendid stone-built COSTAIN BUILDING which, L-shaped,
encloses a court and occupies the NE corner. 1927–30 by *S.
Colwyn Foulkes.* The repeating bay unit, between buttresses,
comprises two mullioned and transomed windows, one above
the other, with the mullions continuing between the storeys.
A low corner tower, which provides the chief accent, has an
oriel on both outer faces, one oriel two-storeyed, the other
corbelled. The inner elevations of the two ranges show particular sensitivity in their simpler use of Tudor elements, and
one has an arcaded walkway. The MEMORIAL HALL, added
by *Colwyn Foulkes*, 1955–7, extends the E range further S.
Lighter and more fanciful than the earlier work, with pinnacled buttresses, but the masonry still of fine quality. Inside is
a coffered ceiling with coloured patterning in the panels. The
entrance corridor is aligned on an oriel of the DINING HALL,
which is by *Lidiard James*, 1900, and has battlemented parapets, flèche, and a roof open to the collar. Also an oriel either
side. Originally the hall continued beyond the oriels for only
one bay, but it was enlarged southwards by *Colwyn Foulkes*,
1957–8. Stained glass includes a war memorial window by
Abbot & Co.

The school has acquired a number of Victorian suburban
villas, the most noteworthy of which are referred to below in
the Perambulation.*

PUBLIC BUILDINGS

CIVIC CENTRE, Abergele Road, the former GLAN-Y-DON
HALL. By *Percy Scott Worthington* of Manchester, and built
1909–10 as a convalescent home.‡ Opened as council offices
1964. Date inscription of 1911. In a picturesque and resourcefully eclectic Arts and Crafts manner, roughcast, with stone

---

* The former Bursar, Mr Wilfred Bartlett, kindly provided much help and
information in connection with the school buildings.
‡ Information from Mr Anthony Pass.

dressings, stone flagged roofs, rustic brick chimneys and sash windows. There is a Scottish feel about the tall, rendered masses. The straight entrance drive differs from the informal approach originally intended. Entrance front with a Neo-Georgian core sandwiched between a gabled chimneybreast and a hipped-roofed tower. From the latter projects an irregular, gabled wing, being the central stroke of what is a T-shaped plan. On the far side of the wing, groupings of gables, dormers and canted bays are revealed, and the long rear elevation (the cross-bar of the T) also sustains interest.

POLICE HEADQUARTERS, Abergele Road. 1972–4 by *E. Langford Lewis*, County Architect. The main block is five-storeyed, with corrugated concrete spandrels.

COUNTY BUILDINGS, Rhiw Road. Built as Police Station and Magistrates' Courts. By *Walter Wiles*, County Architect, 1905–7, though a plan had been made earlier in 1905 by the then County Surveyor, *R. Lloyd Williams*.* Limestone and red sandstone, in free Elizabethan, with Arts and Crafts touches. A low tower is not very well integrated, and an aedicule has an entrance either side of it, rather than within it.

POST OFFICE, Prince's Drive. *c.*1923–1926 by *C.P. Wilkinson* of the Office of Works. Distinguished Neo-Georgian (or rather William and Mary). Seven bays, with modillion cornice, pedimented dormers and a roof of Roman tiles. All ground-floor openings are arched. Rusticated corner pilaster strips of brick. To the r. is a gateway in screen walls between single-storey blocks.

PUBLIC LIBRARY, Woodland Road West. 1902–5 by *Booth, Chadwick & Porter*. Andrew Carnegie contributed to the cost. Public-looking dome, and domestic-looking Elizabethan bows. Enlarged 1960–2.

COLWYN BAY AND WEST DENBIGHSHIRE HOSPITAL, Hesketh Road. Main block by *S. Colwyn Foulkes*, opened 1925, and in very seemly Neo-Georgian. Shallow U-plan front. At the ends of the cross wings are two-storey verandas, with clusters of slender columns and drape-like decoration on their fascias. At the rear, a three-bay Corinthian loggia faces the street.

PIER. 1898–1900 by *Mangnall & Littlewood* of Manchester. Not as long as originally intended. The stanchions have Corinthian caps. Of the superstructure, the only original feature is the gay and frothy iron balustrading. The present pavilion is of 1934. Two predecessors were destroyed by fire.

WAR MEMORIAL, Conway Road/Queens Drive Gardens. 1922 by *John Cassidy*. Bronze figure of a soldier.

PERAMBULATION

First, it must be said that, except for the PIER (such as it is, *see* above), there is no architectural inducement to visit the PRO-

---

* I owe this information to Mr Peter D. Randall.

MENADE. The late lamented Colwyn Bay Hotel stood near the corner of Marine Road, and the original length of promenade of c.1872 may here be discerned. A little sea-front development peters out at the unremarkable WESTBURY by *Booth, Chadwick & Porter*.

The perambulation proper begins in STATION ROAD. On the w side is a row of SHOPS by *Booth, Chadwick & Porter*, the best of their town-centre jobs. Brick, with eight stepped gables. Oriels, and pargetting in tympana. At the lower end is a differently styled unit, with pointed-roofed octagonal corner turret. This was built as public offices and a police station, and has handcuffs in a spandrel. It is of 1892. The shops were completed earlier. On the opposite side, at No. 4, of 1933–7, *S. Colwyn Foulkes* turned his eclectic hand to Romanesque, with detail of great refinement. Ashlar. Arcaded corbel table and arcaded fenestration with ornamented tympana. Above the shop-front are two Art Deco busts on pedestals. Round the corner in ABERGELE ROAD, No. 7, of 116 1930, is also by *Colwyn Foulkes*. This too has a delightful ashlar elevation with detail of great sensitivity and refinement. Tripartite window with Adamish tympanum, slender windows either side, and a couple of paterae containing masks. Circular windows in the frieze. The original shop-front has, of course, gone, but a ceiling with octagonal coffering remains in the porch.*

The NATIONAL WESTMINSTER BANK closes the view up Station Road with unsophisticated Gothic. It was built in or after 1881, not as a bank. In CONWAY ROAD, three more BANKS demand attention. The MIDLAND is an Italianate remodelling by *Woolfall & Eccles*, 1903–4. BARCLAYS, 1896 by *Booth, Chadwick & Porter*, with an under-sized turret, was built to house a club as well as a bank. WILLIAMS & GLYN'S (built as WILLIAMS DEACON'S) is of ashlar. Seven by four bays, with entablatures and moulded surrounds to the ground-floor windows and a Doric doorcase *in antis*. By *Colwyn Foulkes*, 1931, and more strictly revivalist than was usual for him, with only a few details to show that it is anything other than good work of a century earlier. In contrast, the ASTRA CINEMA (formerly ODEON) of 1935–6 by *Harry Weedon*, is thoroughly evocative of its own decade. The auditorium has been divided, but except for changes of lettering the exterior is relatively unscathed. Faience and channelled brick. Curves on plan and a tower with fins. Shops are incorporated.

Exploration of the leafy suburbs may begin in QUEEN'S DRIVE, E of Rydal School, with two houses now both belong-

* *Colwyn Foulkes's* ARCADIA THEATRE, built 1920 in Prince's Drive, was demolished in 1981. In its latter years it was the Wedgwood Cinema, and did not look its best, but it had a refined classical front, redolent of Parisian elegance, with fruitier Frenchified plasterwork in the foyer and auditorium. Like the Colwyn Bay Hotel, it was an asset, which should have been cherished by a town which seeks to attract visitors and provide entertainment.

ing to Rydal and attributable to *Douglas & Fordham*. HEATHFIELD, 1893, is partly half-timbered, and BRENDON is of about the same date, but was later remodelled internally. It has the broken limestone facings occasionally used by Douglas, together with brick and terra-cotta dressings, a shaped gable and shaped-headed window lights. QUEEN'S LODGE, by *William Owen*, was built *c.*1895 for W. D. Houghton, a Warrington wire manufacturer. Of brick and stone, and one of the largest of the Colwyn Bay houses, it has a tower with corner turret and recessed pyramid roof. In 1919 it was bought by Frederick Henry Smith, an india-rubber and cotton manufacturer, who had been ennobled as Baron Colwyn. At the top of PWLLYCROCHAN AVENUE is PWLLYCRO-CHAN itself, a prominent landmark, now Rydal Preparatory School. It was rebuilt when the heiress married Sir David Erskine in 1821, and remodelled or largely again rebuilt after she was widowed in 1841. Stuccoed Tudor, with coped gables, labels, and timber mullions and transoms. E-plan front, formerly with loggias between the cross wings and the storeyed porch. As already noted (*see* p.134), it was opened as a hotel in 1866 by John Porter. A large extension, with machicolated and turreted tower, was added *c.*1886–7 by – need it be said? – *Booth, Chadwick & Porter*. Also by them is BRAE-SIDE (No. 26 Pwllycrochan Avenue), 1891, which was J. M. Porter's own house. Conical-roofed corner turret with terra-cotta frieze. OUTRAM LODGE (Rydal property) is large, many-gabled and has its upper storey half-timbered. Date inscription of 1879 in stained glass. BEECH HOLME (also Rydal premises) looks as though it is of the 1870s, with later C19 internal features. There is record of *T. E. Lidiard James* having designed stables, *c.*1892. In the lower part of the road, THE WHITE HOUSE is by *Alfred Steinthal* of Manchester. The next road along is BRACKLEY AVENUE, where the Edwardian Arts and Crafts COTSWOLD, 1908, is also by *Alfred Steinthal*. Roughcast and gabled, it has half-timbered work with richly ornamented bargeboards and bressumer. Spacious galleried hall and staircase.*

Along LANSDOWNE ROAD is THE WREN'S NEST, Neo-Georgian by *S. Colwyn Foulkes*, 1932. Reeded frieze below the eaves, and over the entrance a recessed balcony with delicate balustrading. A return southwards may be made by way of Walshaw Avenue to OAK DRIVE. Here is the entrance to WALSHAW (another Rydal house). 1891 by *Booth, Chadwick & Porter*. Brick, terra-cotta, half-timber etc. with a small stable block integrated in the spreading composition. The staircase is compactly planned, but has a gallery, and its hefty woodwork includes two storeys of turned posts. Further W, at the corner of KING'S DRIVE, RATONAGH (now Penrhos College Junior School) is also by *Booth, Chadwick & Porter*, and is of similar materials. Dated 1894. Tall, with strong

---

* I owe the Steinthal ascriptions to Mr and Mrs R. Colwyn Foulkes.

vertical emphasis in its pointed-roofed octagonal corner turret and its three scarcely diminishing storeys. Staircase similar in its elements to that of Walshaw, but less complicated in plan. Lower in King's Drive, early C20 houses include WHITE OAK by *Steinthal*.

Much higher, PEN-Y-BRYN ROAD crests the ridge behind the town. Nos. 5–13 were built in stages, 1966–80, as a terrace of five houses, designed individually for separate clients by *Bowen, Dann, Davies*. Dark brick and much timber. The row is staggered on plan and stepped in elevation also, following the fall of the ground. Open-plan living areas. Westwards along the ridge, THE FLAGSTAFF (now WELSH MOUNTAIN ZOO) is reached from OLD HIGHWAY. Walter Whitehead, a Manchester surgeon, commissioned a scheme for a house and extensive gardens from *Thomas H. Mawson* and his then architectural collaborator *Dan Gibson*. The grounds were laid out by Mawson, *c.*1898–1900, and roughcast buildings by *Gibson* include an ENTRANCE LODGE in Llanrwst Road and two GATEHOUSES facing Old Highway, one with battered buttresses and some half-timber. The house itself was never built, and in his autobiography Mawson recounted how Whitehead diddled him out of his fees. Features of the *Mawson* GARDENS may still be recognized, especially that part of the layout in front of the intended site of the house. Lawn, with bowed retaining wall (now overlooking the bear pit) on the axis, and small formal enclosures either end. A higher terrace walk is aligned on GATEPIERS of the former kitchen garden. A GORSEDD CIRCLE of 1909. From LLANRWST ROAD leads the drive to BRYN EITHIN, a most interesting house, built 1889. Its character is that of a large-scale suburban villa. The main block is free Elizabethan and largely of rock-faced masonry, though there are ribbed brick chimneys. It is clearly the work of an able architect, but with signs of immaturity, particularly in the resolving of the elevations, and there is a strong hint of Norman Shaw in the tile-hanging of the service wing. It is by *Gerald Horsley* and was an early independent commission (possibly his very first) after he left Shaw's office. The main interior feature is a central well staircase, late C17 in style, rising through two storeys, and with an arcade at the first-floor landing. Small leaded window between porch and entrance hall. Atop the roof is a viewing platform and a square lantern with cupola.

At the opposite end of the town is another noteworthy house, LLETY DRYW, in ABERGELE ROAD, beside the approach to the Civic Centre. 1893 by *Douglas & Fordham*. Coped and finialed gables, cross wings and, in the angle of one of the wings, a storeyed porch with ornamented lintel; i.e. the house is inspired by C17 vernacular work of northern England. The idea is loosely interpreted and the plan does not follow historical precedent, there being no central living hall, though one is suggested by a range of mullioned and transomed lights.

In GROES ROAD, near the junction with Abergele Road, is a symmetrical Italianate VILLA, of yellow brick with stone dressings and with a belvedere tower. Could it be the 'summer residence at Colwyn' for which *Lloyd Williams & Underwood* were responsible in 1867 (VH)? NANT-Y-GLYN ROAD leads to WERN TYNNO (now FOXHILL YOUTH HOSTEL), amid hanging woods, ½m. beyond the town. 1895 by *Booth, Chadwick & Porter*. Brick and terra-cotta, with half-timbered upper storey and gables. The main front is symmetrical, with a gabled balcony at either corner.

Finally, a further outlying item, GRAENLLYN, ¾m. s of the A55 at Mochdre, w of the town. A BARN with four cruck trusses.

CORNWAL *see* MYNYDD HIRAETHOG

CROSS LANES *see* MARCHWIEL

0050
CYFFYLLIOG

ST MARY. The village is high in the wooded valley of the Clywedog, with the church near to the river. A single chamber with some Dec features, namely the E window with three cusped lights and intersecting tracery, and, on the s, a two-light traceried window (turning Perp), and the easternmost, with two pairs of cusped lights. (Bellcote dated 1874. *P. Howell*.) A Perp N window. A s doorway and porch were done away with in a destructive restoration of 1876 by *Arthur Baker*, and the easternmost N window and the w porch are of 1903–4. At the E end a Perp wagon ceiling, boarded and ribbed, with the main members traceried and with mask corbels and vine trail at the cornice. The chancel is further emphasized by a raised floor (of 1856) and a sort of hammerbeam spere-truss by *Baker*. He introduced ENCAUSTIC TILES. A WALL PAINTING discovered during his restoration was not preserved. It seems that until 1876 the lower part of the ROOD SCREEN remained *in situ*, and that a portion of the loft was incorporated in a w gallery. Whatever may have survived was dismantled and partly discarded by *Baker*, though he worked four tracery heads into STALLS and the head of the screen doorway into RAILS, with in both cases similar pieces being made to match. Also, the PULPIT and adjoining SCREEN reproduce mouldings from the rood screen, and pierced traceried panels from its loft are embodied. – The FONT, probably C14, was retooled and altered, 1904. – CHESTS. A dugout. – Another chest dated 1687. – HEARSE HOUSE dated 1823.

DENBIGH / DINBYCH

DENBIGH CASTLE AND ITS ENVIRONS

The chief stronghold of Dafydd ap Gruffydd was at Denbigh, the centre of the *cantref* of Rhufoniog. In 1282, after the up-rising and defeat of Dafydd, the newly created lordship of Denbigh was granted by Edward I to Henry de Lacy, Earl of Lincoln. Construction of a castle and walled town was imme-diately begun, on the summit of what is a dramatically steep outcrop within the Vale of Clwyd. By 1290 de Lacy had granted a charter to the new town, and work was substantially complete by the time of his death in 1311. Further building seems to have taken place, however, and the castle may never have been finished as intended. Some of the strengthening of defences may date from after the temporary capture by the Welsh in 1294. By the C16 the walled town had been abandoned in favour of a new settlement on lower ground. The move was probably a result of

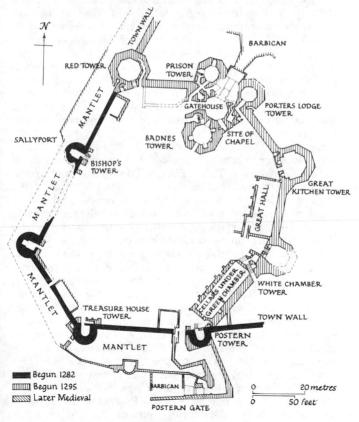

Denbigh Castle, plan
(Department of the Environment)

the inconvenience, for a developing market centre, of the restricted site and excessive gradients, and of the lack of a satisfactory water supply. It may have been precipitated by the sack-
ing of the town in 1468, in the Wars of the Roses. In the Civil
War the castle was surrendered to Parliament, and it was dismantled in 1660.

CASTLE. The enclosure is an irregular polygon in the S tip of
the *enceinte* of the town. It was built in two stages. The
curtain walls on the S and W form part of the system of town
walls put in hand in 1282, but unlike the rest of the circuit
they are regularly punctuated with half-round towers. The N
and E curtains, defining the castle proper, came later, presumably in the mid-1290s. They are thicker, and their towers are
polygonal, most of them octagons. Master *James of St George*
is known to have been involved, and his ingenuity seems
evident in the GREAT GATEHOUSE on the N. This has a
cluster of three octagonal towers, two on the outer side flanking the gateway, and one behind. They enclose a central
chamber, an irregular octagon, which was originally vaulted,
and where the entrance route changes axis. The frontage, Dec
in style, survives only fragmentarily, but includes an arch in
two recessed orders. Above is a trefoiled niche in a rectangular frame decorated with ballflower and containing a statue,
probably of Edward I. Higher again is a band of chequer. In
front was a barbican, and there remain a ditch, crossed by a
causeway, and also drawbridge pits. Murder holes within the
outer arch. The entrance passage had two portcullises and
two sets of doors, in alternation. Visible are grooves of the
inner portcullis and of another one beyond the central octagon. The three towers were each of three storeys, plus a cellar
in two of them. The inner (Badnes Tower) has an octagonal
vice. Virtually nothing remains of the RED TOWER at the
junction with the town walls W of the gatehouse, and only to
the SE does the curtain survive to any great height, either side
of the GREAT KITCHEN TOWER. In the latter are two
(later?) fireplace openings, and between it and the WHITE
CHAMBER TOWER the foundations of the GREAT HALL.
Then follow arrangements which included a postern, and a
range known as GREEN CHAMBERS, possibly mid-C14,
which had two vaulted basement rooms with carved corbels.
At the S junction with the town walls, the POSTERN TOWER,
half-round, belongs to the initial campaign, but was encased
externally in the course of the later work. Additions to the
other towers on the S and W included staircases against the
inner faces, and a MANTLET was introduced to provide a
further line of outer defences below. It is best preserved between the Postern and Treasure House Towers. Similarly
belonging to the later work was the POSTERN GATE, below
the Postern Tower. Drawbridge pits of this and an upper
gatehouse survive, and between them is a steep and tortuous
pathway enclosed within walls, and originally having both

steps and a ramp. An outer barbican is later again. On the w, near the Bishop's Tower, an elaborately planned SALLYPORT leads down from the mantlet. It had murder holes and a portcullis.

TOWN WALLS. The circuit, which has remarkably few towers, is of irregular line, dictated by the terrain. It is largely complete, and much of the wall walk remains, though the EX- CHEQUER GATE, on the w side, has gone. The BURGESS 11 GATE, on the N, is, in its present form, possibly later C13 or C14, rather than belonging entirely to the work initiated in 1282. Two storeys. The battlements are missing, but otherwise it survives to its full height. Its inner elevation has at some time been refaced. The tunnel-vaulted entrance passage was heavily defended, and displays portcullis grooves, arrow slits and murder holes. The gateway is between high battered walls from which rise two engaged round towers. Chequer patterning near the top. In front were a ditch and fixed bridge. Further E, a half-round tower and the COUNTESS TOWER, where later rooms were added within an internal angle. Also post-1282 is an outer line of defence, diverging from the earlier wall, across the steep face of the rock. The purpose of this salient was probably to enclose a well, which is contained in the polygonal GOBLIN TOWER. Between this and the Countess Tower were two storeys of embrasures. Near the castle was a further half-round tower.

ST HILARY. Built c.1300 as a chapel to serve castle and town. It had nave and chancel, the latter with a crypt, and in the course of its development acquired an C18 N aisle. Demolished 1923, except for the w wall and tower, the latter an addition made in the C14 or early C15. It is battlemented and unbuttressed, and has a w doorway with wave mould.

LEICESTER'S CHURCH. Robert Dudley, Earl of Leicester, held 62 the castle and lordship of Denbigh from 1563 until his death in 1588. He began the building of a church to serve the growing town and, it is reputed, with the intention that the see of the diocese be transferred from St Asaph. A foundation stone of 1578 and dedication inscription of 1579 are recorded. Work was abandoned in 1584, and the structure has since been eroded. Nevertheless, it is of remarkable interest as a unique Elizabethan instance of major church-building. Leicester was the leading supporter at court of the extreme protestants, who were already being referred to as Puritans, and his ideals are reflected in the architecture. Much remains of the outer walls, particularly on the N and E, forming a ten-bay rectangle 170ft by 75ft. The section would have been of hall church type, but of the arcades, only the E responds survive. The arcades seem to have been round-arched, with Tuscan columns on rectangular plinths, and the window spacing suggests that single and coupled columns alternated. The windows, looking almost round-arched, are in fact four-centred. There is evidence of uncusped tracery. N doorway in the westernmost bay, with keystone and depressed arch; a corresponding one may have existed on the s. There is no indication of how the interior was to have been arranged, but a plan of preaching-church character may be assumed.

Also within the enclosure of the walls is PLAS CASTELL, owing its stone-faced Italianate front to an Early or Mid-Victorian rebuilding or remodelling. Its main approach was by a long drive skirting the castle on the s, but it also has a four-storey GATEHOUSE of polychromatic brick, with naïve castellations. BRYN AWELON (or FRIESLAND HALL), opposite St Hilary's tower, is a cruck house. Nos. 54–56 TOWER HILL are early C19 cottages of rough masonry, with battlements and Gothic windows.

FRIARY

At the end of Abbey Road. The remains of a house of Carmelite Friars (White Friars) established in the late C13. The foundation has been ascribed to Sir John Salusbury, ancestor of the Salusburys of Lleweni, but it is more probable that John de Sunimore was responsible. Of the church, the walls of the choir and a short length of the N and s walls of the nave still stand. Until burnt in 1898, when the building was used as a malt house, the arched-braced roof of the choir survived. Between the two parts, and separated by screens, was a space with a s doorway to the cloisters and above which rose, in the usual manner of the friars' churches, a spire. This was timber-framed, and there are recesses for the wall-plates of its principals. On the N remain corbels for alternate principals. The walls are of the original C13 build, as are triple SEDILIA and two PISCINAS, one of them for one of the two nave altars. Probably also original are the choir N and s windows, which, as the former shows, were double-mullioned and of five ogee-headed lights. Perp five-light E window, bricked up. (Scanty traces of living quarters, including two C13 doorways, in Abbey Cottage, which occupies the site of the s cloister range.)

CHURCHES

LEICESTER'S CHURCH. *See* p. 145.

ST DAVID, St David's Lane. A church by the younger *Thomas Penson* was built 1838–40, and a w tower added 1855–8, but without the spire that Penson had intended. The tower survives, but the remainder was rebuilt by *R. Lloyd Williams*, 1894–5. Cruciform, with clerestory and narrow passage aisles. Lancets. Red and yellow brick interior. The nave has a boarded ceiling, shaped in section. The chancel is expensively fitted up, with a Last Supper REREDOS in an alabaster setting, ENCAUSTIC TILES, and iron and copper CANCELLI with gates. – STAINED GLASS. E window reused from the previous building. Pictorial representations in early C19 style, but in a Gothic setting, and the commemoration date is 1857. – Some aisle windows by *Ballantine & Gardiner* and *J. Ballantine & Son*; the s transept window, 1895, is probably by the former.

St Hilary. *See* p. 145.

St Marcella. *See* p. 152.

St Mary, Lenten Pool. 1871–4 by *Lloyd Williams & Underwood*. Aisles but no clerestory. se tower of unusual appearance, smooth and solid, with no hoodmoulds, the buttresses stopping short of the top, and the pinnacles, with pierced parapets between, rising flush from the wall face. Unusual also the buttresses of the body of the building, with numerous set-offs. Polygonal masonry. Cusped lancets and Geometrical tracery. Tall n and s windows effectively light the sanctuary, and the capitals of the nave arcades are well carved. Not a specially attractive church, but 'there is a definite and more or less harmonious character about everything that has not come by chance' (Goodhart-Rendel). – font, reredos and pulpit designed by the architects and carved by *Earp*. Controversy over the reredos, with its Crucifixion, delayed consecration. – *Maw* encaustic tiles in the chancel. – stained glass. e window by *Hardman*, 1874. – w window by *J. V. Rowlands & Co.*, 1880, with large areas of sky, unusual for the date. – s aisle second from e by *J. Ballantine & Son*, 1891. – n aisle westernmost by *Christopher Whall*, 1918. – s aisle westernmost by *Veronica M. Whall*, 1933. Of colourful mosaic character, and particularly good.

St Joseph (R.C.), Bryn Stanley. 1968 by *G. Parry Davies & Associates*. Hyperbolic paraboloid. Brick walls and, at the w end, a polygonal glazed baptistery contained under the main roof. – stained glass by *Jonah Jones*.

Baptist Chapel, Henllan Street. Pedimented brick front, of three bays and two storeys, with round-headed windows. The plaque includes reference to 1812, a rebuilding of 1836, and restorations 1884 and 1927.

Trefn y Moddion Congregational Chapel, Swan Lane. Heavily Italianate two-storey brick and stone front. Ornamented plaster ceiling inside. The gallery, on cast-iron brackets and slender columns and with curved corners, is carried round all four sides, though behind the pulpit it is now obscured by an organ, inserted 1891. The pulpit itself, with monumental curved stairs either side, may also be an insertion, though pre-dating the organ.

Pentref Methodist Chapel, Factory Ward. Stone. Three by three bays and two storeys, the upper windows round-arched. Open pediment. First built 1801, but was it later rebuilt or remodelled?

Capel Mawr, Welsh Presbyterian (Calvinistic Methodist), Swan Lane. Rebuilt 1829, but in its present form dating from 1880.* Very large. Restrained Italianate front, of ashlar, with

* I am grateful to Mr E. P. Williams for supplying the reference to the date.

round-headed windows. Six bays, including windows for the gallery stairs. Balustraded porch. Fine interior, virtually square, with beamed ceiling and a steeply raked horseshoe gallery on the usual iron brackets and slender columns. Grand build-up of SÊT-FAWR, PULPIT and ORGAN, with baluster motifs and pierced patterns, and some cast-iron balustrading. The SCHOOLROOM is dated 1892.

ST THOMAS PRESBYTERIAN CHURCH OF WALES, Vale Street. Gothic. Front with a big cusped circular window set in a recessed arch. Stumpy octagonal corner turret and spirelet. By *Owen Edwards* and opened 1880.*

PUBLIC BUILDINGS

COUNTY HALL (Old Town Hall), High Street. Built 1572 under the auspices of Robert Dudley, Earl of Leicester, and remodelled 1780. Market hall on the ground floor. Probably c16 rather than c18 are the Tuscan colonnades (now largely blocked) below relieving arches at the sides, and the internal row of columns down the middle. The c16 roof-line shows on the rear gable. c19 addition along one side.

TOWN HALL, Crown Square. 1914–16 by *C. E. Elcock*. Arts and Crafts eclecticism. The centre is classical in feeling, but has mullioned and transomed windows. Asymmetrical appendages with Scottish Baronial tendencies. The ground floor was a market hall, and the building occupies part of the site of the Tudor Gothic BOROUGH MARKET by *Thomas Fulljames* of Gloucester, fragments of which remain at the back.

POLICE STATION, Vale Street. *See* p. 151.

DENBIGHSHIRE INFIRMARY, Ruthin Road. Founded 1807 as the Denbighshire General Dispensary. The building was opened 1813. Long seven-bay front, rather uninspired, even allowing for later alterations and additions. By *Harrison* of Chester, according to Newcome's *Account of the Castle and Town of Denbigh*, 1829, but this is hard to believe.

WAR MEMORIAL, Crown Square. A winged Peace by *C. L. Hartwell*, 1923. On the site of the Market Cross.

MARKET CROSS, Lenten Pool. Transferred from Crown Square to make way for the War Memorial. Of the mid-1840s by *Fulljames*,‡ replacing the earlier cross which was moved to near the castle.

MARKET CROSS, Vale Street/Hall Square. Moved from Crown Square to a site near the castle, to make way for Fulljames's cross in the mid-1840s, and transferred to its present position 1982. Medieval shaft with a ball finial of 1760.

PIERCE MONUMENT, Vale Street. In a garden. Built in honour of Dr Evan Pierce, a local worthy, in his lifetime. He himself gave the site, opposite his own house (demolished 1953). The

---

* Information from Mr E. P. Williams.
‡ Information from Mr R. M. Owen.

monument is of 1874-6, designed by *Martin Underwood*. Small statue by *W. & T. Wills* atop a slender Tuscan column. Relief panels on the pedestal, by *M. Raggi*, added in the 1880s. Two FOUNTAINS, with cast-iron palm-like leaves and formerly numerous birds, were given by the good doctor to commemorate the 1887 Jubilee.

Former MEMORIAL HALL, now THEATR TWM O'R NANT, Red Lane. Built at the expense of Dr Pierce, probably in 1887 and in memory of his mother. Stuccoed Italianate. Five bays, with a two-column stone porch bearing the Royal Arms in its pediment. Converted to a theatre 1978-9. Pierce was also responsible for the neighbouring LLYS MEDDYG, built as a Wesleyan manse.

The Gothic RAILWAY STATION deserves an obituary note. 1861-2 by *Lloyd Williams & Underwood*, the best of the stations which they designed for the Vale of Clwyd Railway. Demolished after the line had fallen victim to Beeching.

HOWELL'S SCHOOL

The famous girls' school, and its sister foundation at Llandaff, owe their origin to a bequest made in 1540 by Thomas Howell, merchant, for the benefit of orphan girls, with the Drapers' Company as trustees. Under an Act of 1853, the endowment was applied to the establishment of the schools. The original building, of 1858-9, opened 1860, is by *Herbert Williams*. He was also the architect for the one at Llandaff and, ten years later, for the rebuilding of Drapers' Hall. Free Elizabethan, with some traceried windows and other Gothic detail. Central pyramid-roofed tower, forming a lantern over the staircase. Symmetrical on both fronts, except for a clock tower at one end and a bellcote beside the central gable on the entrance front. On this side, C20 additions, in refined collegiate manner, dominate. A large NE wing of 1914, by *Heaton Comyn*, with *Leslie Moore* associated, has three storeys successively set back between gabled projections with canted bays. By *Maurice Webb*, 1929-30, are long Neo-Perp cross wings, projecting from Williams's main front, and well integrated with it, despite difference in style. With classical interiors, they contain great hall and dining hall. The former, together with adjoining parts, was restored by *Edward Playne*, 1950-3, after a fire, with the spire of Williams's clock tower being simplified. Of 1929-30 by *Webb* are three SCHOOL HOUSES, symmetrically arranged opposite the main building. Though still historicist, they are treated freely, with the Tudor styling minimal, and with balconies expressing the use of reinforced concrete. Neat brick SPORTS HALL by *Colwyn Foulkes & Partners*, 1969-71.*

* Information on the buildings was kindly supplied by the Drapers' Company and Mr J. M. Griffiths, Bursar of the school.

PERAMBULATION

The County Hall (*see* Public Buildings, above) occupies the E
end of the broad HIGH STREET, where the market is held.
On the S, No. 22 has a Victorian shop-front, its fascia obscured. Nos. 26 and 28 (BRITANNIA BUILDINGS) have two
separate but closely related façades, both with cornices of
enriched brackets and with arched openings in rusticated
ground storeys. The two upper storeys of No. 26 are fully
glazed, divided into three by pilaster strips, and with vertical
glazing bars, arched at the top. No. 28 is of conventional
solid-and-void type, Romanesque rather than Italianate, and
formerly with a first-floor oriel. The buildings were not existing in 1874, but cannot be much later in date. Mr Vernon
Hughes is disposed to attribute them to *Underwood*. The front
of Nos. 40-42 (THE OLD VAULTS), a post-war reconstruction of an C18 predecessor, is carried above the pavement on
columns. Opposite is a whole row of shops with ground-floor
colonnade – a feature which has been retained through successive individual rebuildings and remodellings, with each
building having its own set of columns. Most are Tuscan,
though those of No. 31, a narrow Victorian front with stepped
gable, are mildly Gothic. The range, which has been curtailed
at the W end, seems to have been built as an island block,
encroaching on the market place, as happened at Ludlow. It
is shown existing on Speed's plan of 1610.*
The enclosures created by the island block are Crown Square
at the E end and BACK ROW behind. In the latter, the GOL-
DEN LION, roughcast over jettied timber framing. Also the
EAGLES, which has a plaster overmantel dated 1643, with
strapwork and heraldic eagle, now walled up in a small space
leading off the gents'. CROWN SQUARE, closed by the Town
Hall, has two tall red buildings with much terra-cotta ornament. The space around the County Hall is HALL SQUARE.
In it the BULL HOTEL. Late Georgian sash windows were
inserted into its earlier three-gable front, and it has received
half-timber and tile-hanging, probably *c*.1900. Compact C17
well staircase, with shaped and moulded flat balusters, strapwork on the string, and the gloved hand of the Myddeltons
on the newels. Building work of 1666 is recorded, which
seems too late for the staircase, though not impossibly so. A
brick extension to the hotel, with shaped gable, is early or
mid-C18. It has a panelled room and a full-height dog-leg
staircase, with string and turned balusters. No. 2 Hall Square
displays a late C18 three-bay brick elevation, with modillion
cornice and pilastered and pedimented doorcase. Tripartite
windows in the outer bays, those of the ground floor Venetian
with Gothic glazing. A gable end shows this to be the refronting of an earlier house, and the well staircase is late C17, with

---

* Mr R. M. Owen notes that colonnades once returned into Crown Square,
though projecting in front of the buildings rather than carrying the upper
storeys.

string and twisted balusters. Up to the first floor the balustrade is repeated against the wall as a dado.

From here, VALE STREET leads down. Odd numbers on the left-hand side, even on the r. Of its Georgian houses, No. 19 has been one of the best, but is marred by bay-windows and a shop-front. It is mid- or late C18, of brick, with three storeys, three bays, a stone cornice, one-bay pediment, and a pedimented doorcase with consoles. On the same side, the NATIONAL WESTMINSTER BANK, stuccoed Italianate. No. 22, early or mid-C19, is stone, with rusticated lower storey and tripartite windows. Nos. 26–32 was the town house of the Heatons of Plas Heaton (see Henllan). Probably mid-C18. Stone, large in scale, and of five bays and three storeys, with three-bay pediment. Much altered. No. 47. Brick, late C18, of three bays and three storeys. Four Venetian windows with Gothic glazing in the outer bays. Doorcase with enriched cornice and consoles. The HAWK AND BUCKLE next door had, in the rear yard, a circular thatched COCK-PIT, possibly C17, which was taken off to St Fagan's in 1964. Terraces below (Nos. 53–59) and Nos. 38–42 opposite are minor, but No. 44, though much altered, has moulded and shaped window surrounds which show it to have been an early C18 five-bay three-storey house of some consequence. Next to it is the POLICE STATION, a late C18 three-bay brick house with tripartite windows in the outer bays. Those of the ground floor are Venetian, and those of the top storey lunettes. Some Gothic glazing. GROVE HOUSE, on the left-hand side, is early or mid-C18, of brick with stone quoins and keystones. Modillion cornice and a doorcase with fluted pilasters. Two storeys and five bays, the centre one projecting, and probably once pedimented. Later dormers. Earlier work at the rear, with a datestone of 1693, but believed to include part of a house built in 1574 by Hugh Clough, brother of Sir Richard.

Parallel with Vale Street is PARK STREET, where, below the road leading through to Howell's School, is BOD GWILYM, an Italianate brick villa by *R. Lloyd Williams* for himself. Now part of the school. BRYN-Y-PARC (Nos. 3–5) is at the top of the street. (It has a room with panelling, moulded beams, and a late C16 or early C17 overmantel with heraldry and an Annunciation scene. NMR)

At the W end of the High Street, the right-hand fork is Portland Place, becoming BRIDGE STREET, where No. 24, looking early C19, has a semicircular columned porch, obscuring a doorcase with consoles. It was the home of William Williams (1801–68), the poet Caledfryn. So to LENTEN POOL, with the former BLUECOAT SCHOOL (closed 1976) by *Henry Kennedy*, 1846–7. Neo-Jacobean, with shaped gables, including a tall thin one and two thin dormers on the main front. Highgate, the left-hand fork at the end of the High Street, continues as LOVE LANE. A house on the r., LYNDALE, was a tiny COUNTY GAOL. The earlier part is of *c.* 1843 by *Sir Joshua*

Jebb, the military engineer and prison specialist. Rock-faced, with rusticated lintels, and of two bays and two storeys, with a pediment. On the l., the former BRITISH SCHOOL, 1843-4, bulky, with large diamond glazing patterns. Above, in TAN Y GWALIA (reached *via* Castle Lane) is a former R.C. church (ST JOSEPH), built in 1863 as a combined church and school. Neo-Elizabethan, with diamond glazing patterns, and a cottage either end. Used until 1968.

OUTER DENBIGH

27-8 ST MARCELLA, Llanfarchell (Whitchurch), in a rural setting 1¼m. E. The parish church of Denbigh. One of the best examples of the local double-naved type, it is a late Perp enlargement and remodelling of an earlier structure. A blocked W doorway, apparently C14, proclaims the S nave as the earlier half. A slender and unbuttressed battlemented W tower has two-light Perp bell openings. It is of the same date as, or slightly later than, the Perp N nave, though it is not in axis with it, and slightly overlaps the S nave. The E windows of both naves are four-centred, of five lights, with cusping, single-light sub-arches and panel tracery, though they differ in size and outline. Three S windows with hoodmoulds, a blocked priest's door, S porch with round-headed arch, and a N doorway with cyclopean pointed head. Five-bay arcade with octagonal piers and four-centred arches, and with mouldings of greater refinement than is usual for the region. Panelled roofs, all the members moulded, with simple arched-braced trusses alternating with hammerbeams. Internal stonecarving includes animal and angel corbels, and string courses containing flowers, animals, heads etc., a fox and hare, and a boy pulling a donkey's tail. Cloth shears are said to refer to a tailors' company.

The FONT is dated 1640. – ALTAR TABLES. One of 1623 with melon-bulb legs and small-scale strapwork. Signed on the underside by *David Rogeres*. – Another, from St Hilary's, of 1617. – SCREENS. By *C. Hodgson Fowler*, who restored the church in 1908. Parts of the rood screen are incorporated, the doorway of the N screen and the flanking tracery heads being old. – RAILS. Chunky C17 turned balusters. The rail itself, with vine trail, is from the rood screen. – PULPIT. With tester and panelled backdrop. Dated 1683. – STAINED GLASS. Fragments in the N nave E window and the porch. – CHANDELIER. Made by *John Thomas* of Chester, 1753. Two six-branch tiers and a dove. – BENEFACTION BOARD. Painted 1720. – CHEST. Dated 1676. – MONUMENTS. In the N nave: Robert Salus-
64   bury. 1802. Elegant. – Humphrey Llwyd, antiquary, †1568. A Corinthian aedicule, with ball finial and heraldry in the tympanum. Renaissance ornament, particularly in the frieze. Kneeling figure in relief, within a classical architectural setting. – A BRASS to Richard Myddelton, governor of Denbigh

Denbigh, Llanfarchell (Whitchurch),
brass to Richard and Jane Myddelton, *c.* 1575
(*Archaeologia Cambrensis*, 5th ser., vol. 1, 1884)

Castle, †1575 and wife Jane †1565. They kneel, facing each
other across desks, with their nine sons and seven daughters.
– Thomas Shaw †1717. Segmental canopy, panelled pilaster
strips, and drapery over the tablet. – Richard Heaton †1791.
By the elder *Westmacott*. Draped urn, the drapery extending
down the sides of the tablet. – In the s nave: Sir John Salusbury of Lleweni †1578 and wife Joan. Erected by her in 63
1588, and executed by one *Donbins*. Alabaster. Tomb-chest
and two recumbent effigies, he in armour. Against the tomb-
chest and facing outward are nine sons and four daughters,
two of the latter swaddled babes. Except for putti bearing
heraldry, all is of excellent workmanship. Some colouring. –
Mary Drihurst †1692. Drapery and a big cherub head. –
Jeanette Octavia Ward. By *Albert Toft*, 1915. Recumbent
figure in relief, and angels with a wreath. – Cotton monument. Hester, daughter of Sir Thomas Salusbury, and her
husband Sir Robert Cotton. 1714, and attributed by Mrs
Esdaile to the workshop of *Edward Stanton*. Spiral Corinthian
columns and a segmental canopy. Heraldry and urns above,
volutes and leafage either side, and cherub heads below. –
Nine HATCHMENTS.

NORTH WALES MENTAL HOSPITAL, ¾m. SSW. 1842-8 by 110
Fulljames & Waller of Gloucester. Grand Jacobethan frontage of ashlar. Three storeys and a basement, and many small
gables, some shaped, some straight. Fifteen windows long.

The three bays at either end project, as do the central three, where there are large first-floor windows and a storeyed porch. Clock tower with shaped gables and octagonal turret. Of successive extensions, the earliest (1867) are by *Lloyd Williams & Underwood*. Neo-Georgian buildings in the grounds include BRYNHYFRYD VILLA, by *S. Colwyn Foulkes*, 1956. Also in the grounds, the CHAPEL, by *Lloyd Williams & Underwood*, 1861-2. (VH) Vigorous in its massing, having cross gables, N and S porches, transepts, and a polygonal E end with flèche and gabled E projection. E window with STAINED GLASS by *James Ballantine*, 1861. (VH)

PLAS CLOUGH, 1 m. NNE. Built for Sir Richard Clough, whose initials are displayed in iron, as is the date 1567. If the latter is to be believed, the house is contemporary with Bach-y-graig (*see* Tremeirchion, p. 451). The date inscription, however, is not shown by Moses Griffith, and it may have been transferred from Bach-y-graig. Though less remarkable than that prodigious house, Plas Clough too was influenced by the Low Countries, and it marks the introduction of stepped gables into Wales, where they soon came to be much used. Renaissance symmetry and the use of brick were also innovatory. The brick is now rendered, and sashes have been inserted. Storeyed porch on Doric columns, originally with a stepped gable. Stepped gables to the cross wings, which do not project as such at the front, though they extend some way back at the rear.

KILFORD FARM, Llanfarchell (Whitchurch), 1½ m. E. In a BARN are three reused hammerbeam trusses, though the hammerbeams themselves are missing.

WYNNE'S PARC, in Brookhouse Road, 1 m. ESE. A fresh and informal house, roughcast and with leaded casements, by *Sir E. Guy Dawber*, 1905. Storeyed porch with coped gable and some reused masonry. A taller gable has a two-storey oriel.

YSTRAD ISAF, 1 m. SW. Late C17 or early C18, of brick. Storeyed porch with splayed corners.

YSTRAD HALL, a large house of early C19 character, has been demolished.

GALCH HILL, ¾ m. SW. Two-unit plan. Timber-framed upper storey. This was the birthplace of Sir Hugh Myddelton, who was responsible for the 'New River' London water supply, and of Sir Thomas Myddelton, Lord Mayor and founder of the Chirk dynasty.

GWAENYNOG, 1¼ m. WSW. A former Myddelton house, basically of H-plan, and complicated in its evolution. Much was done following a change of ownership in 1870, and the last major alterations were carried out from 1914 onwards. There is an *ex situ* date inscription of 1571, and a carved and inlaid chimneypiece may be of this time. The recessed centre of the E (entrance) front, still half-timbered in 1870, is a grand version of the central chimney and lobby entrance plan, with hall to the l. and kitchen on the r. In the kitchen a date inscription of 1762. In 1764 the S cross wing was remodelled

and lengthened, with a fine new room the full height of the
wing formed at either end – dining room to the E, drawing
room to the W, both with a canted bay to the S. Between, the
old storey heights were retained, and a staircase with Venetian
window inserted. In or after 1870 the S elevation was refaced
in stone, in a sort of Tudor Gothic, and the Venetian window
was done away with, but very good C18 interiors remain. The
staircase has swept rail, ornamented stair ends, columnar balusters and Ionic newels. In the (former) dining room a Doric
marble chimneypiece and rococo plasterwork. The drawing
room is later in character, with good Adamish ceiling and
marble chimneypiece. Female figures in medallions on the
ceiling and frieze.* A first-floor room in the central part of
the house has a coved ceiling with excellent rococo plasterwork. Its stalks and flowers, in the round, are noteworthy.
C18 plasterwork also in the hall, especially heraldry and
weapons above the fireplace. In the Evidence Room, or mu-
niment room, is a strong-room door, dated 1784, with a
painted medallion depicting a pastoral scene.

JOHNSON MONUMENT, beside the River Ystrad. An urn
and pedestal, erected in honour of Dr Johnson, at a spot
which he frequented during a visit to Colonel John Myddelton in 1774. He remarked that it 'looks like an intention to
bury me alive'. A further inscription was added after his
death. Restored and resited 1975. Downstream is the so-
called DR JOHNSON'S COTTAGE, ruinous.

ERIVIAT HALL, 2¼ m. W. An enlargement of 1732 is recorded,
but the house assumed its present appearance in 1856, when
remodelled in flat and severe Neo-Elizabethan. Brick with
stone dressings. (Well staircase with shaped stair ends, swept
rail and fluted columnar balusters. The main flights are
doubtless of 1732, though upper parts and some timber arcades look Victorian. NMR)

DERWEN
0050

ST MARY. A single chamber, its exterior whitewashed when
seen by Glynne in 1849. He also noted the double W bellcote
to have been dated 1688. Perp five-light E window with transom at springing level, two-light sub-arches, cusping and
panel tracery. Intersecting tracery of a S window may not be
reliable. The easternmost on the N, a pair of lancets, probably
dates from the Perp period, to which the arched-braced roof
belongs, with struts and cusping above the collars, and cusped
wind-braces. A shallow N projection contains rood-loft stairs,
an arrangement dating from *Kennedy*'s restoration of 1857.
– The church indeed enjoys the rare good fortune of having

---

* Plasterwork below the frieze by the Manchester branch of *Waring & Gillow*,
who were responsible for decoration at the time of the post-1914 work. They
fitted up a new dining room at the N end of the house. I owe this information,
and indeed most of the facts on Gwaenynog, to Captain J. O. Burton.

36   a ROOD SCREEN which retains its loft. Screen of rectangular construction, in the usual Welsh manner, with a continuous middle rail between the end standards. The divisions of the intermediate mullions do not coincide with those of the wainscot panels below. Heavily moulded uprights, pierced traceried panels of differing pattern, and varied open traceried heads to the openings. The loft parapets are also open, with traceried heads. Flat soffits (i.e. no vaulting), panelled and ribbed, with bosses. Vine-trail bressumers and, on the E, cresting. The socket for the rood remains. – FONT. Dated 1665, and the FONT COVER is probably contemporary. – STAINED GLASS. Second from E on S. Designed by *H. E. Wooldridge* and made by *James Powell & Sons*, 1869.* – In the circular CHURCHYARD is a fine mid- or late C15 CHURCHYARD CROSS. Sculpture at the head in niches under cusped and crocketed canopies, the E and W ones double. On the E the Coronation of the Virgin, W the Crucifixion, N Virgin and Child, and S an angel (St Michael?) with scales. The top of the head is missing. Sculpture also, much worn, on the chamfered corners of the shaft and in a band at the neck. – The building to the S was a LYCHGATE. With an upper room once used as a school, the gateway itself was walled in when more accommodation was needed.

COED FOEL, $\frac{3}{8}$ m. SE. A cruck house with inserted central chimney backing on to the entrance passage. A date inscription of 1633 (DOE) probably refers to this adaptation.

FFYNNON SARAH, $\frac{5}{8}$ m. NNW. A stone bath, with steps, fed by a spring. A nearby cottage has vanished, but the well was restored and the setting neatly landscaped, 1972–3. The work was carried out on the initiative of the rector, the *Rev. J. P. Cooke*, and to his design.

DERWEN HALL, $1\frac{1}{2}$ m. ENE. L-shaped. Two timber-framed ranges (brick-nogged) suggest unit planning, with its parts fairly large. One has C19 latticed casements. The other, with sashes, has diagonal bracing, with the infill bricks set at an angle. (It is jettied and under-built in brick. NMR) Lateral chimneys.

DINBYCH *see* DENBIGH

0040   DINMAEL

ST CATHERINE, Maerdy. Aisleless, built in 1878. S porch and W bellcote. The proportions of the lancet windows are wrong, and the church was the work of an amateur, *William Kerr* of Maesmor. A brass records that he also gave the site. Goodhart-Rendel adds, though, that Kerr was credited as 'designer' and *D. Jones* of Cerrigydrudion as 'architect'. –

* Thanks are due to Mr Martin Harrison for this information.

FONT and PULPIT of marble, and quite sumptuous. –
STAINED GLASS. First nave window from E on S, commemorating Mrs Kerr, by *Mayer & Co.* of Munich.

PONT MAESMOR. Two small arches, and full-height cutwaters.

MAESMOR. An ancient site. The present appearance is largely
the result of a Neo-Tudor remodelling of *c.* 1830. Roughcast,
with labels, margin panes, ornamented bargeboards etc. Details characteristic of the style and period inside also. The
staircase is apparently early C18, not *in situ*. Short wings were
added, at either end of the main front, by the firm of *William
& Segar Owen*, 1923.

Here is a noteworthy section of *Telford*'s HOLYHEAD ROAD,
especially the portion in a gorge, ¾ m. beyond Dinmael.

DINORBEN *see* ST GEORGE

EFENECHDYD

1050

ST MICHAEL. A single chamber, and very small, though external evidence of eastward extension shows that it was once yet
smaller. Unusual for the region in having a pre-Perp feature:
the two-light E window is Dec. Also unusual is the roof, in
which arched-braced principals alternate with single common
rafters. W porch with some timber framing and cusped
wind-braces. By *Arthur Baker*, 1873, are N and S windows, W
doorway (containing ancient DOOR), bellcote etc. – Rare
wooden tub FONT, hollowed out of a single block of oak; it
has never been reliably dated. Really circular, but the circumference is worked into fourteen facets. Diminishing downwards in profile, and at the base is a band of large beads or
knobs. – Low SCREEN, from parts of the late medieval rood
screen. Deep beam, with cusped arcading and multi-tier brattishing. – PULPIT. With C17 panelling. – WALL PAINTING.
Fragment of a Welsh inscription. – Circular CHURCHYARD.

Efenechdyd, in its own little valley, is hardly a village, so small
is the settlement around the church. The early or mid-C18
PLAS-YN-LLAN, however, is quite ambitious, having seven
bays and a doorcase with pediment and lugged surround.
Brick with stone dressings, including quoins and keystones.
Coped end gables. (Staircase with columnar balusters. Also
a panelled room. NMR) The GATEPIERS have iron blackamoor
busts as finials.

EGLWSYBACH*

8060

A market once existed, and the village street forms a small but
closely knit entity.

* Transferred to Gwynedd in 1974.

ST MARTIN. Rebuilt 1782, though two w windows, both with
two arched lights, look earlier. The builder, and presumably
designer, was *Hugh Williams* of Conwy. Recognizably C18 is
the w tower with obelisk pinnacles. Also the round-arched s
doorway, lurking in a porch dated 1837. *R. Lloyd Williams*
inserted Gothic tracery into round-headed windows, as part
of a restoration conceived in 1874 and executed 1881–2.
Five-bay arcades of round arches on rectangular ashlar piers.
All else, including the responds and coved ceiling, is plastered. – Tub FONT. Circular, turning octagonal, with
moulded base. Dated 1731, but possibly Norman. – Turned
columnar RAILS on three sides of the altar. – CHANDELIER.
One of a former pair. An exuberant Victorian version of the
traditional form. – Also ornate LAMP BRACKETS. – ROYAL
ARMS. A painted panel dated 1816.

PLAS LLAN, ¼ m. S. Of lateral chimney and inside cross passage
plan, with large stacks. (Indescribably crude chimneypiece
and pilastered overmantel, with initials and heraldry, dated
1684. A further plaster overmantel bears the same date. NMR)

PENNANT, 2¼ m. SSE. A rubble-walled house dated 1749. (P.
Smith) The generously scaled four-bay front and its one-bay
returns must, however, be early C19. Ground-floor windows
in arched recesses. The entrance is also of this period, though
set further back in the less regular earlier part (and there are
contemporary internal features, including a plain but effective
sweeping staircase. DOE).

On the Caernarfonshire border, 1¼ m. SSW, a small CHAPEL,
with cottage.

At CEFN-Y-COED ISAF, 1¾ m. SW, is a BARN with four cruck
trusses, one incomplete.

(A cruck BARN at MEDDIANT UCHAF, ⅝ m. WSW.)

PENRHYD, 1¼ m. NW. The gabled GATEHOUSE is roughcast,
with brick dressings and a semicircular staircase turret. By
H. L. North, 1927.* Its pointed arch is particularly characteristic of his own Arts and Crafts idiom. A LILY POND GAR-
DEN (now a swimming pool) may also be his, though not in
his style. Curving screen walls and a classical loggia, all in
grey brick.

On the summit of Mwdwl Eithin, 2⅛ m. SE (SH 829 683), is a
group of three Bronze Age BARROWS in a line N–S. The
northernmost one is a very prominent mound which can be
seen from miles around. The other two are smaller, the southern one crossed by the field fence. In 1911–12 the central
mound was excavated, revealing that it had been built of
turves and covered a stone wall almost identical in construction to that found recently beneath one of the turf barrows in
the Brenig Valley (*see* p. 254). The wall was built of spaced
upright stones linked by very rough dry walling. Three cremation burials were found in the mound, one at the centre on
the old ground surface, the other two incorporated in the turf

---

* Mr Ian Allan kindly supplied the date and confirmed the attribution.

mound. One was accompanied by an unusual grooved stone, an arrow shaft smoother.

EGLWYSEG

ST MARY. Like the church at Froncysyllte (q.v.), this was built as a school and chapel of ease in Llangollen parish, 1870–1. Quite a decent little lancet job, with E bellcote and polygonal apse. – (STAINED GLASS. A roundel by *Eginton*, transferred from the parish church.)

TAN-Y-GRAIG, 1 m. NNE of the church. (A ceiling with moulded beams of equal depth in two directions, plus stop-chamfered joists. NMR)

World's End is the name given to the head of this remote valley, below the cliffs of the Eglwyseg Rocks. Here is PLAS UCHAF 46 (or Manor House), L-shaped, with a wing projecting forward at the front, and long and low. Partly of stone, though most of the upper storey is timber-framed, with herringbone and lozenge bracing. Close studding at the rear. Doorway with depressed ogee head. The house is traditionally assigned to 1563, but is of more than one build, and the wing is possibly the older part.

There are a number of Bronze Age CAIRNS and BARROWS on the limestone plateau which stretches away behind Eglwyseg Rocks. Some of them are conspicuous mounds and may be recognized at a distance; others have been robbed and scattered and are difficult to find. The most interesting group is close to SJ 228 452, where a circle of boulders may be seen standing in what is now a very boggy depression. The monument has been disturbed and is difficult to classify but is probably best described as a kerb circle. Nearby are two kerb cairns, very small, but with large kerb stones, and there are several other less elaborate cairns in the vicinity.

ERBISTOCK

Once there was a ferry across the Dee, here seen at its most placid. The church, beside the river, lies between the former RECTORY and the charmingly diminutive BOAT INN, now a restaurant. Gardens have replaced the landing stage and river wall.

ST HILARY. Rebuilt 1860–1, as a memorial church. Rather good, and it is a pity that the name of the architect is unknown. E.E. and Dec features. Nave and aisles under one roof, though end windows and buttresses express the aisles externally. S porch, elaborate W bellcote, and polygonal apse. Good carving – head-stops etc. and, especially, the arcade capitals. The piers are polished granite, and the ashlar-lined chancel has the lancets of its apse contained in cusped arcades with polished shafts. – Disused FONT bowl. Square, with slightly canted faces and a rough corner projection. – Six-branch CHANDELIER, with dove. – MONUMENTS. Anne Vaughan †1791. Falling column against an obelisk. – Eliza Jane Robson †1835. By *T. Ashton*. Sarcophagus tablet.

ERBISTOCK MILL. ½m. N. Four-storeyed. (Fireplace with inscription of 1602. DOE)

GROVES FARM, ½m. NE. Early or mid-C18, of brick with stone quoins. Five bays. Dog-leg staircase, with twisted balusters, through two storeys. An earlier wing at the back has timber-framing, brick-nogged.

MANLEY HALL, ⅜m. NW. C17, of H-plan, but much altered. Some brick nogging. One panelled room and a rearranged staircase with turned balusters and square-finialed newels.

ERBISTOCK HALL, ¾m. NNW. Brick, with some stone dressings. Main front of 1720, though a projecting right-hand wing may be later. The house has been greatly remodelled and reduced, and once had steeper roofs (that of the wing hipped) with dormers. A fine large DOVECOTE, brick-built, and circular, with conical roof. Oval windows. It has a vane dated 1737.

ROSE HILL, 1m. NNW. A Late Georgian three-bay three-storey centre, rendered, is recessed between pedimented brick cross wings which look Early Victorian. The return of the right-hand wing forms the entrance front, with one-bay pediment and distyle *in antis* Doric porch. STABLES with a blank Venetian window in a big arched recess. PARKLAND slopes down towards Overton Bridge.

3040
ERDDIG

In 1683 a new house was designed for Joshua Edisbury by *Thomas Webb*, a freemason of Middlewich, and was completed *c.*1687. Edisbury, whose father had bought the estate, was not a provident man, and the upshot of wild borrowing was the sale of Erddig to John Meller, Master in Chancery. Meller, who entered into possession in 1718, enlarged and furnished the house*; on his death it passed to his nephew Simon Yorke, and descended through the Yorkes until given to the National Trust by the last of the line in 1973. Extensive restoration, necessitated to a considerable degree by mining subsidence, was immediately put in hand. The architect for the work was *Robert B. Heaton* of *The Anthony Clark Partnership*.‡

67   Examination of the EXTERIOR should begin with the E or garden front, a long brick façade of nineteen bays.§ The main

---

* The important contents surviving from his time are outside the scope of *The Buildings of Wales*. Marble chimneypieces were made for Meller by *Robert Wynne*.

‡ Mr Merlin Waterson and Mr Gervase Jackson-Stops generously made available the results of their researches on Erddig, and I am also indebted to Mr Waterson for much helpful comment.

§ The description given here is not related to the route by which the public are conducted.

block – *Webb*'s house for Edisbury – comprises the nine middle bays and is of two storeys and a basement. The centre is emphasized by a pedimented doorcase, a moulded surround to the window above it, and balustrading piercing an otherwise solid parapet behind which are hipped dormers. Originally balustrading occurred at each bay. There was also a cupola, characteristic of the Restoration house of the Hugh May and Roger Pratt school of which Erddig, with its lack of enrichment and articulation, is so pared down a version. Yet compared with, e.g., Ramsbury, the omission of a pediment and the substitution of parapet for eaves cornice has a forward-looking character, foreshadowing the early C18. Side wings were added for Meller, *c.*1721–4; one room deep, they have low roofs contrasting with the prominent hip of the double-pile main block. For two bays the wings continue the 1680s storey heights. Then follow three bays with two storeys, intermediate oval windows, and no basement. The N wing contains a chapel, and here a ground floor and oval window merge. Sashes are doubtless of the 1720s, the main block having originally had timber cross windows. All basement windows still have timber mullions. Present central steps *c.*1861–3. Stone chimneystacks rebuilt *c.*1900–1. On the W (entrance) front are first encountered the activities of Philip Yorke (succeeded 1767), for whom much was done in the 1770s. Designs were made by *James Wyatt*, but execution seems to have been by one *Franks* and by *William Turner*. *Joseph Turner* was also involved, and it is impossible to say who did what. Until this time the W front was of similar character to the E, but in 1772–3 main block and wings were cased in stone and a three-bay pediment added. Separate service wings flanking the courtyard were demolished. The C17 proportions look awkward decked out in suave ashlar and with recessed sashes and thin glazing bars. Entrance with Doric doorcase and curving double flight of steps. Iron balustrading, for which the date 1781 is recorded. Basement porch of 1858 on the N return.

INTERIOR. Rooms remodelled in the 1770s are the entrance hall, drawing room (SW room of main block) and the first-floor W rooms. Of the 1680s are dog-leg staircases at either end, between the E and W ranges of rooms. The northern is the main one, spacious, and with turned balusters and flat-topped newels. Many rooms with original bolection-moulded panelling. It occurs, e.g., in the saloon (which occupies the five central bays of the E front) and on the N staircase and landing, and in a narrow first-floor gallery running transversely through the centre of the house. The saloon, however, was originally two rooms, and received its present form in Philip Yorke's time. Previously it consisted only of the three northernmost bays of the present room. An 'apartment' extended S, into Meller's wing, and had the usual progression of drawing room, state bedroom and dressing room. S of the enlarged saloon there now is the dining room, formed by

Thomas Hopper, 1826–7. His somewhat heavy hand is apparent in deeply moulded entablatures and a coffered ceiling. A Doric screen at either end. In the N wing the Chinese Room, named from its C18 wallpaper, extends the enfilade of the E front.* The chapel, beyond, has late C18 fittings and various subsequent embellishments. Its stained glass includes a late medieval figure of St Catherine. Also King David, datable 1755–64 on heraldic evidence. These are both from Wimpole, Cambridgeshire, seat of the Yorkes, Earls of Hardwicke, and were installed here in 1909. A third light is probably of this date. At the S end of the house, the kitchen, with Venetian window and rusticated fireplace and other openings, is of 1772–4. Originally detached from the rest of the house, this was an entirely new building. It will have been noted that Philip Yorke's remodellings of the earlier structure, both outside and in, were confined to the W side. On the E he merely enlarged the saloon, and in doing so he eschewed a complete refashioning and preserved and adapted C17 fittings. Author of *The Royal Tribes of Wales*, he fitted up an emblematic Tribes Room in the basement, and initiated an Erddig tradition of assembling portraits of household servants annotated with descriptive verses. Mr Waterson considers that his selective preservation of earlier work reflects deliberate policy, stemming from antiquarian interest and a sense of history.

The pattern of retention on the E and modernization on the W is further apparent in the GROUNDS. Edisbury's FORMAL GARDENS on the E were, like the house itself, extended by Meller. In their present form they are enclosed by screen walls, and a Victorianized parterre near the house has walls either side, surmounted by shaped gables. Until 1898 they continued W to meet the house, and the gables themselves are of 1912–13. Baluster SUNDIAL from Plas Grono (*see* below). A broader area to the E has its early C18 pattern of pleached limes and fruit trees replanted. Pair of PINNACLES from Wrexham church. The principal element dating from Meller's time is a long CANAL, aligned on the axis, and flanked by an avenue of limes which once were pleached. The vista is now closed by a glorious SCREEN of railings and central gates, of unknown provenance but attributable to *Robert Davies*. Formerly at Stansty Park, Gwersyllt (q.v.), it was set up at the East or Forest Lodge of Erddig in 1908 and transferred to the present site during the 1970s restorations. Scrollwork not only in the overthrow and as cresting to the railings, but in the divisions between every rail. A further length of water, N of the canal, was probably a fish pond. At its E end, a formal pattern of yew hedges has been reinstated. SUNDIAL, with Meller's arms engraved on the plate, and a (later?) octagonal baluster stem. A wooded area S of the canal was originally a bowling green.

---

* Chinese wallpaper also in the first-floor NW room (state bedchamber).

The formal layout, spared by Philip Yorke, contrasts with the PARK, landscaped in the naturalistic manner of the day by *William Emes*, who worked at Erddig between 1768 and 1789, and in 1778-9 continued the canal. The recasing of the w front of the house, and the demolition of the service wings, was accompanied by the removal of the entrance court, together with gates made for Meller by *Davies*. A lush expanse of parkland and distant country now lies before the hall door. Only the colliery, which so nearly did for the house, provides a reminder of the proximity of Wrexham.

s of the house the STABLES, dated 1774. Rusticated and pedimented segmental entrance arch, and Doric arcades inside. In the kitchen yard a CUPOLA from Stansty, erected here 1913.

DOVECOTE, to the E, in the park. Large and octagonal, of brick. Existing by 1739.

The house is approached from the park through two pairs of small GATEPIERS, elegantly ornamented, and possibly of 1780.

CUP AND SAUCER, $\frac{1}{4}$m. NNW. 1774 by *Emes*. The cup is below and inside the saucer. A stream discharges into a disc, and disappears through a hole in the middle, creating an internal cylindrical waterfall. The water emerges a few yards away under a bridge-like arch.

MOTTE AND BAILEY, $\frac{3}{8}$m. N. This was the castle of 'Wristlesham', or Wrexham, mentioned in the Pipe Rolls 1161. Mound within a roughly square enclosure, constructed against WAT'S DYKE on an elevated site at the confluence of two streams. Now heavily wooded. Planting by *Emes* obscured formal yew walks.

At the EAST or FOREST LODGE, the gates moved to the gardens have been replaced by GATES of 1902 from the former Coed-y-Glyn Lodge, which stood at the Wrexham end of the park.

PLAS GRONO, near Plas Grono Lodge. The house which was the home of Elihu Yale and the sporting writer C. J. Apperley (Nimrod) was demolished in 1876.

NEW SONTLEY, $\frac{1}{2}$m. E. Formed from the service wings of an early c18 house, the main block of which was demolished in 1764. Brick, with stone dressings. House of seven bays with a three-bay pediment. Quoins, those at the outer corners of even length. The balancing wing, axially opposite, is converted to farm buildings.

OLD SONTLEY. *See* Marchwiel.

SONTLEY BRIDGE, NE of New Sontley. Segmental lattice arch. Dated 1845, and with the names of (the younger) *Thomas Penson*, County Surveyor, and *R. & W. Jones* of the Ruabon Foundry.

ERIVIAT HALL *see* DENBIGH, p. 155

2050

ERYRYS

St David. 1863 by *T. H. Wyatt*. Lancets. Aisleless, with w bellcote and polygonal apse.

3040

ESCLUSHAM

An area of varied character, extending from the outskirts of Wrexham to the lonely expanse of Esclusham Mountain. A well-preserved portion of OFFA'S DYKE runs s from Bersham, and to the e is WAT'S DYKE, running s from Erddig. The Bersham Colliery at Rhostyllen is the last mine of the Wrexham coalfield to remain in operation.

HOLY TRINITY, Rhostyllen. 1876–7 by *J. E. Lash* of Wrexham. Rock-faced, aisleless but cruciform, and saved from dullness by a perkily tall bellcote above the chancel arch. Geometrical tracery. – PANELLING and CHANCEL FITTINGS of 1916 must surely be a Hamer benefaction and be by *Cecil Hare* (cf. St Peter, Broughton). Especially notable the vaulted and traceried SCREEN. The sandstone REREDOS, in the stylized Perp of the late Gothic Revival, has panels of the Adoration of the Magi and the Shepherds.

CROES FOEL, ½ m. SW of the church, near the by-pass roundabout. Georgian vernacular of 1781. (A dated rainwater head is later.) Three storeys, three bays, pedimented doorcase, but still having broad windows with timber mullions and transoms. Some earlier FARM BUILDINGS. It was at Croes Foel that the *Davies* family had their smithy.

HAFOD-Y-BWCH. Its GATEPIERS, with ball finials, are almost opposite Croes Foel. Three portions, the earliest of which formed part of a timber-framed hall house. The central truss remains – a base cruck with cusped struts above the tie. Also a partition wall and truss and one gable end, though the latter is now internal following the addition of a cross wing. In the wing an early or mid-C17 staircase, from first to second floor, with flat, shaped balusters and square-finialed newels. A brick-nogged further addition, built against the wing, has two gables, timber mullions and transoms and a yet later porch and central gable. Two enormous brick stacks apparently incorporated lateral chimneys of the earlier wing, and have diapering as sunk panels. There are references to dates of 1612 (DOE) and 1615 (P. Smith), and a reset heraldic panel was dated 1590. Late C17 staircase from Five Fords, Marchwiel, reassembled here in the course of restorations by *Robert B. Heaton* in the latter 1970s. Swept rail, twisted balusters and string with pulvinated frieze. In its original form it was a dog-leg, rising through two storeys.

(LLYNTRO. A moated site, w of Croes Foel, with some stones still visible. D. Leslie Davies)

CREMATORIUM, 1 m. WSW of the church. On the site of PENTREBYCHAN HALL, an early C19 house demolished in 1962.

There remains a circular brick DOVECOTE of 1721, with conical roof.

LEGACY WATER TOWER, Talwrn, 1¼ m. W of the church, 1933–5 Circular, of reinforced concrete, with an order of pilasters.

ESCLUSHAM HALL, S of the water tower. This was a timber-framed hall house. There remains the central truss – a base cruck with, it seems, struts above its cambered tie-beam. Also the two partition trusses and walls, with two pointed doorways in the one at the lower end. Inserted lateral chimney and a floor with stop-chamfered beams. Staircase with flat, pierced and shaped balusters and a square finial. These insertions, and the rebuilding of the outer walls in brick, are presumably of 1677, a date inscribed on the stone doorcase.

MONTANA, ⅛ m. S of the water tower. 1966 by *Jon James*. Built on and around a disused circular reservoir tank. This provided garages, an embanked terrace and a base for load-bearing walls. The adjoining part of the house is timber-framed, faced with vertical boarding, above brick piers.

BRONWYLFA, 2 m. W of the church. Remodelled or largely rebuilt 1872. Gothic, with cusped lancets, tracery and a castellated turret. Gothic interior features also, including a top-lit staircase. The porch looks C20. Fanciful ENTRANCE LODGE; its masonry contrasts in both colour and texture, with red and yellow brick, and there is some timberwork. Half-hipped roofs.

TAN-Y-LAN, ⅛ m. S of Bronwylfa. A crude cruck in a gable end.

PLAS CADWGAN remains a happily rare instance of the demolition of a grade I listed building. The deed was done in 1967. The house had had a domino-like growth, and part had previously been destroyed, but it retained an undivided hall, possibly C14, with speres and central arched-braced cruck. Also a C17 staircase with pierced balusters and finialed newels. The central and spere-trusses were re-erected at the Avoncroft Museum, Worcestershire.

HAFOD HOUSE. *See* Rhosllannerchrugog.

A large Bronze Age BARROW covered in gorse can be seen at SJ 309 474. There is a suggestion that it may have been surrounded by a ditch, and there are indications that it has been disturbed but there is no record of any finds. There used to be another barrow, *c*.½ m. away, near Croes Foel.

EYTON

3040

EYTON MANOR FARM, W of the main road. Timber-framed, with brick nogging, and very fetching in appearance. The house provides an instance of traditional planning succumbing to Renaissance influence, and is probably of 1633 (date inscribed on garden wall). Unevenly cruciform in plan, with a two-unit portion having a kitchen wing at the rear (the three rooms sharing a central chimney), and a storeyed porch at the front. The symmetrical front and the gable end returns have close studding, some jettying and diagonal bracing, and diagonal patterning of the brick infill. Two panelled rooms. Staircase with bulbous turned balusters.

EYTON OLD HALL, $\frac{5}{8}$m. sw of Manor Farm. Traces of a MOAT. The area enclosed was of considerable size.

DDOL, $\frac{3}{4}$m. ESE of Manor Farm. A three-bay brick front, proud but unlettered in its use of classical forms. Tripartite ground-floor windows and entrance, the latter with arched fanlight and a sort of pediment. The window above rises into a pediment containing heraldry and an inscription of 1789.

FFOS-Y-GO *see* GWERSYLLT

FOEL FENLLI *see* LLANBEDR DYFFRYN CLWYD

2040

FRONCYSYLLTE

104 PONT CYSYLLTE. *Thomas Telford*'s aqueduct, striding across the valley, became in the C19 as much a part of the wonder and romance of the Vale of Llangollen as Dinas Bran itself. Carrying a canal 127 ft above the waters of the Dee, it earned the nickname 'the stream in the sky', and deserves its reputation as an engineering achievement of consummate mastery.

The Ellesmere Canal was intended to link the Mersey with the Dee at Chester and the Severn at Shrewsbury. With *William Jessop* as engineer, it was authorized in 1793, and *Telford* was appointed 'General Agent, Surveyor, Architect and Overseer of the Works'. The Wirral section, between Chester and Ellesmere Port, was opened in 1795, but of the remainder only a middle portion was built, terminating at basins and wharfs N of Pont Cysyllte. A tramway served local collieries and ironworks. A branch to Llanymynech was, however, completed, and connection with Chester was made by 1806, with the continuing of an Ellesmere and Whitchurch branch to join the Chester Canal at Nantwich. Pont Cysyllte and the Chirk Aqueduct (*see* p. 130) thus form part of what had become a branch.

Proposals for a three-arch masonry aqueduct, approached by locks at either end, were made in 1793-4. When building began in 1795 these were abandoned in favour of a full-height structure, to maintain the level of the canal, consisting of a cast-iron trough on stone piers, and approached from the s by an enormous embankment. Earlier in the year Telford had designed his iron aqueduct (a departure from the puddled channels hitherto used) at Longdon-upon-Tern, on the Shrewsbury Canal, though it seems that *Jessop* deserves to share with Telford some of the credit for Pont Cysyllte as executed. It was completed in 1805. There are nineteen bays, each of 45 ft span, and with four iron arches carrying the trough. The piers are solid to a height of 70 ft, then become hollow, with internal cross buttressing. The height, as has been said, is 127 ft, and the length of the trough 1,007 ft. Framing to carry the tow-path is contained within the trough. There is protective railing on the tow-path side only, making the experience of crossing, either by barge or on foot, all the more exhilarating and vertiginous.

A branch to Llangollen, completed 1808, was built as a navigable feeder, and extends from N of the aqueduct to the Horseshoe Falls at Llandysilio (q.v.).

The Ellesmere Canal subsequently became part of the Shropshire Union system.

CYSYLLTE BRIDGE, upstream from Pont Cysyllte. A date inscription of 1697 is recorded. Full-height cutwaters and three segmental arches. Gratifyingly unwidened.

ST DAVID, on the Holyhead Road. Built 1870–1 as a combined school and chapel of ease in the parish of Llangollen, and similar to that at Eglwyseg (q.v.). A new chancel was added 1914. – (STAINED GLASS. Mr Peter Howell attributes the E window to *Comper*.)

ARGOED HALL, ¾ m. SSW of Pont Cysyllte. A stone-built Early Victorian villa, of simple Neo-Elizabethan style, may be discerned on the S (entrance) front and, more particularly, in the near-symmetrical two-gable part of the E front. It was remodelled and enlarged for Robert F. Graesser, the German-born founder of the Wrexham Lager Brewery and of what became the Monsanto Chemical Works at Cefn Mawr. This later work has Elizabethan and Late Victorian 'Queen Anne' classical elements, as well as some turrets. The brick and terra-cotta STABLES have an octagonal-topped tower.

OFFA'S DYKE is ¾ m. SE.

CLOUD HILL, near Offa's Dyke, on the NE side of the Holyhead Road. 1963–5 by *Mervyn Edwards, Morton & Partners*. The main rooms are at upper level. Open-plan living area at the front, bedrooms at the rear, and the entrance at the side between the two parts. Much use of timber framework and cantilevering. A long veranda projects above a stone podium. Well-landscaped GARDEN.

PLAS-YN-Y-PENTRE. *See* Trevor.

GARTH *see* TREVOR

GARTHEWIN *see* LLANFAIR TALHAEARN

GLYN CEIRIOG / LLANSANFFRAID GLYN CEIRIOG

St Ffraid. On the hillside high above the village. Rebuilt c.1790, but there remains little which is recognizably c18 beyond the broad, room-like proportions, a round-headed window in the w tower, and the front of the w gallery. A remodelling took place 1838–9, and the Dec N and s windows must be of this date. So, possibly, is the archaeologically more convincing Perp E window, though a panelled ceiling over the sanctuary is of 1887. – c18 turned RAILS. – COMMANDMENT BOARDS. Creed, Decalogue and Lord's Prayer in Welsh. – Other FURNISHINGS are of 1887 and not at all bad. – STAINED GLASS. Attributable to *Evans* are first from E on s, and also four heraldic panels, one dated 1843. – ROYAL ARMS of Queen Victoria. – The CHURCHYARD may originally have been circular.

VICARAGE. Neo-Tudor, of 1842.

GLYN VALLEY HOTEL, on the main road. Whitewashed. Still Early Georgian in feeling, with flush sashes, though dated 1835.

CEIRIOG MEMORIAL INSTITUTE, NNE of the hotel, and presenting a half-timbered gable to the street. Commemorating the poet Ceiriog (John Ceiriog Hughes, 1832–87) and other Welshmen and their achievements. By *T. Taliesin Rees* of Liverpool, 1910–11, and extended 1929 by *T. Alwyn Lloyd* of Cardiff. – STAINED GLASS. Ceiriog window in the gable end by *H. Gustave Hiller*. Bishop Morgan and Sir Thomas Myddelton windows by *Herbert Hendrie*. – SCULPTURE. Several plaques. They include a relief portrait of Ceiriog by *Sir W. Goscombe John*.

PLAS NANTYR, 3 m. w. Set high above a stream, in beautifully planted grounds. Gabled, roughcast, and with Gothic glazing patterns. Only a fraction of its former size.

TOMEN Y MEIRW. *See* Llanarmon Dyffryn Ceiriog.

GRESFORD

ALL SAINTS. Rebuilt late in the c15, and one of the finest parish churches in Wales. The absence of structural division between nave and chancel is characteristically Welsh, but, especially in the Perpendicular period, not exclusively so. Indeed, with its tall clerestory, screens of English workmanship and panelled camberbeam roofs, Gresford was aptly described by Crossley and Ridgway as 'the perfect Cheshire church in Wales'. Stained glass of 1498 gives an approximate completion date, and there is record of another window having been given by Thomas Stanley, Earl of Derby, in 1500. It is not known to what extent the rebuilding may have been dependent on Stanley patronage. There is none of the emblematic evidence so profusely scattered at Mold, and an alternative source of wealth apparently lay in the church having possessed a relic or miracle-working image, so that it became a place of pilgrimage.

Some earlier – and later – work at the W end should first be noted. In the angle between W tower and N aisle is a renewed buttress of a towerless, probably C13 church, the roof-line of which may be discerned internally on the E face of the tower. Surviving from a C14 enlargement is the four-light W window of the S aisle, good curvilinear work, with two ogee sub-arches. Also C14 is the lower part of the tower. The tower arch, cut through the earlier W wall, has plain chamfered orders, and the W doorway two orders of wave mould. The upper stages and the SW buttress are Perp, but C16, for it is known from wills that the work had not commenced in 1512 and that as late as 1582 the pinnacles had not been completed. The design, nicely balancing richness with plain surfaces, concentrates elaboration at the crown. Pairs of two-light bell openings (thrown off-centre on the S and W by the vice), transomed and traceried, under pairs of crocketed ogee hoodmoulds. Diagonal buttresses with STATUES in canopied and pinnacled niches. Another such feature against the SW buttress lower down and, at the junction of the C14 and C16 walling, a quatrefoil frieze. Crown with frieze, gargoyles, panelled parapet and sixteen pinnacles, the two intermediate ones on each side in the form of figures. Also C16 is the S porch, with a small STATUE of the Virgin under a nodding ogee canopy. N porch by *Sir Thomas Graham Jackson*, 1920–1, as a war memorial.

The C15 church is to a complete and uniform design. Four-centred windows. Embattled parapets. The aisles have gargoyles and a string course with tablet flowers, masks and animals. Masks etc. as hoodmould stops also. Eight bays, of which three are devoted to the chancel and the two eastern-most in the aisles to chapels. In the rebuilding the nave was widened at the expense of the S aisle, putting the tower arch out of axis. Arcade piers of eight shafts with deep hollows between. Rudimentary capitals with deep octagonal abaci. The arches, which are not four-centred, are more sensitively moulded, but have no hoodmoulds. For reasons to be explained, the arcades are of only seven bays and do not extend to the E end. Also, in the easternmost bay the clerestory windows are of three cusped lights and everywhere else of four. Fine seven-light E window, arranged two-three-two, with cusping and panel tracery and with the two-light sections having sub-arches. Other windows of four lights with panel tracery. The N aisle E window has drop tracery and thus looks more elaborate than the others. Its importance may be explained by an adjoining canopied NICHE, which in all probability held the object of the pilgrims' veneration. It now contains a Virgin and Child STATUE by *William Webb*, 1927. In the S E chapel a cusped ogee PISCINA with crocketed gable. Varied corbels for the glorious camberbeam roofs. All roof

members are moulded, and a pattern of panels is made up with two sizes of purlin and three sizes of rafter. Many bosses and, at the cornice, fluttering angels. Greater richness is given
37   to the chancel by ribs introduced into the panels. Shields date from a restoration by *F. H. Crossley*, 1929–31, when plaster and cast iron, dating from a restoration of *c.*1820, were removed. The aisle roofs are much simpler.

Now for the E end, which was elucidated by the Rev. E. A. Fishbourne, vicar from 1897. In the C14 enlargement, the church was extended E and, facilitated by the fall of the ground, a crypt was built below the end bay. The C15 rebuilding carried the church yet another bay further E. The altar, however, remained in its previous position and the C14 E wall was cut down to provide a reredos. Behind, there was formed a processional way, linking the two chapels, presumably for the circulation of the pilgrims. The arcades stop short of this easternmost bay, where there are solid walls, each pierced by a round-headed arch for the processional way and, above, by a four-centred doorway which must have given access to a gallery over the reredos. These four openings remain. At some post-Reformation date (possibly *c.*1634–5 and in the course of Laudian reforms), the reredos wall was removed and the altar placed against the E wall, at a higher level, the processional passage being boarded over. The original arrangement has been further obscured by changes of level, and the passage is now a vestry.* From it is reached the C14 crypt. This has a segmental tunnel-vault and former windows at either end. The present chancel steps are by *W. D. Caröe*, 1913–14. The sympathetic and self-effacing Victorian restoration of the church was by *Street*, 1865–7.

FURNISHINGS. – FONT. Perp. Panels represent the Virgin and Child, the lion of St Mark, saints and angels. Ribbed patterns below and cusped panels in the stem. – REREDOS. By *Douglas*, 1879, with a Last Supper painting by *Heaton, Butler & Bayne*. Side panels added 1895. – NE CHAPEL FITTINGS. By *Caröe*, 1913, including a REREDOS with figures executed by *Nathaniel Hitch*. – A full set of SCREENS. The ROOD SCREEN is of English type, i.e. with the uprights extending through from sill to head. Loft with lierne vaulting in stellar patterns on the W, and panelled coved soffit on the E. Cresting, friezes of vine trail, much tracery etc., including open traceried cusping in the main arches and arcading on the wainscot. There probably remains some cast iron, dating from repairs in 1820. – N and S CHAPEL SCREENS, one bay further E. Simpler, but of comparable character and with reduced versions of the vaulted and coved loft. Pierced wainscot tracery, and the arches fretted with tiny cusps. – Two bays of N and S PARCLOSE SCREENS. Similar, but without the miniature lofts. – STALLS. On either side are four against the western parcloses and three returned against the rood screen.

*Formed by lowering the floor level in a scheme initiated by *Richard Creed* and carried out by *Douglas & Minshull*, 1908–10.

Elbow knops of angels and animals. Two seated beasts either side of the screen doorway. Eleven MISERICORDS survive. On the S, from E to W and returning N, they include two lions holding a fox, the devil wheeling souls to Hell, angels, a fox preaching to geese and hens, and the Annunciation. In front are panelled desk fronts, their four BENCH ENDS traceried and with figures in the poppyheads. – PANELLING in the vestry, made up in 1910 of wood from pews, with brass PEW PLATES. – PULPIT. By *Street*, contemporary with his restoration. Perp in detail, and with figures under nodding ogee canopies. – Brass eagle LECTERN, 1878. – CHANDELIERS. One of 1747. It has two tiers of eight curly branches. Shaped centre and fine wrought-iron suspension. – Another, from Chirk, of 1796. Out of the ordinary, with gadrooning, and a broad stem between two eight-branch tiers. – Of 1892 a two-tier brass CORONA and pair of CANDLESTANDARDS. – Under the tower two BENEFACTION BOARDS dated 1731.

STAINED GLASS. Disaster struck in 1966, when much of Gresford's glass was treated with detergent by a church cleaning company and appallingly damaged. Restoration was carried out by *Denis King* of Norwich. The E window is the one given by Lord Derby, 1500, though now mostly by *Clayton & Bell*, 1867, with surviving early parts rearranged. All suffered extensively in 1966. A Jesse Tree in the tracery and a Te Deum in the lower parts of the main lights, both introduced 1867, but incorporating work of 1500, and there may well have been a Jesse originally. Large figures in the main lights are mostly original (or rather were until 1966), but only that of the Virgin in the first light entirely so. – N aisle E. Badly damaged in the cleaning. Of 1498 and restored by *Clayton & Bell*, 1872. In the lower tracery row the second light shows St Apollonia (patron of toothache sufferers, with tooth in pincers), followed by the Evangelists with their symbols. In the main light a touching series of ten scenes from the lives of St Anne and the Virgin, with inscriptions. Angel 40–1 appearing to Joachim in the wilderness, angel appearing to Anne, Joachim and Anne meeting at the Golden Gate at Jerusalem etc. In the two lower corners are, respectively, the donor and sons, and his wife and daughters. – N aisle windows from E to W: 1. *c.* 1500. Fragments in the tracery. In the main lights the Entombment, Coronation, Funeral (not restored after 1966) and Assumption of the Virgin. In the latter the head has at some time been replaced by that of Our Lord. – 2. Fragments, including angels, of similar date and later. – (3. Hidden by the organ. Fragments, partly *c.* 1500 and partly C18 continental.) – 4. In the tracery, angels of 1508, damaged 1966. The remainder by *Kempe*, 1905. – 5 and 6. Both by *Clayton & Bell*, the former with commemoration date 1877. – 7. By *Kempe*, commemoration date 1895. – N aisle W by *L. Lobin* of Tours, 1868. In pictorial, transparency manner, with little use of leading.

S aisle E. Glass of *c.* 1500 and later. Arranged by *Clayton*

& Bell under *Caröe*, 1915–16. It escaped harm in 1966. Some jumbled fragments and, in the tracery, kneeling angels. Panels in the main lights depict the execution of John the Baptist, with Salome waiting with her charger, and Salome serving up the head to Herod and Herodias. These two are said to be of 1506. Of 1510 are St Anthony entering the religious life and the burial of St Anthony, his soul being carried away by angels. In the row below are symbols of Evangelists in the first and fourth lights and, in the second, St Apollonia with tooth and pincers again appears. Bottom row, fourth light, includes St George. – S aisle windows from E to W: 1. In the tracery fragments of *c*.1500 and a late C18 or early C19 panel. – 2. In the tracery heraldic and other fragments, *c*.1500. – 3. By *Clayton & Bell*, commemoration date 1880. – 4. In the tracery, angels, saints and a nimbed bishop. *c*.1500. The remainder by *Heaton, Butler & Bayne*, commemoration date 1873. – 5. By *Clayton & Bell*, commemoration date 1872. – 6. Angels and symbols of two Evangelists in the first, second, seventh and eighth tracery lights, *c*.1500. The remainder by *Heaton, Butler & Bayne*, commemoration date 1873. – 7. By *Ward & Hughes*, later commemoration date 1873. – S aisle W by *Clayton & Bell*, commemoration date 1868. – N clerestory easternmost. Commemoration date 1849, and, according to Fishbourne, by *Hardman*, though it does not look like a Pugin design. – That next to it and the S clerestory easternmost both by *Clayton & Bell*, commemoration dates 1882 and 1883 respectively. – N porch. Fragments of *c*.1500. – S porch. Cherubs and cherub heads. Italian, C17 or C18.

SEPULCHRAL SLABS. In an arched recess in the N aisle a heraldic slab commemorating Goronwy ab Iorwerth. Late C14. Behind the shield are a spear and, grasped by a hand, a sword. – In the S aisle a fragment of an early C14 heraldic slab commemorating Gruffydd ab Ynyr.

MONUMENTS. In the chancel: William Egerton. By *Chantrey*, 1829. Portrait bust on a free-standing Grecian pedestal. – Lady Broughton †1857. A BRASS by *Hardman*. – George Warrington †1770. By *Benjamin Bromfield*. Obelisk and ridiculously small urn. – John Parry †1797. A fine early work by *Sir Richard Westmacott*. Free-standing. Urn on a pedestal and a partly draped boy mourner seated at the base. – Rev. Henry Newcome †1803. Also by *Westmacott*. Standing female figure, very small. – John Boydell †1839. By *James Harrison* of Chester. Inferior to his Gothic work. – W end of nave: John Williams. By the younger *Theed*, 1851. Free-standing. A life-size female figure, on one knee, symbolizing resignation. – Anne Goodwin †1842. By *William Spence*. Draped urn, and the tablet simulates drapery. – N aisle. E end first, then from E to W: John Madocks †1837. By *James Harrison*. Gothic. – John Madocks †1794. By *W. Rogerson*. Tablet surmounted by a portrait bust. – Jones monument, 1779. Urn against an obelisk. Coloured marbles. The monument to Susan Price (†1813) at Overton (*see* p. 411) by Alexander Wil-

son Edwards (*see* below) is similar. – Margarette Golightly
†1831. By *Spence*. Awkwardly and heavily Grecian. – Mary
Boydell †1823 and son Richard †1835. By *J. Blayney* of
Chester. Big and Gothic. – A large pilastered and pedimented
C18 tablet with its inscription indecipherable. – Also in the N
aisle the loose fragments of a late C14 male effigy.

s aisle. E end first, then from E to W: John Trevor, builder 43
of Trevalyn Hall (*see* Trefalun), †1589. Three arches with a
Welsh inscription on a panel in the centre one. Behind is a
reclining effigy, or rather just the legs and bust, visible in the
end arches. A similar curious arrangement is to be seen at
Llanarmon-yn-Iâl (q.v.). Heraldry and, below, a winged
death's head. – Sir Richard Trevor and wife Dame Katherine.
Erected 1638, in his lifetime. He wears armour and both
kneel, looking out from arches. Heraldry and Corinthian columns. Jacobean in character. – In addition Dame Katherine
Trevor †1602 has her own separate monument. Relief of her
kneeling, with daughters, under an arch. – Rev. Christopher
Parkins †1843 and wife. Low tomb-chest with encaustic tiles
in the sides. On the top a BRASS, by *J. G. & L. A. B. Waller*,
with canopied effigies. Revivalism which Pugin would have
hailed as the true thing. – Townshend monument. By *Edward
& Richard Spencer* of Chester, 1790. Coloured marbles. Elegant. – Travers and Johnson monument, latest commemoration date 1806. By *Alexander Wilson Edwards* of Wrexham.
Veined marble tablet and a small urn. – Madog ap Llywelyn
ap Gruffydd †1331. In an arched recess. Effigy in mailcoat,
with shield, sword etc., his head on a cushion. – William Pate
†1783. By *S. & F. Franceys*. Goofy-looking female. – Pedimented tablet to John Travers †1748 and wife †1749. – Another to Rev. Robert Wynne †1743. – Anthony Lewis. A
large tablet of 1659. Chaste pilasters and, in lieu of pediment,
heraldry and volutes. Welsh inscription. – John Robinson
†1680. Cartouche with cherub heads and heraldry.

Upright in the s porch the mutilated effigy of a bishop, late
C13 or early C14. – Also a STATUE divorced from an archi-
tectural context, its provenance unknown. – In the s aisle, a
Roman STONE found 1908 in the foundations of the C14 E
end. Atropos, with shears, is shown in relief. – Two HATCH-
MENTS fixed to the aisle roof.

Gresford retains a pleasant and peaceful village centre, grouped
round the church. On the N side modest former ALMSHOUSES
and SCHOOL, both with inscriptions of 1725. The almshouses
have been rendered, and three of the five bays unsympathetically renovated. The school has brick still exposed. Toothed
eaves and leaded casements. Rear extension 1838. THE
GREEN FARM is by *R. T. Beckett*, c.1911.* It replaced an
early C19 house of the Marford type (*see* p. 386) and at the
rear is still a Gothic brick PRIVY.

SCHOOL. 1873–4 by *Edward Jones* of Wrexham. Gothic, with

* Information from Mr D. Leslie Davies.

house incorporated. Separate block, built for girls and infants, by *G. Morrison* of Wrexham, 1905–6.

VICARAGE, in wooded grounds. A brick house of 1850 by *Thomas Jones*. Construction was supervised by his nephew *Edward Hodkinson*, who later claimed the design as his own, and Jones is unlikely to have been entirely responsible for it. Plain coped gables and timber cross windows (paired sashes) with glazing bars suggest an early instance of free vernacular revivalism, and the garden front is symmetrical in a chunky Victorian sort of way. On the other hand a re-entrant angle contains three sides of an octagon (originally with gablets) around which is wrapped a stone entrance loggia harking back to picturesque Regency Tudor. Octagonal vestibule. The house has been reduced in size. STABLES with a chimney above the entrance arch.

At the main road, ½ m. S, the base of a medieval CROSS.

In the valley of the Alun stood GRESFORD LODGE, a villa of great refinement by *James Wyatt* or, possibly, *Sir Jeffry Wyatville*, c. 1790. It had a segmental bow with a ground-floor colonnade and a dome. The colonnade was a very early instance of Greek Doric, though in hybrid form. Demolished in the late 1950s.

Two BRIDGES, one carrying the B road. The other, downstream from it and disused, has three elliptical spans.

The GRESFORD COLLIERY, sunk 1908–11, was closed in 1972 and its PITHEAD BATHS of 1939 were demolished. They belonged to the architecturally progressive series promoted by the Miners' Welfare Committee.

HILLOCK FARM, ¾ m. ESE. One of the Marford-style Gothic houses listed on p. 388. It was altered and renovated, 1918, for Lord Wavertree of Horsley Hall.

GWAENYNOG *see* DENBIGH, p. 154

3050

GWERSYLLT

HOLY TRINITY. 1850–1 by the younger *Thomas Penson*, who lived in the parish and charged no fee for the work. Camdenian plan, with properly arranged chancel. Lancets and, in the E and W windows, Geometrical tracery. NE steeple, with triple lancets as bell openings and a broach spire. The church received a Commissioners' grant. S organ chamber added 1912. – STAINED GLASS. By *Wailes*: E window, 1851; a window reset in the organ chamber, given by Penson, 1851; two S windows, commemorating members of his family, 1858, and a third, commemorating Penson himself, † 1859. – By *Ballantine & Gardiner*, second from E on N, commemoration date 1897. – *Penson* presumably designed a Gothic BRASS, commemorating his wife († 1856) and others.

The earliest part of the SCHOOL (with house), w of the church, is of 1851 and attributable to *Penson*. In 1858 it was enlarged and a further block built (itself later enlarged) in similar style.

GWERSYLLT HILL, ¾m. WSW. *Penson's* own house, and re-modelled by him in his distinctive Neo-Jacobean, with curly shaped gables and pedimented windows. Dated 1841. Two asymmetrical elevations, the chief accent a small tower with ogee roof. The house has been mutilated, and STABLES, in-corporating earlier work, are ruinous.

GWERSYLLT PARK had been demolished by 1910. It was re-modelled or enlarged, probably for John Humbertson Caw-ley, in the mid- or late C18, and had a five-bay front of two and a half storeys, with three-bay pediment. Palladian, but apparently tending towards Neo-Classicism.

HENBLAS, ¾m. SSW. Dated 1694. Now rendered, and with sashes and a frilly Victorian fascia. Hipped dormer, and ancient, small roofing slates.

STANSTY PARK, ¾m. S. A house of *c*.1830–2 has been demo-lished. It was built for Richard Thompson, ironmaster and colliery owner, who paid for the Roman Catholic church at Wrexham (*see* p. 302). Unremarkable STABLES remain. Also two columns which, being Greek Doric but with bases and enriched capitals, suggest that the house was interesting.*
They are reused in a GARDEN GATEWAY adjoining another house within the grounds, now called STANSTY HOUSE. C16 in origin. If ever of H-plan, a later brick portion has replaced one of the cross wings. Ribbed brick stacks. A (reset?) win-dow of two arched lights. (Mr D. Leslie Davies refers to panelling dated 1577.) For the GATES and CUPOLA, *see* Erddig.

(LOWER STANSTY FARM, ⅞m. SSE. Remodelled *c*.1925–6, and Mr Ian Allan suggests that this may be the job which *Ernest Barnsley* is known to have done near Wrexham. Whitewashed brick, coped gables, casements, and a roof of local red tiles. It was an adaptation of late C17 work, and a yet earlier cruck truss remains incorporated.)

OLD HALL FARM, Ffos-y-go, ½m. NNW. Two FARM BUILD-INGS, both with coped and finialed gables and one retaining brick nogging.

GWASTAD HALL, Cefn-y-Bedd, 1½m. N. Built for a colliery owner in 1854. In ecclesiological sort of Gothic, serious and parsonage-like. A wing was added in 1913. Windows were mutilated when the house became a hotel.

GWRYCH CASTLE

9070

One of the most amazing of C19 castellated mansions, and one which the age in which it was conceived would have assigned to

---

* But did they belong to the house? A lithograph shows it as chastely classical, long in proportion, with a seven-bay front and two curved bows. A four-column porch on the return looks Ionic.

the realm of the sublime rather than that of the picturesque. Hanging woods form the background to an extended composition punctuated by numerous circular and rectangular towers and turrets. Its theatricality can best be appreciated from a distance, for this is a gigantic folly as much as a dwelling house, and the relatively tame *corps de logis* accounts for only part of the spectacle. Terraces and the stables contribute something, but the apparent size and complexity result mainly from functionless towers and screen walls, built against the hillside. These now tend to get overgrown, and although this is appropriately romantic up to a point, their effectiveness is reduced.

The castle was created by *Lloyd Bamford Hesketh*, acting partly as his own architect, with professional contributions and assistance. His father had married the heiress of the Lloyds of Gwrych, and he succeeded to the estate in 1816. A castellated scheme had been prepared for him in 1814 by *C. A. Busby*, but in 1816 he turned to *Thomas Rickman*, initially just for the designing of Gothic windows. Hesketh worked on proposals of his own for the building itself, but a full scheme was drawn up by Rickman in 1817.* The foundation stone was laid in 1819. Rickman was still involved in some capacity in 1820, and although the *corps de logis*, or main block, incorporates and adapts elements of his design (which had, in its planning, itself owed a little to Busby's), it can broadly be ascribed to *Hesketh*. It is likely to have been finished by 1822 (date inscribed on the separate Hesketh Tower to the w), but details of subsequent alterations, and of the dating and evolution of the out-works, are obscure. Hesketh continued to produce picturesquely conceived sketches for towers etc. until at least 1853. On his death in 1861, Gwrych passed to his son, Robert Bamford Hesketh (patron of G. E. Street), and subsequently to R. B. Hesketh's daughter, wife of the twelfth Earl of Dundonald. Since 1946 it has served various functions in the cause of popular recreation and entertainment.

The castle looks northward to the sea. The approach to the w (entrance) front of the main block is by way of a broad terrace entered through an arched gateway. On the r. is the Hesketh Tower and an array of further towers and out-works. These include the stables, at a higher level, the drive to which is reached through a further arched gateway. Because of the steeply sloping site, a courtyard behind the main block of the house is two storeys above entrance level. Scenically, the most rewarding progress within the precincts is from the e, through

* For transcriptions from Rickman's diary, and some comments on his contributions to Gwrych, I am indebted to Mr John Baily.

Rickman recorded in 1817 that, when discussing the proposals with Hesketh, they looked at publications by (the elder) Pugin and Lugar. He wrote: 'on now looking at Lugar's work in reference to a larger house, I do not like them so much as I did.' This presumably refers to the design for a castellated mansion in Robert Lugar's *Architectural Sketches* ... (first published 1805). Interestingly, Professor Hitchcock compared this, unfavourably, with Gwrych, considering the latter to be superior as a pictorially organized composition.

a barbican gateway to a terrace and the upper courtyard, with a good big tower on the l., and then through a gatehouse and the stable court to the W approach below.

Nearly all the windows are of cast iron, to standard patterns by *Rickman*, and have affinities with his work elsewhere. They were cast at the Mersey Iron Foundry owned by *John Cragg*, with whom Rickman had collaborated over the two famous cast-iron Liverpool churches of 1812–15. The windows include a three-light traceried Perp design, and a fine six-light one, with use also made of quatrefoiled transoms, and they occur in the out-works and entrance lodges etc. as well as in the main block. Nowhere, however, can they necessarily be regarded as evidence of Rickman's direct involvement in building work. Not only are some *ex situ* as a result of alterations, but the Mersey Iron Foundry apparently continued to supply them long after Rickman's direct association with Gwrych had ended. In 1820 designs for bookcases were sent to Cragg. An unexecuted project of 1841 for an estate inn by *John Welch* (who did some minor work at the castle at that time) utilized one of the window patterns.

The W front is of at least three dates, and the NW corner, containing the entrance, was originally single-storeyed. The upper stage at this point, and the top storey of the portion to the r., are C20 – almost certainly by *C. E. Elcock*, who carried out alterations for Lord and Lady Dundonald in 1914. Part of the E front, including much of its top storey, is by *Henry Kennedy*, 1845–6. In a scheme of 1852, Kennedy continued the axis of his 1845–6 bedroom corridor by means of a new flight of stairs and a porch giving on to the upper courtyard. On the ground floor, classical features in the two northernmost rooms on the E side, and Gothic plaster vaulting in part of the entrance hall, are presumably original work of 1819–c.1822. Much was done by *Elcock*, including the classical treatment of the enormous dining room. A chimneypiece in the entrance hall, of Welsh vernacular character, is dated 1914. The exceedingly grand staircase, a straight cascade of fifty-two marble steps in three flights, is of unknown date and authorship. It replaced a staircase of 1845–6 by *Kennedy*, and links up with his upper flight and porch of 1852. It may from the first have had its delicate scrolly wrought-iron balustrading, but marble dadoes are embellishments by *Elcock*, and stained glass at the head of the stairs (in one of Rickman's six-light windows) is dated 1914. Much heraldic glass of earlier date, some probably of the 1820s. In the hall a six-lighter containing glass by *J. Alexander Forrest* of Liverpool, *c.*1846, with roundels of Works of Mercy. Hesketh clearly took an interest in stained glass, and in submitting a design for flamboyantly foliated tracery lights (not extant), *George Lyon* of Liverpool wrote in 1837: 'I have tried to meet your ideas.' The Hesketh archives also contain references to stained-glass makers *Ward & Nixon* and *Ward & Hughes*. A clerestory window, now incomplete, over Kennedy's 1852 stairs, seems to have been of luscious character, and for Hesketh's glass in Abergele church *see* p. 98.

A series of castellated lodges, gateways and estate buildings must, in whole or part, be by *Hesketh*. Some or all are of the 1830s, and the habitable structures have cast-iron windows to the *Rickman* standard designs. ABERGELE (or KING'S) LODGE, the main entrance to the park. Gatehouse with two round towers, and, absurdly, an inner barbican enclosure. HEN WRYCH, ¾ m. along the Llanddulas road, is the site of the home of the Lloyds. The present farmhouse retains stone mullions, but also has iron windows. Castellated walls and square towers, not all of one build, face the road. TAN-YR-OGO GATEWAY, ¾ m. further on. Gateway and curtain walls set back between round bastion towers. Four tablets record local historical events. Within, a walled enclosure deflects the drive. TAN-YR-OGO HOUSE, opposite, has straight-headed windows with iron labels. Also one of the six-light Perp windows, and at the rear some of the three-light type. Iron gate in a Gothic arch, with the name of the Mersey Iron Foundry, Liverpool, on the lock. Nearby, TAN-YR-OGO FARM, castellated and turreted. The variously turreted PARK WALL continues to Llanddulas. On the hillside is LADY ELEANOR'S TOWER. Across the park, NANT-Y-BELLA LODGE, ⅜ m. SE of the castle, has a tall circular corner turret. BETWS LODGE, ⅝ m. SW of the latter, on the opposite side of the road, with screen walls. MOUNTAIN LODGE, ½ m. S of Nant-y-Bella Lodge.

GWYLFA HIRAETHOG *see* MYNYDD
HIRAETHOG

8060   GWYTHERIN

A remote little village, sheltered in a valley amid bare but cultivated hill country. Legend has it that St Winefride (*see* Holywell, p. 371) became abbess of a convent here.

ST WINIFRED. Rebuilt 1867–9 by *Lloyd Williams & Underwood*. Like its predecessor it is a single chamber. Cusped lancets and a traceried E window. Turret-like bellcote on the ridge, in line with the S porch. – FONT. Octagonal bowl, diminishing downwards in convex profile. – Dugout CHEST. – SEPULCHRAL SLABS. Set in the N wall an early C14 expanded arm cross. – Of similar date, and set in the sanctuary steps, a floriated cross slab commemorating Llaywarch Cappellanus, i.e. chaplain. With representation of a chalice. – In the oval CHURCHYARD, are, N of the church, four C5 or early C6 PILLAR STONES. A Latin inscription on the westernmost commemorates Vinnemaglus, son of Senemaglus.

(TY'N Y LLIDIART, 1⅛ m. N. A late C18 or early C19 single-

storey cottage, one of those which has its roof timbers of
roughly trimmed branches. Later extension either end. DOE)
RHOS DOMEN, Cornwall. *See* Mynydd Hiraethog.

HAFODUNOS *see* LLANGERNYW

HENLLAN   *0060*

ST SADWRN. A single chamber, remodelled 1806–8. The Y-
traceried side windows are probably of this date, but except
for the low-pitched roof the church is otherwise completely
de-Georgianized. *R. Lloyd Williams* is recorded as having
reseated it, removed a w gallery, demarcated a chancel, and
provided a s porch and new w windows, 1878–9. He may also
have exposed the rubble walling inside, but the wagon ceiling
is earlier. Medieval features include a Dec N doorway, now
giving into a NW vestry, and in the vestry a reset two-light
window. Ogee PISCINA. Renewed five-light Perp E window,
with a transom, two-light sub-arches, cusping and panel
tracery. – ALTAR TABLE. Jacobean. Melon-bulb legs and a
pendant in the centre of the front. – At the w end some
Waterhouse PANELLING from Eaton Hall. – STAINED GLASS.
E window of 1878. – Second from E on N by *Whitefriars*, 1935,
commemorating George V's Jubilee. – At the w end of the N
wall a small window with mid-C19 heraldic glass designed by
Charles Winston, the pioneer student of medieval glass, and
made by *Ward & Nixon*. – First and second from E on S by
Miller, commemoration dates 1863 and 1855 respectively. –
Pair of nine-branch CHANDELIERS, bequeathed 1788. –
MONUMENTS. John Jones †1778. Small figure on an obelisk.
Side volutes, cherub heads. – Richard Augustus Griffith
†1831. By *W. Spence*. Clasped hands above a draped urn.
    The TOWER, probably Perp in date, is detached, built on
an outcrop of rock at the head of the steeply sloping churchyard. Battlemented and unbuttressed and starkly rectangular.
Paired lancet bell openings. Opposite the church porch the
octagonal shaft of a CHURCHYARD CROSS.
LLYS MEIRCHION, ¼m. W. Castellated. Remodelled by *Lloyd
Williams & Underwood*, 1867; the centre, with porch block,
canted bay and stepped gable, must be theirs. Other parts
look like an earlier C19 remodelling.
GARN, ⅜m. NNE. This was for long the home of the Griffith
family. A late C17 or early C18 house was burnt in 1738, and
as rebuilt by *Robert West*, 1738–9, was reduced from three
storeys to two. Seven-bay brick and stone front, with pilasters
and a three-bay pediment. Windows with the fluted keystones
met with elsewhere in the Vale of Clwyd. Also aprons, those
of the three middle bays semicircular and fluted. Doorcase
with lugged surround and segmental pediment. The five-bay

right-hand return, of stone, has a rusticated doorcase, and is a pre-fire survival. So too, perhaps, is bolection-moulded panelling in the corner room. Broad staircase with dado, swept rail and fluted columnar balusters. Much plasterwork upstairs and down, not of such good quality as the staircase, but with considerable panache. Patterning is applied variously to cornices, beams and ceiling panels, the motifs including arabesques, leaf trails and tiny heads. Even in the kitchen there are enriched cornices, and over the fireplace (which has a fluted keystone) is a decorative panel dated 1739. Later extensions include a regrettable wing by *R. Lloyd Williams*, 1889, faced in bright red brick and terra-cotta.

GALLTFAENAN HALL, 1m. NNE. A stone-built house of three periods. Three-bay front, early C19, but also owing something to one or both of the later phases. It has tripartite windows, emphasized centre, and a columned porch. The early C19 structure is only one room deep, what lies behind being a rebuilding of the 1860s by *Lloyd Williams & Underwood*, a Mainwaring commission. Extensions, including a long pilastered wing, were made in 1926 for Sir Ernest Tate, of the sugar-refining family, by *F. C. Saxon* of *Lockwood, Abercrombie & Saxon*. At the same time interior work was done by *Waring & Gillow* of Liverpool. By them the entrance screen and the chimneypieces in all the main rooms except one on the main front, where an early C19 example survives. Of the 1860s, a galleried hall and effectively planned staircase. Iron balustrade panels, elaborately scrolled.*

GALLTFAENAN ISAF (Brynwgan), 1½m. NNE. A C16 storeyed house, of end chimney and inside cross passage plan, and originally with an upper room open to the roof. (Its central truss, with cusping above the collar, remains.) A later rear wing had the only known example of a dated cyclopean doorway – 1601 – but this is now obscured.

(DOLBELIDR, 1¾m. NNE, beside the Elwy. Ruinous. A late C16 storeyed house, with open arched-braced roof. Central service room. Large chimneystack either end, and a cyclopean doorway, with arched lintel. Mullioned and transomed windows of timber, the longest having seven lights. NMR)

PLAS HEATON, ¾m. NE. The Heatons came to Denbigh with Henry de Lacy (*see* Denbigh Castle, p.143) in the C13; the present Plas Heaton, previously Plas Newydd, was renamed when bought by the family in 1805 (perpetuating the name of their earlier residences), and it assumed its present form either then or shortly before.‡ This work of *c*.1805 involved the skilful remodelling and enlarging of an early C18 house. Features of the earlier period include a dog-leg staircase, rising through two storeys, with dado panelling as far as the first landing, and splayed columnar balusters. Of the same date a small stone chimneypiece with fluted keystone. Nine-

---

* I am indebted to Mrs E. Jones for help with this entry, and to Mr G. N. S. Mitchell of Lovelock, Mitchell & Partners, successors to the Lockwood practice.
‡ Kindly explained by Mr Richard Heaton.

bay s front, of *c.*1805, in the form of a recessed centre, with
Doric loggia, recessed between three-bay wings. The wings,
though two-storeyed, are of the same height as the centre.
The older work, refaced, lies behind the centre and the
right-hand wing, the latter actually masking three storeys.
The opposite wing is entirely *c.*1805, and has a central segmental bow on its w front. On the N, its return is balanced
by an E addition. Good interiors, with plasterwork and marble
chimneypieces. Suite of three rooms, one of them now dismantled, along the w front. The dining room, behind the
bow, has honeysuckle frieze, Ionic chimneypiece, and a segmental recess in the end wall. (Shorter room above, with fully
segmental inner wall, echoing the bow.) Work of this period
within the earlier fabric includes the main staircase and a
first-floor (former) library.

PLAS HEATON FARM, 1¼ m. ENE. Originally of central chimney
and lobby entry plan. Small well staircase, with shaped flat
balusters, square-finialed newels, and strapwork on the string.
An *ex situ* date of 1680. An earlier two-unit house, now a
FARM BUILDING, has stepped gables and an end chimney.
Traces of a MOAT.

PLAS CHAMBRES, 1½ m. E. Two ranges at right angles, functioning as independent houses, i.e. unit-system planning. The
main part has a lateral chimney with gabled breast, and a
cross passage. In the lower-end room a plaster ceiling with
strapwork on the beams and arabesques in ribbed panels. Its
frieze, dated 1598, is hidden by early C18 bolection-moulded
panelling. In a rear extension a staircase with columnar balusters, doubtless contemporary with the panelling. The other
wing has its own lateral chimney and a staircase with pierced
balusters and square-finialed newels.

FOXHALL, ¾ m. ESE. This was a hall house with an upper-end
room and lower-end cross wing. A blocked first-floor window
of two cusped lights in the wing, and a four-centred doorway
(now internal) to the cross passage. Lower-end post-and-
panel partition, retaining one doorway with moulded arch. A
fireplace backing on to the passage doubtless dates from when
a floor was inserted into the hall. (Original late medieval roof
timbers in the cross wing.) A late C16 or C17 kitchen, extending the wing, had a lateral chimney, since removed. The fireplace arch now forms a window. CART SHED, with four segmental arches and a storey above. Foxhall was the home of
the C16 antiquary Humphrey Llwyd.

FOXHALL NEWYDD, ¼ m. w of Foxhall. Begun by John Panton,
Recorder of Denbigh. He ran into difficulties; the house was
never completed, and only stone outer walls now remain.
Very high, having three storeys, plus a basement and windows in the gables. Mullions and transoms, and a canted bay
and the remains of another. (Date 1608 over a fireplace opening.) If, as seems likely, all this was but one cross wing of an
intended H-plan house, the project was a startlingly ambitious
one. A gabled DOVECOTE.

There are several Early Bronze Age BARROWS near Henllan. One of the best-preserved is a stone cairn in the corner of a field near Plas Meifod (SJ 028 682). Three large trees stand on the mound, which is earth-covered, but the stone structure can be seen where it has been damaged. The large barrow near Plas Heaton (SJ 033 686) was excavated in the last century, when several inhumation burials were found, one of them accompanied by a beaker. The bodies were found both within and on top of a stone cist in the centre. A cremation in an urn was subsequently buried in the top of the barrow. Two other barrows recorded in these fields can scarcely be recognized now.

HOLT

4050

ST CHAD. One of the churches remodelled under the auspices of the Stanley family. In this case the patron was Sir William Stanley, who held the lordship of Bromfield, and with it Holt Castle, from 1483 until his execution in 1495. The five-bay nave arcades, of narrow, sharply pointed arches on octagonal piers, are Dec.* Dec in style though very much later (dated 1679. P. Howell) is the Cheshire-type W tower, battlemented, buttressed and with SE stair turret and two-light traceried bell openings. Its W window belongs to the late C15 Perp remodelling. So does the chancel, which was largely rebuilt, with no structural division between it and the nave. The aisles also were rebuilt and extended E to flank the chancel, and the nave walls and tower arch were raised, but no clerestory was introduced. In the S chancel aisle a reset Dec PISCINA. Graceful two-bay chancel arcades of broad, four-centred arches and octagonal concave-sided piers. The E windows of the chancel and aisles have panel tracery, sub-arches and cusping, but all three differ greatly in design. That of the chancel has a transom, the shallow arched heads of the lights below it reflected by inverted arches on its upper side. Uniform four-light aisle windows, not corresponding with arcade bays. The S aisle is wider than the N, and its E respond – unused, with the arch springing from a corbel – indicates changes of plan. Four-centred N and S doorways, the latter with enriched label and, above it, an Annunciation panel. Arms in the spandrels include those of Henry VII and there are figures in the jamb mouldings, that of a bishop still recognizable. In a restoration of 1871–3, *Ewan Christian*, acting for the Ecclesiastical Commissioners, was responsible for the chancel, and *Douglas* did the rest. The camberbeam roof, with tracery in the panels of its easternmost bay, dates almost entirely from this time. Douglas vaulted the tower space, where springers already existed. – FONT. Each face of the bowl, the stem and the coving is carved in boldly scaled relief. Datable to *c.*1493 by the

* cf. the Dec arcades retained in the remodelling at Wrexham, with which Sir William Stanley may also have been associated.

heraldry, which refers to the history of the lordship of Bromfield over two centuries. – Plank CHEST. – BRASS, or rather
a small copper plate, N chancel aisle. 1666. To Thomas Crue
and signed in Greek by *Silvanus Crue*. Acrostic inscription.
Former BAPTIST CHAPEL, Chapel Street. 1827. Small three-
bay, two-storey brick front, with low-pitched gable.
PRESBYTERIAN CHURCH, Castle Street. 1865 by *T. M. Lockwood*. Tall corner spirelet, and High Victorian touches in the
details.
CASTLE. It stood beside the river, with which its moat was
connected. A lordship castle, built after (probably very soon
after) Edward I granted the lands of Bromfield and Yale to
John de Warenne, Earl of Surrey, in 1282. Master *James of
St George* may have been responsible, and the plan, a regular
pentagon, was unusual. A tower stood at each corner, and
there were buildings against the inner sides of the five curtains. A separate tower rose from the moat. There remain
fragments of walls, on a five-sided plan, poised on the artifi-
cially shaped rock around and against which the castle was
built. There is a pointed doorway.
BRIDGE. Crossing the Dee, which here forms the boundary
with England. The present structure is C15 or early C16.
Eight segmental arches (Pennant referred to ten arches) of
two chamfered orders. Full-height cutwaters. The third arch
from the Welsh bank marks the site of a defensive tower, with
drawbridge. The original arch is visible, higher than the
others, with later masonry inserted below. The parapet is
thicker here, with some moulding remaining on the downstream side.
A modest rectangular layout, suggesting a bastide plan, lies between the bridge and the former market place. At the latter
a MARKET CROSS, with a shaft on a tall and octagonal stepped
base. No town defences are known to have existed.
LODGE FARM, 1¾ m. W. Early or mid-C17 dog-leg staircase,
with flat, shaped balusters and finialed newels.
CORNISH HALL, 1¾ m. WSW. Five-gable front, including cross
wings and a storeyed porch. Now rendered, but before a C20
remodelling there was a fine array of shaped and Dutch gables
of brick. Dog-leg staircase with flat, shaped and pierced balusters, finialed newels, and leaf trail on the string. (Peter
Smith mentions a datestone of 1618.)
CROES YOKIN, Hugmore Lane, ¾ m. SW of Cornish Hall. Possibly 1820s; Soanish local work. Three-bay brick front, the
openings in each bay contained within a two-storey arched
recess. Pediment with lunette window.
There was an important Roman WORKS DEPOT close to the
Dee (SJ 403 547). The remains, excavated at the beginning of
this century, consist of an enclosed barrack block or work-
men's compound, a small bathhouse and a domestic range
which may have been the commandant's house. S of these
living quarters were pottery workshops – a throwing shed and
drying room etc. – and an impressive bank of six large kilns.

Two of these kilns had been used for making tiles, the other four for making coarse pottery together with some unusual green glazed vessels. It is likely that other remains are yet to be found on this twenty-acre industrial site. The evidence of marked tiles and antefixes links this depot with the legionary fortress at Chester, easily accessible by barge down the river. Several necessary raw materials, clay, sandstone and wood, were readily available at Holt and it seems that the depot here was established at the end of the C1 A.D. when the fort at Chester was rebuilt in stone. It was declining in importance by the mid-C3.

Three Bronze Age burial urns were found during the excavations, an instance of the valley-bottom siting which is unusually common in this part of Wales.

IS-Y-COED

4050

ST PAUL. Agreeably rebuilt in 1829. The architect was *John Butler*. A brick rectangle lit by narrow round-headed windows, and having a shallow altar recess at the E end and a small tower at the W. The top stage of the tower is a domed octagon. Blocked N and S doorways. A W gallery, on cast-iron columns, contains BOX PEWS. – A Victorian CORONA.

The church and its rural surroundings, between the Wrexham Industrial Estate and the English border, have a remote and Cheshire-like feel. The PLOUGH INN, opposite the church gates, shows the top of a cruck truss in a gable end (and parts of two pairs of crucks are visible inside. DOE). Cruck frame in the gable end of a rear wing at CHAPEL HOUSE FARMHOUSE, $\frac{1}{4}$ m. W.

JOHNSTOWN *see* RHOSLLANNERCHRUGOG

KINMEL MANOR *see* ABERGELE

KINMEL PARK *see* ST GEORGE

LLANARMON DYFFRYN CEIRIOG

1030

A small village high in the Ceiriog Valley, with two whitewashed inns – the HAND and the attractively gabled WEST ARMS.

ST GARMON. Rebuilt in 1846 by *Thomas Jones*, as a simple box, with windows in his favourite Perp. Splayed corners, those at the W end having two storeys of tiny windows, lighting gallery stairs etc. w tower turning octagonal, and ending in a short slated spire. – PULPIT. Against the E wall, N of the window. Balanced on the S by a two-decker, i.e. a READING PEW and CLERK'S DESK. – Late C17 or early C18 turned RAILS, and similar ones on the gallery front. – Circular CHURCHYARD, with ancient yews and a MOUND of uncertain origin, previously with a sundial on top.

DOLWEN, 1m. NW. C17, with cross wings, the right-hand one comprising farm buildings. The doorway, almost central, has cyclopean jambs and rubble voussoirs. (In the left-hand wing a room with massive moulded beams and some C17 panelling. DOE)

THE TOWERS, ⅜m. NE. A Victorian shooting lodge which belonged to the Wests of Ruthin Castle. It was castellated, of two storeys, with a three-storey polygonal and machicolated corner tower. Now much reduced.

HAFOD ADAMS, ¾m. NE. Of single-storey scale, though it was a hall house with open roof. The chimney may, unusually, have been in the gable end. Cyclopean doorway. (Timber-framed partitions. Heavily moulded beams, with the original arched-braced trusses remaining above. DOE)

The small univallate hillfort known as CERRIG GWYNION, ⅞m. NNW (SJ 152 340), is remarkable for its geology as well as its archaeology, for it surrounds a startling ridge of white quartz. The rubble rampart and ditch are impressive on the southern and western sides. The simple entrance at the E end is obscured by trees. A later bank, conspicuous in its use of white quartz, has been built across the western half of the fort.

Two small Bronze Age CAIRNS can still be recognized on the moorland to the N. One, 2m. N (SJ 157 361), is close to the old track, Ffordd Saeson, while the other, TOMEN Y GWYDDEL, 2m. NNE (SJ 175 355), stands at the junction of two fir plantations. It is crossed by a fence and was damaged by treasure seekers in the last century. TOMEN Y MEIRW, 3¼m. N (SJ 162 381), across a valley, is a much larger barrow and has also been badly damaged – strange stories circulating about what was found when it was dug into!

For the CAIRNS along the crest of the Berwyns to the W, see Llanrhaeadr-ym-Mochnant.

LLANARMON MYNYDD MAWR
1020

ST GARMON. A single chamber, rebuilt, or restored beyond recognition, by *W. H. Spaull* of Oswestry in 1886. He gave it a W bellcote, broad cusped lancets, an Early Dec E window, and a mechanical-looking interior. – FONT COVER. Dated 1723. – Built into the vestry wall a crude FONT BOWL of 1717. – C18 turned RAILS (with end ones of iron).

A scattered settlement pattern. The church, lying just below the 1000-ft contour line, has only one farm as a neighbour. To the SW are three buildings worthy of mention, on the hillside in the valley of Afon Iwrch. First, BRYN-COCH. The wing breaking forward from the main front was a timber-framed hall house, though its walls are now stone. Part of the arched-braced central cruck truss remains, with a later chimney built into it. Also a post-and-panel partition.

Next, PLAS-YN-GLYN. A group of farm buildings and an L-shaped house. Lateral chimney in the range at right angles to the slope. In the other, a counterchanged ceiling, a lesser version of that at Henblas, Llangedwyn (q.v.). Divided unequally into four by large beams, then into twelve by lesser ones, and finally a cross-pattern of joists.

TŶ-DRAW, ⅛ m. beyond Plas-yn-Glyn. Now a barn, but with portions of a four-bay cruck hall house, C15 or possibly late C14. The axis at right angles to, i.e. against, the slope, in customary fashion. Two-bay hall, its central truss arched-braced, with cusped struts above the collar. Lower-end partition truss, and straight-headed central doorway. The lower-end outer gable now rebuilt in stone. When Peter Smith and Douglas Hague described the structure in *Archaeologia Cambrensis*, vol. 107, 1958, the two upper-end trusses remained, with two pointed doorways in the partition, but these had vanished less than twenty years later.

GLAS-HIRFRYN, 1¾ m. NE of the church. Derelict. Lateral chimney and a jettied upper storey. (Moulded beams and joists, and carved corbels. NMR. Also an arched-braced roof. DOE)

HERMON METHODIST CHAPEL, 1⅛ m. ENE of the church. Built 1906. Roughcast, with stone dressings, in a Voysey-inspired manner. Broad window with shallow curving head, and Art Nouveau tracery in the middle.

LLANARMON-YN-IÂL

1050

ST GARMON. Double-naved. Said to have been largely rebuilt in 1736, but late medieval arched-braced roofs remain, with framing for a wagon ceiling at the E end of the N nave. Of 1736 are round-headed windows, S porch with rusticated arch, and S doorway with crude pilasters. Of similarly unsophisticated but engaging character is a timber colonnade between the two naves, the posts octagonal, with circular classical capitals. It replaced a stone arcade, and is of 1733 by *Edward Wettnall*, a Wrexham carpenter.* Diagonal bracing to the colonnade, as well as some Gothic windows, probably date from *Douglas*'s restoration of 1870. – Baluster FONT, dated 1734. – (Good PULPIT, attributable to *Douglas*.) Pre-Reformation brass CHANDELIER. C15 or early C16, and a rare and wonderful treasure. Three tiers of six branches, with stylized foliated ornament on curving stems. Enshrined in the centre is a canopied figure of the Virgin. It has been supposed

34

* Canon T. W. Pritchard discovered this.

that this and a comparable piece at Llandegla (q.v.) came from Valle Crucis Abbey. However, they are possibly of Flemish workmanship, and Canon Pritchard has suggested that they may have been brought from the Low Countries by a member of the family from Bodidris, near Llandegla. – CHEST. Of plank type, with iron bands. – MONUMENTS. A worn effigy of an ecclesiastic. Early C14. – Gruffydd ap Llywelyn ab Ynyr, of Bodidris, c.1320. Effigy in mail surcoat with sword etc., said to have come from Valle Crucis. The plinth (apparently not belonging) has on one side a pattern of trefoiled arcading enclosing shields. – Efan Llwyd, of Bodi- 44 dris, 1639. Triple-arched mural monument. Inside, or so it seems, is a reclining effigy, though only the legs and bust are visible, the central arch being a solid panel. This carries a Welsh inscription. The work is thus a counterpart to the John Trevor monument at Gresford (q.v.). – ROYAL ARMS. A large panel, painted by *David Davies*, 1740. – The CHURCH-YARD is almost circular. – Part of the shaft of a CHURCHYARD CROSS, now a sundial.

The village clusters round the church. The group includes, e.g., the whitewashed C18 OLD VICARAGE, on the W.

To the E, on the r. beyond a BRIDGE, is TOMEN Y FAERDRE. A motte and ditch, possibly the castle fortified by King John, 1212.

Further on, two single-storey houses of white-painted block, with monopitch roofs – BRYN LLWYNOGOD and SWN YR AWEL. By *Anthony Lee*, 1971–3. The former, for himself, is planned round three sides of a landscaped courtyard.

SCHOOL, ⅝m. NE, on the road to Eryrys. Rebuilt 1843, according to Thomas, though this cannot apply to the bargeboards or High Victorian spirelet.

CREIGIOG-ISAF, ½m. SSE, has stepped gables.

PLAS LLANARMON, ¾m. SW. (Plaster ceiling, presumably C17, with floral and leaf motifs, arranged in panels. Staircase with string and turned balusters. NMR)

The road S from the village runs between low cliffs of limestone. There are many CAVES and FISSURES in these cliffs and at the end of the C19 several of them were excavated by Sir William Boyd Dawkins. He found animal remains in most, and communal burials of Neolithic type were found in the crevices of Perthi Chwarae and Rhos Ddigre, the latter also producing evidence of contemporary occupation. The entrance to Perthi Chwarae had been intentionally closed with a wall of earth and stone. The mouth of the cave at Perthi Chwarae (SJ 188 537) can still be seen, but the others have been blocked.

LLANBEDR DYFFRYN CLWYD   *1050*

ST PETER. A neat little High Victorian church, of considerable 92 vivacity. It was built in 1863 at the expense of John Jesse of

Llanbedr Hall. Rock-faced, with polychromatic bands and voussoirs. Stripes also in the slating. Plate tracery. The S porch has stumpy columns with big foliated caps, and beside it rises a bell turret, starting square, diminishing to a hexagon, and ending in a spirelet sprouting weird crockets. The chancel, with iron-crested roof, has a polygonal apse, its windows rising into gables. Lively gargoyles. On the N a vestry with Frenchy pavilion roof. Attributions considered by Goodhart-Rendel included Street, Scott, Prichard, Seddon and Ewan Christian. Finally he settled for Arthur Blomfield, and discovered only later that the little-known partnership of *Poundley & Walker* were responsible. Disappointing interior, but the vestry doorway and an iron GRILLE next to the chancel arch are worth a glance. – ENCAUSTIC TILES by *Maw & Co.* – STAINED GLASS. Chancel windows, contemporary with the building, probably by *Clayton & Bell*. – Two nave S windows, one and two lights, by *Shrigley & Hunt*, 1898. – Second from E on N, commemoration date 1886, looks like *James Powell & Sons* – Several classical MONUMENTS, including that by *S. & F. Franceys* to Ursula Lloyd and others, latest commemoration date 1810. Crouching maiden clutching a cross. – Edward Lloyd. Signed by *John Gibson*, in Rome, 1863. Relief profile in a medallion, the surrounding tablet so plain as to look C20. – Churchyard GATEPIERS in character with the building, and a spired Lloyd MONUMENT suggests the hands of the same architects.

OLD CHURCH, ¼ m. N, near the approach to Llanbedr Hall. Abandoned after the Victorian church was built, and now a ruin. It was a single chamber, with Perp windows and a blocked lancet. W wall with doorway and bellcote, but little else remains above sill level. N and S doorways, the latter with a STOUP. Also the stone base of an added timber-framed S porch.

OLD RECTORY, ⅜ m. NW. Late C17, and of a type rare in the county. A double pile, of brick, with hipped roof and a modillion cornice. Timber cross windows and leaded glazing. The front is of five bays, its lower windows with segmental heads. Central well staircase rising through two storeys, with string, turned balusters and square newels. One room with an original stone chimneypiece and bolection-moulded panelling.

LLANBEDR HALL, ⅜ m. NE. Remodelled or largely rebuilt by *Poundley & Walker*, c.1866–74, for J.F. Jesse, son of John. Yellow brick, some sandstone polychromy, and a seaside-looking corner turret.

CASTELL GYRN, 1¼ m. ESE. On the mountainside, commanding wonderful views of the vale and beyond. A castellated stone tower of cruciform plan, with one arm rising higher than the rest. Not exactly a folly, for it is habitable. Moreover, it was built not in, say, 1777, but in 1977. By *John Taylor*, of *Chapman, Taylor & Partners*, for himself, and extended by him 1982–3.

See p. 24 FOEL FENLLI, 1¼ m. ENE (SJ 163 601), is the southernmost of the chain of great hillforts overlooking the eastern side of the

Vale of Clwyd. Although the site is naturally steep, the artificial defences are large and extensive, with an elaborately modelled entrance at the W end where both the inner and the outer ramparts turn inwards to form a defended passageway. The design of this entrance is impressive, its siting is magnificent, but its actual use must have been awkward even for the inhabitants, for access to it can only be gained by a narrow footpath cut into the steep slopes of the hill. A more accessible gap in the southern defences is not considered to have been original. The fort is not central on the summit of the hill, but is tipped forward to the W, with the highest point, which is occupied by a Bronze Age cairn, just inside the eastern end. In the western half the defences consist of a rampart with ditch and counterscarp bank; around the eastern side an extra bank and ditch have been added. The material for the main rampart was quarried from the interior, where a broad 'quarry-ditch' can be seen just behind the rampart. This feature, which exists at many sites though often difficult to recognize, is particularly clear along the N side of Foel Fenlli. In spite of the growth of heather, platforms recessed into the sloping interior, and often interpreted as hut sites, can still be recognized. Moel y Gaer, a small fort on a spur to the NW, can easily be seen from Foel Fenlli.

This monument commands magnificent views, is easily accessible from a large car park in the pass to the N, and is now suffering considerable erosion because of the simple pressure of human feet. It exemplifies an almost intractable conservation problem.

MOEL Y GAER, 1½ m. N (SJ 149 617). Viewed from Foel Fenlli, Moel y Gaer is the classic contour fort, crowning its rounded spur like a tonsure. Closer inspection shows it to have been rather more complicated in design, the extra ditch and rampart on the N and E perhaps being an addition to the original circuit of rampart, ditch and counterscarp bank. The fort has two entrances. The western one, which gives on to a steep slope, is straightforward – a simple gap in the outer bank with an inturned passageway through the inner rampart. On the E the entrance through the outer defences is placed some 100 ft N of that through the main rampart, which itself is protected by inturned ends. Such a dog-leg entrance is quite a common device with which to check an enemy's charge on the gates, but, strangely, it is not employed at any other hillfort in Clwyd. The NE side of the fort is vulnerable because of the easy access along the neck of the spur. Unfortunately the defences here have been badly damaged and the outermost line, which swept out to enclose dead ground on the NW, has been destroyed. Excavations were carried out here in the C19, but little was found except a quantity of burnt stone, suggestive of timber-lacing in the inner ramparts, and a sherd of Roman pottery.

8060

LLANDDEWI

1¾ m. s s w of Llangernyw

ST DAVID. Rescued from dereliction when converted to a house (ST DAVID'S LODGE); but the work, begun 1975, could have been done more sympathetically. The church was built in 1867 by *J. Oldrid Scott*, largely at the expense of Henry R. Sandbach of Hafodunos (*see* Llangernyw). Grey stone with red dressings. Lancets. A NW tower, which rose above the porch and had a shingled spire, has been truncated, and the SE vestry demolished. – STAINED GLASS by *James Powell & Sons* in the E window and a circular W window. – *Maw* ENCAUSTIC TILES still in the chancel, now a garage. – The LYCHGATE is at Treuddyn (*see* p. 454).

Former VICARAGE, to the E, built 1876.

METHODIST CHAPEL, Pandy Tudur, ¼ m. SW. In its own graveyard. Of 1907, with Edwardian Baroque touches.

8060

LLANDDOGED*

ST DOGED. Double-naved. Said to have been rebuilt, 1838–9, by the rector, the *Rev. Thomas Davies*, with help from the rector of Eglwsybach, the *Rev. David Owen*. Their work, though, was no more than a remodelling. The E windows, both of three round-headed lights, are C16. It may be presumed that others which are stone-framed are of similar date, and that timber imitations are of 1838–9. Most windows were then given timber cover moulds, those at the W end with ogee tendencies. Curly bargeboards add to the *cottage orné* flavour. Arcade of six plastered pointed arches on (renewed) timber posts is also of the remodelling. So are some pre-Camdenian FURNISHINGS. – PULPIT. In the middle of the N wall. Two-decker, and with the CLERK'S DESK in front, i.e. a three-decker. Above is a circular skylight of coloured glass. – PAINTINGS, behind the pulpit. Exhortations, in Welsh, to preach the Gospel and honour the king, respectively accompany panels of Our Lord, with Bible, and the ROYAL ARMS. The latter, of Victoria, is incorrect, apparently adapted from a Hanoverian set. – BOX PEWS focused on the pulpit, and raked PEWS at the W end. – The FONT is ancient. Octagonal bowl of diminishing width in convex profile. – C17 PANELLING behind the altar, with an indication that rails were arranged on three sides. – MONUMENTS. Sir Thomas Kyffin, 1752. Broken curved pediments and a gadrooned base with cherub head below. – Sir Thomas Kyffyn †1784. By the younger *van der Hagen*. Architectural frame with urns above and cherub heads below. – The CHURCHYARD is circular.

The village, in the hills on the E of the Conwy Valley, has a small and compact centre round the church. To the SW a

* Transferred to Gwynedd in 1974.

CHAPEL of 1863. Gable end, but still with two doorways and, between them, two windows above the pulpit.

TOLLHOUSES. One on the A496, 1 m. W; another, 1⅛ m. E, near the junction of the A548 and B5113.

LLANDDULAS

ST CYNBRYD. Rebuilt in 1732 and again in 1868–9 at the expense of Robert Bamford Hesketh of Gwrych. By *Street*. It is a church of subtlety and sophistication, combining complicated and random-looking elements into a coherent and reposeful whole. External walls of random polygonal masonry, displaying sensitivity to scale and texture. The interior is of ashlar. Nave, chancel, S aisle with gable roof, S porch, and a NE vestry, later enlarged. The aisle does not extend as far W as does the nave, and in the angle rises an octagonal spired bellcote. Neither does it reach to the end of the chancel, though the two partly overlap and are separated internally by traceried stone screenwork in two narrow arches. A buttress for the chancel arch encroaches into the aisle. Nave arcade with low and thin circular piers. The N windows are mainly cusped lancets. The others have varying forms of Dec tracery, and those in the aisle are irregularly spaced. Good roofs. – FONTS. An ancient square bowl has been superseded by 'a sentimental but galumphing white angel with a shell that is so comical that it must distract everybody terribly' (Goodhart-Rendel). By *Cecil Thomas*, 1926. – Other fittings by *Street*, including the REREDOS, with a Crucifixion almost certainly carved by *Earp*. Flamboyant stone panelling either side. – As always, *Street*'s metalwork is worthy of note: e.g. iron CHANCEL GATES and the HINGES of the S door. Also five brass CORONAE and the fragment of another. There were originally seven. – (NEEDLEWORK. An embroidered and jewelled FRONTAL, given by Mrs Hesketh, was designed by *Street* and made by a local lady, *Miss Foster*.)*

Timber-framed LYCHGATE, 1898. A CHURCHYARD CROSS, of 1912, marks the burial plot of the Dundonalds of Gwrych. Both were designed by *Harold Hughes*.

CHURCH HALL, ⅛ m. E. Also by *Hughes* (VH) and built 1910–11. Small corner clock tower with a slated spire.

PEN-Y-CORDDYN HILLFORT, 1¼ m. SSE (SH 915 765), occupies a flat-topped limestone hill overlooking the Dulas valley. There are steep cliffs round every side except the N, where the land slopes down in a series of shallow steps. This sloping ground, enclosed by a single stone rampart wherever necessary between the crags, forms an annexe to the large and impressive main fort, which itself had two ramparts set at the break of slope on this N side and a single smaller rampart blocking gaps on the cliffs on the other sides. The main

---

* I am indebted to Mr Paul Joyce for information on this church.

northern defences are still impressive: the inner rampart was once a huge stone wall, more than 16 ft thick, terraced on the inside and probably almost 8 ft high; some distance outside it was a rock-cut ditch 10–13 ft wide, with a second sloping bank of loose stone beyond that. There are two entrances through this main line of defence, one at the NE corner and the other at the NW. Both are approached by hollow ways providing convenient access to the interior. Until recently, when it was extensively damaged by widening the tracks, the NE entrance, with its outworks and long inturned passage incorporating two fine guard chambers, was one of the best-preserved of these constructions, which are such an important feature of the Clwydian and Marcher hillforts. There is a smaller entrance at the southern end of the fort, and a minor gap on the E side, supposedly to give access to a spring at the foot of the cliff. The fortifications were investigated at the beginning of this century by Dr Willoughby Gardner (*Archaeologia Cambrensis*, vol. 10, 1910), who dug several sections across the ramparts and cleared the entrance, which, not surprisingly, he found to have been closed by stout wooden gates. Finds from the excavations were few and can provide no accurate date for the hillfort construction. There are no hut foundations visible within the 23¾-acre interior of the main enclosure, but the northern half, which is relatively sheltered, would be suitable for habitation.

1050

LLANDEGLA

St Tegla. Rebuilt at the expense of Margaret, Lady Willoughby de Broke, 1866, and almost certainly by *John Gibson* (*see* Bodelwyddan, p. 324). Nave but no chancel, reflecting the single-chamber predecessor, but otherwise a conventional Dec job. – FONT. Perp. Roll mouldings, and carving in the panels. – STAINED GLASS. An E window by *Francis Eginton* was installed in St Asaph Cathedral, 1800, characteristic of its period in style and technique. Characteristic also in having three pictorial lights as against eleven containing the arms of the bishop and the nobility and gentry who paid for it. The figurative lights were transferred to Llandegla in 1864 and are now in the E window. Our Lord, in youth, contemplates a vision of the future. Chubby child angels with Instruments of the Passion. One hovers with a Crown of Thorns; below a more fully grown and fully clad angel with a chalice. Strong red and blue robes, but a harmonious haze of greyish pink predominates. – A late medieval brass CHANDELIER is a great enough rarity; to find two in neighbouring parishes (*see* Llanarmon-yn-Iâl) is remarkable indeed. This is the simpler of the two, with only two tiers of branches, one of eight, one of four, but also having Perp ornament (fruit and foliage) on curving stems. Surmounted by a figure of the Virgin, not canopied. Beast head with a ring below. – A plank CHEST.

The village is tucked away w of Llandegla Moor. SCHOOL, 1874, with a clock in its gable below the bellcote. The VILLAGE HALL was a chapel (Sion) of the longitudinal elevation type, with two round-headed windows between a pair of doors.

BODIDRIS, I m. SE. The main range, late C16 or early C17, faces w. At the rear three lateral chimneys with ribbed stacks. Projecting forward at the s end of the front is a taller tower-like block, with gable roof, probably early C16. Never strictly a fortified tower house, and too small to be a dwelling in its own right, this must have originated as an adjunct to a main domestic range on the site of the present one. Mullioned windows, those of the tower contemporary with the later range. Hoodmoulds, heraldic and decorative finials, and, at the angles of the tower, pseudo gargoyles. Some remodelling on the s front. Staircase round an enclosed well. Post-and-panel partition, probably *ex situ*. Moulded and stopped beams in the hall. A more recent N wing has been demolished, and a reset pointed doorway from it has been reassembled, in an E extension. Former STABLE range, with a lintel dated 1581. chimney, and a gable end with three storeys of mullioned windows. Cyclopean lintel. Former FARM BUILDINGS constitute the other three sides of an enclosure. All were subject to restoration and conversion, begun in 1971.

TOMEN-Y-RHODWYDD, 1¼m. WSW. This excellently preserved motte and bailey seem to be the castle known to have been built in 1149 by Owain Gwynedd. Bailey protected by a bank, and the whole enclosed by an outer ditch and bank.

BARROWS. *See* Bwlchgwyn.

LLANDRILLO-YN-RHOS

8080

Contiguous with Colwyn Bay (q.v.) and commonly called Rhos-on-Sea. Development began in the 1860s, and in 1895 a pier was acquired – an importation from Douglas on the Isle of Man, where it had first been erected 1868-9. It was demolished in 1954. Prominent on the sea front is the brick and half-timber RHOS ABBEY HOTEL of 1898, next to which is RHOS FYNACH (or CEGIN Y MYNACH), dated 1717, though earlier in origin.

ST TRILLO, Llandudno Road. High up, above reclaimed coastal land. It was formerly whitewashed and provided a landmark for vessels at sea. The w tower served as a beacon, and may have been adapted as such *c.* 1600 by the addition of the sw turret with stepped merlons, to form part of the chain of watchtowers which includes those at Abergele and Whitford (*see* pp. 100 and 456). The tower itself is said to be of 1552, and earlier in the C16 the church had become double-naved when an extension was added on the s.*

---

* Bequests for a chancel and for a s porch were made in a will of 1540.

Four-centred E window in this new S nave, with cusping, panel tracery and two single-light sub-arches. The S nave W window and the N nave E are not reliable, and probably date from a restoration of 1857 by *H. Kennedy*. Blocked priest's door. Four-bay arcade with octagonal piers. N roof trussed-raftered, and the southern one arched-braced with cusped wind-braces and quasi-hammerbeams. Wagon ceiling in the E half of its end bay. The roof does not correspond with the (later?) angel corbels of the arcade. Arched-bracing in the S porch. At the W end of the N wall are two blocked C13 arches belonging to a former aisle or chapel, and cut through previously existing wall. The work may be associated with Ednyfed Fychan (*see* Llys Euryn, below). – FONT. C13 bowl with a band of nailhead. – STAINED GLASS. Both E windows of 1873, the southern one, and possibly the other, by *Heaton, Butler & Bayne*. (VH) – A W window is by *T.F. Curtis* of *Ward & Hughes*, 1902. – SEPULCHRAL SLAB, in the porch, commemorating Ednyfed, vicar. Floriated cross with petaloid pattern, each arm branching into five lobes. Early C14.

LYCHGATE of 1677. Arched openings.

ST GEORGE, St George's Road. Rock-faced Neo-Perp. 1913 by *L.W. Barnard*. Not as bad as he often was, despite peculiar tracery, but his usual defect of failing to express the chancel arch externally may be seen. Here, though, the transition from clerestoried nave is masked by transepts. The W tower, for which vaulting was apparently intended, was completed in 1965 to a revised design. – STAINED GLASS. Some windows by *A.O. Hemming*.

CAPEL TRILLO, on the foreshore, below Rhos Promenade. A tiny chapel, of boulders, built over a spring. Estimates of its date range from the C6 to the C16. There seems no reason why it should not be early. The roof caved in some time after 1855, and was incorrectly restored by *Arthur Baker*, c.1892. He made the external pitch much lower, and built the tunnel-vault pointed instead of segmental. Again restored 1935; STAINED GLASS by *Morris & Co.* in the slit E window is of that date.

HERMON WELSH PRESBYTERIAN (CALVINISTIC METHODIST) CHAPEL, Brompton Avenue. Built 1903. Red brick and terra-cotta, including terra-cotta plate tracery.

UNITED REFORMED CHURCH (formerly Congregational), Colwyn Avenue. An interesting early C20 Arts and Crafts design, with not a trace of Gothic in the details. Note, e.g., unmoulded mullions and circular clerestory windows with tracery of intersecting curves and diagonals. Transepts were added 1913.

BRYN EURYN (SH 833 799), ½ m. S of the parish church, is a prominent hill commanding spectacular views. On the southern summit are the much-reduced remains of a defensive enclosure. The stone rampart with large facing blocks can still be easily recognized on the N side just below the triangulation point, but the circuit is less clear to the S, where the slope is steeper. On the NW an incomplete outer rampart diverges from the inner one just where the old fence line (and modern path) cross it. The remains of pillow mounds have been observed on the southern slope but they are now overgrown. There is no sign of any defence of the lower southern summit of the hill, but there is a suggestion of an eroded rampart further down the hill on the northern side, from which the ascent is much easier.

LLYS EURYN, at the N end of Bryn Euryn. Ruins of a C15 or early C16 house which consisted of three ranges enclosing a court. Arched fireplace and a chimneystack. A predecessor house was the seat of Ednyfed Fychan, seneschal of Llywelyn the Great, who obtained grant of the *vill* in 1230.

Several works of *S. Colwyn Foulkes* deserve mention. First, MORYN, NO. 27 CAYLEY PROMENADE, for himself. Brick, with steep hipped roof recessed behind a parapet. Canted bay with a Regency-style canopy and serrated fascia. Neo-Georgian is abandoned in a flat-roofed apsidal projection with a large undivided window facing the sea. Forming part of the original build are two attached single-storeyed houses. At No. 23 EBBERSTON ROAD WEST, of 1960–1, classical elements are wittily integrated with a post-war domestic idiom. Asymmetrical, with gable ends, square and horizontal windows, but also a triglyph cornice and a pilastered and pedimented doorcase. HEATON PLACE, nearby, is a layout of old people's homes, 1956–78. It is approached either end between slender, finialed GATEPIERS. Finally, the ELWY ROAD ESTATE, 1952–6, one of the best of *Colwyn Foulkes*'s many local authority housing schemes in Wales. Two-storey houses and three-storey flats. Vehicular service access is at the rear, and in some places there is pedestrian access at the front only, e.g. in the broad and curving MAES GLAS and part of BRYN EGLWYS. Walls are mostly rendered, but the end blocks of terraces are of brick, with classical stone doorcases. Elsewhere are lighthearted porches, with striped coloured canopies, and further delicate touches are provided in glazing patterns.

LLANDYRNOG   *1060*

ST TEYRNOG. Two naves, their roofs arched-braced, with cusped wind-braces. Both E windows have cusping and panel tracery, but otherwise differ in design. The church is thus a typical Perp double-naver of the region, but it is a special one, for *Nesfield* restored and left his mark on it, 1876–8. Pinkish pebbledash and crisp sandstone dressings immediately give a Late Victorian impression. By Nesfield the Gothic double W bellcote (replacing a simpler one) on the N nave, and the W window of the S nave. Also the timber-framed S porch. This displays his favourite decorative roundels ('pies') in a couple of brackets, and similar circular sunflower patterns in the plaster panels. Two roof trusses were reused, one perhaps from the N porch, which he abolished and replaced with a window. Most or all other windows, including the E ones, seem to be faithful restorations, but the five-bay arcade was rebuilt as a neater and more regular version of its predecessor. – FURNISHINGS by *Nesfield*, including FONT, PULPIT and LECTERN. Also the STALLS, sensitively done, strong and simple in their framing and moulding, and with sunflower pies in poppyheads. Best of all a sanctuary BENCH, with incised C17-style patterns in some panels and artfully random pies in others. Like others of the items it is dated 1877. – Good TILES including embossed ones in a dado behind the altar. – Fine IRONWORK on doors. – STAINED GLASS. In the N nave E window work of *c.*1500, restored and rearranged by *Kempe*. In the main lights, some canopy work and remains of a Seven Sacraments window, with central Crucifixion, the Eucharist and Extreme Unction in the second light, and (more complete) Ordination and Marriage in the fourth. Also parts from an Apostles window, with two figures in the first light and two in the fifth, each with their clause of the Creed. Ox of St Luke in the fifth. Canopy work in the tracery, and the Coronation of the Virgin in the two centre panels of the top row with a nimbed bishop to the l. Below, female saints and, in the two centre panels, the Annunciation. – MONUMENTS. Loose in the sanctuary are fragments of a priestly effigy. – Several tablets with heraldry, cherub heads etc., e.g. John Ashpoole †1716, John Ashpoole †1722, Henry Powell †1749. – Dugout CHEST. – The CHURCHYARD seems to have been circular.

RECTORY, ½ m. NNE. Symmetrical brick and stone front, with a tall central gable and canted bays either side. This is an addition by *Lloyd Williams & Underwood*, 1860, to an earlier structure.

CAPEL DYFFRYN, Waen, ½ m. N. Built 1836. Longitudinal elevation. Two doors with fanlights, and between them round-headed windows. Gothic glazing patterns. Now pebble-dashed, as is the accompanying house.

BAPTIST CHAPEL, ¼ m. SW. Also of 1836. In its own graveyard. Longitudinal elevation, with labels. Derelict.

PLAS BENNETT, ⅜ m. WSW. Mid-C18. Double pile, with gable ends and a five-bay front. Pebbledashed, but stone quoins, fluted keystones and a cornice and solid parapet remain exposed. Also a doorcase with lugged architrave and curly broken pediment. (Dog-leg staircase with ornamented stair ends and fluted columnar balusters. NMR)

GLAN-Y-WERN, ¾ m. NW. Seven by seven bays, with the middle three of the return emphasized by slight projection and a raised blocking course. Of ashlar. Date inscriptions of 1813 and 1814 are recorded. A service wing has been demolished. Interior with enriched cornices, mahogany doors, reeded architraves etc. and some original chimneypieces. Ionic screen in the entrance hall. Dining room to the r.; to the l. a suite of three rooms along the return front. Central

top-lit imperial staircase, of stone, with iron balustrade.
Above is a lantern surmounting a dome-like drum with scalloped sides. A later entrance porch has ornament which suggests *Nesfield*. It may well be by him, for P. S. Humberston,
a principal subscriber to the church restoration, lived here.

PENTRE MAWR. 1¼ m. NNW. Early C19. Porch with two pairs
of Tuscan columns. Fine range of brick FARM BUILDINGS,
L-shaped, with tall segmental entrance arch and a cupola. A
cottage occurs at the angle.

PLAS ASHPOOL, 1¾ m. N. Probably early C18. Brick, with stone
quoins. Two-gable three-storeyed front, having four bays of
windows and an off-centre doorway with pedimented hood
on brackets. (Staircase with turned balusters. A heavily
carved Jacobean overmantel, with heraldry. NMR) Attractive
group of FARM BUILDINGS, including a CART SHED with
segmental arches and upper storey, and, opposite, two parallel
BARNS with quoins and coped gables. That next to the yard
contains four splendid cruck trusses with tie and collar beams,
possibly late C16, with the brick walls late C17 or early C18.

LLANDYSILIO

1040

The River Dee is nowhere more lovely than in its wooded
course through the valley which lies between Llandysilio
Mountain and the Berwyns. The church, not far from the
river, has no village close to it, and the simple stone-built
SCHOOL, 1858, is ⅝ m. NNW, and the former VICARAGE, 1859,
¼ m. further on. The LLANGOLLEN CANAL, completed 1808,
which was constructed as a navigable feeder for the Ellesmere
system (*see* Pont Cysyllte, Froncysyllte), has its origin ⅛ m. SE
of the church. Its water is drawn from the Dee at the HORSE-
SHOE FALLS, a crescent-shaped weir for which, as well as for
the canal itself, *Telford* was responsible.

ST TYSILIO. A single chamber, to which in 1718 a N transept
was added at the E end. The transept was rebuilt and enlarged
in a restoration of 1869. The W window is also of this date,
but the design of the three-light Perp E window, with panel
tracery, is probably authentic, and there are three straight-
headed S windows, one with the (renewed) date 1580. Late
medieval roof, arched-braced, with cusped struts above the
collars. Panelled wagon ceiling in the easternmost bay, following the curve of the braces, and with quatrefoil tracery on the
horizontals, brattishing, and moulded ribs. A small round-
headed N window has fragments of SEPULCHRAL SLABS as
dressings: e.g. the lintel and the lower part of the E jamb from
the heads of C13 floriated slabs. Also two portions of a cross
raguly. – FONT, Perp. Stem with cusped panels and the bowl
with quatrefoils containing shields, flowers etc. – LECTERN.
A rare oak eagle of early date. – PULPIT and CHANCEL FIT-
TINGS, including the FLOORING and SCREEN, by *R. T. Beckett*, with work being done both before and after the First

World War.* – STAINED GLASS. In the small N window two
C15 figures, one of them St James the Great. – E window.
Brightly coloured, with strong Aesthetic Movement influ-
ence. Commemoration date 1890. – MONUMENTS. Elizabeth
Jones †1721. Cherub heads, heraldry, volutes, drapery and
gadrooning. – Lady Martin, the actress Helen Faucit, †1898
(*see* Bryntysilio, below). She is depicted seated. Masks of
comedy and tragedy and a portrait medallion of Shakespeare.
A copy by *J. Hughes* of work by *J. H. Foley*, exhibited at the
Academy in 1856.

LLANTYSILIO HALL, ¼m. WNW. A brick-built predecessor
was dated 1723. It had two-bay wings, projecting by two bays

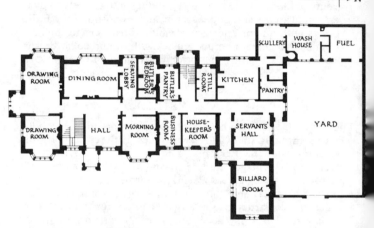

Llandysilio, Llantysilio Hall, 1872–4, plan
(*The Architect*, vol. 15, 1876)

from a three-bay centre with pedimented doorcase below a
tripartite window. This house was bought in the mid-1860s
by C. F. Beyer, a native of Saxony and a partner in the Manchester firm of Beyer, Peacock & Co., locomotive builders.
The present house was built for him on higher ground, behind the old site, by *S. Pountney Smith*, 1872–4. It is a
younger brother of Pale, Merioneth, which Smith rebuilt for
the railway engineer and ironmaster Henry Robertson, 1869–
71. Robertson had a financial interest in Beyer's firm, and
Beyer was godfather to his son, Sir Henry Beyer Robertson,
to whom Llantysilio Hall was bequeathed.‡ Neo-Elizabethan,
with little modelling or ornament. Earlier proposals by Smith
had included more relief, and the severity seems in part to
reflect Beyer's wishes. The walling is ashlar, of high quality,

* Information from the Rev. David Hinge.
‡ It remains with the family. Mr Duncan Robertson kindly supplied information on both the present and previous houses.

and such stonecarving as there is is sharp and precise. The main block is symmetrical on the E (entrance) and narrow S fronts. Service wing to the N, and on the W a tower at the junction of the two parts. The layout provides an excellent and little-altered example of Victorian country-house planning. Double pile, with a central corridor extending for almost the entire length, through both principal and service parts, with a door separating family accommodation from the servants' part of the house. On the ground floor the corridor merges with the hall and staircase area, around which the main rooms are grouped. Behind the hall the dining room. This has direct communication with the carefully arranged service quarters, beyond which, as an isolated male preserve, is the billiard room, with traceried window and open roof. Main staircase with balustrade of freely enriched strapwork. This and other internal woodwork was probably executed by *Cox*, who did that at Pale. Two interconnecting drawing rooms across the S front, their fittings lighter and more feminine than those of the dining room and entrance hall. Their marble chimneypieces, made by *Bennett Bros.* of Liverpool, display portrait medallions. One has Queen Victoria, Mrs Henry Robertson, and Lady Martin, of Bryntysilio. For the other, Beyer chose the German emperor (Wilhelm I) accompanied by Bismarck and Moltke. The S front is aligned on an AVENUE, which belonged to the previous house, and extends down to the river. (STABLES, to the N. Designed in the office of *Beyer, Peacock & Co.*, 1874.) *Waring & Gillow* supplied furniture for both the old house and the new, and though some of it remains in the latter, it is outside the scope of *The Buildings of Wales*. Even the drawing-room piano (by Collard & Collard) was sent to Waring & Gillow for its casing to be made.

BRYNTYSILIO, $\frac{1}{4}$ m. ESE, above the Horseshoe Falls. The country home of Sir Theodore Martin, lawyer, man of letters, and biographer of the Prince Consort. Lady Martin was Helen Faucit, the Shakespearian actress. A three-bay Georgian house, bought in 1865, was in 1870 remodelled as a serene Italianate villa, refined and asymmetrical, with white walls (painted stone, not stucco), shutters, and a cast-iron veranda. The nucleus was extended to the r. by a further bay, and to the l. by a pedimented cross wing. On the left-hand return was the higher pedimented end of a rear service wing. Not at all Mid-Victorian in character, and it is regrettable that the identity of the architect, presumably a London man, is unknown. There was a top-lit hall, separated from the staircase by arches below and columns above. Some later alterations (probably by *Beckett*, 1910) seem to have been fairly minor, but drastic remodelling and partial demolition took place *c.* 1950. What remains is the Georgian nucleus plus its right-hand extension and, reduced in height, the service wing. Little of note left inside, but the Martins' GARDENS have undergone surprisingly little change.

RHYDONNEN UCHAF, 1¼ m. WSW, beyond a great bend of the
Dee. Altered and enlarged 1716, when additions were made
in brick to an earlier stone structure. Rendering now masks
the demarcations, and a room of 1716 has lost bolection-
moulded panelling. Dog-leg staircase, through two storeys,
inserted into the older part. String and turned bobbin balusters. Similar balustrading against the walls, as a dado, returned at the half-landings.

TŶ CANOL, on the Merioneth border, 1⅛ m. NNW of Glyndy-
frdwy. Two cruck trusses partly survive, one with a later
chimney built into it. The range is aligned against the slope
and at the top has a (later?) cross range, also with a cruck.

MOEL Y GAER (SJ 167 463), on Llandysilio Mountain, is a
small univallate fort with an inturned entrance on the E.
Because of its remote position – the walk is a long and arduous one – the site is well preserved, though the fortifications were never very impressive.

CHAIN BRIDGE. See Berwyn.

PENTREFELIN. See Llangollen.

PILLAR OF ELISEG. See Valle Crucis Abbey.

LLANEFYDD

Rolling cultivated uplands, with glimpses of the sea. The village, with a tiny nucleus around the church, is set within a
labyrinth of lanes.

ST NEFYDD AND ST MARY. A double-naved Perp church, and
a particularly pleasing one, light and spacious, and with
greater uniformity of fenestration than most. Side windows
of two and three lights, all with cusping. The five-light E
windows are both the same – two centred, with a transom at
springing level and panel tracery. Five-bay arcade, the arches
with a hollow and a chamfer, the piers octagonal with heavy
caps. Arched-braced roofs, with cusping to the wind-bracing
and the struts above the collars. A priest's door (blocked) and
a S porch with cyclopean inner doorway. Double W bellcote
on the S nave, apparently renewed in a restoration of 1859.
Restoration in 1908–9 by *Harold Hughes*. – FONT. Dated
1668. – Against the N wall the tester and pilastered back of
an C18 PULPIT. – STAINED GLASS. Jumbled fragments in the
tracery of the E windows. – Pendant OIL LAMPS. – SEPUL-
CHRAL SLABS. At E end of N nave: part of an early C14
four-circle cross head. – Fragment of a decorated heraldic
slab. – At E end of S nave: early C14 circular-headed cross
slab (concentric rings) with sword. – MONUMENTS. Edward
ab Iorwerth. Late C14. Part of a miniature effigy, now set in
the sill of the easternmost S window. – Some C17 and C18
vernacular tablets, and a couple of well-engraved BRASSES,
particularly that to William Brown †1773. – Pre-1801 Hanoverian ROYAL ARMS, painted on plaster.

s of the church, OLD VICARAGE, 1871, probably by *Lloyd Williams & Underwood*. They definitely did the OLD SCHOOL, 1866, ¼m. ESE. Its windows have been mutilated.

PLAS HARRI, 1¼m. W. L-shaped, and (as pointed out by Mr Vernon Hughes) an example of unit planning. The longer wing, with sashes, is dated 1764. Group of FARM BUILD-INGS, including a two-arch cart shed.

PONT-YR-ALED, 1¾m. W. Two arches, the smaller one for flood water.

PLAS UCHAF, 1m. WNW. Evidence of former mullioned win-dows and of a cyclopean doorway. Large stacks. Irregular plan, and a wing, with end stacks, which touches only at one corner, is an instance of unit planning. Late C17 or early C18 staircase, beginning in a straight flight and continuing round a solid well. Dadoes of twisted balusters, and baluster motifs applied to the newels. Dog-gate. The house also has some later woodwork, and panelling is said to have gone to Coed Coch, Betws-yn-Rhos (q.v.).

BERAIN, 1¾m. ESE. The main range contains two hammerbeam trusses belonging to a late medieval hall, together with a frag-ment of the moulded beam of a dais canopy. The original form and size of the house are unclear, and an extension at the N (lower) end is now a farm building. Of the late C16 or early C17, and not necessarily all carried out simultaneously, are the subdivision of the hall, the insertion of a lateral fire-place with heavily moulded ingle beam, and the addition, at an angle, of a wing to the E. The wing abuts the lateral chim-ney, and at its opposite end has a similar square stack, but set diagonally and with a gabled breast. Though obviously an instance of the unit system, the wing has been given internal communication with the main range through two stone door-ways in the NE angle. The wing has a pointed cyclopean doorway, and a post-and-panel partition containing a door-way with ornamented head. On the first floor is another par-tition, and a room with moulded beams and stop-moulded joists. Other rooms in both parts of the house have only chamfering. Signs of former mullioned windows in both parts. On the E side of the main range a blocked cyclopean doorway, and on the W an enriched timber lintel, now inside a porch.

This was the home of Katheryn of Berain (1535–91), mar-ried successively to John Salusbury of Lleweni, Sir Richard Clough, Maurice Wynn of Gwydir, and Edward Thelwall.

PONT-Y-GWYDDEL. *See* Llanfair Talhaearn.

PONT Y DDÔL. *See* Cefn Meiriadog.

PONT NEWYDD. *See* Cefn Meiriadog.

BRYN-Y-PIN. *See* Cefn Meiriadog.

The hillfort called MYNYDD Y GAER, ⅞m. NW (SH 973 717), occupies a splendid site and, though badly damaged, is not without interest. The defences surrounding the top of the hill (which is of some ten acres) once consisted of an inner stone wall rampart (now almost entirely removed, leaving only a

spread of small stones to indicate its line) with an external
ditch and counterscarp bank (which still survives to a considerable height in places). The fort appears to have had two
entrances: at the SE, where access is easy but where subsequent quarrying has confused the original arrangement, and
at the N, where the hill slope is steep and the bank/ditch
terminals are staggered. The ditch ends abruptly *c.*100 ft to
the E of the N entrance where the geology of the hill changes
from a friable shale to a hard igneous rock. This rock has
been quarried in the recent past, making the original earthworks in this sector very difficult to interpret. The western
side of the hill is more hospitable and is occupied by the ruins
of a small *tyddyn* and its fields.

8070

LLANELIAN-YN-RHOS

A small but coherent village group on high ground, with a view
of the sea from the churchyard.

ST ELIAN. A double-naved church, which continued to be
whitewashed into the C19. The earlier N portion shows evidence of eastward extension, probably prior to the Perp remodelling and enlargement to which the S half belongs. E
windows of differing design, that of the N nave straight-
headed, though both have cusped lights. Most other windows
renewed. (Restorations of 1859 and 1903 are recorded.) W
bellcote to the N nave, and three cyclopean pointed doorways,
two of them blocked. Crude five-bay arcade, its chamfered
arches rising from thin octagonal piers without caps (cf. Llysfaen). Arched-braced roofs with cusped wind-braces. Wagon
ceilings at the E end, the northern one with arcading above
the wall-plate and other embellishment. The colouring is
probably Victorian. On the ceiling in the S compartment are
traces of paintings which included the Magi, and St Anne
with the Virgin. Arched-bracing and cusped wind-braces in
the S porch. – FONTS. A C17 piece with quatrefoils on the
octagonal bowl. – Also an early circular bowl. – REREDOS. A
Last Supper, carved in 1873 by *John Yorke*, i.e. General
Yorke of Plas Newydd fame (*see* p. 222). – ROOD SCREEN.
The lower part, extending across both naves, has been reinstated. Moulded uprights and middle rail, and random
squints. Against the N wall nine PAINTED PANELS from the
rood loft W parapet, depicting the Last Judgement, the Ascension, and the legend of St Hubert. They show the cusped
pattern of the original framing. – STAINED GLASS. W and
both E windows by *Ballantine & Son*, 1862. (VH) – MONU-
MENTS. Classical tablets include that to John Holland †1784.
It is by *Benjamin Bromfield*.

LLAN FARM, in the village. Thatched. A three-unit, four-bay
cruck hall house. Outer walls rebuilt in stone in the late C15
or early C16 (though all five cruck trusses survive in part.

NMR). Lateral chimneys and a wing have been added. Some timber framing in a gable end.

TEYRDAN, ½m. ESE. C18 sashes and roof hips. A moulded stone doorcase looks C17, and in a gable end are mullioned windows with arched lights which are presumably C16. Axial layout of late C18 or early C19 FARM BUILDINGS, their arched entrance under a gable.

Beyond the SCHOOL (1865), 1m. ESE, is PLAS UCHAF, or PLAS LLANELIAN, with a cyclopean lintel. Two-unit plan, with end chimney and inside cross passage. Lower-end parlour and service room, now one. Chamfered beams and stop-chamfered joists. Also the partition truss and arched-braced central truss of an upper room once open to the roof. Cusped wind-braces.

PLAS LLEWELYN, 1m. SE. In the grounds a GATEHOUSE, attractively converted from a farm building.

LLANELIDAN   1050

ST ELIDAN. The N nave, with double bellcote, extends further W than does the S. Otherwise this is a characteristic Vale of Clwyd church. All features are Perp and later, except for a Dec two-light N window, and, possibly, the N doorway, with head-stops, which may be of similar date. It is partly obscured by a later porch, with timber arch. N nave E window of five lights with cusping and panel tracery. S nave E of four lights, the two middle ones with transoms. Cusping follows the line of the arch. Blocked W doorway in the S nave, with cyclopean lintel forming a Tudor arch. A N window is dated 1618; a straight-headed and cusped three-lighter on the S is of 1626, and the N nave W window was introduced in a restoration of 1890. Five-bay arcade with octagonal piers. Arched-braced roofs with struts above the collars and wind-bracing, that of the S roof cusped. At the E end are four-centred wagon ceilings, the southern one following the curve of the arched-braces. Their horizontal members are brattished and traceried and have vine trail etc. In the N nave an ogee PISCINA. – FONT. Low and spreading, with roll mouldings. Probably C15. – REREDOS. Made up of Jacobean work. – BOX PEWS, with dates of 1760 and 1769. Rearranged by *Gronwy R. Griffith*, c.1938. – PULPIT. Jacobean, with its own carved panels and a couple of beasts, and also with fragments of the ROOD SCREEN, applied by *Griffith*. Including reeded uprights, vine trail, traceried panels etc., these had previously been incorporated in a clerk's desk. Also from the rood screen are two beams, one with quatrefoil, the other traceried, now in a vestry screen at the W end, together with carving of a crown and two beasts. – Late C17 turned RAILS round two sides of the altar. – STAINED GLASS. Late C15 or early C16 pieces, including patterned quarries in the tracery of the N nave E window and Emblems of the Passion in its main lights.

Also a jumble in the s nave E, and the Ox of St Luke, with other fragments, in the vestry screen. – Gothic COMMANDMENT BOARDS inscribed in Welsh. – MONUMENTS. Humphrey Jones †1676. Sumptuous, with Corinthian columns, wreathed volutes, gadrooning, cherub heads, drapery and urns. Volutes form a pediment. – Eubule Thelwall †1694. Architectural surround, gadrooned base, poor lettering. Added tablet, with drapery and simulated folds, to wife Mary †1698. – Richard Kenrick †1820. Neo-Classical, with sarcophagus. – Lt George Vivyan Naylor-Leyland, killed in action 1914. Signed by *Gaffin*. Heavily classical, overlaid with trophies.

The CHURCHYARD was originally circular.

s of the church the stone-built LEYLAND ARMS, dated 1844. Diamond glazing patterns and wavy bargeboards. Alterations at the rear by *Sir Clough Williams-Ellis*, *c*.1966.

NANTCLWYD HALL, ¾m. N. The remodelling of the house and the embellishment of the grounds were of a magnitude and lavishness rare in the latter half of the C20. Under *Sir Vivyan Naylor-Leyland* and his architect, *Sir Clough Williams-Ellis*, the transformation evolved in a series of schemes extending from the mid-1950s into the 1970s. The *ensemble* fully displays the colourful theatricality of Sir Clough's style, and in his autobiographies he wrote graphically of the collaboration with his exceptional client. The house also figures in a story of prodigious Victorian patronage, the estate having been inherited by Richard Christopher Naylor. He and his brother John were partners in the Liverpool banking house of Leyland & Bullins, and were great-nephews of Thomas Leyland and nephews of Richard Bullin, the founders.* It was John who, from *c*.1849, created the vast and wondrous domain of Leighton near Welshpool (*see The Buildings of Wales: Powys*), and in the 1890s his son, C. J. Leyland, put in hand gargantuan works at Haggerston Castle, Northumberland, to the design of Norman Shaw. From the 1850s R. C. Naylor gave employment to *J. K. Colling*, best remembered for his books on Gothic and foliated ornament. Commissions included the Albany in Liverpool, the *Rundbogenstil* church at Hooton, Wirral, and the equally spectacular altering and enlarging of Hooton Hall, as well as additions to Nantclwyd and work at both the church and the mansion at Kelmarsh in Northamptonshire. Nantclwyd was further enlarged – indeed doubled in size – by *David Walker* of Liverpool, after Naylor had made the estate over to his nephew Tom Naylor-Leyland.

The earliest surviving part is a late C17 wing, with three-bay front and three-bay left-hand return, breaking forward from the NW front. Brick, with stone quoins and pedimented windows. Timber cross windows, modillion cornice, and hipped roof. C18 views show four return bays, and that the then remainder of the house was of indeterminate character.

*The banking Leylands are not to be confused with F. R. Leyland, the Liverpool shipowner and patron of Rossetti and Whistler.

The Victorian work took its cue from the wing, and reproduced its elements (but not its disciplined proportions) *ad lib*.
To the l. extends a range by *Colling*, 1857. Into it was inserted
a new main entrance, by *Clough Williams-Ellis*, with classical
doorcase. The portion to the r. of the wing, with a symmetrical (former) entrance front facing SW, is by *Walker*, 1875-6.
His SE continuation, which included service quarters, stables,
and a huge water tower, has been demolished, and the house
now has a rendered SE front of 1958-9 by *Sir Clough*. Frontispiece with a Venetian window and a shaped gable between
urns. Replanning and reconstruction took place inside, with
decorations by *John Fowler*. The room in the C17 wing has
original bolection-moulded panelling. Also a chimneypiece
(not original?) with Corinthian pilasters. (Panelling too in the
room above.) Walker did away with a C17 staircase, but incorporated work from it (including, it seems, scrolled balustrading) in his own more grandiose affair. It no longer exists,
and a two-storey great hall, which occupied the full length of
his entrance front, has been divided up. This had been altered
at an intermediate stage, and other interiors may have undergone early C20 refitting and redecoration.

Now for work carried out in the GROUNDS by *Clough
Williams-Ellis*. A CLOCK TOWER, *c*. 1964, has a gateway in its
base forming the entrance to a service yard. Corner pilasters,
swept pyramid roof, and a cupola. In the GARDENS a formal
axis is aligned on the 1950s frontispiece. It is flanked by two
LOGGIAS and also has a pair of GAZEBOS. These are not large,
and neither is, e.g., a castellated TOWER, within the informal
part beyond, for although the layout is extensive, much of the
treatment is finically small in scale. Other buildings include
an open ROTUNDA beyond a LAKE. In a lane to the S are two
pairs of massive GATEPIERS, and, facing the main road, a
triple-arched GATEWAY. The latter serves a drive which, for
part of its length, follows the course of a railway which ran
through the park. The drive approaches the house aligned on
the entrance in the NW front and crosses the River Clwyd
(which was specially widened) over a BRIDGE of *c*. 1964. This
has an elliptical arch and balustraded parapet with obelisks,
and is possessed of some dignity.

STATUARY, brought from Scarisbrick Hall, Lancashire,
following the sale held there in 1963, includes the bronze
Stag at Bay and *Wild Boar at Bay*, with pedestals by *E. W.
Pugin*.

Of the older planting, some is contemporary with the
mid-1870s enlargement of the house, when the grounds were
laid out by *F. & A. Dickson* of Chester. A drive formed at
that time is now abandoned, but its ENTRANCE LODGE by
Walker remains.

CWM, 1½ m. SSW. Chalet-style farmhouse by *Clough Williams-
Ellis*, *c*. 1966.

TŶ BRITH, 1⅜ m. N. Timber-framed. Gable end with diagonal
bracing and some quatrefoil patterning.

DRILLAU, $\frac{3}{8}$ m. W of Tŷ Brith. Two cruck trusses. Derelict.

ZION CHAPEL, $\frac{3}{4}$ m. ENE. Rebuilt 1852. Two windows between two doorways, all round-headed. A couple of cottages attached.

47 PLAS UCHAF, $1\frac{1}{4}$ m. NE. A C15 or early C16 stone-built, three-unit hall house. Adapted in the C17 by the insertion of a floor, a lateral chimney at the front with gabled breast, and windows with timber mullions and (in the lower storey) transoms. The fireplace opening has a stone arch. Other additions, not necessarily of the same date, include end chimneys, one of them diagonal, and a rear service room. Pointed doorways to the cross passage belong to the original build. Timber-framed FARM BUILDINGS alongside.

GLAN HESBIN, $1\frac{1}{2}$ m. ENE. Date inscriptions of 1641 and 1698. Dog-leg staircase, presumably of 1698, through two storeys, with flat-topped newels and twisted balusters. An internal 'preacher's door' is a relic of C18 nonconformity. Approached by three steps, it is in two halves, like a stable door, with a desk fitted to the lower part.*

1050

LLANFAIR DYFFRYN CLWYD

ST CYNFARCH AND ST MARY. Double-naved, with no pre-Perp features discernible. The northern half has a W tower, its upper stage unbuttressed, and with battlemented parapet. It is mentioned in a will dated 1535-6. Blocked N doorway, set in which, upside-down, is the four-circle cross of an early C14 SEPULCHRAL SLAB. The N nave E window is four-centred, of five lights, with panel tracery and cusping. The S nave E and a S window are of four lights and have transoms which, in the two middle lights, are stepped up and brattished. Another S window, with panel tracery, is dated 1626. Arcade with slender octagonal piers. The church was restored by *J. D. Sedding*, 1870-2, and the S porch is his. The arched-braced roofs, with cusping above the collars, were reconstructed by him and raised in height, but with old timbers reused. By *Sedding* the FONT, REREDOS, STALLS, PULPIT and a LECTERN. They have Perp tracery, but are chaste in character, with large areas of plain wood. – *Godwin* ENCAUSTIC TILES in the sanctuary also date from the time of the restoration. – SCREENS. Of the rood screen there remain, in the S nave, the wainscot, with traceried panels, and, much renewed, the middle rail, with horizontal reeding arranged like brattishing. – N screen by *Sedding*. – STAINED GLASS. Second from E on S. Fragments, including Crucifixion, Apostles with clauses of the Creed, canopy work, and also part of a date which may be inferred to have been 1503. – Westernmost on S. Middle light by *Christopher Whall*, 1893. Ancient quarries in the side lights. – N aisle E by *Westlake*, 1872. – Easternmost on S by *Kempe*, commemoration date 1890. – Huge iron-bound CHEST. –

* Colonel Jones-Mortimer drew attention to this.

SEPULCHRAL SLAB. Early C14, commemorating Dafydd ap Madog. Heraldic shield with inscription. Diagonal sword and a pattern of leaves etc. – MONUMENTS. Lewis monument, with commemoration dates 1820 and 1845. By *W. Spence*. Draped urn. – John Hughes †1830. By *Solomon Gibson*, younger brother of John. A curious design, Grecian in detail, and with the elements including a sarcophagus poised in front.

The exterior was whitewashed when seen by Glynne.

CHURCHYARD with yew trees. The SUNDIAL is the base and part of the shaft of a churchyard cross. Timber-framed LYCHGATE of 1708, looking a century older. The VESTRY HOUSE, dated 1831 on an attractive plaque, is of three bays. Doorway, with Gothic glazing in its fanlight, between two storeys of windows.*

In the village, the SCHOOL, 1859 by *Lloyd Williams & Underwood*, and a row of former ALMSHOUSES, looking mid-C19, but in existence before 1835.

JESUS CHAPEL, 1⅛ m. SSE. A sweet little building, set back from the road with fields on three sides. Founded 1619 by Rice Williams, a native of the parish and verger of Westminster Abbey, for 'a curate to read prayers and teach school in'; i.e. it was an office church, and originally had no altar. As first built it was of timber, and the present stone structure is of 1787. L-plan, with an eastern N transept. The SE corner is hipped, but elsewhere there are coped gables. W bellcote, stone cross windows, and a N doorway with elementary columns and an inscribed lintel. Open roof. – From the parish church are the FONT, dated 1663, and Jacobean PULPIT, with arched panels, strapwork etc. – (Also from the parish church a Jacobean-style ALTAR TABLE of 1816.‡)

LLWYN YNN, 1¼ m. S, has been demolished. It was a large house, partly step-gabled, and was of Jacobean character and probably earlier than an inscribed date of 1672. There remain a pair of C18 GATEPIERS, with urn finials and iron GATES. Also surviving are low service ranges, including a half-timbered portion.

PENTRE CELYN HALL, Pentre Celyn, 1⅝ m. SE. A Neo-Tudor villa, of ashlar, dated 1852. Steep coped gables, labels etc., but the windows are sashes. Symmetrical entrance front.

LLYSFASI (College of Agriculture), 2 m. SSE. A former Myddelton house, of irregular H-plan, with lateral chimney. Altered and enlarged, with much being done in 1911. An upper room in the right-hand cross wing has a barrel-vaulted ceiling with early or mid-C17 plasterwork in the tympana. Strapwork, heraldry, trails, tassels etc. Staircase with reused C18 columnar balusters.

Across the road are FARM COTTAGES by *D. T. Fyfe*, 1913. A stone-built block, looking like a semi-detached pair, in fact consists of four.

*I am indebted to Mr Peter D. Randall for advice and comments on the church.

‡ Information from Mr Randall.

THE DINGLE, 1⅜ m. SSE. Single storey, with a large end stack. (Three cruck trusses, two of them exposed internally. An original partition. DOE)

EYARTH HOUSE, ⅝ m. SW. Built 1812–14, and extensively re-modelled for J. Lever Tillotson, of the Bolton family, who bought it in 1929. Five-bay stuccoed entrance front, and a stone porch with two pairs of Tuscan columns. OUTBUILD-INGS with Gothic touches and a cupola. Beautifully planted GARDENS. Rock garden by *T. R. Hayes*, 1933–4, and a wider layout, *c.* 1937–8, by *C. H. Taudevin*, with much improvement from 1954.

PWLLCALLOD, 1¼ m. SW. In the FARM BUILDINGS is the cen-tral cruck truss of a former hall house, arched-braced, with cusped struts above the collar. Also part of a partition cruck. This was the birthplace of Richard Parry (1560–1623), Bishop of St Asaph, whose revision of the Welsh Bible of 1588 was published in 1620.

FFYNOGION, ½ m. NW. Patterned timber framing has been plas-tered over. Lateral chimney, and a ribbed brick central chim-ney.

CEFN COCH, 1⅛ m. NNE. A group of house and FARM BUILD-INGS, displaying much timber-framing. One range, though partly half-timbered, also has a five-bay C18 portion, of brick, with a cupola. Segmental archway under a pediment-like gable. Brick-nogged BARN, with its framing in square panels and curved bracing in the gable end. It retains a row of panels of undaubed wattle for ventilation.

PLAS NEWYDD, ½ m. NE. A C17 double-pile house, with an *ex situ* date inscription of 1678 inside. Now rendered, and with many later features, including Georgian windows on the gar-den front, but the five-bay entrance front retains stone cross windows, and there are windows with arched lights in the coped and finialed end gables. The entrance hall has a bolection-moulded chimneypiece of slate, with Welsh inscrip-tion. Mid-C18 dog-leg staircase, through two storeys, with ornamented stair ends, swept rail, and columnar newels and balusters.

CAPEL SEION, ½ m. E. A Baptist chapel of 1840. Five-bay longi-tudinal elevation, with diamond glazing patterns and a four-centred doorway. Converted into a dwelling 1982–3.

PENTRE COCH MANOR (formerly TŶ MAWR), 1 m. E. Probably C16 or early C17 in origin. Almost all trace of a Victorian remodelling was done away with in a further transformation from 1933 onwards. Of the 1930s are stepped gables and mullioned windows with arched lights. The front door, stud-ded with the initials RC and the date 1568, may well be from Bach-y-graig, Tremeirchion (*see* p. 452).

GARTH GYNAN, ½ m. ESE. The three-bay entrance front, of brick, looks late C18 or early C19. Two and a half storeys, pedimented doorcase, and the windows of the outer bays tri-partite. This is, though, a re-windowing, and possibly also a raising in height, of an earlier, C18, façade. The structure

behind is earlier still, being a C17 double pile house – possibly
of 1658. (Date inscribed in farm buildings.) Some mullioned
windows. The original walling must all have been of stone,
but there is now some brickwork, as well as a set of enormous
ribbed brick chimneys, of star plan. (C17 staircase, with string
and bulbous turned balusters. NMR) Ranges of brick and
stone FARM BUILDINGS.

PLAS UCHAF. *See* Llanelidan.

CRAIG ADWY WYNT, 1m. SW (SJ 123 545), is a narrow hillfort
on the southern half of the limestone ridge through which the
River Clwyd cuts an impressive gorge at Pwll Glas. It is a
spectacularly sited fort using high natural cliffs for its defence
on the western side and enjoying majestic views of the Clwydian range to the E. The defended area is divided into two by
steep cliffs. The defences of the lower shelf consist of a stone
rampart at the N and S ends, with an inturned entrance
through the northern one which is just S of Graig Isaf Cottage, the highest of the cottages on the NW corner of the hill.
The main camp above is defended by a large stone rampart
on the N, E and S sides. The entrance is in the N side, but the
area has been confused by the construction of a number of
C19 miners' huts with walled gardens. The incurved rampart
on the W of the entrance can still be recognized, as can a
lower bank projecting northwards to cover the path as it
approaches the entrance. At the southern end the fort is defended by two ramparts, the outer one a good deal smaller
than the main rampart. Below the cliff the southern end of
the lower annexe exactly corresponds with the fort above.

LLANFAIR TALHAEARN

9060

On the Elwy, with a short but intriguingly tortuous village
street. The church is on higher ground, immediately above.
LLANFAIR BRIDGE, of rubble masonry, has three elliptical
arches, the middle one twice as wide as the others. Full-height
cutwaters, semicircular on the downstream side. A reinforced
concrete skew BRIDGE, of 1927, was designed by *Considere
Constructions Ltd.*

ST MARY. Double-naved. The sole surviving late medieval
features are the arched-braced roofs, though even these are
only partly old. The six-bay arcade was rebuilt in inappropriate Dec style in 1876, and the windows are of this date,
replacing C17 and C18 ones.* – In the NW corner a TANK,
now under trap doors. Constructed 1841 for adult immersion
baptism, and last used in 1933. – Disused FONT bowl.
Square, changing to an octagon at the top by means of
cushion-like corners. – PAINTING. King David playing the
(Welsh) harp. – Many MONUMENTS, mostly to the Wynnes
of Garthewin. John Wynne. 1692. Large tablet with fruit

* The restoration was possibly by *J. Oldrid Scott.*

garlands above and volutes. – Robert Wynne and others.
1707. Pilasters, entablature rising segmentally, volutes,
cherub heads and heraldry. – John Wynne. 1720. Sumptuous,
with Corinthian columns, an urn in a broken segmental pediment, volutes, cherub heads, and leaf and flower garlands.
– Robert Wynne †1771. Pedimented tablet and an urn. In
differing coloured marbles. – That to Robert Wynne †1798
is similar. – Elizabeth Wynne †1816. By *S. & F. Franceys*.
Infant crouching against a draped urn. – Elizabeth Fleming
†1831. By *James Hatchard* of Pimlico. Draped urn and
sarcophagus-like tablet. – Robert William Wynne †1842. By
Holmes of Pimlico. Neo-Jacobean, in white marble against a
black ground.

   In the churchyard is buried John Jones (1810–69), the poet
'Talhaiarn'.

The RECTORY, ⅛m. SSW of the church, is of 1863. Stone, and
gabled, with sashes. The parsonage manner at its simplest,
and thoroughly sound and sensible. W of the church a
SCHOOL with octagonal spired bell turret.

ST JOHN BAPTIST, Pont-y-Gwyddel, ¾m. NE, in the steep and
wooded valley. Of 1882–3, with chancel, nave and N porch.
Cusped lancets.

Below St John's Church, PONT-Y-GWYDDEL itself. Two segmental arches and full-height cutwaters. It has been widened
on the upstream side.

GARTHEWIN, ¾m. WNW. In the C17 Robert Wynne married
Margaret Price, the Garthewin heiress, and the house still
remains with the Wynnes. It was rebuilt early in the C18,
incorporating substantial older portions. Now stuccoed. Nine
bays, with quoins and a three-bay pediment. The shallow top
storey is an addition, and belongs to alterations of 1767–72
by one of the Turners, probably *Joseph Turner*. Later Georgian is a single-storey left-hand wing containing a drawing
room with marble chimneypiece and broad, mahogany doors
in a consoled surround. In a first-floor room early C18
bolection-moulded panelling. Work by *Sir Clough Williams-
Ellis*, 1930, included de-Victorianization in the form of rein-
stating glazing bars and remodelling a service tower. Circular
and round-headed windows in the tower light the (1767)
staircase, and a new main entrance was contrived at the base.
Some shutters were added and, on the main front, a loggia to
balance the drawing-room wing.

   A tiny CHAPEL (R.C.) was converted from an outbuilding
by the owner, *R. O. F. Wynne*, 1932. Bellcote, and arched
openings with rubble voussoirs.

   FARM BUILDINGS. A GATEHOUSE is dated 1772. Tall
centre, with low-pitched gable and a cupola. Lower hipped
blocks abut either side. A barn, spanned by two impressive
brick arches, both with a lunette above, was converted by
T. S. Tait (VH) in 1938 to a THEATRE. One of the arches
became the proscenium. In its day this was a notable home
of Welsh drama.

MELAI, 2¼ m. SW. The house is eclipsed by FARM BUILDINGS of 1804, forming an enclosed courtyard. Of stone. Two-storey front range of eleven bays, with three-bay pediment-like gable, a cupola, and elliptical entrance arch. The group also includes a BRIDGE and a CART SHED with four tall segmental arches.

PLAS NEWYDD, 1 m. N. A three-unit lateral chimney house with inside cross passage. The plan has been altered, but there remains a fine post-and-panel upper-end partition 50 screen, dated 1585 and with *anno mundi* date and other inscriptions. Guilloche pattern on the middle rail and main uprights; the other uprights heavily moulded. Two doorways, with ornamented heads, to former service rooms. Ceiling partly framed in three ways, with stop-chamfered beams and joists. (A post-and-panel partition on the first floor. DOE)

(BRON HEULOG, ¾ m. NNE. Stone, of nine bays, including projecting two-bay end wings. Two-column porch. The front seems late C18 or early C19, but a dog-leg staircase, with columnar balusters, must be older. DOVECOTE. NMR)

CAIRNS, probably Bronze Age, can be seen on the summits of Mynydd Bodrochwyn, 1⅝ m. NNE (SJ 939 724), and Moelfre Isaf, 2½ m. NNE (SH 952 734).

BRYNGWYLAN. *See* Llangernyw.

SIRIOR GOCH. *See* Betws-yn-Rhos.

LLANFARCHELL *see* DENBIGH, pp. 152, 154

LLANFERRES   *1060*

ST BERRES. Rebuilt 1774 with a datestone of 1650 reset.* The present external character is due to *Thomas Jones*, who in 1843 added a S transept and a W tower with perky little octagonal bellcote. Neo-Perp windows are doubtless his as well. Inside, *John Douglas* predominates. His activities of 1891–2 included the removal of plaster from rubble walling, and the provision of characteristic *Douglas* timber FURNISHINGS. – FONT. Bowl, with quatrefoils, dated 1684. A dugout CHEST. – SEPULCHRAL SLABS. Slab with checky shield and a diagonal sword behind. Late C13. – Fragment of an early C14 four-circle cross slab. – MONUMENTS. Mutilated effigy with lion at feet and inscription at head. Late C14. – John Meredith, rector, †1660. Inscribed with Welsh pedigree. – Edward Jones †1685 and wife Jane †1711. Cartouche with draperies and, at the base, flowers and a cherub head.

GLAN-YR-AFON, ¾ m. NNE. A roughcast villa of *c.*1810, beside

---

* Canon Pritchard notes that payment was made to 'Mr Turner', presumably *Joseph Turner*, and that in 1768 plans and estimates for rebuilding had been made by *John Jordan*, mason, and *Thomas Rathbone*, carpenter.

the River Alun. Soffited eaves and a low-pitched hipped roof.
Five-bay garden front, of which the middle three bays project
and have an iron trellis veranda. The centre of the entrance
front projects as a semi-octagon, and a stone porch with two
pairs of unfluted Greek Doric columns introduces a serious
and scholarly note. Indeed, the architect was almost certainly
Thomas Harrison. Service wing and internal alterations, 1890.
In the grounds, a HOUSE by *J. Quentin Hughes*, 1964.

COLOMENDY, Loggerheads, 1¼ m. NE. Now Liverpool's GLAN
ALYN SCHOOL and ENVIRONMENTAL STUDIES CENTRE.
The house, now much altered, was rebuilt 1810–11. Stuccoed, hipped and of five bays. The end bays project as shallow
cross wings, and they both have a tripartite window within a
segmental arch. SCHOOL BUILDINGS are by *Colwyn Foulkes
& Partners*, 1967–8. They include a teaching block with
assembly hall emphasized in the centre. Varied low-pitched
roofs are exploited in section. Five square, four-storey dormitory blocks. They are concrete-framed and have timber
cladding, low pyramid roofs and spreading eaves.

Richard Wilson spent the last years of his life at Colomendy,
and the sign at the LOGGERHEADS INN on the main road is
said to have been painted by him.

THE LEETE. *See* Rhydymwyn, p. 428.

₉₀₄₀   LLANFIHANGEL GLYN MYFYR

The whitewashed CROWN INN stands next to an early C19
BRIDGE by the elder *Thomas Penson*. The lofty arch spans
the Alwen. The church is beside the river, a short way upstream.

ST MICHAEL. A single chamber, which includes an eastern
extension, slightly broader than the rest, and probably contemporary with C15 or early C16 arched-braced trusses. The
easternmost bay of the roof has a ribbed wagon ceiling, following the curve of the arched braces. Round-headed windows perhaps date from after part of the E end was swept
away by a flood in 1781. Their tracery, and the E window, are
of 1853, when the church was apparently extended slightly
W. *Harold Hughes* altered the new W wall. His restoration,
1901–2, was a sympathetic one, and he permitted internal
plaster to remain. W gallery, with flat, shaped and pierced C17
balusters. They may be former ALTAR RAILS. – In the sanctuary a BENCH, viz. 'Hugh Davies's Bench 1753'. – Plank
CHEST.

BODTEGIR, 1¼ m. SE. The present farmhouse is C17 to C19.
Linked is an older house, single-storeyed, of end chimney
and inside cross passage plan. Cyclopean doorway dated 1655,
and two-light mullioned windows. Byre under the same roof.
A CART SHED has three elliptical arches and a granary above.

CAER DDUNOD, 1⅝ m. NNW (SH 986 520), is a small isolated hill
on the W side of the Alwen Valley. The top appears to have

been fortified by a stone rampart, already completely collapsed by the C17. Considering its ruined state, small size and
obscure setting, the site received an extraordinary amount of
attention from early antiquaries, and was even (implausibly)
identified as the site of Caractacus's last stand (Tacitus, *Annals* XII).

LLANFWROG   *1050*

Close to Ruthin, but with its own village character and identity.

St Mwrog. Double-naved. A massive embattled tower at the
w end of the N nave has two-light Dec bell openings, probably not reliable. Arched-braced s roof with uncusped wind-
braces. The N nave was rebuilt by *J. D. Sedding* in a restoration of 1869–70. Except for a two-light cusped s window,
all windows are his, and include Perp tracery of a type alien
to the region. Timber-framed s porch. It retains old work,
but the slate-hanging and the bottle-glass and diamond
leading, very Nesfieldian, must be *Sedding*'s. The puzzling
feature of the church is the three-bay arcade. Two chamfered
orders and the piers consisting of four clustered shafts each
with a square cap chamfered to an octagon. Small arch at the
E end, partly a wall passage. The main arches are wide, suggesting the reconstruction of an arcade originally of four bays,
and a post-Reformation date is probable. – FONTS. Disused
octagon, splayed inwards towards the base. – Another is High
Victorian, and if by Sedding it contrasts strangely with the
later character of the porch. – Parts of the middle rail and
uprights of the ROOD SCREEN are worked into PANELLING
in the easternmost bay of the arcade. – STAINED GLASS. N
and s easternmost by *Lavers & Barraud*, contemporary with
the 1869–70 restoration. – N nave E window, 1907, looks like
Burlison & Grylls. – MONUMENTS. Hughes monument, last
commemoration date 1799. A simple Grecian tablet signed by
(the elder?) *R. Westmacott*. – Jane Hughes †1829. By *John
Wright* of Chester. Sarcophagus-like Grecian tablet. – The w
LYCHGATE is timber-framed.

Our Lady Help of Christians (R.C.), Mwrog Street. The
front portion was built as a little school, and is by *Clutton*,
contemporary with his work at Ruthin Castle.

A row of ALMSHOUSES of 1708, ¼m. wsw, was spoilt when
converted to two houses.

LLANGADWALADR   *1020*

St Cadwaladr. Like that at Llanarmon Mynydd Mawr
(q.v.), this church is a single chamber, and remote, with no
village. Like that one also it was ruthlessly gone over by
Spaull. He gave it a polygonal apse, broad cusped lancets,

and ENCAUSTIC TILES etc., all in 1883. Much had already been done in 1840, but early features nevertheless remain. Blocked N doorway and, in the vestry, a reset single light with depressed trefoil head. Medieval work in the arched-braced roof with cusped wind-braces. A cruder truss is set against the W gable.

HAFOD ADAMS. *See* Llanarmon Dyffryn Ceiriog.

TOMEN Y GWYDDEL. *See* Llanarmon Dyffryn Ceiriog.

LLANGEDWYN

2020

ST CEDWYN. Rebuilt 1869–70 by *Benjamin Ferrey* under Williams-Wynn patronage (cf. Wynnstay). S aisle, W bellcote, windows mostly lancets. There is no structural division for the chancel, doubtless a concession to the previous church, and inscribed woodwork of 1527 is reused in the chancel cornice. Ferrey retained an earlier Victorian W porch, with Romanesque features in terra-cotta. Church restored by *H. L. North*, in or before 1907, and a pair of dormers are his.* – In the porch the bowl of a plain octagonal FONT. – PULPIT. C17, with incised diamond pattern. – STAINED GLASS. E window 1853. Bright colours and geometrical patterns predominate. A more proper use of the medium than the second from W on the N (1884 by *Ward & Hughes*) with angels and a podgy and sullen little girl. – Pair of brass CANDLE STANDARDS and a CORONA. – CHEST. Panelled front with Jacobean ornament. – Wooden pillar ALMSBOX, 1741. – MONUMENTS. Recumbent effigy of a vested ecclesiastic, with missal. C14. – Edward Vaughan †1718 and wife Mary †1722. Apparently erected in their lifetime. Corinthian surround. Open segmental pediment and garlands meeting above an urn. Three cherub heads. – John Wynne †1722. Cherub heads and a cartouche in folds. – Many classical tablets on the W wall; e.g. Richard Maurice †1802. By *John Carline II* of Shrewsbury. Fulsome inscription on a wreath, and a book and gristly ornament at the foot. – Also Jane Bonnor †1830. By *William Spence* of Liverpool. Conventional weeping maiden and draped urn.

In the porch a WAR MEMORIAL of wood and copper, with Art Nouveau detail. Designed by *John Haughton Maurice Bonnor* (1875–1916) of the Bonnors of Bryn-y-Gwalia, Llangedwyn. He worked in an excellent Arts and Crafts manner, and his skills as a craftsman embraced jewellery, stained glass, sculpture and woodwork. His widow maintained his studio in Chiswick and its staff, and the War Memorial was carried out after his death. ALTAR RAILS in his memory were also posthumously executed to his design. The supports of the timber rails are panels of foliated trail, in brass. In the churchyard, E of the church, are two TOMBSTONES carved by *Bonnor*.

* Information from Mr Ian Allan.

They are those of his father, G. H. Bonnor †1912, and the latter's half-brother, R. M. Bonnor †1913.*

Also in the churchyard a graceful CROSS, 1886, commemorating Sir Watkin Williams-Wynn, sixth Baronet. Against the E wall of the church a CROSS SLAB, incised, with a circle in the head.

LLANGEDWYN HALL. Sir Watkin Williams-Wynn, of Wynnstay, third Baronet, inherited Llangedwyn on the death of his father-in-law, Sir Edward Vaughan, in 1718. The house, which is now the seat of the tenth Baronet, has had a complicated evolution. It is rendered, with cornice, sash windows and hipped gables, and a service range extends at an angle to the l. of the main S front. Extensive alterations and demolitions took place in the 1950s, before which the S front was of irregular E-plan, with three projecting wings, the recessed portion on the l., i.e. W of the central wing, twice the depth of that on the E. The entrance, with classical doorcase, was in the end of the central wing. It seems certain that this wing and the parts E of it represented the structure of an Elizabethan or Jacobean H-plan house, which underwent considerable enlargement and remodelling, probably in more than one stage, from, say, the late C17 to the mid-C18, involving both Vaughan and Williams-Wynn work.‡ The mid-C20 alterations included the removal of everything E of the central wing; i.e. what remains is one cross wing of the original building plus the westward extensions. The main entrance, with doorcase of 1959, is now on the E. A spacious well staircase, late C17 or very early C18, with string and turned balusters, was transferred from the demolished portion. Its present landing has timber cornice and enriched doorcases. The previous setting had good C18 plasterwork. A little heraldic plaster has been reused, and a minor staircase, also with string and turned balusters, remains *in situ* in the internal angle of the (former) central wing. Chimneypieces include one, *ex situ*, of grey marble with top volutes. Also a Victorian confection of marble and bronze.

The GARDENS are of particular interest in retaining features, including the TERRACING, of a late C17 or early C18 formal layout. The main parterre, E of the house, had fountains and a pyramid-roofed gazebo. Above is a narrow walled terrace against the hillside, and there are two further levels below. At the lowest stage was a bowling green. A further parterre lay W of the AVENUE, which is aligned on the former central wing and main entrance. Semicircular steps lead up to the house from a walled FORECOURT, which retains a version of its original oval sweep. At the opposite end of the

* Information on J. H. M. Bonnor was kindly supplied by Mrs C. Easton, his daughter. An appreciation by J. Romney Green appeared in *The Studio*, vol. 79, 1920.

‡ Sir Watkin comments that work by the third Baronet, c. 1725, included refenestration and the rendering of the brickwork, but there was not, he thinks, any alteration then to the shape of the house.

avenue (now replanted but whose original limes survived
until the late 1970s) is a fine set of iron GATES with overthrow, between rusticated PIERS with ball finials.

To the E, a stone-built octagonal structure comprising four
LOOSE BOXES. Segmental-arched doorways, circular openings
above, and a pointed roof. The paddock in which it stands
used to be divided by walls into four enclosures, with a loose
box opening from each.

The village lies in the delectable valley of the Tanat, and the
river is crossed by a late C18 or early C19 BRIDGE, of ashlar.
Broad segmental arch and broad pilaster strips. On the downstream side are niches and a dentil course.

PLAS UCHAF, on the hillside, ¾ m. WNW. A stylish early C18
house of brick with stone quoins. Hipped roof with modillion
cornice and hipped dormers. Six bays of windows, the central
two more widely spaced. On the ground floor these two
middle windows are narrower than the rest, and between
them is a doorway with bracketed hood.

Across the river are three buildings of note, here listed from E
to W:

HENDRE, on an elevated site ½ m. S of the church. Now a
stone-walled barn, with cottage attached, but preserving the
central arched-braced truss and lower-end partition of a cruck
hall house.

TÝ-NANT. Three-bay brick front, probably mid-C18, but still
with timber mullioned and transomed windows of two and
three lights.

HENBLAS. L-shaped. The front is faced with brick older than
the Georgian character suggests. Behind is a range which,
though now stone-clad, contains traces of a large C15
timber-framed hall house. There survives the upper part of
a central arched-braced cruck truss, now with a chimney
against it. Also the top of a box-framed spere-truss, with
speres (which had attached shafts and moulded caps) and
arched braces meeting a cambered tie-beam. Decorated
bosses and cusped wind-braces. Trusses in the front part of
the house, if *in situ*, belonged to an upper-end cross wing.
The subdivision of the hall, possibly *c.* 1600, was accompanied
by the insertion of a counterchanged ceiling of great complexity. Divided first into four compartments by two enormous beams crossing at right angles, then into twenty-eight
by secondary beams. These cells are in turn treated in chequer fashion with a system of joists – two joists running in
one direction crossed by a single one running in the other,
and the system reversed in alternate cells. Some chamfering
but no moulding.

LLWYN BRYN DINAS (SJ 172 247), 1 m. WNW of the village.
The steep-sided isolated hill, commanding the centre of the
Tanat Valley, is an ideal defensive site, and it is in fact
crowned by a single rampart with ditch and counterscarp
bank along the NW side. The rampart swings inwards along
either side of a natural gully which makes an easier approach;

there is some indication of a recessed guard chamber where the gate might have been. Recent excavations indicated Late Bronze Age metal working on site.

LLANGERNYW

ST DIGAIN. Unusual for Clwyd in being cruciform. The transepts and E arm are perhaps a late medieval enlargement of an earlier single chamber. Most features are Victorian, from the crested ridge tiles downwards, and including the N porch and flowing Dec transept windows. Work is known to have been done in 1849 by one of the Pensons, presumably *R. K. Penson*. The design of the three-light Perp E window is, though, authentic, and the arched-braced roofs are old. So is the S doorway, reopened in 1881 to give access to a vestry. Beside it a STOUP. Present vestry 1898. – FONT. Perp. Quatrefoils in circles in squares on the bowl, and cusped panels on the stem. – Flat baluster-shaped C17 RAILS. – STAINED GLASS. S transept window by *Ballantine*. It commemorates Margaret (†1852), wife of H. R. Sandbach of Hafodunos. – MONUMENT. Samuel Sandbach †1851, and his wife Elizabeth †1859. Portrait medallions in a large pointed frame. According to Thomas it is 'by *Smith*, a deputy of Gibson'. – S of the church two PILLAR STONES, C7–9, with incised crosses. – LYCHGATE. Lintel dated 1745.

PONTFAEN, E of the village. A good-looking bridge, gently cambered, with three segmental arches, the middle one the largest.

In the road leading W from the church a pair of late C19 Hafodunos ESTATE COTTAGES. By *William & Segar Owen* of Warrington. Partly half-timbered, like much of their Port Sunlight work.

HAFODUNOS, $\frac{1}{2}$ m. WSW. Bought in 1831 by Samuel Sandbach, a Liverpool merchant and shipowner. The house was rebuilt for his son, Henry R. Sandbach, 1861–6, by *Sir Gilbert Scott*, at a cost of £30,000. Second in importance only to Kelham Hall, Nottinghamshire, among Scott's country houses, it is in the immediately recognizable style in which, for large buildings, he interpreted the principles and precepts of his own persuasive *Remarks on Secular and Domestic Architecture*. It is a Venetian-inspired style, with late C13 or early C14 detail, and is characterized by bold versatile massing and varied skylines. Much use is made of foliated stonecarving, particularly for the capitals of the slender shafts which profusely adorn windows. At Hafodunos, the walling is of brick, with diapering, and with stone dressings generous enough to imply polychromy. The S (garden) front is nearly symmetrical, with a 107 gabled projection either end, but with that on the r. having a canted bay, and the l. counterpart a smaller oriel rising from vaulting. Timber dormers. To the r. is a windowless octagon, suggesting a medieval kitchen, but built as a top-lit billiard room and to receive sculpture. On the E another oriel and, at the NE corner, a tall spired clock tower rising above the porch.* N front punctuated by traceried staircase windows and continued W as a service wing. Though lacking the grandeur and richness of Kelham, the interiors possess features typical of Scott's domestic style, e.g. Puginesque doors, and the main rooms along the S front have ribbed ceilings, marble and stone chimneypieces etc. Panelled and coved ceiling below the lantern of the billiard room. A central corridor running the length of the main block results in the solecism of separating the dining room in the SW corner from the service quarters. An arcade with polished granite shafts, foliated capitals and enriched cusped arches between the entrance hall in the NE corner and the corridor. Simpler arcade between corridor and staircase. Encaustic tiles, heraldic stained glass etc., and the staircase with iron balustrading. Simpler detailing upstairs, but there is elaborate woodwork in the bay windows. Early C17 secondary staircase, reused from the previous house. It has flat, shaped balusters, pierced and moulded, and a patterned string, and strapwork on the newels.

The house contained H. R. Sandbach's collection of sculpture, including items by *John Gibson*, with whom he and his first wife were on terms of friendship. She was a granddaughter of Gibson's early patron William Roscoe, of Liverpool. Gibson work built into the structure consisted of marble reliefs in the billiard room, now at the Walker Art Gallery. Also casts on the staircase and in an adjoining room, where, in addition, *Hector reproaching Paris* is after *Thorwaldsen*; these still remain.

At the W end of the S front a large CONSERVATORY, added 1883 by *Messenger & Co.*, under *J. Oldrid Scott*.

Gorgeous and luxuriantly-planted GROUNDS. Said to be by *Hooker*, but (whether referring to the botanist and horticulturist *Sir William Hooker* or his son *J. D. Hooker*) this seems improbable.

Single-storey ENTRANCE LODGE by *Scott*, in the same style as the house. Original oak and iron GATES.

BRYNGWYLAN, 1¾ m. NNE. A three-unit storeyed house, with chimney backing on to an outside cross passage. Stop-chamfered beams and joists framed in three stages, and a beautifully cut date inscription of 1589. At the rear a tiny COTTAGE, suggesting humble unit planning.

AINON CHAPEL, ⅜ m. W of Bryngwylan. 1862. Two windows between two doors in the gable end. Cottage at the rear, under the same roof.

On the B5382, 1 m. ESE, a small CHAPEL, with cottage under the same roof, and a graveyard.

---

*The topmost stage, with lantern and spirelet, has been removed.

LLANGOLLEN

The little town beside its salmon river has, since the late C18, been a haunt of travellers and tourists. Its two largest hotels were once the leading coaching inns; it is celebrated as the home of the Ladies of Llangollen, is steeped in the romance of the Holyhead Road, and since 1947 has enjoyed the glamour of its International Eisteddfod. Set below Dinas Bran in the much-admired Vale of Llangollen, and hailed by generations of writers as picturesque, its reputation takes some living up to, and it has disappointingly little to offer in the way of urban charm and character. Much of the centre belongs to a nevertheless interesting piece of mid-C19 town planning. The main shopping thoroughfare, CASTLE STREET, continues the axis of the bridge southwards. Together with a rectangular pattern of streets to the w, it belongs to a scheme of c.1860. An intended informally planned set of villas further w was never built. The idea was conceived by *Morris Roberts*, a local builder,* and the layout was probably designed by *W. H. Hill* of Oswestry. Previously, traffic crossing the Dee was deflected E (by way of Bridge Street, the old main road) into what is the historic core of the town, with winding streets between the river and Telford's new Holyhead Road, and with the church as its nucleus. Though façades have been rendered, BRIDGE STREET remains largely Georgian. Datestones of 1764 and 1775. CHURCH STREET has a half-timbered survival.

ST COLLEN. W tower, nave, gabled aisles, and a chancel flanked by short aisles forming vestry and organ chamber. It was double-naved, without eastern division, before a remodelling by *S. Pountney Smith*, 1864–7, in which the s aisle and chancel and chancel aisles were added. A NW vestry came in 1876. The tower, mid-C18, with round-headed openings and urns as pinnacles, was not such as to endear itself to Mid-Victorian taste. *The Builder* remarked that it would 'require considerable outlay to make [it] worthy of the new work', and Smith merely formed a Gothic window and a new w entrance in its base. An E.E. s doorway, retained *in situ* in the new aisle, has groups of shafts in two rectangularly arranged orders. Corner shafts keeled, and arch mouldings continuing the same profile. Elementary foliated caps are similar to early C13 ones at Valle Crucis (q.v.). Perp N arcade with octagonal piers and four four-centred arches. A fragmentary arch at the E end is of the 1860s. Smith renewed the aisle windows, though in part to previous designs. The former Perp E window was apparently reproduced in the new chancel aisle. A pre-Perp aisle may have existed, for the design of the present easternmost window is authentic, and of earlier character. Also, a nearby C14 TOMB RECESS is probably *in situ*. It is heavily moulded and has a cinquefoil inner arch, and a group of short

* According to Miss Sara Pugh Jones.

shafts with fleurons in their caps. Crocketed gable and end pinnacles.

Fine late medieval roofs in the nave and N aisle, their members beautifully moulded. Hammerbeam trusses (which hardly function as such) alternate with principals which have collars but no arched-bracing. Much carving, especially in the nave. Bosses, angels, cusping above the hammerbeams. Cornice of trail motif, and linenfold frieze. Masks, beasts and figures, and both secular and sacred subjects at the feet of the alternate trusses. The two easternmost hammerbeam bays are very elaborately treated. Many of their members are enriched, and at collar level is an exquisite panelled ceiling of filigree Celtic intricacy. The nave roof is said, most improbably, to have come from Valle Crucis. Curious wall-post brackets do suggest the possibility of some post-Reformation re-assembly, but there is no other evidence of importation apparent, and nave and aisle roofs seem to belong together.

Gigantic and exuberant Victorian FONT. – REREDOS. 1876–8, carved by *Earp*, and given by R. B. Hesketh of Gwrych (q.v.). – Iron CHANCEL SCREEN, 1902. – STAINED GLASS. In the porch a light of 1833, still in pictorial transparency style. – N aisle E. 1849. According to Thomas it is by Rowland of Warwick, presumably meaning *Holland*. – E window by *Done & Davies*, 1867. (VH) – (In the N chancel aisle a window by *Alexander Gibbs*, 1879. – By the same, Baker memorial window, S aisle, commemoration date 1875.) – MONUMENTS. A BRASS to Margaret Trevor †1663. By *Silvanus Crue*. – Susanna Price. By *Joseph Turner*, 1796. Urn on a corbelled-out casket. – Lady Eleanor Butler and Sarah Ponsonby, the Ladies of Llangollen (*see* Plas Newydd, below). Of 1937, at the expense of Dr Mary Gordon, feminist, disciple of Jung, and author of a biographical novel about the Ladies. Relief portraits, for which the donor and the sculptor, *Violet Labouchere*, were the models. – ROYAL ARMS. Post-1801 Hanoverian. Painted panel.

In the churchyard, and designed by *Thomas N. Parker*, the triangular Gothic TOMBSTONE of the Ladies of Llangollen and their housekeeper. Erected following the death of the latter in 1809.

ST JOHN (Welsh Church), Abbey Road. Built 1858 as a cemetery chapel. Cusped lancets and a small W bellcote. – Marble FONT of 1796 from the parish church. Small bowl on a slender column.

BAPTIST CHAPEL, Castle Street. 1860. Two-storey front of brick with stone dressings. Three arches on pilasters beneath a pediment. Round-headed openings more Romanesque than Italianate.

Former PRITCHARD MEMORIAL BAPTIST CHAPEL, Abbey Road. 1895 by *John Wills* of Derby. (CW) Brick and stone. Gothic. A corner steeple was demolished c. 1979.

GLANRAFON CONGREGATIONAL CHAPEL, Princess Street. The main elevation faces the river and is stuccoed Italianate, pedimented, with Corinthian pilasters, round-headed windows and margin panes. Of 1902–3, and astonishingly retrograde, even by the standards of chapel architecture.

METHODIST CHURCH, Princess Street. 1903 by *W. & J. Morley & Son*. (CW) Churchy-looking, of stone, with transepts, polygonal apse, octagonal spire, and Geometrical tracery.

SEION METHODIST CHAPEL, Berwyn Street. Stone and Ruabon brick. The windows are in two storeys, but Gothic. Built 1903,* and with typical detail of the period.

REHOBOTH WELSH PRESBYTERIAN (CALVINISTIC METHODIST) CHAPEL, Victoria Square. Round-arched stone front of 1874. Of the sort with one-bay hipped wings either side of a gabled centre.

TOWN HALL, Castle Street. 1867 by *Lloyd Williams & Underwood*. Gothic, with tall roof, plate tracery, and some polished granite shafts. Originally with a market hall at street level. The end elevation is the more lively.

POLICE STATION, Parade Street. Next to the Town Hall, and also by *Lloyd Williams & Underwood*, 1867. Simpler Gothic.

OLD TOWN HALL, or SHIRE HALL, Victoria Square. Now Eisteddfod Office. Built 1835 in blunt C17 vernacular. Is it survival or revival?

LIBRARY, Parade Street. 1970–2 by *R. A. C. MacFarlane* and *E. Langford Lewis*, successive Denbighshire County Architects. A building of quality and character. Sixteen-sided, and faced with rough-textured reconstructed stone. Only the lower storey has windows, and they are pointed, with shallow triangular heads. The impression is not so much medieval as early industrial. Galleried interior with a branching staircase. Timber ceiling and radiating beams.

SCHOOL, Regent Street. 1840, with alterations and additions of 1871, including a flabby Gothic tower.

SCHOOL, East Street. 1874. Polychromatic brick and other High Victorian traits. Margin panes too, for the architect was the chapel specialist *Richard Owens*. (VH)

Former SCHOOL, Brook Street. 1846. Like the preceding, this was built as a British (i.e. non-Church) School, and it is chapel-like. Two superimposed Venetian windows, and a doorway either side of the lower one.

BRIDGE. Four unequal pointed arches, each with two chamfered arch rings. Tradition ascribes a bridge to the first Bishop Trevor of St Asaph in the mid-C14, though one existed in the C13, and the present structure is probably *c.*1500. It was widened on the upstream side in 1873 and, sadly but perhaps necessarily, again in 1968–9. The now defunct railway impinged heavily on the riverside scene, and a further span, with castellation, was added as a RAILWAY BRIDGE, 1863. It was remodelled in the last widening, and an adjoining castellated tower had earlier been demolished, though the nearby STATION remains.

* I owe the date to Miss Pugh Jones.

The LLANGOLLEN CANAL (*see* p. 197) is to the N. Near it the early C19 castellated front of SIAMBR WEN in Wern Road overlooks the town. Rendered, with Gothic windows and slender corner turrets. (Set in an outbuilding, fragments of two early C14 SEPULCHRAL SLABS, with vine trail and inscriptions, and one with intertwined dragons.)

WOODLANDS HOTEL, Mill Street. Built beside the river, as the vicarage, 1816, but sold for the railway to be cut through the grounds. Roughcast. Hipped roofs and soffited eaves, and symmetrical on both fronts.

In Queen Street a Holyhead Road TOLLHOUSE. T-plan, the front wing with the usual splayed corners.

PLAS NEWYDD, Butler Hill. The story of the Ladies of Llangollen is well known. *Lady Eleanor Butler* (1739–1829) and *Miss Sarah Ponsonby* (1755–1831), both of noble Irish families, left their homes together in 1778. After touring in Wales, they settled in 1780 in what was then a three-bay stone-built cottage which they renamed Plas Newydd. Professedly living in retirement from the world, they moved in local society, received successions of distinguished visitors *en route* to and from Ireland, espoused eccentricity, and made it their business to become a legend in their lifetime.

The gradual transformation of the house and the treatment of the grounds was in strongly romantic spirit. A right-hand extension of the front contains a Gothic library, canted at the rear. The earlier part received Gothic windows, including three oriels, below which the porch and two tripartite canopies display some of the fruits of the Ladies' mania for collecting carved oak. Pieces from Jacobean furniture were pressed into service, but much else besides, British and continental, Gothic and Renaissance, ecclesiastical and secular. The porch and door are a riot of fragments, and the tiny entrance hall and the staircase are indescribably encrusted. So too is the Oak Room, which in addition has Spanish leather, and is dated 1814 above the fireplace. More carving in the library and upstairs. In every room there is stained glass, again of diverse dates and origins.

In 1876 Plas Newydd was bought by General John Yorke, of the Erddig family. He devotedly enlarged and embellished it, and fostered the cult of the Ladies. It had passed through the hands of *Richard Lloyd Williams*, whom he may have employed as architect, though it is more probable that *Yorke* did his own designing. He added a long gabled and half-timbered rear wing, intensively enriched outside and in with yet more carved oak, both new and imported. He also gave the overall black-and-white treatment to the main front, which had hitherto remained whitewashed stone. Later the front was further extended to the r., but this addition and, most regrettably, the Yorke wing itself were demolished in 1963, and the ornament from the latter dispersed. Of work executed by *Yorke* himself, there remains carving in the pedimented sham doorway on the left-hand gable end return.

GARDENS. A parterre is of late C19 and early C20 evolution, and was planned in relation to the full length of the now curtailed front. Part of the shaft of the C15 CHESTER HIGH CROSS, and a GORSEDD CIRCLE of 1908. Fields extended up to the front of the house in the Ladies' time. They had a garden behind. Also, with wild planting, rustic timber bridges, and pools and cascades, they developed the potential of THE GLEN, a deep dell containing a stream. Essentially complete by c. 1800, this was an early instance of the picturesque at its more extreme. No recognizable original features remain except a Gothic NICHE, with screen walls and seats, and containing a FONT said to come from Valle Crucis.

J. C. Loudon in his *Encyclopaedia of Gardening*, 2nd ed., 1824, wrote of Plas Newydd: 'An elegant residence fitted up in the cottage style, and the grounds beautifully laid out by the elegant and accomplished proprietors.'

Scant respect has been shown to the memory of General Yorke. THE HERMITAGE, a house which he built nearby, has also been demolished.

CASTELL DINAS BRAN, ¾ m. NE of the town and 750 ft above it. The ruins on their commanding hilltop are the distinguishing landmark to which the Vale of Llangollen has owed much of its romantic appeal. A C13 native castle, possibly built by Gruffydd ap Madoc (†1270), son of the founder of Valle Crucis Abbey. In the war of 1277 it was burnt by the Welsh themselves. Although it was included in Edward I's grant of Bromfield and Yale to John de Warenne, Earl of Surrey, in 1282, a new castle was built at Holt (q.v.), and Dinas Bran remained abandoned. On the E and S are deep ditches, but not on the precipitous N and W sides. The curtain walls enclosed a roughly rectangular area, aligned E–W. Gatehouse at the N end of the E side, with two towers (the southern one retaining its barrel-vaulted lower room). The entrance passage may have been rib-vaulted. A rectangular block at the S end of the E side, separated from the rest of the works by its own ditch, was the keep. Indications of the stair which would have led to its main room. Cutting across the line of the S curtain is a Welsh D-tower. Its inner part stands to a fair height, and E of it is a length of curtain with two windows, eroded into great gashes, probably marking the site of the hall. At its W end the S curtain contained a postern.

The summit now occupied by the medieval castle was originally the site of an Iron Age HILLFORT. It appears to have been a fort with a large rampart with external ditch and internal quarry ditch. Only the southern and eastern sides have survived the later remodelling.

PLAS DINBREN, ¾ m. N. Stuccoed. Seven bays and a pedimented doorcase. (The doorcase is dated 1820. Portions of a timber-framed house survive in a rear wing. NMR)

Beside the canal at Pentrefelin, 1 m. NNW, was the terminus of a TRAMWAY, built in 1852, serving slate quarries above the Horseshoe Pass. Belonging to it a stone-faced embankment, pierced with arches, set back from the opposite side of the road near the B5103 junction. Near the site of the quay, a *Telford* CANAL BRIDGE, with elliptical arch, typical of a number still surviving on this branch.

PENGWERN, $\frac{7}{8}$m. SE. The house, facing W, is C17, much altered. H-plan, with lateral chimney. Medieval work in the present FARM BUILDINGS. The main range, running N–S, has a flat-headed three-light Dec window in its S end. Also a single-light cusped window on the E side and one of two lights on the W, together with a pointed doorway. A short and narrow two-storey range forms a link with the house. Its lower room has a stone barrel-vault on chamfered ribs, and springers show that a similar arrangement existed above.

TYNDWR, $1\frac{1}{8}$m. ESE. A substantial villa of *c.*1866–70, now a youth hostel. Some brick with stone dressings, and the upper storeys almost entirely half-timbered. A little early for true vernacular feel, the black-and-white being spiky, and the detailing of the masonry Gothic. Service wing at an angle, with a tower at the junction and a gable marking a first-floor billiard room.* Gothic staircase, but there are features of greater character and elaboration, suggesting that the fitting up and decorating were entrusted to a different designer. Exuberant and freely designed chimneypieces, incorporating Jacobean motifs. That in the drawing room is of marble, and there is a massive one in the billiard room. Plasterwork, stained glass etc., and in the hall a panelled ceiling. Good doors and ceilings extend to the bedrooms.

VIVOD. *See* Berwyn.

LLANGWM

ST JEROME. A rebuilding or remodelling of 1747 is recorded, and a restoration and refurnishing of 1873–4. Round-headed S windows must be of the earlier date, and pointed N ones could be so as well. Structurally a single chamber, but there is a plastered C18 chancel arch, rusticated and depressed, on pilasters. A ceiling in the chancel. The E window and the exposing of the nave roof may be ascribed to 1873–4. Set over the N porch is the shield of a C14 heraldic SEPULCHRAL SLAB. – STAINED GLASS. E window by *Ward & Hughes*, 1882. – MONUMENT. Robert Wynne †1757. The elements include three cherub heads against an obelisk.

A stream runs through the village, crossed by a tiny BRIDGE.

GARTHMEILIO, $\frac{1}{2}$m. WNW. An H-plan house, doubtless early C17 in origin, successively enlarged and altered. The front is a remodelling in C19 Tudor, looking *c.*1830–40, though family history suggests a somewhat earlier date.‡ Once it was rendered, with labels and heavy finials, and it still has wavy

---

* Beyond this point there seems to have been some alteration or addition, made before 1890.

‡ As Mr and Mrs D. H. Griffith explained.

cusped bargeboards, windows with stepped lights in the gables, margin panes and a Gothic entrance loggia of timber. Some work of this period inside, and also of the early or mid-C18, especially a dog-leg staircase, its lower flights with dado, swept rail and columnar balusters. A crude C17 staircase has pierced shaped balusters.

LLANGWYFAN 1060

ST CWYFAN. An endearing little single chamber, rendered. Victorian crested ridge tiles surmount its wobbly roof, but it escaped Camdenian restoration. A N window (two segmental-headed lights) is dated 1684, and the S porch 1714. W bellcote of two piers spanned by a flagstone. Vaguely Gothic E window, and the plastered interior is of rustic Georgian character, with curved ceiling (presumably concealing late medieval timbers), reeded window surrounds, and BOX PEWS. – Baluster FONT, its bowl decorated with Biblical scenes and angel heads. – STAINED GLASS. E window by *Alexander Gibbs*, commemoration date 1853.

Outside the churchyard are, unexpectedly, STOCKS. No village, but the church was joined in its hillside isolation by the former LLANGWYFAN HOSPITAL. Built 1918–20, as a sanatorium, forming part of the Welsh memorial to Edward VII, and closed 1981. Neo-Georgian, by *T. Taliesin Rees*. The main building, brick and roughcast, has pediment-like gables either end, and hipped dormers.

VRON IW, ¼m. N. A rebuilding, c.1906, by *Percy Scott Worthington*, with date inscriptions of 1655 relating to a predecessor house.* Very simple in its elevations. Battered chimneys express the underlying Arts and Crafts character.

LLANGYNHAFAL 1060

The church is on the lower slopes of Moel Fama, with a farm and the partly half-timbered PLAS-YN-LLAN (where Wordsworth stayed with his friend Robert Jones) as neighbours.

ST CYNHAFAL. Vale of Clwyd type, Perp and double-naved. Whitewashed when seen by Glynne in 1864 and now rendered. At the W end the S nave has a diminishing rectangular bellcote, and the N nave a round-headed C18 window. Uniform S windows and a differing one on the N; and, as usual, the two E windows differ. Both have sub-arches and panel tracery, but the northern is two-centred and of four lights, whereas the other, with cusping, is four-centred and has five lights. S doorway with the figure of an ecclesiastic in the

---

* Information from Mr W. J. Oliver. The house is not to be confused with another in Denbighshire which Worthington designed for a relation, Dugald Scott, and which has not been identified.

hollow of its moulding. The porch dates from a restoration of 1869–70. Five-bay arcade with octagonal piers. In the roofs, tentative hammerbeam trusses (on which a few angels remain) alternate with principals which have masks at their feet and curved collars. Moulded purlins and rafters. In the N nave cusped struts above the collars, and above the wall-plate a frieze of cusped and traceried panels. In the s a cornice of elongated tracery. – Plain octagonal FONT. – REREDOS. Of 1902, incorporating old wood, some of which, with vine trail, seems to be roof timbering. Above is a PELICAN in her Piety, said to be C17, though that at Llanrhaeadr-yng-Nghinmeirch (q.v.) is of 1762. – PULPIT. 1636.* Arched panels, and carved ones which include a lion, cockatrice and pelican. – LECTERN. Brass, and a rather splendid piece. Latter commemoration date 1882. – Fluted columnar RAILS, C18, round three sides of the altar. – C17 BOX PEW with open arcading and turned balusters. – Other PEWS characteristic of *Arthur Baker*, who carried out a restoration in 1884. – MONUMENTS. Several Neo-Classical tablets, the biggest the Jones monument by *J. Blayney* of Chester. Latest commemoration date 1836. – Thomas Davies †1829. By *Edmund Ashcroft* of Liverpool. Draped urn. – Plank CHEST. – The CHURCHYARD seems to have been circular.

At TŶ-COCH, ⅜ m. NW, is a C17 BARN with four cruck trusses. Tie and collar beams. Walls with timber framing, brick-nogged.

PLAS DRAW, ¾ m. s. Stuccoed front. The centre is of two and a half storeys, and above the ground floor it is of three bays punctuated by two pairs of pilasters carrying a pediment. First-floor windows with moulded surrounds, and the middle one pedimented. Two-storey wings. This is all a refacing, probably early C19, of an early or mid-C18 brick façade, the windows of which had stone keystones and aprons. The pilasters occupy the position of former windows, as the five-bay ground storey still indicates. Of the earlier period are quoins, and the doorway with fluted keystone. Also a compact well staircase, with dado, swept rail, and columnar newels and balusters. Attractive group of former FARM BUILDINGS, including a partly half-timbered range and a stone barn.

HENDRE'R YWYDD UCHAF. A late C15 five-bay cruck house, retaining its timber-framed outer walls, is now at St Fagan's.

LLANHYCHAN
¾ m. ESE of Llanynys

ST HYCHEN. A single chamber. Perp W doorway, moulded and four-centred. Also an arched-braced roof, with diagonal struts

---

* According to Thomas. This date cannot be seen on the pulpit, but it does appear on one of a set of panels in the reredos.

above the collar, and cusped wind-braces. A restoration of 1877–8 by *Arthur Baker* was paid for John Taber (*see* Clwyd Hall, below). Baker seems to have changed the disposition of windows, but in rebuilding the s wall reused a three-light one dated 1626. His timber-framed s porch had a predecessor, though of course without the cusped bargeboards and Nesfieldian pies. The E window and its STAINED GLASS are of 1925, the gift of (Sir) Crosland Graham of Clwyd Hall and his first wife, as a thank offering. The glass, by *J. Dudley Forsyth*, includes a portrayal of the donors, nimbed, and their son. – Second window from E on the N obviously by *Kempe*; commemoration date 1891. – Octagonal baluster FONT. – Woodwork, probably from a former wagon ceiling over the sanctuary, with cusping and tracery, is worked into the REREDOS of 1846 and READING DESK of 1730. – Good brass LECTERN of 1899. – C18 columnar RAILS. – Brass CANDLESTICKS on desk and pulpit. – COMMANDMENT BOARDS. – MONUMENTS. Some competent classical tablets of the second quarter of the C18, but all with poor lettering.

No village. Next to the church the former SCHOOL, by *Lloyd Williams & Underwood*, 1866. Brick, with stone dressings. Traceried windows and a bellcote and chimney combined. The teacher's house is included in the composition.

CLWYD HALL, originally called CLAREMONT, ¾m. SSE. 1867–9 by *Lloyd Williams & Underwood*, for John Taber, a London wine merchant. The grounds and buildings, now much changed, were created as a very complete Victorian domain, with LODGE GATES, STABLES, WALLED GARDENS and VINERIES, as well as PLEASURE GARDENS. Even the outer boundary wall formed part of the operations. *Ewing* of Chester laid out the grounds. The house – a villa rather than a mansion – had a conservatory floored with *Maw* tiles; stone-carving was executed by *Edward Griffith* of Chester, and the fitting up and decorating was by no less than *J.G. Crace*. The house, of brick with stone dressings, has straight-headed mullioned and transomed windows with labels. Otherwise it is fully Gothic in feel, asymmetrical and with a tower. The tower, the tank in which supplied both house and gardens, originally had an oriel above the entrance, a band of half-timbering at the top, and a crested spire. Early alterations included the extending of the s (entrance) front to the r., possibly *c.*1880; and on the w front an addition was made above a single-storey wing at the N end. This upper room has panelling, a wagon roof and embossed fireplace tiles, and is possibly by *Arthur Baker*. The conservatory has vanished, and in the 1920s Sir Crosland Graham reduced and remodelled the tower and made internal alterations. Except perhaps for parquet flooring, little or nothing by Crace remains. The flowing staircase balustrade of wrought iron, rich in flowers and leafage, is a *Lloyd Williams & Underwood* design, executed by *Thomas*, a Denbigh blacksmith.

Former RECTORY, ½m. SE. A three-bay house of 1785, with

alterations of 1927, for which Sir Crosland Graham was responsible.

(PLAS-YN-RHOS, $\frac{5}{8}$m. ESE. H-plan, though the centre and cross wings are probably of different periods. A beam dated 1594, with Welsh inscription. Also date inscriptions of 1611 and 1621, the latter on a heavily carved overmantel which may be *ex situ*. Timber-framed BARN.*)

PLAS LLANYCHAN, $\frac{1}{2}$m. SSE. 1881 by *Arthur Baker*, with John Taber as client. Brick and half-timber, with traceried bargeboards. Foundations of a predecessor house were used, and as a result difficulty was met in fitting in the staircase. A feature was made of its soffit, carried through into an adjoining room as an oak canopy on turned posts. Baker ruefully recalled that the device lost him a commission, rumour having identified him as the mythical architect who forgot the stairs.

GLAN CLWYD, $\frac{5}{8}$m. S. This was a timber-framed house of 1619. Remodelled, but the original two-unit plan is discernible. It had lateral chimney, inside cross passage, and a lower-end room with end chimney. Post-and-panel partition.

LLANNERCH HALL *see* TREFNANT

1020 # LLANRHAEADR-YM-MOCHNANT

ST DOGFAN. The site of a *clas* or Celtic monastery. The present church has a W tower, its battered base of indeterminate date, and its upper stage, with obelisk pinnacles, C18. No chancel arch, and the building was a lengthy single chamber until three-bay chancel aisles were added. Some eastward extension also took place, though not the full length of the chancel, for at least the westernmost bay of the aisle arcades was cut through earlier walling. Arcade piers, with brattished caps, are largely C19. The N aisle E window, straight-headed, is probably Dec, though the easternmost bay of the chancel has a wagon ceiling of Perp date, panelled, and with crow's foot bosses. Its section is continued W by a plaster vault, and it is remarkable that this survived Victorian restoration, especially as it conceals medieval timbers.‡ In 1872 Lloyd Williams and Underwood referred to all windows except the N aisle E having been spoilt in a restoration, and much was done by *W. H. Spaull*, 1879–82. A N porch is his, as are the E and the S aisle S windows, and the raised chancel floor with ENCAUSTIC TILES. – FONT. Dated 1663. – ALTAR TABLE. Dated 1749. – SEPULCHRAL SLAB. C9 or C10. Wheel cross of

---

* Lady Graham informed me that the house was altered by Sir Crosland to serve as a bailiff's residence, but that it was never used as such.

‡ The Rev. J. E. Jones told me this.

Celtic type, with fragments of a Latin inscription. Spiral ornament in the upper spandrels. Plait pattern l. of the shaft, and fret on the r. – SCULPTURAL FRAGMENTS. Part of a cylindrical shaft, C9 or C10, with angular fret. – Fragments of a Romanesque shrine. Comparable with that at Pennant Melangell of c. 1160 (see The Buildings of Wales: Powys). – Part of a small effigy of a praying woman, in relief. – A number of MONUMENTS, e.g. Sydney Bynner †1694. Crude architectural frame and skull and cross bones.

The parish is celebrated as the place where Bishop William Morgan worked on his translation of the Bible into Welsh during his incumbency (1578–88). Dr William Worthington, vicar 1747–78, was an early devotee of romantic fashion, for he built SHAM RUINS, no longer in evidence, on high ground s of the church. The VICARAGE, E of the church, where Dr Johnson visited him, dates partly from his time. The front, though, is of 1852, and the core much older. (The Rev. J. E. Jones mentioned hidden traces of crucks.)

SCHOOL, E of the vicarage. Neo-Tudor, of 1858. Window of stepped lights in a central gable, and girls' and boys' entrances under smaller gables either side.

N of the church the WYNNSTAY ARMS. 'In the modern Gothic style', thought Borrow, who stayed there. Ornamented bargeboards and a storeyed porch with timber columns. The village, though not large, has an urban air. Its w end is in Montgomeryshire, across a BRIDGE of c.1770 over the Rhaeadr. On the Montgomeryshire side is a huddle of chapels and cottages. SEION METHODIST CHURCH, by Shayler & Ridge, 1904 (CW), in a massive Arts and Crafts Gothic, has two stumpy towers and bold buttressing down the sides.

TAN-Y-FFORDD, 1⅛m. WNW. In the FARM BUILDINGS are two cruck trusses, surviving from a timber-framed hall house. A chimney, with long ingle beam, has been built into one of them, doubtless at what was the cross passage end.

CAPEL CARMEL, 1⅝m. WNW. A tiny vernacular chapel, with central entrance in a three-bay longitudinal elevation. Built 1836, enlarged 1861, according to the inscription.

PISTYLL RHAEADR, 3¾m. WNW. A famous waterfall, and a sight which Dr Worthington (see above) appreciated, for he built a shelter, or cottage, nearby. This was, wrote Torrington, 'for tea drinking'. Sir Watkin Williams-Wynn, fifth Baronet (1789–1840), was responsible for the present COTTAGE, a splendid essay in the rustic picturesque. Rubble walling, and a tetrastyle portico, its columns unwrought tree trunks, and its pediment faced with bark. With the cottage happily restored from dereliction for use as a café, the site is again 'for tea drinking'. External restoration was commendably faithful, involving little change, but exposed masonry now predominates in what previously was a plain plastered interior with simple Gothic touches.

(TOMEN Y MAERDY, 2m. SE. A motte and ditch. There was an enclosure SE of the mound.)

HENBLAS. *See* Llangedwyn.

TŶ-NANT. *See* Llangedwyn.

A fine MENHIR stands at the SE end of the village (SJ 125 259). It has had a chequered history and is not in its original position. Tradition states that it came originally from further up the valley (SJ 11 31) near Maengwynedd. In the C18 it was set up by the vicar, i.e. Dr Worthington, on a mound in the village, then when the school was built it was moved to the road and used as a lamp-post until 1925. The stone has a Latin inscription added by Worthington in 1770 and was also used as a milestone, 26 m. from Shrewsbury and 180 m. from London.

Another tall STANDING STONE at the centre of the valley floor, $1\frac{1}{8}$ m. SE (SJ 138 248), is said to have been moved in 1772 from a site at the head of the valley near Pistyll Rhaeadr. However, air photographs have recently revealed Bronze Age sites in this area between the two rivers, so it is possible that this stone might be in its original position. Folklore relates that the stone, draped in a red cloth, was used to lure a troublesome flying serpent to its death.

The Denbighshire boundary runs along the crest of the Berwyns, and many of the peaks are marked by CAIRNS of Bronze Age date (many of them now with small modern cairns atop). A cremation burial in a food vessel has been found in the most northerly cairn, on Moel Ferna (SJ 118 398), but, though the others have obviously been disturbed, there are no records of any other finds. The central spine, between Cadair Bronwen (SJ 077 346) and Moel Sych (SJ 066 319), has four cairns, one of which contains a lot of quartz (SJ 072 327), while part of the kerb can be recognized at Moel Sych. The most southerly cairn at SJ 041 309 has been very badly ruined. Less prominent cairns can be seen in the pass, Bwlch Maen Gwynedd (SJ 080 337), and in the valley below Moel Sych, which contains an interesting monument group, RHOS Y BEDDAU (SJ 059 302), with stone circle, avenue and kerb cairn. This is just in Montgomeryshire, and is more fully described under Llanrhaeadr-ym-Mochnant in *The Buildings of Wales: Powys*.

0060   LLANRHAEADR-YNG-NGHINMEIRCH

30   ST DYFNOG. A characteristically double-naved Vale of Clwyd church. A battlemented and unbuttressed W tower to the S part. Except perhaps for the tower doorway, no features are pre-Perp. Stained glass dates of 1508 and 1533 may either or both represent the Perp remodelling, or stages of it. Timber-framed N porch, with arched opening, ornamented tie-beam, and in the gable a niche with (renewed) canopy work. Also cusped and traceried side openings, an arched-braced truss and (though possibly not authentic) elaborate bargeboards. Both nave E windows are four-centred, with

five lights, two two-light sub-arches, panel tracery and cusping, though they differ in outline and the southern one has a transom at springing level. A single-light s window marks the site of the roof loft. Inappropriate Y-traceried N windows date either from *Arthur Baker*'s restoration of 1879–80, or from very shortly after. Four-bay arcade with crude octagonal piers. Nave roofs arched-braced, with cusped struts above the collars and alternate trusses with hammerbeams bearing angels. Moulded rafters and purlins, carved bosses, and a frieze of cusped and traceried panelling. Part of the N roof is simpler, and apparently renewed. The two easternmost bays of the southern one have a wagon ceiling following the curve of the arched-braces, with cusped and traceried panels, bosses, vine trail etc.

Some typical *Baker* FURNISHINGS, including refinedly Neo-Jacobean STALLS. – FONT. Probably C17. – REREDOS. By *C. M. O. Scott*, 1930. – A carved PELICAN, of 1762, was formerly above the altar, as at Llangynhafal (q.v.). – STAINED GLASS. In the N nave E window is some of the finest glass in Wales, a wonderfully complete Jesse. Dated 1533 at the foot of the fifth light. It is said to have been hidden during the Civil War and put back in 1661. The curving stems form subdivisions and frame the Virgin and Child at the head of the centre light within a vesica. Full-length figures in the centre light. Those in the side lights (for some of which the same cartoons were used, reversed) emerge from flowers. Renaissance spirit is heralded in luxuriant flowers and foliage. In the tracery are four prophets, and also some patchwork, with fragments from other windows. – N nave W. Fragments (including a date of 1508), partly of an Annunciation. Found at a farmhouse in the parish c.1830, and possibly from the S nave E window. – Dugout CHEST to which a pillar POORBOX has been attached. – MONUMENTS. Maurice Jones of Llanrhaeadr Hall †1702. Attributable to *Robert Wynne*. Large and Baroque. Reclining bewigged effigy, and curtains draped from an arch, all between a pair of Corinthian columns. Much higher is a segmentally-curving canopy surmounted by urns. Gadrooning, heraldry, volutes etc., and four good-sized putti. – Watkins Edwards Wynne †1796. Severely Neo-Classical. Weeping female recessed in an oval.

Overlooking the churchyard, and approached from it between stone GATEPIERS, is a single-storey row of ALMSHOUSES. Built in 1729 by Jane, widow of Maurice Jones (of the sumptuous monument) and daughter of Sir Walter Bagot of Blithfield. Three-gabled front, of whitewashed brick and stone, with cross wings and a central arch. Diamond glazing belongs to alterations made by Lord Bagot in 1820. From the churchyard a bridge leads to FFYNNON DYFNOG in the adjoining wood. A spring and rectangular bath tank.

LLANRHAEADR HALL, ¼ m. E. Schemes for rebuilding were prepared by *Robert Adam* for Richard Parry, who had inherited in 1759. Nothing came of these, and instead the old house was, in the 1770s, altered and enlarged, with a new range by an unknown architect added at the rear. The old part, probably C16 rather than C17, was shown by Moses Griffith as having cross wings, coped gables, and mullions and transoms. It was remodelled, 1841-2, by the younger *Thomas Penson*, in his distinctive Jacobean style, in ashlar, with pediments to some of the windows, and scrolly shaped gables. He formed an E-plan front, with storeyed porch and with a loggia (removed *c*.1939) extending between the wings. His side elevation, to the r., is also symmetrical, but meets a canted bay which is the return of the seven-bay 1770s range. This C18 work has rubble walling which was (see the raised dressings) or was meant to be rendered. Features inside include a mahogany staircase with dado, swept rail, and Adamish ornament on the stair ends. Also a good chimneypiece in the drawing room. Of Neo-Jacobean work by *Penson* in the front part of the house, there is a ceiling and a staircase, though only its upper flights survive. His transformation was superficial, for the entrance hall is C18, and there are two roof trusses, one with arched-bracing and struts above the collar, being the central and a partition truss of a former first-floor hall. Wind-braces also.

Group of BARNS, LAUNDRY and STABLES. The latter, of the 1770s, have a cupola and three-bay pediment, and the centre recessed between two-bay wings.

An ambitious scheme for the GROUNDS was prepared, 1771, by *Emes*. Though it was not fully implemented, something must have been done, for in 1784 that not uncritical observer Lord Torrington noted that Mr Parry's 'plantations and laying out of his grounds bespeak him a man of taste.' A later AVENUE, aligned on the entrance front, was severed by a by-pass road in 1971. The piers and strapwork balustrading of *Penson*'s LODGE GATES were resited, but the lodge itself was subsequently demolished and the avenue replanted after succumbing to Dutch elm disease. Forecourt GATEPIERS by Penson remain *in situ*.*

VICARAGE, ¼m. SW. A beautifully neat stone-built house of 1820, restored by *Robert B. Heaton*, 1960-1, when later additions were removed. Three bays, with shallow recesses in the outer ones, and tripartite ground-floor windows. Low-pitched hipped roof and a central chimney. Both side elevations are asymmetrical, with off-centre gable. Simple but elegantly curving staircase. STABLE with cupola.

CARREG-Y-PENNILL, ⅝m. SSW. Storeyed porch with coped gable and Tudor-arched doorway. Some mullions and labels.

LLEWESOG HALL, 1¼m. SW. Rendered. A late C18 or early C19 front with one-bay pediment and tripartite windows. Rear wing with a shaped gable. (Late C17 staircase, with string, swept rail and heavy turned balusters of complex profile. NMR)

* Mr D. O. Winterbottom kindly communicated the results of his researches on Llanrhaeadr Hall.

LLANRHUDD

ST MEUGAN. The mother church of Ruthin, a mile or so from the town, and with no village of its own. A single chamber, with double W bellcote, and Perp in its earliest datable features. Arched-braced roof, with cusping to the wind-braces and the struts above the collars. Cusped struts also in the gable of the S porch. The S doorway looks late. Over-sized E window. This, and the westernmost on the N, must either or both belong to a restoration by *Kennedy* (VH) in 1852. A traceried four-light N window is dated 1626, though renewed. Unusually elaborate for C17 work in the Vale of Clwyd, it is similar to the E windows of some double-naved churches, and may not be *in situ*. In 1844 Glynne described it, perhaps erroneously, as being on the S.W gallery, dated 1721, with turned balusters. – Plain octagonal FONT. – ALTAR TABLE. C17. The front legs are beasts, supposedly lions. – ROOD SCREEN. Of Welsh type, i.e. framed entirely rectangularly, and with continuous middle rails. Open traceried heads, and tracery in wainscot panels, some of it pierced. Top beam with trail enrichment. – STAINED GLASS. Late C15 or early C16 quarries in second window from E on S. – Two vesical medallions in the E window by *Clayton & Bell*.* – Numerous MONUMENTS, mostly to the Thelwalls of Bathafarn. John Thelwall †1586 and wife Jane †1585. They kneel at a desk, facing each other, in a recess flanked by Corinthian columns. On a frieze below kneel ten sons and four daughters, all named and some holding skulls. – Ambrose Thelwall †1653. Bust, coloured, in a niche. He wears a ruff. Below is a tablet with volutes and fruit garlands. – John Thelwall †1664. Drapery above and either side. Heraldry and two cherub heads. – John Thelwall †1686. In the form of a banner, with drapery above and either side, and the tablet itself with simulated folds and a fringe. – Thomas Roberts †1708. Cartouche. Heraldry and cherub heads. – In the SE corner two Thelwall tablets at right angles, in massive surrounds. Broken pediments containing heraldry, and a cherub head where they meet. Painted inscriptions in which dates of 1670–1729 are legible. – Price monument. Draped urn of 1777, i.e. before it had become a Neo-Classical cliché. – Jemima Clough †1812. By *Sir Richard Westmacott*. Grecian tablet with inverted torches. – Stanley John Weyman, the author, who lived at Llanrhydd Hall, †1928. In the form of an open book. – CHURCHYARD CROSS. On each of the chamfered corners of the shaft is a tablet flower and mask head, much worn.

Opposite the church the entrance to LLANRHYDD HALL, with GATES attributable to *Robert Bakewell*. Shamefully neglected and now only fragmentary. At the time of writing the over-throw lies on the ground.

BATHAFARN HALL, ½m. E. Rendered. Three bays, pilasters,

pedimented doorcase and, on the right-hand return, a segmental bow. Moses Griffith showed it as a late C17 or early
C18 house, with solid parapets and seven bays of segment-
headed windows. Lewis referred to it as 'Grecian', so there
may have been an early C19 remodelling. Today there are
features and details which look early C20. A long C18 range
of brick FARM BUILDINGS, with a projecting wing either end.
The five-bay return of the right-hand wing has a cupola and
a three-bay pediment containing a clock. Single-storey ashlar
ENTRANCE LODGE, early C19. T-plan, the corners of the
upright stroke splayed. Against one splay a Tuscan porch,
with no entablature.

BATHAFARN FARM, ¼m. s of Bathafarn Hall. Late C18, of
brick. There were two storeys of Venetian windows, with
lunettes above, arranged in three irregularly spaced bays.
Now somewhat mutilated.

8060   LLANRWST*

ST GRWST. Once a single chamber and still with no structural
division between nave and chancel. The rood screen remains
in situ and, what is more, retains its loft. Perp s doorway and
some Perp windows, including the four-light E window with
panel tracery and brattished transom. Arched-braced roof
with small cusped wind-braces. Early C19 w tower, replacing
a weather-boarded bellcote. The s porch is a C19 rebuild.
The church was restored and a N aisle added in quiet and
conventionalized Perp by *Paley & Austin*, 1882–4. The work
included new rood-loft stairs. For the SE Gwydir Chapel,
see below. Some *Paley & Austin* FURNISHINGS, e.g. the
STALLS. – The ROOD SCREEN of c.1500 is something of a
hybrid – largely Welsh in its detail and ornament but English
in its construction, with vaulting and continuous uprights.
Some traceried openings in the wainscot panels and, in the
heads of the main divisions, elaborate filigree tracery depicting Emblems of the Passion and pigs eating acorns. On both
sides are canopies of tierceron vaultings plus an extended
panelled soffit. On the w side is a row of straight-sided pendant arches in front. Crested bressumers with vine trail and
acorn and oak-leaf bands terminate the rood-loft parapets.
The w parapet has vaulted niches and remains of canopy
work above and between them. – FONT. Bowl of weird
organic forms. Square on plan, on a later stem. Were it not
for the good state of preservation, a very early date might be
supposed. It is possibly C17. – Columnar turned RAILS. C18.
– MONUMENTS. Hughes monument by *C. Bromfield* of
Liverpool. Latest commemoration date 1767. Pedimented,
with doves and, at the foot, a cherub head. – In the chancel,
some C17 and C18 BRASSES. – Pre-1801 Hanoverian ROYAL
ARMS. A painted panel.

* Transferred to Gwynedd in 1974.

The Gwydir Chapel was added in 1633-4 by Sir Richard Wynn of Gwydir (*see The Buildings of Wales: Gwynedd*). With its fascinating contents it is a little treasure box of a chapel, in urbane Perp. Externally, the contrast with the more homely body of the church must have been even greater when the nave was towerless and whitewashed. Broad, of two bays, with pinnacles and embattled parapets. Panel tracery, and the main lights of the windows are cusped. Low-pitched camberbeam roof, panelled and with bosses. Only a round-headed doorway and details of the roof, particularly strap-work, betray the late date, though elliptically arched windows also hint at it. An over-wide arch with SCREENWORK separates chapel from chancel. – Other woodwork includes PANELLING with characteristic early C17 unmitred mouldings. It also has pierced and traceried patterns, Late Gothic in effect, though not in detail. – DESK FRONTS with guilloche are more thoroughly Jacobean, though grotesquely so, with pierced patterns in round-headed arches and funny heads as finials. – Further SCREENWORK, apparently reused from a PEW. – Also a READING DESK. – A stone COFFIN, with sunk quatrefoils, is said to be that of Llywelyn the Great †1240. – MONUMENTS. Hywel Coetmor, c.1440. Recumbent effigy in mail and plate armour, with sword. Head on cushion, lion at feet. – Sir John Wynn †1627 and wife Sydney, and also commemorating other members of the family. Remarkable for its barbaric exuberance. The main elements, creating a duality, are two obelisks adorned with trophies of war and peace and with heraldic finials. Equally archaic tablet between. Cherub heads below do not seem to belong. – Sydney Wynn †1639. Small alabaster slab with raised effigy of an infant. – A marble tablet records the building of the chapel by Sir Richard Wynn and gives his pedigree. Broken segmental pediment. It is by *Nicholas Stone*,* and has a crude outer frame, obviously the work of the local mason who fixed it in place. – A series of BRASSES, mostly lozenges with portrait busts. Sir John Wynn †1626. – His wife Sydney †1632. – Sir Owen Wynn †1660. – Katherine Lewis †1669. Half figure standing in a tomb. – Mary Mostyn †1653. Signed by *Silvanus Crue* and different from the others in its layout. – Dame Sarah Wynn †1671. By *William Vaughan*. Three-quarter-length portrait, framed by a superbly engraved cartouche, winged putti etc.

The CHURCHYARD lies beside the River Conwy. It is entered through a C19 ARCH, between the steep-gabled SEX-

---

* Mr Howard Colvin's discovery. Stone's account book (*Walpole Society*, VII, 1919, p. 110) records the receipt in 1636 of £15 for 'the monument for Sir Richard Wynn ... being the first and all I have received towards it.' The tablet is so characteristic of Stone's work that, although it cannot positively be identified as this 'monument', the proof of his having been employed by Wynn in at least some capacity is sufficient evidence of its being his. Wynn was Queen Henrietta Maria's Treasurer and thus responsible for payments to Inigo Jones and various London craftsmen on the Queen's behalf, so Stone would have been well known to him. I am indebted to Mr Colvin for the reference, and for helpful comments on the ascription.

TON'S COTTAGE and the gable end of JESUS HOSPITAL. These almshouses, with their frontage to Church Street, were founded by Sir John Wynn, or possibly by John Williams, with Wynn acting as his agent or trustee, c.1610–12. The buildings were erected at about that date. Mullioned windows, those of the ground floor of three lights, with six dormers, each containing a two-lighter, above. There were originally twelve dwellings in all, those on the upper floor reached by steps at the rear. The westernmost ground-floor apartment became a passageway in 1812, to give access to the then warden's house, which was being remodelled.

ST MARY, Betws Road. By *Kennedy*. Built 1841–2 for English residents and visitors. Now largely demolished, with only fragments of wall remaining. It was ignorant in its detail, but not without charm. The w tower might almost have been C18 Gothic.

GOOD SHEPHERD (R.C.), Llanddoged Road. 1956 by *S. Powell Bowen*. Steep slate roof on a reinforced concrete portal frame.

Unusually for Welsh Methodism, HOREB CHAPEL in Station Road has a Gothic front, and is unusual also in having no plaque or memorial stone. TABERNACL INDEPENDENT CHAPEL, Parry Road, 1882, is more thoroughly Gothic, though not, of course, churchy in form.

SEION WELSH PRESBYTERIAN (CALVINISTIC METHODIST) CHAPEL, set back from Station Road. Rebuilt 1881–3. It is of exceptional size and grandeur, and has a broad two-storeyed front of five bays, with a three-bay pediment. Recessed three-bay loggia of rusticated arches, and with stumpy Doric columns above. Urns on the parapet. The side elevations are also long and impressive, and the interior is magnificent. Curved gallery on iron columns with Corinthian caps. Boarded ceiling in big panels, with enrichment. Triple-arcaded end wall with a huge ORGAN, which dates from the time of the First World War. Ornament includes scroll patterns (gallery front), fretwork (tympana of arches flanking the organ) and incised patterns (PULPIT, SÊT-FAWR etc.). A lecture room, with caretaker's dwelling below it, are incorporated within the main body of the structure, behind the chapel proper.

In the grounds is a building of longitudinal elevation; it is not, as might be supposed, the predecessor chapel.*

SCHOOL, Conway Terrace/Watling Street. 1896–7 by *Grierson & Bellis* of Bangor. Fresh and free, with shaped gables and Renaissance touches. Octagonal bellcote with recessed spirelet.

In Schoolbank Road, the SENIOR DEPARTMENT of YSGOL DYFFRYN CONWY has buildings of 1960–5 by *R. A. Mac-Farlane*, Denbighshire County Architect. The LOWER HALF of the same school, in Nebo Road, is set in wooded grounds, with a Victorian house as its nucleus. Timber curtain-walled

_____
* Thanks are due to the Rev. Gwilym I. Davies for information on Seion Chapel.

blocks on the *Vic Hallam* prefabricated system, with some slate-hanging. A glazed link forms a bridge across a stream. 1960-3 by *R. A. MacFarlane*.

Former SCHOOL, Schoolbank Road. Tudor Gothic of 1846. Symmetrical, with an entrance loggia between cross wings. The adjoining teacher's house is composed with intersecting axes, and has tiny oriels.

RAILWAY STATION, Station Road. Built 1863. Of indeterminate style. Some good foliated stone carving.

BRIDGE (PONT FAWR), spanning the Conwy. Steeply cambered and very graceful, with a high proportion of void to solid. Three segmental arches, the middle one of *c.*60 ft, the others *c.*45 ft. That on the W was clumsily rebuilt in 1703. Full-height cutwaters and straight parapets with plaques at their apexes. The upstream plaque contains the date 1636 and the Royal Arms, within crude aedicular framework. The date appears also inside the downstream parapet. The work of rebuilding had been authorized in 1634.*

TU HWNT I'R BONT groups with the bridge on the W (Caernarfonshire) bank. Early C17 in origin (see roof timbers and other woodwork) but altered in the C18.‡

At the E (Denbighshire) end of the bridge, in BRIDGE STREET, is the stuccoed VICTORIA HOTEL, Early Victorian and large, attesting to the long-standing importance of the tourist trade. The EAGLES HOTEL incorporates C18 parts, though the main block, with an Italianate tower-like portion, is Mid-Victorian. ANCASTER SQUARE forms the heart of the little town and is a lively place on market day. A small and simple TOWN HALL, with bellcote, once stood at the N end. It was early C19, replacing a predecessor of 1661. Some C18 fronts remain in the square and nearby streets, but none calls for special mention. For JESUS HOSPITAL in CHURCH STREET, *see* p. 236. The local C19 tradition of pebbledash with flat, cement-rendered surrounds may be noted. At the NW corner of the square is the MIDLAND BANK, big-boned and large in size. The top storey is half-timbered. Heavy doorcase with a corbelled-out canopy. By *Edmund Kirby* of Liverpool, 1880, for the North & South Wales Bank. It was built to house a public hall and magistrates' court as well as the bank. At the same time, *Kirby* was building a house in Birkenhead for George Rae, pre-Raphaelite patron and chairman of the North & South Wales Bank. Effective townscape alongside, where STATION ROAD is funnelled round a corner past the

---

* It would be pedantic to refrain from mentioning the popular traditions which connect Inigo Jones with Llanrwst and, in particular, credit him with the design of the bridge. Except for the link provided by Sir Richard Wynn of Gwydir (*see* p. 235*n.*), he had no known association with the town. Nevertheless, one would like to think that he might have had something to do with the bridge, and this is less wildly impossible than other Jones attributions in Wales.

This fine structure has happily escaped widening, and long remained free from the indignity of traffic lights. With its camber preventing a view from one end to the other, it exercised strict discipline on its modern users.

‡ This entry is by Mr Haslam.

NATIONAL WESTMINSTER BANK (the former National Provincial), by *Shayler & Ridge*, 1922–4. A refined job, of ashlar, two-storeyed. Mainly early C18 in its elements, but a French flavour results from a steep roof and dormers with alternating pediments. The KWIKSAVE DISCOUNT STORE, behind Horeb Chapel, is the former LUXOR CINEMA, by *S. Colwyn Foulkes*, 1936–8. Gently curving brick front between lower bastions. The canopy still has its original fascia.

CYFFDY, 1½ m. SE. Now of Georgian character, but with a beam dated 1596 over the door. Inside is a beam with an inscription, in excellent lettering, also of 1596, and with *anno mundi* date as well.

Near the house is a curving AVENUE of Wellingtonias.

SOFLEN, 3¼ m. SSE. A good example of an early C17 end chimney and inside cross passage plan. (Staircase, now blocked off, beside the chimneybreast.) Lower-end service room and parlour, the latter also with end chimney. Cyclopean doorway. Post-and-panel partitions to the cross passage. A partition doorway and the rear outer door have depressed ogee heads.

HENDRE HOUSE, 2 m. SSE. Early C19, of ashlar, with moulded cornice. Three bays, with Doric porch, and the ground-floor windows set in arched recesses. Segmental bow on the left-hand return. Contemporary STABLES.

CAER BERLLAN, 1 m. SSE. An early or mid-C17 staircase has flat, pierced balusters and finialed newels. A ceiling with stop-chamfering is framed in three stages. Upstairs, a post-and-panel partition. Extensive C20 alterations, including new windows, were done sensitively and attractively, in Arts and Crafts tradition, with which the GARDEN is in happy accord. (Cruck construction in a former BARN.)

PLAS TIRION, 1¾ m. SSE. The front was, or was to have been, of E-plan, with three-storeyed cross wings and porch, but the left-hand wing is missing. In a ground-floor room, a plaster overmantel, with heraldry and strapwork, is dated 1626. The same date, with initials and heraldry, occurs above an upstairs fireplace. A further first-floor chimneypiece has heraldry and strapwork, and there is a more elaborate one of 1628.

58 A cruck BARN from HENDRE WEN, ¼ m. SW of Plas Tirion, has been transferred to St Fagan's. Of four bays, partly of stone, partly weather-boarded timber-framing, it was erected in the C18, reusing C16 or early C17 materials.*

PLAS MADOC, ¼ m. N, has been demolished. It was a plain Georgian house, remodelled and enlarged 1893 by *Dawes & Hoyland* of Manchester, in thorough-going half-timber revivalism, with rich interior woodwork.

LLAN SAIN SIÔR *see* ST GEORGE

* Information supplied by Mr Eurwyn Wiliam.

LLANSANFFRAID GLAN CONWY* ₈₀₇₀

St Ffraid. 1839 by *John Welch*, replacing a Perp double
naved church. Broad and aisleless, with shallow altar recess
and a low-pitched roof. Two tiny w towers, their top stages
open. A porch stands between them. Doorway of two orders
in which chamfered and plain voussoirs alternate. Equally
curious is the chamfering of windows, which stops short at
the springing. – FURNISHINGS, including a weak Neo-Jacobean SCREEN, belong to a restoration of 1907–8 by *Hoare &
Wheeler*. A w gallery was at that time removed, and the
FONT, claimed to be C17, was recut and carved. – STAINED
GLASS. In the w window are figures of St John the Baptist
and St Catherine, probably *c.*1500. – Heraldic glass in first
and second from w on N, and first from w on s, attributable
to *Evans*. – Second from w on s by *Clutterbuck*, 1846. – Third
from w on s by *Edward Woore*, 1943, but just as it might
have been fifty years earlier.

CHURCH HOUSE (i.e. Church Hall). 1932 by *S. Colwyn
Foulkes*. Whimsically *moderne*, of brick, immaculately detailed. A quadrant porch in an internal angle has a concave-
profiled roof rising into an octagonal brick chimney.

(CEFN GARLLEG, 1¼ m. NE. Of end chimney and inside cross
passage plan. A post-and-panel partition. P. Smith. A ceiling,
framed in four stages, has all its members moulded, with
some of them stopped. NMR)

MORIAH CHAPEL, 1½ m. ESE. At the rear, a house forms a cross
wing. The plaque refers to dates of 1826 and 1856.

PLAS ISAF, ¾ m. ESE. A C16 storeyed house now serves as an
OUTBUILDING. Lateral chimney and a fireplace with corbels.
Upper-end post-and-panel partition and a ceiling framed in
four stages, its beams and joists chamfered. The upper room
has an open roof. Arched-braced central truss with diagonal
struts above the collar, and there is a former partition truss.

PLAS UCHA, 1⅛ m. SE. Probably late C17. Leaded cross windows with timber mullions and transoms. Five-bay front.
The hall extends to the r. of the entrance and has a gabled
lateral chimney at the rear. Right-hand cross wing, also with
a gabled chimneybreast. A dog-leg staircase with turned
balusters occupies the internal angle between the two ranges.
Upstairs is a post-and-panel partition.

HENDRE WAELOD BURIAL CHAMBER, ¾ m. SSW (SH 793 747),
stands in a small wood close to the River Conwy. This is an
interesting Neolithic monument, a Portal Dolmen with a low
square chamber covered by an enormous capstone with tall
portal stones just in front of it. These stones must originally
have been spanned by a separate lintel. The chamber is divided from the portal area by a full-height septal, but as it is
beneath the capstone it is in fact very low, and the two parts
of the tomb seem strangely ill-matched. This is because of

* Transferred to Gwynedd in 1974.

the cumbersome capstone over the chamber, which is propped up on a number of small stones, unlike the usual construction with a few large slabs.

The remains of a LONG CAIRN can be seen running westward behind the stone chamber.

LLANSANFFRAID GLYN CEIRIOG *see* GLYN CEIRIOG

LLANSANNAN

ST SANNAN. Double-naved, but rebuilt or remodelled in 1777–8, and Victorianized in 1879, possibly by *R. Lloyd Williams*. Of the former date a round-headed S window. Of the latter, the W bellcote, timber porch, Geometrical windows, boarded ceilings etc. Also the timber arcade posts, replacing C18 fluted timber piers. – PULPIT. Given in 1894, and from a Liverpool church, supposedly St Luke's, but a century or more older than that building. Late C17 or early C18, and formerly a three-decker. Square, with bolection moulding, rich flower and leaf carving, and stairs with twisted balusters. – CHURCHWARDEN'S BENCH. Dated 1634. – STAINED GLASS. N nave E by *Jones & Willis*. – S nave E by *H. Gustave Hiller*, 1910. – BENEFACTION BOARD and later COMMANDMENT BOARDS inscribed in Welsh. – MONUMENTS. Ridgeway Owen Meyrick †1773. Draped medallion of a seated maiden beside an urn. Refined ornament around the tablet. – The following, to the Yorkes of Dyffryn Aled, are all by *W. Spence*: Diana Yorke †1805. Female figure with cross, against a rocky background. – Rev. Brownlow Yorke †1813. – Pierce Wynne Yorke †1837. Female figures, including two seated with their backs to an urn.

LLANSANNAN MONUMENT. 1899 by *Goscombe John*. A girl in Welsh dress, with a garland, seated in front of an obelisk. Commemorating five writers born here: Tudur Aled (*c.* 1470–1526), William Salesbury (a translator of the New Testament into Welsh, *c.* 1520–?1584), Henry Rees (1798–1869), William Rees ('Gwilym Hiraethog', 1802–83), and Iorwerth Glanaled (1819–67).

SARACEN'S HEAD. Early or mid-C18 well staircase, through two storeys. Columnar balusters, but still with a string.

Former SCHOOL, ⅛ m. E. 1857 by *Lloyd Williams & Underwood*. Cusped lancets.

PLAS ISAF, 1¾ m. NE. Lateral chimney and inside cross passage plan, but originally of two units only. The lower-end room is a later addition, as is a wing in front of the original entrance. An early C14 SEPULCHRAL SLAB serves as a lintel. Of four-circle type, the circles are interlaced with a quatrefoil. A sword beside the stem.

DYFFRYN ALED was demolished *c.* 1920. Its entrance front had a two-and-a-half-storey seven-bay centre, with one-bay pediment. Lower and very elegant three-bay wings and three-bay links. On the other side was a basement storey. Begun 1777 by *Joseph Turner*. The wings and the interior were by *John Woolfe*, joint author, with James Gandon, of the fourth and fifth volumes of *Vitruvius Britannicus*.

PLAS NEWYDD BARROW (SH 947 666), a large mound in an unusual valley-bottom situation, was disturbed in the last century, when human bones were found beneath a central cairn.

The BARROW near Deunant Isa (SH 968 649) has been badly eroded by agriculture but can still be recognized in the corner of the field.

LLANSILIN

2020

A far-flung parish in the southern tip of Denbighshire, beyond the Berwyns. It is a place of extreme beauty, and no main roads disturb the peace of its hills and fertile valleys.

ST SILIN. A double-naved church, Perp in its main features. A tower, at the W end of the S nave, replaced a timber-framed spire in 1832. It seems that a *clas* (Celtic monastery) existed, and Dr Ralegh Radford has shown* that there was an early C13 cruciform church, with aisled nave, comparable with the somewhat earlier example at Tywyn, Merioneth. The S wall of the S nave is in line with the position of that of the former transept. The N nave extends a little further E than the site of the W crossing arch, but otherwise coincides with the position of the C13 nave, the W wall of which remains. In it a blocked doorway cut into by a later window. Also E.E. and *in situ*, the W respond of the arcade, i.e. that of the former S arcade. Its capital has roughly carved stiff-leaf. A further survival of the cruciform building occurs at the E end of the S wall, where a short length of the transept walling is incorporated. Quoins and a vertical joint mark the transept's SW corner, and another break, further W, indicates the addition of a chapel in the angle between transept and S aisle. A lancet is probably reset. The remainder of the S wall belongs to the Perp remodelling, carried out after the church had, in all probability, been laid waste in the time of Owain Glyndŵr. Blocked S doorway of E.E. work, reset, and stiff-leaf is worked into the arcade E respond. Arcade itself Perp, of four bays, with thick octagonal piers. Fleurons in the easternmost cap. N nave E window with cusping and panel tracery. The southern is of four lights with two sub-arches, a transom at springing level, cusping, and panel tracery. An incongruous N window is perhaps of 1864, when an C18 S porch was removed. The major restoration was by *Arthur Baker*, 1890. He exposed the C15 arched-

* *Archaeologia Cambrensis*, vol. 115, 1966.

braced roof of the s nave, and the wagon ceiling at its E end. Following the curve of the arched-braces, this has cusped and traceried panels, bands of vine trail etc. C16 or C17 W gallery. Its balustrade must be *Baker*'s, as he removed an C18 panelled front to make a SCREEN at the E end of the N nave. Also by him the STALLS and PEWS, in his Aesthetic Movement interpretation of Jacobean, with some old pieces in the stalls. Lots of little turned finials.

The plain, octagonal FONT is probably C17, like the spired FONT COVER. – Carolean ALTAR TABLE. One end is uncarved, showing it was to have been aligned E-W, table-wise, with its end against the E wall.* – PULPIT. With an C18 tester. – STAINED GLASS. s nave E by *James Powell & Sons*, 1866. Evangelists designed by *H. Casolani* and the Ascension in the tracery by *E. J. Poynter*.‡ – Two-tier CHANDELIER of great sumptuousness. Dated 1824. – COMMANDMENTS, painted on canvas. Now at the back of the gallery, but formerly a reredos, and combining, as was common in the C17 and C18, the Decalogue with figures of Moses and Aaron. – BENEFACTION BOARD, s wall at E end of N nave. An endearing and quaint painting of 1740, which, like the Commandments, is of real historical importance. – Dugout CHEST, from Llangadwaladr. – Pillar POORBOX. 1664. – MONUMENTS. Sir William Williams † 1700. Architectural surround, its entablature rising in a segmental curve. Urns and cherub heads. – David Maurice † 1719. Pedimented and heavily decorated. Small wrought-iron screen at the base, its design related to the inscription panel and group of cherub heads behind. – Foulkes monument. Original commemoration dates 1761–71. Crudely painted architectural surround. – Thomas Davies † 1810. By *S. & F. Franceys*. Draped urn. – ROYAL ARMS of Queen Anne, in plaster. Encroached upon by the Foulkes monument. – The W doorway, in the tower, has C18 iron GATES.

Opposite the church a MALTHOUSE, dated 1822. Curving village street, and, at its N end, the OLD VICARAGE, early C19 Tudor, with cross wings.

SALEM BAPTIST CHAPEL, ¼ m. N, in its own graveyard. Of 1831 with longitudinal elevation and a pair of cottages attached.

SYCHARTH, in the valley of the Cynllaith, 1½ m. s of the village, and behind the farm of Bryn Derw. Motte and bailey. Here stood the chief residence of Owain Glyndŵr, described in the famous poem of Iolo Goch, *c.* 1390. The well-preserved earthworks, possibly of Norman origin, include the mound, with

---

* In his decision in the Grantham case of 1627, John Williams, Bishop of Lincoln and later Archbishop of York, ruled that the altar was to be placed in this way when not in use. Addleshaw and Etchells (*The Architectural Setting of Anglican Worship*, 1948) note that the practice was continued in a number of Welsh churches into the C19, and suggest that it may have been encouraged by Williams, who was born at Conwy and spent his last years in Wales.

‡ Information from Mr Martin Harrison.

ditch and outer bank, and the bailey, also with ditch. Traces of buildings were revealed in excavations of 1962–3.

MOELIWRCH, ½ m. NW. Late Georgian and, at right angles, an earlier house with lateral chimney. This was storeyed from the first (though having an open roof with wind-braces. DOE). A pointed doorway, originally external, connects the two parts.

TYDDYN CYNNAR, 1½ m. N, SE of the farm of Rhydleos. A cruck hall house, with an upper floor and a chimney backing on to the cross passage as later insertions. Doorway with pointed timber head. (Arched-braced central cruck truss. Wind-braces. Mr Smith, who investigated the house at a time when it was derelict, illustrates lower- and upper-end post-and-panel partitions, the former with one doorway, the latter with two. The latter also has mortices providing evidence of a dais bench and a canopy.)

YSGWENNANT, 1¾ m. NNW. H-plan. Timber framing remains exposed at the rear of the right-hand cross wing. Cruck trusses. The floor subdividing the former hall has massive beams.

HAFOD, 2½ m. N. Two ranges, on the unit system. The part aligned against the slope was a C15 box-framed house, i.e. no crucks. Not only did it have a spere-truss, but the hall was fully aisled, with aisle posts and arcade plates. Now about half its original length, and divided up, retaining only the central and upper-end partition trusses. The former has wavy arched-braces and, above the collar, cusped struts and a king-post of clustered shafts. The other part of the house, at right angles, is C16 or early C17, with some later extension. Doorway with a pointed head formed in the lintel. Heavily moulded beams and joists. Also a poor C17 staircase, with flat, pierced balusters.

PEN-Y-BRYN, 1⅜ m. SSW of Hafod. Ruins of a cruck-framed hall. Not to be confused with another house of the same name. *See* below.

MOELFRE HALL, 1⅜ m. W of the village. Tall, whitewashed and gabled, a landmark on the lower slopes of Gyrn Moelfre, at the limit of cultivation. It has been reduced in size. Quite a wide C17 dog-leg staircase, through two storeys. Large and heavy flat, pierced balusters.

CARMEL CHAPEL, below the road, ¼ m. ESE of the secluded little Llyn Moelfre. A small, whitewashed vernacular chapel, with a graveyard. Longitudinal elevation, with adjoining schoolroom. Built 1826, rebuilt 1862, according to the inscription.

GLASCOED, 1⅛ m. SE of the village. Cruciform. The main ridge runs E–W, and lower wings project N and S. Materials include stone (with some mullioned windows), brick, and brick nogging, suggesting successive reconstructions of a C17 timber-framed building. Central cluster of brick stacks, and the S wing has a lateral chimney. C17 well staircase, through two storeys. Pierced, flat balusters, and square, finialed newels. An ornamented plaster ceiling in an upper room is recorded, but no longer exists. BARN of two parallel ranges, the walls of stone below, brick above. (Dated 1689. DOE)

PONT-Y-GLASCOED, W of Glascoed. Unusual among local bridges in being of two arches. Parapet of vertical slabs.

TŶ-NEWYDD, ¾m. S of the village. The group of house and farm buildings is approached across a bridge. H-plan house, with a five-bay central range, of brick. Facing S this has timber cross windows, and is consistent with the inscribed date of 1684. The E wing is earlier, for its long E front is timber-framed, in close studding, now brick-nogged. The W wing is puzzling. The lower part of its W wall is stone, the rest of C17 brick. There are several arbitrarily placed decorative blank brick arches of small size, and, to add to the confusion, some later stone-mullioned windows. All three parts have internal woodwork which is probably of 1684. Bolection-moulded panelling, a staircase with sturdy turned balusters and square newels, and a grander staircase in the W wing, rising through two storeys, with broad rail and vase-shaped turned balusters.

PEN-Y-BRYN, ⅜m. W of Tŷ-Newydd, S of the B4580. A C15 hall house. When modified by the C17 insertion of an upper floor and a chimney, the latter was placed in the former cross passage, creating a lobby entry. Outer walls now largely of stone, but some close-studded timber framing was revealed and partly renewed in a restoration of 1970–2. C17 timber-framed dormers. The central truss of the hall is an arched-braced base cruck, with struts forming a cusped quatrefoil above the collar. Cusped wind-braces. There is also a spere-truss, with cusped quatrefoil, and the upper- and lower-end partitions are of aisle truss type, i.e. they contain posts in line with the two spere posts. Arcade plates spring from the several posts. All this is virtually intact, though threaded round with the floor and chimney. Aisle trusses existed in the two gable ends. Post-and-panel partition at the upper end of the hall, retaining one of a pair of doorways. Chamfered beams in the room beyond. C17 staircase with flat, shaped and moulded balusters. BARN with a cruck truss.

LLORAN ISAF, 1¼m. WSW of the village. Derelict, and a fine early or mid-C17 well staircase is in a deplorable state. Flat, pierced balusters, and square newels with tall finials.

BRON HEULOG, ⅝m. WSW of Lloran Isaf, near the B road. Mid- or late C17. Central chimney and lobby entry. Stairs, behind the chimney and housed in a gabled rear projection, wrap around a bread oven. Turned balusters.

LLORAN UCHAF, ⅞m. W of Bron Heulog. Differing cross wings, one with lateral chimney. The five-bay centre, now rendered, has casements and a segmental door hood which could be C17. Inside, however, is a good mid-C18 staircase. Panelled dado, swept rail, and columnar balusters.

A lane runs S of, and roughly parallel with, the B road, from near Bron Heulog eastwards towards Sycharth. The following four houses are on its N side, from W to E.

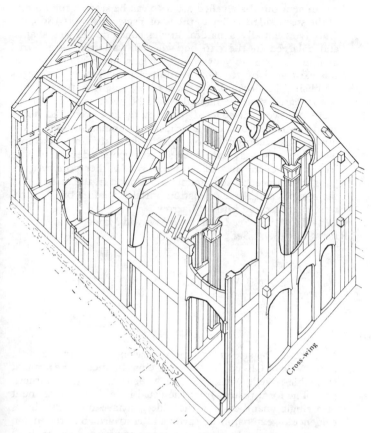

Llansilin, Pen-y-Bryn, fifteenth century
(Royal Commission on Ancient and Historical Monuments in Wales)

PRIDDBWLL BACH. Central chimney and lobby entry, approached through a storeyed porch. The surviving lower portions of a cruck show that this was a hall house. The date 1632 is inscribed internally; this is probably when the chimney and intermediate floor were inserted. Two upper-end service rooms.

PRIDDBWLL GANOL. A pleasing Late Georgian vernacular front. Stone-built, with a Doric pilastered doorcase.

PRIDDBWLL MAWR. Gabled, of grey rubble, and from a distance looking like a Victorian parsonage. In fact dated 1687, of H-plan, and apparently once with a lateral chimney.

HENDY. Single storey plus dormers. Central chimney and lobby entry. (Post-and-panel partition. NMR)

Finally, GOLFA ISAF, 2 m. SSE of the village, on the road to Llangedwyn, with timber-framing in closely set panels.

A prominent but dishevelled MOUND can be seen in the bottom of the steep-sided valley to the w of Ysgwennant (SJ 189 305). This is essentially a natural gravel bank, but it was shaped and enlarged in the C16 bc, when it was used as a burial monument, probably over quite a long period. The mound was excavated by the Offa Antiquarian Society in the 1950s (published in *Archaeologia Cambrensis*, vol. 121, 1972), when it was feared that the mound would be destroyed. Two large grave pits were discovered, both containing cremated bones and long-necked beakers (an unusual combination); one of the burials was accompanied by a fire-making kit – flint and iron pyrites in what may have been a leather pouch decorated with jet beads. Several hearths and sherds of earlier pottery (perhaps from a nearby settlement) were found in the make-up of the mound, and three cremation burials (one in a broken urn) were later inserted into the barrow.

GLAS-HIRFRYN. *See* Llanarmon Mynydd Mawr.
RHYDYCROESAU. *See* p. 266.

LLANTYSILIO *see* LLANDYSILIO

1060
LLANYNYS

ST SAERAN. The site of a C6 monastery and a *clas*, in the heart of the Vale of Clwyd. The present church, once whitewashed, is double-naved, with a double w bellcote on the southern part. The form results from the usual Late Perp enlargement of a single chamber, and the older, N nave not only shows evidence of extension upwards and eastward, but retains an E.E. w doorway. This has two orders of grouped shafts, with fillets, continued up into the arch, but with caps, probably once foliated, intervening (cf. Llangollen, p. 219). Of a five-bay Perp arcade, only raised responds and some bases remain, having been replaced by fluted square Doric columns of oak, *c.* 1768. Reliably renewed Perp windows in the N nave, where the four-centred E window has five lights, two single-light sub-arches, and panel tracery. The s nave E is Victorian, as is tracery inserted into three round-headed s windows, which are probably of *c.* 1768. Also on the s a priest's door, and a timber-framed porch with moulded roof timbers and dated 1544. Earlier, and belonging to the Perp work, is the four-centred doorway and the DOOR itself, with applied mouldings forming four vertical panels, their heads cusped and traceried. Arched-braced roofs, the alternate trusses with hammerbeams, some of which retain shafted wall posts. Trusses, purlins, and large intermediate rafters are moulded.

Perp FONT. Cusped panels on the stem and quatrefoils on the bowl. – ALTAR TABLES. High altar with lions bearing shields dated 1637. – Another C17 table in the s nave. – Much

reused WOODWORK, from pews etc. It includes work with
C17 and early C18 dates in the STALLS. Also some of 1613 in
the sanctuary PANELLING, together with panels of 1570, il-
lustrating fables and bestiaries, thought to have come from
Bachymbyd Fawr (see below). – PULPIT. Post-Jacobean.
Square-within-square panels. Others arched, with little baluster motifs. – WALL PAINTING. A St Christopher, in the
usual position opposite the s door, discovered in 1967. Pre-
dating the Perp remodelling, and considered by Mrs Eve
Baker to be of the first third of the C15. Windmill and swimming fish, and patterned with the monogram of the Virgin.
The saint's staff is shown as already bearing leaves. The work
had been covered by C17 painting, with a text in Welsh, and
this has been removed and preserved. – STAINED GLASS. s
nave E by *Wailes*, 1855. – CHANDELIERS. Two of wood, one
with a painted inscription of 1749. – A secular C19 brass one,
from Rhug, Merioneth. – Panelled CHEST dated 1687. – Part
of a heraldic SEPULCHRAL SLAB, much worn, forms the
threshold of the priest's door. Early C14. – SEPULCHRAL 42
CROSS. A rare memorial stone, mid-C14, from the churchyard.
Hexagonal slab, on a short stem, representing the Crucifixion
on one side and a bishop on the other. – MONUMENTS. Mutilated effigy of a priest, early C14, his head canopied. Placed
on a tomb-chest with C16 or C17 fragments incorporated. –
Rev. William Williams Edwards †1829. By *W. Spence*.
Female figure beside an urn on a pedestal. – ROYAL ARMS.
Painted on canvas and dated 1661. – Two HATCHMENTS. –
DOG TONGS.

There is no village, the church having as neighbours just a pub
and the VICARAGE. Built 1807–8, this is of brick, with
splayed corners at one end.

PONT PERFA, ⅜m. NNE. Two segmental arches with central
cutwaters. The river is the Clwyd.

RHYDONNEN, ¾m. NE. The gable end of a cross wing is half-
timbered, with patterns of diagonal bracing. Central chimney,
and the wing has a lateral one with gabled breast. Panelled
GATEPIERS with obelisk finials.

At Rhewl, 1½m. SSE, the Clywedog is crossed by a BRIDGE of
1819, inscribed with a Welsh poem. Upstream, PONT
RHYD-Y-CILGWYN, earlier, is of two spans with central
cutwaters. RHYD-Y-CILGWYN itself is early C19 Neo-
Tudor, stuccoed. Its ENTRANCE LODGE, similar in style,
has little oriels and a former porch on posts. The property
was part of Lord Bagot's estate (see Pool Park), so the architect may well have been *Buckler*. Timber-framed FARM
BUILDINGS.

PANT GLAS ISAF, 2m. SSW. A four-bay cruck house is now a
BARN. The central truss of the hall is jointed, and has tie-
beam and king-post. Partition trusses with arched collars.
Wind-braces.

BACHYMBYD FAWR, 1¼m. SW. A house which belonged to the
Salusburys of Lleweni (q.v.). It was rebuilt in 1666, of brick

with stone dressings. Seven bays and, to the r., a hipped two-bay wing, projecting one bay. A matching left-hand wing was intended, and may have existed. An orderly Restoration house, with cross windows and moulded stone cornice. The mullions and transoms are, though, still of stone, and there is ornament of Jacobean flavour around the heraldry and inscribed date above the entrance. This work was reset in alterations which involved the loss of the original doorcase. The roof, too, is not in its original form, and interiors are early c20. The gable end, where the missing wing should be, was effectively remodelled by *K. W. Favell*, *c.*1960. Rear staircase wing. BARN with two crucks and some timber-framed walling.

LLAY
1 m. NW of Gresford

A c20 mining village. Its formal layout, begun in 1920, was planned by *Barry Parker*. The Llay Main Colliery, sinking of which started in 1914, was closed in 1966, and factories occupy the pithead site. Llay Hall Colliery, dating from 1873, closed in 1947.

ST MARTIN. On the central axis. 1923–5 by *R. T. Beckett*, his only fully completed church. Brick, outside and in. Perp tracery, and the aisle windows straight-headed. The aisle roofs continue that of the nave, but at a lower pitch. Flèche over the chancel. Timber-framed N and S porches, and the arcades are also of timber, consisting of posts and beams with curved bracing. No chancel arch. The easternmost bay of the chancel is ashlar-lined and has a wagon ceiling.*

SCHOOL. 1925 by *W. D. Wiles*, County Architect. Single-storey, with a low central tower, and some Leonard Stokesian touches.

MINERS' INSTITUTE. At the NW end of, but outside, the axial layout. 1929–31 by *F. A. Roberts*. Not pure Neo-Georgian so much as Edwardian Baroque Survival. Done with real swagger, but more refined than the Institute at Rhosllannerchrugog (q.v.), especially the rear elevation, with urns and balustraded parapet. Roughcast, with stone dressings.

LLAY PLACE. Also near the NW end of the layout. Low, gabled and symmetrical. Further parts, apparently additions, include a tower-like pavilion roof, dated 1865, on the garden front.

LLAY HALL, ½ m. W. A c17 remodelling left it with mullioned and transomed windows, and a hall range between tall cross wings with coped and finialed gables. In the 1930s the E wing and part of the hall were demolished, and the rest was altered, but enough remains of the hall to show that it originally had a spere-truss and, unusually for the region, a crown-post and

---

* This account is based on material kindly supplied by the Rev. David Hinge.

collar purlin. (Traces of a MOAT to the S.) C18 brick FARM
BUILDINGS round three sides of a yard.

LLEWENI   0060

Once the seat of the Salusburys, Lleweni was in 1810 bought
by the Rev. Edward Hughes of Kinmel (*see* p. 280). In 1816–
18 it was almost entirely demolished by his son, the future
Lord Dinorben. A previous owner had been the Hon.
Thomas Fitzmaurice, who established nearby a Bleach Works
for treating linen produced on his Irish estates. By *Thomas
Sandby*, *c.*1785, this was an early industrial building of remarkable grandeur, on a crescent plan, with the upper storey
set back above an arcaded loggia and with a central giant arch
and a cupola – thirty-five bays in all. The house itself had a
late medieval hall with hammerbeam roof. A long wing, late
C17 or early C18, was intended as the first stage of a complete
rebuilding. Much was done later in the C18, probably all in
Fitzmaurice's time, and some of it in the form of curious
Gothicizing. New service quarters were built, and these partially survived the demolition, though the fragment was
further reduced in 1928. The remaining part is of brick, with
round-headed ground-floor windows and a three-bay pediment. To the l., five further bays and, formerly, a second
pediment. Two stone Doric columns in the kitchen. Present
FARM BUILDINGS, with blank arcading, were stables. Now
reroofed and bereft of a large cupola. Impressive CARRIAGE
YARD, attributable to *Sandby*. Two parallel ranges of brick
stables etc. Main elevation of seventeen bays, with blank
arches, and including three-bay two-storey corner pavilions.
Similar but simpler rear elevation, and the yard is entered
between the pavilions at one end.*

LLYSFAEN‡   9070

ST CYNFRAN. Like that at Llanelian-yn-Rhos (q.v.), this is a
double-naved church high above the sea. The N chamber is
the earlier, with its narrower E end representing an intermediate extension. Cyclopean S doorway with a (reset?) mask
corbel above. Four-bay arcade, its chamfered arches springing direct from octagonal piers, as at Llanelian. It was retooled in a drastic restoration by *Street*, 1870, to which R.
Bamford Hesketh of Gwrych was a principal contributor. By
Street the S porch, W bellcote, and all the windows. He renewed the arched-braced roofs, reusing some old work.
Cusped wind-bracing. – Pierced wainscot panels from the

* Research by Mr Peter Howell threw light on the mysteries and complexities
of Lleweni. *See Country Life*, vol. 162, 1977, p. 1966.
‡ Formerly a detached part of Caernarfonshire. Transferred to Denbighshire
in 1923.

ROOD SCREEN behind the N stalls and on the N of the sanctuary. Reeded mouldings were reproduced by *Street* in his new CHANCEL SCREEN. – A full set of other *Street* FURNISHINGS. – In the chancel he used *William Godwin*'s ENCAUSTIC TILES.

CHURCH HALL, E of the church. Built 1929–30. Roughcast. Pointed windows and twin gables suggest H. L. North. In fact by *S. Colwyn Foulkes*.

SCHOOL, SW of the church. 1870–1* by *Street*, and again Hesketh was among the subscribers. Massive-looking, and with the school house incorporated. Tile-hung gables. Gothic in spirit, and one window is pointed and traceried, though the rest are straight-headed.

BETHEL CHAPEL, $\frac{3}{8}$m. SSE. Dated 1834. Continued as a cottage at one end, and meeting a row of cottages, at right angles, at the other.

Former TELEGRAPH STATION, on the summit of the hill. Single-storeyed, with half-hipped roof. Like that at Prestatyn (*see* p. 419), it was built in 1841, originally for semaphore, by the Trustees of Liverpool Docks.

LOGGERHEADS *see* LLANFERRES

MAEN PEBYLL *see* CAPEL GARMON

MAERDY *see* DINMAEL

MAESHAFN

2060

The Maeshafn Lead Mine, first established in the C18, was reopened in 1823, and enjoyed a mid-C19 boom. Rows of MINERS' COTTAGES are grouped near the site of an engine house, and the pub is the MINERS' ARMS. The CHAPEL was, according to its inscription, built in 1820 and enlarged 1843 and 1863. (Two large early C19 WHEELPITS, $\frac{5}{8}$m. WNW on the E bank of the Alun. The larger (S) pit was probably overshot to supply power by rods to a shaft *c*. 500 yards E. The other was probably undershot to work ore-dressing machinery.‡)

PONT-Y-MWYNWR, a house $\frac{1}{2}$m. W, was the residence of the mining agent.§ Early C19 Neo-Tudor.

* I owe the dates to Mr Joyce.
‡ Information from Mr Christopher J. Williams.
§ Information from Canon Pritchard.

YOUTH HOSTEL, ½m. SE. 1931 by *Sir Clough Williams-Ellis*. The first purpose-built youth hostel. Weatherboarded Neo-Georgian, with pediment and shutters.

MARCHWIEL

ST MARCELLUS. Of crisply detailed ashlar. The nave is a re-building of 1778. On the S it has a pilastered and pedimented doorcase, handled with restrained Neo-Classical freedom,* and three round-headed windows. The W tower was added by *James Wyatt*, 1789, under the patronage of Philip Yorke of Erddig (q.v.). Round-headed bell openings, corner pilaster strips, and balustrading with urns. Its former W doorway has unusually large consoles. N transept of 1829. A polygonal-apsed chancel, attached to the pedimented E end of the nave, must be a Victorian addition. It is a sympathetic one, and the nave retains its flat plaster ceiling. – STAINED GLASS. Nave, first from E on S by *Hardman*, 1860. – Next to it, heraldry in roundels by *Francis Eginton*, 1788. – MONUMENTS. John Meller, of Erddig. By *Scheemakers*, 1736.‡ Side volutes and a shield in a cartouche against a pyramid. – Anne Jemima Yorke †1770, aged sixteen. By *William Tyler*. Seated figure against an obelisk, and a rose bush with a serpent coiled around the flowers. – Elizabeth Yorke †1779. By the elder *Robert Aston*. Sarcophagus-like tablet against an obelisk. Shield and drapery below. – Philip Yorke. By *Sir Richard Westmacott*, 1805. Inscription on a column-like shaft, with a willow draped above and a weeping maiden and broken harp at the base. – BRASSES include one by *Evans & Gresty* of Chester to Captain Thomas David Ellis †1858.
DEINIOL COUNTY PRIMARY SCHOOL, NE of the church. Single-storeyed, and of informal plan and differing heights, with clerestories. Deep corrugated timber fascias. 1972–4 by *E. Langford Lewis*, County Architect.
BRYN-Y-GROG, ¾m. NW. Late C18, of brick, with some stone dressings. Three-bay central block of two and a half storeys. Four-column Doric porch and a tripartite pedimented door-case with good fanlight. Two-storey wings have three-window segmental fronts. Above them, the return ends of the main block are pedimented, and the return of the left-hand wing has blank arches and a pediment below the cornice. Victorian rear additions.
MARCHWIEL HALL, ⅞m. WNW. Stuccoed. Eight bays, the two at either end pedimented and with Corinthian pilasters. On the right-hand return another pediment and a four-column Ionic porch.

---

* Inappropriate doors belong to a restoration of 1977–8.
‡ Mr D. Leslie Davies kindly drew attention to the reference among the Erddig MSS.

OLD SONTLEY, 2 m. SW. Timber framing, with brick nogging and diagonal bracing. Internal chimney and lobby entry plan.

THE GROVES, 1¾ m. SSW. Late C17, of brick. Segmental-headed casements and a three-bay front. Staircase with flat, shaped balusters and finialed newels. Among the farm buildings is a HORSE ENGINE HOUSE.

GERWYN HALL, 1¼ m. SE. Late C18 or early C19 three-storey front of ashlar, with two tripartite segmental bows. Four-column Tuscan porch and above it a tripartite window, with Wyattish consoles, set in a segmental-arched recess. Central pediment. This is a remodelling or enlargement, for the other façades are brick, and the rear, which has quoins and segmental-headed windows with brick aprons and stone keystones, is early or mid-C18. The entrance hall, with segmental barrel ceiling, leads to a top-lit staircase, with iron balusters. Pleasing brick STABLES, probably Early Victorian.

Former WESLEYAN CHAPEL, Cross Lanes, SW of the A525/B5130 intersection. Built 1834. Small longitudinal front, altered.

BEDWELL, Sesswick, ¼ m. N of Cross Lanes. Late C17 or early C18. Brick, with cross wings and segmental-headed windows.

PICKHILL HALL, 1½ m. ENE of Cross Lanes. A most distinguished brick and stone façade, added to an earlier structure, in the provincial Baroque of the early C18. It is of the 1720s, and may tentatively be attributed to *Richard Trubshaw*. Three storeys, surmounted by a balustraded parapet. Seven bays, articulated as two-three-two by two fluted Ionic pilasters. Quoins of even length at the corners. Segmental-headed windows, emphasized in the middle bay with moulded surrounds and, on the first floor, side volutes. The parapet rises, pediment-like, in the middle bay. A Corinthian porch is probably a later addition, and a discreetly done wing to the r. is dated 1866. (Good staircase and panelling. DOE) The house has regrettably fallen into extreme disrepair. Round-arched High Victorian ENTRANCE LODGE, with a conical-roofed turret.

See p. 519

PICKHILL OLD HALL, ¾ m. E of Cross Lanes. C18. Brick, with some toothing and segmental-headed casements. Distyle-*in-antis* porch, of Laugier-like simplicity, the stone columns completely plain, with stone abaci, and the antae of brick. Ruinous four-gable DOVECOTE. Domestic-looking C17 FARM BUILDINGS, with quoins, coped and finialed gables, and former mullioned windows.

FIVE FORDS has been demolished, but the staircase is re-assembled at Hafod-y-Bwch, Esclusham (q.v.).

NEW SONTLEY. *See* Erddig.

WREXHAM INDUSTRIAL ESTATE. *See* Wrexham, p. 311.

MARFORD *see* Flintshire

MINERA

St Mary. Rebuilt by *Kennedy & Rogers*, 1864–5, in a spiky sort of Dec, with polygonal masonry. Cruciform, but nave and transepts are of equal length, and there is a detached tower in the angle between nave and s transept. Its base forms the porch, but the entrance link connects with the transept, not the nave. Crossing arches on clustered shafts, with carved caps and corbels. – STAINED GLASS. E window by *A. Gibbs*, commemoration date 1860.

School, ¼m. ESE of the church, on the B road. A many-gabled Gothic group by *R. K. Penson*, 1849–51. Enlarged 1875.

The Vicarage, ⅛m. NW of the school, is of 1849, so perhaps also by *Penson*, Neo-Elizabethan. Varied massing, but severe, unrelieved wall surfaces.

W of the school is Plasgwyn. Mid-C18. Pedimented doorcase and segment-headed windows with rusticated lintels. Tŷ-Brith, ¼m. further W across a valley, has been overprettified (but Mr Smith refers to cruck construction and a dais canopy). SSE of this, on the B5426, Caemynydd, early C19, with pedimented doorcase. Door and reveals have octagonal panels.

Minera was an important lead-mining centre. Amid scarred landscape, ½m. S at New Brighton, is the engine house of the Meadow, or City, Shaft of the Minera Lead Mine. Mid-C19, with separate chimney. Ruinous.

MOEL FAMA

The highest mountain of the Clwydian range. At the summit (1,820ft), on the boundary of Denbighshire and Flintshire, the Jubilee Tower was built 1810–c.1812 to commemorate George III's fifty years as king. The architect was *Thomas Harrison*, who produced the first Egyptian-style monument to be built in Britain. His design was modified in execution, resulting in three diminishing stages, the top one an obelisk, and the lowest a battered podium, with a blank doorway on each face, and square corner bastions. In 1862 it was blown down, but much of the podium remains, amid rubble. Tidied up 1970, and a viewing platform made.

At least two Bronze Age cairns can be easily seen on the path from Bwlch Pen Barras to the Jubilee Tower. They occur in a group just N of a point where the upper and lower paths join (SJ 158 612). The best-preserved is a small heap of stones on a rise to the W of the path; the path itself may have destroyed another where it crosses a circular patch of stony ground, and the third is a little to the S, just to the E of the wire fence. A quarter of this large cairn has been almost entirely removed, but there is no information about what was found during this excavation. A good deal of stone has been removed from the centre of the cairn, leaving a stone bank around the fringes. However, the centre is obviously filled with stone, and this is a good example of a destroyed cairn, not a ring cairn. Smaller cairns may be concealed in the heather in the vicinity of these larger ones.

MOELFRE *see* LLANSILIN

9050

MYNYDD HIRAETHOG

Moorland country, between the Conwy Valley and the Vale of Clwyd.

At 1,627ft, and a landmark for miles around, is GWYLFA HIR-AETHOG, 3m. SSW of Bylchau. Built as a shooting lodge for the first Viscount Devonport, politician, one-time senior partner in the firm of Kearley & Tonge, and first Chairman of the Port of London Authority. It took its present form in 1913, when enlarged by *Sir Edwin Cooper*,* who received a number of commissions from Lord Devonport, besides being architect of the Port of London Authority Building. Three-gabled front in C17 vernacular, with cross wings and long mullioned windows. Stone flagged roof. Sold in 1925, and now fallen into ruin.

Much land has been given over to afforestation and reservoirs. ALWEN RESERVOIR was built for Birkenhead, 1911–16, with *Sir Alexander Binnie, Son & Deacon* as engineers. Curved dam of concrete blocks, rock-faced on the outer side. Asymmetrically placed valve tower, like an Italianate belvedere. The scheme, initiated on the advice of *G. F. Deacon*, designer of Vyrnwy Reservoir, Montgomeryshire, was authorized in 1907. The same Act empowered the impounding of the River Brenig, but LLYN BRENIG, by *Binnie & Partners*, is larger than was then intended. Authorized 1972 and constructed 1973–6. The functional and sculpturesque head of the draw-off tower contrasts with the Gothic mysteries at Vyrnwy, and the dam differs from those of earlier generations in being a gigantic bank. Landscape architects: *Colvin & Moggridge*.

The northern end of the Brenig Valley (SH 98 57) – now part of Llyn Brenig – contains an interesting Early Bronze Age CEMETERY, and a group of HAFODYDD of the C16 A.D. All the monuments were excavated before the valley was flooded and they have been rebuilt as part of a historical trail on the NE side of the lake. There is an interpretative exhibition with casts of the best finds at Canolfan Brenig, close to the dam, where leaflets for the trail may be obtained.

The CEMETERY consists of four large turf barrows (three on the western side of the lake), three small stone cairns, a large platform cairn, a ring cairn, a kerb cairn and, above Bwlch

---

* I owe this information to the present Viscount.

Du, outside the Water Authority's estate, a small cairn set at the apex of the group but without evidence of burials beneath it. Within this cemetery there are fine examples of several of the more unusual forms of Bronze Age cairns, and thus the trail provides what might almost be called a gallery of Bronze Age architecture. The platform cairn, which was originally a broad ring with a hollow centre, is the most striking monument and a very rare variant on the normal burial cairn; the ring cairn is a splendid example of a quite common Welsh ceremonial site. This one provided evidence of ceremonies involving the burial of charcoal. Radiocarbon dates show that it was in use for c.500 years – throughout the life of the cemetery (1700–1200 bc). The barrows were built of turves and had covered a number of circles of stakes, each with a cremation burial at the centre. Only the more complex mound next to the ring cairn had more than one burial in it. The latest monument in the group is the very small kerb cairn, quite a long walk up a side valley, but a very good example of this distinctive type of small cairn. Just across the stream is the large stone, Maen y Cleddau, which legend says was split by a sword blow.

HEN DDINBYCH is a large square earthwork with the remains of a long narrow stone building in the southern half. There has been a good deal of controversy about the date of this enclosure, estimates ranging from Roman to late medieval. Small-scale excavations have not satisfactorily resolved the problem, but it is likely to have been a medieval settlement of some kind, though its economy in this remote moorland valley can never have been secure.

The group of HAFODYDD in the Nant Criafolen reflects the post-medieval economy of this region – the transhumance system whereby the young people of the district would live for the summer months in these simple stone huts while tending the cattle on their summer grazing lands. This system died with the change to sheep farming, for sheep do not need to be milked. Several of these huts and their banked yards were excavated and pottery and iron knives of C16 date were found, together with a spur and part of a sword which hint at some brigandage, preying on travellers on this lonely road.

RHOS DOMEN, Cornwal (SH 900 640). A linear cemetery comprising three large Bronze Age barrows and a fourth one which has been almost flattened. They stand in a line, N-S, on either side of the road.

BONCYN CRWN (SH 919 622). A very prominent barrow, probably built of turves, standing close beside the road. This monument is visible on the horizon for miles around. Further down the ridge to the N is the CAE DU barrow (SH 926 631). On either side of the valley W of Rhiwiau are two large BARROWS (SH 939 609 and 945 607). The eastern one was dug into in the last century, when three cremation urns were found, one containing a bronze dagger. A summerhouse was built on the top of the mound at the beginning of this century.

There are two groups of Early Bronze Age BARROWS on the prominent ridge of Gorsedd Bran, a pair on the southern tip, where the triangulation point stands on the larger of the two, and another pair in the centre (SH 969 597 and 974 602). Cremation urns and small stone cists were found in four barrows in this area which were dug into by quarrymen *c.*1850, but it is not certain from which the small urn in St Asaph Cathedral Museum was obtained.

TWR YR HILL (SJ 013 583) is a fine turf barrow covered in heather and very similar in appearance to the Brenig barrows before they were excavated. It stands on a ridge and would have commanded wide views before the surrounding forest was planted.

NANTCLWYD HALL *see* LLANELIDAN

0060

NANTGLYN

ST JAMES. A single chamber with s porch and w bellcote. Drastically restored by *Lloyd Williams & Underwood*, 1862. Except for arched-braced trusses, all the features are theirs. Cusped lancets and a w window with quatrefoils in a circle. In 1870 Glynne saw traces of a w doorway, now hidden by slatehanging. – STAINED GLASS. E window by *O'Connor*, 1861. – Four s windows by *Alexander Gibbs*, the westernmost 1895, the others 1872.

The village rises on either side of a stream. PONT-Y-LLAN, a little bridge near the church, has two miniature arches and splayed parapets. PONT NEWYDD, ¼m. NE, is of wide segmental span.

PLAS NANTGLYN, ½m. S. Some post-and-panel partitioning, dated 1573, with a doorway. Also a beam with inscription of 1574, its lettering reversed, mirror-wise, and in the same room a moulded ingle beam.

NEWBRIDGE *see* CEFN MAWR

NEW BRIGHTON *see* MINERA

8070

OLD COLWYN

Following the establishment of Colwyn Bay (q.v.), the village of Colwyn came to be known as Old Colwyn, and in due course was engulfed by its new neighbour.

1. *Landscape:* Vale of Clwyd and Clwydian Hills
from Denbigh (D), looking east
2. *Landscape:* Llangollen (D), looking south from Horseshoe Pass
with Eglwyseg Rocks on left

3 | 5
4 | 6

7. Nannerch (F), Pen y Cloddiau hillfort, Iron Age, aerial view from
the north in light snow. Third rampart in foreground, entrances on left
8. Whitford (F), Maen Achwyfan, late tenth or early eleventh century
9. Rhuddlan (F) Castle, probably by Master James of St George,
begun 1277, aerial view from the south-east
10. Denbigh (D) Castle Gatehouse, probably by Master James of St George,
late thirteenth or early fourteenth century
11. Denbigh (D), Burgess Gate, probably late thirteenth
or early fourteenth century

12. Chirk (D) Castle, probably by Master James of St George,
begun *c.* or after 1282, aerial view from the south-west
13. Greenfield (F), Basingwerk Abbey, refectory west wall,
mid- or late thirteenth century
14. Gresford (D) church, south aisle west window, fourteenth century
15. Bryneglwys (D) church from the north-east, nave late fifteenth
or early sixteenth century, side chapel Elizabethan

16. Valle Crucis Abbey (D), east end, early and mid-thirteenth century
17. Valle Crucis Abbey (D) from the west, early thirteenth to
late fourteenth or early fifteenth century
18. Valle Crucis Abbey (D), west doorway, mid-thirteenth century
19. Valle Crucis Abbey (D), cloister and east range, early thirteenth
to late fourteenth or early fifteenth century

20. Holywell (F), St Winefride's Well, well chamber with well
chapel above, from the north, probably early sixteenth century
21. Holywell (F), St Winefride's Well, well chapel looking east,
probably early sixteenth century
22. Mold (F) church, nave north arcade, probably early sixteenth
century

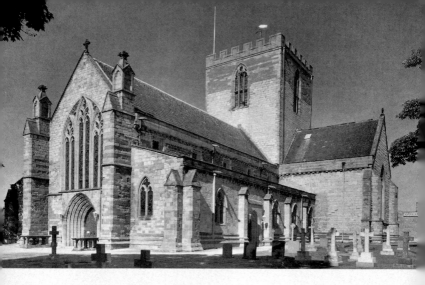

23. St Asaph (F) Cathedral from the south-west, nave and transepts possibly by Master Henry of Ellerton, *c.* 1310–20, tower by Robert Fagan, 1391–2
24. Wrexham (D), St Giles, from the south-west, aisles and clerestory late fifteenth century, tower sixteenth century, and probably by William Hort
25. Gresford (D) church, from the north-west, nave late fifteenth century, tower completed late sixteenth century
26. Gresford (D) church, nave looking east, late fifteenth century

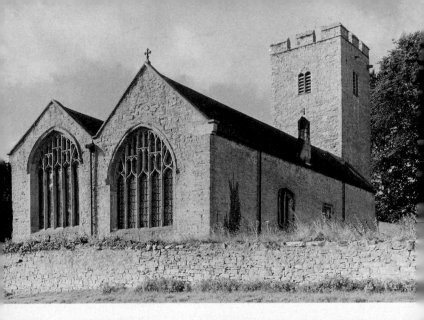

27. Denbigh (D), Llanfarchell (Whitchurch) church, from the north-east,
late fifteenth or early sixteenth century

28. Denbigh (D), Llanfarchell (Whitchurch) church, south nave looking east,
late fifteenth or early sixteenth century

29. Cilcain (F) church, south nave roof, late fifteenth or
early sixteenth century

30. Llanrhaeadr-yng-Nghinmeirch (D) church, east end,
probably early sixteenth century

31. Efenechdyd (D) church, font, date unknown
32. Llanynys (D) church, south door, early sixteenth century
33. Nercwys (F) church, pulpit, probably early sixteenth century
34. Llanarmon-yn-Iâl (D) church, chandelier, late fifteenth or early sixteenth century
35. St Asaph (F) Cathedral, stalls, late fifteenth century, altered by Sir Gilbert Scott, *c.* 1867–75
36. Derwen (D) church, screen, late fifteenth or early sixteenth century

31 32 | 35
33 34 | 36

37. Gresford (D) church, chancel roof, late fifteenth century
38. Llangollen (D) church, chancel ceiling, late fifteenth or
early sixteenth century
39. Llanrhaeadr-yng-Nghinmeirch (D) church, north nave east window, 1533

bic angelus mandat ut ucmat
obuiari Joachim porta aurea

Obuiacio Joachim et
anne in porta aurea

Presentacio marie in templum

Salutacio marie per s abrielem
archangelum

Presentacio marie in templum

Natalis Christi
nw ben nrastram fert

40. Gresford (D) church, north aisle east window, with series depicting the lives of St Anne and the Virgin, 1498, partly renewed by Denis King after 1966. Details: top left, Angel appears to Anne: top right, Anne and Joachim meet at the Golden Gate; bottom left, Presentation of the Virgin in the Temple; bottom right, Annunciation

41. Gresford (D) church, north aisle east window, with series depicting the lives of St Anne and the Virgin, 1498. Detail: Birth of Christ, largely renewed by Clayton & Bell, 1872

42. Llanynys (D) church, sepulchral cross, mid-fourteenth century

43. Gresford (D) church, monument to John Trevor †1589

44. Llanarmon-yn-Iâl (D) church, monument to Efan Llwyd, 1639

45. Mold (F), Rhual, barn, possibly fifteenth century
46. Eglwyseg (D), World's End, Plas Uchaf (or Manor House),
possibly 1563 in part
47. Llanelidan (D), Plas Uchaf, fifteenth or early sixteenth
century, altered seventeenth century
48. Cilcain (F), Brithdir Mawr, medieval, altered 1589 and 1637

45 | 47
46 | 48

49. Cefn Meiriadog (D), Plas Newydd, 1583
50. Llanfair Talhaearn (D), Plas Newydd, post-and-panel partition, 1585
51. Eyton (D), Eyton Manor Farm, probably 1633
52. Cerrigydrudion (D), Llaethwryd, partly 1668

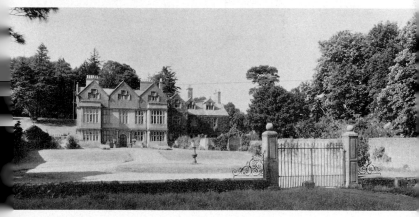

53. Trefalun (D), Trevalyn Hall, 1576
54. Bodelwyddan (F), Facnol Fawr, 1597,
photographed before the fire of 1984
55. Nercwys (F), Nerquis Hall, by Evan Jones, 1637–8
56. Mold (F), Rhual, 1634, staircase
57. Mold (F), Rhual, 1634

59. Hope (F), Plas Teg, probably 1610
60. Mold (F), Pentrehobyn, hall overmantel, early seventeenth century
61. Hope (F) church, pulpit, mid- or late seventeenth century

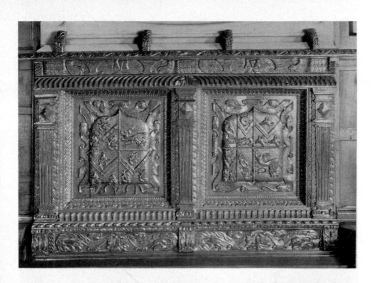

62. Denbigh (D), Leicester's Church, 1578-84 and left unfinished
63. Denbigh (D), Llanfarchell (Whitchurch) church,
monument to Sir John and Joan Salusbury, by Donbins, 1588
64. Denbigh (D), Llanfarchell (Whitchurch) church,
monument to Humphrey Llwyd †1568

62
63 | 64

65. Chirk (D) Castle, Long Gallery looking north, *c.* 1667–78,
probably by Lady Wilbraham, woodcarving by Thomas Dugdale,
ceiling by A. W. N. Pugin, 1847
66. Chirk (D) Castle, south end of Long Gallery, *c.* 1667–78,
probably by Lady Wilbraham, woodcarving by Thomas Dugdale,
fireplace surround mid-eighteenth century,
ceiling, grate and tiles by A. W. N. Pugin, 1847
67. Erddig (D), east front, central nine bays by
Thomas Webb, 1683–*c.* 1687, wings *c.* 1721–4
68. Erddig (D), by Thomas Webb, 1683–*c.* 1687, north staircase

65 | 67
66 | 68

69. Betws-yn-Rhos (D), Coed Coch, by Hakewill, c. 1804, staircase
70. Hawarden (F) Castle, possibly by Samuel Turner, c. 1750-7,
landing, plasterwork probably by Thomas Oliver
71. Chirk (D) Castle, Saloon, by Joseph Turner, c. 1771-2,
plasterwork by Kilmister, 1772, chimneypiece by Benjamin Bromfield, 1773

72. St Asaph (F), former Bishop's Palace (Plas yr Esgob),
east front, 1791, probably by Samuel Wyatt
73. Erddig (D), dining room, by Thomas Hopper, 1826–7
74. Tremeirchion (F), Brynbella, 1792–5 by C. Mead,
wings enlarged mid-nineteenth century
75. Wynnstay (D), Dairy, by Lancelot ('Capability') Brown, 1782–3

| 72 | 74 |
| 73 | 75 |

76. Wynnstay (D), Newbridge Lodge, by C. R. Cockerell, 1827-8
77. Worthenbury (F) church, by Richard Trubshaw, 1736-9
78. Ruabon (D) church, font, by Robert Adam, 1772

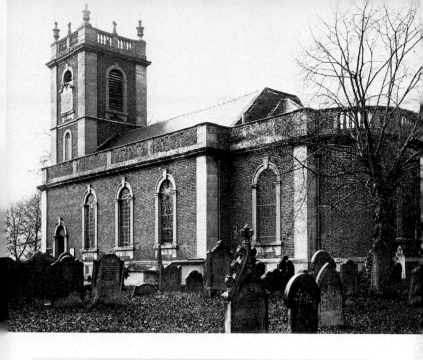

Here lies
MAURICE JONES of BLANKHAYRE Esq.
Son of HUMPHREY JONES [...] Esq. by JANE his Wife
Daughter of EDMUND [...] of NANTGLYN Esq.
He married JANE Daughter of [...] BAGOT of STAFFORD-SHIRE Bar[...]
By whom he had [...] who died an Infant
He was a Gentlem[...] [...] Body and Mind
His Conversation was divert[...] [...] pleasant and instructive
His Hospitality was diffusi[...] [...] charity unbounded though secret
The former gain'd him tho[...] [...] that knew him here
And he now en[...] [...] the latter
He died y[e] 1st of January in th[...] [...] of his Age N[...]
[...] of a pious Respect to his [...] [...] to beg[...]

79. Chirk (D) Castle, gates, by Robert and John
Davies, 1712 and 1718–20
80. Leeswood (F), Leeswood Hall, White Gates, c. 1726,
probably by Robert Davies
81. Llanrhaeadr-yng-Nghinmeirch (D) church,
monument to Maurice Jones † 1702, possibly by Robert Wynne

82. Nannerch (F) church, monument to
Charlotte Mostyn † 1694, by Grinling Gibbons
83. Nannerch (F) church, monument to
Charlotte Mostyn † 1694, by Grinling Gibbons, detail
84. Wrexham (D), St Giles, monument to
Mary Myddelton, by L. F. Roubiliac, 1751-2

85. Chirk (D) church, monument to Sir Richard, Lady and
Sir William Myddelton, by Robert Wynne, c. 1718–22
86. Gresford (D) church, monument to John Parry †1797, by
Sir Richard Westmacott
87. Gresford (D) church, monument to the Rev. Henry Newcome †1803,
by Sir Richard Westmacott
88. Marchwiel (D) church, monument to Philip Yorke,
by Sir Richard Westmacott, 1805

89. Hawarden (F) Castle, south front,
remodelled by Thomas Cundy, 1809–10
90. Marford (F), Yew Tree Cottage, probably c. 1813–15,
altered c. 1963 and 1979–81
91. Trefnant (D) church, by Sir Gilbert Scott, 1853–5, looking east
92. Llanbedr Dyffryn Clwyd (D), New Church, by Poundley & Walker, 1863

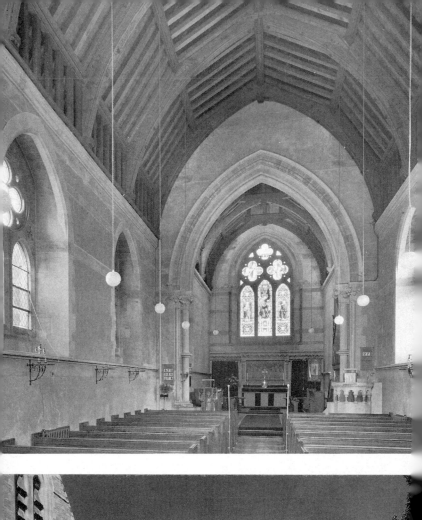

93. Rhydymwyn (F) church, by J. L. Pearson, 1860–3, looking east
94. Towyn (D) church and vicarage, by G. E. Street, 1872–3, looking north
95. Towyn (D) church, 1872–3, and former school, 1871,
by G. E. Street, looking east
96. Towyn (D) vicarage and church, by G. E. Street, 1872–3, looking east

93	95
94	96

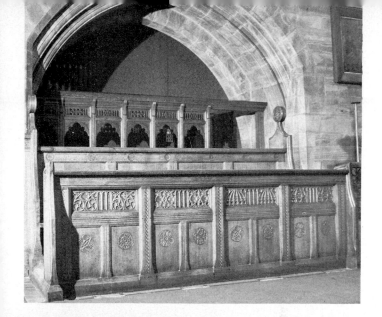

97. Bersham (D) church, by John Gibson, 1873, looking east
98. Northop (F) church, altar table, by John Douglas, c. 1876–7,
enriched 1879. Reredos panels painted by Hardman & Co., 1877
99. Halkyn (F) church, by John Douglas, 1877–8,
vestry screen and choir stalls
100. Halkyn (F) church, by John Douglas, 1877–8, from the south-west

101. Hawarden (F) church, west window, by Sir Edward Burne-Jones, 1898
102. Hawarden (F) church, monument to William Ewart Gladstone and
Catherine Gladstone, by Sir William Richmond, *c.* 1901–6
103. Chirk (D), railway viaduct, by Henry Robertson, 1846–8,
and beyond it, canal aqueduct, by Thomas Telford and
William Jessop, 1796–1801
104. Froncysyllte (D), Pont Cysyllte, by Thomas Telford and
William Jessop, 1795–1805

105. Llanrhaeadr-yng-Nghinmeirch (D), Llanrhaeadr Hall,
remodelled by the younger Thomas Penson, 1841–2
106. Chirk (D) Castle, Cromwell Hall, remodelled by A. W. N. Pugin, 1845
107. Llangernyw (D), Hafodunos, by Sir Gilbert Scott, 1861–6, garden front
108. St George (D), Kinmel Park, remodelled by W. Eden Nesfield,
c. 1868–74, east front, photographed before the fire of 1975 and
subsequent restoration

109. St George (D), Kinmel Park, Golden Lodge,
by W. Eden Nesfield, 1868
110. Denbigh (D), North Wales Mental Hospital,
by Fulljames & Waller, 1842–8
111. Hawarden (F), St Deiniol's Library, by
Douglas & Minshull, 1899–1902 and 1904–6

112. Ruthin (D), Pendref Chapel, 1827, altered 1875
113. Llanrwst (D), Seion Chapel, 1881–3, interior
114. Mold (F), Bethesda Chapel, by W. W. Gwyther, 1863
115. Mold (F), Bethesda Chapel, by W. W. Gwyther, 1863, interior

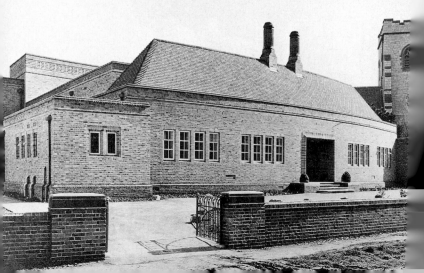

116. Colwyn Bay (D), No. 7 Abergele Road, by S. Colwyn Foulkes, 1930
117. Old Colwyn (D), St John's Church House, Cliff Road,
by S. Colwyn Foulkes, 1935–7
118. Rhyl (F), Regal Cinema (demolished), High Street,
by S. Colwyn Foulkes, 1935–7
119. Rhyl (F), Plaza Cinema, High Street, by S. Colwyn Foulkes, 1930–1

| 116 | 118 |
| 117 | 119 |

120. Queensferry (F), Williams & Robinson Factory,
by H. B. Creswell, c. 1901–5
121. Mold (F), Theatr Clwyd, County Civic Centre, by R. W. Harvey, 1973–6
122. Rhosllannerchrugog (D) Library, by R. A. MacFarlane, 1961–2
123. Towyn (D), Christ the King (R.C.), by Bowen, Dann, Davies, 1973–4, interior
124. Wrexham (D), Capel-y-Groes Chapel, by Bowen, Dann, Davies, 1981–2

120	123
121	
122	124

125. *Seaside scenery:* Colwyn Bay (D)

St Catherine, Abergele Road. Built 1837. Aisleless, with a short chancel. Lancets and intersecting tracery. The w tower has obelisk pinnacles. (stained glass. e window by *Clutterbuck*, commemoration date 1844. P. Howell)

St John Baptist, Station Road. A fresh and breezy seaside church by *Douglas & Minshull*, 1899–1903. Outer walls of local limestone. Dressings and ashlar interior are of red Cheshire sandstone. The elements are Perp. There is variety in the size and disposition of windows, and those of the clerestory are untraceried, with the wall-plate continuing as a lintel. Arcades with conventionalized caps and the arch mouldings springing from little brackets. Chancel arch with continuous mouldings and no caps. Roof a form of double hammerbeam. w tower, the original design for which had an octagonal upper stage with flying buttresses and a low spire. As built, by the firm of *Douglas, Minshull & Muspratt*, 1912, the proposals were much improved. The tower has a squared-off effect, with battlements stepped up towards the corners. An octagonal sw vice turret throws the bell openings off-centre and has the same effect on the w window, and this looks odd inside. – stalls with baluster motifs as well as tracery. – stained glass. s aisle e by *Kempe & Tower*. Commemoration date 1914.

St John's Church House, i.e. Church Hall, Cliff Road. 117 1935–7 by *S. Colwyn Foulkes*. Fine brickwork, including moulding on the long convex front, and an ornamented frieze, built up in brick, on the stage tower behind. Also two fluted chimneys.

Baptist Church, Abergele Road. 1905 by *A. Hewitt* of Llandudno. (cw) One of those all-red chapels – red in wall and roof, in terra-cotta tracery and in octagonal spirelet.

Methodist Church, Wynn Avenue. 1908–9 by *J. M. Porter & Elcock*. Low, rock-faced and arty-looking, with continuous dormers as a clerestory. Enlarged 1932.

United Reformed Church (formerly Congregational), Berthes Road. Built 1924–5. Limestone, with sandstone dressings. Neo-Perp windows in the gables, and a square spirelet near the w end of the ridge. A room with a big mullioned and transomed semicircular bow was added by *Colwyn Foulkes*, 1935–9.

Bethel Chapel, Miners Lane, Penmaenrhos. 1935 by *Colwyn Foulkes*. Rendered, and in the gable is a tall mullioned and transomed window with segmental head. To the l. is a hipped porch, and low screen walls either side end in ball finials. The whole façade recalls the work of Edgar Wood.

In Station Road, The White House is a witty response by *Colwyn Foulkes* to the modernism of the 1930s. White-painted rendered walls, courses of green pantiles at the parapet, and a small pantiled belvedere turret. As with so many houses of the thirties, the windows have been altered. Nearby, at the corner of Abergele Road, is the Midland Bank. 1912 by *Woolfall & Eccles*, in Mannerist free classical. The

QUEEN'S HOTEL, further E in Abergele Road, is by *J. W. & R. F. Beaumont* of Manchester, *c.*1893.

In LLANELIAN ROAD, and by *Brian Lingard & Partners*, 1963–7, is KENNEDY COURT. Two-storeyed ranges of old people's flats, of brick, with concrete first-floor and roof fascias. Nicely scaled, and most successfully planned around existing trees. Further out, the BROOKLANDS DEVELOPMENT, off DOLWEN ROAD, built 1975–82, provides an example of one of the private housing schemes designed by *Bowen, Dann, Davies*.

PANDY TUDUR *see* LLANDDEWI

PENMAENRHOS *see* OLD COLWYN

PENRHYD *see* EGLWSYBACH

PENSARN *see* ABERGELE

PENTRE BROUGHTON *see* BROUGHTON

PENTRE CELYN *see* LLANFAIR DYFFRYN CLWYD

PENTREFELIN *see* LLANGOLLEN

8050

PENTREFOELAS

CHURCH. 1857–9 by *Sir Gilbert Scott*, at the expense of Charles Griffith Wynne of Voelas (*see* p. 259). It replaced a church of 1766 to which a S transept had been added in 1774. The transept was repeated in what is otherwise a very ordinary lancet and bellcote affair, with none of the usual panache of an estate church. External rendering has not helped. – CHANCEL FITTINGS. 1905–6 by *Sir Charles Nicholson*, including Neo-Jacobean REREDOS and red and white stone and marble FLOOR patterns. – STAINED GLASS. E window by *F. W. Oliphant*. – W windows by *Clayton & Bell*. – By *Comper*, a pair of S lancets, 1912, and a horribly insipid N window opposite, 1935. – MONUMENTS. John Griffith †1794. By *Westmacott*, presumably the elder. A maiden, holding a rose, sits in front of a draped urn and clasps its base. - Colonel C. A. Wynne-Finch. 1905, as part of *Nicholson*'s chancel scheme. Tablet with strapwork turning curly. Executed by *R. Davison*. - CORONA and CANDLESTANDARDS.

C.W.G. Wynne also paid for the little (former) SCHOOL, NW of the church. Dated 1852 and with a tiny bellcote over the porch like that at Capel Garmon (q.v.).

Pentrefoelas is a grey stone village on the Holyhead Road with ESTATE HOUSING and the three-storeyed VOELAS ARMS. The latter has two three-bay fronts of different date, one meeting the single-bay return of the other. The enlargement took place in 1839, when the licence was transferred from CERNIOGE, 2¼m. towards Cerrigydrudion, where there was a well-known posting house. (Hence the appearance of Cernioge on mileposts.)

(VOELAS, 1½m. w.* In a picturesque park with river walks either side of the Conwy and approached by PONT RHYD-DYFRGI, a bridge with a level roadway on three arches built in 1781. The present rectangular white plastered house, built by *Sir Clough Williams-Ellis* for Colonel John Wynne-Finch in 1957–61, is the third on the site. Nine bays and two storeys, the central three projecting beneath an armorial pediment and with tautly curved pediments on the doorcases. Deep plan based on a transverse gallery 50ft long. Fine Baroque chimneypiece and other details from Lindsey House, Chelsea, inside. The SUMMERHOUSE contains Elizabethan panelling from Old Voelas (*see* below). To the E, the Victorian STABLE YARD and large terraced GARDEN.

The first house here, called Lima, was a long Regency Gothic villa, also white and plastered, built 1813–19 by the Hon. Charles Finch, who had married the Wynne heiress. Wyattish rooms with coved ceilings and bowed ends. This was engulfed in a much larger Ruabon brick house, built for his grandson Charles Wynne-Finch, who inherited the Kirby Hall portraits, and who revived the name of the old family house. This was constructed to a massive E.E. design by *Richard Coad* in 1856–8. Subsequent internal work (*c.* 1884) and a garden porch by *Hungerford Pollen*, who was the brother of Charles Wynne-Finch's first wife and architect of the now demolished church of the Assumption at Rhyl (*see* p. 430*n*.).

BRIDGE and LODGE, ½m. w of Voelas.‡ Victorian romanticism; a 40-ft span high above the Conwy, with the lodge, dated 1862, perched over the gorge at the N.

Opposite the park wall of Voelas, and previously in Caernarfonshire but now in Gwynedd, is a Holyhead Road TOLL-HOUSE.

---

* The entire entry for Voelas is by Mr Haslam.
‡ Previously on the boundary between Denbighshire and Caernarfonshire, but wholly transferred to Gwynedd in 1974.

HEN FOELAS MOTTE, ½ m. NNW. Perhaps made by Owain Gwynedd c.1164. A very tall earth castle, perhaps a natural hillock but scarped into concentric rings, on top of which foundations for a square stone tower were found in 1882. Its history ceased in 1185, when the manor of Hiraethog became a grange of Aberconwy Abbey. At the bottom the pool for Pentrefoelas Mill.

OLD VOELAS, ½ m. NNW. Remains of the principal house of the Pentrefoelas uplands, the home of the Wynnes from 1545 to 1819, when it was demolished. Moses Griffith's watercolour of c.1770 shows a large unit-system group of rectangular C16 and C17 buildings just below the motte, with twelve chimneys. Of this, one small altered cottage remains, together with fragmentary carved window traceries which suggest that the house built c.1550 by Cadwaladr ap Maurice was a hall like that at Gloddaeth in Gwynedd. As hereditary stewards of Aberconwy Abbey, he and his son received grants of its lands from Henry VIII and Elizabeth. Two overmantels and panelling with classical motifs (a frieze of semicircles, fluted pilasters) and painted heraldry of c.1600 are preserved in a summerhouse at Voelas (see above). Two AVENUES of beeches and limes lead to the site from the W, past a late C18 walled GARDEN. The early C13 LEVELINUS STONE, now in the National Museum, was moved near the house, to the present site of its replica, in 1790.)

MAES GWYN, ¾ m. NW. (Dated 1665. DOE) Storeyed porch and, at the rear, mullioned windows. FARM BUILDINGS on either side of the yard in front and on the opposite side of the road.

PLAS IOLYN, 1 m. SE. Cruciform in plan with an C18 S wing, and an early C20 one to the N. House and buildings are dominated by the so-called GREAT BARN. Long and massive, built high up on a rock, and mysterious in its dating and purpose. At its S end, at ground level, is the lower stage of a square tower. Opposite, on the N of the yard, is a splendid lofty BARN, with queen-post trusses. (One collar dated 1572. DOE)

GILER, 1¼ m. SW. Whitewashed stone. The N front is unbroken except for a porch and is unusually long. The house was, in fact, built in two stages, end to end, on the unit system. First came the E half, c.1560, the home of the poet Rhys Wynn. Lateral chimney and inside cross passage, with the hall to the l., i.e. to the E of the entrance. Lower-end post-and-panel partition partly original, and a later one separates the passage from the hall. The W house, with a cyclopean doorway on the S, was built c.1600 for one of Wynn's sons, who secured the whole building for himself and made a single dwelling of it. Some diagonally set timber mullions remain. The son probably added the staircase wing which partly obscures the gabled lateral chimney of the E house, and it was definitely he who was responsible for the charming little GATEHOUSE which provided access to a N entrance court. Square, with mullioned windows and a gable on each face and an upper room approached by an outer staircase. Fireplace in the upper room, with heraldry and the date 1623 above it. C17 FARM BUILDINGS back on to either side of the forecourt.

Two remarkable monuments of a type very rare in Wales are to be found – with luck and perseverance – on the enclosed moorland w of Hafod Dinbych. The first, at HAFOD Y DRE (SH 885 537), consists of a small cairn set at the SW end of a line of small stones forming an area of 'dragons' teeth' *c.*52ft square. All these stones and the cairn are very low, and the group is extremely inconspicuous. However, it would originally have been easier to find, for at the centre of the NW line is a fallen monolith which would have stood *c.*5ft high. The date of their erection is probably Bronze Age. Not far away at SH 878 536, in Ffridd Can-Awen, is another larger but less regular area of low set stones. At the beginning of the century excavation exposed three small cists with cremated human bone on the western edge of this group. The full extent of the arrangement of upright stones has probably been reduced by field clearance in both ancient and modern times.

A small but complex RING CAIRN of Bronze Age date occurs 2m. NNW of Pentrefoelas at SH 859 547 in a field N of the track to MAES MERDDYN. The monument consists of a small mound surrounded by a ditch and low bank. On the inner edge of the bank seven small upright stones can be seen poking through the turf. The ruins of a cruciform lambing shelter and an old cottage can be seen nearby, and there is a tradition that the ring cairn had been regularly used as a cock-pit; cockfighting was once very popular in this part of the world.

PENTRE MAELOR *see* WREXHAM, p. 311

PENYCAE

2040

ST THOMAS. 1877–8 by *Sir Aston Webb*. Polygonal rock-faced masonry. Lancets and circles. The roof of a N aisle continues that of the nave. At the E end of the nave a slate-hung pyramid-spired bellcote. N porch with timber framing. Nothing is handled well, though the local press reported that an architectural journal (which?) considered it 'a perfect model of a church for a mountainous district like Wales.'* – The ENCAUSTIC TILES in the chancel are by *William Godwin*.

VICARAGE, W of the church. Of 1893, with Douglas-like features outside and in, though more likely to be by a former pupil or assistant than his own work.

SALEM BAPTIST CHAPEL, ⅛m. E. 1878. The front has a tall central gable flanked by hips.

WYNN HALL, 1m. ESE. Two *ex situ* date inscriptions of 1649. Some exposed half-timbering with cusped lozenge and other

---

* Information from Canon Pritchard.

patterns. Two late C17 staircases. Much was done in the C19, particularly embellishment with carved oak from furniture, doubtless inspired by Plas Newydd, Llangollen (*see* p. 222). The work included the porch, and also a chimneypiece, the latter now dismantled. Rusticated GATEPIERS.

3040
PEN-Y-LAN

A house in fine parkland, an estate church, and a small village.

PEN-Y-LAN, the house itself, was bought in 1854 by Thomas Hardcastle, a Bolton cotton manufacturer, of the firm of Ormrod & Hardcastle, and it subsequently passed to his brother-in-law James Ormrod. Said to date from *c.*1690, it was remodelled in 1830, and is stuccoed and castellated. It was enlarged and further altered later in the C19, and although the additions were demolished in the 1950s, features of this phase remain, including probably the cusped windows on the entrance front.

ALL SAINTS. Built at the expense of James Ormrod in memory of his wife, and originally a private chapel. 1889 by *R. Knill Freeman* of Bolton. Polygonal apse and a bellcote over the chancel arch. A costly building, of red sandstone ashlar throughout, and enriched with elaborate oak FURNISHINGS, STAINED GLASS in the apse, and PAINTED DECORATION on the chancel roof. The N porch is vaulted. It is just the sort of thing which would have been done superbly well by Paley & Austin, whom Ormrod employed for the church at Scorton, built to commemorate his brother. As it is, it fails to hang together, and great variety of window design (mostly Early Dec and tending to straight-headed Perp in the chancel) makes for restlessness.

The former SCHOOL bears the date 1885 and Ormrod's initials.

BRYN HOUSE, ½m. NNW of the church. Brick, of 1749, and instructive as a dated vernacular example. Three bays, the first-floor middle window set higher than its fellows. Still with timber cross windows in small panes, and the staircase has a string and heavy rail, even if the balusters are comparatively slender.

PICKHILL HALL *see* MARCHWIEL

PLAS CLOUGH *see* DENBIGH, p. 154

PLAS NANTYR *see* GLYN CEIRIOG

PONTFADOG 2030

St John Baptist. 1845–7. Begun by an architect named *Wehnert*, who went bankrupt, and the execution was entrusted to *R. K. Penson*. Commissioners' type, with lancets and a shallow altar recess, and in fact in receipt of a Commissioners' grant. Thin w tower and pyramid spire. Dressings of terra-cotta and yellowish brick are doubtless due to Penson.

Tan-y-Garth, ½m. NE. 1915–16 by *Philip H. Lockwood*, for Mrs Bertram Brooke of the Sarawak rajahship family. Her husband, who died in the Great War, was His Highness the Tuan Muda B. W. D. Brooke, a captain in the Royal Horse Artillery. A many-gabled Arts and Crafts house, stone-faced, and with sturdy timber mullions. At one corner a large two-storey veranda, its upper stage timber-framed and intended as a sleeping balcony. Terraced GARDEN and a circular DOVECOTE.*

Offa's Dyke. *See* Chirk, p. 131.
Yr Orsedd Wen. *See* Chirk, p. 131.

PONT-Y-GWYDDEL *see* LLANFAIR TALHAEARN

POOL PARK 0050

Rebuilt 1826–9 for the second Lord Bagot. The designer was *John Buckler*, who is believed to have worked also at the Bagot seat of Blithfield in Staffordshire. *Benjamin Gummow* too was involved at Pool Park, but was probably responsible only for supervision. Neo-Elizabethan, and suggesting the pages of a pattern book rather than a house which actually got built. The service quarters, as well as the main rooms, are all contained within one symmetrical block. E-plan front, with three big gables and a storeyed porch set against the middle one. The porch, with Jacobethan embellishment, is of stone, as is all the ground-floor walling and the upper-storey dressings. Originally the upper parts were faced with sham half-timbering, an early instance of its use for so large a building. The black-and-white patterning was small in scale and complicated. Only quatrefoil motifs in bargeboards survive as a reminder, for it was regrettably done away with in the 1930s, and the surface is now rendered and the masonry below painted to match. Symmetrical right-hand return, with central gable and three oriels. Interior much altered, and the imperial staircase may be an early C20 remodelling. It is splendidly strong and solid, and incorporates enriched C17 vase-shaped balusters, figurative panels, and other reused woodwork. A pair of angels serve as newels. At the former

---

* Information on the house was supplied by Mr J. F. Smout.

main gates, 1m. NNE, a highly picturesque ENTRANCE LODGE, of stone and half-timbering. Jettied and gabled overhangs, each with an oriel, and one carried on posts to form a porch.

PRION

0060

ST JAMES. A church without a village, among the hills W of the Vale of Clwyd. 1859 by *R. Lloyd Williams*. The usual formula for a small country church, with lancets, and a nave, chancel, S porch, and W bellcote.

RHEWL *see* LLANYNYS

2040

RHOSLLANNERCHRUGOG

Rhosllannerchrugog grew up as a mining community. Ruabon brick predominates, except in the older part, which lies along a ridge to the E. There is a great concentration of chapels; most of them, though not all, are mentioned below.

ST JOHN EVANGELIST, Church Street. In a wooded churchyard. 1852–3 by the younger *Thomas Penson*, and later than his ecclesiologically more advanced church at Gwersyllt (q.v.). Aisleless and cruciform, with a slender SE tower and pyramidal stone spire. The style is Norman, carried through with thoroughness. Carved enrichment, and a S portal in three orders. There are transept and chancel arches, the former superfluous, as the roofs of nave and transepts intersect. Arcading against the ashlar-faced E wall. – PULPIT and STALLS also Norman. – STAINED GLASS. By *H. Walter Lonsdale*, 1882, are the E window, with figurative work set in grisaille, and chancel N.

VICARAGE, Gutter Hill. A remarkably unremarkable early work of *Sir Aston Webb*, 1875.

ST DAVID (Welsh Church), Broad Street. Nave and a N aisle, built 1892, without the intended chancel and SE steeple. By *Douglas & Fordham*. Ruabon brick inside and out, with some sandstone dressings. Broad Perp W window, and a S porch with timberwork in its gable. Brick arcade and sturdy roof timbers. Chancel by *J. H. Swainson*, 1935–6. – Two sets of C18 domestic PANELLING.

ST MARY, Merlin Street, Johnstown. 1926–8 by *E. Glyn Wooley*. Seemly conventionalized Perp. Rustic brick with stone dressings externally, and white-painted plaster and dressings of a harder brick inside. Spacious and lofty, but no clerestory, and a S but no N aisle. An intended NE tower was never built, and the E end of the chancel was completed by *H. Anthony Clark, F. C. Roberts & Partners*, 1957.

MOUNT PLEASANT BAPTIST CHAPEL, Chapel Street. 1891 by *J. G. Owen* of Liverpool. Brick, with lancets.

PENUEL BAPTIST CHAPEL, Market Street. Large, two-storeyed. The main structure is presumably of 1859. (Reset datestone.) Exuberant brick and terra-cotta façade, added 1891, with Ionic pilasters and much else.

SION BAPTIST CHAPEL, Bank Street. By *J. G. Owen* (CW), 1900. Brick. Gable front, and the main upper windows round-headed.

TABERNACL BAPTIST CHAPEL, Chapel Street. Polychromatic brick gable, 1883, fronting an earlier stone body.

BETHLEHEM INDEPENDENT CHAPEL, Hall Street. Spectacular rock-faced *Rundbogenstil* front of 1889. Asymmetrical, and with a pyramid-spired clock tower. It masks a massive structure of earlier date, but can this be as early as 1812? (Reset datestone.) Interior fittings of the later period.

MYNYDD SEION INDEPENDENT CHAPEL, Chapel Street. 1891. Brick and terra-cotta. Round-arched.

SALEM INDEPENDENT CHAPEL, Bank Street. 1896. Brick, stone and terra-cotta. In a mixed style. It is probably the chapel known to have been designed by a Gummow (CW), presumably *M. J. Gummow*.

(There is or was a CONGREGATIONAL CHAPEL at Johnstown by the noted chapel designer *Sir John Sulman*, 1881 (CW), but this has not been traced.)

BETHEL METHODIST CHAPEL, Chapel Street. Stuccoed. Round-arched windows at the front.

HOREB METHODIST CHAPEL, Johnson Street. 1875. Red brick, with yellow brick dressings.

BETHEL WELSH PRESBYTERIAN (CALVINISTIC METHODIST) CHAPEL, Johnson Street. 1903. Brick and terra-cotta. Slightly Arts and Crafts.

JERUSALEM WELSH PRESBYTERIAN (CALVINISTIC METHODIST) CHAPEL, Brook Street. 1770, enlarged 1837, according to the inscription. Of the latter date, the stuccoed two-storey front, round-arched. Pediment and four-column Tuscan porch.

PUBLIC LIBRARY, Princes Road. 1961–2 by *R. A. MacFarlane*, 122 County Architect, and exceptionally good. Clean, precise and immaculately detailed. Flat-roofed. Glazing and dark brick panels, with the bookshelves backing on to them, alternate in the outer walls. The fascias are of slate. A central clerestory is raised on four columns. Contained in a lower wing is an intimately scaled children's library. The structure is unusual and ingenious; the brick panels are non-loadbearing; all windows are suspended from the roofs, with the lower roof cantilevered from the four steel columns which also carry the upper one.

MINERS' INSTITUTE (Plas Mwynwyr Rhos), Broad Street. By *John Owen* of Wrexham and *F. A. Roberts* of Mold. Very large, with the end elevation facing the street. Of 1924–6, though in the brick and stone 'Queen Anne' Baroque of the turn of the century. Fairly elaborately treated, with a clock cupola crowning the roof.

LLANERCHRUGOG HALL, ½ m. w of the built-up area. Mid-C18. Three storeys, five bays. Now rendered, but with quoins exposed. Tuscan porch.

HAFOD HOUSE, ¾ m. E of Johnstown. Five bays, two and a half storeys. Of brick, with stone dressings. Parapet and coped gable ends. Pedimented doorcase, and the windows above it have shouldered architraves with keystones. Rusticated lintels elsewhere. Said to be 1720, and this is possible, though interior features, including the staircase, are early C19. A wing behind is said to be of 1690. (It contains a staircase with turned balusters, string with pulvinated frieze, and square double newels at the landings. DOE)

To the E is WAT'S DYKE.

RHOSNESNI see WREXHAM, pp. 311–12

RHOS-ON-SEA see LLANDRILLO-YN-RHOS

RHOSROBIN see WREXHAM, p. 312

RHOSTYLLEN see ESCLUSHAM

RHOSYMEDRE see CEFN MAWR

2030
RHYDYCROESAU

The River Cynllaith forms the boundary between Wales and England.

CHRIST CHURCH. The small w tower is of 1838. The nave was remodelled (new roof, new windows etc.) and the chancel added by *W. H. Spaull*, 1886.

3050
ROSSETT / YR ORSEDD

CHRIST CHURCH. By *Douglas & Fordham*. Designed 1886 and built 1891–2, replacing a predecessor of 1841. 'Inside and out,' Goodhart-Rendel rightly noted, 'this building has real charm, and is beautifully thorough in detail.' Neo-Perp, of ashlar throughout, and cruciform, with a sturdy central tower. Tower buttresses on the N and S only, flush with the

E and W faces. One of them rises from a vice projection, with good sculptural effect, if lack of structural logic. An aisle on the N only. It opens into the transept, which serves as a chapel, and the S transept is a vestry. The choir occupies the crossing, the arches of which all differ, and beyond is a short sanctuary with a fine, broad E window. Good woodwork, not least the roofs, and characteristic and consistent Douglas FURNISHINGS, e.g. REREDOS, STALLS, PEWS and ORGAN CASE. – STAINED GLASS. By *Kempe* the E window, 1905, and nave easternmost on S, 1904.   Chancel N by *Morris & Co.*, 1907. – Two three-light windows in the N transept show the depths to which *Heaton, Butler & Bayne* had sunk by the late 1920s.

VICARAGE, W of the church. A splendid High Victorian period piece, with polychromatic brick, built 1866.

PRESBYTERIAN CHURCH OF WALES, Station Road. 1875 by *Douglas*. Lancets, timber porch at the gable end, and a flèche.

ROSSETT HALL, ¼ m. NE of the church, close to the main road. Early or mid-C18, of two and a half storeys. Brick, with parapets and flush long-and-short quoins. The centre is recessed between projecting wings with splayed corners. One-bay pediment. A curving stone staircase is later in date.

ROSSETT MILL, on the main road, S of the church. Brick-nogged, the framing in large squares. Diagonal bracing, and a dormer, dated 1661, has some patterning. Cross wings, that on the l. largely rebuilt in brick. The other is a C19 addition, entirely of brick. Undershot wheel.

MARFORD MILL, opposite Rossett Mill. Rebuilt in brick, 1791, incorporating some earlier masonry. Two undershot wheels and, at the opposite side, a long C19 addition. Rescued from dereliction when converted to offices by *John K. Bellis & Robert B. Kay*, 1972–3. The older part was extensively re-windowed and had its brickwork rendered, and the C19 addition was made to look thoroughly modern. Its iron window frames with glazing bars were replaced with large panes, and the topmost openings were enlarged upwards into new dormers. The scheme received two conservation awards from bodies which should have known better. However seemly the end result, it is preposterous that radical adaptation, greatly transforming the character of a building, should be called conservation.

In STATION ROAD, W of the Presbyterian church, is the half-timbered ROSSETT INSTITUTE and NATIONAL WESTMINSTER BANK. 1881 by *Douglas*. It was built as a coffee house for the Liverpool merchant and shipowner Alexander Balfour, a noted philanthropist and temperance campaigner. By *P. H. Lockwood** the CHURCH HALL, 1911. The stone-built RAILWAY STATION, with margin panes and curly bargeboards, now demolished, was one of the last to remain

* Information from Mr Howell.

of *T. M. Penson*'s original buildings for the Shrewsbury and Chester Railway, opened 1848.

MEIFOD, further W, on the B road. In the Gothic manner of Marford (*see* p. 386). Dated 1818, but this must refer to the addition of the non-Gothic upper storey.

Further out are STONELEIGH and STRATHALYN, two of the prosperous C19 villas which appeared around Rossett and Gresford. Strathalyn, free Elizabethan, is dated 1862. Almost opposite, at YEW TREE FARM, are two COTTAGES, semi-detached but asymmetrical, with half-timbering. 1881 by *Douglas*, for Alexander Balfour, who lived nearby at Mount Alyn (now demolished). One was for the farm bailiff, the other for the use of members of a Liverpool mission. Piquantly asymmetrical OUTBUILDING, with a pyramid-like roof ending in a gabled dovecote. At CROES HOWELL, a set of large brick FARM BUILDINGS, with date inscriptions of 1735–58. Pointed arches.

BALLS HALL, ⅝m. NNW. Date inscription of 1650, and traces of a cruck truss. Brick-nogged BARN.

IVY COTTAGE (formerly Ravensbourne), ¾m. NW. Another Marford-style house, and a very charming one. Ogee windows, some of them tripartite. Symmetrical. Three bays of two storeys, with a shallow, curved bow in the centre, and single-storey one-bay wings.

BURTON HALL, 1¼m. NW. Of H-plan and sizeable. Date inscription of 1632 in plaster on a beam. In the same room a stone chimneypiece with Tudor arch and fluted Doric columns on pedestals. Panelled room above, and an C18 staircase.

LYNDIR, ⅝m. NNE. Early C19 Gothic, with a quatrefoil frieze and, at one corner, a three-bay loggia.

RUABON

3040

ST MARY. C14 W tower, related in type and probably in date, though not in detail, to those at Holt and Overton. In other words, a Cheshire type, with buttressing, battlements, no pinnacles, and a (NE) vice turret. Two-light bell openings and W doorway with characteristically Dec wave moulding. The body of the church is largely of 1870–2 by *Benjamin Ferrey* (plans prepared 1868), who was set loose on it by Sir Watkin Williams-Wynn, sixth Baronet (*see* Wynnstay). Chancel, gabled aisles, and a clerestoried nave in a version of Dec. Except for the tower and a blocked S doorway, the earliest surviving features date from a Perp remodelling; they are a N window, the aisle W windows with cusping and panel tracery, a pair of crocketed buttresses at the E end, and cusped niches either side of the E window internally. Also N and S doorways, their depressed arches indicating late date. *Ferrey* replaced a perfectly good Perp E window with his own bastardized idea of one. A pre-Perp roof-line is visible over the tower arch. In

1755 a SE chapel was added to house a monument to the third Baronet; a faculty for a matching NE chapel was obtained in 1769, and there followed a remodelling of the church by *T. F. Pritchard*, 1769–70. It seems he retained the piers of a Perp arcade and added his own semicircular arches and circular clerestory windows. Of this C18 work, there survives some masonry at the E end, and a blocked window of the N chapel, with Gibbs surround. N and S porches added subsequent to Ferrey's reconstruction.

(Opened in 1984, a CHURCH HALL by *TACP* was built as an extension abutting the N aisle, both for church purposes and for the use of the wider community. This followed the inauguration in 1980 of a scheme whereby St Mary's became a 'shared' church, used by the Roman Catholic Church as well as the (Anglican) Church in Wales. The former N porch was dismantled and its masonry reused as an E-facing porch for the new extension.)

The FONT, given by the fourth Baronet in 1772, was de- 78 signed by *Robert Adam*, with all the refined and delicate intricacy of the Adam style. Small marble bowl and wooden cover in the form of an urn, and a wooden tripod stand, Gothic in its detail.* – PULPIT. Transferred from the chapel at Wynnstay in 1819. Like the reredos in the present chapel there (*see* p. 315), it can probably be identified with *Francis Smith*'s work at the house in the late 1730s. Hexagonal stem. Much good carved enrichment. – RAILS. Fluted columns in the style of the pulpit. Of 1845, designed and made by *William Davies* of Cefn Mawr. – WALL PAINTING. Works of Mercy. Of the first half of the C15. Over 15ft long, though of the seven scenes only four are complete, with portions of two others. A different person performs each deed, one of them a woman. Each is inspired by an angel. Bent ribbon ornament. A border and Welsh inscription were added after the discovery of the painting in 1870. It can perhaps be associated with the poet Maredudd ap Rhys, who was vicar from 1430, and who wrote a poem on the subject of the Works of Mercy. – STAINED GLASS. N aisle westernmost by *T. F. Curtis* of *Ward & Hughes*, 1898. – N aisle W by *Gibbs*, commemoration date 1872. – S chapel by *H. Hughes* of *Ward & Hughes*, 1888. – CHANDELIERS. A pair, both with six branches and some enrichment. One was given by the sixth Baronet and the vicar in 1781, and an earlier one was then recast to match it. – CHESTS. One of 1709, encased in iron, and in the tower gallery a plank chest of 1637. – SEPULCHRAL SLAB. In the S chapel a fragment of an early C14 shield and sword heraldic slab, commemorating Llywelyn.

MONUMENTS. In the N chapel: John ab Ellis Eyton †1526 and wife Elizabeth. Alabaster tomb-chest and recumbent effigies. Their heads on cushions and he, in armour, with SS collar, an animal at his feet and gauntlets at his side. On all four sides are angel weepers, under elaborate canopies, bear-

---

* Church PLATE was also designed by *Adam*.

ing shields. – Henry Wynn. By *Robert Wynne* of Ruthin,
1719. Three life-size effigies. He stands on a pedestal, in lu-
dicrous posture, wearing lawyer's robes. His wrists point outwards in blessing of his son, Sir John, and daughter-in-law,
who was the heiress through whom Wynnstay came to the
family. Awkward-looking surround, of Corinthian pilasters
and a big semicircular canopy, with drapery in folds. – In the
N aisle: Edward Lloyd Rowland †1828. By *W. Spence*.
Draped urn. – Ellis Lloyd †1712. Cartouche. – Anne Rowland and Edward Rowland † 1815. By *S. & F. Franceys*.
Tablet with simulated folds. – Lady Henrietta Williams
Wynn. By *Nollekens*, 1773. A free-standing life-size figure of
Hope, holding an anchor, leans against an excellent draped
urn. The good detail of the pedestal should also be noted. –
In the S chapel: Sir Watkin W. Wynn, third Baronet. By
Rysbrack, 1751–4. Vast and splendid, with sarcophagus, pyr-
amid, and reclining effigy. An angel holds a medallion show-
ing a female figure with an upturned vessel and in the back-
ground a circular temple. – William Watkin W. Wynn †1763.
Adamish tablet of great refinement, with sarcophagus and
oval medallion. The style and detail and the fact that *Robert
Adam* received patronage from the Wynns suggest that he
may perhaps have designed this monument. – Iorwerth ab
Awr ab Ieuaf. Early C14 effigy. Shield with inscription.
Sword. – Hywel. Effigy, also early C14, with an inscription
on the shield. – In the S aisle: Edward Lloyd Kenyon †1843.
By *Edward Bowring Stephens*. Poor relief, in a Gothic frame.
– Lloyd monument, 1871. Gothic, of brass and other inlay,
with a long inscription. – Charlotte Eva Edward †1889. By
Gaffin. Amid attendant angels she rises up to meet the child
who predeceased her.

ROYAL ARMS. Painted on wood, 1780.*

CONGREGATIONAL CHAPEL, W of the railway. 1858 by *W. I.
Mason* of Liverpool. Gothic.

PROVIDENCE WELSH PRESBYTERIAN (CALVINISTIC METH-
ODIST) CHAPEL, SW of the church, below the main road.
Built 1834. Pedimented at the end and in the middle of one
side. The chapel itself is at upper level.

CEMETERY. Arched Gothic GATEWAY, 1858–9, by *T. M.
Penson*.

ROUND HOUSE, on the main road, against the churchyard retaining wall. An C18 circular lock-up. Tooled masonry, and
with entablature and an ashlar-faced dome. (Inside, the dome
is of brick.)

RAILWAY STATION. The original station by *T. M. Penson* for
the Shrewsbury and Chester Railway, 1848, has been replaced. The present Neo-Tudor building is by *Henry Robertson*, 1860. (DOE) *Penson*'s building was reportedly Italianate,
as is his surviving station at Gobowen, Shropshire, the best,
and virtually the only, original remaining one on the line.

* This account of Ruabon church owes much to the researches of the Rev.
Canon T. W. Pritchard.

This was a colliery region. In the latter C19 the brickmaking industry developed rapidly, and flourished on an extensive scale well into the C20.* Yet the centre of Ruabon still has something of the character of a Wynnstay estate village. PARK STREET, really a square, frames the RUABON GATEWAY of Wynnstay (*see* p. 316) with sets of stone COTTAGES, probably built *c*.1840. Windows now altered. On the corner the three-storey WYNNSTAY ARMS, late C18, of brick. Facing Park Street it has a semi-octagonal bay with tripartite windows. Also a stone-faced wing, dated 1841, with arched gateway and one-bay pediment. Village-like character also in CHURCH STREET. Here a group of ALMSHOUSES, with a row of ten, *c*.1711, and others added later in the C18.

PLAS NEWYDD, in Pont Adam Crescent, W of the railway. Derelict. H-plan, with lateral chimney and brick-nogged gables at the rear. (Though almost entirely reconstructed as a storeyed house, there remain roof timbers of a box-framed hall, possibly C14. The hall was of two subdivided bays. One subdivision formed the passage bay, with spere-truss. Peter Smith illustrates the three trusses, all of them different and of unusual form, and with much cusping.)

Beside the A483, ½ m. SW, the stone winding-engine house of the former WYNNSTAY COLLIERY, with tall round-headed openings. *c*.1855. Now roofless.

Y GARDDEN FORT, ¾ m. NNW, occupies the summit of a low hill overlooking Ruabon. The hilltop (SJ 297 448) is surrounded by an inner stone rampart with a second, earthen, rampart outside it on the S and E sides, where there is also an intermittent third bank. The series of banks and ditches are well preserved and easily seen on the S side, where a modern track gives access to the interior. The position of the original entrance is not clear but may be represented by a gap in the defences on the E side.

OFFA'S DYKE forms one side of the present road up to Y Gardden and is particularly well preserved at SJ 297 440. The parallel line of WAT'S DYKE, to the E, is also well preserved. It can be seen as it approaches the main road, ½ m. E (SJ 310 434) of Ruabon.

RUTHIN

1050

RUTHIN CASTLE

Like Denbigh, the town stands on an eminence which rises from the floor of the Vale of Clwyd. The castle, at its S end, was begun as part of the royal building programme of 1277, at the same time as those at Flint and Rhuddlan. The *cantref* of Dyffryn Clwyd, with its centre at Ruthin, was then held by Edward I's ally, Dafydd ap Gruffydd, brother of Llywelyn the

---

* For the Penybont Works of *J. C. Edwards*, the most notable of the manufacturers of Ruabon terra-cotta and red pressed brick, *see* Cefn Mawr.

Last. In 1282, following Dafydd's revolt, the castle was retaken
for the King by Reginald de Grey, and building seems to have
been resumed under Master *James of St George*. In the same
year, Dyffryn Clwyd was granted by Edward to de Grey as the
new marcher lordship of Ruthin, and any subsequent continuation of building would have been the responsibility of the
lordship, rather than royal work. It was a quarrel with the third
Lord Grey of Ruthin which precipitated the rising of Owain
Glyndŵr, who signified his displeasure when, in 1400, he attacked
the castle and the town.

The present house stands within the confines of the medieval
castle, which had been laid waste in the Civil War. The earliest
part was built in 1826 for Frederick West and his wife Maria,
who was a Myddelton heiress, Ruthin having been acquired by
the Myddeltons of Chirk in the C17. Much was done by *Henry
Clutton* for their son, Frederick Richard West. With the next
generation came the name Cornwallis West – a name to conjure
with for followers of Edwardian society. Ruthin Castle was sold
in 1920, and became a private clinic, in connection with which
large additions were made. It is now a hotel.

First, the RUINS of the medieval castle. The plan is aligned SW–
NE, along the crest of the hill. An upper ward formed an
irregular pentagon – a square plus a triangle with its apex at
the NE end. Rectangular lower ward to the SW. The S corner
of the upper ward, and much of the lower, are respectively
occupied by the two separate blocks which comprise the C19
house. There are ditches on the SE and SW, and the ground
falls steeply away on the NW. At the E corner of the upper
ward is a gatehouse, which, together with other parts, received C19 romantic embellishment. Originally, D-towers
flanked the gateway, and their basement chambers remain,
connected by a passage. One retains its segmental vault, and
is reached by a staircase roofed with a vault of stepped chamfered ribs. Portions may be seen of SE, N and NW curtain
walls; also of the E, N and W corner towers of the upper ward,
and the W one of the lower. The lower ward has, in its N
corner, a postern approached by a vice, and in its NW curtain
is an arch with portcullis grooves. Corbelling for some form
of tower above this.

Disregarding the C20 additions, the HOUSE consists, as has been
said, of two separate blocks. They are linked by a bridge
corridor, and, as built in 1826, both were castellated, irregular
in massing, and of white limestone. *Clutton*'s work was carried out 1848–53. His alterations to one of the two parts
included the insertion of new windows, and the capping of a
slender octagonal turret with a square clock stage. This had
a saddleback roof with stepped gables, now removed. All
sandstone dressings are by Clutton. The main block he
largely demolished, and replaced with a three-storey castellated *corps de logis* of an intensely red local sandstone. At the
W corner, a big octagonal tower, with vice turret. The SE end

(the entrance front) is, with large areas of blank wall, an early instance of High Victorian composition. The ground storey has canted corners, and an off-centre arch with animals as label stops. Above, all is symmetrical, with three slender two-storey oriels, the outer ones of complicated plan and embracing the corners. A pair of chimneystacks rose from the parapet, but have been removed. *William Burges* had a hand in fitting up the interior from the time of entering into association with Clutton in 1851, and he was still designing furniture for the castle in 1856. *J. G. Crace* was probably also employed for the decorating. The ground floor consists of a set of five rooms, including an octagonal library in the tower, with ribbed ceilings, ornate chimneypieces etc. In the hall, a stone chimneypiece (possibly by *Burges*), and a stone Gothic screen. An especially elaborate chimneypiece in the dining room. The drawing room, 56ft long, has an intricate and delicate ceiling pattern, and still retained its original wallpaper when the clinic sold up in 1963. The oak chimneypiece, recalling the filigree quality of Welsh Late Gothic woodwork, was made by *Wynne & Lumsden* to *Clutton*'s design, and in 1851 was shown at the Great Exhibition.

ENTRANCE LODGE, in the form of an asymmetrical castellated gatehouse. By *Clutton*. Limestone, with sandstone dressings. Wide archway, and the house, with tower and a small corner oriel, is set at an angle to it.

Set back from the drive, opposite the medieval gatehouse, is a small GATEHOUSE folly. Early C19.

s of the house, a GORSEDD CIRCLE of 1973.

SCOTT HOUSE, ½m. S. Built as a nurses' home, 1933. Asymmetrical E-plan front, pebbledashed, with tall gables and big, hipped dormers.

CHURCHES

ST PETER. A chapel, then in the parish of Llanrhudd (*see* p. 233), was built in the time of Reginald de Grey, and in 1310 his son, John de Grey, founded a collegiate parish church. It seems that at some stage a community of Augustinian Bonhommes existed, and the establishment was suppressed, not with the houses of secular clergy, but at the dissolution of the lesser monasteries in 1536. The church begun in 1310 consisted of aisleless nave, chancel, and central tower. There never were transepts, and the N and S arches which appear internally below the tower have always been blank. The domestic buildings abutted on the N. A S aisle was added in the latter half of the C14, creating a double-naved form. It extends as far E as the E tower arch of the earlier part, and nothing now lies beyond this point, for the original chancel was demolished in 1663. Much which was done in the C18 and early C19 was obliterated in two separate restorations by *R. K. Penson*, 1854–9.

At the E end, the stage of the tower above the blocked E arch is C18. *Penson* rebuilt the higher belfry storey, and added the broach spire. The tower looks precariously balanced, lacking the visual support of the buttresses which he intended. By him, the steep roofs, the S porch, and Late Geometrical windows, including tracery in the S nave E window, which he reopened. The S nave W window, of three lights, with a sexfoil, is not only earlier in style, but looks ancient in date, and could be work of 1310, reset. The W walls themselves were rebuilt in 1722 – see, as elsewhere, the neat quoins. Some realignment has taken place – see the partial obscuring of a cusped STOUP in the NW corner of the S nave, and a Perp doorway in the SW corner. Five-bay arcade, its piers octagonal and with notches in the diagonals, and with the capitals having the characteristically Dec scroll mould. Hoodmoulds and head-stops. Of the earlier C14 tower arches, the E and W have orders so strongly articulated as almost to be separate arches. Some wave moulding – an early instance. Filleted shafts with foliated capitals. The blank N and S arches have two orders, the inner one on corbels. Hoodmoulds and some head-stops. Smaller arches set in the recesses, and an external hoodmould shows that that on the N was always a doorway. (PISCINA for the parochial altar, W of the W tower arch, now hidden by the organ.) A Perp N window. Perp also, and late, the camberbeam roofs. That of the S nave, all its members moulded, consists of panels, each sub-divided into four. Richly carved bosses. Painted decoration at the E end dates from a restoration of 1965–6. The N nave roof is exceptionally elaborate. The camberbeams themselves are decorated, and the numerous small panels are (except for some at the W end which are painted) carved with traceried circles, and with arms, badges, and inscriptions. Families represented include the Stanleys.

Ornate FONT, dating from the 1850s restorations, and Perp in style. – ALTAR TABLE. (Dated 1621 at the back.) Turned baluster legs, and a guilloche pattern to the top rail. – Four BENCH ENDS, incorporated in seats in the sanctuary. Tracery and drooping poppyheads. – STAINED GLASS. E window by *Wailes*, 1855. – By *James Powell & Sons*, the N nave westernmost window, 1855, designed by *Bouvier*,* and quarries in five S windows, c.1854–5. – MONUMENTS. In the vestry, loose: Fragment of the effigy of a priest. Early C14. – Headless effigy of a lady, her hands in prayer, a lion at her feet. Late C14. – In the chancel: Gabriel Goodman, Dean of Westminster, †1601. Crudely carved bust, coloured, set in an arched niche, with heraldry above. – John Parry. Heraldic tablet of 1636. – Gabriel Goodman †1673, and Roger Mostyn †1712. Attributable to *Robert Wynne*. Two panels, with a Corinthian column either side, and another, twisted, in the middle. Cherub heads, gadrooning, swags etc., and an urn and her-

---

* Information from Mr Harrison.

aldry above. – Thomas Roberts †1713. Draperies, cherub heads, and urns and heraldry above. – John Wynn †1725. Not large, but rather grand, and of good quality. Side volutes, cherub heads, heraldry at the top. It commemorates the brother of *Robert Wynne*, to whom it can be attributed. – Mary Hughes †1798. By *Joseph Turner*. Elegant urn against an obelisk. – Hughes and Newcome monument, last commemoration date 1803. By *Sir Richard Westmacott*. Plain tablet and inscription. – Rev. Edward Jones †1811 and wife Mary †1823. By *Franceys & Spence*. Symbolical scene and female figure. – Joseph Ablett †1848. By *J. H. Foley*. Circular panel, with relief of a kneeling, weeping maiden. Set in a tall, diminishing tablet. – In the N nave: Wynne monument, latest commemoration date 1694. Cartouche. – Also the following BRASSES in the N nave: Edward Goodman, father of the Dean, †1560. Figure and inscription mounted in isolation. – Another brass to the same, with wife Ciselye †1583. They are depicted kneeling, with three sons and five daughters. – Archdeacon Richard Newcome †1857. By *J. Hardman & Co.* – Plank CHEST.

The churchyard and its buildings form a remarkable parochial close. Dr Gabriel Goodman, Dean of Westminster and a native of Ruthin, purchased the collegiate buildings and their precincts, and in 1590 founded CHRIST'S HOSPITAL, for a priest (the warden) and twelve poor persons. The incumbency of Ruthin still goes by the title of warden. The almshouses, rebuilt 1865, are single-storeyed, with cross wings, and a touch of polychromy.

Under the Dean's foundation, the domestic buildings of the college became the warden's residence. They remained such, known as The Cloisters, until a new parsonage was built in the 1950s. They are now THE OLD CLOISTERS. Two-storeyed, adjoining the church on the N, and almost certainly contemporary with the 1310 foundation. Much altered, not least by early C19 Gothicizing; but externally the arches of some openings, including those of two doorways on the E, seem original. Five-bay vaulted undercroft, now divided, and the tierceron vaulting, with wave-moulded ribs, is visible only in the middle bay. Further N is a transverse passage, with pointed tunnel-vault and chamfered ribs, and containing blocked doorways with hoodmoulds. A room of early C19 Gothic character has STAINED GLASS incorporating a pair of medallions which are probably early C16 and Flemish. WOODWORK, presumably from the church, includes traceried panels worked into shutters. Staircase with C18 columnar balusters. It is not known how far N the range originally extended, and a smaller-scaled addition at the end is post-Reformation.

Ruthin School was refounded by Dr Goodman in 1574, and endowed twenty years later. For its present buildings, *see* Public Buildings, below. The OLD GRAMMAR SCHOOL, L-shaped, closes the churchyard on the N. A stone-built range dates from 1700, but is C19 in its features. Work of 1831–2 is recorded, and some by *Lloyd Williams & Underwood* (VH) in 1867. The porch must be theirs. A five-bay brick block, of two and a half storeys, was built in 1742 as dormitories and headmaster's house. Staircase with columnar balusters, and a chimneypiece with fluted keyblock.

Further N, THE NEW CLOISTERS. The warden's house. Neo-Georgian, by *H. Anthony Clark, F. C. Roberts & Partners*, 1953–4.

CHURCHYARD GATES. 1727 by *Robert Davies*, restored 1928. Main gates between two-dimensional piers. Smaller side gates, the work above them building up to the central overthrow. Much scrollwork.*

BAPTIST CHAPEL, Park Road. Stepped-gabled front. 1934 by *S. Colwyn Foulkes*.

112 PENDREF CONGREGATIONAL CHAPEL, Well Street. Built 1827, with work of 1875. Elegant ashlar front, gently embayed. Three bays, the central one pedimented and slightly advanced, all on the curve. Balustrading, two storeys of round-headed windows, and a Tuscan porch. (Ceiling with five floral motifs linked by bands. Gallery on three sides. – PULPIT with open pediment on consoles. DOE)

BATHAFARN METHODIST CHAPEL, Market Street. Built 1869. Gable front of brick and stone, with a debased mixture of round arches and Gothic detail. Ceiling with bold plasterwork. Gallery on iron columns round three sides.

Y TABERNACL WELSH PRESBYTERIAN (CALVINISTIC METHODIST) CHAPEL, Well Street. 1889–91 by *T. G. Williams*. Strange-looking convex front, with a big traceried window in the gable, plus a pyramid roof to the l. and, to the r., a pinnacle rising from a flying buttress. The plan is a shallow horseshoe, with trusses radiating across the wide roof. Internal ornament is concentrated on the PULPIT and SÊT-FAWR. Fretwork, miniature balusters etc.

PUBLIC BUILDINGS

COUNTY HALL, Record Street. By *Joseph Turner*, and completed 1790. It was begun in 1785 to house records of the Courts of Great Sessions (which had jurisdiction similar to that of Assizes in England), but the scheme was amended the following year to serve also as a county hall, i.e. courthouse. Ashlar front, monumental in character but modest in scale. Tetrastyle pedimented portico with triglyphs and wider middle intercolumniation. The unfluted columns have Greek Doric capitals and Attic bases. Screen walls either side contain arches rising into segmental pediments. The courtroom has a Venetian window either side, and is separated by a

---

* Mr Randall provided much help and advice regarding the church and its precinct.

Roman Doric screen from a laterally elongated octagon beyond.

TOWN HALL, Market Street. Together with the adjoining
MARKET HALL, it is by *Poundley & Walker*, 1863–5. High
Victorian Gothic, rock-faced. The main building is tall and
compact, with a hipped roof abutting against a corner tower,
which itself has a steep Mansard top. Capitals and spandrels,
carved by *Edward Griffith* of Chester, include leaves, birds,
and a harvest scene.

DISTRICT COUNCIL OFFICES, Market Street. Built 1907–8 as
the Denbighshire County Council Offices. By *Walter D.
Wiles*, County Architect. Baroque, with polychromatic masonry. Two pedimented fronts, and between them a diagonal
corner with an Ionic order and segmental pediment.

RUTHIN SCHOOL, Mold Road. The Grammar School, refounded by Dr Gabriel Goodman, moved from the churchyard (*see* Churches above) to new buildings of 1891–3 by
Douglas & Fordham. Long front of rock-faced white limestone with sandstone dressings, and with variously shaped
heads to the lights of the mullioned and transomed windows.
A range of gables is punctuated by a square, squat tower, its
pyramid roof recessed behind a parapet, and with an off-
centre doorway. The headmaster's house, with two shaped
gables, forms the right-hand end of the façade. An unworthy
and all too large extension to the l. is of 1980.

At opposite ends of the town are two Neo-Elizabethan
SCHOOLS, the former British School, Rhos Street, 1848, and
the former National (i.e. Church) School, Borthyn, *c.*1849–
50.

OLD COUNTY GAOL, Clwyd Street. It ceased to be used as a
prison in 1916, and now houses departments of the County
Council. Rebuilt to the design of *Joseph Turner* in 1775, probably as an early response to John Howard's campaigns. Of
this date the broad, five-bay front, with three-bay pediment
and central arched recess. Extension of 1803 to the r. Much
successive extension and rebuilding took place behind, and a
four-storey cell block, with prominent ventilation tower, is by
Lloyd Williams & Underwood, 1867–8. Its galleried interior,
which was lit from a canted staircase window in the end wall,
has been floored in.

PONT HOWKIN, formerly Pont Newydd, Clwyd Street. A
three-arched bridge of 1771 by *Joseph Turner* (DOE), badly
mutilated in 1969.

PEERS MONUMENT, St Peter's Square. *See* Perambulation.

PERAMBULATION

Some good townscape may be enjoyed, particularly along the
ridge on which Castle Street and the market place (St Peter's
Square) extend between the castle and the church. The streets
on either side fall away steeply, and those to the E afford

glimpses of the Clwydian Hills. The commanding building in
ST PETER'S SQUARE is the early or mid-C18 CASTLE
HOTEL (formerly White Lion), of three storeys plus a blank
half-storey below a modillion cornice. Four bays. Brick, with
stone quoins, keystones (some fluted) and aprons, and an entablature and lugged surround to the window above the off-
centre entrance. Staircase with swept rail and columnar balusters. On the first floor, some panelling, and three separate
pairs of fluted pilasters, one set flanking a chimneypiece with
fluted keystone. The MYDDELTON ARMS is traditionally associated with Sir Richard Clough, but perhaps only on the
strength of the three tiers of dormers which, climbing its tiled
roof, impart something of the alien character of Bach-y-graig
(*see* Tremeirchion, p. 451). Internal timber framing includes
part of the spere-truss of a medieval hall house, clearly visible
upstairs. A chimneypiece with strapwork and heraldry is
dated 1657, and a staircase with turned balusters may be
contemporary. In front of the hotel, the PEERS MONUMENT,
by *Douglas*, 1883. A combined clock tower, horse trough and
drinking fountain, Jacobean in its motifs. Erected as a testi-
monial to a local worthy, within his lifetime. It is on the site
of a free-standing TOWN HALL, built 1663 and demolished
1863. Free-standing at the s end of the square is the timber-
framed NATIONAL WESTMINSTER BANK, once the courthouse of the lordship of Ruthin, and ascribed to 1401. It had
been much altered, but was excellently restored and fitted up
for the National Provincial Bank in 1925–6, seemingly by
F. H. Shayler. Four bays, with curved top braces. Box-frame
construction, i.e. no crucks. The trusses have curved struts
between ties and collars. Cusped wind-braces. On the w gable
end, the remains of a gibbet. BARCLAYS BANK is by *F. A.
Roberts*, 1928, but reproduces features of the timber-framed
Exmewe Hall, which it replaced. Completing a trio of half-
timbered banks is the MIDLAND, 1925 by *T. M. Alexander*
of *Woolfall & Eccles*. Of the single-storeyed and diagonal
corner entrance type, decked out with carved woodwork and
twisted brick chimneys.

CASTLE STREET, which begins with the Tuscan colonnade of
the WINE VAULTS, presents a picture of varied materials,
styles and shapes, in recession and advance. On the l., SIR
JOHN TREVOR HOUSE has a timber-framed gable end to a
projecting wing, with quatrefoils and diagonal bracing.
(GORFFWYSFA, opposite, retains roof timbers of a timber-
framed hall and cross wing. Curved bracings to collars and
wallplates. NMR) NANTCLWYD HOUSE is a cruck hall house,
much altered, of course, but with attractive C17 and early C18
features. Timber-framed porch, its upper storey jettied over
a cluster of posts, of which the outermost are Ionic columns.
A further projection also has exposed framing with, in the
gable, a diagonal pattern of concave lozenges. The hall, with
central arched-braced truss, remains undivided, though an
inserted chimney forms a lobby entry, and a ceiling, roughly

following the curve of the arched-brace, hides cusping and wind-braces. It continues into a further bay on the upper floor. The hall has also received a gallery round two sides, its turned balusters heavier than those of the C17 staircase. The house has panelling, some of it bolection-moulded, and a pair of fluted pilasters flank a chimneypiece. Star pattern of plaster strapwork in the ceiling of the porch chamber. A GAZEBO in the garden behind. BRON-Y-GAER, with ashlar front, is dated 1823. Two projecting wings with coped and finialed gables, and a Tudor Gothic porch slotted between. Labels. Here the street widens, giving a view of the early C19 COL-OMENDY on the corner of Record Street. Brick, of three bays plus another to the l., and with tripartite ground-floor windows and a tripartite pedimented doorcase. Nos. 16 and 18 are early to mid-C19 in character, stuccoed, and with curly bargeboards. Structurally they are probably older, with timber framing. This is certainly the case with No. 20, which has a storeyed porch on Ionic posts. The entrance lodge of Ruthin Castle (*see* above) marks the end of the town, and splendidly closes the view at the end of the street.

Down RECORD STREET, where No. 1 has a pedimented doorcase, to Well Street, at the further end of which is RAILWAY TERRACE. Cottages of 1864, in front of which the Vale of Clwyd Railway once ran in a cutting. N from here, at the junction of WERNFECHAN and BRYN GOODMAN, are two *Douglas & Fordham* villas – COETMOR and DEDWYDDFA, the latter dated 1886. In WELL STREET itself, PLAS COCH, built 1613, is at the junction of Dog Lane. Of sandstone obtained from the castle. With labels, but rewindowed. The WYNNSTAY ARMS (formerly Cross Foxes, mentioned by Borrow) is partly timber-framed. Central chimney and lobby entrance. The shop-front of No. 16, at the Record Street fork, retains a fascia with big consoles. No. 10 has its early C19 stone front at right angles to the street. Three bays, with most windows tripartite, and a tripartite pedimented doorcase. Next, the former CROSS KEYS, probably Early Victorian. Symmetrical, but with the windows differing on all three storeys. The lowest stage is rusticated. Some timber-framed gables include No. 4A, now carried on cast-iron columns, and No. 2. Between is No. 4, Mid-Victorian and of brick, with exuberant consoles, both to the shop-front and to the cornice. Much timber framing survives behind plaster and refrontings in CLWYD STREET, which leads down from St Peter's Square on the w. Nos. 32 and 34, symmetrical in massing, have a central projection with some framing exposed. (Nos. 47 and 49 were a storeyed house with open roof. Wind-braces and a collared truss. DOE) PORTH (No. 65) has timber balustrading embedded at the rear (and cusped roof trusses. DOE). The TOWN MILL, in MILL STREET nearby, is believed to have been the late C13 mill of Ruthin Castle. Largely rebuilt, but the original gable ends, each with a lancet, are clearly seen, and there is a pointed-arched opening on the N.

Now landlocked, but water and a wheel survived into the
C20.

Finally, one outlying item, CAE'RAFALLEN, $\frac{7}{8}$m. NNE.
Timber-framed, partly brick-nogged, with jettying and close
studding. Ribbed brick chimneys. Built in two stages, perhaps as unit planning. The earlier, which is of three units,
has herringbone bracing in the gable end, and a lateral chimney. Later range at right angles, with central chimney and
lobby entry. FARM BUILDINGS round two sides of a court.

LLANRHUDD. *See* p. 233.

9070   ST GEORGE / LLAN SAIN SIÔR

KINMEL PARK. The remodelling by *William Eden Nesfield*
holds a notable place in the history of Victorian architecture,
and it is grievous that, in 1975, the house was seriously damaged by fire. Fortunately, destruction was largely confined to
the roof and service parts, and most of the main interiors
escaped. In 1978 Kinmel was acquired for use as a Christian
conference centre, and was opened as such in 1982. The admirable long-term programme of repair and reinstatement
begun late in 1978 is being continued, and it is hoped that
the use of the present tense in the following description will
be justified, even though not fully applicable at the time of
writing.

The estate was bought in 1786 by the Rev. Edward
Hughes. His marriage had brought him property in Anglesey
and thus, following the discovery of the copper resources of
Parys Mountain, an immense fortune.

A new house at Kinmel by *Samuel Wyatt* was of *c.*1791–
1802 (with a typically Wyattish bow to the N) and seems to
have been later enlarged. It was burnt in 1841, and rebuilding, completed in 1843, was by *Thomas Hopper*, apparently
incorporating at least part of the shell of the Wyatt building
as its N end. Hopper's work was for Edward Hughes's son,
who was created Lord Dinorben in 1831. The title became
extinct on the death of his own son in 1852 and Kinmel
passed to his nephew, Hugh Robert Hughes.

From 1865, *Nesfield* was designing estate buildings for
H. R. Hughes, and must have been engaged on designs for
the remodelling of the mansion itself by 1868, when Hughes
and family visited Hampton Court with him. Construction is
known to have been in progress 1872–4, but was probably
begun earlier. Much of the previous structure was retained,
though enlarged and completely transformed in a way which
foreshadowed C20 Neo-Georgian and was of key importance
in the development of the so-called Queen Anne style – the
style soon to be made fashionable by Norman Shaw, with
whom Nesfield long shared an office and was for a while in
partnership.

Not until the time of Shaw's Bryanston, twenty years later, did Queen Anne again appear in terms of such palatial grandeur. The EXTERIOR, clad in brick, with generous stone dressings, owes much to Wren and Hampton Court. It also has features which are earlier C17 and French in derivation, especially the steep hipped roofs, which perpetuated Mid-Victorian taste, and which contain tall pedimented dormers. There had been C19 precedent for revived William and Mary combined with continental elements, but the immediate precursor was Nesfield's own Temperate House Lodge at Kew of 1867. It may be wondered if inspiration for the Queen Anne Movement, and for Kinmel in particular, may have sprung from unexecuted schemes prepared by Nesfield in 1863 and 1866 for work at Croxteth Hall, Lancashire, where he took his stylistic cue from the genuinely Queen Anne w front.

The classical dress is very different from the vernacular revival idiom evolved by Nesfield and Shaw also in the 1860s, and which they termed 'Old English'. Yet the house possesses much of the picturesque grouping associated with that style. Hopper's house had a long E (entrance) front and a W (garden) front. Both elevations had a pedimented Ionic portico. These two porticoes were not in axis, for the E front was longer than the W – a feature which Nesfield retained and exploited while at the same time introducing strong elements of asymmetry but keeping a symmetrical central feature on each elevation. The porticoes, in their non-aligned positions, were first introduced in the course of the alterations to the Wyatt house.* The E front comprises fifteen bays (with some varied rhythm 108 of fenestration) and extends 190ft. It includes end pavilions and, rising a storey higher, a broader middle pavilion. Corner pilaster strips are of banded brick and stone, and pilasters – some of brick, some stone – articulate the central pavilion. In contrast to this disciplined formality, a service wing wanders *ad lib* up the hillside to the l., and has a pyramid-roofed tower. What is more, the central pavilion itself is crowned by cheerful and unmonumental white-painted balustrading and flaunts an off-centre chimneystack. An enriched but homely-looking entrance canopy is in the same engaging Carolean spirit. Detailing is also highly individual, with much excellent stonecarving executed by *James Forsyth*. Nesfield's vocabulary of ornament included the sunflowers, lilies and decorative roundels redolent of the Aesthetic Movement, and sunflowers appear in plaster coving on the service range. The roundels (which he called 'pies') had medieval precedent as well as appearing on Japanese porcelain and Jacobean furniture.

The symmetrical portion of the garden front has seven bays, counting a central pavilion as one. To the r. are the staircase windows (with a frieze of pies in lead above and originally with a conservatory below) beyond which projects

* I owe this information to Mrs Elaine Boxhall, who kindly communicated the results of her research on Kinmel. I also received help from Mr R. Fred Roberts.

the tall, narrow mass of the former chapel, with cupola and an elaborate Venetian composition in its end wall. Reinstatement of the chapel roof after the fire was in a simplified form. At the opposite end of the façade is a pavilion being the return of a shallow addition made to the earlier structure, and which presents a totally asymmetrical N elevation.

The stonecarving of the garden front, concentrated on the central pavilion and the heads of the segmentally-pedimented ground-floor windows, is of Renaissance character, but with sunflower and other floral patterns, deeply undercut. Beyond the chapel, the service range pursues a long informal course, embracing a courtyard. Attractive features include the four tall windows of the servants' hall, which face the court and rise into pargetted gables.

INTERIOR. There are ornately treated chimneypieces and overmantels, pedimented doorcases and plaster ceilings. The style is predominently classical, but everywhere there is eclecticism (e.g. Jacobean motifs in the library and dining room), and a coherent whole is not fully achieved. Extensive use is made, as a decorative device, of flowers growing from pots. The layout of the main rooms was largely inherited from Hopper, but interlocking L-shapes, as found in the Old English vernacular houses of Nesfield and Shaw, were introduced. The ballroom which, like the drawing room and library, is almost 60ft long, rises two storeys in height, and has an elliptical barrel ceiling and an end gallery. Its marble Ionic chimneypiece must be either an importation or a survival from the *Samuel Wyatt* house. In the entrance hall (the fine chimneypiece from which is now at Kinmel Manor, Abergele; *see* p. 100) is a three-bay arcade with marble-faced piers. Also panelling, with pies randomly disposed in Japanese manner. On the half-landing of the staircase, a similar arcade opens to the former conservatory. At this level is the entrance to the chapel, whose simple interior was the only important room completely gutted in 1975. The staircase itself was extensively damaged. Its ceiling has potted sunflowers in its patterned cove; there are Corinthian pilasters to the upper stages of the walls; the dado panelling and turned balusters have the flavour of Nesfield's Old English interiors, and this is even more markedly true of a minor, second-floor staircase, its dado adorned with pies. It rises direct from the panelled first-floor corridor, which in its simple classicism is one of the most consistent and successful interiors. A staircase with spiral balusters serves a private set of family rooms at the S end of the entrance front.

FORECOURT GATES by *Nesfield*, 1868. With overthrow, and probably inspired by Tijou's work at Hampton Court. Rusticated piers.

STABLES. Built c.1855 and attributable to *William Burn*.* Very swagger, of ashlar, and with much rustication. Raised and pedimented end pavilions, and a large and heavily

* Schemes by *Burn* for ESTATE BUILDINGS seem not to have been executed.

Baroque clock cupola. Except for pedimented stone dormers, there is little to suggest that the frontage is not early C18.

An extensive FORMAL GARDEN, aligned on the W front, is almost certainly a *Nesfield* layout, and landscaping in the PARK was carried out by his father, *W. A. Nesfield*. Designs for some garden work were made by *Edward Milner*, 1883.

In the Kitchen Garden, ¼ m. SE of the mansion, across the Flintshire border, are the ruins of OLD KINMEL, i.e. the predecessor of the Wyatt house. C17, with mullioned and transomed windows, storeyed porch and lateral chimney.

LODGE GATES, in the village. The asymmetrical lodge – an octagon plus a wing and a Greek Doric porch – is early C19. Tall gatepiers with ball finials have ornament which suggests *Nesfield*. Gates with overthrow.

By *Nesfield*, 1868, the gorgeous little ENTRANCE LODGE (GOLDEN LODGE) on the Bodelwyddan road (A55). Road 109 improvements have isolated it from the park. It is a more playful and ornate version, in ashlar, of the Queen Anne lodge built at Kew the previous year. Single storey, with sprocketed hipped roof, off-centre panelled chimney and segmentally-pedimented dormers, one of them stone-faced and with Corinthian pilasters and a miniature iron balcony. Heavily enriched with carving, mainly sunflowers, some of them in pots, intertwined with H for Hughes. Also a panelled frieze of great big pies.

For ESTATE BUILDINGS in vernacular revival idiom, *Nesfield* here sensibly and properly substituted slate for the tiling more usually associated with 'Old English' and its Home Counties roots, and he used stone as the main walling material, with brick being restricted to chimneys. TERFYN COTTAGES, on the A55, E of the lodge, consist of four semi-detached pairs with hipped gables, and they group with a conical-roofed WELL. They are so simple as not to be fully fledged examples of the style, but at the same time they show how much it owes to Butterfield and Street. At TALRYCH SMITHY (dated 1867 but possibly designed 1865), W of the lodge, the upper storey of a pair of cottages is partly over-sailing and has incised pargetting. Subtle composition, with a central slate-hung gable, but asymmetrical in fenestration and in its other roof shapes. The forge itself is at the side. On the Rhuddlan road (A547) MORFA LODGE of 1868. This has jettying and some half-timber, as well as slate-hanging. Ribbed brick chimney. Further W, BODORYN COTTAGES, 1867, simple in treatment. The adjacent CHAPEL, though built 1866 at the expense of the Hughes family, can hardly be Nesfield's. By *Nesfield* is TOLL-BAR COTTAGE, single-storey, probably of 1865, at the junction of the two main roads. Brick ribbed chimney, half-timber and a slate-hung gable on massive stone corbels.

In the 1920s the mansion was abandoned as the family residence in favour of Hendre Gyda, near Abergele, which was renamed Kinmel Manor (*see* p. 100). In the 1950s this was itself superseded by COED BEDW, which became PLAS

KINMEL. Sited between the main roads, this delectable place had been built in 1866 as the home farm with dairy and bailiff's house. For it, *Nesfield* used a version of Old English tinged with Gothic, the walling of stone, and with mullioned windows and brick chimneys. The front of the house has a most sophisticated grouping, permeated by the diagonals of porch, chimneybreast and coped and finialed gable. Two touches of stonecarving including heraldry and the sunflower motif and the ironwork of the door are of artily aesthetic character. On the return, facing a GARDEN originally laid out by *W. A. Nesfield*, is a canted stone-roofed bay. Then follow a portion altered *c.*1934, a range of farm buildings and a circular DOVECOTE with conical roof and a timber dormer on stone brackets. More relief carving – an H intertwined with flowers and a panel with heraldry and sunflowers in pots. Inside the house, floral patterns appear also in stained glass.

St George was the Kinmel estate village. Near the lodge gates in the village (*see* above) are the Neo-Elizabethan KINMEL ARMS and the VILLAGE HALL, the latter displaying heraldry, and proclaiming that it was provided by Lady Florentia Hughes in 1899.

ST GEORGE. Rebuilt 1887–94 by *C. H. M. Mileham* at the expense of H. R. Hughes. The previous church on the site was double-naved. The replacement is rendered, and of consciously vernacular character, with straight-headed windows under labels. The lights are cusped. Big s porch carried up as a bellcote, and, near the E end, a s transept. The building occupies a steep part of the churchyard, and there is a lower storey on the N. Simple and not unpleasing interior with crown-posts and a wagon ceiling. – Across the W end a panelled FAMILY PEW. Hughes HATCHMENTS of 1815–1911. – ROYAL ARMS. A rare Stuart example. William and Mary. In plaster, flanked by Jacobean-looking Ionic pilasters. – A painted panel comprises a post-1801 Hanoverian set.

In the churchyard a MAUSOLEUM by *Thomas Jones*, 1836, commissioned by W. L. Hughes, first Lord Dinorben. Square, with pinnacles and four gables, and with Jones's characteristically crisp and scholarly Tudor Gothic detail. Contained within a pointed arch is a finely carved coat of arms. Blank Perp windows on the other three sides.

DINORBEN, ¾ m. SSW of the village. A three-unit house with inside cross passage. (Medieval roof timbers, including wind-braces and the arched-braced central cruck truss of the hall.) Sub-divided in the C17 and given end stacks as well as a gabled lateral chimney. It was presumably at the same time that stepped gables, which no longer exist, were added.

FAERDRE, ¾ m. WSW of the village. C16. Tall and austere, with small mullioned windows devoid of mouldings. Formerly there was a stone dormer which may have been C17. Three-unit plan. Outside cross passage in the lower-end room with two cyclopean doorways (one now blocked) and an internal chimney backing on to it. Upper-end post-and-panel partition with Tudor-arched doorways. Hall ceiling with stop-chamfered joists, and moulded beams framed in two stages.

DINORBEN HILLFORT, ¾m. WSW (SH 968 757), which once overlooked the broad marshes at the mouth of the Clwyd, has now been totally destoyed by quarrying for limestone; only the white scar remains visible from the road below. But although there is nothing now to visit, the site must not be forgotten, because it was probably the most important fort in the area, providing evidence for what may have been almost continuous occupation from the Late Bronze Age into the Dark Ages. The fort was a small one by comparison with others in the area, but the multiple defences which cut across the neck of the craggy promontory were impressive – three large ditches and ramparts, the inner of which saw many alterations in the course of its long history. Excavations were carried out here in 1912–22 (Dr Willoughby Gardner), in 1956–69 (Dr H. N. Savory) and finally in 1977–8 (Mr G. C. Guilbert). Together these excavations have revealed a re- markable sequence of palisade and rampart building, destruc- tion and replacement with considerable remodelling of the entrance, which, in its later stages, was built with rectangular guard chambers at the end of the passage as in so many Clwydian hillforts. Excavation also revealed many postholes, which suggest that the interior was densely occupied, though for the most part it is difficult to interpret particular building plans. The question of the date of occupation and the associa- tion of this occupation with the construction of the ramparts has been the subject of much discussion, for radiocarbon dates from the site have been widely quoted. The first dates, obtained by Dr Savory, suggested that the earliest rampart around the hilltop, an earth and stone bank with timber- lacing, belonged to the C9 bc (Late Bronze Age), an exception- ally early date for such complex fortifications. However, the more recent series of radiocarbon dates have failed to confirm this and suggest instead that the timber-laced rampart was built in the C5 bc. The earlier dates could derive from habi- tation behind wooden palisades, of which traces were found beneath the ramparts, or they could refer to old, reused tim- bers. The presence of wealthy individuals in the neighbour- hood in the C7 bc is evidenced by the large hoard of fine horse harness found in the last century at the foot of the promontory; but it must be admitted that there is virtually no Late Bronze Age material from the fort itself. The bulk of the artefacts found inside the hillfort date from a prosperous period of occupation during the later centuries of Roman rule, with more tenuous evidence of continued activity in the post-Roman centuries. This late occupation is particularly interesting because there is documentary evidence for a medieval *llys* or court at Dinorben (exact site unknown), which may suggest that the centre of power and administration in

this district remained essentially the same through generations of social and political change.

SESSWICK *see* MARCHWIEL

SOUTHSEA *see* BROUGHTON

STANSTY *see* GWERSYLLT

TANYFRON *see* BROUGHTON

9070

TOWYN

ST MARY. Few expressions of Victorian ecclesiology are more
moving and evocative than a complete parochial group by
Street. There are six such groups, and except for that at
Boyne Hill in Berkshire, Towyn's is the most dramatic and
closely knit.* It is strange to see it now, amid bungalows and
caravans. The school came in 1871, and the church and vicarage, which may have been intended from the first, were
built together in 1872–3. All were paid for by Robert Bamford Hesketh of Gwrych (q.v.), and all are of similar
materials, with the masonry polygonal, and polychromatically
patterned slating.

95
  The SCHOOL, E of the church, is of sensitively contrived
simplicity, and the most relaxed of the three. A projecting
gable at one end, the teacher's house under a gable at the
other, and a lateral chimney between. Tall flèche.

95
  The CHURCH has Geometrical tracery, and a vigorous
saddleback central tower, with traceried bell openings E and
W, and a NE vice turret which rises only to the ringing chamber, and ends in a conical roof. Internally, walls are of coursed
rubble, with darker grey dressings. The choir, below the
tower, is vaulted, and has a large S window. To its N is an
organ chamber, in which the vice begins. The nave is aisled
only on the N. Unusually enough, for a single-aisled church,
there is also, on the N, a clerestory. The task of balancing the
traceried S windows in terms of proportion and scale is,
though, adequately handled. Aisle windows with central
free-standing shafts. Small clerestory windows of three
cusped lights, with the pattern in two layers, duplicated internally. Wagon roof in the sanctuary, and crown-posts in the
nave. – A full set of *Street* FURNISHINGS, including the PUL-
PIT, diapered FONT, and good chunky SCREENS and STALLS.

* I owe this observation, and many facts in the following account, to Mr Joyce.

Also the REREDOS, with a Crucifixion carved by *Earp*. It has, regrettably, been painted. – The RAILS and the HINGES (the s door has splendid ones) were executed by *James Leaver*. – *Godwin* ENCAUSTIC TILES in the chancel. – STAINED GLASS. E window of 1873, designed by *Street* and made by *Hardman*. – Brass CORONAE made by *Hardman* have, alas, vanished. – (*Hardman* also supplied PLATE. – FRONTALS were designed by *Street*.)

A linking corridor extends N from a NE vestry to the SW 94 corner of the VICARAGE, communicating with the study. The house has a three-gable s front, not completely symmetrical. Chequerwork in the middle gable, tile-hanging on the others, and a broad, arched doorway all give a friendly, domestic touch. Simple mullioned and transomed windows and, at the rear, a gabled projection for the staircase, with a traceried window. Streetian chimneys.

The three buildings group round the front garden of the vicarage. There is, though, another enclosure, and the rela- 96 tionship of its elements is arranged no less skilfully and sensitively. It is bounded on the s by the church, on the E by the vestry and the corridor and vicarage, and on the N by a COACH HOUSE and the wall which (masking outbuildings) links it to the vicarage.

CHRIST THE KING (R.C.), Gors Road. 1973–4 by *Bowen,* 123 *Dann, Davies*. A century after Street, and what a difference! Yet here too is a carefully considered though seemingly effortless style, handled with confidence and sensitivity, and with a feeling for the quality of materials. Small and simple, in a modern vernacular idiom. Low-pitched roof of interlocking tiles, harmonizing in colour with the sandy brick of the low walls. The roof rises to a clerestory over the sanctuary, and is of varied shape, following as it does the ins and outs of the plan. Boarded ceilings. The main body of the church may be opened, not only into the adjoining hall, but also to an external paved area, by means of sliding doors. A free-standing vertical structure incorporates a cross.

TREFALUN
3050

TREVALYN HALL. Dated 1576, and possessing the best Eliza- 53 bethan frontage in the county, the present house was built for John Trevor. His great-grandfather, of the Brynkinalt Trevors (*see* p. 112), had married the Trevalyn heiress, and ownership remained in the hands of his descendants until 1980. John Trevor did well for himself in London. He owed much to the patronage of Thomas Sackville (Lord Buckhurst and Earl of Dorset), and the resulting connections were also of service to his younger son, Sir John Trevor of Plas Teg (*see* p. 376). Among the several armorial bearings at Trevalyn, Sackville's appears above the entrance. The house is of brick with stone dressings, but has been rendered, which is a pity, though the quoins have been re-exposed, which helps. H-plan, with a storeyed porch. The recesses between the porch and the cross wings are gabled, i.e. the front has five gables in all. Mullions and transoms, mullions only in the gables. Renaissance awareness not only in the symmetry, but also in the use of pediments over windows – a feature which gives an East Anglian flavour. The coped and finialed gables are, however, straight, rather than of the stepped variety which might be expected in Norfolk, and which had been introduced into Wales the previous decade at Plas Clough (*see* p. 154). The rear elevation is also symmetrical, with some pediments, but is less disciplined. A surprise comes with the discovery of what at first sight looks like a duplication of the house a short way further back, presenting almost a mirror image of the rear of the first block, though with its brick still exposed. The two parallel ranges are connected at their mid-points by a single-storey corridor, in the centre of which is a tiny gabled gatehouse, the so-called Porter's Lodge, with an upper room perched above the doorway. It has two-light pedimented windows and a Doric aedicule framing the arch. This structure originally stood in line with the ends of the two ranges, but was moved backwards as part of alterations by *Thomas Jones*, 1836–8. He remodelled the interior of the main house, adapted the other range as service quarters, and built the linking corridor. The work was for Dr Thomas Griffith and his wife, who was a Boscawen and the Trevalyn heiress.

The usual explanation of the curious layout is that the two ranges are contemporary and were to have been connected by a further block, thus enclosing three sides of a quadrangle, with the Porter's Lodge on the fourth. The subsidiary range, so it is claimed, would have been a service wing, with the missing portion containing the great hall and great chamber, absent in the present main house. This cannot be correct. The main house was clearly complete in itself, and in its shape is typical of Elizabethan planning; the large kitchen chimney in what was obviously the service wing may be recognized, and the lack of the usual accommodation is attributable to successive alterations, from the C17 to the early C20. Moreover, the entrance front is designed for display, and it is inconceivable that the less carefully considered rear could have been intended as one side of a symmetrical entrance court. The mysterious subsidiary range has undergone change, and its back and interior are nondescript. Whatever its purpose – perhaps it is a grand instance of unit planning – it is likely to be later than the main house, as is the Porter's Lodge. In the latter is a corbel dated 1606 and inscribed 'SRT' for John Trevor's son Sir Richard. It is probably *in situ*, and one of the Lodge's sets of doors has strapwork and the initials RT.

Inside the main house, the lower rooms show only *Jones*'s and subsequent work, and the staircase is late C17 and unremarkable. Upstairs is a panelled gallery running between the cross wings at the rear, and said, improbably, to be an unaltered feature of John Trevor's house. The panelling may be genuine enough (if not all the doors), but is not necessarily *in situ*, and it is strange to find what amounts to a bedroom corridor where the great chamber is likely to have been. C20 work, including the drawing-room chimneypiece, is possibly by *R. T. Beckett*.

A C17 building to the NE, now known as MARFORD MILL-HOUSE, is aligned on the Porter's Lodge, i.e. on the axis created by the two parallel ranges. Symmetrical, with pedimented windows and doorcase. No stone dressings, all mouldings etc. being of brick, but now regrettably rendered.

TREVALYN HOUSE, ⅜m. SE of Trevalyn Hall. Built 1754. Three-storeyed, of brick. Stone dressings include quoins and rusticated lintels. Seven bays, the centre three deeply recessed, and a seven-bay return, the centre three closely spaced. A large wing, bay windows and a Doric porch are later additions, and use as a hospital has resulted in accretions. Spacious well staircase with ornamented stair ends, swept rail and columnar balusters. Some plasterwork and a couple of good chimneypieces, including an elaborate Corinthian one, of marble. The STABLES look Early Victorian.

ALLINGTON FARM, Cox Lane, 1 m. SW of the hamlet of Trefalun. A folly-like GATEHOUSE with ogees (cf. Marford, p. 386); and nearby are three COTTAGES with diluted Marford elements.

(TREVALYN FARM, ¼m. N of the hamlet. Panelled room with carved overmantel dated 1588. DOE)

TREFNANT

0070

HOLY TRINITY. 1853–5 by *Sir Gilbert Scott*. It commemorates Colonel and Mrs Salusbury of Galltfaenan Hall and was paid for by their two daughters. Being a memorial church, nothing was stinted; features which are out of the ordinary, and proclaim it as being of more than average interest, include aisle windows rising into cross gables, a double bellcote above the chancel arch, and a narrow two-light W window. Geometrical tracery, head-stops, and crisp detail. Vestry by *Sir Giles Gilbert Scott*, 1906. Rich internal effect owes much to polished shafts and foliated capitals, especially those of the arcades. The stonecarving marks a notable and early following of Ruskinian precept, for *J. Blinstone* of Denbigh, who executed it, 'studied for some days under Mr Scott's direction, the specimens of the French carving of the 13th century, collected in the Architectural Museum in London, and on his return successfully applied the same principles to his own work, arranging every group of leaves from natural specimens, gathered as they were needed from the woods and hedges around'.* – Elaborately treated FONT and PULPIT.

* John Williams, *Ancient and Modern Denbigh*, 1856.

(By *Giles Scott* the War Memorial tablet and N aisle screen, 1921. Also C20, the refitting of the chancel. P. Howell) – STAINED GLASS. Contemporary with the church are the E window and S aisle E, both by *Wailes*, and several with grisaille by *James Powell & Sons*.

The church forms the centre of a *Scott* parochial group. His RECTORY, to the W, is in good and true Victorian parsonage manner, with Elizabethan elements freely grouped on the principles of Pugin's picturesque utility. The SCHOOL, built 1860, is also informally composed, with the teacher's house integrated.

LLANNERCH HALL, 1m. N. Dour Italianate, cement-rendered, with stone dressings. A tall and compact Jacobean house was, wrote Pennant, 'spoiled by modern alteration and frittered into an errant villa', in a remodelling of 1772. It assumed its present appearance c.1862–4, but something of the C17 structure must survive, for the original arrangement of a central entrance between rectangular projections is preserved. Staircases of the 1770s. A chimneypiece in two colours of marble may also be of this time, though the same room has a ceiling which is so profuse that it cannot be genuinely C18, at least in its entirety. (Adamish ceiling in the room above.) Four stained-glass windows, dated 1862, incorporate some earlier pieces. Nothing remains of the prodigious GARDENS, laid out in the 1660s, with parterres, gazebos etc. in a series of enclosures on four successive levels. They gave place to C18 landscaping. Work by *Percy Cane*, c.1928, included terracing near the house, with canal, arcades, and a loggia.

PERTHEWIG, ¾m. ENE. Dated 1594 internally. The upper storey is largely of timber framing, some of which, with diagonal bracing, is exposed inside, though the exterior is rendered. Timber-framed porch. End chimneys, and a three-unit plan, unusual in that the centre consisted of two service rooms, and an internal lateral passage between them. Cross passage, its two post-and-panel partitions with moulded vertical members and ornamental door heads. On one side is the kitchen, and on the other the internal passage leads to the hall. Stopmoulded beams and joists in the hall and room above, stop-chamfered in the kitchen. Plasterwork with heraldry and strapwork over a fireplace. A mullioned window with arched lights is perhaps reset. Early C18 brick addition, with quoins and sashes. Two brick FARM BUILDINGS, one dated 1687.

TŶ COCH, 1¼m. E. Brick with stone dressings. Five bays and a Tudor-arched doorway, its lintel dated 1683 and inscribed in Welsh. Later sashes. Brick dormers and a coped and finialed gable end. Altered and enlarged, and there is some Douglas-like diapered brick and a rainwater head dated 1902.

MAES HEULYN, 1¼m. ESE. 1907 by *Sir E. Guy Dawber*. A suburban-looking roughcast house, with casements and glazing bars. Coped gables on the entrance front, bargeboards facing the garden.

PLAS NEWYDD, ¾ m. S. Rebuilt 1840–1 for *Edward Humphrey Griffith*, a younger son of the Garn family (*see* Henllan, p. 179). He designed it himself, but perhaps with some assistance, for the detailing bears a professional stamp, outside and in. Neo-Elizabethan, with coped and finialed gables, and the two main elevations asymmetrical. Entrance loggia of three four-centred arches. A rear wing and the ENTRANCE LODGE are by *William & Segar Owen*, 1901.*

TREVALYN *see* TREFALUN

TREVOR

TREVOR HALL. A mid-C18 front proudly looks out across the Vale of Llangollen. Brick, with stone quoins and other dressings. Nine bays, including two-bay wings advancing one bay. Two and a half storeys and solid parapets. Pedimented doorcase approached by branching flights of steps. A rainwater head is dated 1742. The rear and sides reveal all this to have been a remodelling and enlarging of an earlier house, with lateral chimney. (Hall chimneypiece, dated 1743, with urns, heraldry, and segmental pediment. Full-height staircase, a narrow well, with shaped stair ends, swept rail, and columnar balusters. NMR) The house, now derelict, was bought by the Ruabon brick and terra-cotta manufacturer J. C. Edwards (*see* Penybont Works, Cefn Mawr, p. 117). Additions made for him were probably by *G. C. Richardson*.

TREVOR CHURCH. Consecrated 1772, but built earlier in the C18 as a private chapel for the Lloyds of Trevor Hall – *c.*1717 according to Thomas, though Lewis says 1742. It is in the grounds of the house. Later traceried windows are likely to be of 1841, when refurnishing took place. – The PULPIT looks Jacobean, but is probably made up from fragments. – BOX PEWS include a large one for the Trevor Hall family. – Two-tier CHANDELIER with dove and wrought-iron suspension. – STAINED GLASS. Imported medieval fragments in N and S windows. – Two HATCHMENTS.

BRYNHYFRYD WELSH PRESBYTERIAN (CALVINISTIC METHODIST) CHAPEL, Garth, ½ m. N. The fall of the ground permits two domestic storeys below the chapel proper.

TREVOR TOWER. A hilltop castellated folly, ¾ m. N, now hidden by trees. Circular three-storey tower, plus a higher turret. (Rainwater head dated 1827.)

PLAS-YN-Y-PENTRE, between the canal and River Dee. Dated 1634. Three-gable front, including tall and thin cross wings. The upper parts retain exposed half-timbering, with cusped patterns. The entrance is in the left-hand wing. Thus there are no lower-end rooms.

* Information on Plas Newydd was kindly supplied by Mr E. G. E. Griffith.

On either side of the lane are attractive FARM BUILDINGS, and beyond is TREVOR MILL, dated 1848, and still with its waterwheel. Quite stylish, of four storeys, and with a low-pitched roof, and a gabled projection over the hoist.

BRYN HOWEL, s of the A539. Built 1896 for the younger J. C. Edwards, who followed his father into the brickmaking business. With bright red brickwork, terra-cotta, tile-hanging, and tiled roof, their products are much in evidence. There is also half-timbering. A room in a wing which is perhaps a later addition has a bold stone chimneypiece and elaborate plaster ceiling. Elsewhere is imported woodwork, including panelling and a Jacobean overmantel. The staircase looks mid-C18, with swept rail, ornamented stair ends, Corinthian newels, and slender twisted balusters. The house has been extended, as a hotel, and the original main entrance obscured.

Typical and pleasing *Telford* CANAL BRIDGES at Bryn Howel and beside the main road at Trevor Uchaf.

⁸⁰⁷⁰   TROFARTH

Hilly country, with views of the sea. There is no village, and the church stands alone.

ST JOHN. An unassuming little lancet job by *Sir Gilbert Scott*, 1873. Small chancel, s porch, and a turret-like bellcote near the w gable. In 1899 *Douglas & Minshull* added a NE vestry and organ chamber, and replaced the internal plaster with a veneer of random limestone fragments. The chancel was re-fitted to extend into the nave, and given recognizable Douglas FURNISHINGS.

TYDDYN BLEIDDYN *see* CEFN MEIRIADOG

²⁰⁴⁰   VALLE CRUCIS ABBEY

¹⁷ Founded by Madog ap Gruffydd Maelor in 1201 as a colony of Strata Marcella. The site is a typical Cistercian one, in a secluded valley, beside a plentiful supply of water. It is to be deplored that a caravan site now compromises the picturesque charm of the impressive ruins.

Characteristically Cistercian also is the plan of the early C13 CHURCH, with aisled nave (of five bays), two-bay transepts with eastern aisles as chapels, and an unaisled two-bay presbytery. Presbytery and s transept survive to a considerable height, and the w wall of the nave is virtually complete. The N transept and the aisles are fragmentary, and of the arcades there is little more than bases. Much of the work is that which was put in hand following the foundation, but

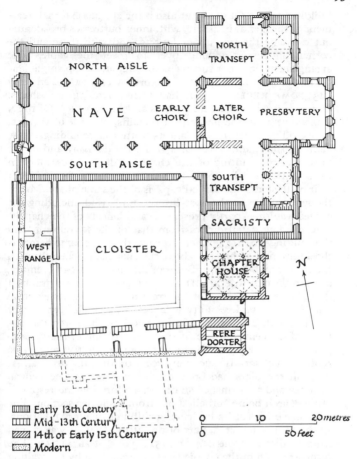

Valle Crucis Abbey, plan
(Department of the Environment)

some reconstruction, and a heightening, took place in the mid-C13, after a fire. The rubble masonry of the later walling is of generally smaller stones. The two stages are clearly seen superimposed in the PRESBYTERY, where wallshafts indicate that vaulting was intended from the first, and may well have been built. With the raising of the walls the shafts were abandoned, and a vault constructed independent of them. See the fragment of a rib in the SE corner. Of the earlier build are N and S lancets in the easternmost bay and a group of three in the E end. Their jambs and heads have roll mouldings inside and out, and these were returned externally as moulded sills. The central E window has shafts also, and originally rose higher. It was curtailed, and its foliated caps were reset, when a pair of lancets was introduced above, during the second

building period. Of the latter also is the curious external treat-
16   ment of the E end, in ashlar, with inner buttresses broadening
out to frame the two upper lancets, and with these and the
corner buttresses arching over to meet the gable. The
arrangement does not survive complete, and a top single lancet has vanished. On the N of the presbytery, part of an early
C13 TOMB RECESS, which had blank arcading and shafts.
Opposite is a reconstructed recess and an AUMBRY. Of the N
TRANSEPT only the lower part remains, all of it of the first
period. There are two E lancets with roll mouldings, a W
vaulting shaft, and traces of a shafted N doorway and of the
quadripartite vaulting of the chapels. Also an AUMBRY. In
the S TRANSEPT the upper-level doorway to the former night
stair, with shafts and carved caps, is of the same phase. Much,
though, belongs to the post-fire second period, including the
arches, vaulting (partly preserved) and lancets of the chapels.
The window detail differs from that of the N transept, and
the vaulting ribs are thinner. Apparently of the same date was
the addition of a chamber above the chapels, reached through
the conventual buildings. Bases of the chapel ALTARS remain,
and a reset DOUBLE PISCINA. The S gable, with its group of
three lancets, is gone, but the transept preserves its external
(later?) corbel table. A lofty W lancet, into which Perp tracery
was inserted. The fire would seem to have impaired the sta-
bility of the central tower (if such existed) and of the CROSS-
ING, for the SW pier, and the S respond of the NW pier, were
rebuilt. The work is cruder in execution than the original. At
first, all the piers had on each face a broad keeled central
member and two smaller shafts, those forming the responds
of the E arch being corbelled out from a smaller section. The
caps, like others at Valle Crucis, exhibit elementary foliations.
In the W crossing arch, part of the PULPITUM. It was moved
from further E in the C14 or C15. Against it an ALTAR. The
reconstruction of the SW pier was accompanied by the walling
up of the easternmost arch of the S arcade of the NAVE, showing that the choir then extended thus far W. A clerestory jamb
is preserved in this bay. Traces of abandoned vaulting shafts
in the N aisle, with masonry of the second period above them,
indicate that the church was far from complete at the time of
the fire. In the S aisle the doorway to the E cloister walk is of
the first period, and has three orders of shafts and deep
mouldings. The caps are further basic versions of stiff-leaf.
Also of the first period, the simply moulded bases of the
arcade piers and, though later in the campaign, the W re-
17   sponds. Finally, the W FRONT, the well-known face of Valle
Crucis. The doorway (inserted into earlier walling) and W
window are of the second period of construction. The door-
18   way, in four orders, displays something of the luxurance of
which the E.E. style was capable. Heavy mouldings, creating
deep shadow, and enriched with dogtooth. Shafts with stiff-
leaf capitals which are a little freer than those elsewhere. The
window consists of three two-light openings, the central one

higher than its fellows, and all contained within a single arch.
Similar rere-arch inside, now incomplete. Embryonic bar tracery, missing in the centre. In the gable, rebuilt in the mid-
C14, is a small Dec rose window, with eight radiating trefoiled
lights.

CONVENTUAL BUILDINGS. S of the church. Of the cloister
walks and the S and W ranges, only foundations remain. The
E range is well preserved, for although it is known to have 19
been roofless in the C18, it has been put to various domestic
and agricultural uses both before and since. Putlog holes remain. Next to the S transept a barrel-vaulted sacristy. It is of
the first building period, and its round-headed doorway has
shafts with caps of intertwined foliage. The CHAPTER HOUSE
and passage (or slype), and the dorter extending above, together with the much changed reredorter block at the S end,
form a rebuild. The junction of ashlar with earlier rubble is
clear. The date is C14 or even early C15, though the chapter
house is thoroughly Dec in style. It is square, of three by
three vaulted bays, with wave-moulded piers and vaulting
ribs. The mouldings are continuous, with no intervening capitals. Three reticulated E windows, the middle one renewed.
The doorway also has continuous wave moulding. Next to
the door a vaulted book recess with a screen of curvilinear
tracery showing externally as three sub-arches within intersecting ogees. In the slype are vaulting ribs similar to those
of the chapter house, and at its E end is a reset C13 doorway
with shafts and foliated caps. The dorter has reverted to being
a single room, though it was first partitioned in the late C15.
Its N end then became an abbot's hall, and an inner chamber
(the Abbot's Camera) was built beyond it, over the E end of
the sacristy. Both rooms were given fireplaces, and these significant changes reflect a remarkable relaxation of monastic
rule. The hall was provided with an outer door, its position
showing that the E cloister walk was then no longer intact.
Hall fireplace with corbels and moulded jambs. That in the
Abbot's Camera, which externally has its original circular
chimneystack, now uses a sepulchral slab as a lintel (see
below). The original fireplace, similar to that of the hall but
smaller, is reset in a room above. This attic room is post-
Suppression, as are an addition above the E end of the chapter
house and the renewal of the hall and Camera doorways. In
the S cloister range the fragment of the refectory includes the
base of a staircase and doorway, with shafts and dogtooth,
and apparently of the mid-C13 period.

The poet Gutun Owain not only praised the choir of the
abbey but also mentioned the fretted ceiling of the abbot's
house, doubtless referring to the late C15 rooms.

Among many SEPULCHRAL SLABS are the following: Worn
fragments in the presbytery include a rare dated example,
1290, commemorating Gweirca ferch Owain. – Also an early
C14 semi-effigy commemorating Ieuaf ab Adda. – Built into
the chapter house S wall a fragment of a late C13 cross head

with interlaced pattern. – Forming a lintel in the Abbot's Camera, and trimmed, an early C14 slab commemorating Maruruet. Vine trail and a stem branching into interlaced patterns. – Loose in the dorter: Fragment of a splendid slab which may have commemorated Madog ap Gruffydd Maelor, founder of the abbey, †1236. Central shaft with trilobes, branching stems with trilobed leaves and bunches of fruit between. – A very fine and well-preserved shield and sword heraldic slab commemorating Madog ap Gruffydd, †1306, great-grandson of the founder. Heraldic shield, vertical spear, diagonal sword and naturalistic foliage. Found *in situ* in front of the high altar. – Late C13 expanded arm cross, with three ribs in each arm overlapping in the centre. – Late C13 expanded arm cross with a sword incised in the cross, and a pattern of lobes at the base. – Late C13 expanded arm cross with circles between the arms and spear and sword either side of the shaft. – Four-circle cross, probably *c.*1300. – Built into

Valle Crucis Abbey,
slab to Madog ap Gruffydd, *c.* 1306
(Colin Gresham, *Medieval Stone
Carving in North Wales*)

the vaulting below the dorter floor, and covered now by trap-doors, are several slabs and fragments of various c13 dates.

PILLAR OF ELISEG, ¼ m. NW. The cross from which the abbey got its name. It is a pillar cross of the 'staff rood' type, standing on a burial mound. Rounded shaft, becoming square at the top. The transition is marked by a roll moulding, drooped swag-like on each face, with a collar below. The upper portion, including the head, is missing, as is the lower part of the shaft, and the original height would have been about twice the present 8 ft. Re-erected in this form in 1779, having been knocked down and broken during the Civil War. The original Latin inscription, transcribed in 1696, celebrated the glories of the royal house of Powys and recorded that the stone was erected by Cyngen, in honour of his great-grandfather Eliseg. The latter reigned in the mid-c8 and Cyngen died in 854, and it may thus be dated to the first half of the c9. In all probability it is linked with the north Mercian staff rood crosses, though their dating is in dispute. The tumulus is likely to be c5 or early c6, rather than the burial place of Eliseg himself.

WAEN see ABERWHEELER and LLANDYRNOG

WHITCHURCH see DENBIGH, pp. 152, 154

WHITEHURST see CHIRK

WREXHAM

3050

INTRODUCTION

A market existed in the Middle Ages, and as early as Tudor times local gentry were maintaining town houses in Wrexham. Thus long established as a place of commercial and social importance, the town became a centre of industry following the c18 development of coalmining and iron manufacture in the region. In 1848 the *Wrexham Recorder* noted that 'Other interests sprang up, mineral discoveries were extended, smoking engine chimneys peeped out of neighbouring hills, and during the last 25 years or so, the wealth accumulated among the tradesmen, assisted by that of the neighbouring gentry, has been gradually converting the town out of a decayed "genteel" one into something like an improved and improving commercial one.' Brewing, introduced in the late c18, became an important industry, with nineteen breweries in the town by the 1880s. A

charter of incorporation was granted in 1857, when the population was *c*.7,500. It had increased from 2,575 in 1801; in 1901
there were nearly 15,000 inhabitants, and in 1981 there were
40,000.

C19 and C20 prosperity produced some good architecture, but
brought disasters, too. Some losses are mentioned in the following pages, and the quality of much redevelopment has left a lot
to be desired. Especially grievous was the obliteration of part of
the ancient centre of the town by, and following, the driving
through in the late 1880s of a railway. It runs immediately s of
the parish church, which also suffers the indignity of a brewery
(one of the few which are left) as a close neighbour. Also, it is
sad that a well-intentioned opening up E of the church by demolition in Yorke Street is a questionable success in terms of
townscape.

Nevertheless, the church has a worthy approach from the N;
the town centre retains a surprising amount of character, and
Wrexham has much which is well worth seeing and well worth
preserving.

CHURCHES

St GILES. The church has a short chancel with three-sided
polygonal apse, a seven-bay clerestoried nave, and a w tower
which is justly famous. The nave arcades are of only six bays,
for the westernmost bay – the so-called ante-nave – is aisleless. On its N side, though, is a storeyed porch, which forms
a continuation of the aisle. A porch in corresponding position
on the s is an addition of 1822. Restoration by *Ferrey*, 1866-
7, did not seriously interfere with the fabric, and, except for
this sw porch, the exterior presents itself as entirely Perp. It
is Perp of several stages, which followed each other in close
succession. Internally, the arcades are Dec, and have been
ascribed to rebuilding which may have followed the fall of
the tower in 1330 or 1331. The major Perp remodelling is
said to have taken place after a fire of 1457 or 1463, but a
later C15 date is more probable. To this remodelling belong
the aisles and, except for that of the ante-nave, the clerestory.
Also the N porch with a STATUE of the Virgin in an ogee-
canopied niche. A vice to the upper chamber is continued as
a turret above the clerestory. Porch vaulting of 1901 by *H. A.
Prothero*, who restored the church exterior 1901-3. In the
aisles windows of four lights, with panel tracery, the side ones
four-centred. Three-centred, with two lights, in the clerestory. All have cusping. Five bays of windows in the N aisle,
but six in the s, corresponding to the arcade bays. The westernmost replaces a small s doorway. Tablet flowers, masks
etc. in string courses, and on the s are gargoyles and, at the
bases of pinnacles, grotesques. On the N, gargoyles appear on
the porch. The major remodelling allowed for no structurally
distinct chancel, and the present apsidal extension represents

a separate, and later, stage of work. Its windows, the E one of
five lights with sub-arches, have crocketed ogee heads. Like
all the windows which post-date the major remodelling, they
are not four-centred, and have very wide casement moulds.
This feature also occurs, e.g., in the S aisle easternmost window, in a bay which, together with its E return, differs greatly
from its fellows in design and detail. The disparities are hard
to explain, but it is possible that C14 features survived the
major remodelling (to which the return window belongs, set
in earlier walling) and that only later were they obliterated.
Animals now abound in the string course.

Turning to the interior, the C14 arcades have octagonal
piers, two chamfered orders, and no responds. Disused corbels are mementoes of the C14 roof, though most in their
present form date from *Ferrey*'s restoration, and some of
those which they replaced were themselves not original. The
present camberbeam roof, with bosses and with patterns of
diagonal ribs in its panels, belongs to the major Perp remodelling. Arched braces, traceried, with outer cusps carrying
angels. The aisle roofs have been renewed, except for traceried arched-bracing in the N aisle. The corbels for the nave
and aisle roofs may be original. They include in the N aisle a
suckling sow, and in the S an *Agnus Dei* and the Legs of
Man.* A large E window, dating from the remodelling, became the chancel arch when the church was later extended E.
It retains fragments of tracery, in a symmetrical arrangement
of stalactiform stumps. Either side are the canopies, with
ogees and tracery, of former corner niches. In the chancel
itself, luxuriant vaulted and canopied niches rise into crocketed pinnacles. Luxuriant also the triple SEDILIA, with vaulting and nodding ogees, and with heads, foliation etc. in its
spandrels. A blocked upper-level doorway, at the E end of the
S arcade, is less likely to have belonged to the rood loft than
to have been in connection with a gallery which Elihu Yale
received permission to erect in 1707. In it is set anachronistically one of the unused corbels. (Below the chancel is a
crypt.)

In the SE corner of the S aisle is a vaulted and canopied
niche (and near it, but hidden, the remains of a simple ogee
PISCINA). Both might be C14. The puzzling nature of this
end bay has already been noted, and those of its features
which post-date the major Perp remodelling are probably
contemporary with the ante-nave. The line of redundant corbels has been continued into the ante-nave – misleadingly, for
the masonry of the C14 arcades clearly meets later work at a
straight joint, possibly the site of a former tower arch. The
windows of the ante-nave clerestory have four lights. En-

---

* Suggesting that the church was one of those with which the Stanleys were
associated. Sir William Stanley was lord of Bromfield (in which Wrexham was
situated) 1483-95 (*see* Holt). Mr D. Leslie Davies notes also that either side of
the chancel arch at Wrexham are heads of Lady Margaret Beaufort, Countess of
Richmond and Derby, and her husband Lord Derby.

closed within the C19 SW porch is a blocked and mutilated window, with affinities to the odd one of the S aisle. Adjoining it an *ex situ* corbel.

Last of all, of separate build from the ante-nave, came the TOWER. It has an inscription of 1506, but wills of 1518 and 1520 suggest that work was then still continuing. It has been ascribed to Hart of Bristol, who, according to Mr John Harvey, may be identified with *William Hort*. Though the pinnacles and parapets of the Wrexham crown are not pierced, the tower is an outlier of the series, mostly in Gloucestershire and Somerset, which owe their inspiration to that of Gloucester Cathedral. Hexagonal corner pinnacles set back behind the face of the parapet. Sixteen subsidiary pinnacles. W doorway with label, a W window and, above, three stages of paired openings. All windows, and the bell openings, have crocketed ogee hoods. Clasping buttresses, except at the top storey, where they are diagonal, and have canopied niches. Similar niches in three stages against three pilaster strips, and much blank panelling, quatrefoil banding etc. Variations occur on the other faces, e.g. panelling on the S, in place of tiered niches. On the E the treatment below the topmost stage is simpler, making effective contrast. Indeed, like that of Gloucester itself, the tower has been criticized for its indiscriminate over-all ornamentation. The fault was avoided in other Gloucester derivatives, but the crustaceous richness has a character of its own, and the recessed pinnacles continue the diminution of outline provided by the buttresses, giving a craggy, organic quality, with a marvellous feeling of strength. Of a total of thirty niches, twenty-seven still contain SCULPTURE, but how much of it is original is unclear. The central statue of the nine on the W is a Virgin and Child. Inside is tierceron vaulting with grotesque corbels. Panelled internal reveal to the W window. The tower arch and its responds have identical moulding, though separated by capitals.

Elihu Yale lies buried within a few feet of the tower, a reproduction of which was erected at Yale University in the 1920s.

FURNISHINGS. The chancel was partly refurbished by *Sir Thomas Graham Jackson*, 1914, and the REREDOS, RAILS and marble FLOORING are his. In 1918–19 he fitted up the E end of the N aisle as a WAR MEMORIAL CHAPEL, and he also intended that STATUES, of which only three materialized, be placed on the disused corbels of the nave. – FONT. An ancient bowl, retooled when brought back into the church in 1843. – PULPIT. By *Ferrey*, 1867. High Victorian Dec. – Brass eagle LECTERN, given in 1524. Moulded stem, and three lions at the base. It is probably of East Anglian make, and, among forty or so surviving pre-Reformation lecterns, it belongs to the same group as those at Cavendish and Woolpit, Suffolk; Croft, Lincolnshire; Chipping Campden, Gloucestershire; Upwell, Norfolk, and Corpus Christi College, Oxford. – Iron CHANCEL SCREEN, with gates. Scrollwork, twisted bars and vine trail, foliage, orange trees growing from urns etc. Two cherub masks. Said to have been given by Elihu Yale, and thus possibly dating from 1707, i.e. from the same time as his gallery. The work has been attributed both to *Hugh Davies*, who died in 1702, and, more convincingly, to *Robert Davies*, his son.* – Above the chancel arch, there are traces of a late medieval Last Judgement PAINTING. Figures rise from their coffins in front of Our Lord in Majesty (head and bust missing) with the Virgin and St John.

STAINED GLASS. The three apse windows are by *James Powell & Sons*, 1914, as part of Jackson's refitting, and replaced glass of 1841 by *Evans*. Medallions from Evans's E window are reused in the chancel N. – W window by *Clayton & Bell*, 1895. – S aisle easternmost by *A. Gibbs*, 1867. – Further S aisle windows by *Kempe* and the firm of *Kempe & Tower*, commemoration dates 1892–1920.

MONUMENTS. In the chancel: Hugh Bellot, Bishop of Chester, †1596. Fragment of an effigy, set in a windowsill. – Mary Fitzhugh †1784. Draped urn. – Lloyd monument. By *Sir Richard Westmacott*, 1816. Inscription on a convex bow. Female figures either side, one with two children, the other holding a chalice. – E end of nave: Rev. Thomas Myddelton †1754 and wife Arabella †1756. By *Roubiliac*. Overlapping portrait medallions, under a canopy from which drapery is drawn back. – W end of nave: Inscriptions to three generations of parish clerks, including Daniel Jones †1668:

> *Here lies interrd beneath the's ſtone[s]*
> *The Beard ye Fleſh and eke ye Bones*
> *of Wrexham Clark old* Daniel Iones

– Mary Ellen Peel. By *Thomas Woolner*, 1866–7. Reunited with her infant son, who is held by an angel. – Sir Foster Cunliffe †1834 and wife Harriet †1830. By *John Davies* of Wrexham. Gothic, with tripartite canopy. Very large and elaborate. – In the tower: Monument to those of the Twenty-Third Royal Welch Fusiliers who died in the 1873–4 Ashanti Campaign. By *Gaffin & Co.*, 1874. – N aisle: William Johnson Edensor †1829 and daughter Joana Thomasine †1830 by *Millers & Derome* of Manchester. Sarcophagus tablet against an obclisk. – Ann Fryer †1817. By *Sir Richard Westmacott*. Grecian touches. – Cynwrig ap Hywel. Early C14. Worn recumbent effigy. Shield, with inscription, and sword. Head on a cushion, and at the feet two animals and a snake. – Frances Puleston †1804. By *Peter Mathias Vangelder*. Little urn, big background, columns carrying nothing. – Mary Puleston †1802. Also by *Vangelder*. Draped

* Mr Davies suggests that both may have contributed, and cites a reference to a 'lychgate' being transferred into the church in 1720. He suggests that this may represent the simple railings, which could be by Hugh, and that the Baroque enrichment was added by Robert in 1720, i.e. at the same time as making the new churchyard gates (*see below*).

urn. – Philip Puleston †1776. By *C. Bromfield*. Heraldry
against an obelisk. Use is made of contrasting marbles. –
84 Mary Myddelton. By *Roubiliac*, 1751–2.* In its spirited de-
piction of the Last Trump and a resurrection and falling
pyramid, Roubiliac anticipated his Hargrave monument of
1757 in Westminster Abbey. A child angel in clouds sounds
the trumpet, and the lady, who died in middle age, clambers
youthful from a shattered sarcophagus. The pyramid crashes
in fragments, and a vigorous plant springs up. – s aisle: Sir
Richard Lloyd †1676. Erected in his lifetime, but with the
inscription dating only from 1877. Achievement of arms and
barbaric architectural surround. – Jones monument. Latest
commemoration date 1797. Adamish urn. – Ann Wilkinson
†1756, wife of the ironmaster John Wilkinson. By *T. F. Pritchard*. Pedimented tablet. – Owen Bold †1703 and wife Margaret †1705. Either by *William Stanton* (Gunnis) or *Edward
Stanton* (Esdaile). Twisted Corinthian columns, gadrooning,
side volutes and garlands, urn in a broken scrolly pediment
etc.

BRASSES include that at the e end of the nave to Elizabeth
Lloyd †1665. Emblems of mortality. – Some by *Silvanus
Crue*, also of the latter half of the c17, attached to arcade
piers; unremarkable. – In the s aisle Sir Evan Morris †1890.
Ostentatious, by *Jones & Willis*.

ROYAL ARMS of Queen Anne.

CHURCHYARD GATES. Documented work by *Robert Davies*, 1720. Restored 1900, and probably extensively renewed,
but authentically. A beautiful frothy *clair-voie* with much
scrollwork. Central pair of gates, side wickets, and short
screen lengths, all separated by two-dimensional piers. Each
portion has its own overthrow. Pair of rusticated stone PIERS
with urns.

OUR LADY OF DOLOURS (R.C. CATHEDRAL), Regent Street.
Built 1857 at the expense of Richard Thompson, ironmaster
and colliery owner. In 1907 it became the pro-cathedral of
the diocese of Menevia. By *E. W. Pugin*. In neither the brick
PRESBYTERY nor the church itself, with late c13 features,
was he as aggressive and heavy-handed as often he was. The
windows with straight pointed heads are characteristic.
Clerestory and sw broach spire. e rose window set within
tracery internally. – MONUMENT. Ellen Thompson †1854,
wife of the donor. Tomb-chest and a good recumbent effigy.

ST DAVID (Welsh Church), Rhosddu Road. 1889–90 by *Howel
Davies* of Wrexham. Rock-faced and red-roofed. Cruciform
but aisleless. Polygonal apse and a bellcote over the chancel
arch. Altered internally.

ST JAMES, Rhosddu Road. By *William Turner* of Wrexham.
Cruciform but aisleless. Begun as a 'school church' 1874, and
made more churchy by the addition of vestry, polygonal apse

---

* In an agreement of 30 April 1751, the work was undertaken to be completed
within sixteen months. Discovered by Mr D. Leslie Davies.

and s porch, 1875. Rock-faced, with cusped lancets and bar tracery, and a tall E bellcote. – STAINED GLASS. N transept E by *I. A. Gibbs & Howard*, commemoration date 1882.

ST JOHN BAPTIST, King's Mills Road, Hightown. Built at the expense of John Jones, a brewer, in memory of his wife. 1908–9 by *L. W. Barnard*. Neo-Perp, but without a scrap of the refinement and scholarship associated with the style or the period. Rock-faced. No structural division between nave and chancel, even though only the former has aisles and clerestory. On the S this awkward transition is masked by a steeple with broach spire. The only really good thing is the STAINED GLASS of the E window, by *Morris & Co.*, 1910, incorporating *Burne-Jones* designs.

ST MARK, Regent Street, demolished 1959, was cruciform and lofty, in Geometrical Dec. By *R. K. Penson*, 1856–8, with its spire completed 1862. Goodhart-Rendel considered it 'one of the best provincially designed town churches of its epoch'. There was stencilled decoration supposedly by *Owen Jones*.

ST MICHAEL, Poyser Street. 1910–12 by *Barnard*. Ruabon brick. Perp tracery. Timber porch (ungainly) and timber arcades. Cross-gabled nave aisles, and although there is a chancel arch, this is scarcely expressed externally, and the chancel windows are in the same plane as the (thoroughly incongruous) ones of the clerestory. Originally there was a flèche. As at St John's, the redeeming feature is *Morris* STAINED GLASS in the E window, with work by *Burne-Jones*. Of 1912.

BAPTIST CHAPEL, Chester Street. 1875–6 by *Morrison* of Wrexham. Gothic.

PEN-Y-BRYN BAPTIST CHAPEL, Chapel Street. Built as Congregational (Independent), 1789. Remodelled 1881. Coved ceiling, possibly of the earlier date, though no features can definitely be recognized as original.

EBENEZER CONGREGATIONAL CHAPEL, Queen Street. Built 1862–3; demolished 1979. It had a small stuccoed front, of three bays, with pediment, Ionic pilasters, and round-headed windows.

EBENESER CONGREGATIONAL CHAPEL, Chester Road. 1974–5 by *G. Raymond Jones & Associates* of Wrexham. Wedge-shaped plan, presenting to the street a series of articulated blocks.

WREXHAM METHODIST CHURCH, Regent Street. There were two predecessors. Bryn y Ffynnon Wesleyan Chapel, Gothic, with a spire, by *William Waddington & Son*, 1889–90, itself replaced a building of 1855–6 by *James Simpson*. The present church, 1970–2, is incorporated at upper level in shopping redevelopment of 1970–4. A cumbersome free-standing affair contains the staircase. Architects for the scheme *G. Raymond Jones & Associates*, in collaboration with *John Laing Design Associates*. Church interior by *Design Group Partnership* of Chester.

METHODIST CHAPEL, Poyser Street. Built 1911–12. Ruabon

brick and yellow terra-cotta. Perp tracery. Slender corner tower, with battered corner buttresses of unbroken outline.

Built 1867 and demolished 1979 was SEION WELSH PRESBY-TERIAN (CALVINISTIC METHODIST) CHAPEL, Regent Street. A sad loss, for it was by *W. & G. Audsley* of Liverpool, and had fanciful capitals (carved by *Stirling*) and some polychromatic brick. Round-arched, and a frontage with two towers surmounted by slated spires, into which tall louvred openings rose as lucarnes.

124 CAPEL-Y-GROES WELSH PRESBYTERIAN (CALVINISTIC METHODIST) CHAPEL. Built 1981–2 and characteristic of *Bowen, Dann, Davies* with its low, spreading roofscape expressing the plan shape. Steel frame, clad in brick, and the facings, the roofing tiles and the stained hardwood of the windows accord harmoniously together. A free-standing sculpturesque brick tower carries a cross. The building is a replacement for the *Audsley* Seion Chapel, the PULPIT from which has been reused.

TRINITY PRESBYTERIAN CHURCH OF WALES, King Street. Built 1907–8. Ruabon brick and some stone. Perp tracery and a tower. Front with pepperbox corner turrets and a broad window containing Art Nouveau tracery. A pair of corbelled buttresses serve as mullions and continue up to become pinnacles.

By *Ingall & Son* of Birmingham, 1898 (CW), SALISBURY PARK UNITED REFORMED CHURCH (formerly Congregational), Salisbury Road, was demolished 1981–2. Of Ruabon brick and some stone, it had a wayward front, with a peculiar octagonal corner tower and spirelet.

CEMETERY, Ruabon Road. Of 1874–6. The layout by *Yeaman Strachan*, the LODGES and a pair of CHAPELS by *William Turner*, both of Wrexham. The chapels, with Geometrical tracery, are linked by an arched gateway above which rises a vigorous broach spire. Original iron GATES and RAILINGS.

PUBLIC BUILDINGS

GUILDHALL, Rhosddu Road. 1959–61 by *Stephenson, Young & Partners* of Liverpool. Brick, with three storeys of freely proportioned sash windows. Neat and clean, and cautiously modern, of Scandinavian inspiration, owing much to Stockholm Town Hall, rather than being thoroughly Neo-Georgian. Wing with a low-pitched copper roof and rectangular lantern. Higher than the original building, and less satisfactory, is an extension at one end, 1980–1 by the *Borough of Wrexham Maelor Public Works Department* (*G. O. Evans*, Principal Assistant Architect).

COUNTY BUILDINGS, Regent Street. Built as militia barracks, 1856. Converted for magistrates' courts and police station,

1879, and now council offices. Neo-Elizabethan, with Gothic bits. The recessed centre has an oriel and arcaded loggia, and the left-hand cross wing a spired octagonal turret.

OLD LIBRARY, Queen Street. A Carnegie Library, built 1906–7 and now council offices. Won in competition by *Vernon Hodge* of Teddington. Brick and stone. Modillion cornice and one-bay segmental pediment. Edwardian Baroque in character, but with fresh and free detail. The first-floor windows form virtually a continuous band.

MAGISTRATES' COURTS, Bodhyfryd. By *Colwyn Foulkes & Partners*, 1975–7. Well finished. Sandy brick, with pairs of windows recessed between buttresses. Copper-clad top storey. An entrance on three of the four fronts.

POLICE HEADQUARTERS, Bodhyfryd. 1973–5 by *Eric Langford Lewis*, Denbighshire County Architect. Linked to the Magistrates' Courts. Reinforced concrete frame with storey-height pre-cast corrugated cladding panels. Spreading two- and three-storey base, from which rises, adjacent to a glazed entrance hall, a hefty stalk containing lifts etc. Cantilevered out from this is a tower block rising a further eight storeys and vying with the parish church in distant views of the Wrexham skyline.

SWIMMING BATHS, Bodhyfryd. 1965–7 by *F. D. Williamson & Associates* of Bridgend. An enormous hyperbolic paraboloid rising to four storeys over the entrance. The opposite end, where the diving boards are, is fully glazed. Three pools, with spectators' galleries passing as bridges over the spaces which separate the pools.

PUBLIC LIBRARY, Rhosddu Road. By *James Roberts* of Birmingham. The handling of internal space and the quality of finishes and detail make this building a pleasure to visit and to use. Reinforced concrete frame, and brick and travertine facings. The library proper, 1971–2, is articulated by two-light two-storey slit windows. Inside is a mezzanine with a central well, above which is top lighting. Aligned on the axis of the mezzanine is the entrance and, at the opposite end, a glazed apsidal projection. An Arts Centre, added 1973, is attached to the main block by two glazed links, enclosing a small courtyard.

COLLEGE OF ART, Regent Street. Ashlar front of nine bays, with a three-bay pediment and a four-column Greek Doric porch. The capitals are enriched. Built as the Infirmary, 1838, and by *Edward Welch*.

SCHOOLS, Madeira Hill. Gothic, symmetrical and spreading. By *Edward Jones* of Wrexham, *c.*1884–6. Smaller, symmetrical block facing Poplar Road (built as Girls' School) by *John Morrison* of Wrexham, 1895–6.

Former BRITISH SCHOOL, Brook Street. *See* Perambulations, p. 308.

WAR MEMORIAL HOSPITAL, Rhosddu Road. Begun 1923. The nucleus is a Mid-Victorian Italianate villa with crested roof.

HIGHTOWN BARRACKS, King's Mills Road, Hightown. Built
as militia barracks, 1877. Several sombre brick ranges, most
with purple banding.

The earliest MARKET HALL (BUTCHERS' MARKET), 1848, is
by the younger *Thomas Penson*, and has a frontage to the
High Street in his unmistakable and cheerful Neo-Jacobean.
Shaped and finialed gables, pedimented mullioned and transomed windows and an oriel over the entrance arch. Behind,
in Henblas Street, is the GENERAL MARKET, 1879. It occupies the site of Manchester Square, one of the many courts
built by visiting tradesmen for use during the Wrexham
March Fairs. The hardware dealers' New Birmingham
Square has been replaced by the VEGETABLE MARKET,
partly in Henblas Street. A large extension by *John England*,
Borough Engineer and Architect, 1927, has frontages of
half-timbered shops to Queen Street and Lambpit Street,
recalling late C19 Chester.

ROYAL WELCH FUSILIERS MONUMENT, Bodhyfryd. A First
World War memorial by *Sir W. Goscombe John*. An C18 sol-
dier holds a banner and laurel wreath behind a figure of his
C20 counterpart.

QUEEN VICTORIA MONUMENT, Parciau, Bradley Road.
Figure by *Henry Price*, 1904.

PERAMBULATIONS

1. The Town Centre

From a crossroads at the head of High Street, the short length
of CHURCH STREET is closed by the gates of the parish
church and dominated by the tower beyond. Nos. 3–4 are
C18, minor. Nos. 5–6 of 1974–5 by *Raymond Jones & Associates* respect the scale of Nos. 7–10 next door. Inside the latter
may be seen the upper (straight) portions of four crucks with
king-posts and cambered ties. Arched-bracing to the one
which was the central truss of the hall. Date inscription of
1681, probably referring to the addition of the timber-framed
gables which face the street. More timber framing (rendered)
at Nos. 3–7 TOWN HILL, w of the crossroads. (In a range
running back at right angles, behind No. 7, is a cruck. Discovered by Mr D. Leslie Davies, who refers also to linenfold
panelling.) Nos. 17–19 are an Italianate frontage, Mid-Victorian, with big arched window openings embracing two storeys. Pathetic fragments in ABBOT STREET hint at the
character which must have prevailed in this part of the town
before the devastation wrought by the railway and subsequent
despoliation. BRYN-Y-FFYNNON, a large timber-framed
house in Priory Street, was a notable early C20 loss. Its
three-storeyed brick gatehouse, with side wings and pedimented windows, survived long enough to be listed; and
much good that did.

The demolition most to be deplored is perhaps that of the
TOWN HALL. Built 1715 and destroyed 1939, it stood at the
head of Town Hill and crowned the view up HIGH STREET.
The street itself is notable for dignified C19 and early C20
office buildings. On the corner of Church Street, the TRUS-
TEE SAVINGS BANK (originally Parr's Bank), by *J. H. Swainson* of Wrexham, *c.* 1896–9. Red ashlar, in a free Renaissance,
with octagonal corner turret. Next, BARCLAYS BANK, a
five-bay, three-storey palazzo of brick and stone. Then Nos.
38–9, mid-C18, with rusticated lintels. No. 33 by *Grayson
& Ould*, formerly MARTINS BANK, was built *c.* 1906–7 for
the Bank of Liverpool. Red ashlar, with attached pedimented
tetrastyle Corinthian portico, much ornament and enrichment, but not at all coarse. Best of all is the SUN ALLIANCE,
originally Provincial Welsh Insurance Co., by *R. K. Penson*,
1860–1. Balustraded ashlar palazzo of three storeys and five
bays. First-floor windows with balusters and alternating segmental and triangular pediments. Iron railings to the windows above. Opposite is the Market Hall (*see* Public Buildings), below which is the MIDLAND BANK by *Woolfall &
Eccles*, 1910–12. Brick and stone and opulently Baroque. Five
bays, with segmental pediments, to the two end bays, carrying
chimneys. The vista down the broad street is closed by the
mid-C18 façade of the CREST HOTEL in YORKE STREET.
The Wynnstay Arms (as it previously was) had been
threatened with demolition, but fortunately reconstruction
took place behind the frontage, in a redevelopment scheme
of 1970–3. Two and a half storeys. Asymmetrical, but including five bays symmetrical about the former entrance. Later
extension to the r. Brick with stone dressings. Brick aprons,
rusticated lintels and moulded surrounds to the windows
above the doorway. That of the first floor is pedimented also.

Now for two early or mid-C17 staircases.* The first is in
the offices of BORDER BREWERIES in MOUNT STREET, near
the foot of Yorke Street. Well-plan, rising through two storeys. Small newels and flat, shaped balusters, moulded on the
outer sides and flush facing the stairs. At No. 2A CHESTER
STREET (set back from the street) the parts are *ex situ*, reused.
HOPE STREET, leading N from the High Street crossroads, has
a number of Victorian façades in a miscellany of styles. Also
the CENTRAL ARCADE (formerly Wrexham Arcade) by *A. C.
Baugh*, 1890–1. (VH) Brick and terra-cotta front and a narrow
glass-roofed arcade. The NATIONAL WESTMINSTER BANK
was one of *Gibson*'s branches for the National Provincial.
Built 1876. Ashlar, of three bays. Restrained Italianate with
rusticated pilaster strips and four-column Doric doorcase.
The axis of the street is closed by the Douglas-like polygonal
roof of the former TALBOT HOTEL, 1904–5 by *John H. Davies & Son* of Chester.‡ Half-timbered.

* To which Mr Davies drew attention.
‡ The ornamented chimneys are a standard type, in purpose-made brick, designed by *Douglas & Fordham*, *c.* 1895, for production by *J. C. Edwards* of Ruabon.

A glimpse of the OLD LIBRARY (*see* Public Buildings) makes for good townscape. Further down Hope Street, No. 35, with No. 2 REGENT STREET, is tall, Gothic and of yellow brick, with a gateway through. It is by *H. Kennedy*, 1875. (VH) The thatched HORSE AND JOCKEY on the corner of Priory Street is timber-framed and rendered but is not as old as it looks.*

Off to the l. into HILL STREET for a fragment of cinema history. The LITTLE THEATRE has a projection box built out at the front when an earlier hall was converted. Regent Street is notable for ecclesiastical destruction. St Mark's and the Bryn y Ffynnon and Seion Chapels have vanished, and of the former array of spires, only that of the R.C. Cathedral remains (*see* Churches).

In KING STREET, to the r., Nos. 55–67 form an early C19 brick terrace of two and a half storeys. Shop fronts occur within segmental arches which alternate with oval cast-iron medallions; being an integral part of the elevational composition, they indicate that the block was intended as shops from the first. It has a return to RHOSDDU ROAD, where No. 4, PARK LODGE, *c.*1863, is by *William Turner*. (VH) It does him little credit, and more interesting work by a local architect is to be found among the remaining villas in GROSVENOR ROAD and its continuation. *J. R. Gummow* designed the Italianate GROSVENOR LODGE of 1869, on the corner of Regent Street. Brick and stone. Its longer front is symmetrical and has Corinthian pilasters and shell tympana to its first-floor windows. His ABBOTSFIELD, built 1863, is stone and thorough-going Gothic, with cusping, tracery, patterned slating etc. and an apse-like projection at the side. Houses in GROVE ROAD known to be by *Gummow* include FERN BANK, 1873. PLAS GWILYM may also be ascribed. (It is similar to one of his of 1860 which has been demolished.) Gothic, with traceried bargeboards and a pyramid-roofed tower. Also Gothic, but probably of different authorship, is EPWORTH LODGE, built 1865 as the manse for Bryn y Ffynnon Chapel. Nos. 5–7 are simple and stuccoed Italianate and contrast with the plummier fare offered by their neighbours. Further on, along PENYMAES AVENUE, No. 1 is a sizeable house, set back from the road. 1934 by *Baillie Scott & Beresford*.‡ It can be seen as harking back to better things, though it is less readily associable with the name of the famous Arts and Crafts architect than is Cherry Hill (*see* p. 313).

See p. 519

2. *To the South*

Individual items rather than a sustained perambulation.

In BROOK STREET, the former BRITISH SCHOOL has, in the course of a varied history, acquired a misleading datestone. The building is of 1844 by the younger *Thomas Penson*.

---

* Mr Davies mentions that it is not shown on a map of 1790.
‡ Information from Mr Ian Allan.

Stone. Tall gable-ended façade with pedimented mullioned and transomed windows. The centre is corbelled out and rises as the top-piece of the fancifully shaped gable. Beyond Bridge Street, PLAS-Y-BRYN in CHAPEL STREET is early C19 with a pedimented Ionic doorcase. Along Poplar Street to SALISBURY ROAD and OTELEY HOUSE, a stone-built Gothic villa of the 1860s. It has tall gables, cusped lancets, tracery and an oriel above the entrance. Salisbury Road leads to BENNIONS ROAD, where, on the corner of KING'S MILLS ROAD is BEECHLEY, described as new in 1726.

Finally, some suburban houses further s, beginning in FAIRY ROAD. Nos. 5–7 by *E. A. Ould*, 1881, comprise a semi-detached block, but asymmetrical and well composed. Brick and pebbledash, and *J. C. Edwards* supplied terra-cotta. Stepped gables and sashes. Also turrets clearly inspired by Douglas, whose pupil Ould was. No. 9, with turrets and a coved terra-cotta cornice, and No. 11, STRATFORD HOUSE, are doubtless also by *Ould*. The latter, dated 1879, is Douglas-like and particularly striking, though not large. Partly half-timbered, with pargetted patterns in the panels of the framing, and typical Aesthetic Movement motifs in stonecarving around the doorway.

Nearby, and further s again, in SONTLEY ROAD, is TŶ'R ESGOB (formerly PLAS TIRION and now the residence of the R.C. Bishop). It is by *J. R. Gummow*, 1865. At the corner of HILLBURY ROAD is NAZARETH HOUSE (R.C. Convent), with a Victorian villa as its nucleus and large additions by *Weightman & Bullen*, 1964–6.

OUTER WREXHAM

EAST AND SOUTH-EAST

ST ANNE (R.C.), Prince Charles Road, Queen's Park. 1960–2 by *Patrick M. White*. Shallow copper-covered dome above an octagon, its drum glazed, as a clerestory. Built with the altar against a wall, thus conflicting with the concept of the centralized plan, as well as being liturgically dated for the early sixties.

ST MARK, Bryn Eglwys Road, Queen's Park. Built 1961, and unworthy of its commanding hilltop site.

Radburn planning, first applied at Radburn, New Jersey, was conceived in the United States in the 1920s as a development of English garden-city ideals in providing for traffic segregation. The principle is that of inward-looking superblocks served by vehicular ring-roads and cul-de-sacs, and with pedestrian routes within and between the superblocks. The idea was introduced into Britain with the s part of the QUEEN'S PARK HOUSING ESTATE, by *J. M. Davies*, Wrexham Borough Engineer and Surveyor, with *Gordon Stephenson*, later of *Stephenson, Young & Partners*, as consultant.

The scheme dates from 1950, and the first superblock (COED ABEN at the E end of the site, N of Anthony Eden Drive) was completed in 1954. In all there are seven N of Queensway and one (of two which were intended) to the S. They are of modest size, enclosing little more than sets of footpaths and grass verges, as against the parkland at Radburn, and there is no separate pedestrian access between them. There is some open space around a brook which crosses the site, and separating off the more conventionally planned N part of the estate. The architectural quality is not high, and it is a pity that more attention was not given to the landscaping of the larger open areas.

KING'S MILLS, near the junction of King's Mills and Abenbury Roads, Abenbury. Four-square C18 stone mill. Later gable with balustraded balcony to the hoist. Two BRIDGES nearby, one with rusticated arch.

BRYN ESTYN, Bryn Estyn Lane, Abenbury. Rebuilt 1903–4 for F. W. Soames, a Wrexham brewer. Much half-timbering handled convincingly, the richly carved bargeboards being particularly effective. The garden front suffers from the removal of a timber loggia and balcony.* Disappointingly plain and unremarkable interior. In connection with present use as a community home (i.e. what was formerly called an approved school), extensions, including a special secure unit, were made by *R. W. Harvey*, County Architect, 1975–7. To the W of the house is a GARDEN TEMPLE, or what is probably no more than an Edwardian reusing of columns from the predecessor house to create an ornamental feature.

CEFN PARK, E of Cefn Road, Abenbury. A country house still in family occupation. Early or mid-C18, much altered and enlarged after a fire, *c.*1830, and again altered subsequently. The original house, of brick with rusticated lintels, was of two and a half storeys and five bays, with one-bay pediment, plus two-storey one-bay wings. Now rendered, and with an Ionic loggia added in front. The left-hand wing is swallowed up in Victorian extensions (possibly the work for which *Ferrey* is known to have been responsible) and to the r. is a single-storey Victorian billiard room. On this side also, but belonging to the garden front, is a full-height addition of *c.*1830 containing a drawing room. Interior features of this date include mahogany doors and an apsidal stone staircase. Also a coffered ceiling and a marble chimneypiece in the drawing room. A dining-room wing added 1910, projecting outwards on the garden front, has been demolished. Victorian brick STABLES (and further N a domed brick ICEHOUSE).

LLWYN ONN HALL, Abenbury, S of Cefn Park. An early C18 double pile, existing by 1724. Now rendered, and with later sashes and veranda, and with the left-hand return (the present entrance front) extended. Staircase, through two storeys, with dado, swept rail, turned balusters, and still with a string.

* The name of the architect is not recorded, but there exists a plan for the GARDENS, not entirely as executed, by *W. Goldring* of Kew, 1903.

WREXHAM INDUSTRIAL ESTATE, 3 m. E of the town. Developed from the Marchwiel Royal Ordnance Factory, which
had been built for munition manufacture in the Second
World War. Among the best of the smaller new factories is
that of WEDDEL PHARMACEUTICALS LTD, Red Willow
Road, near the main approach to the estate. 1970 by *Colwyn
Foulkes & Partners*. Curtain walling and a landscaped setting.
FIBREGLASS LTD, in Bryn Lane, to the E, successfully demonstrates broad landscaping and the neat treatment of large
masses of industrial buildings. By *Charles Andrews & Sons*,
consulting engineers. Built 1970–1 and later extended. Main
building steel-framed, with plastic-coated cladding. (A landscaped courtyard within the office block.) Near the road is a
circular glazed entrance unit (a so-called 'gatehouse') alongside a security moat.
At PENTRE MAELOR, beyond the Firestone Factory, is a
HOUSING ESTATE by *S. Colwyn Foulkes*, *c*. 1949–52. Linked
semi-detached blocks, rendered, around a spacious green.
Central axis, though the over-all plan is informal.

SOUTH AND SOUTH-WEST

ERDDIG. *See* p. 160.
RHOSTYLLEN. *See* Esclusham.

WEST AND NORTH-WEST

ASTON COLLEGE (formerly DENBIGHSHIRE TECHNICAL
COLLEGE), Mold Road. The main building is by *Saxon Smith
& Partners*. Its date is 1950–3, and it is characteristic of the
immediate post-war years, before the lightness and delicacy
of the Festival of Britain style began to exert influence. Long
and blocky, with a corner tower. Attention is focused around
the entrance by cinema-like channelled brickwork and sculptural panels on the segmental wall of the lecture theatre.
CROESNEWYDD. *See* Broughton.
LOWER BERSE. *See* Broughton.

NORTH AND NORTH-EAST

ST JOHN EVANGELIST, Herbert Jennings Avenue, Rhosnesni.
1973–4 by *John L. Jones* of *Barnard & Partners* of Cheltenham, and a good deal better than many of the other churches
for which the practice had previously been responsible in
Clwyd. Octagonal, with laminated timber trusses reaching to
the ground, some externally. Others are enclosed within the
low blocks which cluster round the central core and which
include the sanctuary. Steep, slated roof, with folded gables
on alternate faces.

ST MARGARET, Chester Road. Built in connection with the Garden Village (*see* below). By *T. Alwyn Lloyd* for the Welsh Town Planning and Housing Trust Ltd. Built 1927-8, but left incomplete, only chancel and transepts having been erected. A narthex was added 1976-8. Round-arched. Of rustic brick externally, plastered within. Arcaded screen walls across the transepts carry framing for the high roofs. Flèche.

ST PETER, Rhosrobin, beyond the by-pass. 1897-8 by *J. H. Swainson*. Ruabon brick and terra-cotta, with a spired octagonal turret. Chapel-like except for the articulated chancel.

SCHOOL, at the corner of Borras and Dean Roads, Rhosnesni. By *Ferrey* (VH), 1868, and not up to much. Polychromatic brick.

WREXHAM GARDEN VILLAGE. One of the many garden suburbs belonging to the movement which began in 1901 with Ealing Tenants Ltd. Wrexham Tenants Ltd was founded in 1913 under the auspices of Co-Partnership Tenants Ltd, but was soon taken over as the first project to be sponsored by the Welsh Town Planning and Housing Trust. Axial layout by *G. L. Sutcliffe*, architect to Co-Partnership Tenants. The earliest buildings, some of them brick, some roughcast, and with gables and casements, are in the simple and informal vernacular style which characterizes so much of the best housing of the first half of the C20.* Some are by *Sutcliffe*, 1913-14, e.g. Nos. 157-167 CHESTER ROAD and others in CUNLIFFE WALK. Many more were built, 1914-17, by *T. Alwyn Lloyd*, architect to the Trust, e.g. those looking across open space from WAT'S DYKE WAY. After the Great War, nothing more was built by Wrexham Tenants, and although the Trust continued to sell off plots and to exercise a degree of control, much inferior later work is now interspersed. Also the plan was not fully completed, and churches, shops and an institute were not built as intended. Among the first houses were some larger ones by *Sutcliffe*, e.g. Nos. 63-69 ACTON GATE.

ACTON PARK, the home of the Cunliffes, was demolished in 1956. It was partly by *James Wyatt*, 1786-7, and had undergone Victorian alteration. There remains the fine Greek Doric ENTRANCE SCREEN on Chester Road; Mr Howell attributes it to *Thomas Harrison*.‡ It is shamefully slighted by housing which encroaches behind. A Douglas-like LODGE is dated 1887, and there are others in Box Lane and, dated 1876, in Jeffreys Road. A further one in this road has been demolished. A pair of COTTAGES in Dean Road is in similar vernacular revival style.

The S part of the ACTON PARK HOUSING ESTATE is by *Sir Patrick Abercrombie*, then of *Lockwood, Abercrombie & Saxon*. Planned 1918 and begun 1920. Seemly two-storey Neo-Georgian houses face RHOSNESSNEY LANE and the pleasant roads behind it. The layout apparently forms part of an in-

* The reprehensible practice of removing glazing bars is taking its toll.
‡ Mrs Ockrim accepts the attribution.

tended larger scheme, the central axis of which would have
been opened by MARSH CRESCENT, and which, with
NEVILLE CRESCENT, would have included a circus.* Post-
war housing further N is by *J. M. Davies*, Borough Engineer,
Surveyor and Architect, and is of quite good quality.

In BORRAS PARK ROAD, CHERRY HILL (No. 91) of *c.* 1936 is
indistinguishable from countless other suburban houses of its
date designed by architects still able to handle with conviction
the Edwardian Arts and Crafts idiom of Baillie Scott. This
one, however, is by the firm of *Baillie Scott & Beresford*, with
Edgar Beresford responsible.

Cherry Hill is the last house in Wrexham, and the following are
in the country beyond:

BORRAS FARM, ¼ m. N. C17. Brick. Central chimney and lobby
entrance. Staircase with flat wavy balusters. Later plaster heraldry (1706) and porch (1707).

BORRAS HEAD, 1¼ m. NE of the edge of the town. Late C17 or
early C18, of brick, with flush quoins. Five bays and two
storeys plus a high basement. The original doorway, with
moulded surround, is now blocked, and its steps removed.
Timber cross windows and C19 margin panes. Single-span
roof, though the plan is a double pile, arranged round a well
staircase at the rear. The stairs rise through four storeys.
Square, capped newels and turned balusters.

BORRAS HALL, ½ m. SSE of Borras Head. H-plan, with lateral
chimney. Brick outer walls, and internal timber-framed partitions. Early or mid-C17 staircase in the upper-end cross
wing, with flat, pierced and moulded balusters. Newels with
octagonal finials.

WYNNSTAY‡

3040

Wynnstay was the principal seat of the Williams-Wynns, a
family which, with immense estates, was in the C18 and C19
the richest, most powerful and most profusely hospitable in
North Wales. The house is magnificently sited in an enormous park, high above the River Dee, with views to the Berwyns and into the Vale of Llangollen. Though now largely
agricultural, the park retains something of its character, and
Ruabon (now more than a mere estate village at the gates)
and the industrialization of Cefn Mawr are invisible from the
house. Seen from across the valley, château-like towers look
promising. Nearer to, the mansion, rebuilt by *Benjamin Ferrey* after a fire, reveals itself as stark and prosaic. A High
Victorian version of French Renaissance, it has much of the
coarseness and little of the gusto associated with the genre.

The estate passed by descent from Madog ap Gruffydd
Maelor, founder of Valle Crucis Abbey. Formerly Watstay

* Mr G. N. S. Mitchell of Lovelock, Mitchell & Partners supplied details of
Abercrombie's involvement.

‡ Now a school, having been occupied since 1950 by Lindisfarne College.

(Wat's Dyke runs through the park), it was renamed by Sir John Wynn, who in the mid-C17 married the heiress. The house was then of half-timber, but was greatly enlarged by *Francis Smith*, 1736–8, for Sir Watkin Williams-Wynn, third Baronet and the first Sir Watkin. The new work, which was only a portion of a more ambitious scheme, had its main front facing W, and there was a longer S elevation. In 1770 a 'Great Room' was added, probably by *T. F. Pritchard*, extending S from the E end of the S front. It was intended for the coming-of-age festivities of the fourth Baronet, who also bore the name Watkin, as have all his successors. Schemes for total rebuilding commissioned by him, including one from *Robert Adam*, remained unexecuted. So did plans for alterations by *Capability Brown*. Adam was, however, responsible for the font in Ruabon church (q.v.) and for Sir Watkin's London house, 20 St James's Square. *James Wyatt* carried out work for both the fourth Baronet and the fifth, who succeeded in 1789, and for whom the house was recased in a Wyatt-looking way, *c.*1820, probably by *Benjamin Gummow*. In 1827–8 the Great Room was redecorated by *C. R. Cockerell*. Work by *Ferrey* was in hand for the sixth Baronet when, in 1858, the building was burnt. Reconstruction, under Ferrey, continued until at least 1865.

EXTERIOR. *Ferrey*'s S front, two-storeyed and roughly symmetrical in massing though not in detail, is punctuated by towers with steep pavilion roofs and iron cresting. A tower of three storeys plus roof at the W corner and another, smaller one, at the E. From the centre projects a wing containing a two-storey great hall and ending in a four-storey tower. The main entrance was formerly in the base of this tower, through a *porte cochère* now walled up. The W front had a loggia, and two of its piers remain, as a porch for the present entrance. Beyond the E tower a conservatory (later reconstructed as a billiard room) linked the main block with the family's private wing, which presents a pair of conical-roofed turrets to the E. The plan was influenced by what previously existed, with the great hall occupying the site of the Great Room. The façade W of it and the W return respectively represent the S and W fronts of the Smith house. Facing N is a two-storey, eleven-bay range, with a three-bay pediment. A survival of the late C18 or early C19 works, it is squeezed between two chunks of Ferrey, though one of these is in part older, as may be seen from the service court behind the private wing. In fact the court presents a jumble of dates and materials, some pre-Ferrey, some probably later. Now built around, and partly embedded in the pedimented range, is the STONE TOWER. It was built in 1706, in Sir John Wynn's time, in the court-yard of the half-timbered house. It is extremely old-fashioned for its date, of Jacobean character, with a staircase turret ending in an ogee stone roof square in plan. Ball finial.

As for the INTERIOR, ineptitude in planning is apparent, as well as some of the heavy-handed Frenchiness of the exterior. Elaborate ceilings with polygonal coffering in the principal rooms, one retaining colouring. Top-lit staircase hall; its exuberant chimneypiece, like others formerly in the house, has now vanished. Main corridors with encaustic tiles by *Maw & Co.* (floors) and *W. B. Simpson* (dadoes). Vaulted ceilings visible in corridors and some smaller rooms indicate fire-resisting construction, said to be concrete. Groining in what is now the headmaster's study has a good all-over pattern of stencilled decoration. It is probably by *Charles Hudson*, who did the stencilling in what was the boudoir in the private wing. This is on a small scale, and is applied to doors etc. and to the beamed and boarded ceiling. The room has a stone chimneypiece with architectural framework loaded with rich and fanciful ornament, and rather incongruously incorporating copies of *Thorwaldsen*'s roundels *Night* and *Day*. Imported woodwork includes a made-up chimneypiece in the billiard room, and oval panels of Old Testament scenes in the SW room and staircase hall. In the great hall, a splendid treasure – a Snetzler organ of 1775, its case by *Adam*. Brought in 1864 from the music room of 20 St James's Square, and still with its original colouring. Circular panel of pipes with elegant maidens following the curve on either side. They were carved by *Richard Collins*, 1777, replacing earlier figures.

Immediately N is the STABLE BLOCK of the *Smith* house. Built 1738–9, it is of one and a half storeys, with seven bays and a three-bay pediment. Ground-floor windows with Gibbs surrounds and heavy triple keystones. Pedimented doorcase. A range enclosing the fourth side of the court was added 1845–7, possibly by *George Tattersall*. It is heavier than the C18 work, with scrolly keystones and a giant arch under a pediment.

CHAPEL, E of the stables. Formed *c.*1876 by *Edmund B. Ferrey*, utilizing an earlier structure. This was almost certainly the GREENHOUSE which is known to have been built to designs by *John Evans* and *James Wyatt*, 1785. Ferrey retained a five-bay pilastered S front, gave it round-headed windows, and added a N aisle and steep roof. – REREDOS. A large, pedimented Corinthian aedicule, probably from the chapel of the *Smith* house. It may be compared with the pulpit, now at Ruabon (*see* p. 269).

An AVENUE to Ruabon (now almost entirely vanished) was planted *c.*1777 – an unusual date for a formal scheme. At about the same time *Capability Brown* was called in. His activities included the laying out of pleasure grounds, probably E of the house, where planting is now predominantly Victorian. After his death in 1783 landscaping was continued till 1785 by *John Evans*. It was probably he who converted a formal canal of *c.*1771–4, W of the house, into the present LAKE. Certainly he formed a further lake, no longer existing, on a lower site to the NW.

Many noteworthy buildings remain in and around the park. They are here listed in relation to the house, though not all are now directly accessible from it, and ownership is fragmented.

To the E, beyond the chapel, a fine example of an C18 ornamental DAIRY. 1782–3 by *Brown*. Doric tetrastyle temple front, with wider middle intercolumniation. Groined plaster ceiling. The building has been modified, and is devoid of its *Wedgwood* tiles.

COLUMN, $\frac{3}{8}$m. NW. By *Wyatt*, commemorating Sir Watkin Williams-Wynn, fourth Baronet, †1789. Doric, with Roman capital and base, but Greek Doric fluting. Surmounted by a railed walkway and an urn on a pedestal.

BATHHOUSE, $\frac{1}{2}$m. NW. Existing by 1784 and said to be by *Harrison*. Mrs Ockrim suggests he may have refaced it. Tetrastyle Doric portico with wider middle intercolumniation. Niches in the walls either side. Steps lead down into a large bath-tank in front. The setting was formerly an open slope, above the later, now vanished, lower lake.

RUABON GATEWAY, $\frac{3}{4}$m. NW, at the end of the former avenue. Of *c*.1783. Arch flanked by niches, all under a pediment. By *John Jones*.

SCHOOL LODGE, $\frac{1}{4}$m. E. The gateway, no longer complete, had unfluted Greek Doric columns carrying lengths of entablature. Later cottages, Victorian, in free Elizabethan, are placed asymmetrically either side. Attached to one is a chapel-like SCHOOL. Set of four GATEPIERS, $\frac{1}{4}$m. NNE of School Lodge. Rusticated, with ball finials.

BELAN PLACE, $\frac{3}{8}$m. S. A mid-C18 house of brick, with quoins and gable ends. Two and a half storeys and three bays, with one-bay pediment. Late C18 or early C19 single-storey extension in front.

NANT-Y-BELAN TOWER, 1m. SSW, on a precipitous site above the confluence of the Belan Stream and the Dee. By *Wyatville*, as a memorial to the officers and men of the fifth Baronet's regiment of 'Ancient British Fencibles' who fell in the Irish rebellion of 1798. Existing by 1812. Only a fragment remains, for the cliff has given way and taken most of the structure with it. A circular tower, based on the Tomb of Caecilia Metella at Rome, and containing a sarcophagus, stood on a rectangular platform below which were habitable vaulted chambers, built against the hillside. Now heavily wooded, the site originally commanded splendid views.

NEWBRIDGE LODGE, $1\frac{3}{8}$m. WSW. 1827–8 by *C. R. Cockerell*, and bearing eloquent witness to his brilliant originality and the essentially Mannerist nature of his inspiration. Long, low frontage, rusticated, the ground storey pierced by three arches. The middle arch is cavernously recessed, the outer ones frame small segmental-headed windows. The upper storey, with three circular windows, is less strong and solid in character. It does not extend for the full length of the lower façade, and is slightly recessed. The building is parallel with the drive, and integrated with a set of heavily rusticated gatepiers. Iron gates and railings.

See
p. 519

See
p. 519

WATERLOO TOWER, 1½m. WSW, on high ground. Built to *See* p. 519 commemorate the battle. Castellated and irregular. Basically two-storeyed, with a strikingly tall and slender octagonal turret, tapering and machicolated. The masonry suggests that the turret may originally have been shorter.

PARK EYTON LODGE, 1¼m. ESE. A little temple-like *See* p. 519 building, with tetrastyle Greek Doric portico, unfluted.

KENNELS, SW of Park Eyton Lodge. 1843 by *George Tattersall*. Brick and stone, of nine bays, with a giant rusticated arch under a steep pediment. Bell cupola.*

Y WAUN *see* CHIRK

YR ORSEDD *see* ROSSETT

YSBYTY IFAN‡

8040

ST JOHN BAPTIST. As the place name attests, there was here a hospice of the Knights Hospitallers (Knights of St John of Jerusalem). Founded *c.*1190; its endowments were increased by Llywelyn the Great, 1221-4. On the Suppression, the church became parochial, and pre-Reformation parts seem to have survived in a building demolished only in 1858. The replacement, by *George Benmore*, was opened in 1861. Nave, chancel, S porch, W bellcote, N vestry. Cusped lancets. – REREDOS. By *E. B. Ferrey*, 1882 (VH). – SEPULCHRAL SLABS. Shield, from a shield and sword heraldic slab, commemorating Cynwrig, son of Llywarch, *c.*1330. A hare below the shield. – Three fragments of a late C14 foliated cross slab commemorating Maruret verch Hywel. Inscription on border. Vine trail. Fragment of a late C14 slab with base of cross and vine trail. – MONUMENTS. Three mutilated early C16 effigies, comprising torso fragment, female figure and headless ecclesiastic. Said to be respectively Rhys Fawr ap Meredydd, standard bearer of Henry VII at Bosworth; his wife Lowry; and their son Robert ap Rhys, chaplain to Cardinal Wolsey. – Peter Price, 1792. Two winged heads in a pediment and an urn on top. – BRASSES. Robert Gethin and wife Anne, both †1598. Clasped hands. Below are a shrouded infant and, kneeling, two sons and four daughters. A further plate to Robert Gethin, their grandson, added above, its inscription completed by the earlier one. Both are contained in a crude stone frame.

* Thanks are due to Mr Peter Howell for help and advice in connection with Wynnstay. Articles by him and the Rev. Canon T. W. Pritchard appeared in *Country Life*, vol. 151, 1972, and by Canon Pritchard in *Transactions of the Denbighshire Historical Society*, vols. 29-30, 1980-1.
‡ Transferred to Gwynedd in 1974.

This stone-built village is the highest in the Conwy Valley and
is divided by the river, which until 1974 formed the boundary
with Caernarfonshire. The two parts are linked by a little C18
humped-back BRIDGE, with two arches and cutwaters. In the
C19 the village had an important upland sheep fair; it belonged to the Penrhyn Estate, and most of its COTTAGES were
rebuilt. It has now been transferred to the National Trust.
On the Caernarfonshire side, the early C19 MILL has an
overshot wheel; the inn stood opposite. A little higher up are
the SCHOOL and VICARAGE of 1857, and the single-storey
ALMSHOUSES of 1880, replacing six founded by Captain
Richard Vaughan in 1600.*

PLAS UCHAF, ¾m. NE. An end chimney and inside cross passage house, much altered (but preserving a ceiling with
moulded beams framed in two stages. NMR).

* This paragraph is by Mr Haslam.

FLINTSHIRE

SIR FFLINT

AFON-WEN *see* CAERWYS

ALLT MELID *see* MELIDEN

BABELL *see* YSGEIFIOG

BACH-Y-GRAIG *see* TREMEIRCHION

BAGILLT

ST MARY. Built 1837–9 with the aid of a Commissioners' grant. In 1836 a design by *John Lloyd* was rejected in favour of that by *John Welch*. Cruciform, with lancets and low-pitched roofs. W tower, its parapet of stepped battlements, corbelled out. The transepts and E end have pairs of buttresses carried up as octagonal pinnacles. Shallow and broad crossing arches and a W gallery.

Thomas Pennant owned BAGILLT HALL, 1½ m. WNW, and partly demolished it because 'the thick smoke of a great smelting-mill for lead and of a great calcining-house for calamine, just beneath, must have ever deterred my descendants from making it their residence'. Bagillt was the oldest centre of the Flintshire lead smelting and manufacturing industry – an industry which, as elsewhere along the Dee coast, led to the establishment of collieries and a port. Gadlys, ¾ m. SW, is now wholly rural, but the London Lead Company built a large smelting house here in 1703–4. GADLYS FARM and a nearby HOUSE were used by the company, and BRYN MADYN HALL was the house of their agent.

SCHOOL, 1¼ m. NW, near an A-road junction. Brick, with a tower (altered) between two gables either side. By *John Hill*, 1878, as a Board School. (VH)

BASINGWERK CASTLE was 1 m. S, at Coleshill. The site was refortified by Henry II in 1157 and taken by Owain Gwynedd in 1166. A C12 motte and bailey were largely levelled in the C13, and foundations of this date and later were revealed in excavations of 1954–7. A chapel here seems to have been the first building assigned to the monks of Basingwerk Abbey (*see* Greenfield).

BANGOR IS-COED*

There was here a great Celtic monastery (*clas*), existing in the C6 and possibly founded earlier, and said to have had 2,000 monks. In a massacre following the Battle of Chester in 615, 1,200 of them (as recounted by Bede) were put to death by Ethelfrith, King of Northumbria. The exact site of the monastery is not known.

ST DUNAWD. Much was done in 1726–7 by *Richard Trubshaw*, and C19 work included restorations by *Douglas* in 1868 and 1877. Douglas was married here in 1860. W tower by *Trubshaw*, three-storeyed, of brick and stone, with pilaster strips, round-headed bell openings, and urn-like finials. C14 five-light E window, and a two-light straight-headed chancel S window is also probably Dec. Dec nave arcades, the capitals of their octagonal piers with the characteristic scroll moulding. The S arcade was originally of only three bays, but the N continued beyond its present length of four. See the fragment of a further arch at the W end. Two four-light Perp windows in the chancel, that on the S with cusping. The roofs are probably of the same date, arched-braced, with wind-bracing and cusped struts above the collars. At the E end of the chancel a panelled and traceried wagon ceiling, with bands of leaf trail on the main horizontals. No chancel arch, and just a slight contraction on plan. The N aisle, in its present form, with windows Perp in style, dates from 1832. Previously its three E bays had cross gables and Y-tracery, and the westernmost bay was narrower. E extension to the aisle, forming a vestry, 1913. N porch with half-timbered gable and Nesfieldian pies in the brackets. It is by *Douglas*, 1877, as is the Neo-Perp S aisle, replacing work by *Trubshaw*. Douglas extended the aisle W, adding a fourth bay to the arcade.

Gothic STALLS and RAILS by *Douglas*, 1868. They may be compared with his mature woodwork, exemplified by the PEWS and PULPIT, 1877. These are more refinedly Gothic and, like the N porch, reflect the Aesthetic Movement (see the incised flower patterns of the pulpit) and possess a stronger sense of craftsmanship. – His ORGAN SCREEN was resited in 1913. – FONTS. A disused octagonal bowl, with rudimentary roll moulds. Also a Late Perp piece. Corner mouldings continuous from stem to bowl, following an ogee profile. Cusped panels on stem, Instruments of the Passion and symbols of

* In Maelor Saesneg.

the Evangelists on shields in panels on the bowl, and ornament also on the soffit. – FONT COVER. Like the stalls at
Overton (q.v.), it is the work of *Evelyn Wythergh*. Gorgeous
tabernacle work. – Former REREDOS, 1725, now at the w end.
Urn in a broken pediment, swags, and enriched pilasters.
Four panels for the Commandments etc. – Also at the w end
the bressumer and brattished rood beam of the ROOD
SCREEN. – Brass LECTERN, commemorating three brothers
who died in the First World War. Arts and Crafts elements
in its lower stage, with an angel in a canopy formed by stems
and branching foliage. – STAINED GLASS. Early fragments in
the tracery of the chancel easternmost on S. – E window by
Gibbs, 1868. – Two BENEFACTION BOARDS. – Dugout
CHEST. – Part of an early C14 SEPULCHRAL SLAB. Curling
volutes in pairs. – MONUMENT. Rev. John Fletcher †1741
and wife Mary †1777. By *John Nelson*. Slender columns and
an urn.

Near the church the BRIDGE, cambered, and of five unequal
elliptical arches. Formerly dated 1658. Slab parapets and
splayed (not triangular) full-height cutwaters.

Opposite the church, in HIGH STREET, an urban-looking
three-storey block, probably early Victorian, and with an
early shop-front. Nearby, the drive to the RECTORY. By
Douglas, 1868. Rather stark, though relieved by a storeyed
porch with half-timbered upper stage. The house has been
reduced in size. Its ENTRANCE LODGE is more suave. By
Douglas & Fordham, 1897, at the expense of the Duke of
Westminster, patron of the living. CHAPEL HOUSE, a cottage
further E, was originally a small chapel.

ALTHREY HALL, 1 m. SW, beyond Bangor Racecourse. H-plan,
with a storeyed (former) porch in the angle of the lower-end
cross wing. Further small gables in the angles of both wings
at the rear, with lateral chimney between. This was a C15 hall
house, with spere, hammerbeams, and open hearth, though
nothing of this remains readily visible, and much reconstruction has taken place. Surviving half-timbering, with much
diagonal bracing, is probably contemporary with the insertion
of the lateral chimney, and with panelling and a staircase of
the early C17. Stairs with pierced, flat balusters. In an extension built against the upper-end wing is a first-floor chapel.
It has a painted ceiling representing the Celestial City, and
Sacred Monograms in end tympana.

BASINGWERK ABBEY *see* GREENFIELD

BASINGWERK CASTLE *see* BAGILLT

BERTHANGAM *see* LLANASA

BETTISFIELD*

ST JOHN BAPTIST. 1872–4 by *Street*, at the expense of Lord
and Lady Hanmer. Dec tracery. Only the E and W windows
have hoodmoulds. Nave, chancel, S porch. A small tower rises
at the SE corner of the nave, turns from square to octagonal,
and ends in a spire. In the angle between tower and chancel
is a lean-to chapel, and a combined vestry and organ chamber
occupies the angle between the chancel and a N transept. The
complicated massing, small in scale, is most successfully handled, and even a chimney looks happy and well thought-out.
Ashlar externally, but hammer-dressed coursed rubble inside.
The tower opens into the nave, the chapel (not used as such)
into the chancel. Crown-post roof. The interior is one of quiet
and subtle sensitivity, and is profoundly satisfying. – Except
for a later transept screen, all the FURNISHINGS are by *Street*.
They include the Caen stone REREDOS, with embossed *Minton* TILES either side. – STAINED GLASS. E and W windows
by *Clayton & Bell*. – By *Street* the LYCHGATE, with steep
tiled roof, tile-hung gable ends, timber arches spanning between the stone side walls, and a little lean-to either side.‡

BETTISFIELD OLD HALL, E of the church. A curious early C17
house, of brick. Tall and compact, with a lower gabled projection to the r., and a later rear wing. Lateral chimney.
Traces of mullioned windows and, on the second floor,
several large mullioned and transomed windows, now
blocked. The larger of the rooms which they lit formerly had
a barrel-vaulted ceiling and moulded cornice. Tradition states
that it was a chapel, but in a recusant house (which this was)
it is unlikely to have been so prominently displayed.

HAULTON RING, 1 m. NNE. A deserted moated site.

THE ASHES, 1¼ m. NW. Brick nogging is visible on the W, on
the N gable end, and in a later rear wing. Timber bracing in
diagonal patterns.

BETTISFIELD PARK, 1 m. N. The seat of the Hanmer family.
Elucidation of a complicated building history has not been
helped by extensive demolitions, and at the time of writing
further reduction of the house is proposed. Moses Griffith
showed it with a compact and symmetrical early C17 S front.
The immediate E return was also symmetrical, but extending
back from it was a collegiate-looking range, perhaps earlier in
date, forming a long E front punctuated by gables and chimneystacks. It is difficult to imagine what the plan arrangement
can have been, but it is possible that there was already an
enclosed courtyard. Wyatt-like Late Georgian additions were
made, late in the C18 or early in the C19. This work has a
long S front (involving, at its right-hand end, the remodelling
or replacement of the old front) and a return to the W. Next,
an Italianate belvedere tower was planted against the middle
of the E front, apparently in the 1840s, though it underwent

* In Maelor Saesneg.
‡ Most of the facts relating to the church were supplied by Mr Joyce.

later alteration. Further Victorian additions, of differing
dates, included a billiard-room block on the w, and a small
tower with steep roof of elongated octagon plan at the SE
corner. The elevation between this and the belvedere tower
was refaced, and this part of the house peppered with mass-
produced heraldic plaques and given pyramid-roofed turrets
clinging to the towers. At the NE corner was built a Tudor-
style tower with French pavilion roof, and between this and
the belvedere something of what Moses Griffith depicted still
peeped out. With its three disparate towers, the E front was
astonishing; but soon after the Second World War everything
to the r. of the belvedere was demolished, together with a
service court behind. Inside are two heavily carved early C17
chimneypieces, possibly from another Hanmer house. A mullioned and transomed window survives in the cellar.

The Late Georgian additions are cement-rendered and of
one and a half storeys, with the lower windows in arched
recesses. The right-hand end of the s front (with the end bay
masking earlier storey heights) is symmetrical in itself, and
has a pedimented Greek Doric porch of stone. The remainder
is asymmetrical, with two semicircular bows, one with a shallow dome, the other effecting the w return. More exciting are
the interiors, with particularly good ceilings and friezes. The
plasterwork, some of it quite heavy, is of different character
in each room. Three ceilings with figurative painted panels,
that in the drawing room with four roundels as well. Here the
plasterwork includes big scallop patterns. Marble chimneypieces in the library and morning room, the latter with
maidens in relief. Screens of scagliola columns in the dining
room (based on the Tower of the Winds) and entrance hall
(Erechtheion Ionic). Spacious well staircase with ornamented
stair ends and slender brass balusters. Except for the renewal
of the drawing-room chimneypiece, Victorian alterations preserved the integrity of the rooms.

The STABLES have pediment and cupola, and, although
dated 1787, are vernacular in character. Kneelers and finials
to the pediment and to the coped gables of cross wings. A
WATER TOWER, dated 1842, has a pyramid roof which may
be later. Steep pyramid roofs on a couple of buildings by the
KITCHEN GARDENS, and the penchant for such features, so
strongly exhibited at the house itself, is further marked by a
turret attached to FARM BUILDINGS.*

BISTRE see BUCKLEY

* It may be noted that in 1864 both the church and school at nearby Bronington
(q.v.) were given pyramid-roofed towers, with the school also receiving heraldic
plaques like those at the house.

BODELWYDDAN

ST MARGARET. The ultimate in splendiferous estate churches. Built 1856–60 at the expense of Margaret, Lady Willoughby de Broke, daughter of Sir John Williams of Bodelwyddan Castle, in memory of her husband. The architect was *John Gibson*, who had worked in Warwickshire for her and her husband at Compton Verney and for her sister and brother-in-law at Charlecote. With an exterior of white local limestone and an indiscriminately lavish interior, it has achieved fame and popularity as 'The Marble Church'. The discerning would prefer Street's church three miles away at Towyn, or Douglas's at Halkyn, which the coast-bound crowds pass twenty minutes before stopping at Bodelwyddan to raise their cameras and buy their postcards and souvenir ashtrays. The style is Dec, with Late Geometrical tracery. Aisles with gable roofs, and a W steeple more than 200ft high. Open turrets with crocketed pinnacles at the E end of the nave. The spire is based on that of Kings Sutton, Northamptonshire, but with bands of pierced tracery, which contribute to the icing-sugar delicacy of the exterior. Subtle optical corrections are introduced, e.g. an entasis of 6 in. on the spire. The ashlar-lined interior is opulent with foliated and other carving, and with numerous marbles used as flooring, wallshafts etc. Marble quatrefoil arcade piers, very clumsy, with foliated caps carved by *Henry Smith*. In the chancel, banded marble forms a background to an arcade of cusped and crocketed nodding ogee canopies, the carving executed by *Harmer*. The same motif, even more profusely treated, forms the REREDOS. Bosses of the panelled chancel ceiling carved by *Thomas Earp*. The nave roof is dimly but dramatically lit by lucarnes, high up, and by a row of cusped triangular clerestory windows (hidden externally by the aisle roofs) between the bases of the trusses. Within the tower, a W gallery on two arches. – FONT. By *Peter Hollins*, 1862. Given by Sir Hugh Williams, brother of Lady Willoughby de Broke. It represents his two daughters holding a shell. – *Earp* carved the bench-ends of the STALLS, and also the ambitious PULPIT, with a base of kneeling angels, and Evangelists peering out under nodding ogees. – LECTERN. By *T. H. Kendall* of Warwick, *c.*1882–3. An eagle perched on what is meant to be a rock. – Elaborate, but disciplined and free of such bombast, are CHAPEL FITTINGS in the S aisle, by *W. D. Caröe*, as a war memorial. – Much good STAINED GLASS. By *O'Connor*, contemporary with the building, are the E window; the easternmost on either side of the chancel; S aisle E; W rose window; N aisle E rose window, and probably the westernmost on either side of the chancel. – By *Ward & Hughes*, the middle windows on either side of the chancel, 1880s, and the N aisle W, 1881. – By *T. F. Curtis* of *Ward & Hughes*, the S aisle W, 1896, and N aisle westernmost, 1910.*

*Mr Howell states that in the church is a bust of Lady Willoughby de Broke by *Matthew Noble*, 1855, presented in 1879.

W of the church, the VICARAGE, institutional-looking, and
the SCHOOL, dated 1857, symmetrical, with a central flèche
and a gabled house either end. Both were paid for by Lady
Willoughby de Broke, and are presumably by *Gibson*. Also
contemporary with the church are two gabled terraces of
ESTATE COTTAGES.

BODELWYDDAN CASTLE. (Formerly Lowther College, it has
been acquired by Clwyd County Council and at the time of
writing is being adapted for a museum.) Totally asymmetrical, and effective and intriguing when seen from a distance,
in its landscape setting. A Neo-Classical remodelling of an
Elizabethan or early C17 house was carried out for Sir John
Williams some time between 1800 and 1808. A new five-bay
E front was of two and a half storeys and had a recessed
three-bay centre with a Greek Doric loggia. Castellated form
was assumed when the house was further remodelled and
greatly enlarged by *Hansom & Welch* for Sir John Hay
Williams. The work was begun *c.*1830–4 and completed before 1842.* Many turrets etc. Though refaced, the earlier C19
façade remains recognizable, forming the N end of the enlarged E front. Long N front also, extending W to a gatehouse
with two octagonal towers. Castellations continue yet further,
forming a large enclosure within curtain walls. There are
towers at the W end of these outworks bigger than any on the
house itself. Set in the N front of the house is a statue of a
knight, and near a gateway in the S curtain is another.
Features of the *c.*1800–8 remodelling survive inside. There is
also a marble chimneypiece earlier in style, and a curious one
representing trees and agricultural scenes. Of the 1830s, a
large Gothic room with canted bay, plaster vaulting, and castellated chimneypiece. It is not known what may have been
done in 1886, a date which appears on encaustic tiles in a
corridor. Of this time could possibly be the axial fireplace and
flight of Neo-Jacobean stairs in the entrance hall (of 1830s
build), and the main staircase, similar in style, which is set
within the older fabric.

A miscellany of buildings stands within the W enclosure.
C17 work appears in one almost opposite the gatehouse, and
in the former school library.

(Work was done in the GARDENS by *Mawson*, *c.*1910. He
noted: 'I replanned the upper part of the gardens behind the
Castle, and carried out some necessary improvements ...')

ICEHOUSE, behind the entrance lodge, ⅛ m. NW of the
house. Ruinous, with the brick dome partly revealed.

FELIN-Y-GORS, ½ m. ENE of the house. A mill with symmetrical Gothic end elevation. Its battlemented parapet continues over a central gable. Probably early C19.

---

* Thomas Roscoe (*Wanderings and Excursions in North Wales*, 1844) states that
it was started by *Edward Welch* (J. A. Hansom's then partner) and was continued
under the direction of the agent of the estate. Does this mean that the agent was
responsible for some designing, or did he merely supervise the execution?

GLAN CLWYD HOSPITAL, ⅜m. N. By the *Percy Thomas Partnership*. Begun 1972 and opened 1980. With 360 beds it is the first stage of a scheme designed ultimately to have 750. Two-storey podium, planned around courtyards. Above are three storeys of wards, arranged in an H-plan, with standard Department of Health and Social Security layouts. Steel frame construction. The massing is disciplined, and the elevations are neatly done. Continuous bands of windows and pre-cast facings. Separate from the main buildings are a geriatric unit (built 1980–1), laundry (completed 1983), and boilerhouse and works department. Also a residential area to the S, with flats and bedsitting rooms for staff.

FAENOL BACH, 1m. WNW. L-shaped, with one range dated internally 1571 and the other 1627. Stepped gables, including stepped chimneybreasts and, on the later wing, dormers. Square chimneys with moulded caps. The older portion is the earliest known dated example in Wales of a storeyed house with lateral chimney. It is of three-unit plan. The lower-end room, as well as the hall, has a lateral chimney, but on the opposite flank of the house. Internal cross passage, one of its doorways now blocked, the other with cyclopean arch. Stop-chamfered beams and joists. An upper-end post-and-panel screen has guilloche patterns and heavily moulded vertical members. It is incomplete, and only one doorway (doubtless one of a pair), with decorated head, remains. The inscription of 1571 appears on a beam above the screen, together with an *anno mundi* date. FARM BUILDINGS, round three sides of a yard; beyond is an exceptionally long range of late C19 HAMMELS, i.e. loose boxes for cattle, with open yards in front.

PEN ISA'R GLASCOED, 1m. SW. Another three-unit house with stepped gables. An upper-end post-and-panel screen is dated 1570, along with an *anno mundi* inscription. Two storeys plus stepped dormers. A rear projection, later extended laterally, contains a newel staircase. Stop-chamfered beams and joists and, on the first floor, heavily moulded post-and-panel partitions. Much seems to have been done in the C17 and C19, and the original plan is unclear. There is a central chimney with square stack, and there was a cross passage, its cyclopean doorway now blocked. An arched-braced truss indicates that an upper room was once open to the roof, so the dormers must be additions. A separate small HOUSE, probably a humble instance of the unit system, also has a stepped gable.

54 FAENOL FAWR, ½m. NNW.* A much grander stepped-gabled house, built in 1597 for John Lloyd, registrar of the diocese of St Asaph, and with C18 alterations. It has a third storey in the gables, and there are stepped dormers. Square chimneys with moulded caps. Front with cross wings and a central gable. Some sashes, and remaining mullioned and transomed windows have entablatures and crude classical detail. With a

---

* This entry was written before Faenol Fawr was seriously damaged by fire in 1984.

hall planned in traditional fashion, symmetry was broken by the entrance, which adjoined the right-hand wing. The present doorcase, also crudely classical and dated 1725, is at the opposite end, and is *ex situ*, having initially been inserted in the middle. A rear wing, obscuring the lateral chimney of the hall, does not belong to the original build, but it is not much later, and has stepped gables. It probably contained the well staircase which now rises from the hall. This cannot be *in situ* and is too advanced for 1597. Flat, shaped and moulded balusters, panelled newels with bulbous square finials, and, at the top, a dog-gate. The former kitchen in the right-hand wing has a wide fireplace with C17 and C18 date inscriptions. In the opposite wing is a chimneypiece, dated 1597, with strapwork and scrolly decoration, heraldry, and freely shaped foliated columns. An exceptionally good C18 well staircase – possibly of 1725 – rises through two storeys. Swept rail, bulbous turned balusters, and ornamented stair ends. The balustrade breaks forward in segmental bows on both landings, one bow above the other. As far as the first floor there is full-height (i.e. continuing above dado level) bolection-moulded panelling, between pilasters which have Corinthianesque foliated capitals. (Tudor and bolection-moulded panelling in first-floor rooms. Arched-braced roof trusses. DOE) Behind the house, and linked with it by a later brick range, is a DOVECOTE with four stepped gables. FARM BUILDINGS include a block with stepped dormers and end gables. Also a six-arch cart shed.

GWERNIGRON, 1¼ m. E. A DOVECOTE, now roofless, has four stepped gables.

FAENOL BROPER, ¾ m. ESE. Late C18, of brick, with toothed cornice. Three bays, and a one-bay pediment with lunette window.

BRYN-Y-PIN. *See* Cefn Meiriadog, p. 119.

PENGWERN. *See* Rhuddlan.

BODFARI

0070

A village on a hill. The DINORBEN ARMS, the lychgate and, on higher ground, the church tower and an early C19 stuccoed house with labels (HAFOD TAN EGLWYS) form an attractive group. The inn has, though, become a busy restaurant, and spawned a set of tiered car parks behind.

ST STEPHEN. Medieval W tower, with Perp bell openings, a battered base, battlemented parapet and no buttresses. The rest was rebuilt by *T. H. Wyatt*, 1865, replacing a whitewashed church which had S aisle, timber arcade and undivided nave and chancel. The windows of Wyatt's effort are presumably meant to be Perp. He is said to have followed the old plan, but introduced a chancel arch. – FONT. Perp bowl with quatrefoils. – ALTAR TABLE. 1635, with carved melonbulb legs. – PULPIT. Dated 1635 as part of a painted inscription. Elaborate woodcarving, with strapwork, grotesque terms etc. and panels representing Virtues. – STAINED GLASS. E window by *Clayton & Bell*, commemoration date 1866. – S aisle W and nave easternmost on N by *Burlison & Grylls*, 1909. – MONUMENTS. Thomas Eyton †1837; the commissioner †1873. By *H. W. Wilkins*. Grecian motifs with Victorian flavour. – Hughes and Chambers monument. Anne Hughes †1810. Draped urn and foliated consoles. Signature of *Wright* of Chester, but probably referring to a later interpolation, commemoration date 1831.

Former SCHOOL, to the E. 1858–9 by *H. John Fairclough* of St Asaph. Gothic details. Octagonal turret with spirelet at the junction of school and teacher's house.

PONTRUFFYDD, ¾m. WSW. It seems that a C16 structure underwent early C19 Gothicization and extension. Then came a total rebuilding, in Neo-Elizabethan, by *T. H. Wyatt*, and a subsequent enlargement. This mansion is demolished, but a further successor house occupies the site. A BRIDGE carrying one drive across another, and an ornate ENTRANCE LODGE, dated 1858, are doubtless by Wyatt. Earlier is a Gothic ARCHWAY of grotto-like character. At PONTRUFFYDD HALL FARM – referred to by Pennant as a *ferme ornée* – the house has pointed windows and the buildings have a cupola.

GEINAS MILL. *See* Aberwheeler, p. 101.

See p. 24 MOEL Y GAER, ½m. NNE (SJ 095 708), is the lowest of the hillforts on the Clwydian range, but even so it enjoys fine views and formidable natural defences. The entrance is at the northern end, where the access is less steep but still awkward, especially for any wheeled vehicle. The gap in the outer rampart is a simple one, but the inner rampart has a T-shaped eastern end, just short of a steep natural drop, leaving space for only a narrow path. A similar arrangement may be seen at Moel Arthur a few miles to the S (*see* Cilcain). The inner rampart is high at the N, where it incorporates a good deal of rock outcrop, but becomes progressively less impressive towards the S and dies to nothing part-way along the steep eastern side. Much of the material for the rampart was gained from an internal quarry ditch. The outer defences – a ditch and counterscarp bank – do not exist at all on the E.

0070

BODRHYDDAN

The entrance front, approached axially from the W, belongs to *Nesfield*'s remodelling. His survey plans are dated 1872; a scheme simpler than that carried out was prepared the following year, and the completed fabric is dated 1874 and 1875. The work thus overlapped with his transformation of Kinmel (*see* p. 280), and the W front, both cheerful and stately, is a particularly happy creation in the so-called Queen Anne style which he developed there. C17 rather than C18 in its elements, and showing Dutch influence and Aesthetic Movement detail, it is of brick, with stone dressings and white-painted wood-work. Five bays and three storeys, with a four-storey porch and a pair of pedimented dormers in the steep hipped roof. The porch forms a frontispiece, each stage differently and resourcefully treated, and is crowned by a shaped gable, semi-circular shell pediment and heraldic pelican. Single-storey screen walls, carrying white balustrading, extend either side of the façade.

The first house on the site was probably built by Richard Conwy early in the C15, and Bodrhyddan is now the seat of his descendant, the Baron Langford. On the strength of a doorway of 1696 and rainwater heads of 1700, it has been assumed that a rebuilding for Sir John Conwy took place at that time. The work was, however, no more than a remodel-ling, and was probably begun soon after 1689. The s front consists (though no longer obviously so) of a recessed centre, projecting cross wings and extruded corners, i.e. blocks in the re-entrant angles. These extruded corners are flush with the wings, but were differentiated by the window spacing and a system of quoins. Behind is a room with (repositioned) lateral fireplace and still known as the great hall. The room above is of similar dimensions. All this suggests the late C16 or early C17, with the upper room the great chamber and the left-hand extruded corner forming a porch. An inscription of 1601, with the initials of the John Conwy of the time, appears *ex situ* inside. The structure may thus well be of this date, with (as irregularities in plan would suggest) some medieval walling incorporated. The *c.*1696 remodelling included the insertion of sashes (though some mullions and transoms re-mained) and the adding of straight parapets (doubtless re-placing gables), a cupola and a central doorcase, the latter carrying the 1696 inscription. Some time between 1784 and 1810 a single-storey dining room was added at the e end. Next, probably *c.*1840, windows and the roof-line of the s front were again altered; a pediment-like gable and a pair of small projections obscuring the junctions between wings and extruded corners were added. Finally, *Nesfield* returned his w front treatment, refacing as far as and including the pro-jection, and repeating the process at the other end for the sake of symmetry. With his transferring the entrance to the new w front, the 1696 doorcase became redundant and was reproduced in facsimile as a garden door in the dining-room wing. (Part of the original is reused as a chimneypiece.) With armorial shield and broken pediment, the design of the new w doorway was based on it. It should be added that the remodelling involved the removal of complicated additions, the banishing of the kitchen from the w end, and the building of a very pleasing service wing, of stone with brick chimneys, at the NE corner.

At the foot of cellar steps on the N is a reset doorcase,

which could be of 1601 or earlier. Tudor arch within Doric columns and entablature.

The principal interiors of the 1870s are the front hall and the remodelled great hall, both in Nesfield's 'Old English' vein. Heavily moulded woodwork and a rich, mellow character, particularly in the great hall, which is fully panelled and has an inglenook. Also by him the staircase, in the upper flights of which are reused twisted balusters, probably of the 1696 period. In the drawing room above the great hall is a confection of carved oak, probably installed c.1840. Painted cream and gold in a redecoration of 1955, it now looks curiously light and frothy. Continental, with much of it ecclesiastical, it is doubtless of C16–18 date. Biblical panels in the two chimneypieces. Dining-room chimneypiece made up of similar work. Some of the collection, in the form of a pair of Baroque twisted columns, was evidently left over, and was used by Nesfield in the inglenook of his billiard room. The room is top-lit and lies behind the left-hand screen wall of the W front; the right-hand counterpart neatly masks a conservatory.

To the S a Nesfield FORMAL GARDEN. Previously the house was approached from this direction, and beyond the parterre is a vista to a pair of GATEPIERS, probably of the 1696 period, with heraldic blackamoor busts.

ST MARY'S WELL, NW of the house. An octagonal little wellhouse with arched doorway and a lantern carrying a pelican. A rectangular bath adjoins. A later inscription may be more reliable in dating the structure to 1612 than in ascribing it to Inigo Jones.

(A domed ICEHOUSE, ¼ m. ESE.)

STABLES. Vernacular C18 work. Gatehouse with coped gables and a cupola.

By *Sir Clough Williams-Ellis* the GATEPIERS at the main entrance, 1963. Also by him a MONUMENT, 1959, on the axis of the farm entrance. It incorporates fragments from a drinking fountain by *T. M. Penson*, erected in Rhyl in 1862. This commemorated the coming of age of Conwy Grenville Hercules Rowley-Conwy, the young man who had the good sense later to employ Nesfield for the remodelling of the house.[*]

BRANCOED see MOLD, p. 397

3060

BRETTON

Formerly part of the Eaton estate, and although the hamlet never had the quality and character of the villages across the border (*see The Buildings of England: Cheshire*) there may be

[*] I received valuable help and advice in connection with Bodrhyddan from Lord Langford, and also from Mr Clive Aslet.

seen a little of the distinctive estate work which Douglas carried out for the first Duke of Westminster. By *Douglas &
Fordham*, and with diapered brick, half-timbering, twisted
chimneys etc., are, to the S, BRETTON LODGE, 1898 (which
in the mid-1970s got squeezed between the Chester by-pass
and a WATER TREATMENT PLANT), and, to the E, HOPE'S
PLACE FARM, 1890–2, and BRETTON HALL FARM, 1891–
3. Near the latter a MOAT, complete and containing water.
Traces of foundations in its enclosure. An adjacent brick
structure is C16 or early C17, incorporating earlier masonry.

BRONINGTON*   4030

HOLY TRINITY. An artlessly endearing brick-built church. It
began life as a barn, hence the long, high proportions and
king-post roof. The conversion was by *William Smith*, 1836,
and transepts were added. Windows mostly of four-centred
lights, with brick dressings. The N transept has a little porch.
Sanctuary added 1864, together with a pyramid-spired tower
in the E angle of the S transept. W gallery. – Stone PULPIT,
LECTERN and FONT, 1864, the latter originally at the crossing. – BOX PEWS remain in the transepts.
Church and former vicarage stand on their own. In the village,
¼ m. WNW, is the SCHOOL. It has the armorial plaques which
were used so extensively at Bettisfield Park (q.v.). Like the
church it has a tower with steep pyramid roof, and the building is largely of 1864.
BRONINGTON CHEQUER METHODIST CHAPEL. *See* Iscoed.
HAULTON RING. *See* Bettisfield.

BROUGHTON   3060

ST MARY. 1823–4 by *John Oates* of Halifax. Two-light cusped
windows, a steep roof and a W tower with pyramid spire. The
more serious chancel, added 1876–7, is in Perp and has an
ashlar interior and a panelled roof with painted decoration.
– WOODWORK. Much imported carving, some of it worked
into the PULPIT, including figurative panels. Also parchemin
panels in the vestry door. On the W gallery front, St Anne
with the Virgin and Child, probably German. The gallery
itself is carried on two pairs of posts, apparently from an early
four-poster bed.‡ Their motifs include bizarre capitals, vertical trail and arms and badges. – STAINED GLASS. Chancel N
and S by *Kempe*, 1876. – ROYAL ARMS. Hanoverian, pre-
1801.
PLAS WARREN, 1½ m. WSW. Stuccoed Italianate, of five bays.
Alterations designed by *Goodhart-Rendel* (a Gladstone commission) seem never to have been carried out.

* In Maelor Saesneg.
‡ The suggestion has been made that it belonged to Henry VII (*Transactions
of the Historic Society of Lancashire and Cheshire*, vol. 66, 1914).

BRYNFORD

ST MICHAEL. One of the two churches built in lieu of that at
Pantasaph (q.v.). 1851–3 by *T. H. Wyatt*. Aisleless, with lancets. Double W bellcote growing from the W front, pierced
in its lower stages by a two-light window and a multifoiled
circle.

SCHOOL, S of the church, 1852–4, also by *Wyatt*. The OLD
RECTORY, opposite, is of 1857, Gothic and symmetrical.

EBENEZER CHAPEL, 1¼ m. ESE. Built 1841. Longitudinal
three-bay elevation with two round-headed windows. Cottage
(later?) under the same roof.

HENBLAS, Pen yr Henblas, 1¼ m. SE. Dated 1651. Central
chimney and lobby entrance, and the staircase in a rear wing.
Symmetrical three-bay front with some mullioned windows,
labels and a Tudor-arched doorway.

There used to be a number of Bronze Age BARROWS on the
high ground above Holywell, but none of them can be easily
recognized now. This is because of C19 mining and quarrying
all over the area and, more recently, the development of a golf
course where one of the more interesting groups stood (SJ 173
750). When one of the tees was redesigned in 1933 an important grave group was discovered containing a unique spacer
bead of faience (Brynford Barrow). The only surviving monument is the pair of small STONES standing beside the road at
Naid y March (The Horse's Leap; SJ 168 753), but recent
excavation has shown that they are probably not ancient and
certainly not *in situ*. The large mound on the opposite side of
the road is spoil from a mine shaft.

BRYNGWYN HALL see TREMEIRCHION

BRYN IORCYN see CAERGWRLE

BUCKLEY

Manufacture of firebrick began in 1737, and brickmaking, together with earlier-established pottery manufacture and coalmining, enjoyed a long period of prosperity. Buckley's most
notable industrial monument, THE SMELT, was demolished
in 1966. For the smelting of lead, it is said to have been built
c. 1790 as an enterprise of John Wilkinson.

ST MATTHEW, Church Road. A church of 1821–2 by *John
Oates* (the only Commissioners' church in Wales of the First
Parliamentary Grant) was gradually rebuilt during the incumbency of Canon Drew, son-in-law of W. E. Gladstone. The
architects were *Douglas & Minshull* and the style Neo-Perp
with Arts and Crafts touches. NE vestries came 1897–9, and

then, as the first stage of a planned rebuilding scheme, a polygonal-apsed chancel, 1900–1. In 1902 Oates's w tower was remodelled, its height being reduced to produce more acceptably squat proportions, and a baptistry formed within.* At the same time a richly treated sw porch was added, its doorway on the diagonal. Mrs Drew paid for it with the proceeds of publishing letters written to her by Ruskin. Finally, the nave was reconstructed, 1904–5. It is wide and has a half-timbered clerestory. The arcades are also timber (though the posts enclose steel columns), and below the clerestory the infill panels have cheerful PAINTED DECORA-TION of 1910, restored 1963. Decoration also in the baptistry, 1903, designed by *Douglas* and executed by *W. F. Lodge*. Ash-lar walling elsewhere. – FURNISHINGS include characteristic Douglas woodwork in STALLS, PULPIT etc. Different are Art Nouveau SANCTUARY FITTINGS, of oak with copper embel-lishment, including REREDOS and copper CROSS and CANDLESTICKS. Also belonging to the set a pair of PEDES-TALS, but on them stand mid-C19 brass CANDLESTICKS by *Butterfield*. – STAINED GLASS. N aisle easternmost by *H. J. Stammers*, 1953, not one of his best. – A rewarding set by *Holiday* comprises that in the apse, 1899–1901 (the five-light Crucifixion particularly good), baptistry, 1901–2, and N aisle westernmost, 1909–10. – Timber-framed LYCHGATE of 1902.

EMMANUEL, Mold Road, Bistre. 1841–2 by *John Lloyd*; said to have been modelled on Casterton church, Westmorland. 'It seems odd that anyone having seen anything like it should want another,' remarked Goodhart-Rendel. A Commission-ers' box (it received aid from the Second Grant) with lancets, low-pitched roof, and an altar recess which is matched by a w porch. From the porch rises a little tower. Refitted by *W. H. Spaull*, 1881, with the w gallery removed, E recess remodelled, new FURNISHINGS etc. (Also ENCAUSTIC TILES from *J. C. Edwards*.) – STAINED GLASS. E window by *Ballan-tine*, 1881. – Third from w on N by *A. E. Child*, 1930.

ST JOHN'S UNITED REFORMED CHURCH (formerly Congre-gational), Hawkesbury Road. 1872–4. Yellow brick façade, with polychromy and a square, slated spirelet. Not a brilliant effort. One of the many chapels in Wales designed by the *Rev. Thomas Thomas* of Landore (VH), himself a Congrega-tional minister.

BETHEL WELSH PRESBYTERIAN (CALVINISTIC METHOD-IST) CHAPEL, Mold Road, Bistre. 1878 by *Richard Owens*. Round-arched, with polychromatic brickwork.

WAT'S DYKE. A fragment 1¼ m. w. Then longer sections to sw and s, and continuing towards Hope.

---

* According to Mr Howell, the w window belongs to alterations of 1845 by *James Harrison*.

CAERGWRLE

HOPE CASTLE. Granted in 1277 by Edward I to his then ally Dafydd ap Gruffydd, brother of Llywelyn the Last. The castle was slighted by Dafydd, following his revolt in 1282, and repairs, initiated under Master *Richard of Chester* and continued by *James of St George*, were put in hand for the King. In 1283, after being granted by Edward to Queen Eleanor, it was damaged by fire, and probably never repaired. It is not known to what extent the present remains are of 1282-3 or to what extent earlier parts are incorporated, though the likelihood is that they are substantially Dafydd's. They occupy a hilltop site, with embanked ditches on the N and E. Curtain walls enclosed an inner bailey of irregular plan, and there survive considerable portions of those on the N and E, and of a tower at their junction. The latter is suggestive of the Welsh D-towers, though having a segmental rather than semicircular end. The length of E curtain immediately S of it, where the gateway must have been, is missing. Parts of the S curtain remain, between fragments of a SE tower and yet scantier traces of one to the SW. Nothing survives of masonry defences on the W, where the ground falls steeply, if indeed any ever existed. The ruins are still largely as shown in Buck's view of 1742.

The top of the castle hill is surrounded by a low bank; only on the S side is there an external ditch. The impressive earthwork which runs E-W across the flat top of the hill is certainly associated with the C13 castle, and it is possible that the larger enclosure is also of medieval date, though it is normally considered to be a prehistoric HILLFORT. Immediately across the valley, ½m. ENE, is another, lower hill, CAER ESTYN (SJ 315 575), which is also crowned by a HILL-FORT. The pair would command the river, but such tactical siting is rare and difficult to prove amongst prehistoric forts. Caer Estyn has a dense tree cover, and the E end has been destroyed by quarrying.

METHODIST CHURCH, Castle Street. 1914. Red brick and yellow terra-cotta. Small tower with spirelet recessed behind swept battlements.

POLICE STATION, Wrexham Road. 1970 by *R.W. Harvey*, County Architect. Single-storeyed and flat-roofed. Beam ends emerge through a clerestory, and there is a deep, far-projecting fascia. Three houses introduce different materials and a larger scale.

PACKHORSE BRIDGE, Fellows Lane, crossing the Alun. Probably C17, but of more than one build. The W end has two segmental arches and sets of cutwaters, no longer complete. The remainder, not in line, now has two unequally spaced arches.

RHYDDYN HALL, E of the river, at Bridge End. 1749, but altered. Doric porch and, behind, a C19 cast-iron veranda. Pennant mentioned salt springs at Rhyddyn, and a short-lived

Edwardian spa was established around a sulphur well and saline spring. One building with a Ruabon brick tower survives. A GATEWAY, formerly arched, with battlemented screen walls, looks early C19.

BRYN IORCYN, ½m. W of the castle, on the E side of Hope Mountain, and aligned against the slope. H-plan. Encased in stone in the C17. Storeyed hall with cross passage and lateral chimney. Porch in the angle of the right-hand wing, and the opposite wing, which extends further, has a staircase projection in its angle. Mullioned windows. Diagonally set chimneystacks. Embedded within are three crucks, being the central (arched-braced) and the upper- and lower-end partition trusses of an earlier timber-framed hall house. The lower portions of the two posts of a spere truss also remain. Forecourt entered between ball-finialed GATEPIERS. The FARM BUILDINGS contain a cruck, and the group includes a DOVECOTE.

CAERWYS

1070

Following the granting of a charter by Edward I in 1290, a rectangular street plan was laid out. There were no defences, the foundation being commercial rather than military. The market place was in the centre, and the crossing of the two main village streets still has a townish air, though the gridiron was never fully built up, and only in the 1970s did housing appear in its NE corner.

ST MICHAEL. Nave and later chancel. Later again the addition of a gabled N aisle. Not a true double-naved church, though, for there is a chancel arch, and a W tower reduces the N compartment to little more than a chancel aisle. The tower is battlemented and unbuttressed, and battered at the base. Top stage said to be 1769, but this must refer to a repair. On the S of the nave a pair of cusped lancets, and in the chancel a good two-light C14 window. Below this is a TOMB RECESS, also Dec, with cinquefoil arch and sub-cusping. Five-light E window which, if its renewed masonry is to be trusted, is of transitional design, with Dec reticulated tracery turning rectilinear. Arches upon arches, with their verticals stressed. In the aisle, the E window is more thoroughly Perp, and the arched-braced roof is doubtless contemporary with it. They belong to a remodelling, not to the initial building of the aisle – see the earlier and steeper roof-line on the tower. Two post-Reformation windows in the chancel and one in the aisle. Internal plaster escaped the rigours of Victorian restoration, but a two-bay chancel arcade is of 1894–5, replacing three timber posts or columns. W entrance formed 1904, when the S porch became a vestry. – FONT. Dated 1661. Simple cusped panels. – Iron-bound FONT COVER. – ALTAR TABLE. Dated 1620. – Old woodwork in the PULPIT, low CHANCEL SCREEN

and chancel and aisle PANELLING. It includes roof timbers
(still *in situ* when seen by Glynne) with vine trail and quatrefoils under brattishing. Also panels from pews, two with dates
of the 1680s. – STAINED GLASS. Fragments of various dates
in easternmost on S of chancel, including canopy work in the
tracery and angels facing each other. – E window by *Joseph
Bell & Son*, commemoration date 1908. – Third from E on S
is a late one by *Morris & Co.*, 1936. – SEPULCHRAL SLABS.
Early C14 four-circle cross slab, in two pieces. – Part of the
head of another, of similar date, with four open-ended circles
back to back, interlaced with a quatrefoil. Fleurs-de-lys and
a flower in the centre. – Late C14 slab, set upside down,
commemorating Gyean Fach. Foliated pattern and part of a
sword. – MONUMENTS. In the Dec recess is an earlier (C13 or
early C14) incomplete female effigy in relief, the head framed
by an arch. Tradition identifies her as the wife of Dafydd ap
Gruffydd, brother of Llywelyn the Last. – Two tablets, both
with a cherub head at the base, respectively to Thomas Mostyn and the Rev. Thomas Lewis, both †1751. – In the churchyard a thin baluster SUNDIAL, its plate dated 1830. –
LYCHGATE. Stone side walls, and spanning between them a
beam, on which the medieval lych cross stood.

THE OLD COURT, High Street. An early C19 refacing, with
Victorian touches, belies a longer history. It is believed that
this may be the site of a court of the Welsh princes; a rebuilding by the Mostyn family took place in the C15, and their
manorial courts were held here; until 1672 it was a place of
meeting of the courts of Great Sessions, and it remained a
magistrates' court until 1882. The present structure is early
C17, with nothing that can definitely be identified as being
older. Mullioned windows at the rear. Indications of symmetrical fenestration on gable end and a rear wing (both obscured by later building) suggest that before the early C19
refacing the Jacobean front must have been quite a grand one.
The plan is of the internal chimney and lobby entry type, but
with a tunnel-vaulted passage burrowing through the chimneybreast to the staircase at the rear. Stairs, with turned balusters, rising through two storeys, but with the lower flights
realigned at an early date.*

CAERWYS HALL, ⅞ m. NNE. A massive gabled chimneybreast.
(Built as a storeyed house with first-floor room open to the
roof, and of lateral chimney and inside cross passage plan. P.
Smith)

MAES-Y-COED, Afon-Wen, ¾ m. S. Five-bay C18 front with
flush sashes. Earlier rear wing.

Industrial relics at Afon-Wen include a three-storey former
FOUNDRY, ⅛ m. W of Maes-y-Coed.

---

* I am indebted to Mr Tom Lloyd-Roberts for his help relating to The Old
Court.

CHWITFFORDD *see* WHITFORD

CILCAIN   *1060*

ST MARY. Double-naved. The E part of the central division is a three-bay Dec arcade, the responds of which indicate it to have been cut through an earlier wall and also suggest premature cessation of work. A cruder arch further W is Perp, and also made in existing walling. It doubtless dates from the time when the N nave and its W tower were built, in place of the previously existing or intended aisle. The W end of the division remains solid. Perp E windows with cusping and panel tracery, three-light in N nave, five in S. Round-headed N windows and doorway are of 1764. S windows, S porch, and the upper stage and buttresses of the tower belong to *Douglas*'s restoration of 1888-9. This was instigated by W. B. Buddicom of Penbedw, Nannerch (*see* p. 402), and carried out after his death at the expense of his widow. Blocked priest's doorway. The glory of the church is the S nave roof, of alternating 29 arched-braced and hammerbeam trusses, and with all its parts moulded in excellent Late Gothic manner. Obviously brought from elsewhere: it does not relate to the arcade; it is said to show signs of having been reassembled, and the scale suggests it should be at a greater height. Nevertheless there is no evidence to support a tradition of its having belonged to Basingwerk Abbey. Static (non-fluttering) angels on the hammerbeams carry shields bearing emblems of the Passion. Secular subjects and grotesques on bosses and at the feet of the arched-braced trusses. Wagon ceiling at the E end.* – *Douglas* FURNISHINGS include STALLS and PEWS, with some C17 carving reused at the W end and in connection with the stalls. – SCREENS in the arcade also by Douglas. – STAINED GLASS. Figures in the E window, which is said to have been dated 1546. In the centre a Crucifixion with the Virgin and St John. St George and St Peter in the outer lights. – BOARDS with the Creed and Lord's Prayer in Welsh, painted and signed by *Robert Jones*, 1809. – SCULPTURAL FRAGMENTS include a font bowl with interlacing and other ornament. – Also parts of C14 SEPULCHRAL SLABS, with effigies and crosses, and one which is of the heraldic shield and diagonal sword type. – MONUMENTS. Mostyn monument. By *T. Wynne*, 1731. Broken segmental pediment, but in the middle an isolated fragment of pediment is raised up higher on a group of cherub heads and drapery. Heraldry above and urns either side. – Thomas Mostyn Edwards †1832. By *Reeves & Sons* of Bath. Neo-Classical but quite vigorous. – In the porch, iron GATES from Mold church (q.v.) and identifiable as belonging to the earlier set of *c.*1726, attributed to *Davies*. – Circular, or rather oval, CHURCHYARD. – Adjoining the lychgate a HEARSE HOUSE of 1810.

* The roof was restored 1845-6 by *Ambrose Poynter*, 1888-9 by *Douglas*, and 1935-7 by *F. H. Crossley*.

The village, on the lower slopes of Moel Fama, has miniature townscape E of the church. To the W, PLAS YN LLAN has a Tudor-arched doorway with label, and a late C17 staircase with turned balusters. Opposite the lychgate a COTTAGE built in 1799 as a school.

MAES-Y-GROES, 1⅛m. SSE. An early C17 two-unit storeyed house, with end chimney and end entrance. Neat little elevation, with four three-light mullioned windows. Post-and-panel partition. The larger of the first-floor rooms was open to the roof, and its central truss remains above a ceiling, arched-braced, with struts above the collar. Later rear wing. (A BARN is dated 1682 internally.)

48 BRITHDIR MAWR, 1⅜m. S. A hall house, now, of course, with a floor inserted, but its central arched-braced truss remains, and an open hearth shows that the present lateral chimney is also an insertion. Cross passage and screens partition. Upper-end post-and-panel partition dated 1589. This has been taken as the original building date, but is incredibly late for a hall arranged in so thorough a medieval way. It may be supposed that it refers to a remodelling, and that the lateral chimney is of this date, rather than contemporary with the introduction of the floor, which, on the evidence of a dated dormer, took place in 1637. Indeed, the hall fireplace, with timber beam on corbels, differs from that in the room above, which has a stone Tudor arch. The inserted floor has ovolo beams and incised mouldings to the joists. Heraldry of 1642 in the lower-end room is no longer *in situ*. Large windows with timber mullions and transoms of diagonal section, probably of 1589. Timber mullions also, but different, in a rear wing which apparently pre-dates the lateral chimney.

LEDROD (formerly Cefn Isaf), ¾m. NE. Two truncated crucks in the barn.

TŶ ISAF, 1⅜m. N. An excellent example of a late hall house. The main room was open to the roof, but the lateral chimney, unlike that at Brithdir Mawr, is part of the initial build. Gabled breast and long ingle beam. The hall has had a floor inserted, but the central truss remains, as do timber-framed partitions. Cross passage with screens partition. There were two lower-end service rooms (now in one) and an upper-end parlour. C19 addition at the lower end.

FFYNNON LEINW, 1⅝m. NE, immediately S of the main road, in a wood. A shallow, rectangular well basin.

FFAGNALLT, 3m. N. An early or mid-C17 staircase, with shaped flat balusters and strapwork on the string and the newels.

TRELLYNIAU FAWR, 2¾m. N. A two-unit end-chimney house, with lateral entrance at the fireplace end, and outbuildings under the same roof at the other. Two mullioned windows, one with transom. Probably a storeyed house from the outset, with the larger of the two first-floor rooms open to the roof. A wing at right angles, once with no internal communication, is an unmistakable instance of unit planning.

CILCAIN HALL, 2m. NNE. 1875 by *Douglas*. Elizabethan in its elements, of stone with a red-tiled roof. The client was W. B. Buddicom of Penbedw. Former ENTRANCE LODGE on the main road.

BETHEL CHAPEL, Penyfron. *See* Rhydymwyn.

COED DU. *See* Rhydymwyn.

MOEL ARTHUR, 2m. WNW (SJ 145 660), is a small but prominent hillfort with impressive defences on the more accessible N side. The rest of the circuit needs little artificial defence and it is marked by just a terrace and scarped slope. The northern defences consist of two enormous banks and ditches with a third (counterscarp) bank outside for most of their length. The most comfortable living areas lie in a broad flattish area behind these multivallate defences, for the southern side of the hill is fiercely exposed. The single entrance is along a narrow track from the NE passing under the linked ends of the ramparts, a hazardous passageway for any attacker, for the S side of the track drops steeply away. This passageway is lengthened by inturning the inner rampart on either side. Marked hollows in these inturns probably betray the presence of guard chambers. *See* p. 24

An important hoard of Early Bronze Age copper flat axes was found within this hillfort in 1962.

In the fields between Glust and Pen-y-Gelli, 2m. N, are three prominent mounds and two less conspicuous ones (SJ 182 685). It is difficult to be certain whether or not all these are Bronze Age BARROWS, but it is likely that two or three are.

CONNAH'S QUAY   2060

In the belt of industrial Deeside, there is no break between Connah's Quay, Shotton and Queensferry.

ST MARK. 1836-7 by *John Lloyd*. Aisleless nave, sharply pointed lancets, W tower with recessed pyramid roof, W gallery on slender iron columns, very heavy roof timbers. *Douglas* refitted the church and added a new chancel in a discreetly more competent lancet style, 1876-8. – MONUMENT. Trevor Owen Jones †1839. Draped urn. By *William Spence*.

VICARAGE. 1839-41, but still with the flush sashes of early C18 vernacular tradition.

ST DAVID, Mold Road. 1907 by *L. W. Barnard*. Set well back from the road. Of rock-faced sandstone, and intended as the church hall for a large church which was to have been built in front.

WEPRE PRESBYTERIAN CHURCH. Built 1901. Red brick, with all dressings including Gothic detail and an octagonal spirelet of yellow terra-cotta.

CIVIC CENTRE, Wepre Drive. The idea is commendable. Public buildings of two storeys (i.e. intimately scaled) form three sides of a landscaped enclosure. Sadly, the architecture is uninspired, and the SWIMMING BATHS, 1961–4, and AS-SEMBLY HALL, 1959–61, are particularly poor. They are by *J. G. L. Poulson* of Pontefract. LEARNER POOL, 1972–5, by *William Gower & Partners*. Opposite is a BRANCH LIBRARY, 1963–4, by *R. W. Harvey*, Flintshire County Architect, and between them are the COUNCIL OFFICES, 1964–5, also by *Poulson*. Dignity is aspired to by projecting the council chamber forward on piers, with the main entrance below. A coat of arms, now joined in its splendid isolation by an equally carefully placed burglar alarm, adorns the blank front wall. Older suburban houses close the fourth side of the layout.

KELSTERTON COLLEGE OF TECHNOLOGY (formerly Flintshire Technical College). Low and spreading, of brick, with a matchbox clock tower, it is typical of the degeneration of the International Style between the end of the war and the Festival of Britain. 1952–4 by *R. W. Harvey*, County Architect, with *Sir Howard Robertson* as consultant. To the r. are extensive pitched-roofed ranges of different character. Various large extensions are in the fashions of subsequent years.

POWER STATION, almost opposite the College. One of the series of post-war plants. The first stage was built 1950–4; completion took place 1958. By the Engineers of the Merseyside and North Wales Division of the then British Electricity Authority, *A. R. Cooper*, Divisional Controller, and *Mouchel & Partners*, Civil Engineering Consultants. The enormous mass of the main building, steel-framed and clad in brick, is very decently done.

KELSTERTON HOUSE, NW of the College. A two-storey front of *c.*1800 with quoins. Four bays and a later ground-floor insertion between projecting one-bay wings.

TOP-Y-FRON, ½m. SW of the College. An early C18 double pile house, of brick. Three-storey front, of five bays on the upper floors and three below. Patterned fanlight (and some internal features of the 1760s. DOE).

CWM

ST MAEL AND ST SULIEN. The village (though it is hardly a village) is on a hilly site, and the church follows the slope of the ground. The nave is on two levels, and the chancel higher again. No structural division between the parts, i.e. a single chamber. Double W bellcote. Perp four-centred E window of five cusped lights. Of similar date two S windows and the W and S doorways, moulded, with hoodmoulds. The S porch is later. Post-Reformation N windows and a round-headed S one dated 1769. In the chancel a tomb recess, or possibly an EASTER SEPULCHRE, of reused stones, with C14 floral motifs in the soffit. By the S door a STOUP. Restorations of 1881 and by *Harold Hughes*, 1901, though the interior is not as he left it. NW vestry 1946. – FONT. The bowl is square, outside and in. – STAINED GLASS. Late medieval fragments in the E window. – Plank CHEST. – SCULPTURE. Portion of a cross head with virtually identical Crucifixions on either side. – SEPULCHRAL SLABS. Early C14 four-circle cross slab. Open-ended circles back-to-back. – Late C14 foliated cross slab. Maltese cross and a pattern of lobed leaves on one side of the shaft and an inscription on the other. – Base of a late C14 cross slab commemorating Hywel ap H... ap Maredudd. Inscription up the middle with lobed leaf patterns on one side and a sword on the other. – Outside, by the S wall, the TOMBSTONE of Grace Williams †1642. The most elaborate of the Welsh hooded tombs. Base of two by one open arched bays, with fluted columns, decorated spandrels and strapwork frieze. Open semicircular canopy enriched with volutes and, under the soffit, an angel and skull and shields.

The church was whitewashed when seen by Glynne in 1839.

VICARAGE. Built 1847, a crisp and refined version of the Italianate villa of the time. Of ashlar, with intersecting axes to the two asymmetrical fronts, a boldly scaled arched porch, and little arches piercing the chimneystacks.

PLAS IS-LLAN, ¾ m. W. Dated 1765. Brick, with three bays, two and a half storeys, one-bay pediment and a small (blocked) lunette window. This description belies the true character, for here is a curious fusion of fashion with vernacular tradition. The windows, of two lights, have stone mullions and, on the lower floors, transoms. The doorcase and its mouldings are also of C17 type. FARM BUILDINGS define a symmetrical forecourt.

PENTRE CWM, ½ m. NW. Coped gable ends with ball finials. A central storeyed porch has a four-centred doorway and a chimney on its gable. (The first stage has hall with lateral chimney, and a parlour with chimneypiece dated 1632. To this was added the porch, dated 1636, and a rear service wing. Later again came a kitchen, forming a further part of the rear block. NMR)

TERFYN, 1¼ m. ENE. Lateral chimney, its fireplace with corbels dated 1577. (Arched-braced truss of a former open roof. DOE) At right angles is an earlier range with end chimney and an inside cross passage retaining post-and-panel partitioning.

PWLLHALOG, 1¼ m. E. L-plan, of different builds, with, at the end of one of the ranges, a taller cross wing, which may once have extended further. This has stepped gables and mullioned and transomed windows with labels. Some mullioned windows elsewhere. Though now a single house, it probably evolved on the unit system. FARM BUILDINGS include one with stone mullions.

Several Bronze Age BARROWS are clustered around the pass above the village. One on the S side (SJ 078 772) is very easily recognized and has been excavated, producing a cremation burial in an urn with a small bone pommel. Another very large mound may be seen right in the centre of the pass (SJ 074 775), but it is of natural origin, not a barrow.

See
p. 24 MOEL HIRADDUG, ½ m. NNW (SJ 063 785), the long bony limestone ridge at the northern end of the Clwydian range, is a
landmark for many miles around, even though the N end has
been almost entirely removed by quarrying. This narrow
ridge is occupied by an important multivallate hillfort which
has been the scene of intermittent excavation over the last
thirty years, mainly in the area now destroyed by the quarry.
The area within the fort may be divided into three: the northern plateau (now almost gone), where several round stone
huts and wooden 'four-post' structures were recorded; the
narrow southern ridge, which provides little suitable living
space, though 'four-posters' can be recognized there; and the
eastern shelf, which is relatively sheltered, being lower than
the ridge which lies to its W. The defences consist mainly of
thick limestone walls, some with rock-cut ditches outside
them; the outermost line of defence on the eastern side, however, is a more earthy rampart with internal ditch. The walls
now appear tumbled and spread, but their facings can be
discerned in places among the rubble; the ditches have largely
silted up. The plan of the fort follows the contours closely
and on the very steep western side there is only a single
relatively feeble stone rampart. On the more vulnerable side,
four ramparts could once be seen at the NE end; three of them
continue around the flank of the eastern shelf, and the innermost one separates the shelf from the ridge. Altogether there
are six entrances to the various parts of the fort. That at the
NW has been totally destroyed, but the others can still be
seen, though the entrance giving access from the shelf to the
plateau has been very badly mutilated and the guard chambers revealed by excavation in the 1970s can no longer be
recognized. Those at the S include an overlapped gateway on
to the ridge, an inturned gateway into the shelf, and an outermost one giving access through earthworks which appear to
be later additions. The gate into the shelf is large and, with
the remodelled inner entrance, must have formed the main
approach to the fort. The sixth entrance is an interesting one,
perhaps blocked in antiquity, through the eastern side of the
shelf defences. The excavations have shown that the defences
are not all of the same date; the innermost rampart on the NE
seems to be later than at least one of those outside it and may
represent a division of, or a reduction in, the fort area. The
inner entrance had certainly been remodelled, the original
arrangement being a simple, gated gap through the rampart,
while the later building of guard chambers is a modification
found in other hillforts of NE Wales, and marks a horizon of
considerable historical importance. Several round stone huts
have been excavated (and some regrettably have not been
filled in, giving the hillside a disreputable look which cannot
benefit the long-term preservation of the archaeological
remains); the finds have been few but indicate occupation
during the Iron Age. In 1872, however, a remarkable collection of decorative bronze fittings for a La Tène shield was

found buried in the inner ditch on the NE side of the fort. It is very seldom that such parade armour has been found in the context in which it might have been used.

DDOL *see* YSGEIFIOG

DISERTH   *0070*

Tourists come to see the waterfall.

St Ffraid, Waterfall Road. One sees first the w front, with bellcote, window and doorway by *Sir Gilbert Scott*. He restored the church in E.E. to Dec manner 1873-5, and added a N chancel aisle (as vestry etc.), N transept and s porch. Massive buttresses give an air of antiquity, though, and the E window is Perp, with five lights, two single-light sub-arches and panel tracery. A chancel s window dated 1636, with four curved-headed lights. Arched-braced roof with small cusped wind-braces (dated 1579 on a collar). A truss with angels, at the chancel entrance, must be *Scott*'s. No structural division, but the chancel is marked by a slight contraction and by inclination to the N. – STAINED GLASS. E window. An inscription of 1450 is recorded. Possibly of this date are the twelve Apostles in the tracery lights, each with a clause of the Creed on an arched scroll. The remainder, with a Jesse Tree in the main lights, resulted from a bequest in the 1530s. First and fifth and second and fourth lights respectively are from the same cartoons, but not reversed. Figures in groups of three, the outer ones emerging from flowers. Jesse himself is missing, the lower lights being jumbled fragments. Virgin and Child at the top of the middle light. – SEPULCHRAL SLABS. In the nave floor against the chancel steps part of an early C14 incised cross slab. Flower at base of shaft. – Against the nave s wall a slab of *c*. 1400 with two foliated crosses and two separate inscriptions. The heads differ in design. Patterns of lobed leaves up either side. – CHURCHYARD CROSS, now inside. Wheel head (incomplete) with cusped trefoils between the arms, which project only slightly. Central raised bosses, that at the back moulded. Much crude ornament – spiral, double-bead and three-cord triple-bead plait etc. Not pre-Norman, and Dr Nash-Williams dated the work as late as the C12 or C13, citing the cusped wheel head and the degenerate character of the decoration as indicating this to be one of the last Welsh crosses, and one which suggests debased hybridity between a true wheel cross and the ring-headed Anglo-Viking type. – A CROSS BASE, with socket, is of similar date and style. Roughly semicircular and tapering, it has ornament in four panels.

E of the church a group of C17 tomb-chests and TABLE TOMBS, two of them of the hooded type. One of these, 1676, has a base with open arches and architectural features. The hood, once with a finial, has an angel on the underside. The other, similar but slightly earlier, no longer retains the canopy intact.

Former VICARAGE, almost opposite the church. Centre of 1799 between later cross wings.

DYSERTH CASTLE, ½ m. NE of the church. Built in the time of Henry III, following the defeat of Dafydd ap Llywelyn in 1241, and completed by 1250. Taken by Llywelyn the Last in 1263 and soon superseded by Edward I's new castle at Rhuddlan. Remains existing c. 1900 were destroyed by quarrying, but a bank and ditch, defences of the outer ward, may still be seen.

CRAIG-Y-CASTELL, W of the castle site. C20 Tudor character, but incorporating a C16 range with mullioned windows of two curved-headed lights. A few pieces of carving, said to have come from the castle, are built in at the rear.

SIAMBER WEN, in a field, ⅛ m. S of the castle site. Ruined walls of a medieval house. T-plan, consisting of hall and service range, and an upper-end cross wing.

TALARGOCH LEAD MINE. Beside the A547, ⅜ m. N of the church, is the Clive Shaft engine house, built 1862 for a hundred-foot pumping engine. Abandoned 1883.*

DYSERTH HALL, N of the junction of the A547 and B5119. The three-bay stone front looks early C19, but there is a blocked mullioned window of three curved-headed lights, i.e. C16. Similar two-light blocked window in the gable of the left-hand return, though the gable is stepped, i.e. later C16 or C17.

LLEWERLLYD, ¼ m. W of Dyserth Hall. Brick. Three bays. Central pediment-like gable with a small lunette window. Datestone of 1783. A similar plaque, bearing the same date, is at LLEWERLLYD MILL, ¼ m. S. Stone. The wheel remains, but the machinery and mill race have been destroyed, and the adjoining miller's house, of brick, nastily tarted up.

EMRAL HALL see WORTHENBURY

3060

EWLOE

EWLOE CASTLE. The ruins of a native Welsh castle, in a secluded and wooded setting. The site is a promontory above the confluence of two streams, and has a steep fall on the N. On the S the castle is overlooked by higher ground, and there are ditches on the E and S, the latter with counterscarp. Curtain walls enclose a lower ward on the W and an eastern upper ward. Circular West Tower at the extremity of the lower,

* Information from Mr Christopher Williams.

surviving in part to a considerable height. Traces of a building on the s of the upper ward, and at the NE corner the
position of a bridge across the ditch may be seen. The castle
remains dominated by the so-called Welsh Tower, standing
free within this ward. It is of the Welsh D-plan, a rectangle
with apsidal end. With the possible exception of this tower,
the building works may be ascribed to Llywelyn ap Gruffydd
(Llywelyn the Last), c.1257, following his recapture of the
district from the English. The Welsh Tower may be earlier
C13, and the work of Llywelyn ab Iorwerth (Llywelyn the
Great). On the s and w its walls largely stand to their full
height, and the line of a pitched roof shows that they were
carried above roof level. External stair to a first-floor doorway.

HOLY SPIRIT, Aston Hill. 1937-8 by *Goodhart-Rendel*, at the
expense of Lady Gladstone. Of Byzantine derivation. Brick.
The interior, vaulted in reinforced concrete, is plastered.
Nave and sanctuary are variously enclosed by porches, vestries, choir, transepts and chapel. Freely arranged barrel and
groin vaulting. The result is spatially ambiguous inside and
uncoordinated externally. Numerous low-pitched roofs build
up to a shallow drum and low conical roof, surmounted by a
lantern, over the sanctuary. – ALTAR CROSS. A C17 Italian
Crucifix, the figure of ivory. From the Certosa, Pavia. It once
belonged to C.E. Kempe. – CANDLESTICKS designed by
Goodhart-Rendel to match. – ORGAN CASE from Hawarden
Castle. By *Beresford Pite*, but altered.

ASTON MEAD COTTAGES, between Lower Aston Lane and the
railway, and now dominated by an elevated road. An exercise
in economical housing, with roofs of corrugated asbestos, by
Goodhart-Rendel, 1933-4. Grouped round a green.

ASTON HALL, Lower Aston Lane. H-plan. Much altered. An
exuberantly carved overmantel, *ex situ* but belonging to the
house, with marquetry and painted heraldry, is dated 1615.
Earlier linenfold panelling arranged in connection with it. In
a garden wall an aedicular ARCHWAY dated 1617 (recut), now
lacking its columns.

FFERM *see* HOPE

FFRITH *see* LLANFYNYDD

FFYNNONGROYW   *1080*

ALL SAINTS. Beside the main road in an unlovely village at the
extremity of industrial Deeside. One could be forgiven for
passing it by without a second glance, along with several
nearby chapels. Yet it is by *George Edmund Street*, and his

very last church, designed in 1881 and completed posthumously the following year. Dull and poverty-stricken, it is a strange end to Street's career, but it repays examination, and the form is skilfully contrived. Nave and aisles are contained under one low-pitched roof which continues without a break over the narrower chancel. w bellcote and lean-to porch. Lancets. Recognizably Streetian three-bay arcades, with rock-faced arches, circular shafts, and the transition between them effected by heavily moulded stop-chamfered caps.* – Big, chunky FONT by *Street*. – Good STAINED GLASS of 1889 in the E window.

Further W a former SCHOOL of 1869–71 by *Richard Owens*, the chapel specialist. Asymmetrical, with bellcote. Built as the British (i.e. not Church) School.

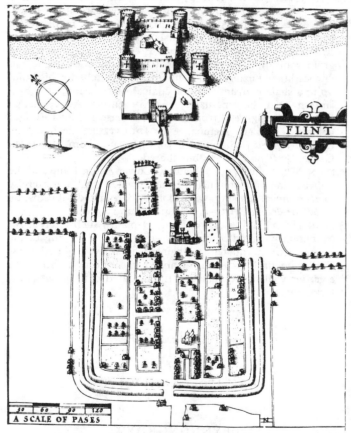

The town of Flint in 1610, plan
(John Speed, *The Theatre of the Empire of Great Britaine*, 1611–12)

---

*Practically the same design, Mr Joyce points out, had been used by Street in his early church at Wheatley, Oxfordshire, 1855.

FLINT

Flint was among the first group of Edward I's castles in Wales. 2070
Together with its attendant town (one of those inspired by the
bastides seen by the King during his sojourn in France) it was
begun during the campaign of 1277. A market was established
in the town the following year, and a charter granted in 1284.
There was no town wall, the defences consisting of ditch, bank
and palisade, curved at the corners nearest the castle. An entrance occurred on each of the four sides, that on the NE communicating with the castle. The plan had six parallel streets
aligned NE-SW and one cross route; the principal thoroughfare,
Church Street, still runs SW from the direction of the castle and
market place. The NE part of the layout, where the railway

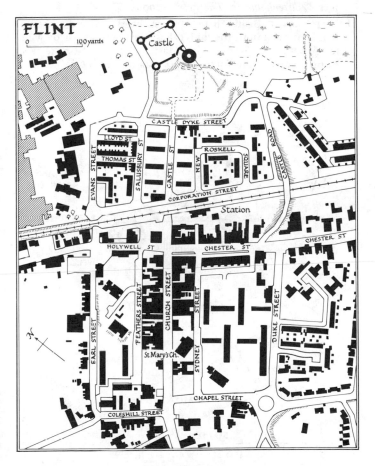

Modern Flint, plan
(Department of the Environment)

crosses, has been obscured, and dreary blocks of flats have encroached on the pattern either side of Church Street. Earl Street on the NW and Duke Street on the S mark the sites of the defences.

Speed's plan of 1610 shows that very little of the layout had by then been built up, but growth came with the development of industry from the late C18 onwards. Besides exporting coal, Flint became a centre for lead smelting and associated manufacture, leading in turn to the establishing of chemical works. By the 1970s the skyline had become dominated by flats and by the chimneys and multistorey factories of Courtaulds Ltd (now largely demolished). Best visually was their ABER WORKS in Aber Road, with a number of subsidiary buildings in attractively textured brick. Built for the German-based British Glanzstoff Co., makers of artificial silk, it was by *F. G. Briggs* of *Briggs, Wolstenholme & Thornely*, *c.*1908.

FLINT CASTLE. Begun in 1277, as has been said, and construction continued until the mid-1280s. Supervision was by Master *James of St George*, with Master *Richard of Chester* also being involved, and further work was carried out by Richard

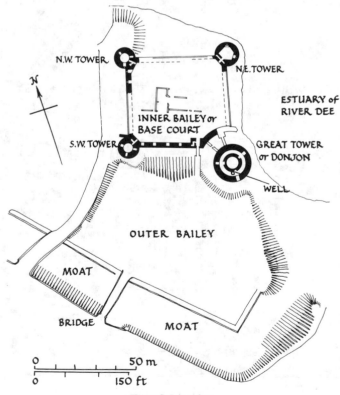

Flint Castle, plan
(Department of the Environment)

early in the C14. The OUTER WARD is approached across a former moat, where there is a small fragment of the OUTER GATEHOUSE. To the N a further moat separates off the INNER WARD, a roughly square enclosure, which was protected on its three other sides by the tidal waters of the Dee Estuary. It was approached by a drawbridge, and traces of the GATE-WAY remain. Some CURTAIN WALLING with embrasures survives on the s and around the NW corner. Attached circular TOWERS at all corners except the SE; the NE TOWER is the best-preserved. Basement plus three hexagonal upper storeys. Traces of two hooded fireplaces, and another in the NW TOWER.

The special and extraordinary feature of the castle is the circular GREAT TOWER or DONJON, free-standing outside the SE corner of the inner ward, commanding the entrance to it, and once entirely surrounded by water. The curtain assumes a segmental re-entrant, concentric with the tower, and against it is the substantial abutment of some form of bridge, which supplied a link. The concept of a keep was, by the late C13, outmoded, though there are comparable continental examples. A desire to emulate them seems not unlikely, particularly on the part of a king who was to endow Caernarfon with such symbolical and associational significance, and the direct prototype was undoubtedly the Tour de Constance at the great bastide of Aigues Mortes. The lower storey of the Flint donjon is encircled by a broad tunnel-vaulted wall passage with embrasures and arrow slits. On the inner side three sets of steps lead down, through pointed arches, to a central circular chamber to which there is also direct access from the tower's entrance. The wall passage drops in level to pass below this entrance passage. The prosaic, but likely explanation of the curious plan is that the chamber was intended for storage. On the upper floor a series of apartments were arranged radially about the central circular space, and if the latter was an open light well rather than a roofed chamber, comparison may be made with the Emperor Frederick II's Castel del Monte. A well in the tower and the provision of three garderobe shafts indicates planning to withstand siege, and the carrying up of the surviving shafts shows that at least one further storey was intended and (though there is some uncertainty) in all probability built.

On the upper floor, immediately w of the newel stair, was a CHAPEL, and evidence of barrel vaulting and a PISCINA may be discerned. It would have been here that Richard II heard Mass while he was awaiting the arrival of Henry Bolingbroke in 1399.

The castle was dismantled after being surrendered to Parliament in 1646. The Flintshire COUNTY GAOL, erected in the outer ward, was by *Joseph Turner*, 1784–5; in the cause of tidying up the castle and its surroundings, it was demolished in 1969.

ST MARY, Church Street. Still occupying the medieval site,

though the church was rebuilt by *Ambrose Poynter*, 1846–8.
Large, with clerestory and a NW tower and octagonal spire.
Light and spacious interior, falling woefully short of Camdenian standards. Arcades in the forbidden Third Pointed, a
camberbeam roof and no structural division for the chancel
all suggest a genuine attempt at regional character, though
there is a W gallery and the windows are cusped lancets. –
STAINED GLASS. In the S aisle a version of Holman Hunt's
'The Light of the World' by *Ward & Hughes*, 1885. – In the
chancel, MONUMENTS to members of a Liverpool family who
established alkali manufacture in Flint. On the S, Julia Jose-
phine Muspratt †1857. By *Spence*. Full-length figure in
Gothic frame. On the N, James Muspratt †1886 and Richard
Muspratt †1885. By *E. J. Physick*. Angel, writing a verse
from Revelation in a more strongly Gothic frame. – ROYAL
ARMS of Queen Victoria. A painted panel.

ST DAVID, Chester Road, Pentre. 1871–2 by *Daniel Lewis* of
Manchester. The main feature is its polychromy, the walls
being of red brick with yellow brick patterning, and there is
yellow terra-cotta plate tracery. Polygonal apse, and over the
chancel arch a bellcote. The interior, also of polychromatic
brick, has misguidedly been painted. Later baptistry and
organ chamber with terra-cotta arches. – *Minton* ENCAUSTIC
TILES include lettering on a chancel step, providing details of
the building and those concerned with it.

ST THOMAS, Flint Mountain, 1¼ m. S. 1874–5 by *John Hill*.
Rock-faced, with nave, chancel, S porch and W bellcote. Lancets.

ST MARY (R.C.), Coleshill Street. 1884–5 by *J. B. Sinnott*.*
Polygonal apse, lancets, and the interior largely faced in red
brick. Unusually, there is aisle, arcade and clerestory on one
side of the nave (the N) only.

ENGLISH METHODIST CHURCH, Holywell Street. Wildly improbable. Like a child's drawing of a church actually built,
tower and all, and given restless polychromy and glazing patterns. 1881 by *Joseph Hall*, a member of the congregation.

TOWN HALL, Trelawny Square. Tudor Gothic, of 1840, by
John Welch. As built, less ambitious than he originally designed it. The two ends are symmetrical, but the long sides
less regular, as a result of additions. At the SE end, an arch
spanning between octagonal turrets carries a stepped gable.
Big former entrance arch with decorated spandrels. The
ground floor originally served as a market. The assembly hall
(now council chamber) on the upper floor has a hammerbeam
roof. The ceiling of the Mayor's parlour (added as council
chamber) has heraldry of the Tribes of Wales, executed by
the versatile *Joseph Hall*.

GUILDHALL, Chapel Street. The name is ominous, suggesting
one of those attempts at grandeur and monumentality incom-
patible with a modern idiom on a limited budget. In fact the

* So said Goodhart-Rendel, but should this not be J. & B. Sinnott?

building is a clean and unpretentious set of council offices with a rectangular elevational grid, and slight emphasis given to the entrance bays. By *The Anthony Clark Partnership*, 1965–6.

SCHOOL, Northop Road. 1859 by *T. M. Penson*. Four-gable front, symmetrical except for one of the porches carrying a bellcote. Traceried windows in two larger gables. School-house at the end of the left-hand return.

RAILWAY STATION. 1847–8, one of *Francis Thompson*'s Italianate stations for the Chester and Holyhead Railway. A simple one, and its brickwork has been painted, but it is essentially complete, even to the main members of the original iron canopies. And, what is more, it is still in use. The centre of the entrance front is recessed, with a canopy spanning between projecting end bays, as at Mostyn (q.v.). Also as at Mostyn, the platform canopy was planned between projecting single-storey blocks.

PERAMBULATION is neither necessary nor desirable, and in the town centre only CHURCH STREET calls for any sort of mention. No. 34, once the SESSIONS HOUSE, has a stuccoed gable front with rusticated quoins (and C17 work inside including two mullioned windows. DOE). The former PLAZA is one of the two cinemas which Flint was once able to support, with another at Bagillt. It is now the MECCA SOCIAL CLUB, i.e. bingo. 1936–8 by *S. Colwyn Foulkes*. Emphatically rectangular brick front relieved by two-dimensional mythological figures set against heavily framed grille panels. A decorative brick frieze runs immediately above a canopy which preserves its Art Deco fascia.

OAKENHOLT HALL, 2m. SE. Dated 1808. A brick house of three bays and two and a half storeys. Two-column porch. Next to it at OAKENHOLT FARMHOUSE the surviving lower portion of a cruck truss has been revealed.

PLAS-Y-MYNYDD, Northop Road, 1¼m. S. A farmhouse of 1883, almost certainly by *John Douglas* for the first Duke of Westminster. Asymmetrical gabled front of warm red brick, with diapering. Stone dressings include mullioned windows.

BRYN EDWIN, 2m. S. A three-bay stuccoed house of one and a half storeys, with hipped roof and soffited eaves. Iron veranda and a fine doorway with recessed and enriched columns below a delicate fanlight. The door has octagonal panels. Although the house must be early C19, it is not, on the evidence of internal details, quite so early as the exterior suggests.

CORNIST HALL, 1m. WSW. Neo-Jacobean, of brick and stone. The rebuilding of a smaller house was begun by *Douglas* c.1884 for the alkali manufacturer Richard Muspratt, on whose death in 1885 it remained incomplete. Only the pyramid-roofed tower with its canted bay appears in Douglas's published perspective. The rest of the elevations are later and probably not by him. Since 1953 the house has belonged to the local authority, and much has been lost in remodelling the interior for catering purposes. Of features which do remain, only the staircase can be recognized as being by *Douglas*.

Over the years a number of Roman finds have been made on the E side of Flint, and recent rescue excavations revealed Roman buildings at PENTRE FARM, ¾m. SE (SJ 254 723). The earliest building was a courtyard house built of timber *c*.A.D. 120 and replaced in stone in the mid-C2 A.D. Details of the construction show links with military buildings in the legionary fort at Chester, and a likely interpretation is that this was the residence of an official involved in the mining of lead on Halkyn Mountain. Roman exploitation of the local mineral resources is evidenced by finds of several stamped lead pigs, and the connection of this large house with the industry is shown by its degeneration into a lead-processing workshop in the C3.

GLAN-Y-DON *see* MOSTYN

GORSEDD

ST PAUL. 1852–3. One of the two churches designed by *T. H. Wyatt* following the Pantasaph controversy (*see* p. 414). Aisleless, with NW steeple. Cusped lancets and Geometrical tracery – plate and (in the E window) bar. The W front has curious tendencies, with an asymmetrically placed baptistry projecting between buttresses. Though not a success, this is an interestingly early piece of High Victorian 'roguishness'.

The former SCHOOL, contemporary, is also by *Wyatt*, and so, probably, is the awkwardly-gabled VICARAGE.

Near the crossroads, ½m. W, is a winding-engine house of the former LLOC LEAD MINE.

Two large Bronze Age BARROWS stand in the garden of a house (SJ 150 766) W of the church. The western one has been damaged, but the other is untouched.

In the field just behind Lower Stables Farm, ½m. S (SJ 152 753), is an interesting group of EARTHWORKS – an Early Bronze Age barrow surrounded by a circular bank and ditch against which abuts a low bank believed to be part of Offa's Dyke. The barrow, which was excavated by Sir Cyril Fox in 1925 (*Archaeologia Cambrensis*, vol. 81, 1926, pp. 48 ff.), can be quite easily recognized from the road. It covered a large grave pit surrounded by an outer ditch. Three later cremation burials had been dug into the mound. Minor excavations failed to reveal the date or purpose of the circle, to which the barrow is not central. The area enclosed is *c*.330ft across, but the bank and the ditch outside it are quite slight (best preserved on the eastern side). It is by no means certain that it is contemporary with the barrow but it is certainly earlier than the linear bank. Recent work on the Dark Age dyke system in

Clwyd has shown that Offa's Dyke cannot be traced N of
Treuddyn, but the frontier further E, Wat's Dyke, does reach
the sea, running below Halkyn Mountain to Holywell and
Basingwerk.

There were several Bronze Age BARROWS on this plateau
but most of them have been badly damaged by ploughing.
One can still be recognized from the road at SJ 153 743.

FFRIDD Y GARREG WEN, I m. WSW (SJ 136 759). A small but
prominent barrow in the centre of a large field, to the S of the
main road. It was excavated in 1923, when several cremation
burials and a small dagger and a whetstone were found. The
mound had been enlarged on two occasions to accommodate
the extra burials.

In a wood SSE from Ffridd y Garreg Wen is the earthwork
enclosure called BWRDD Y RHYFEL.

A fine BARROW, on the top of a hill (SJ 112 758), stands in the
corner of the field behind the Travellers' Inn, 2½ m. WSW of
Gorsedd. It can be easily seen from the main road. Another
barrow in this area, PANT Y DULAITH, was excavated in the
1950s, when a complex internal structure of stake and stone
circles was revealed beneath the mound. This monument can
no longer be seen.

GREDINGTON see HANMER

GREENFIELD

2070

BASINGWERK ABBEY. Founded as a house of the French Savigniac order, probably by Ranulf II, Earl of Chester, in
1131. It seems that the first building assigned to the monks
was a chapel at the Castle of Basingwerk, near Bagillt (q.v.),
but that the present site had been adopted when in 1157 the
foundation became affiliated to the Cistercian Abbey of Build-
was in Shropshire.

The CHURCH, early C13, had a seven-bay nave and a characteristic Cistercian E end of transepts, each with a pair of E
chapels, and aisleless presbytery. The nave S and W walls
stand a few feet high, but there is more of the S transept W
wall, together with the SW crossing pier. Double-chamfered
arch between transept and aisle, triple-corbelled springing for
the W crossing arch, and a semicircular respond of the nave
arcade. Higher up, the line of the aisle roof, and a single
lancet. Until its collapse in 1901, the transept gable contained
three lancets. The doorway to the cloisters, at the E end of
the S aisle, had, on its outer side, three orders of detached
shafts.

CONVENTUAL BUILDINGS. The E range, though retaining
older masonry, is contemporary with the church in its architectural features. Next to the S transept was the sacristy. Then

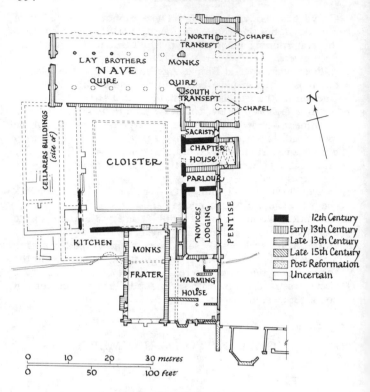

Greenfield,
Basingwerk Abbey, plan
(Department of the Environment)

came the chapter house. Its E end, forming an early C13 extension to a C12 chamber, had two bays of rib vaulting, and is separated off by a pair of semicircular arches, with central octagonal column and semi-octagonal responds. S again was the parlour, its doorway with two orders of detached shafts. Next followed the novices' lodging, a long room extending beyond the S walk of the cloister. Lancets and a doorway in the E wall. Three lancets above belonged to the dorter, which extended over the E range. The warming house, yet further S, was a mid-C13 addition, and the change of build is seen at the SE corner of the novices' lodging. Originally vaulted in four by two bays. Its column bases, with E.E. waterholding moulds, were central prior to a C15 remodelling, which included the building of a fireplace on the S. Mid- or late C13 is the REFECTORY, belonging to the N claustral range, but with a N–S axis. The end splays of what was a group of four lofty lancets remain at the S end. Along the W wall is a set of tall openings in the form of arcading, under hoodmoulds, and having various shafts with rings and moulded caps. Three

13

arches contain lancets, another is blocked, and a group of
four, now blocked, were respectively the reader's pulpit (with
cupboard door below), a pair of lancets belonging to its staircase, and the doorway giving access to the stair. Wall cupboard at N end of E wall, and opposite it a hatch which communicated with the kitchen. Nothing of the latter or of the W
range is to be seen. At the angle of the S and E ranges is the
base of the day stair.

Post-Reformation buildings extending E may occupy the
INFIRMARY site.

HOLY TRINITY, Basingwerk Avenue. 1870–1 by *Ewan Christian*. Lancets and plate tracery. An aisle on the S only. Christian intended an apsidal chancel and a SE vestry, but the
chancel as built, by *Douglas*, 1910–11, is simpler. Similar in
style to the nave, but neater and better.

HOLYWELL (later HOLYWELL JUNCTION) STATION (closed),
¼ m. N of the main road junction. Of 1847–8, and the best
remaining of *Francis Thompson*'s Italianate brick and stone

Greenfield,
Holywell (later Holywell Junction) Railway Station, 1847–8
(*Illustrated London News*, 13, 1848)

stations for the Chester and Holyhead Railway. Professor
Hitchcock compared its elegance with that of the villas by
Persius at Potsdam. Compact two-storey central block with
three-bay entrance and platform fronts, their ground-floor

openings round-headed. Single-storey side wings, originally with little tower-like pavilions at the four corners, though those on the entrance front have gone. The platform pair remain, but the canopy which spanned between them is missing. The stone dressings display some fine detailing, e.g. paterae on the frieze of the main block.

THE LODGE (or VALLEY LODGE), Greenfield Road. Late C18 or early C19. Five bays plus single-storey wings. Large and good fanlight.

PLAS-Y-MORFA, NW of the main road junction. Early C19, stone-built, with Gothic windows. Fanlight, door with octagonal panels, and a Victorian porch. Gable end returns, but otherwise the low-pitched roofs are hipped, as are those of the STABLES.

The once copious flow from St Winefride's Well (*see* Holywell) led to the establishment of water-powered industry in the GREENFIELD VALLEY, immediately below. As a development from the local lead mines Holywell had, in the second half of the C18, become an important centre of metallurgical industry, with lead and copper smelting and manufacture, and the making of brass and wire. Pennant referred also to paper and snuff mills, and Dr Johnson, on his visit with Mrs Thrale in 1774, counted nineteen works within two miles of the well. In 1777 textile manufacture was introduced by John Smalley, a former associate of Arkwright, and by 1790 four cotton mills had been built. They were impressive buildings. One was of seventeen bays and six storeys, with a pediment and cupola. Nothing remains of all this enterprise except a succession of DAMS and RESERVOIRS, a few fragmentary survivals, and the more substantial ruins of the BATTERY WORKS, below the B road, ¾ m. SW of the main road junction. This was a copper and brass works, and the structures include part of a metal shearing shop, with steep brick pediment, and a later engine house built in front. Also several wheelpits.

GREENFIELD HALL has been demolished. It was late C17 or early C18, of five bays and three storeys, and with hipped roof and modillion cornice.

GRONANT *see* TALACRE

GWAUNYSGOR

A high-up village, close to Prestatyn, but seeming remote.

ST MARY. A single chamber, remodelled and probably extended E in the C15. Perp are the three-light E window, with cusping and panel tracery, and the easternmost S window. Former N doorway earlier, its pointed arch of rubble voussoirs. Restorers have been kind, permitting the interior plastering to remain. In 1931 *Harold Hughes* exposed the roof –

arched-braced, with struts above the collar. Barrel-vaulted s porch and a round-arched s doorway. The arch has been contracted by the insertion of a timber-framed doorway, with straight-sided pointed head and curious incised carving in the spandrels. Now free-standing within the arch, but the inter-mediate space was formerly built up. C16 or C17 dates may be ascribed to porch, arch and timberwork. – FONT. Early C13. Square bowl, circular inside. Pattern of lobes and inter-secting stalks and, at one corner, a head. Five supporting shafts have been renewed, but the characteristically E.E. waterholding base mould is original. – ALTAR TABLE. Dated 1637. – SEPULCHRAL SLABS. An early C14 incised slab. Cross with circular head enclosing a pattern of four smaller circles. A sword to the r. of the shaft. – Fragment of another, of similar date. – Many fragments of further cross slabs, C13 to early C14, set in window sills, and one in the porch. – In the SW corner of the churchyard a former SUNDIAL, dated 1663, but possibly the shaft of an earlier cross.

KING CHARLES'S BOWLING GREEN, Bryn Llwyn (SJ 072 815), is one of several rounded summits along the western edge of the limestone plateau. On the eastward sloping front, away from the strong prevailing winds, evidence of Neolithic occupation has been found. The excavator in 1913 claimed that banks across the area were of this ancient date, but later work showed these to have been much more recent. They can still be recognized between the modern hedge and a line of small quarry pits. There is a small but prominent Bronze Age BARROW on the very top of the hill. A cremation burial was found beneath it.

ST ELMO'S SUMMERHOUSE (SJ 085 818) is now no more than a pile of broken brick but its foundations stand on what is almost certainly a Bronze Age BARROW, set in a magnificent position on the very top of the hill. The ditch and bank and stone revetting belong to the summerhouse and the stone with the enigmatic inscription 'Alafs Poor Frisk 1797' might be the tombstone of a dog. In the saddle just below St Elmo's Summerhouse is a very large, smooth-profiled BARROW which appears to be undisturbed. Both these mounds can be seen on the horizon from many miles around.

GWERNAFFIELD

2060

HOLY TRINITY. 1871–2 by *David Walker*. Broad nave and chancel. Square bellcote set back from the W gable, rising into a circular spirelet. N and S windows consist of lancets, with quatrefoils in bar tracery above. E window inserted 1876. The previous one, with intersecting tracery and reused from a predecessor church of 1838, was then moved to the W. It has STAINED GLASS of 1850, with geometrical patterns and a grisaille ground. – ENCAUSTIC TILES in the chancel by *Malkin, Edge & Co.* – MONUMENT. John and Jane, children

of Thomas Lloyd. They died within a few days of each other, and a relief shows them naked, on a bed, with hovering angel above. Signed by the younger *Theed* in Rome, 1848. A later inscription has been interpolated, and the surround perhaps altered. – Churchyard GATES. From the ironwork made *c.*1726 and 1732 for the interior of Mold church (q.v.).
The church of 1838 was by the unaccomplished *John Lloyd*. His SCHOOL, immediately N, survives.

GWESPYR *see* TALACRE

GWYSANEY *see* MOLD, p. 399

4040
HALGHTON*

HALGHTON HALL. Of brick with stone dressings, and built in 1662. Clearly the house was intended to be of five bays, with a central entrance, plus two cross wings projecting to a depth of two bays. The E (right-hand) wing and the easternmost bay of the centre are missing, and were probably never built. Two-light mullioned windows, those of the ground floor with transoms. The gable end of the W wing is coped and finialed and its windows are of three lights – the lower one with arched motifs to the centre light and with side volutes which are quite advanced for vernacular work of the date. In contrast, the doorcase, very large and with Doric pilasters, is more crudely Jacobean in style. Interior much altered, with a mezzanine inserted at an early date. The room into which the entrance led had a plaster ceiling in four compartments, with strapwork, still visible in the mezzanine. Lateral chimney to a separate room. The staircase, altered, has both flat and turned balusters.
There is neither church nor village. The following are listed in relation to Halghton Hall.
HALGHTON LANE FARM, $\frac{3}{4}$m. E. A dated example of simple vernacular work – 1780.
PEARTREE FARM, $1\frac{1}{8}$m. ESE. Brick-nogged, and unusual for the region in that the brick remains unpainted. Of T-plan, with an eye to Renaissance order. Strictly it is cruciform, for a chimneybreast, with two massive brick stacks, forms a further arm. The roofs have at some stage been reduced in pitch. Rescued from dereliction in a restoration of 1979–80 by *Robert B. Heaton*.
THE DUKES, $1\frac{5}{8}$m. SE. Also brick-nogged and unpainted.

* In Maelor Saesneg.

THE BRYN, 1¼m. SSE. Two separate houses, i.e. unit system, later joined together as one. The main building was re-modelled as an C18 double pile, but retains a timber-framed gable end (and the trusses and cusped wind-braces of a first-floor room which was open to the roof. P. Smith, DOE). The later, smaller dwelling is timber-framed, with brick nogging. Linking portion altered in the 1960s.

Finally, two houses at Horseman's Green, 2m. ESE. WEST VIEW, at the SW end of the hamlet, is late C18 vernacular classical, of brick, with casements, small pediment, and a pediment hood over a Venetian doorcase. HORSEMAN'S GREEN FARM, towards the main road, is faced in C17 brick (but retains fragments of a C14 timber-framed hall house. They include a spere truss with arched-bracing and with cusped members above the collar, and the upper-end parti-tion truss. Arched-braced trusses in a later N wing. P. Smith, DOE). Part of a MOAT.

THE BUCK. See Tallarn Green.

HALKYN / HELYGAIN 2070

HALKYN CASTLE. Halkyn, with its lead mines, formed an im-portant part of the Grosvenors' Flintshire estate. (The rich mineral resources of Halkyn Mountain had been worked since Roman times.) The house was built 1824-c.1827 by *John Buckler* for the second Earl Grosvenor (later first Marquess of Westminster). As first designed, it was a small specimen of a basically symmetrical (i.e. classically conceived) early C19 castellated mansion. In execution, it was much simplified, with a concentration of Tudor Gothic elements being diluted: e.g. straight parapets were substituted for battlements, and the lights of the mullioned and transomed windows have straight heads, instead of being arched or shaped. On the other hand, corner turrets – some polygonal, some castellated and some ogee – did materialize. Strict symmetry was eschewed by a battlemented and polygonal tower, with stair turret, and the main front is extended leftwards by the STA-BLES with their four-centred entrance arch. Further irregu-larity came in 1886, when *Douglas & Fordham* added a wing containing a new drawing room at the right-hand end of the main front. This was for the first Duke of Westminster, and the enlargement was accompanied by alterations to windows of the hitherto symmetrical entrance front on the right-hand return. Interior features by *Douglas & Fordham*, other than those of the new wing itself, include the chimneypiece in the dining room and the staircase.

Two early C19 castellated ENTRANCE LODGES.

ST MARY. Rebuilt 1877-8 by *Douglas* at the expense of the 100 Duke of Westminster; one of the best Victorian churches in Clwyd. Consisting of chancel, four-bay nave, S porch, N aisle and NE tower, it is not large, but was a costly and thorough job of ashlar inside and out. With some Geometrical tracery, the style is predominantly that of *c.*1300, but by no means slavishly so. The tower, in particular, seeks to be original, and not only in its siting. Strong and confident, it is (despite its Early Dec tracery) of sensitive Neo-Perp character, with a quatrefoil frieze and a pyramid roof recessed behind battlements. Piquantly placed slits and quatrefoils light the vice in its NW turret. On the S of the chancel six cusped lancets form a continuous arcade, with free-standing shafts internally. Sumptuous are deep and generous mouldings and the use of polished granite. Nice balance between windows of three lights in the nave and two in the aisle. Arched-braced nave roof. That of the chancel is boarded. – FURNISHINGS display Douglas's facility for joinery detail in a style composed of elements from Late Gothic (traceried panels etc.), C17 furniture (unmitred mouldings) and the Nesfieldian pies and sunflower motifs of Late Victorian aestheticism. – STAINED GLASS. A complete set by *Heaton, Butler & Bayne*. – SCULPTURE. Reset in a S buttress is a Crucifixion panel, with figures of the Virgin and St John, the whole under a cinquefoil canopy and on an angel corbel. Doubtless from a C14 CHURCHYARD CROSS.

In the village, ESTATE HOUSING and the BRITANNIA INN, with labels.

SCHOOL, opposite the church. Built 1849, but enlarged and refronted 1898–9, almost certainly by *Douglas & Minshull*.

THE OLD HALL, ⅛m. W of the church. Its five-bay rendered front, with two-column porch, may be of *c.*1910. To its NW, HALKYN OLD HALL is also of five bays but of exposed rubble walling, with some early C19 detail. Behind the two houses is a castellated FOLLY, with screen wall, a pair of corner turrets and a lean-to structure behind.

THE OLD RECTORY, ⅜m. NNW. Built 1885, and by Douglas's former pupil *Edward Ould* of *Grayson & Ould*, at the expense of the Duke of Westminster. Stone-faced ground storey. Norman Shavian tile-hanging and white-painted casements above. The entrance front is asymmetrically grouped.

SION CHAPEL, Pentre Halkyn, ⅞m. NW. Built 1839. Longitudinal elevation with two round-headed windows and, originally, a door either end. One door is blocked, indicating internal rearrangement.

LYGAN-Y-WERN, Pentre Halkyn, 1m. NNW. An early or mid-C18 double pile, split-level in section, with the rear rooms at half-landing level. Five-bay front of two and a half storeys, now rendered. C19 additions include labels, finialed kneelers and a reeded doorcase. Staircase with dado, swept rail and fluted columnar balusters. Ornamented stair ends. Newels of four clustered balusters. Brick DOVECOTE with pyramid roof.

BRYN EITHIN, Pant-y-Gof, ¾m. S. 1974 by *Malcolm Edwards* for himself. A sloping site, and the house is planned on different levels and has separate and neatly articulated monopitch roofs. The principal living room, at the highest point, extends across the garage and entrance at the front. Black window frames contrast with white concrete block walling.

HANMER*

4030

ST CHAD. Late Perp, and Cheshire-like. Broad battlemented aisles, with gargoyles and grotesques. Four-centred windows of four lights (five at the E ends) with panel tracery above transoms, and cusping. No clerestory. Tall w tower with buttresses below the belfry stage, paired two-light bell openings, and gargoyles. Springers inside show that vaulting was intended. The chancel was built in 1720, and has classical detail and round-headed side windows. It also has a battlemented parapet, and this carries the date 1720, so the pointed E window may be of this time, even if the tracery must be later. In 1889 the church was burnt, and little more than the tower and outer walls remained. Restoration by *Bodley & Garner* was completed in 1892, though the chancel remained open to the sky until restored by *Caröe* in 1936. The s porch is a post-fire rebuild, as are the arcades, with broad four-centred arches on clustered shafts. The capitals are a Bodleyesque refinement of what existed previously. Panelled aisle roofs are correct reproductions, and there was precedent for the design of the PARCLOSE SCREENS. These are, however, uniform and mechanical, and lack the merits either of full historical authenticity or of the zest of original Bodley work. – RAILS. 1936, in stylized Arts and Crafts manner. – STAINED GLASS. E window by *Shrigley & Hunt*, 1936. – By *Kempe* the s aisle E and easternmost, 1901; also N aisle westernmost, 1908. – CHANDELIERS. One which was given to Bangor church in 1727. Two six-branch tiers. Not hung. – Also an elaborate Victorian piece. – Many MONUMENTS perished in the fire. Much damaged is that by the younger *Bacon*, 1806, to Lloyd, Lord Kenyon. He is seated in his robes of Lord Chief Justice, accompanied by figures of Faith and Justice. – CHURCHYARD CROSS. Slender octagonal shaft on a stepped base. The head is worn, but a Crucifixion on the w and a Virgin and Child on the E may be discerned. Also figures (bishops?) at the ends. – CHURCHYARD GATES. The former chancel gates and screen, presumably of 1720, and attributable to *Robert Davies*.
The village stands beside Hanmer Mere, between which and the church is the WAR MEMORIAL, designed in 1919 by *Sir Giles Gilbert Scott*. E of the church, the early C18 brick VICARAGE, and to the SE, close to the mere, MAGPIE COTTAGE, thatched and brick-nogged.
To the sw, beyond the mere, is the park of GREDINGTON. The main block of the previous house was by *Thomas Harrison*, 1808-11, for the second Lord Kenyon. Its w front was of

*In Maelor Saesneg.

seven bays, the middle three emphasized by paired Ionic columns to the ground storey and panelled pilaster strips above. The E (entrance) front, partly of brick, had a four-column Doric porch and two segmental bows. That on the l. belonged to work of 1785 for Lloyd, first Baron Kenyon and Lord Chief Justice. A service wing may have been partly C 17. Much was done in the time of the fourth Lord Kenyon (succeeded 1869 as a minor), including work by *H. T. Hare*, 1916; but the house was demolished by the fifth Baron, in part *c*.1958, the remainder *c*.1980.

Brick STABLES, round three sides of a court, survive.* A cupola and pedimented entrance arch are of 1886. In the centre of the open fourth side, a square DOVECOTE with pyramid roof and cupola.

THE CUMBERS, ¾m. WSW. 1887–8 by *Lockwood*.‡ Brick, with sashes, but also with half-timbered gables.

WERN, ¾m. WNW. Some brick nogging. (Two cruck trusses and a staircase with flat, shaped balusters and finialed newels. DOE)

HANMER HALL, ½m. ENE. A large brick farmhouse, being a remodelling by *William Baker*, 1756, for Humphrey Hanmer of Bettisfield. Roof behind parapets, and the whole so starkly rectangular as to have a C20 look. U-plan, open to the E. Three-bay S and W fronts, the latter with pilastered and segmental-pedimented doorcase. On the N, three two-light mullioned windows. Extensive Georgian FARM BUILDINGS, much altered.

CROXTON, 1m. NNE. Georgian vernacular, dated 1793. Three bays, two and a half storeys, and a classical doorcase. Broad casements.

A large Bronze Age BARROW may be seen on the summit of a low hill, 1m. NE (SJ 465 409). Digging during the Second World War revealed evidence of a stone kerb.

3060   HAWARDEN / PENARLÂG

HAWARDEN CASTLE

The castle of which the ruins are known as Hawarden Old Castle was in 1453 granted to Sir Thomas Stanley. It formed part of the property of the Earl of Derby sequestrated following the Civil War, and in 1653 was sold to John Glynne, serjeant-at-law. His son was created a baronet, and Sir John Glynne, sixth Baronet, not only inherited the castle but acquired by marriage the neighbouring Broadlane Hall. This he rebuilt, *c*.1750–7. The builder, and possibly the designer also, was the

---

* According to Lewis, they date from the Lord Chief Justice's time, but Lord Kenyon, to whom I am indebted for information on the house, ascribes them to the 1808–11 period.
‡ Information from Lord Kenyon.

elder *Samuel Turner* of Whitchurch. *Joseph Turner*, believed to have been his nephew, may also have been involved. The new house, of brick, with stone dressings, had two side pavilions (or was to have had them) and a main block of three storeys, seven bays and a three-bay pediment. It forms the nucleus of the present building. Nothing of this is immediately obvious externally, for enlargements and recasing were carried out in castellated style by *Thomas Cundy*, 1809–10, for Sir Stephen Richard Glynne,* a young Regency man of romantic tastes who renamed the house Hawarden Castle. In his son, also Stephen Richard, interest in the Middle Ages took a more serious and scholarly turn, for he was Sir Stephen Glynne, the ecclesiologist and antiquary. This Sir Stephen's sister married W. E. Gladstone, who, with the help of other members of the family, made successful efforts to save the estate from the consequences of the unworldly baronet's financial imprudence. Hawarden became the Prime Minister's home, and after Sir Stephen's death it passed to him and his descendants.

Cundy transformed the EXTERIOR of the Palladian house with stone veneer, mullioned windows, labels and battlements. On the s (then entrance) front, the centre (corresponding with the position of the pediment) was raised and given sham machicolations, and a two-storey canted bay was added to the two right-hand bays, and a circular turret to the left-hand (i.e. sw) corner. The façade was extended to the r. by an irregular service wing with octagonal turret and to the l. by a w wing, containing a library, with Gothic windows and a canted bay on its w return. Cundy also provided a porch, which was removed when the entrance was transferred to the N in 1830 – a change for which *Blore* may have been responsible. An addition in the NW corner, in the angle between the C18 house and Cundy's w wing, is of the mid-1860s by *George Shaw* of Saddleworth. Although its windows are of dour and serious Gothic, it has a varied and castellated skyline. It contains Gladstone's study (the 'Temple of Peace'); a stone-roofed octagonal strongroom, by *Douglas & Fordham*, was built out to the N, 1887–8, to house his papers. Despite turrets and a canted bay, the N front of the C18 house is more tamely castellated than the s. Entrance is by a *Douglas & Fordham* porch with internal stairs, built in 1889 to commemorate Mr and Mrs Gladstone's golden wedding. It stands in front of a porch of 1830, beyond the Gothic vaulting of which the INTERIORS are classical. They include excellent work of the 1750s, with carving by *Phillips* and plasterwork by Oliver, presumably the *Thomas Oliver* who worked at Chirk Castle. Of this period is the staircase. Cantilevered stone steps with scrolled ends. Swept rail and iron balusters, those on alternate steps with scrollwork. The doorcases of the staircase hall have lugged architraves and enriched mouldings, and are conser-

89

* A scheme for castellation by *Nash*, 1807, was abandoned.

vative for their date compared with rococo swags above them.
70 At landing level, ornament is yet freer and more elaborate,
both on the ceiling and in and around wall panels. The landing chimneypiece is fairly staid in its lugged and open-pedi-
mented overmantel and its fireplace surround, both with side
volutes, but it is enlivened by delightful rococo detail. Back
on the ground floor, the drawing room in the SW corner of
the C18 house has a rococo ceiling and two doorcases by
Cundy with honeysuckle friezes. One was adapted as a china
cabinet by *H. S. Goodhart-Rendel*, and the other communi-
cates with the library in *Cundy*'s W wing – a large room
decorated in white and gold and with a screen of fluted Ionic
columns either end. Severely Grecian tops to the bookcases.
Cundy remodelled the dining room in the SE corner of the
C18 house and gave it an Ionic screen of scagliola columns.

Immediately E of the house is a GATEWAY with four-
centred arch and a pair of circular turrets. It is attributed to
John Buckler. Near to it is a house still known as BROAD-
LANE, in which Mrs Gladstone conducted an orphanage. (It
retains a Jacobean dog-leg staircase, with flat, shaped balusters and square, finialed newels. DOE) It was remodelled in
1757 and has a five-bay two-storey front with rusticated
lintels. A clock in its three-bay pediment and a cupola give
it a stable-like appearance, but separate pedimented brick
STABLES exist. Two cottages known as DIGLANE used to
be bakehouse and brewhouse.

TEA HOUSE, at the SW corner of the lawn. A summerhouse
with Gothic glazing, designed by *Goodhart-Rendel*, who carried out much work for the Hawarden estate, as well as receiving personal commissions from the Gladstone family, to
whom he was related.*

Until it was diverted in 1804, the Chester road ran between
the house and the Old Castle, passing through a fosse which
had formed part of the defences. In 1771 an elegant little
BRIDGE was built to span it. This still remains, with segmental arch and moulded archivolt, over which the parapet gently
rises.

HAWARDEN OLD CASTLE. A Norman castle was established
in the time of Hugh Lupus, Earl of Chester, on the site of an
earlier settlement. The present buildings replace a castle destroyed by Llywelyn the Last in 1265, and construction was
probably in hand when, in 1282, Llywelyn's brother Dafydd
launched his rising with an attack on Hawarden. Since this
was one of the lordship castles with affinities with the royal
works, Master *James of St George* is likely to have had something to do with it. A large mound stands in a concentric
enclosure formed on a steeply sloping site, by a ditch and

---

* Sir William Gladstone thinks that he was a nephew of Maud Ernestine Rendel, Lady Gladstone, daughter-in-law of W. E. Gladstone and daughter of his
friend Lord Rendel. Maud Rendel's husband, Henry Neville Gladstone, first
Baron Gladstone, lived at Hawarden Castle 1920–35, and it may be assumed that
the *Goodhart-Rendel* works there date from those years.

double banks. Large ditches on the N and E (the latter the one through which the Chester road ran) formed outer defences. The motte is crowned by a circular two-storey tower or KEEP, on the E of which curtain walls enclosed a WARD of irregular plan. Although the concept of a keep had by the late C13 been superseded, the building of one here would have been dictated by the existing earthworks. Portcullis grooves at its entrance. On the upper storey the central room is octagonal, and a mural chamber provides a small CHAPEL with PISCINA and cinquefoil-headed doorway. A wall passage extending round most of the circumference looks out in the directions not protected by the ward. Of the CURTAIN, the portion climbing the motte to meet the keep on the NE remains, as do sections on the E side of the ward, where the GREAT HALL abutted. Two lofty cusped lancets belonged to the hall, corbels for the floor and roof of which, and a moulded door jamb, may also be seen. At the foot of the motte and again outside the E curtain are fragments of buildings apparently of later date. Also later are the puzzling arrangements extending NE between the N and E outer ditches and the site of a BARBICAN. Axial layout, executed in ashlar, and thought to have been a subsidiary route below the main form of access. From the direction of the ward, a narrow staircase leads down between enclosing walls to a deep (drawbridge?) pit. Across this is a small chamber with outer doorways to l. and r., and beyond is a stair rising into the barbican site.

After two sieges in the Civil War, the castle was dismantled on Parliamentary orders in 1647. A ready-made and genuine ruin on an elevated site close to his house must have been valued by the elder Sir Stephen as a great picturesque asset. It was doubtless he who increased the romantic appeal by adding an irregular skyline where previously the top of the keep had been straight. Restoration was carried out in the 1860s by *George Shaw* and after the Great War by *R. S. Weir*.

SIR JOHN'S LODGE, in the park, ½m. SW of the house. A pair of mid-C18 lodges, one of which has been raised in height. Rusticated GATEPIERS.

For the ENTRANCE GATE in the village, *see* p. 369.

WYNT LODGE, ¼m. NW of the house where, because of its diversion in 1804, the main road takes a sharp turn. By *Goodhart-Rendel*, completed 1923. Of ashlar, with a steep roof. A half-round staircase turret has a window with Gothic glazing. GLYNNE COTTAGE, nearby, is a fair-sized house, mysterious in its origins but probably built for a Glynne spinster. Ground storey of brick. Half-timber above, with carved bressumer and bargeboards. On the entrance front is a tower, with Douglas-like pyramid roof. The house is likely to be of the 1860s, for, despite the style and materials, the detailing looks Mid- rather than Late Victorian.*

---

* I am indebted to Sir William Gladstone, present and seventh Baronet, for much help in connection with Hawarden Castle.

THE VILLAGE

ST DEINIOL. Interest and importance are largely C19 and early
C20, not least as a result of Gladstone associations.

Restored by *James Harrison*, *c.*1855-6. After being burnt
in 1857 (with some woodwork and stained glass surviving at
the E end), restoration was entrusted to *Sir Gilbert Scott*, and
was completed 1859. The s porch is his. Perp s and w doorways have been totally renewed, possibly by Scott. The Dec
character of all the windows seems to date only from the
1850s. Most of them are probably by Scott, but reticulation
at the w end of the aisles and in the chancel s aisle (the so-
called Whitley Chancel) may be ascribed to *Harrison*. A short
lead-covered spire, originally with hipped lucarnes, was
added to the Perp tower by *Scott*. Though central, it is not
a crossing tower, for there are no transepts, and it was inserted into the easternmost bay of the nave, in front of a Dec
chancel arch. Pairs of transomed bell openings. The Perp N,
s and w tower arches remain, with strainer arches spanning
the aisles in line with the latter. The arches of the nave arcades are apparently Dec, though all the piers, including
those of the tower, are by *Scott*. Also his are the nave corbels.
Above the chancel arch is the line of a steep pre-tower roof
and, on the E side, a low-pitched (i.e. Perp) roof-line. The
position of its predecessor is visible externally. Courses of
plain rounded corbelling to the chancel s wall, probably C13,
are now enclosed within the chancel aisle. Ogee PISCINA, *ex
situ*, at E end of N aisle. Chancel SEDILIA of 1846, but said to
be a restoration of an E.E. original. By *Douglas & Fordham*,
1896, is a PORCH to the chancel aisle, in memory of W.H.
Gladstone, son of the Prime Minister. Its gable contains a
kneeling angel in relief, either side of a figure in a canopied
niche.* NE VESTRIES by *Douglas & Minshull*, 1908-9.

At the E end of the N aisle is the small GLADSTONE ME-
MORIAL CHAPEL. By *Douglas & Minshull*, 1901-3. Ashlar-
lined and rib-vaulted, and with a three-sided apse, it was
102 built to receive the MONUMENT to William Ewart Gladstone
and his wife Catherine. By *Sir William Richmond*, and completed 1906, this is of luxuriant Arts and Crafts character,
with the variations in materials typical of the 'New Sculpture'
of the turn of the century. Literary and other references, as
well as Christian symbolism. Recumbent effigies in Carrara
marble, with a Crucifix resting between them. At their heads
is a canopy of two winged prows (a Homeric allusion) formed
by an angel. The tomb-chest base, classical in detail, is of a
different marble, and has figures and oval relief panels in
silvered bronze. The altar CROSS and CANDLESTICKS of the
chapel are also by *Richmond*, and the STAINED GLASS was
made to his design by *James Powell & Sons*.

* Canopied NICHE of s porch probably by the same and also 1896. Of 1901
and probably by *Douglas & Minshull*, the SCULPTURAL PANELS in Gothic framing under the E window, and CANOPIED NICHE of N porch. *Arthur Walker* is
recorded as the sculptor of the STATUE in the latter.

Of the other FURNISHINGS of the church, the FONT is by *Scott*, dating from the time of his restoration. - REREDOS. Of 1873 and (according to Mr Howell) also by *Scott*. A dramatic Last Supper behind a tripartite arcade, and with canopy work above. - ROOD BEAM. By *Sir Giles Gilbert Scott*, 1915-16. - A heraldic BENCH END of the first half of the C16 has carving of markedly Renaissance feel, free and flowing. Pelican in the poppyhead. It has been worked in as the E end of a CLERGY STALL made by *Harry Hems*, with a new W bench end made to match. - CHOIR STALLS are of *James Harrison*'s 1855-7 restoration and survived the fire. - Of many fittings for which *H. S. Goodhart-Rendel* made designs, the only one executed is the PULPIT, in a simplified Wren style, c.1951. - Except for two fragments at the E end, WALL PAINTINGS, in the chancel S aisle by *Edward Frampton*, 1884, have disappeared. - STAINED GLASS. Many windows are Glynne and Gladstone memorials. In the chancel aisle, the E (1859) and S windows (one 1852 and two with dates 1854) are by *Wailes*. - By *Frampton*: N aisle easternmost, 1896, given by the Anglo-Armenian Society in tribute to Gladstone; N aisle centre, commemorating Frampton's own wife †1885; N aisle W; S aisle easternmost, commemoration date 1904, and S aisle W, 1891. - W window. Made by *Morris & Co.*, 1898 and, in the 101 year of his death, the last stained glass ever to be designed by *Burne-Jones*. It is one of the best of his late works. A Nativity scene, with Magi, angels and shepherds. The composition, including the roof of the shed, extends across four lights. In the tracery are angels and the characteristic irregular and horizontally-emphasized leading. - By *Morris & Co.*, reusing *Burne-Jones* designs: E window, 1907, the Crucifixion adapted from a design for St Philip's (i.e. the cathedral) at Birmingham; chancel easternmost on N, 1907; chancel westernmost on N, 1908; (chancel middle on N by *Holiday*, 1908); N aisle westernmost, 1911; S aisle centre, 1911; and S aisle westernmost, 1913. - In the S porch, the eastern, by *Haswall*, and the better, western one by *Eden*, both with commemoration date of 1925.

MONUMENTS. Roger Whitley, 1722. Architectural surround, with Corinthian columns, scrollwork etc. - Sir Stephen Glynne, the antiquary, †1874. Recumbent effigy by *Noble*. Tomb recess designed by *Douglas*. (On the window sill above is a portrait roundel.) - William Henry Gladstone †1891. Alabaster and mosaic tablet by *Douglas & Fordham*. - By *Goodhart-Rendel* are tablets to the first Viscount Gladstone †1931; Gertrude Gladstone †1935, and Rev. S. E. Gladstone †1920, with a further tablet added to his widow †1931. - WAR MEMORIAL. By *D. T. Fyfe*, 1919-24. - Palimpsest BRASS. On part of what had been a larger plate (perhaps taken from a church during the Civil War) is an inscription to John Price †1684. The reverse, now displayed in a frame, carries the upper part of the figures of a man and wife, c.1630, under canopies of Jacobean character beginning to go more classically scrolly. – (PROCESSIONAL CROSS and CHURCHWARDENS' STAVES by *Bodley*.)

The CHURCHYARD may have been circular. – Inelegant baluster SUNDIAL. – SOUTH AFRICAN WAR MEMORIAL. In the form of a churchyard cross, 1901 or 1901–2, and probably by *Douglas & Minshull*. – Churchyard S GATES. By *Douglas*, 1877. – To the NW is a LYCHGATE by *Sir Herbert Baker*, 1929. Pyramid roof on ogee timber framing.*

SACRED HEART (R.C.), The Highway. 1966–7 by *Weightman & Bullen*.

ST DEINIOL'S LIBRARY was founded by W. E. Gladstone in 1895 as a place for study and a centre of Christian learning. He set up a trust and transferred some 30,000 of his own books to a temporary building on the site. After his death the present building was commenced, the library portion being erected 1899–1902 as part of the National Gladstone Memorial. It was completed by the addition of hostel accommodation, 1904–6, at the expense of the Gladstone family, and to a design different from that originally intended. The architects for both stages were *Douglas & Minshull*, and although coming late in John Douglas's career, St Deiniol's was his only commission for a major public building.

The plan is of H-form, the style a Douglas-like blend of Tudor Gothic and Jacobean, executed in warm Runcorn sandstone and immaculately detailed. The main (S) front is long and spreading, with a storeyed central porch, and is asymmetrical in all but its basic massing. The scale, i.e. the size of the parts, is deceptively small. All that part to the E of the porch (i.e. to the r. of and excluding it) is the second, residential building phase. The remainder, constituting the initial portion, is more richly treated, with battlemented parapets and some pinnacles as well as with variety introduced into the shaped heads of window lights. Over the porch is a canopied niche, and another occurs between a pair of oriels in the gable end of the W cross wing. The W elevation of the wing has a storeyed porch with oriel and staircase turret. This wing contains the LIBRARY itself. Its five-bay interior has a complicated roof, open to the collar. With curved struts and arcade plates below tie-beam level, it is treated as that of an aisled hall, for a gallery all round the room forms two-storey aisles on the long sides. Two storeys of octagonal oak columns (not in themselves load-bearing, but with steel or iron cores) ornamented, as is the fascia of the gallery floor, with elaborate and delicate tracery, foliations etc. The balustrading of the gallery consists of sturdier ogee patterns. The Divinity Library adjoins. It is a shorter room, but similar in its construction and treatment. *Goodhart-Rendel* made designs for decorating and fitting up the chapel in the E wing, but only simple STALLS seem to have been executed.

---

* I am most grateful to Mr Donald R. Buttress for assistance, comments and advice in connection with this church.

C20 extensions have been made to both Library and hostel.

A WARDEN'S LODGE was built near the S front in 1971. In its relationship to the main building it is objectionable in massing, scale and materials. Douglas deserved greater sympathy and respect

The MONUMENT in front of the Library is one of three commissioned by the National Gladstone Memorial Committee in 1910 and intended for erection respectively in London, Edinburgh and Dublin, the latter, by *John Hughes*, as the Irish National Memorial to Gladstone. This is the one now at Hawarden, for the Dublin City Council refused to accept it, and, having been completed in 1923, it was placed on the present site in 1925. Bronze figure of Gladstone on a tall stone pedestal which has Renaissance ornament and a Doric column at each of the four corners. Four attendant allegorical figures.

THE OLD RECTORY, Rectory Lane, is a plain brick building of several dates, now housing the Clwyd County Record Office and a branch library. On the E front is first a long Neo-Georgian range of 1927, added when the house was used as a college. Next is a mid-C18 canted bay, added to the E return of a late C17 or early C18 block, the main front of which faced S. Then comes a partly two- and partly three-storey portion dating from the rectorship of Sir Stephen Glynne in the 1770s.* Windows were altered and the parapet raised in height in connection with the making of strongrooms, 1958, for the then Flintshire Record Office. Internal alterations and substantial additions had been made in 1814, and the remainder of the E front is of this date. The work included a *porte cochère* on the W and the main staircase; it is stark, sparse and amateurish, suggesting that the rector, *George Neville*, may have been his own architect.

To the E, adjoining the boundary wall, is an ICEHOUSE.

At the road junction in the centre of the village is an early C19 castellated ENTRANCE GATE of Hawarden Castle, attributable to *Buckler*. It has a four-centred arch, screen walls and a pair of round turrets. A big shaped gable adjoins, being the end return of a row of stone COTTAGES which face GLYNNE WAY. The early C19 GLYNNE ARMS, opposite, also of stone, has five bays, plus another to the l., and a two-column porch. A debasedly Baroque DRINKING FOUNTAIN in the middle of the road junction commemorates the golden wedding of Mr and Mrs Gladstone in 1889. Designed and carved by *Edward Griffith*.

In RECTORY LANE, which leads N from the road junction, is KENTIGERN, ascribed to 1767. Brick, with rusticated stone lintels. Doorcase with segmental hood on consoles. W of the road junction, and itself sited at a fork, is the WAR MEMORIAL, designed by *Sir Giles Gilbert Scott*, 1919–20.

---

* At the same time the GROUNDS were planted by *Emes*.

s of the main junction is the drive to THE SUNDIAL, built for Miss Helen Gladstone, 1907. By *Douglas & Minshull*, but Douglas himself is unlikely to have had much of a hand in it. It is one of those rare instances of a building to which his name is attached which does not exhibit his characteristic detailing, either outside or in. Brick ground storey, with pebbledash and half-timber above. On the garden front are two broad canted bays under half-timbered gables.

At the far (i.e. N) end of GLYNNE WAY are the COUNCIL OFFICES, by *J. H. Davies & Sons* of Chester, 1929–31. Neo-Georgian, with the middle bay strongly emphasized. Beyond is the HOUSE OF CORRECTION or LOCK-UP. Of stone, with embayed front and, to one side, a wing with rudimentary Doric doorcase. Ascribed to the 1740s and to *Joseph Turner*, but as he was born *c.*1729, this is questionable. THE ELMS, C18 but much altered, was Turner's own house. The former HAWARDEN GYMNASIUM, with diapered brick, pebbledash and a Norman Shavian oriel, is by *T. M. Lockwood*, 1891. For GLYNNE COTTAGE and WYNT LODGE, further on, *see* p. 365.

A return to the centre of the village may be made by way of, first, ASH LANE, in order to see DEINIOL'S ASH, a picturesque jumble, $\frac{3}{8}$m. N. Of two periods, C16 and/or C17, and with subsequent alterations. Timber framing, brick-nogged, with some diagonal bracing. Two lateral chimneys. Later and of brick, and all originally with mullioned windows, are a storeyed porch, a small wing at the left-hand corner and a large rear wing with massive chimneystack. Continuing *via* GLADSTONE WAY, a SCHOOL is passed. Built 1911–12, in memory of Canon Harry Drew, Gladstone's son-in-law. With roughcast walls and broad bargeboarded gables, its C20 domestic character contrasts with a Neo-Elizabethan former SCHOOL built 1834, and converted to a MASONIC HALL, 1913.

The main road W is THE HIGHWAY, and $\frac{1}{2}$m. out is the HERBERT GLADSTONE PLAYING FIELD with a CRICKET PAVILION by *Goodhart-Rendel*, 1934, its clock cupola added 1936, but the whole ruined by a horrible later extension.

Further on is HAWARDEN HIGH SCHOOL of 1905. Red brick and terra-cotta, Tudorish. House with a half-timbered gable. Respectable new buildings added 1976–8 by *R. W. Harvey*, County Architect.

THE RED HOUSE, by *Lockwood*, for William Henry Gladstone, 1883, has been demolished. It stood near the railway station and was a simple brick-built rectangle with a hipped roof.

HELYGAIN *see* HALKYN

HIGHER KINNERTON

3060

ALL SAINTS. 1893 by *Douglas & Fordham*. Ruabon brick out-side and in. The chancel is carried up as a pyramid-spired tower, with buttresses N and S, flush with the E and W faces, as at Rossett (*see* p. 266). Polygonal E apse. This promising description is belied by diminutive scale and commonplace detail.

HOLYWELL

1070

ST WINEFRIDE'S WELL

The well marks the site of the reputed martyrdom and mira-culous restoration to life of St Winefride early in the C7. Together with the parish church it was in the possession of Basingwerk Abbey from 1240 until the Suppression, but the first recorded reference to the shrine as a place of pilgrimage occurred in 1115, and, continuing as such after the Refor-mation, it remains one to this day. The flow of water was formerly greater, but mining operations at Halkyn cut off the supply to the spring in 1917, and the well was connected up to a less prolific source. The well chamber, open to the N, has a bath in front. The well chapel forms an upper storey, though its entrance, which is on the S, is at ground level, owing to the steeply sloping site. The building is late Perp, probably very early C16. It is assigned to the patronage of Margaret, Countess of Richmond and Derby, and besides displaying Stanley emblems in the carving, possesses similar-ities of detail to the church at Mold (q.v.), with which she was associated. There are, e.g., arches into which casement moulds continue, independent of adjoining shafts and their capitals. Also, animal string courses occur below the battle-mented parapet, and there is one at intermediate level on the N. All arches are four-centred.

The CHAPEL underwent mutilation from the C18 onwards, but a lengthy restoration was completed in 1976. Nave of four bays, the three easternmost of which are aisled and clere-storied. One-bay chancel plus three-sided apse. Windows with curved-headed and ogee lights. Some transoms and panel tracery. Camberbeam roof, with arched braces. Its beams, purlins and rafters are moulded, and there are lozenge bosses and a cornice of quatrefoils. Carved corbels, both stone and timber, include figure subjects.

The vaulted WELL CHAMBER, of three by three unequal bays, lies below the aisle and the three easternmost bays of the nave of the chapel. The well basin itself is in the centre, and the three outermost bays, i.e. those below the aisle, are treated as a sort of narthex, open to the N. Of the three moulded arches of the elevation, the middle one is the widest. The other two, and that of the W return of the narthex, occur

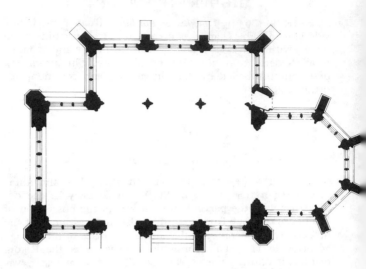

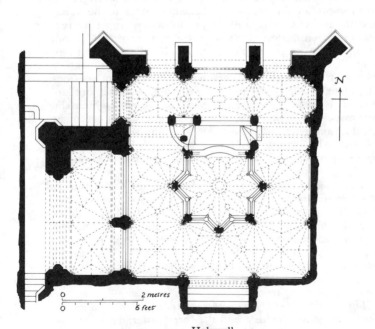

Holywell,
St Winefride's Well, probably early sixteenth century.
(*Top*) plan of chapel. (*Bottom*) plan of well chamber
(Department of the Environment)

above screen walls, which are themselves each pierced with an arch. The arches separating the narthex from the rest of the chamber are deep on plan, and virtually form three tunnel-vaulted small intermediate bays, defined on the E and W walls of the chamber by cusped panelling. Below the W bay of the chapel is a high-level vaulted recess, with a clerestory window. The basin is a rectangle with triangular projections on three sides, producing a stellar pattern, and moulded shafts rise from the points into the vaulting. Traceried screenwork, of which only fragments remain, spanned between the shafts, and the effect must have been that of Perpendicular at its most delicate and crystalline. The vaulting, with ridge ribs and tiercerons but no liernes, is rendered complicated by the stellar plan. The basin extends N into the intermediate tunnel-vaulted bay, and steps leading down into its NW corner are reached from the narthex through a curious ogee screen, from which rises a further shaft. A balancing NE feature was lost in measures taken, at an early date, to correct the weakness of transverse arches carrying the short tunnel vaults. Carved decoration includes spandrels, head-stops, bosses, and a pendant over the basin depicting scenes from St Winefride's life. At the E end of the narthex is an elaborately canopied niche. It contains a STATUE of the saint, dating from 1886, designed by *Edmund Kirby* and executed by *R. L. Boulton* of Cheltenham. (VH)

CHURCHES

ST JAMES. Near St Winefride's Well. Embraced W tower with some Perp detail, much renewed. E and (lower) N and S tower arches with wave moulds. The body of the church was rebuilt 1769–70. Two-storey elevations, with segmental windows below, round-arched above. Aedicular S doorway. Doric columns at gallery level inside. The piers below them are said to have been old work retained. This is possible, for they do not correspond with the window bays, though in their present form they must belong to the remodelling of 1884–5 by *Matthew Wyatt*. He added a classical polygonal apse, inserted Italianate tracery, and curtailed the galleries and gave them new staircases. PANELLING from BOX PEWS was reused around the walls. NW vestry of 1905–6. – PAINTED DECORATION in the apse and the spandrels of its arch is by *Louie Johnson Jones*, 1908–22. – STAINED GLASS in the apse is a War Memorial by *Clayton & Bell*. – MONUMENTS. Mutilated effigy of a priest, now placed upright, with chalice. Late C13. – Robert Edwards †1694. Cartouche. – Edward Pennant †1741 and wife Mary †1750. Three cherub heads, the background of concave profile. – Paul Panton. By *Flaxman*, 1805. Grecian tablet, like a tall sarcophagus, draped with a laurel garland. – Some C17 heraldic tablets. – Plank CHEST dated 1679.

St Winefride (R.C.), Well Street. The earliest part is by
J. J. Scoles, 1832–3. Dignified Neo-Classical w front of ashlar. Pedimented central projection, and a battered doorcase
with entablature and consoles. The projection was originally
balanced by an altar recess with lunette window, but this was
swept away when the church was extended and E transepts
were added, 1909. The side windows of the nave give an
indication of the original length. sw Lady Chapel added
1911–12 by *James Mangan* of Preston. It is of Byzantine
flavour, and the similar Shrine of St Winefride, off the NE
transept, is presumably also by him. – Large STATUE of
St Winefride by *M. Blanchart* of Ghent, 1881.* – Heavily
Neo-Grec MONUMENT to Mary (†1817) and Charles (†1834)
Sankey. By *W. Spence.* – Five BANNERS depicting saints.
Painted by *Frederick Rolfe*, Baron Corvo, during his eventful
sojourn in Holywell.‡

REHOBOTH WELSH PRESBYTERIAN (CALVINISTIC METH-
ODIST) CHAPEL, Whitford Street. A rebuilding or remodelling by *T. G. Williams* (CW), 1904, of a chapel of 1827. A
longitudinal two-storey elevation in Ruabon brick, and of
considerable scale, is set high above the street. Tall thin tower
at the right-hand end, its top stage circular and domed and
embraced by four circular pinnacles. This is balanced on the
l. by a projection with upper-level one-bay loggia. A central
gable and single-storey arcade occur between.

CEMETERY CHAPEL, Coleshill Street. 1848–9 by *Ambrose
Poynter*. Lancets and a w bellcote.

PUBLIC BUILDINGS

TOWN HALL, High Street. The MARKET HALL behind is by
R. Scrivener & Sons of Hanley, 1878, and the same firm
prepared designs for the Town Hall itself. As built, it is by
R. Lloyd Williams, c.1894–5, in High Victorian Gothic, well
behind the times. Asymmetrical, with a lively-looking turret
corbelled out over the entrance. Projecting clock.

COUNTY COURT, Halkyn Street. Built 1855, in robust Italianate. Single-storeyed. The front is divided into three by short
rusticated portions containing arched doorways. In the
middle is a Venetian window, and a pediment contains the
Royal Arms.

LLUESTY HOSPITAL, ¾m. SSE. The former workhouse. The
original building, by *John Welch*, is of 1838–40. Cruciform
plan with central octagon, the rear stroke of the cross lower
than the others. In front is a range with a three-storeyed and
pilastered ashlar façade. There is one bay on either side of
the centre, and the latter is pedimented and has three
round-headed first-floor windows and a tripartite window
above. An unusual composition, but neat and disciplined.

* Information from Mr Denis Evinson.
‡ The story is well told by A. J. A. Symons in *The Quest for Corvo.*

Former CHAPEL by *Douglas*, 1883–4. E end with five stepped lancets, the middle three, between buttresses, forming one window. Shingled flèche.

COTTAGE HOSPITAL, Pen-y-Maes Road. Built 1907–8. Nicely domestic, with red-tiled roof, timber porch, and touches of pargetting in the gables.

HOLYWELL JUNCTION STATION. *See* Greenfield.

PERAMBULATION

The cheerful and varied HIGH STREET has many Georgian fronts, albeit rendered, and also displays the regional motif of flat and shaped cement-rendered window surrounds. The HOTEL VICTORIA, presiding at the head, is Italianate, with bold detail. On the S side, and earlier, but probably still post-Georgian, is the KING'S HEAD, with the best frontage in the street, now marred by roughcast. Three bays, three storeys, with some tripartite windows, a modillion cornice, and a porch with two pairs of square piers. The ground storey is rusticated in stucco. Quoins and tripartite windows at the BELL AND ANTELOPE. Nos. 4–6, dated 1702, has vermiculated surrounds, those of the first floor with masks on the keystones. Hipped roof and moulded timber cornice. Across the street is the MIDLAND BANK (former WHITE HORSE), said to be *c*.1820 (DOE), but surely a full century earlier. Large in scale, and with hipped roof and heavy timber cornice. A side door has a reset hood on scroll-like brackets, presumably once at the front.

PANTON PLACE, off High Street to the S, consists of two-storeyed terrace cottages, dated 1816 in brickwork. The puzzling disposition of doorways is explained by the front rooms of alternate houses having been workshops or single-unit dwellings with separate access. Rehabilitated and converted for old people's homes, with a warden's house provided, by *Lingard & Associates*, 1968–70. A commendable scheme, but with unnecessarily fussy paving textures.

At the foot of High Street, CROSS STREET to the l. funnels a view of the FEATHERS, which is dated 1796 in the brickwork of the gable end. To the r. is WELL STREET, which has lost some Georgian houses and is disorderly. The brick-built, five-bay VICARAGE is of 1760. Lintels with emphasized keystones, and a pedimented doorcase. The door has octagonal panels, as have those of Nos. 44 and 46 opposite.

(Immediately W of the parish church is BRYN-Y-CASTELL, a small motte, with ditch. It was a castle built by Randle III, Earl of Chester, in 1210.)

Of housing schemes in the town by *Brian Lingard & Partners*, the best is AEL-Y-FFYNNON, a terrace in WHITFORD STREET, completed 1977.

At Pen-y-Maes, ⅜ m. E, is the stone tower of an C18 WINDMILL.

GRANGE, ¾m. WNW, was a grange of Basingwerk Abbey. A
house, now used as outbuildings, retains the arched-braced
central truss and one partition truss of an open hall. Wind-
braces. A later cross wing has a yet later Elizabethan corbelled
fireplace, and, set in a once-larger opening, a mullioned window with three arched lights.

For the industry of the GREENFIELD VALLEY *see* Greenfield.

3050   HOPE

ST CYNGAR. Double-naved, the wider N vessel being a Perp
addition. The S portion, with blocked S and priest's doorways,
shows traces of having been extended E and W. At its E end
part of an E.E. DOUBLE PISCINA (and a crypt below). A
straight-headed W window could be either Dec or Perp, but
the S roof, arched-braced, with cusped struts above the collar
and with wind-bracing, is of the latter period. So too is the
arcade, with octagonal piers and crude caps. Perp E windows,
that of the S nave of four lights, the other of five. Both have
two two-light sub-arches and panel tracery. Broad tower,
later than the N nave and slightly W of it, with a connecting
portion. Bell openings with intersecting tracery and a W window of three lights with depressed ogee heads. S and N windows of the naves of 1859. N porch replaced by a vestry 1967.
– SCREEN. Dating from *Oldrid Scott*'s restoration of 1884–5.
61   – PULPIT. C17. Jacobean style becoming classically tamed,
with Ionic pilasters and a frieze not so much of strapwork as
of free foliations. – WALL PAINTINGS. Fragments, including
texts, over the arcade. – STAINED GLASS. In the N nave E
window much of *c.*1500. Evangelists in four long tracery
lights, probably *in situ*. Inscriptions show this to have been
a Te Deum window. Remains also of scenes from the life of
the Virgin, formerly in S nave E. These include canopy work
in first, third and fifth lights, and St Anne praying in the
fifth. – MONUMENT. Sir John Trevor of Plas Teg †1629 and
wife. Kneeling effigies facing out from a mural tablet with
border of shields. Inscription on a separate tablet with strapwork surround, beginning to go scrolly. – ROYAL ARMS. In
plaster. Hanoverian and pre-1801, but with the painted date
1825. – The Perp FONT, which implies possible Stanley
patronage, is now at Llanfynydd (q.v.).

RECTORY. Simple Neo-Elizabethan, built 1851, with margin
panes in somewhat earlier C19 fashion. Diagonally placed
chimney shafts.

59 PLAS TEG, 1¾m. NW. Built probably in 1610 for Sir John
Trevor, second son of John Trevor of Trevalyn (*see* p. 287).
Inheriting his father's powerful connections, he became secretary to Lord Howard of Effingham, a post which led to a
goodly share of lucrative positions and perquisites. Entering
Parliament in 1597, he was appointed Surveyor to the Navy
the following year. In 1603 he was knighted and became

steward and receiver at Windsor Castle, keeper of the fort at
Upnor on the River Medway, and keeper of Oatlands Palace
and Park, Surrey, and he saw to it that he continued to pros-
per. His house is memorable, and utterly different from other
early C17 work in the locality. Cold and grey against the
hillside, it is like some strange exotic, which has barely taken
root, let alone been propagated, in the Flintshire soil.

A three-storeyed central block has a tower at each corner.
With ogee roofs and square cupolas, these four towers overlap
the front and rear elevations. The great hall ran through the
centre of the ground floor, from front to back, and was entered axially. Above it is the great chamber, with windows
either end. The plan, somewhat similar to one in John
Thorpe's book and with precedent in Palladio, also shows
features typical of Robert Smythson, the corner towers of
Wollaton and the transverse hall of Hardwick. The latter feature occurs also at, e.g., Charlton House, Greenwich, of 1607,
but is a rarity. So sophisticated a scheme must have emanated
from the court circles in which Trevor moved, and it is probable that a plan was provided by some official in the Royal
Works, with which he was connected through his Windsor
and Oatlands posts. The hand of a competent designer is also
apparent in the entrance (NE) front. The central portion, containing the hall and great chamber, is recessed, and the resulting tripartite arrangement is crowned by three shaped
gables. Mullioned and transomed windows, some of four
lights. (The pair belonging to the great chamber have been
reduced.) Also two-light cross windows of classical proportion, all those in the towers being of this type, as are all except
one on the SE side. Like the main front, this elevation is of
ashlar, but is less carefully considered. The other façades are
of rubble, and vernacular in character, showing that even if
the plan and one or two elevations came from London, much
was left to local masons in execution. The top storey was
rebuilt during the course of C18 or early C19 alterations, and
the main block, but not the towers, was raised in height. The
changes were greatest on the SE and NW, and the character
of the main front was not radically impaired, though the
design of the gables may not be fully reliable. The doorcase,
with Tuscan columns and a pair of volutes forming a
broken pediment, looks late C17. At one time the flanking windows were taller, and encroached in the form of a
clerestory.

The slice of the plan to the r. (i.e. NW) of the hall includes
the kitchen. On the opposite side is the staircase, which is of
the newly evolved spacious well type, as befitted so ambitious
a Jacobean house. Turned balusters, big square finials to the
newels, and strapwork on strings, handrails and newels. Other
original features include doorcases and a clumsy stone chimneypiece in the great chamber, but most remaining fittings
are early C19. (Some work was carried out or contemplated
in 1823.) The hall is subdivided, and there is no evidence to

confirm if a gallery which runs longitudinally across the top floor replaced an original long gallery.*

Of a forecourt with arched gateway, one of two GAZEBOS or corner pavilions survives. Of later landscaping an AVENUE. Beyond it, across the main road, is an ICEHOUSE.

HARTSHEATH, 2m. NW. Rebuilt in 1825 for the resident director of a short-lived mineral company. The company entrusted its building operations to *Charles James Mathews*, better remembered as an actor than for his youthful career as an architect. The main block, five by five bays, is rock-faced, though the service wing is ashlar. Porch with two pairs of unfluted Greek Doric columns. Marble chimneypieces were supplied by a Liverpool firm. Also by Mathews a BRIDGE, with iron balustrade in fish-scale patterns, and STABLES with a nine-bay unfluted Greek Doric colonnade between higher end blocks.

FFERM, 2⅜m. NW. Late C16 or early C17, with mullions and transoms, and coped and finialed gables. Ribbed brick chimneys. The hall, with lateral chimney, has been partitioned. There is a lower-end cross wing, and an upper-end counterpart probably existed,‡ making the house a smaller version of Pentrehobyn (*see* p. 396). A storeyed porch on the same side of the hall as the chimney is an addition, and its inscribed date of 1506 not to be trusted. Inner doorway with depressed ogee head. Between cross passage and hall is a post-and-panel screen, its uprights moulded, and with two segmental-headed openings containing later doors. Beams, framed in two directions and with stopped moulding in the hall, chamfered in the former kitchen. Several fireplaces with Tudor arches, that in the hall the best. Late C17 staircase with turned balusters. BREWHOUSE with coped gable, and some brick-nogged FARM BUILDINGS.

On the A5104 ¾m. NE of Fferm is a late C18 TOLLHOUSE, with the usual splayed projection. Remarkably, the TOLLGATE has survived, with its stone piers and separate pedestrian gate. It is now to be found, reused, ¼m. E, on the S side of the road.§

Extending NNW from Hope is a well-preserved section of WAT'S DYKE.

HORSEMAN'S GREEN *see* HALGHTON

---

*The casements also have been altered. The few which look right, namely those with leading instead of glazing bars, and no internal woodwork, had been blocked. They were reinstated in the course of work carried out after Mr Patrick Trevor-Roper saved his ancestral home from demolition by purchasing it in 1958.

‡ Colonel Jones-Mortimer drew attention to evidence for this.

§ Shown to me by Colonel Jones-Mortimer.

ISCOED*

ST MARY, Whitewell. Formerly a chapel of ease in the parish of Malpas, Cheshire. Cruciform, and ingenuously Gothic, of whitewashed brick. It replaces a timber-framed building demolished in 1830. w tower with pyramid spire. Some Y-traceried timber windows. Stone windows are possibly of 1872 and by *R. Dodson*. w gallery, and another in the unusually deep N transept. Open roofs, that of the chancel incorporating timbers from the predecessor chapel. Also reused is PANELLING on the gallery fronts and in the chancel. – STAINED GLASS. Chancel s window by *O'Connor*, 1871. – MONUMENTS. A tablet to Philip Henry, the theologian, †1696. Brought from the church at Whitchurch in 1841. – Rev. Richard Congreve †1782. By *Van der Hagen* of Shrewsbury. Contrasting marbles. Obelisk and an elegant draped urn in high relief. – Martha Congreve †1809. Obelisk and draped urn. – John Parsons †1800 and wife Grace †1855. Classical tablet by *James Harrison*.

The church is at the end of a lane, in a secluded little vale. At the gates a C17 CARRIAGE SHELTER, with shallow pyramidal thatched roof on timber posts. Also a Victorian COTTAGE, and a STABLE, which is dated 1849 and carries the initials of P. L. Godsal of Iscoyd Park.

BRONINGTON CHEQUER METHODIST CHAPEL, $\frac{3}{8}$m. S of the church, on the main road. Of brick, 1822. Tiny, with a cottage under the same roof, but aspiring to classical regularity. Three bays. Pedimented centre, with a window above a reeded doorcase. The symmetry is not strict, for there is a single window to the l., whereas the right-hand bay is the cottage, and this has two storeys fitted in.

ISCOYD PARK. A brick-built house, with parapeted roofs and comprising two rectangular blocks which, for a short distance, overlap. There is little or no difference in date between these two parts, though that at the rear may incorporate earlier work.‡ The front block, at the least, was built *c.*1740. Its façade is of only two storeys and five bays, but is large in scale and raised up on a basement. Corner pilaster strips. C19 two-column porch with pedimented upper storey, probably of the early 1840s, following the purchase of the estate by Philip Lake Godsal of Cheltenham. To the r., a single-storey dining room, occupying the angle between the two blocks. Added for P. L. Godsal, it was existing by 1854.§ On the left-hand return, a large canted bay, added for Philip William Godsal by *S. Pountney Smith*, 1872–3, and most carefully done, with bricks specially made to match up. A rear extension, providing bathrooms, came in 1893–4. Original staircase in the front block, with columnar balusters, clustered as

---

* In Maelor Saesneg.

‡ The Jacobean-style balustrade of a service stair is not authentic.

§ I owe this, together with further helpful information, to the late Major Philip Godsal.

comprise the ALUN HIGH SCHOOL and YSGOL MAES GARMON, and a four-storey block as well as single-storey portions. Prominent at a corner of the site is a SPORTS CENTRE, used by the public as well as by the schools. It is of brick and concrete, with deep corrugated fascias. On a hill behind is TRE BEIRDD. Dated 1716, with later sashes and doorcase.

Attractive and extensive sets of brick SERVICE BUILDINGS and GARDEN WALLS. N of the house a square pyramid-roofed DOVECOTE. The STABLES include a range, C17 in character, with coped gables, timber cross windows, and a hexagonal cupola.

MANNING'S GREEN, S of Iscoyd Park. A mid-C19 version of a *cottage orné,* bearing the initials of P. L. Godsal. Two estate cottages of the 1840s or 50s, grouped as an asymmetrical block, with a spikily half-timbered upper storey and of stone and brick below. Two highly ornamented brick chimneys.

WOLVESACRE HALL, N of Iscoyd Park. Three sides of a MOAT, still partly containing water.

In the parish are many half-timbered houses and farm buildings. The framing of the front of the upper storey at BROOK FARM, 1¼m. N of the church on the Cheshire border, has bracing in ogee patterns.

PEN-Y-BRYN, 1½m. NNW of the church. An early C18 double pile, gable-ended. Of brick, with stone quoins of even length. Five bays. The ground-floor windows are round-headed, the upper ones segmental. Bolection-moulded doorcase, and the window above it with a moulded surround.

REDBROOK HUNTING LODGE HOTEL, at the A-road junction, ¼m. W of the Shropshire border. In the grounds a rectangular ICEHOUSE.

THE BEECHES, ¼m S of the hotel. Mid-C18, of three bays. Well staircase rising through two storeys. Shaped stair ends, columnar balusters, and swept rail ending in a swirl.

REDBROOK BRIDGE, taking the main road into England. Early C19. Modest in size, but with rusticated arch and splayed parapet.

THE GELLI. *See* Tallarn Green.

The large BARROW (SJ 495 416), ¼m. N of the church, was dug into in the last century when cremated bones and fragments of two or three urns were found. The urns seem to have been straight-sided jars and perhaps belong to a later period of the Bronze Age when burial monuments of this kind are relatively rare. Another BARROW stood on this broad ridge, a little to the W, and two more MOUNDS may be seen to the E. That at SJ 500 420 may be a natural hillock, but the unmarked one at SJ 501 424 seems more convincing.

KINMEL PARK *see* ST GEORGE, Denbighshire

LEESWOOD

2050

LEESWOOD HALL. Built for George Wynne, to whom a lead mine on Halkyn Mountain had brought sudden wealth. Of *c*. 1724–6 and attributable to *Francis Smith*, it was of eleven bays (the centre five slightly recessed) with a third storey above the main cornice. There were, moreover, side wings of no fewer than thirteen bays each, with cupolas and three-bay pediments. Glory was short-lived, for the mine became exhausted in Wynne's lifetime and he died in poverty. On the death of his daughter in 1798 the house was bought by the Rev. Hope Eyton who drastically reduced it and whose descendants have retained it. The wings were demolished, and the present building seems to be the original main block, shorn of its top storey and remodelled with eight bays, the centre four of which are recessed. The brick has been rendered, but the stone cornice and fluted Corinthian angle pilasters are probably original. Inside, some plasterwork and one or two chimneypieces must belong to Wynne's house, but most features, including the imperial staircase with iron balustrade, date from the remodelling.

Contemporary with George Wynne's house were PLEASURE GROUNDS which (according to Loudon) *Stephen Switzer* designed. An early proponent of landscape gardening, he here provided an informal layout of glades, groves and yew walks. The original plan and character are now obscured, but a notable feature survives in THE MOUND, just N of the house. At the top, approached by a spiral pathway, are a stone table and two (originally four) stately canopied seats. Further N a SUNDIAL on a tall Ionic column.

Also of *c*. 1726 is IRONWORK which has long and convincingly been attributed to *Robert Davies*, though in the absence of documentation *Robert Bakewell* may also be suggested. Some ¼m. in front of the house and conceived as a great screen or *clair-voie* is the stunning 100-ft expanse of the WHITE GATES, the parkland vista to which was related to 80 *Switzer*'s informal layout further N. Five bays, the centre one consisting of gates and overthrow. The others are screens, each sub-divided, and surmounted by a pair of broken pediments. Some motifs are similar to those of the Black Gates (*see* below), but the four openwork iron piers which separate the bays are three-dimensional, rather than flat, and are surmounted by urns and flowers on solid ogee domes. At either end are rusticated stone PIERS with entablatures and fluted Doric corner pilasters. They carry lead sphinxes. All in all, a perfect back-drop for the last act of *The Marriage of Figaro*, and if the pair of lodges or pavilions were still *in situ* the set would have been complete. The BLACK GATES, the former main entrance on the Mold road, have overthrow and flat, two-dimensional iron piers and two bays of lower screenwork either side. Besides scrolls, decorative motifs include wave bars, tassels, diamond fret patterns and spear-headed scrolled dogbars. The gates originally stood in the forecourt of the house but were moved to their present site when a new drive was made some time after 1809.* At the same time, the two single-chamber LODGES or PAVILIONS of c.1726, formerly at the White Gates (where they faced the house), were resited to face each other either side of the Black Gates. They have tetrastyle aedicular Doric fronts with sculpture in the pediments. Though they have been attributed to *Smith*, this is not accepted by Dr Mowl, who considers that a member of *Switzer*'s team may have been responsible.

(Near the White Gates a circular domed ICEHOUSE, of brick. DOE)

DOVECOTE, to the S. Of brick, with stone quoins of even length. Pyramid roof, now minus its cupola. Stylish, and doubtless of the 1720s period.

LEESWOOD OLD HALL, ¾m. SSE of the Black Gates, was the home of the Wynnes before the windfall of mineral wealth. A C17 H-plan house underwent Georgian remodelling and is now rendered. Staircase with columnar balusters and swept rail.

PLAS ISAF, Llong, ⅝m. NNE of the Black Gates. Rendered late C18 front. Pedimented tripartite doorcase and a tripartite window either side. Four windows above.

LEESWOOD GREEN FARM, ¼m. W of Leeswood village. A four-bay cruck house, with its three internal trusses remaining, though the outer walls have been rebuilt in stone. The two middle bays, which formed the open hall, have a floor inserted and also a chimney against the central arched-braced truss, creating an outside cross passage. Original upper-end post-and-panel partition with two doorways. Two doorways also for lower-end service rooms.

1080

LLANASA

ST ASAPH AND ST KENTIGERN. Double-naved and of Perp character. E windows both with panel tracery, though they differ in their details and the southern one has five lights and the northern one four. Arched-braced S roof with cusped struts above the collar. The six-bay Perp arcade was reconstructed in 1739, and the present N roof is probably that referred to in an inscription as being of the same year. It is an updated version of the southern counterpart, having straight braces below the collars and king-posts above. At its E end *Street* added cusping and a boarded ceiling in his restoration of 1874–7.‡ All N and S windows, except for a three-lighter on the N, must be by Street, replacing C18 ones. His contributions also included the S porch and the blocking of a W entrance, though a round-headed N doorway, dated 1750, remains. W bellcote to the N nave. On a giant buttress,

*Dr Tim Mowl, who kindly communicated his discoveries concerning Leeswood, informed me of this.

‡ I owe the dates to Mr Joyce.

The Publishers apologize for the following errors:

PAGE 380 *The first seven lines should read:*

newels at the corners and swept rail. The finest room is the library, extending across the end of the rear block, at first floor level. High, and with a Venetian window at one end and a semicircular bow at the other. Rococo chimneypiece. Another chimneypiece with rococo motifs in the Victorian dining room, brought from elsewhere in the house.

Attractive and extensive sets...

PLATE 58 *The missing caption should read:*

58. Llanrwst (D), Plas Tirion, chimneypiece, 1628

PLATE 60 *is shown the wrong way up.*

it rises into a rather amorphous spirelet. – Perp FONT with traceried panels on the bowl and splayed stem. – PULPIT. C17. Open scroll brackets in the form of profiles of dragon-like beasts. – In the E window early C16 STAINED GLASS, rearranged and with much new work added by *J. Bell* at the time of Street's restoration. In the s window a Crucifixion with Virgin and St John. Also Emblems of the Passion. In the N a bishop and St Catherine, St James the Great and St Lawrence. – CHANDELIER. Dated 1758. Only a single tier, but there are twelve branches and the design is elaborate. Scrolled iron suspension, with dove at the junction. – Plank CHEST. – SEPULCHRAL SLABS. Early C14 shield and sword heraldic slab, in the floor, near E end of s nave, partly obscured. – Fragment of a C14 cross raguly in a quatrefoil, in s wall of sanctuary at E end of N nave. – Outside, at the SE corner of the church, the TOMBSTONE of Sir Peter Mostyn †1605. A tomb-chest, formerly of the hooded type, and the first to emulate the original one of Robert Wynne (†1598) at Conwy. – Baluster SUNDIAL, its plate date 1762. – LYCH-GATE dated 1735.

As Clwyd villages go, Llanasa is a good one. The group around the churches includes the former SCHOOL, 1857–8 by *H. John Fairclough*. It has mullioned and transomed windows, and the teacher's house attached. To the w the whitewashed RED LION. Also GLAN ABER, C18, with pedimented cross wings and a broad, rusticated doorcase.

HENBLAS, above the church, is a fine-looking house, dated 1645, and reminiscent of the limestone belt of England. Tall, with a third storey in the (coped) gables. Ball finials, mullions and transoms, labels. The three-gable asymmetrical front includes a storeyed porch. Four ornamented panels above the doorway are separated by columns from which rise brackets carrying a rectangular oriel. The front is ashlar, the rest rubble. The plan is virtually a double pile, with service parts at the rear. (Top-floor long gallery, with arched-braced trusses. NMR)

GYRN CASTLE, $\frac{3}{8}$m. ENE. A castellated mansion, rebuilt 1817–24 (DOE) for John Douglas, a Holywell cotton manufacturer. Earlier parts are incorporated. Amateurish and uncoordinated, though this results in a degree of authenticity and a sense of artless accretion. The left-hand portion contains a top-lit picture gallery, and in front of it is a tall, slender clock tower. There are views across both Dee and Mersey to Liverpool.

LODGE GATES. By *Culshaw & Sumners* for Sir Edward Bates, a Liverpool merchant and shipowner. Castellated arched gateway with a circular turret, 1866, and a steep-roofed octagonal lodge added 1868.*

---

* The Culshaw practice was responsible for Gyrn estate commissions at Llanasa for Sir Edward, as well as work in Liverpool both for him and for other members of the family. I am indebted to Mr Colin Stansfield for references to the Culshaw firm.

Llanasa, Henblas, 1645
(Royal Commission on Ancient and Historical Monuments in Wales)

(In the hall of the castle is C19 panelling from Beechenhurst, Childwall, Liverpool. This was a Bates house in connection with which the *Culshaw* practice was employed. The staircase in the castle, with turned balusters, is possibly partly C18. DOE)

GROES FARM, ¼ m. NE. Cyclopean doorway, and date inscription 1674 above.

GOLDEN GROVE, 1⅛ m. W. A step-gabled house with mullions and transoms and a two-column storeyed porch. There is a right-hand cross wing at the upper end of the hall, and a corresponding service wing must once have existed. In an upstairs room is a chimneypiece with corbelled brackets and, above it, the date 1604. This is just as likely a date for the house as 1578, which is inscribed over the entrance. In the rear angle of the wing is a late C17 dog-leg staircase with twisted balusters. A Corinthian screen in the hall, and some bolection moulding, are probably contemporary with it. Beyond the wing is what must once have been a separate house (i.e. unit system) with its own stepped gable. In it a roughly ornamented ceiling and a plaster frieze with two figurative panels. The house has a fine setting, with GARDENS arrayed on the slope below.

Two Bronze Age BARROWS on the eastern end of the ridge above the village (SJ 101 819). The western one was badly damaged in 1934, when an Enlarged Food Vessel and cremated bones were found, but the surviving hump can still be recognized from a distance. The other mound has not been disturbed except by ploughing, which has reduced its height considerably.

There is a group of fine BARROWS strung out along the top of Axton Mountain (SJ 105 803). The group is divided by the road. On the W there are two large mounds still almost 6ft high in spite of ploughing; on the E the two barrows in the summit field have been badly damaged by waterworks. One is very close to the road and now surmounted by public seats. When the reservoir was built in 1929 an urn burial in it was destroyed; the second barrow has now been almost destroyed by the new reservoir.

A large spread BARROW may be seen close to the road at Berthangam (SJ 116 797).

For a BARROW at SJ 096 804, see Trelawnyd.

LLANELWY see ST ASAPH

LLANEURGAIN see NORTHOP

LLANFYNYDD

CHRIST CHURCH. 1842–3, one of *John Lloyd*'s efforts. Lancets, low-pitched roof, puny W bellcote and no chancel. J. H. Good, surveyor to the Church Building Commission, noted that 'both the drawings and the specification appear very inaccurate.' – Perp FONT, from Hope. Carvings on the panels of the bowl include the Stanley eagle's claw badge, though they look retooled and may not be reliable. Stem also retooled or renewed.

PENUEL CHAPEL, ¼m. NW. 1828. Longitudinal elevation, with two doors and a pair of windows between. Cottage under the same roof.

TRIMLEY HALL, on the hillside, ½m. SSW. An abandonment of traditional form in a vernacular attempt at Renaissance centralized planning. A square, stone-built house of 1653, with low pyramid roof and a central chimney. Storeyed porch, the ridge of its gable below the main eaves level. The doorway is set off-centre in the porch, and the disposition of mullioned windows is also irregular. (Staircase with flat, shaped balusters and square-finialed newels. NMR)

The course of OFFA'S DYKE is here followed by the B5101, and to the NW, towards Treuddyn, a stretch of the road is carried on the ridge of the dyke.

At Ffrith, $\frac{7}{8}$m. SSE, and a few hundred yards E of the road, is a single-arch PACKHORSE BRIDGE across the Cegidog. Just downstream from it a paved FORD. Across the B road a five-arch VIADUCT sprouts trees where once the trains ran.

A Roman hypocausted building was found at Ffrith (SJ 285 553) in the C16, and other ROMAN REMAINS have come to light there on several subsequent occasions. The site is at the confluence of two streams, at the bottom of a narrow valley. It is unlikely to have been a fort, but the discovery of tiles marked 'LEG XX' suggests a link with the garrison of the legionary fort at Chester. The most probable explanation is that the settlement was connected with lead mining at nearby Minera. Such military-controlled establishments have been found near the gold mines at Dolaucothau, Dyfed, and on the coast near Flint. A great deal of lead slag has been found at Ffrith, and the coin evidence suggests that the settlement lasted from the C1 well into the C4 A.D. Offa's Dyke comes down the Cegidog valley and overlies some of the Roman remains. Modern housing now covers the area, and nothing can be seen on the ground.

LLANNERCH-Y-MOR see MOSTYN

MAEN ACHWYFAN see WHITFORD

MANCOT see QUEENSFERRY

MARFORD*

A fascinating village of Trevalyn ESTATE HOUSING. (For Trevalyn Hall, see p. 287). Comprising some dozen blocks of cottages and an inn, it is like a set of Gothic *cottage orné* patterns come to life.‡ Work may have begun as early as 1803, but much seems to have been done *c.*1813–15. In 1814 *Julius Flower* was paid for travelling from Hungerford to construct

---

*Until 1974, Marford and Hoseley formed an enclave of Flintshire, surrounded by Denbighshire.

‡ Mr D. Leslie Davies kindly communicated the results of his researches on Marford, and gave much help in connection with both the village and Horsley Hall.

a pisé cottage, and some of those buildings which are rendered are of this material. Others are of exposed brick, painted. At least some may originally have been thatched. Ogee windows with cast-iron casements are almost universal, and use is made of brick cogging and dentil courses. Especially delightful are apsidal projections and gentle bulges on plan, curved eyebrow pediments, and circular and double-ogeed eye windows. There is nothing of the extreme variations of massing and materials seen at Nash's Blaise Hamlet, and many of the blocks are symmetrical, for although Marford is a notable essay in the Picturesque, classical discipline is apparent.

The identity of the designer is not known, but credit for at least the inception must go to *John Boydell*, nephew of the engraver, and who was agent to George Boscawen. Boscawen chose not to live at Trevalyn, and Boydell had a free hand in running the estate. After Thomas Griffith and his wife decided to take up residence in the 1830s, Boydell built for himself ROFT CASTLE HOUSE, *c.* 1833, in Springfield Lanc. It is stuccoed, with labels, Gothic glazing, and canted bays, and formerly had battlemented parapets, but is not such as to suggest that Boydell was himself the architect of the earlier buildings.

The character and unity of the village can no longer be fully enjoyed, and not only on account of motor traffic, for C20 fragmentation of ownership has led to some alterations, and one cottage has been demolished.

Some older work is incorporated, notably at SPRINGFIELD FARM, which has an arched-braced cruck. The heart of the layout is a former crossroads, where the road level has unfortunately been raised. BEECH COTTAGE and HOLLY COTTAGE are set at angles symmetrically either side of what was the entrance to a lane. Both have apsidal projections either end, and open curved pediments. Opposite is a long block, probably of the 1830s, with shallow concave front, and a near-symmetrical return to Springfield Lane. It is answered by a similar range, probably once identical. In the lane PISTYLL BANK FARM, with tall gable and lean-to wings. YEW TREE COTTAGE, small and very endearing, has a concentration of the characteristic motifs. Altered by *R. Cresswell Lee c.* 1963, when internal replanning took place and a porch with slender columns was added. Enlarged and further altered 1979–81 by *TACP*, who added a rear wing and provided new Gothic glazed entrance doors. On both occasions the original basic symmetrical form with curves was preserved.

Opposite is BEECH MOUNT, an elegant little house, superior in status to the others, and with Gothic touches to the hall and staircase. At the rear, two of the village's few surviving and modestly Gothic brick PRIVIES. Until *c.* 1820, the road continued past the TREVOR ARMS instead of turning as now. The inn, existing in 1812, has ogee windows in three storeys of three bays and two-storey single-bay wings. STABLES of similar character. Though larger than the cottages, the Trevor Arms is treated more simply, as are a number of further buildings beyond the village. In them, ogees and brick dentils are in evidence, but the curved massing is almost entirely absent. Did Boydell obtain some designs from an architect, while himself responsible for the less subtle work? In any case it would seem that a special show was made in the village, and that something less playful, as well as less costly, was considered appropriate for larger or more remote buildings.

The outliers of the genre include, to the S, MARFORD HALL, of Y-plan, built using bricks from a house demolished 1805. (Mr Davies mentioned a staircase similar to that at Beech Mount.) In Hoseley Lane the former MARFORD HALL COTTAGE, and, 1¼m. further SSE, HOSELEY BANK FARMHOUSE. HILLOCK FARM, 1m. SSW of the village, is just across the Denbighshire border in Gresford parish; see p. 174.

For references to further examples, see The Green Farm, Gresford, p. 173; Meifod and Ivy Cottage, Rossett, p. 268; and Allington Farm, Trefalun, p. 289.

HORSLEY HALL, partly in Denbighshire, 1m. SSE, was enlarged and remodelled in Jacobethan style by *G. H. Kitchin* of Winchester, *c.*1904–6. Demolished 1963, and invasive woodland has taken over the terraced and walled gardens. Ruinous STABLES. A garden GATEWAY, in the form of a screen wall, was blown down in 1978. According to an inscription, it came from the house in Buckingham Street occupied by Peter the Great in 1697. Pedimented, and the doorway, between shell niches, had consoles and a broken segmental pediment. The stone dressings may have been C17, but the bricks were early C20 – post-1917 if, as is believed, the structure was erected in the time of Lord Wavertree, who bought Horsley in that year.

MARFORD MILL. *See* Rossett, p. 267.

MELIDEN / ALLT MELID

0080

Suburbia crawls up the hillside behind Prestatyn.

ST MELYD. A single chamber, probably enlarged to its present length in the C15. Intimate and inviting character, with a feel for the quality of materials, though this results from a sweeping and opinionated restoration by *Arthur Baker*, 1884–5. He remained unrepentant, and cocked a snook at the SPAB when referring to the church in a lecture to the Architectural Association in 1887. By him a half-timbered NE vestry, the rebuilding of the S porch, also using timber, and a W bellcote. Also a pair of W lancets, introduced on the evidence of one arch and reveal. Internal plaster was removed, destroying painted texts in the process, and the roof renewed. That of the nave, trussed rafters with arched-bracing, seems to have been on the old lines, but the panelling of that of the chancel, and the separating of the two by a sort of hammerbeam arch, were new. Five-light Perp E window, its tracery renewed, probably unreliably. Authentic N and S windows, Perp or later. Also earlier S and (blocked) N doorways. – FONT. The bowl looks late C12 or early C13. It has eight panels, each containing a pointed arch. Crude roll mouldings delineate panels and arches, and along the top is a series of stepped recesses. Found during the restoration, it displaced a bowl of 1686. – By *Baker*, in C17 manner, the STALLS and the PULPIT, replacing a three-decker. – His PEWS replaced box pews. – Good STAINED GLASS contributes to the mellow Late Victorian atmosphere, particularly W windows and a three-light S by *T. F. Curtis* of *Ward & Hughes*, 1899. – The CHURCHYARD was formerly circular.

PLAS NEWYDD, $\frac{7}{8}$m. WNW. C17, with mullioned windows. (Arched truss of an open roof, and a corbelled fireplace.)

MOEL ARTHUR *see* CILCAIN

MOEL FAMA *see* p. 253

MOLD / YR WYDDGRUG

2060

ST MARY. One of the Stanley series of churches, being a Late Perp rebuilding commenced under the patronage of Margaret, Countess of Richmond and Derby. The work was never completed as intended, but there was a post-Reformation continuation of building (albeit a sporadic one) with contributions made by Robert Wharton (Bishop of St Asaph 1536–54) and William Hughes (Bishop 1573–1600). A stone bearing the latter's initials and the date 1597 is said to have been found, and the inner DOORWAY of the S porch is patently Elizabethan. Otherwise the exterior of the seven-bay NAVE is late C15 or early C16 at any rate in design. Four-centred side windows with cusped lights and supermullions. More elaborate tracery in the aisle end windows. There is entertaining carving (partly renewed, especially on the S) including animals in the string course, gargoyles and animal heads etc. at the top corners of buttresses. Battlemented parapets and crocketed finials. The W TOWER, replacing a pre-Perp one, is by *Joseph Turner*, 1768–73. Despite some thinness and oddity of detail which betray the true date, the proportions and the continuation of the procession of animals render this a creditable C18 attempt at Perp. W doorway in the tower, 1864. The CHANCEL was added tactfully by *Sir Gilbert Scott*, 1853–6. Taking his cue from Wrexham and the Well Chapel at Holywell, he made it of one bay plus a three-sided apse. Stone carving, including more animals, is by *J. Blinstone*.

A medieval chancel had at one stage been intended, but it got no further than short lengths of wall up to and including the w reveals of side windows. This is clearly seen externally on the N, and on the s is a vice turret which would have provided access to the rood loft across the intended chancel arch. The s PORCH, doubtless C17, was made Neo-Perp externally by *Prothero, Phillott & Barnard* in their restoration of 1911, but it retains a barrel-vaulted roof on transverse ribs. The really special thing is the nave arcades, reminiscent of those at Lavenham and beautifully displaying the rationality and capacity for systematic ornament inherent in Perpendicular. There are, though, carved capitals, rare for the date. Their effect, together with that of the heavy mouldings of the four-centred arches, is uncommonly sumptuous. Piers with concave corner chamfers rising into the arch mouldings, and four attached shafts which alone carry capitals. The spandrels are divided by roll mouldings which spring from angels bearing shields and rise to the roof as thin wallshafts. Cusped compartments in the spandrels, including multi-foiled circles containing a smaller series of shields. The two series include Emblems of the Passion and insignia of the Stanley family, e.g. arms, the Eagle and Child Crest, Eagle's Claw badge, arms of the Isle of Man and the Three Legs of Man. Stanley emblems occur also among the foliage and diverse subjects depicted in the pier caps. Between the spandrels and a frieze of quatrefoils in lozenges, the animal procession has invaded from outside. With the frieze, the Perp elevation terminates. The present shallow clerestory, of unknown date, is a poor substitute for the tall and grand one which would have been projected. The easternmost bay indicates a start having been made. The nave elevation was, though, to have continued further E as well as further up. See the wallshafts partly buried in the chancel arch. The rectory of Mold was appropriated to Bisham Priory in Berkshire, whose responsibility the chancel would have been. Canon Maurice Ridgway and the late F. H. Crossley suggested* that plans for an undivided church were abandoned as a result of the house's refusal to participate in building so ambitious an E end. Thus, as has been seen externally, a modified chancel was put in hand, but this was itself abandoned, doubtless due to the Suppression. The chancel arch had been built, and it remained, blocked, and containing a seven-light window, until opened up by *Scott*.

N aisle windows have a blank light either side. In the aisle is a camberbeam roof, all its members moulded, and with a close texture of cusped tracery patterns in panels. Stanley emblems on bosses. An appropriate nave roof, replacing post-Reformation work, is by *Scott*, and dates from his restoration of the mid-1850s. At the E ends of the aisles are vaulted and canopied NICHES. No specifically Renaissance motifs, but their free luxuriance foreshadows departure from

* *Archaeologia Cambrensis*, vol. 99, 1946-7.

Gothic tradition. N of the S aisle E window is one incorporating the arms of Bishop Wharton, and on the S is one with a Jesse Tree up the side. Another in the S wall. In the N aisle, one with angel corbel at the base, angels punctuating angle shafts, vine trail up the side, David playing the harp and the Stanley Eagle and Child as a finial. This niche probably held an image of the Virgin which is known to have been discovered – and destroyed – in 1768.

FURNISHINGS. – FONT. Perp in style, dated 1847. – The FONT COVER is suspended from reassembled ironwork belonging to an C18 CHANDELIER. – Alabaster REREDOS of 1878, designed by *Douglas* and made by *Hardman & Co.* – PEWS with profusion of poppyheads, PULPIT and STALLS all by *Scott*, 1856. – NE chapel fittings, including REREDOS and black and white marble FLOORING, by Sir *Thomas G. Jackson*, 1921, as a War Memorial. – ORGAN CASES. In the chancel (altered) and at the W end. Both by *Jackson*, 1923. – STAINED GLASS. S aisle, fifth from E. Jumble of fragments. – N aisle, sixth from E, i.e. over N door. Heraldic, commemorating a vicar †1576 and third Earl of Derby †1572. Apparently partly a C19 restoration, but a rare instance of Renaissance design, with balusters, garlands and sea monsters. Legs of Man in the tracery and Eagle's Claw quarries. – Yet more Stanley insignia in N aisle, seventh from E. – Also among fragments in N aisle W. – By *Wailes*, the five chancel windows, 1857, with strong jewel-like colouring. – Also by *Wailes*, S aisle E, 1863, and N aisle second from E, commemoration date 1865. – By *Clayton & Bell*: S aisle first from E, 1872; and third from E, commemoration date 1876. – Also by *Clayton & Bell*, N aisle, third from E, commemoration date 1870. – By *Lavers & Barraud*, S aisle, second from E, commemoration date 1863. – By *Alexander Booker*, S aisle, fourth from E, commemoration date 1891. – N aisle, fifth from E, commemorates the painter Richard Wilson, buried in the churchyard. The two centre lights and tracery 1889 by *Burlison & Grylls*, the remainder 1924. – MONUMENTS. At E end of S aisle, a BRASS to Robert Davies †1602. Kneeling figure. – Several cartouches, some with cherub heads etc.: e.g. Catherine Wynne, 1711, set in the niche at E end of S aisle, and Robert Davies †1666 nearby. – Among Baroque ones at the W end are: William Wynne, 1757, signed by *Rysbrack*. Cartouche with three cherub heads below a moulded canopy. – Robert Davies †1728. By *Sir Henry Cheere*. Life-size figure, *en négligé*, leaning against an urn. In a niche with Ionic aedicular surround. Broken scrolly pediment.

Iron GATES and SCREENWORK were made for the N aisle of the chancel *c.*1726, probably by *Robert Davies*, and a matching set for the chancel S aisle in 1732 by *Thomas Cheswise*. Removed in the 1850s restoration, some of this work is to be seen at Gwysaney (*see* p. 399) and at the churches at Cilcain and Gwernaffield (qq.v.).

ST DAVID (R.C.), St David's Lane. 1964 by *Weightman &*

Bullen.* Built of a beautiful brick, and better inside than out, with segmental arches and deep internal buttresses using the material logically and well.

ST JOHN EVANGELIST (former), King Street. Built as a Welsh church, 1878–9, by *Douglas*. Harmonious use of brown rubble walling, red Helsby dressings and a red-tiled roof. The E end, facing the street, has battered buttresses and five stepped lancets under one hoodmould. A NE steeple was intended. The broad, aisleless interior has been divided up for use as a CHURCH HALL.

PENTREF WELSH METHODIST CHAPEL, at the corner of Denbigh and Gwernaffield Roads. The date is 1828, the style the attractive papery Gothic of the early C19. Three-bay two-storey ashlar façade. Corner buttresses end in obelisks, and in the low-pitched gable there is a circular panel with petaloid pattern.

114 BETHESDA WELSH PRESBYTERIAN CHAPEL, New Street. Rebuilt 1863 by *W.W. Gwyther* of London (VH), with an inscription of 1819 reset. Grand two-storeyed five-bay frontage, with the three middle bays set back behind a pedimented tetrastyle Corinthian portico. There is real Neo-Classical dis-
115 tinction in the detailing. Good and characteristic interior.

UNITED REFORMED (formerly CONGREGATIONAL) CHURCH, Tyddyn Street. Also of 1863 by *Gwyther* (VH), but in lancet style.

CASTLE, Bailey Hill. A Norman motte-and-bailey site on a natural hill. Remains include the mound, a ditch and bank on the E, and, to the S, a ditch separating inner and outer wards.

PUBLIC BUILDINGS. *See* Perambulation.

PERAMBULATION. Excursions may be made from the crossroads in the centre of the town. The most inviting of the four routes is that up HIGH STREET towards the church. The market is held in the wide, lower part of the street.

The MARKET HALL, with Assembly Room above, stands on the left-hand corner. Chunky Italianate of 1849–50, with an over-heavy third storey added later in the C19. Next is MARKET VAULTS in the Chester half-timbered style of *c.*1900, and scattered up the whole of this side of the street are buildings of the 1880s onwards, displaying Douglas influence, but not all black-and-white. Some or all may be by the same hand as suburban houses in the town, e.g. a group in and near GROSVENOR ROAD (*see* p. 394).

Further up is the MIDLAND BANK by *The Anthony Clark Partnership*, 1976. Sculpturesque, with resourceful use made of brick. Lead fascias and canopies. No. 24, of brick with stone dressings, is the only Georgian house of any note remaining in the town. Early or mid-C18, three storeys, with five irregularly but symmetrically spaced bays of windows. Rusticated lintels and sill bands which jump up unexpectedly. The TRUSTEE SAVINGS BANK, brick and stone of 1868–9 (with alterations), is Italianate and has a squat clock tower. The

* Information from Mr Evinson.

Midland Bank stands at an entrance to the DANIEL OWEN SHOPPING PRECINCT. 1974–6 by the *Mountford Piggot Partnership*, and friendlier than most of its kind; its intimate scale and first-floor oriels recall post-war New Towns and L.C.C. estates. There is a ragged open end, unsatisfactory in terms of townscape, towards New Street. Closing the layout at the opposite end, and with a route through below a first-floor bridge, the DANIEL OWEN CENTRE, housing a BRANCH LIBRARY and YOUTH CENTRE. By *R. W. Harvey*, County Architect. Of darker brick than the shops, and with a system of pre-cast fascias, floor bands and window frames. Beyond it, a resited STATUE of Daniel Owen (Welsh novelist, 1836–95) by *Sir W. Goscombe John*, 1901. So into EARL STREET, for an Edwardian Baroque group of limestone and bright red brick, with 'Queen Anne' detail, all by the local architect *F. A. Roberts*, especially the TOWN HALL, 1911–12, only five bays but effectively proud and confident. Display is concentrated on the centre (balustraded balcony curving forward between Ionic columns, etc.), rising to a little tower with four aedicules and a cupola.

Later, and of more domestic scale, is the TERRITORIAL ASSOCIATION BUILDING, the difference in character emphasized by leaded glazing. Four free-standing columns to the first-floor centre window. Vermiculated rustication. Opposite is EARL CHAMBERS, of nine bays, the centre three emphasized. CAMBRIAN HOUSE, the former COUNTY COURT OFFICES, with end pediments, is dated 1910. *Roberts* also designed a POST OFFICE (now demolished) in similar style.

KING STREET is the continuation of Earl Street across High Street, and here is the three-storeyed POLICE STATION, by *R. W. Harvey*, 1976–8. Built of brick. Backing on to the OLD COUNTY HALL (*see* Chester Street, below) was a MILITIA BARRACKS building by *T. M. Penson*, 1857–8. It was converted for use as COUNTY OFFICES by *Grierson & Bellis*, 1897–8, and was demolished when superseded by the SHIRE HALL at the COUNTY CIVIC CENTRE (*see* p. 395).

The view at the top of High Street, beyond the church, is closed by PENTREF CHAPEL (*see* p. 392). Now l. into GWERNAFFIELD ROAD and past *Douglas*'s COTTAGE HOSPITAL of 1877–8. Some way out, on the l., is a group of HOUSES in the International Style as developed in the late 1930s. Brick, with flat roofs. Windows of glass brick follow curved corners. Four houses arranged with alternately reversed plans, and a fifth of different plan. Built *c.*1941, possibly in connection with a government factory managed by I.C.I.

Back to the central crossroads and NE into CHESTER STREET. On the l. the former POLICE STATION, 1881, typical of those for which *Lockwood* was responsible. Domestic-looking Elizabethan, with a red-tiled roof. Behind, in the neat and crisper Elizabethan of earlier in the century, the OLD COUNTY HALL, 1833–4 by *Thomas Jones*. Cruciform. A Gothic lantern rendered unsafe by mining subsidence was removed shortly after completion. R. into TYDDYN STREET and r. again into GROSVENOR ROAD for suburban houses by *F. Bellis*, later of *Grierson & Bellis* of Bangor. GROSVENOR MANSE, on the corner, may well be the minister's house which he is known to have done in 1889, and TŶ GWYN, 1896, is his. This is on the corner of VICTORIA ROAD, where CEUFRON, 1909, brick and roughcast with shaped gables, and BRON HEULOG, 1929, are by *F. A. Roberts*, the latter house strangely hard and in-stitutional for its date. From Grosvenor Road into WREX-HAM STREET, the route leading SE from the crossroads. Glance to the r. into GLANRAFON ROAD for a SCHOOL built 1845, perhaps by *Ambrose Poynter* (P. Howell), and succes-sively enlarged. One stage is by *Douglas*, as is the former TEACHER'S HOUSE, 1875-6. Further out, set back from the main road on the r., educational buildings assert themselves in less humble form. MOLD HIGH SCHOOL CAMPUS. The parts of architectural value are by *R. W. Harvey*, 1972-6, and comprise the ALUN HIGH SCHOOL and YSGOL MAES GARMON, and a four-storey block as well as single-storey por-tions. Prominent at a corner of the site is a SPORTS CENTRE, used by the public as well as by the schools. It is of brick and concrete, with deep corrugated fascias. On a hill behind is TRE BEIRDD. Dated 1716, with later sashes and doorcase.

In 1833 the most spectacular piece of prehistoric goldwork from Britain was found beneath a Bronze Age CAIRN in a field beside the River Alun (SJ 242 640). This is the elaborate ceremonial cape now in the British Museum – the Mold Cape – which was found around the shoulders of an unburnt male skeleton lying, without further protection, on the old ground surface beneath the cairn. When it was found, remains of leather or cloth were noticed under the thin gold and there were a great number of amber beads near the neck. The cape itself, which is beaten without seam from a single nugget of gold, covers the breast, shoulders and upper arms – a garment in which it would be difficult to move robustly – and is decorated with an embossed design imitating a many-stranded bead collar. The date of this masterpiece is difficult to estab-lish, since it is a unique survivor (another may have been found near Wrexham in the C16), but it is most likely to belong to the earlier Bronze Age (*c.* 1500–1400 bc), a period of rich warrior graves in several parts of Britain (*see* T. G. E. Powell in *Proceedings of the Prehistoric Society*, XIX, 1953). The cairn has been levelled and the site built upon, but a plaque recording the discovery survives on a garden wall in Chester Road. This plaque describes the cape as a breast-plate for a warhorse, reflecting an aberration of over-academic scholarship which long held sway. When it was first found it was recognized as a 'corselet' which had been worn by a man, but the scholars at the British Museum failed to reconstruct it satisfactorily to fit the human frame and it was placed rather incongruously around the chest of a pony until its true form, a cape covering both front and back of the shoulders, was rediscovered by Professor Powell in 1953.

OUTER MOLD

COUNTY CIVIC CENTRE, ¾m. NNE. A group of buildings, each one commendable in itself, set in parkland, with views of the town and the Clwydian Hills. The extent of subsequent growth was not initially foreseen, and the splendid site has suffered from the lack of a comprehensive plan and from overcrowding, with too much space sacrificed to car parking. The site was originally the grounds of LLWYNEGRYN, which Philip Davies-Cooke of Gwysaney (*see* p. 399) built in 1830 for his widowed stepmother. By *Thomas Jones*, the house is in simple Tudor, with curly bargeboards. It was originally symmetrical and stuccoed, but it has been extended and its rubble walling exposed. LODGE GATES remain at the main road.

Of the new buildings, the SHIRE HALL was begun first. By *R. W. Harvey*, then Flintshire (later Clwyd) County Architect. Pre-cast concrete construction, with a pattern of projecting concrete window frames, reminiscent of Saarinen's United States Embassy in London. The first phase, 1966–8, consists of a seven-storey slab and, abutting against it, a three-storey block enclosing a landscaped courtyard. Later extensions mar this classical simplicity. A glazed bridge links a three-storey portion of 1970–2, and in 1973–5 there came some higher ranges ending in another slab.

LAW COURTS, housing Magistrates' and Crown Courts. 1967–9 by *R. W. Harvey*. Brick cladding. Some monumentality is achieved by symmetry and with much of the elevation being occupied by the glazing of an upper-level entrance hall, approached by central steps. SCULPTURE by *Jonah Jones*, 1969, at either end of the hall.

COUNTY LIBRARY HEADQUARTERS. 1967–9 by *John Laing Design Associates* in collaboration with *R. W. Harvey*. Vertically emphasized pre-cast slabs above a brick base.

THEATR CLWYD. 1973–6 and also by *R. W. Harvey*, but 121 departing from the disciplined rectangularity of the earlier buildings. Here, at the top of the site, irregularity of massing has been adopted, expressing individual elements of the varied accommodation. Different from the others also in being faced with bright red brick and lead-clad fascias. The brick is hand-made and pleasingly textured, and the finishes and detailing throughout are good. Construction is partly of the load-bearing walls which the strength and blockiness of the exterior imply, though steel-framing is used for the wider spans. The MAIN AUDITORIUM, with walls lined with multi-coloured and faceted tiles, seats 550. Its stage may be adapted from an open apron to one with proscenium arch and orchestra pit. MAIN FOYERS are fully glazed, and a RECEPTION AND

BALLROOM SUITE stands in front of the STUDIO THEATRE. The latter is designed for maximum flexibility, with no fixed furnishings, and has all its steelwork exposed. There is a TELEVISION STUDIO and a FILM THEATRE, both of them associated with the COUNTY EDUCATIONAL TECHNOLOGY CENTRE.

Underground CAR PARKING in front of the building, with a façade against the hillside, has cut a great gash across the parkland.

BRYN-YR-HAUL, $\frac{7}{8}$m. NNE, near the County Civic Centre, and an A-road junction. Early C19. Stuccoed, with a veranda on two sides.

On the A494, $1\frac{3}{4}$m. NE, is a TOLLHOUSE. T-plan, with all its corners splayed, not only those of the central projection.

PENTREHOBYN, $1\frac{1}{8}$m. SE. One of the most appealing of the early C17 houses in this part of Flintshire, and one of which the ownership has descended through numerous generations. H-plan. Coped and finialed gables. There is no concession to regularity in anything but the massing, for the generous mullioned and transomed windows are almost totally asymmetrical in their disposition, and the hall, spanning between the cross wings, is entered in medieval manner, through a screens passage and off-centre doorway in the angle of the lower-end wing. Third storey with windows in the gables of the cross wings, and low untransomed windows below the eaves between the gables. In the hall are chamfered beams framed in two stages, panelling and an overmantel with heraldry and Ionic pilasters. The dining room (formerly the kitchen, in the lower-end wing) has stop-chamfered beams framing nine compartments, a later carved frieze copied from one in the upper-end chamber and an exuberant chimneypiece brought from elsewhere in the house. This displays the arms of James I, but also the date 1546, which is not to be trusted. Neither is the inscription 1540 over the entrance, for the house may be ascribed to Jacobean date and to Edward and Margaret Lloyd, whose son was High Sheriff in 1679. Reused windows with arched lights at one end and at the rear could, though, be mid-C16. The conversion of the kitchen into a dining room was carried out by *Thomas Jones*, who at the same time added a rear service range. In a restoration by *Robert B. Heaton* of *The Anthony Clark Partnership*, 1969–70, the original post-and-panel screens passage partition with depressed ogee arch was revealed; the late C17 staircase was moved and a newel for it was formed from *y-spûr*, i.e. 'the spere'. This is a barbaric-looking Late Gothic post and finial which once belonged to low screenwork. Though it is preserved at Pentrehobyn, a note which had been attached implied that it came from Glanhafon Fawr, Llangynog (*see* Penybontfawr, Montgomeryshire, in *The Buildings of Wales: Powys*), another Lloyd house.*

60

*I am indebted to Mr Heaton for this information and also for telling me about Thomas Jones's work.

LLETTYAU, E of the house. A stone-roofed row of eight cells,
each with segmental tunnel vaulting, said to have been accommodation for poor travellers. A two-storey building at one
end is the supposed overseer's house. Some of the details of
this are Jacobean in character (coped gable, ball finial, square
chimney), but a doorway and arched window lights suggest
earlier origin.

Just beyond the entrance lodge a large Bronze Age BAR-
ROW may be seen in the field next to the road (SJ 248 625). It
was investigated c.1900, but nothing was found. The Alun
valley between Llong and Hope used to contain several barrows and standing stones, indicating a considerable population here in the Bronze Age. However, some caution should
be exercised, because the area also contains natural mounds
of glacial gravels.

THE TOWER (Brancoed), 1¼m. S. A fortified tower house built
by Rheinallt Gruffydd ap Bleddyn in the mid-C15 and the
scene of an incident recorded by the poet Lewys Glyn Cothi.
The main axis is aligned N–S, and at the SE corner (i.e. at the
E corner of the short S end) is a vice turret projecting as a
semicircle and ending in a stone pyramidal roof. There is a
projection also at the S end of the W side. (Shallow vaulted
basement) and the ground-floor chamber has a segmental tunnel vault and a fireplace on the W. The first-floor hall has
been divided up; the original low-pitched roof and embattled
wall walk have gone, and the present parapet is late C18 or
early C19. Elliptical-arched cross windows look later than
this, but seem to have existed when the building was described in *Archaeologia Cambrensis* in 1846, and as it was then
a farmhouse they are not likely to have been very new.
Ground-floor panelling was mentioned, but that now existing
looks late C19. A lower wing abuts against the E side of the
tower, doubtless on the site of a medieval domestic range.
Indeed two corbels (albeit extravagantly renewed or recut)
may be seen inside, on what was an external wall of the tower.
The S front of the wing was remodelled early in the C18, and
the main staircase incorporates early C18 balusters.

(Circular stone DOVECOTE, probably C15.)

A pool to the S provides a picturesque adjunct.

In a road named UPPER BRYN COCH, ⅞m. SW, is a fragment
of a short-lived COUNTY GAOL, demolished shortly before
the Second World War. Of 1868–70 by *Martin & Chamber-
lain* of Birmingham, it was built to replace that at Flint, but
became redundant under the Prison Act of 1877. Subsequent
users included a Jesuit college. A high wall encloses the site,
and there remains a three-gable Gothic gatehouse, not at all
fearsome as prison entrances went.

RHUAL, 1¼m. NW. Built in 1634 by Evan Edwards. His fore-
bears had held Rhual since beyond the limits of its recorded
history, and except for a period of sixteen years following the
death of the heir at Waterloo, ownership has remained in the
hands of descendants. It is more advanced in its plan form

than is the later Nerquis Hall (*see* p. 405). It is a compact double pile, with a single longitudinal roof span (not two) and with no cross wings and no upper-end rooms to the hall. There is still a notional cross passage, leading direct to the staircase in the rear portion. The drawing room, i.e. the great chamber, is above the hall. Alone among the series of early C17 Flintshire houses, Rhual is of brick. It is now rendered, and although this is a pity, it has not destroyed the consider-

57   able charm of the symmetrical E front. Three coped and finialed gables, each containing a window of three stepped lights. Five bays of windows below, the outermost as five-light projecting rectangular bay windows (not in axis with the gables). The first-floor windows are taller than those of the ground floor, though also with only one transom. The central doorway is arched, with a fluted Doric order. Near-symmetrical s end with a single gable like those of the E front except that its windows are not stepped, and at the back, where brick is still exposed, are three gables, with irregular fenestration below. A much altered N wing probably incorporates earlier

56   work. Of 1634 is the full-height well staircase, with flat, shaped and pierced balusters, finialed newels and lozenge pattern on the string. Other interior features are C18 and early C19. The treatment of the hall is of *c.*1730, and there are two later rococo chimneypieces. Other work, including the rendering of the exterior, and new internal doorcases, dates either from the period of alienation or from immediately after the purchase back into the family in 1832. Brick walls enclose a deep FORECOURT, probably late C17, with segmental-arched alcoves. Front walls either side of the GATEPIERS are low and may have been reduced in the course of C18 landscaping to provide views to and from the house. *Stephen Switzer* was responsible for work in the GARDENS, 1739, but what he did has not been established, nor what may survive. His plans seem to have included landscaping to the E. A BOWLING ALLEY on the slopes behind the house may be earlier.

     Among farm buildings is a magnificent six-bay cruck
45   BARN, though owing to sub-division it cannot now be appreciated as such. Arched-bracing to the central of the five trusses, and the structure may have originated as a four-bay hall house.

ALLELUIA MONUMENT, $\frac{1}{8}$m. SSE. A small obelisk raised in 1736 to mark the reputed site of the C5 'Alleluia Victory' of Britons over Picts and Saxons.

A spring and BAPTISMAL TANK, $\frac{3}{8}$m. E. It is of 1685.* The rectangular tank is set in an oval enclosure.

A large BARROW, topped by a clump of lime trees, may be seen in the parkland (SJ 226 648). It stands in the relatively low-lying situation of many barrows in this valley.

---

* Major Basil Heaton drew attention to this.

GWYSANEY, 1½m. NNW. Possession has passed by descent
since beyond the time of John ap David, a descendant of the
royal house of Powys who in the mid-C16 took the surname
of Davies. Either his son or his grandson was responsible for
the present house, dated 1603 in a first-floor room. As built,
it was in many ways similar to, but larger than, Pentrehobyn.
It was of H-plan, symmetrical in massing only, with the cross
wings differing, and the hall, extending between them, entered in traditional way by a door in the angle of the lower-
end (W) wing. The house was unusually tall, having four
storeys in the gable of the E wing, and three elsewhere plus
stone dormers in the recessed centre, and all this raised upon
a tall basement. Broad windows under labels in the wings,
and five bays of cross windows for the two main storeys between. Coped and finialed gables. The plan was hardly a
double pile, as at Rhual, but the centre was two rooms deep,
with the space between the wings and behind the hall being
filled, and providing deeper accommodation than the comparable arrangement at Nerquis. In c.1823 the E wing was
demolished, together with some of the rooms behind the hall.
The dormers were removed, and internal changes included
the subdividing of the hall. The estate had by this time de-
volved upon Philip Davies-Cooke, of Owlston Hall, Yorkshire. In 1862 his son, Philip Bryan Davies-Cooke, married
the daughter of Sir Tatton Sykes, of Sledmere, builder of
churches and patron of Pearson and Street. *Pearson*, who had
already been entrusted with the church at Rhydymwyn (*see*
p. 428), was employed, 1863–5, to enlarge the truncated house
for P. B. Davies-Cooke's occupation. Ambitious proposals,
which included the rebuilding of the E wing, were not carried
out. Instead, a simple and self-effacing two-storey W extension was built, with cross windows (some now altered) and
reusing stone preserved from the 1820s demolitions.* Further
additions in the early C20, some or all by *F. A. Roberts*.

In the former kitchen in the W cross wing a chimneypiece
from elsewhere in the house, probably the hall. Deep frieze
and free scrolly pilasters. It stands in front of the wider original opening. Part of the original staircase, which was
apparently a dog-leg, remains. Flat shaped balusters, pierced
and moulded, and finialed newels. Its lower stage is by *Roberts*, 1911.

GARDEN, to the N. In it two re-erected three-light WIN-
DOWS from the chapel in the demolished E wing. Jacobean
Perp, with ogee-headed lights and panel tracery. E of the
house a screen of three small GATES (and a further one at the
head of the garden), from the ironwork made for Mold church
c.1726 and 1732 (*see* p. 391). Each has cresting in the manner
of a miniature overthrow. Repoussé ornaments as well as
scrollwork etc.

---

* I owe information on Pearson's work to Dr Anthony Quiney and to drawings
to which Captain Peter Davies-Cooke kindly drew attention.

STABLES. C17 with mullioned windows and stepped gables. Stepped gables also on later buildings.

Attributable to *Thomas Jones* the ENTRANCE LODGE, in simple Tudor, dated 1841. There is ESTATE HOUSING in similar style, e.g. some to the E, on the road to Northop.

FRON HALL. *See* Nercwys.

MOSTYN

1080

MOSTYN HALL. It is not known how long there has been a house on this site. In the C15 Ieuan Fychan married the heiress Angharad, daughter of Hywel ap Tudor ab Ithel Fychan, and their great-grandson, Thomas ap Richard (†1558), took the surname of Mostyn. The family became one of the most prominent and powerful in Wales, and the house is one of the largest in the county. A baronetcy was granted in 1660; on its expiry in 1831 the Mostyn barony was created, and Mostyn Hall remains the seat of the present Baron. It was extensively remodelled for the first Lord Mostyn by *Ambrose Poynter*, mainly 1846–7. Inspired by work already existing, the style is vernacular Jacobean rather than Elizabethan; with its free grouping and use of leading instead of plate glass, it looks Late rather than Early Victorian.

The great hall in the centre of the SE front was rebuilt by *Poynter*, but reproducing the former external appearance, which was that of a C16 or C17 remodelling or recasing of the medieval hall. Low-roofed, and with double-storeyed and gabled porch and upper-end bay. Inside, the reconstruction is probably less authentic, but with open roof (its central truss a C15 survival), minstrels' gallery and reused panelling, and with its furniture and fittings, the hall has an ancient and ancestral air. To the NE, early parts survive internally, and a large gable adjoining the lower end of the hall is a close copy by Poynter of its predecessor, though raised in height, with an extra storey inserted. The corresponding gable at the opposite end of the hall belongs to a new block, formed by him at the S corner of the house, there having previously been no upper-end rooms. On its first floor is a library, Neo-Jacobean, lined with bookcases, and with heraldic stained glass, a rich plaster ceiling, and a big overmantel and stone chimneypiece.

Except for its C19 roof, the recessed centre of the SW front is work of 1631–2, carried out for Sir Roger Mostyn, knight. Two rooms, doubtless intended as parlour with great chamber above, and now dining room and drawing room respectively. Both are panelled and have generous mullioned and transomed windows, including a central canted bay. In the lower room a crude plaster overmantel with heraldry, and figures growing from pilasters. Doorcase pedimented on its outer side. In the room above, vine-trail plasterwork to frieze and ceiling. Ground- and first-floor corridors separate these rooms from the lateral wall of the great hall. The upper corridor leads also to the library, and was treated by *Poynter* in similar style.

Left of the recessed centre, a gable on the sw front is also c17. Beyond it, the w corner is of c.1832–3, and the main range of the NW front was added c.1855. A square tower, with truncated pyramid roof, rises from the centre of the house, and must date from the time of the second Baron (succeeded 1854). It is a Frenchified paraphrase by *Poynter* of a feature shown as existing in 1684, but later removed.

PORTH MAWR. Dated 1570, and bearing also the initials of William Mostyn and an *anno mundi* date. A long two-storeyed range, somewhat altered. Mullioned windows, and also some round-headed openings. Central gatehouse, a storey higher, with gable. A clock and bell cupola added near one end. At right angles to the SE front of the house, the range now loosely defines one side of an entrance court.

Opposite the SE front, GATES by *Douglas*, 1896. Ironwork in early c18 style executed by *James Swindley*, and stone piers.

(To the w, beyond the gardens, a domed brick ICEHOUSE.)

DRYBRIDGE LODGE, $\frac{3}{8}$m. SSE. By *Poynter*, 1849. It is not unusual for an approach drive to bridge a public road; here, though, a two-storeyed castellated lodge is poised upon the bridge. The road tunnels below the lodge and the drive tunnels through it.

PENNSYLVANIA LODGE, $1\frac{3}{8}$m. S, at Whitford. Also early or mid-c19 and castellated.

CHRIST CHURCH, Glan-y-Don. 1844–5 by *Poynter*, at the expense of the Mostyn and Pennant families (cf. Whitford, p.454). E.E. Nave, chancel, and NW steeple with porch below. W gallery.

SCHOOL. Near the church, and also of 1844–5 by *Poynter*. Originally symmetrical, with master's house at one end and mistress's at the other, but later enlarged.

Former CHURCH HALL, on the main road. 1923–5 by *Grayson & Barnish* of Liverpool.* Striking Neo-Georgian. Good brickwork and a modillion cornice. Pedimented end, its features including a colonial-looking clock turret with bell cupola.

Mostyn Quay was of importance for the exporting of Flintshire coal to Ireland, and although the Mostyn mines and iron-works are defunct, MOSTYN DOCK flourishes as a port.

RAILWAY STATION, near Mostyn Dock. Erected 1847–8; derelict at the time of writing. This is regrettable, for it is one of the few remaining *Francis Thompson* buildings between Chester and Holyhead. Italianate, two-storeyed, of brick and stone. Recessed centre, with the original iron canopy still extending across it. Above the canopy, and between the ground- and first-floor windows of the end bays, are panels, boldly ornamented in relief. Simpler elevation to the platform, where the canopy spanned between projecting single-storey blocks.

* Information from the Rev. D. T. Richard.

Mostyn Arms, almost opposite the station. Neo-Elizabethan, probably of the 1840s.

Old Tavern (Hen Dafarn), Llannerch-y-Mor. A single-storey thatched portion has three crude and thin cruck trusses. End chimney (its ingle beam dated 1664. doe).

1060   NANNERCH

St Mary. Rebuilt 1852–3 to a conventional design by *T. H. Wyatt*. Cusped lancets and plate tracery. sw steeple with a porch at its base and broach spire. – *Minton* encaustic tiles in the sanctuary. – Later organ case attributable to *Douglas*. – A splendid chandelier, in two tiers of eight branches, their trails Late Gothic in character. Dove at the top. Bequeathed 1826. – Victorian candlestandards. – stained glass. Royal Arms, *c.* 1500, in easternmost window on n of nave. – Early quarries in window e of organ. – e window by *Charles Gibbs*, 1853. – monuments. Charlotte

82   Mostyn †1694. A proud Baroque piece by none other than *Grinling Gibbons*. Above a plinth, with inscription, is a gadrooned sarcophagus. Cherubs at the side. Flaming urn on top, its plinth displaying heraldry, and flanked by weeping cher-

83   ubs. Cherub heads on the sarcophagus are recognizable Gibbons details, and he himself possibly executed the monument. – Watkin Williams †1808 and wife Elizabeth †1825. By *S. & F. Franceys*. Draped urn. – Annabella Puleston †1824. By *J. Carline* (presumably *J. Carline II*). Gothic. – brasses to William Barber Buddicom †1887 and his wife Marie Jeanne †1892. By *Cox & Buckley*.

In the village street, s of the church, Tai Cochion, a pair of cottages of 1877–8. By *Douglas*, as is Station Lodge, near the by-pass, 1874–5, with half-timbering. Both were built for the railway engineer William Barber Buddicom. He lived at Penbedw, the park of which extends to the s. Now demolished, it was a three-storey c18 house with central canted bay, and underwent considerable Victorian remodelling.

Walgoch, ½m. sw. Symmetrical, with two bays of three-light mullioned windows and a central entrance. Labels and a cyclopean doorway. Porch with heraldry, and an end chimney, are later additions. Also an addition, and creating an L-plan, is a wing at the rear. This too has stone mullions, labels and an end chimney, and its own symmetrical entrance front. Its first-floor room was open to the roof, and three arched-braced trusses remain. This was not a true unit-system plan, or at least did not function as such for long, as a staircase, occupying the inner angle, is common to both parts. It either belongs with the new wing or came soon afterwards. Dog-leg, with flat, moulded and pierced balusters, square-finialed newels, and guilloche patterning.

Penbedw Uchaf, ½m. wsw of Walgoch. House, farm buildings and a pool form an attractive group. Near-symmetrical front. Four bays of three-light mullioned windows and a central entrance. Labels. The doorcase, with Tudor arch, is dated 1652, and formerly had elaborate enrichment. A central chimney backs on to the entrance passage, and there is also an end stack. The date 1653 above an upstairs fireplace. A wing, originally separate, is attached by a first-floor link (formerly half-timbered) carried at one corner on a stone column.*

At Pen-y-Felin, ¾m. W, is PEN-Y-FELIN CHAPEL. 1830. A cottage is included, not alongside but, owing to the fall of the ground, below. At Waen, ⅜m. NE from here, a CHAPEL of 1816 was mutilated when converted to a house. Traces of central Venetian window, two doors and end cottage may be discerned.

PEN Y CLODDIAU, 2¾m. WSW (SJ 128 676), is one of the largest hillforts in Wales. The enclosed area is 52 acres, and the defences cover a further 11⅛ acres. Both the siting – dipping down off the top of the ridge – and the layout of the ramparts – main rampart constructed from a conspicuous inner quarry ditch, with a ditch and counterscarp bank outside and additional intermediate banks at vulnerable sections – are similar to Foel Fenlli (see p. 188), a few miles S. The steepness of the slope and, consequently, the strength of the artificial defences vary around the circuit. At the narrow southern end there is an inturned entrance, which, unusually, is asymmetrically designed, the eastern inturn being much longer than the western one, although, outside the main rampart, it is the western defences which are more elaborate. The claw-like ends of the eastern inturn suggest that here, as in so many Clwydian hillforts, there may be at least one guard chamber. East of this entrance the slope is steep and only one rampart has been built. Midway along the E side this rampart crosses a deep gully, on the northern edge of which the inturned eastern entrance is perched – an arrangement which is reminiscent of the skilfully designed entrances at Moel Arthur (see Cilcain) and Moel y Gaer, Bodfari (q.v.), but with the addition here of a hornwork flanking the steep drop into the gully. From this point on, the defences become multivallate right round to the S entrance. The one other entrance which seems likely to be original lies only 400ft N of the E entrance, and is just a simple gap through the defences. At the northern end of the fort the defences cross the summit of the hill and there is an additional short length of bank and ditch, perhaps an unfinished project further to strengthen this, the most vulnerable end of the fort. No hut sites are visible in the interior, but in places the quarry ditch has been dug in a series of platforms which could have made useful building emplacements.

In the park of Penbedw, standing on the floor of the valley, is a fine Bronze Age BARROW with the remains of a STONE

---

* Thanks are due to Mr Anthony Kyrke-Smith for help with this entry.

CIRCLE close by (SJ 170 682). The barrow is undoubtedly a genuine antiquity, for cremated bone and some pieces of a food vessel were found in it in 1860; there is some doubt about the authenticity of the circle, for it is not mentioned by early writers such as Edward Lhuyd, although the owner of Penbedw was a friend and frequent correspondent of his. At present there are five stones in the circle, which is completed by six oak trees set on the same circumference. A short way away is a large stone which might have been an 'outlier' to the circle.

MOEL ARTHUR. *See* Cilcain.

2060   NERCWYS

ST MARY. In 1847 transepts and an altar recess were added. The latter was swept away when, in 1882–4, *J. Oldrid Scott* added a chancel and also a cross-gabled N aisle. The work of 1847 was by *Thomas Jones*,* and shows something of the neat Tudor Gothic in which he specialized, e.g. panelled ceilings and the N transept window. The late medieval roof, arched-braced, with cusped wind-braces, was continued by *Scott*, who provided no structural division for his chancel. On the S a three-light Perp window. Also, W of the doorway, a two-light Dec one, renewed, but probably reliably. A W tower arch of two unmoulded orders is apparently Norman, though a doorway in the wall above it, and the round-headed S doorway, are C17, as is the DOOR itself. The tower, with battered base, is of indeterminate date. Work of 1723 was a repair, and the chamfer spire (on which Scott substituted shingles for slates) is medieval in origin.

Jacobean ALTAR TABLE. Ornamented legs at one end, plain at the other; i.e. it was intended to be placed table-wise, E and W (cf. Llansilin, p. 242). – SEDILIA. Made up with fragments of the late C15 or early C16 ROOD SCREEN. It includes a section of the loft parapet, with canopied niches, fretted pedestals for statuary, and pinnacled buttresses. Also part of the rood beam, with vine trail. Traceried panelling etc. in the lower portion may be partly old. C19 colouring. – A rare specimen of a late medieval PULPIT, probably contemporary with the screen. Octagonal. On each facet a cusped panel under a crocketed ogee and tracery. – C17 turned RAILS in the baptistry below the tower. – PANELLING in the baptistry. Made up by *Scott* from pews etc. – STAINED GLASS. E window 1883 by *Burlison & Grylls*, but incorporating early work, at least some of which may be dated *c.* 1483–5 on the strength of the badge of Richard III (boar, at foot of fifth light). Also old are, e.g., in the first light, St David and lion; in the third, angel; in the fourth, head of St John; and in the fifth, angel, near the top. – CHANDELIER. Given 1761. Ten branches. – In the baptistry SCULPTURAL FRAGMENTS and a STOUP. –

* According to Canon Pritchard.

SEPULCHRAL SLABS, in the S porch. Part of a coffin lid with foliated cross. Mid-C13. – Foliated cross slab, with head set diagonally in a circle, its arms branching into lobes, c.1300. – Fragments of three further foliated slabs, c.1250–1300. – Fragment of inscribed slab commemorating Athunyd ferch Dafydd, c.1300. Upper part of an interlaced cross slab with shield and vertical sword. Early C14. – Ornamented slab with lion's head at top and foliations. Late C14. – MONUMENT. Robert Roberts †1705. Architectural frame, its entablature rising segmentally. Urn and heraldry and, below, a medallion flanked by kneeling weepers.

In the churchyard the NERQUIS HALL VAULT, marked with a gadrooned urn-like sarcophagus. Earliest commemoration dates 1737 and 1749. – Baluster SUNDIAL.

OLD VICARAGE, ¼m. NNW. Dated 1877. Free Elizabethan, of brick, and in its motifs attributable to *Douglas*.

NERQUIS HALL, ⅜m. SE. Dated 1638, and the building con-   55 tract, by which *Raffe Booth*, a Chester freemason, undertook work to a design by *Evan Jones*, carpenter, is of 1637. The contract mentions Rhual (*see* p. 397) in accordance with the custom of citing an existing building as a model of standards to be observed; but unlike Rhual, Nerquis is of stone, and is thoroughly traditional in plan. It is endowed, though, with order and regularity, being more polished and sophisticated than Gwysaney or Pentrehobyn (*see* pp. 399 and 396). H-plan, with the hall occupying the full length between the cross wings. Porch and upper-end bay are in the form of 'extruded corners' (to use Sir John Summerson's term) and are flush with the face of the wings. The doorway is at the side of the porch, thus allowing traditional lower-end entry to be combined with external symmetry. The same arrangement is found at, e.g., Chastleton, Oxfordshire, Dorfold Hall, Cheshire, and Ludstone Hall, Shropshire. Five-gable front, with larger gables for the wings than over the extruded corners and the central recess. Mullioned and transomed windows, those in the gables with stepped lights (again cf. Dorfold and Ludstone). Symmetrical end elevations, on both of which is a gable, with stepped window, between a pair of chimneystacks. Slight disruption at the service end, due to the larger size of the kitchen stack. The chimneys, plain and rectangular, contribute to the disciplined nature of the whole. At the rear are four gables, each with a stepped window, but the lower fenestration is irregular. This elevation is flush, for the shallow space behind the hall and its lateral chimney is enclosed. It contains a later staircase. Early or mid-C18 garden door, with fine iron balustrading. Original interior features include doorcases in the great hall, and a ceiling with ribbing and foliated patterns in an upper-end room. An adjoining room has C18 panelling with shell niches; and there is also C18 panelling, but of different character, in the great chamber above the hall. On the top floor a long gallery. The house also contains good rococo chimneypieces.

In 1797 elephantine Gothic wings, Jacobean in style on the garden front, were added either end, and, somewhat later, a more delicate Gothic porch, the latter probably by *Benjamin Gummow*. All were removed, *c.*1966, in an admirable restoration scheme by *Robert B. Heaton* for Mr and Mrs A. W. Furse. The original entrance arrangement was reinstated, and the porch is now at Portmeirion (*see The Buildings of Wales: Gwynedd*). A chimneypiece, still in the great hall, may be contemporary with the porch.

Similar in style to the wings, battlemented, with Gothic touches, are screen walls and a gatehouse belonging to the STABLES. Also similar, but smaller in scale, is a FOLLY, to the N. Now ruinous, and its builders would surely have approved. W of the house a Gothic ORANGERY, by *Gummow*, *c.*1814. Semi-octagonal, with cast-iron tracery.

PLAS UCHA, ¾m. SSW. A late C17 staircase rises through two storeys. Turned balusters and finialed newels. A long ingle beam is heavily moulded.

HENDRE UCHA, ⅝m. NNW. Small, dated 1635. A two-unit house with lateral chimney, later extended. Labels.

PLAS ONN, ¼m. NW. Remodelled 1833, symmetrically, in stuccoed Elizabethan. Partial demolition in the 1960s unfortunately involved the destruction of the arched-braced central truss of a C15 hall house.

HENDRE ISA, ¾m. N. Brick, of T-plan. The cross member is C17 and earlier than the rest. It has blocked stone cross windows and, in the gable, a small window of two arched lights.

FRON HALL, 1¼m. NNW. Five-bay main block of 1765 (DOE) with a three-bay pediment. Now shorn of entablatures. Balustraded panels between ground- and first-floor windows, and the central upper window has a segmental pediment. Entrance in the right-hand bay. An earlier portion to the r. has been much remodelled and successively reduced.

NEWMARKET *see* TRELAWNYD

NORTHOP/LLANEURGAIN

60

ST EURGAIN AND ST PETER. Nave with no structurally separate chancel, a N aisle, and a Perp W tower. The tower, four-storeyed, is arbitrarily divided by quatrefoil friezes (all different) and by string courses. Eight pinnacles, paired two-light traceried bell openings, and a four-light W window with cusping and panel tracery. The detailing of the W doorway is of 1965 and not authentic. Tower arch with panelled jambs and intrados. Like Gresford tower (*see* p. 169) it may not have been completed until well on in the C16, for it is said to have been dated 1571. Like Gresford church also (though lacking the refinement to be found there), it is English in style and quality. Similarly the camberbeam panelled roof of the nave is suggestive of Cheshire. Perp also, though earlier than the tower and roof, is the nave arcade. At the E end of the arcade is a C14 cinquefoil arch within an ogee, possibly a TOMB RECESS. It is not *in situ*, for the arcade was once of seven bays, as against the present five, with this arch at its E end. The length of the church was reduced, the arch reset, and the outer walls rebuilt in Perp style by *Thomas Jones*, 1839-40. Plaster vaulting in the tower also by him. Very different is the broad and assertive Geometrical E window. It is by *Butterfield*, 1850, when the E wall was rebuilt as a memorial scheme.* The internal exposing of rubble walling probably dates from *Douglas*'s restoration of 1876-7, when work included the removal of Jones's W gallery, and the removal of box pews, a three-decker etc. to make way for a complete set 98 of Douglas FURNISHINGS. They include the ALTAR TABLE and the particularly good ORGAN CASE, and are similar in character to his contemporary fittings at Halkyn (q.v.). *Hardman & Co.* painted the REREDOS panels, 1877, and carved enrichment was added to the altar in 1879.

STAINED GLASS. By *Clutterbuck*: N aisle E, commemoration date 1839, of which only tracery lights remain; first and second from W on S, commemoration dates 1855 and 1856. – By *O'Connor*: E window (i.e. the Butterfield window), 1850; first from E on S, 1867. – By *Ballantine & Son*: third from W on N, commemoration date 1839. – By *James Powell & Sons*: third from W on S, commemoration date 1876; second from W on N, commemoration date 1892; W window, commemoration date 1907. – By *Hardman*: second from E on S, commemoration date 1881.

MONUMENTS. Four effigies in recesses provided for them by *Jones* in the N aisle. From E to W: 1. Knight. Possibly late C14. Very crude, and perhaps unfinished. 2. Ithel ap Bleddyn, knight. Late C14. Unusually small. 3. Lleucu †1382. Possibly the wife of Ithel ap Bleddyn. Her head on a cushion, framed in an arch with canopy work. Lion at her feet. Square headdress and pleated dress. 4. Knight. *c.*1400. – In one of the recesses, fragments of two SEPULCHRAL SLABS. One commemorates the wife of Bleddyn. Late C13. The other, early C14, commemorates David. Part of a circular cross head, and a sword hilt. – Several C19 BRASSES, e.g. Howard monument, N aisle, by *Hardman*. Latest commemoration date 1858.

In the churchyard, the OLD GRAMMAR SCHOOL. Built in or soon after 1608, but the mullioned windows still have arched lights. Two storeys of windows, though the schoolroom is open to the roof. At one end, at upper level, is what is thought to have been the master's lodging, with its own door in the gable end. Reused roof trusses, two of them C15 or C16 and arched-braced. The building was altered when it became a Sunday School in the C19. Restored 1975-8.

*Canon Pritchard's discovery.

s of the church, the VICARAGE, 1826. Stuccoed, and with broad, soffited eaves. Canted projecting centre on the garden front. Also to the S, a brick and half-timbered COTTAGE by *Douglas*, 1877. It was a Bankes commission (*see* Soughton Hall, below), and was built as a newsroom, sessions house, and police station. (PLYMOUTH HOUSE, further W, has a full-height Jacobean staircase, with flat, shaped balusters and finialed newels. DOE) The village has been cut about with road works. s of the A55 is PARKGATE FARM, mid-Victorian, built for the Soughton Hall estate.

WAT'S DYKE. A good section ¾m. W.

COED-Y-CRA UCHAF, 1½m. NW. Dated 1636. Symmetrical three-bay front. Two- and three-light mullioned windows, those of the ground floor transomed. Central chimney and lobby entry. The first floor was open to the roof, with two trusses on console-like corbels. A chimneypiece with crude Doric entablature. According to Mr Kyrke-Smith, there is evidence of the C17 work being a reconstruction of an earlier timber-framed house.

(LLYS EDWYN, ⅞m. NW, and to the ESE of Coed Llys. A site with ditch and bank, identified with Eadwine and the C11. Excavated 1931. Traces were found of a stone hall, probably early C13.)

HIGHFIELD HALL, 1m. E. Early C19. Stuccoed, and with broad, soffited eaves. Only three by three bays, but large in scale. Four-column Doric porch.

LOWER SOUGHTON (SYCHDEN) HALL, ¼m. SSE. Rebuilt or remodelled 1865–6 by *J. W. Walton*. Asymmetrical Elizabethan, of brick with stone dressings. (Carved oak chimneypieces were supplied by *Brown & Lamont* of Chester, and old work was incorporated in that of the entrance hall.)

SOUGHTON (SYCHDEN) HALL, ¾m. SSE. An extraordinary house, and it is regrettable that its development is not more fully documented. The structure is early C18, though externally there are no longer any features to indicate this. Evidence exists to suggest a building date of 1714 or 1727; as there could well have been more than one campaign, both may be correct. Further work seems to have been done after the house was bought in 1732 by John Wynne, Bishop of Bath and Wells, who had previously been Bishop of St Asaph. His daughter married Henry Bankes, of Kingston Lacy in Dorset, and Soughton has remained with the family ever since.

The C18 house was of three storeys, and its eleven-bay S (entrance) front was strongly Baroque, with complicated articulation, a Corinthian order, and much rustication. The N front, of brick, was plain and simple. Remodelling, in supposedly Spanish style, was carried out for *William John Bankes*, collector, romantic and friend of Byron. He was himself partly responsible for the designs, though *Sir Charles Barry* was also involved, at least as executant architect. The two had met in the course of their Egyptian travels; Barry did not return to England until 1820, and his activities at Sough-

ton date probably from later in the decade.* It was not until
1835 that he began to remodel, for Bankes, the Roger Pratt
house at Kingston Lacy. At Soughton, pavilions were added
above the two outermost bays at either end, extending back
for the full depth of the house, and consisting of an arcaded
storey and steep hipped roofs with bracketed eaves. The N
front received not only the rear returns of the pavilions, but
mullioned windows and a canted porch (intended as a new
main entrance) rising into a hexagonal belvedere turret with
ogee roof. Two large first-floor rooms were formed in the
course of the alterations. The saloon, in the centre of the S
front, rises through two storeys and was given tall mullioned
and transomed windows, and the adjoining dining room is of
equal height. A prominent pitched roof, with a cupola, was
added above the saloon. C18 features remained, but these
were obliterated in a further remodelling, carried out 1867–9,
for W. J. Bankes's nephew. It was almost certainly by *Douglas*. A facing of hard, red brick, with stone dressings, was
provided, and the character of the earlier C19 work was extended and heightened, in High Victorian manner. On the S
are rows of mullioned windows, grouped with vertical emphasis, and with the topmost having round-arched tympana.
The saloon roof and pavilions were retained, with some of
their original detail, though a spikier turret replaced the cupola, and on the N the recasting included giving a more massive base to the storeyed porch, and a spire-like and less
playful roof to its turret. Some good carving, e.g. the saloon
tympana and the Romanesque arch of the S porch. The effect
of all this is astonishing, more like a generously endowed
institution than a country house, but undeniably impressive.

C18 work survives inside, especially the full-height well
staircase, with swept rail, ornamented stair ends, and fluted
columnar balusters; 1727 would be a more likely date than
1714. The entrance hall is also basically C18, but with some
woodcarving, doubtless collected by W. J. Bankes, worked in.
Further old work was incorporated by *Barry* in the doors of
the saloon above. From 1841, Bankes found it expedient to
live abroad, but work continued at Kingston Lacy, and it was
at this time that a set of Gobelin tapestries and a Rubens
cartoon copy were transferred from Dorset to Soughton.
Though the saloon and dining room were undoubtedly
formed in the 1820s remodelling, they may possibly have
been altered to receive these items. The ceiling of the saloon,
with beams and stencilling, could be of the 1840s, whereas
that of the dining room has a central feature which looks like
progeny of the Royal Pavilion, and could be exotica of the
1820s. Both rooms have High Victorian chimneypieces. On
the same storey a room with Chinese silk hangings and another C19 chimneypiece.

*That Barry worked at Soughton was discovered by Mr Peter Howell. I am
grateful also to Dr David Blissett and to Mr W. A. Mitchell of the National Trust
for supplying information.

A scheme for a billiard-room wing by *Lockwood*, 1884, remained unexecuted.

On the s is a FORECOURT. Its brick walls and panelled stone GATEPIERS with urn finials are C18. The iron GATES are probably contemporary. The approach is by an AVENUE of limes, ¼m. long. *Barry* added Islamic-looking TURRETS, with naturalistic rock bases, to the court (which Bankes contemplated surrounding with a cloister) and to screen walls on the N. (SCULPTURAL FRAGMENTS from the C18 exterior, built into a terrace W of the court. Corinthian capitals, coat of arms, a mitre etc.)

STABLES, SW of the house, with separate coach house. Both are C18 and were originally detached. The stable block displays Bankes heraldry, so must be mid- rather than early C18. One and a half storeys, six bays with the middle two emphasized. Gibbs surrounds to the lower windows, quoins of even length, and a cupola.

To the NW, a delightful little brick-nogged octagonal GAME LARDER of 1872. It is documented as being by *Douglas*, as is the LOWER LODGE, ½m. NNW. Of 1868, and thus contemporary with the refacing of the house, it has High Victorian touches. Nevertheless it is vernacular revival in style, with half-timbering and patterned pargetting, foreshadowing the mature Douglas.

NORTHOP HALL

2060

ST MARY. Rock-faced, of 1911–12. Typical of its architect, *L.W. Barnard*, in being Perp and in having a chancel arch but no external break between nave and chancel. N aisle and a W tower, its upper stage added 1962 according to Mr Howell.

NORTHOP HALL FARM (Llyseurgain), ½m. NNW. Built in the C15 by Dafydd ab Ithel Fychan, and mentioned by the poet Gutun Owain. Not strictly a tower house, for it was not defensible; rather it was a first-floor-hall house, with its lower storey vaulted. Extended and much altered, but the segmental barrel-vault is visible. (Below the S end is a well chamber reached by a vice. Arched-braced trusses and cusped windbraces of the hall roof remain.) Late C16 or C17 pedimented mullioned and transomed windows, blocked.

OVERTON*

3040

ST MARY. Battlemented Dec W tower of Cheshire character. NE vice turret ending octagonally, and a W doorway with head-stops and sunk wave mouldings. Five-bay nave, its Perp arcades of four-centred arches on octagonal piers, except for the westernmost bay, where narrow arches are cut through

* In Maelor Saesneg.

earlier walling. N aisle rebuilt 1819. It was at the same time widened, to line in with the easternmost bay, which had hitherto projected as a transeptal chapel, and which retains a Perp window, formerly with an ogee hoodmould. s w vestry also of 1819, though the s aisle is a rebuilding of 1855, its windows more archaeologically convincing than those on the N. The chancel of 1710 was recast in a version of Perp by *W. M. Teulon* in association with *E. E. Cronk*, in a restoration of 1870. His is the steep hammerbeam roof of the nave, harbouring clerestory windows as dormers, and sending down detached shafts to big corbels, horribly out of scale and out of character with the arcades.

Two FONTS, a mid-C18 baluster, and a High Victorian piece of 1872, made by *Cox & Sons*. - Parts of the Perp ROOD SCREEN worked into N PARCLOSE SCREENS by *Gronwy Robert Griffith*, 1921. - CHOIR STALLS. Elaborately carved, 1935, by *Evelyn Wybergh*, a local lady. - By her also the WAR MEMORIAL. - STAINED GLASS. E window and chancel N by *Clayton & Bell*, 1870. - Three middle windows of s aisle by *Kempe*, 1890. - CHANDELIER. Given 1746. Two six-branch tiers. - Dugout CHEST. - SEPULCHRAL SLABS. Lower part of a slab. *c.*1300 commemorating Angharad ferch Einion. Inscription on the border and a pattern of stems and leaves. - Fragment of an early C14 four-circle cross slab. - Part of a slab with a recessed bust, in relief. Possibly early C13. - Fragment of an early C14 expanded arm cross, built upside down into the westernmost pier on the s. - MONUMENTS. In the chancel: Lloyd monument (Thomas Lloyd †1730). Corinthianesque pilasters and a segmental pediment, the centre of which, surmounted by an urn, has been pushed upwards by cherub heads and heraldry. - Phillips monument, 1713. Unsophisticated, bitty. Includes two cartouches of drapery. - Thomas Hanmer †1794. By *John Nelson* of Shrewsbury. Oval tablet and two columns. - Mrs Hanmer. By the younger *van der Hagen* of Shrewsbury, *c.*1770. Urn and oval tablet. - Phillips Lloyd Fletcher †1808. By *Sir Richard Westmacott*. Chaste, with no architectural or figurative elements. - Francis Parry Price †1787. By *Benjamin Bromfield*. Urn against an obelisk. - Owen Wynne †1780. By *van der Hagen*. Draped ornamented urn against an obelisk. Consoles flank the tablet. - In the N aisle: Francis Price †1749. By *Daniel Sephton* of Manchester. Heraldry against an obelisk. - Francis Richard Price †1858. By *J. Bedford*. Heraldry above a classical tablet. - Susan Price †1813. By *Alexander Wilson Edwards*. Contrast of coloured marbles. Urn against an obelisk. Similar to the Jones monument of 1779 at Gresford (*see* p. 172). - In the s aisle: Thomas Bennion † 1803 and wife Mary † 1840. By the *Patent Marble Works* of Westminster. Large, and lavishly Gothic. Canopied relief of three daughters mourning at their parents' tomb.

(OUR LADY AND THE WELSH MARTYRS (R.C.), Wrexham Road. 1958 by *Weightman & Bullen*.)

No trace remains of a CASTLE, sited near the river, known to have existed in or soon after 1138. Overton received a charter from Edward I in 1292.

Laid out on a rectangular plan, and with a broad High Street, the village has an urban air. At the N end are early C19 Gothic
5 brick COTTAGES in WREXHAM ROAD, and opposite the end of the street THE QUINTA, early or mid-C19, rendered, with an oriel and fanciful bargeboards. PENDAS, with pedimented doorcase, closes the end of HIGH STREET, and there is much C18 brick in the street itself. Date inscriptions of 1739 and 1741. Also the WHITE HORSE, in the Chester half-timbered style of the turn of the century, and, before reaching the yews of the churchyard, a tiny timber-framed COTTAGE. The timber-framed OVERTON HALL, opposite the church, was demolished 1961. On the site a decent HOUSING SCHEME by *Paterson & Macaulay*, 1961, with pyramid-roofed detached units. Next, the early C18 BRYN-Y-PYS ESTATE OFFICE, with timber cross windows, leaded, and the taller RECTORY, its off-centre doorway with a hood on carved brackets. Staircase with columnar balusters and swept rail. Rear extensions by *Teulon*, 1870. (VH) Thanks to PENYLLAN HOUSE the view along the street is closed at the S end, as at the N by Georgian brick and a pedimented doorcase. Disruptive, though, is the municipalized space in front of the COUNCIL OFFICES, 1956, by *H. Anthony Clark, F. C. Roberts & Partners*. Characteristically 1950s, showing Scandinavian influence, and domestic-looking, with a low-pitched roof. Round the corner in PEN-Y-LLAN STREET, the premises of J. SCOTT, a large late C17 or early C18 H-plan house of brick, with coped gables and later sashes. Later too, a porch with attached Ionic columns and brick pilasters.

Further S, in ELLESMERE ROAD, delightful little Tudor Gothic ALMSHOUSES, built 1848. Single-storeyed, of ashlar. E-plan front, with crocketed and coped gables, battlemented parapets and stone-roofed oriels, all diminutively scaled.

Opposite is a former METHODIST CHAPEL, dated 1816, now cottages.

CEMETERY, ⅜m. WNW. Opened 1872. A small, steeply sloping site arranged in terraces, and largely enclosed by trees. The CHAPEL, by *W. M. Teulon*, is integrated with the terracing. It is now bricked up and roofless. Rock-faced, with lancets and an E.E. portal, beside which rises a square turret with stone spirelet. Foliated caps and ashlar interior. There was STAINED GLASS by *O'Connor*. The layout still has its original GATES and timber inner LYCHGATE.

OVERTON BRIDGE, 1¼m. WNW, crossing the Dee into Denbighshire. A single arch, designed by the elder *Thomas Penson*, County Surveyor, in 1810, collapsed in 1813, apparently while still under construction. Penson was then requested to design a two-arch structure and deposit security for its building. Having failed either to do this or to complete the original contract he was dismissed in 1815, and the work was entrusted to the younger *Penson* and the second *John Carline*. Large and stylish, with two wide rusticated arches, lower-stage cutwaters and a string course below the parapet. The downstream parapet continues as a buttressed retaining wall on the Maelor side.

BRYN-Y-PYS, ⅝m. NNW, was demolished in 1956. It had been rebuilt or remodelled in the mid-C18 with three storeys, a W front which had a five-bay centre between two semicircular bows, and a seven-bay S front. The Georgian massing survived a remodelling of the 1850s, in Italianate fashion, and another by *Waterhouse*,* 1882–3. He decked the house out in a sort of Jacobean dress; his additions included a tower above a *porte cochère*. *See* p. 519

Parts of the STABLES remain. An C18 portion, with pediment and cupola above a rusticated arch, is connected by a later range to an octagonal DOVECOTE with cupola. (A NMR photograph shows a doorcase dated 1739.)

Two ENTRANCE LODGES, both dated 1875 and Douglas-like. In the village is a Neo-Elizabethan one. The other, towards the bridge, is of brick and half-timbering with some pargetting. *See* p. 519

LIGHTWOOD FARM, 1⅛m. ESE. (Nearby is a MOATED SITE.)

ASH GROVE, ¾m. SSW. Early C19. Of ashlar. Three bays with recessed centre and a projecting porch of two Ionic columns *in antis*. Blocking course above the cornice.

KNOLTON HALL, 1½m. SW. Altered and enlarged 1868 for Charles Robert Cotton of the Combermere family. Previously there was a recessed centre, with one gable to the l. and two to the r., all half-timbered (or seemingly so) and with Georgian sashes. The remodelling included rewindowing and the piling on further back of more gables and a pyramid-roofed tower. Though it is so no longer, the whole front was painted black and white in imitation of half-timbering, except for the original left-hand gabled projection, which is of genuine exposed framing. The 1868 garden front may have been intended to be painted in this way, though seemingly never was. Imported carved woodwork in the hall, and early C18 iron balustrading, said to be from Overton church. Early or mid-C18 staircase with swept rail and fluted columnar balusters.‡

Half-timbered ENTRANCE LODGE dated 1862.

LLAN-Y-CEFN, 1⅛m. WSW. (Crucks. Also a staircase with flat shaped balusters and finialed newels. Vaulted brick ICE-HOUSE. DOE)

* Mr Stuart Smith's ascription.
‡ Mr R. H. Hilton Jones kindly provided information on the house.

PANTASAPH

ST DAVID (R.C.). In 1846 Viscount Feilding, later eighth Earl
of Denbigh, married Louisa Pennant, the heiress of Downing
(*see* Whitford, p. 455). They resolved to build a church in
thanksgiving for their marriage, and work began in 1849 to
designs by *T. H. Wyatt*. Though originally intended for the
Establishment, it became Roman Catholic following the donors' conversion in 1850. The transference was unsuccessfully
opposed in the courts by the Bishop of St Asaph, and
churches in lieu were built at Brynford and Gorsedd (qq.v.)
with subscriptions collected throughout Wales and England.
At Pantasaph, *Pugin* was called in to give a 'Catholic finish',
and the church was opened in 1852. *Wyatt*'s building is superior to his usual level of attainment. Bar tracery, spikily
cusped. S aisle with gabled roof and porch. In the angle between aisle and chancel is a tower which, despite the early
date, has an assertively High Victorian vice turret, and is
surmounted by a stone stepped pyramid spire, articulated at
each course. Below the tower a vaulted SE chapel. Nave roof
timbers of curious and restless profile, and carved corbels
alternating in level. Some of *Pugin*'s FURNISHINGS, of 1850–
1, were exhibited in his Medieval Court at the Great Exhibition. Designed by him, STATUES either side of the E
window, the SE chapel REREDOS and the FONT, the latter
octagonal and heavy, on a cluster of shafts, and with Emblems
of the Evangelists etc. in quatrefoil panels. As elsewhere,
though, his work has not fared well. His BAPTISTRY SCREEN
has been dismantled (though partly reused in a confessional
in the S aisle and in a screen between it and the organ); his
PULPIT and – who would be surprised? – his ROOD SCREEN
have gone. Remaining is a suspended CRUCIFIX which belonged to it, and which seems to have been resited as early as
c. 1893, when alterations were made by *A. E. Purdie*. (VH)
Pugin's HIGH ALTAR was then replaced by one which has
now itself lost its elaborate tabernacle. – STAINED GLASS.
Four N windows apparently by *Hardman*, 1852. – Good and
characteristic work by *Harry Clarke*, *c.* 1931–4, in the S aisle
W and westernmost. – MONUMENT. Eighth Earl of Denbigh
† 1892. Recumbent effigy on a tomb-chest under an elaborate
vaulted canopy. Designed by *Purdie* and executed by *Boulton
& Sons*. (P. Howell)

FRANCISCAN FRIARY (R.C.), adjoining the church on the N.
Together they enclose three sides of a court, and form a
pleasing group. A Capuchin community was established
under the auspices of Lord Feilding in 1852, and the building
is of 1858–65. Puginian in spirit, with steep roofs, some Perp
tracery, and many gables, including a rhythm of four in the
N range. Turret, with octagonal spirelet in the angle. The
identity of the architect has not been ascertained, but *T. H.
Wyatt* may have been responsible, for he continued to be
employed for estate work and on the house itself at Downing.

Out of sight is an E extension of 1899. The GUEST HOUSE, to the W, is connected by a single-storey link. Begun by *Wyatt* at the same time as the church, and intended as a parsonage, it has cusped lancets and, on the E gable return, a rectangular oriel.

A set of STATIONS OF THE CROSS on the hill behind. Of 1875, their relief panels replaced with mosaic in 1963. Below the summit a CHAPEL built into the hillside. Above this a CALVARY, its cross of iron, the figures bronze. Plinth dated 1879.

ST CLARE'S CONVENT (R.C.) was established in 1861. An extensive set of buildings followed, in some half-dozen stages, most or all by *Edmund Kirby*, and the latest begun in 1907. They included originally a boarding school and an orphanage. All were closed down in 1977. Partly of H-plan. The convent proper forms the SE stroke, and this and the cross-piece (with unusual brick dressings and built as part of the orphanage) possess the most character. One or other, probably the cross-piece, was begun by *Kirby* in 1868. The NE stroke is the CHAPEL (St Joseph), built 1881, with pairs of lancets between buttresses. Aisleless, but the apsidal E end has an ambulatory with polished granite columns and a clerestory.

PANT-Y-GOF see HALKYN

PENARLÂG see HAWARDEN

PENGWERN see RHUDDLAN

PENLEY*

4040

ST MARY MAGDALENE. Rebuilt by *C. Hodgson Fowler*, 1899–1901. Sandstone, with a red-tiled roof. Dec windows, straight-headed on the N and S. W bellcote growing from a central buttress. The chancel is marked by a slight contraction and a differentiated roof truss. – Baluster FONT.

VICARAGE, NW of the church. Built 1841. Recessed centre between pedimented cross wings. Painted brick.

Almost opposite the church the MADRAS SCHOOL, i.e. one which was run on Andrew Bell's monitorial system. A plaque records its foundation by the second Lord Kenyon in 1811.

*In Maelor Saesneg.

It is a remarkable *cottage orné* of a school, thatched and stuccoed, with casements (renewed) and glazing bars. Symmetrical, with hipped roof and a half-hip over the porch. Rear extensions of 1905 and by *Sir Percy Thomas & Sons*, 1966-7.

LLANNERCH PANNA (regrettably renamed TUDOR COURT), ½ m. S. An admirable half-timbered house of 1878-9 by *Douglas* for the Honourable George T. Kenyon, younger son of the third Baron (*see* Gredington, p. 361, and Tallarn Green, p. 445). There is no truth in the story that it was built as a wedding present. Ruabon brick chimneys and roofing tiles, but the plan form and the handling of the timberwork owe more to historical precedent than was usual for Douglas. Cross wings, a storeyed porch in one of the angles, and a hall with lateral chimney. The hall is, however, handled freely, rising through two storeys, encircled with a gallery, and having window recesses either side of the fireplace, one of them a polygonal bow. Old panelling was worked in; the interior has an aura of antiquity, and there is a splendid front door, with ribs, ironwork and little slit windows. An intended service range, which would have replaced an earlier house, never materialized. The present kitchen wing is c20, and the predecessor building partly remains, as a separate house.

HOLLYBUSH LANE FARMHOUSE, ⅜ m. N. An early c18 double pile, of brick. Five-bay front, and segmental-headed timber cross windows, with glazing bars. Staircase with columnar turned balusters, but still with a string.

(Beyond the Hospital and Penley Hall is a deserted MOATED SITE, ⅜ m. NE.)

A BARN from STRYT LYDAN is at St Fagan's. In two parts, of *c.* 1550 (cruck) and *c.* 1600 respectively, joined by a drift house.

PENTRE *see* FLINT

PENTRE HALKYN *see* HALKYN

PENTREHOBYN *see* MOLD, p. 396

3060 PENTROBIN

ST JOHN BAPTIST, Penymynydd. 1843 by *John Buckler*. Lancets, no aisles, short chancel, and a spindly W steeple. However, the church is set apart from the starved Commissioners' type by some costly touches, especially a W gallery front on arcading, all of stone, and an octagonal SE vestry (with stone vault). It was indeed paid for by Sir Stephen Glynne of Hawarden. Enrichments were executed by the *Rev. J. E. Troughton,* curate-in-charge 1843-64. They include PAINTED DECORATION with patterning designed by *R. P. Pullan,* and paintings, some of them copied from work by *Friedrich Overbeck*: the Expulsion from Eden, scenes in the life of Our Lord, and a Last Judgement. Stencilling over walls and roofs. Also figure paintings on altar, pulpit and the SCREEN, itself made and coloured by *Troughton.* He painted and fired the STAINED GLASS (except the E and W windows); the nave easternmost on S, dated 1850, has his monogram.

The decorations have suffered fitful restoration, with inferior over-painting, but the colouring of the chancel roof was improved in a restoration by *Robert B. Heaton,* 1979-80, following fire damage.

NW of the church the former PARSONAGE, of 1846, in picturesque Elizabethan. Symmetrical S front with an oriel. Is it by *Buckler*? SCHOOL, to the E. Of 1844, but altered.

WHITE COTTAGE, Drury Lane, 1m. NNW. A three-bay cruck house, its outer walls reconstructed, and with a later building adjoining at the W end. The central hall bay has a floor inserted and a chimney built against the E partition. The framing of the W partition truss remains.

PENYMYNYDD *see* PENTROBIN

PEN YR HENBLAS *see* BRYNFORD

PLAS TEG *see* HOPE

PONTBLYDDYN 2060

CHRIST CHURCH. 1836 by *John Lloyd.* Diminutive W tower and tallish pyramid spire. W gallery. *Lloyd Williams & Underwood* added the chancel, 1865-6, and it looks as if they also reroofed the nave. Their E window has Geometrical tracery. W porch of 1906.

PRESTATYN 0080

CHRIST CHURCH, High Street. 1863 by *T. H. Wyatt,* with N aisle and stunted NW broach spire. Lancets and rudimentary plate tracery. A S aisle was added by *Prothero & Phillott,* 1905, and the N arcade was altered to match the new one.

The chancel, 1926, is in what *L. W. Barnard* understood as Perp. – STAINED GLASS. E window by *Shrigley & Hunt*, *c.* 1933. In the churchyard a Perp WAR MEMORIAL by *Barnard*, *c.* 1919–23. The former VICARAGE, by *Wyatt*, 1866, is N of the church and separated from it by a newer successor.

ST PETER AND ST FRANCIS (R.C.), Plas Avenue. 1903 by *Edmund Kirby*. The brick, terra-cotta and roofing tiles, all brightest red, and the timberwork around the heavy-roofed porch are typical of Kirby. Apsidal E end and a W rose window of seven cusped circles. Groups of cusped lancets. Brick mullions and some diapering. PRESBYTERY also by Kirby.

TRINITY METHODIST CHURCH, Gronant Road. In the Arts and Crafts Perp of the turn of the century. Small corner tower and recessed spire.

PRESBYTERIAN CHURCH OF WALES, Nant Hall Road. Built 1902. Brick, with tracery of terra-cotta. Octagonal corner turret with spirelet.

REHOBOTH WELSH PRESBYTERIAN (CALVINISTIC METHODIST) CHAPEL. High Street. Built 1894. An enterprising front, asymmetrical either side of a central shaped gable.

This was just a village straggling up the High Street before H. D. Pochin of Bodnant (*see* p. 107) initiated development and the reclamation of the foreshore. He had begun buying up land in the district in the late 1870s. Work continued in the time of his son-in-law, the first Lord Aberconway, including (unidentified) building and town planning by *Michael Bunney* (best-remembered as joint author of a book on C17 and C18 domestic architecture) and work by *Sir Howard Robertson*, then of *Easton & Robertson*. There is nothing of real architectural value to show for this, and Prestatyn is now more popular in character than once it was. It is a place favoured for retirement, as well as holidays, with consequent bungaloid sprawl. Caravans plug the gap left between Prestatyn and Rhyl.

In the 1930s, the W half of the foreshore was developed as a HOLIDAY CAMP, one of the first to be purpose-built. PONTIN'S HOLIDAY VILLAGE, E of Bastion Road, came later.

Commendable was the grandstand of a short-lived TROTTING STADIUM. It was by *Garnett & Cloughley*, 1962–3, and made much use of exposed steelwork. It has been altered and incorporated in Pontin's Holiday Village.

CASTLE. A motte and bailey, existing in the 1160s, was sited $\frac{1}{2}$ m. E. Nothing is now visible.

Associated with Pontin's Village is the prominent GRAND HOTEL (formerly GOLF HOUSE HOTEL). In its present form it is of 1925 by *Easton & Robertson*. By them the left-hand wing added to an existing golf clubhouse with two shaped gables (once a school). An intended matching right-hand wing was never built.

By *Easton & Robertson* some houses at the top of the town, e.g. No. 2 PLAS AVENUE, 1922, and some behind the sea wall in BEACH ROAD EAST. Here No. 56 stands out from its neighbours, with deep fascias and a cantilevered steel balcony thrusting forward. By *T. O. Pottinger & Partners*, 1964–5. (VH) BEACH ROAD WEST has more houses by *Easton & Robertson*. Also by them was a BEACH PAVILION and BATHING POOL, 1922–3, with a CAFÉ added in 1924. The group was bought by the U.D.C. in 1958, and the genteel classicism was subsequently remodelled into the present architecturally confused and unattractive ROYAL LIDO.*

(In CLAYTON DRIVE, No. 11 is a split-level house of 1962 by *Garnett & Cloughley*. Like a house in Rhuddlan Road, Rhyl (*see* p. 434), it was built for a brother of Patrick Garnett. It has been slightly altered by a subsequent owner.)

The VOELNANT TELEGRAPH STATION, 1 m. SE, was built as a semaphore station, 1841, by the Liverpool Dock Trustees, and may be ascribed to *Jesse Hartley*. Similar to that at Llysfaen (*see* p. 250).

The topography of the coast at Prestatyn has changed a good deal over the centuries, and it is the line of what is now the 50-ft contour that was important for early settlement. Finds made during the 1930s by the town's surveyor, Gilbert Smith, indicate considerable activity during the Mesolithic and Neolithic periods, and his watchfulness also revealed the site of a small Roman FORT near St Chad's School (SJ 062 819). Excavation here in 1934–7 exposed the foundations of two stone buildings outside the fort and indicated that, in the very wet conditions in the lower part of the site, wooden buildings might also survive. Pottery suggested a date for this occupation in the C2 A.D., and the discovery of boar antefixes (the symbol of the XXth Legion) links this small military station with the Roman garrison at Chester. One of the buildings was a bathhouse, traditionally placed outside a fort, but the other is more difficult to explain. Small-scale excavations have been carried out there more recently, and the erection of new houses led to a new campaign of work (1984–5) which has been able to deal more fully with the wooden buildings.

QUEENSFERRY   3060

The silting up of the Dee estuary, which brought an end to the port of Chester, has extended over several centuries and still continues. The river here flows through the long, straight 'New Cut' excavated *c.* 1734–7, and the extensive, flat areas of Sealand etc. are reclaimed land. Two BRIDGES stand close to each other at Queensferry; a gawky opening bridge (1924–6 by *Sir Basil Mott* and the County Surveyor *R. G. Whitley*) contrasts with a quite elegant three-span structure by *Mott, Hay & Anderson*, forming part of a by-pass scheme of 1960–2. Of welded plate girders, it comprises cantilevers and a central slung span.

*Mr J. H. Bradbury told me much about the development of Prestatyn.

ST BARTHOLOMEW, Sealand, 2m. ENE. By *Douglas*, 1867, and belonging to his early, i.e. High Victorian, period. The site was given and the church partially paid for by the River Dee Company. Windows Early Dec. Aisleless and not large, but expensively done with ashlar interior and a SE tower and pyramid spire. A feature is made of a vice turret, against the lower part of the tower, and it is also visible inside, where a door from it gives access to the pulpit. – STAINED GLASS. E window, by *Hardman & Co.*, contemporary with the building and donated by the architect. – W window by *Kempe*, 1880.

ST ETHELWOLD, Shotton. Built partly at the expense of W. E. Gladstone, but not begun till after his death. 1898–1902 by *Douglas & Minshull* and thus a Douglas church thirty years later than St Bartholomew's. Refined Late Victorian Gothic, of sandstone ashlar, outside and in. Very eclectic, being largely free and fresh E.E., rather than completely in the conventionalized Perp of the day. Clerestory, NW turret and apsidal chancel. The latter is higher than the nave, and the steep gabled roof of a NE chapel is much higher than the N aisle. A broad SE tower and spire were intended to adjoin the chancel, and the lower stage was built 1924. Their completion would have made the varied massing even more interesting. Nave arcades with arch mouldings dying into the piers. W gallery. STALLS (1908) incorporate traceried panels and turned balusters. – STAINED GLASS. Three small lancets at the W end by *Frampton*. Good glass in the apse. By whom?

See p. 519 ST ETHELWOLD'S VICARAGE. Built 1907. Pedimented Neo-Georgian. Pebble-dashing divided by brick pilaster strips.

ST FRANCIS, Sandycroft. 1912 by *Nicholson & Corlette*, i.e. *Sir Charles Nicholson*. Gothic, but with no historicist motifs, except for tracery of the very simplest kind. Dark brick outside, plastered within. Sandstone dressings. Square bell turret with steep pyramid copper roof at the junction of N aisle and NE chapel. No S aisle. Only two bays of the nave were built, and a W termination was added 1934–5. Balcony in the chancel, doubtless intended for the organ.

MANCOT PRESBYTERIAN CHURCH, Hawarden Way. 1929. Low and chapel-like in form. Much conventionalized and mechanical Perp tracery.

DEESIDE LEISURE CENTRE. First phase 1970–2 by *F. D. Williamson & Associates*. Phase two 1972–4 by *Rothera & Litherland*, Incorporated Building Surveyors. Huge windowless bulks are neatly handled, with corrugated cladding above brick lower storeys. As an example of the highly ambitious provisions made at that time by even quite small local authorities, together with its modish name, this is a true period piece. Besides licensed restaurant, cafeteria and free car park it offered, when opened, according to the proclamation at the entrance, ice rink, floodlit tennis and games area, badminton, table-tennis, squash and a children's play area, none of which sounds particularly leisurely.

What was until its closure the works of the BRITISH STEEL CORPORATION, STRIP MILLS DIVISION, was formerly that of John Summers & Co. Ltd. The firm originated at Stalybridge and first opened up here in 1896, but steel-making ended in 1979. An unconventional but pompous OFFICE BUILDING, 1907, stands on the N bank of the river. Symmetrical with castellated central tower. Brick and yellow terracotta. Art Nouveau detail. Further upstream, near the bridges, is SEALAND GARDEN SUBURB for company employees, begun 1910 as one of the many contemporary ventures associated with Co-Partnership Tenants Ltd. Only the SW half was laid out in accordance with the original plan, and the central axis was to have had a club at its end.

H. B. Creswell is best-remembered for *Honeywood* and for the FACTORY of *c.* 1901–5 which he designed for Williams & Robinson, makers of water-tube boilers. Faced with dark local brick, it is between the railway and the S bank of the river, E of the A494. Writing in the *Architectural Review* in 1942 ('Nine Swallows – No Summer'), Sir Nikolaus Pevsner described it as 'the most advanced British building of its date', and asked 'Why is it not just as famous as Peter Behrens's turbine factory of 1909?' A square flat-topped tower, with broad, battered corner buttresses, housed hydraulic accumulators. Long, low blocks, also straight-topped, were aligned asymmetrically on either side, articulated in accordance with the original departments and processes. A repeating bay unit consists of a screen wall, with horizontal window band, between piers. Designed to carry the weight not only of roofs but of overhead travelling gantries, the piers are battered to counteract resulting lateral pressures. Their form also obviated the need for the broad footings which the shallow foundations (dictated by ground conditions) would otherwise have required. A band of brick corbelling above the windows has equal functional justification, being pierced for ventilation. The building is not so revolutionary as to be completely divorced from its period; the tower particularly has a feeling of, say, pared-down Leonard Stokes. However, *The Builder* in 1901 rightly described it as 'a highly creditable attempt to give a certain amount of character ... in a manner naturally arising out of structure, and without any introduction of superfluous and unmeaning ornament.' The present condition of this important building leaves much to be desired, for the clear-cut concept has been compromised by additions and mutilations, and the top of the tower has been removed.

In HAWARDEN WAY, CROSSWAYS and MANCOT WAY, Mancot, is housing built for war-time munition workers, as part of a scheme, 1916–18, which also included hostels, a church hall and a hospital. Plain, decent brick pairs and short terraces, some with sash windows and some with casements. Designed by the *Housing Branch of the Ministry of Munitions*, whose director was *Sir Raymond Unwin*.

RHES-Y-CAE

CHRIST CHURCH. The row of lancets and the rectangular plan unbroken by any form of chancel suggest the awkward and ignorant Gothic elsewhere in Flintshire of John Lloyd. But no. *Ambrose Poynter*, 1846–7.

RHOSESMOR

ST PAUL. 1874–6 by *John Hill*. Rock-faced, with a w bellcote, and lancets set high up. Aisleless nave, and a chancel with semicircular apse, under one continuous roof. Crown-post construction.

METHODIST CHAPEL, NE of the church. Built 1910. Rock-faced. Shaped gables, and a characteristically early c20 segmental hood above the door.

PLAS-YN-RHOS, ¼ m. N. Now enlarged, but originally a two-unit storeyed house, with lateral chimney and a first-floor room open to the roof. Some mullioned windows. (Mr Kyrke-Smith noted an arched-braced roof truss, and, in the cross passage, a post-and-panel partition dated 1619. Cruck BARN.)

Former VICARAGE, ½ m. N. Built 1880, in Elizabethan style with Gothic elements. Symmetrical front set on a bank.

An engine house of the RHOSESMOR LEAD MINE, ¼ m. S, W of the B5123, has been converted to offices.

JERUSALEM CHAPEL, ⅞ m. S. Small and vernacular. Longitudinal elevation, with two windows, two doors (one blocked, indicating internal rearrangement), and a cottage under the same roof. Built 1841.

PLAS WINTER, 1 m. WNW. (Thistles and acorns in plaster, dated 1633, over a fireplace. DOE)

MOEL Y GAER, ¼ m. NNW (SJ 210 690), on the southern end of Halkyn Mountain, does not appear to be a very prominent hill, but, when seen from a distance, its commanding position is obvious. Similarly, the surface remains appear simple and perhaps unimpressive when compared to the dramatic forts further W, but the results of recent excavations have shown that it is a site of great interest and importance. As it stands, the fort consists of a single rampart with discontinuous external ditch and a low and intermittent bank outside the ditch. There are two entrances, on the N a simple gap, which may be secondary, and on the E a more complex entrance with inturned banks and possible guard chambers. Excavation has shown that the main rampart incorporates two periods of construction and was first built in the c4–3 bc, succeeding a timber palisade built some time in the c7–5 bc. This palisade had surrounded a village of roundhouses built with substantial posts. The first rampart, which overlay the site of some of these earlier houses and enclosed a formally planned series of stake-wall roundhouses and four-post structures (buildings which are normally interpreted as granaries), comprised a bank of material quarried from the external ditch, piled inside an elaborate timber framework and given an outer face combining vertical timbers and drystone walling. Some time after *c*.200 bc, this was buried beneath a wider construction, capped with stone and probably supporting a timber breastwork. It is probable that an outer bank and ditch had been planned at this stage too, for the present intermittent outer bank incorporates a wooden fence which might have been intended as a facing for a more substantial rampart whose full circuit was never completed. The nature of the occupation inside the final fort is uncertain, but there was tenuous evidence (only preserved because the interior has never been ploughed) for some rectangular sill-built structures overlying the earlier roundhouses. The excavations also revealed evidence for occupation of the hilltop during the later Neolithic and Early Bronze Age, when two burials were made, one under a surviving mound in the NW. More recently, during the Napoleonic Wars, the hill was used as a beacon site, and the postholes for two timber towers, dug with military precision, were found.

RHUAL *see* MOLD, p. 397

RHUALLT   *0070*

On the A55. The gradient of Rhuallt Hill was eased by *Telford* as part of his improvement of the route between Chester and Bangor.

RHUALLT HALL, N of the main road, E of the crossroads. A three-bay, three-storey house. Approached between fluted C18 GATEPIERS with spreading rectangular steps in front, and gadrooned urns. Gabled DOVECOTE, now roofless.

PENNANT LEAD MINE, ¾ m. ENE. Ruinous three-storey engine house and a tall chimney.

RHUDDLAN   *0070*

Rhuddlan was the site of the palace of Gruffydd ap Llywelyn, destroyed by Earl (later King) Harold in 1063. A Norman stronghold was built in 1073 by Robert of Rhuddlan, relative and deputy of Hugh Lupus, Earl of Chester, and under their joint lordship a borough was founded. Possession alternated between Welsh and English until the final capture by Edward I in the war of 1277. The building of a castle on a new site was initiated, and a new borough established. Laid out on bastide lines, the town received a charter in 1278, though its defences were not complete when attacked in the uprising of 1282. A deep navigable channel was formed as a link with the sea, over two miles away, by ambitiously diverting and canalizing the River Clwyd. It was in 1284 that the King issued the Statute of Rhuddlan, creating counties which survived until 1974, and laying down an administrative and legal system. Nothing came of his plan to transfer the see of St Asaph to Rhuddlan. The Edwardian town forms the nucleus of the present one, the Norman site being largely deserted.

TWT HILL, ¼m. SE of Rhuddlan Castle. The site of the CII Norman castle. Large motte, created from a natural hill. The river is to its SW. To the N was a bailey with bank and outer ditch, and a deep ditch remains E of the mound. Running in from the river, this utilizes the steep cliff-like bank which, following the river, formed a natural W boundary for the Norman town.

Norman TOWN DEFENCES, of bank and ditch, may be seen. On the N the line has been built upon, but from the E end of Dyserth Road, ¼m. E of Rhuddlan Castle, it runs for c.⅜m. S before turning SW towards the river. The street layout was rectangular, and the site of the church is known.

RHUDDLAN CASTLE. Begun in 1277, and contemporary with Edward I's castles at Builth, Aberystwyth and Flint, the latter, like Rhuddlan, with a dependent town. Work continued until the mid-1280s and, it seems, included the making good of damage inflicted in the attack of 1282. The chief master mason was *James of St George*, and, as at Flint, some early
9   CI4 work was done by *Richard of Chester*. The plan is concentric, with a moat on three sides (the Clwyd was formerly close in on the SW), and outer and inner wards. The INNER WARD, an imperfect lozenge, has circular towers at the N and S corners, and double-towered gatehouses at the E and W. Its regularity was unprecedented in English medieval military architecture. The curtains, with embrasured slits at ground level, are largely intact. On the NE wall is a fragment of battlement, and the SW and SE walls show indications of the positions of central corbelled turrets. The towers were fourstoreyed, with variations in internal shape above the ground floor. Except for their parapets, the S tower (with basement) and those of the W gatehouse (with some fireplaces) survive to their full height. E gatehouse with portcullis grooves and gate chases. Also the original system of loopholes in its N guardroom – that on the S was obscured by the insertion of a fireplace in 1303. Timber-framed structures backing on to both gatehouses originally extended into the ward. These would have linked up with the vanished domestic buildings of timber, which included the King's Hall and Chamber, Queen's Hall and Chamber, the kitchen, and chapel. The sides of the MOAT were revetted in stone, and largely remain so. The lower portion, to the S, was open to the river, and probably served as a dock. The remainder was dry, cut off by two embankments. At these two points were entrances to the

OUTER WARD. The Town Gate, the present entrance, has a
pit, initially for a turning bridge. The corresponding Friary
Gate was abandoned in 1300 and a turret formed. Though
the outer curtain is not well preserved, there are remains of
turrets containing steps descending to sallyports (most of
them blocked) in the moat. The ward slopes down to the river
on the SW, and at the furthest point of the curtain is the
square, four-storeyed Gillot's Tower. Beside it was a postern,
called now the Dock Gate. Traces of another postern (River
Gate) further N. It adjoined massive retaining walling at the
NW corner, the rebuilding of which formed part of work carried out by *Richard of Chester*, 1301–4.

The castle surrendered to Parliament in 1646, and was
slighted in 1648.

The C13 town plan is represented by the High Street and two
roads crossing it – Castle and Church Streets, and Parliament
and Gwindy Streets. The TOWN DEFENCES of ditch, bank
and palisade encompassed it on the three sides away from the
river, and the earthworks of the N corner may be seen near
the foot of Gwindy Street.

ST MARY. Built *c.*1300 within the rectangular layout, and converted into a double-naved church by a Perp extension on the
N. Later again is the battlemented tower, encroaching on the
N nave and the westernmost bay of the arcade. The arcade,
with octagonal piers, has the three easternmost of its six
arches taller than the rest, and the third from the E asymmetrical in elevation, doubtless in connection with the rood
screen. A watercolour by Moses Griffith shows the S nave
articulated as nave and separate chancel, both E.E., and the
single-chamber form dates only from a reconstruction in
1812. S buttresses mark the length of the original nave, and
a PISCINA suggests that the chancel was a slightly later addition. The S porch is largely by *Sir Gilbert Scott*, who restored
the church in 1868–70. Lancets were introduced as well as
renewed by him, but the triple W group of the S nave is
known to be authentic. Of the original build, but reset, is a
(blocked) doorway on the N, with head-stops. Also on the N
a two-light Dec window, either designed by *Scott* or else his
renewal of reset work. He seems to have had nothing to do
with the five-light E window of the N nave. With four intersecting ogee sub-arches and a tendency to reticulation, the
design is likely to pre-date the Perp enlargement, but its origin is difficult to account for. Griffith's view implies that it
cannot, as has been suggested, have belonged to the former
chancel. Projecting to the N is a battlemented mausoleum,
added in 1820 by William Davies Shipley, of Bodrhyddan,
Dean of St Asaph. E of this a surviving Perp window, and W
of it a later straight-headed one. – Many FURNISHINGS by
Scott. – The STAINED GLASS of the N nave E window, and
probably more, is contemporary with his restoration. – Centre
light of easternmost on N by *A.J. Davies* of the *Bromsgrove
Guild*, 1919. – WALL PAINTING. Fragments of C17 Welsh

texts on the N and S walls. – A plank CHEST dated 1710 but looking older. – SEPULCHRAL SLABS. A floriated cross, c.1250–80, with curling leaves in a circle. With moulded edge, it was probably a coffin lid. – Two early C14 four-circle cross slabs, one with a sword. – MONUMENTS. William de Freney, Archbishop of Rages (Edessa), †c.1290. When the Muslims overran Syria he was obliged to return to England (where his uncle Gilbert de Freney had been sent by St Dominic to establish the Dominican order) and he spent the rest of his life assisting British bishops. Slab with incised effigy, and an inscription in French round the border. Brought from the Dominican Friary site at Abbey Farm (*see* below). – Mutilated effigy of a priest, now upright. Head on a cushion, feet on an animal. Probably early C14. – Lower part of another C14 priestly effigy. – Conwy and Shipley monument. Large, tripartite. Erected by Dean Shipley, presumably in 1820, at the same time as the mausoleum. 'Designed and executed by Mess. *Carline*, Shrewsbury.' (Quoted by Mr Howell) In Gothic more serious than might have been expected for the date. – CHURCHYARD CROSS. 1873, on a medieval circular base. – LYCHGATE by *Scott*, c.1868–70.

ST ILLTUD (R.C.), Maes Onnan. 1975–6 by *Bowen, Dann, Davies*. Rather domestic in character, long and low, with white roughcast walls and a roof of artificial slates. The windows are mostly narrow bands, vigorously detailed, with emphasized vertical divisions. Boarded ceilings internally. The accommodation is flexible, with intercommunicating church and hall. The width diminishes towards the W, with divisions of the plan marked on the N by set-backs. This progression is expressed also in the ridge of the roof, and at the highest point is a clerestory, over the sanctuary. Instead of being a dreary sea of tarmac, the car park is gravelled and landscaped.

EBENEZER WELSH PRESBYTERIAN (CALVINISTIC METHODIST) CHAPEL, Parliament Street. Built 1819, enlarged 1869. Of the latter date the exuberant and shockingly debased entrance gable, and the stuccoing of one side. Rubble walling elsewhere possibly of 1819. (Ceiling with beams forming four panels, each with a central roundel. DOE)

GORSEN INDEPENDENT CHAPEL, Rhyl Road. 1835. Small, with half hips. End elevation with two doors and, between them, two windows.

BRIDGE. A stone bridge replaced a timber one in 1358. Remodelled 1595; the present structure is partly of this date. Two unequal spans, and splayed-corner (not triangular) cutwaters. Unsightly former footways on iron brackets, and there is now a separate footbridge.

PARLIAMENT HOUSE, Parliament Street. There is no foundation for the tradition and inscription associating Edward I with this site or with a parliament. Facing High Street a late C13 doorway and a C14 cusped ogee (both blocked), but *ex situ*, and doubtless from the castle.

VICARAGE, Vicarage Lane. Hipped-roofed and neat, of 1819–20. Porch with pointed arch.

BANQUET HOUSE, Princes Road. Dated 1672. Tall and compact, with coped gable ends, one obscured by an extension. Mullions, labels, and a Tudor-arched lintel.

ABBEY FARM, ½m. SE, within the area of the Norman town. The site of a Dominican Friary (Black Friars), founded in or before 1258. The farmyard occupies the site of the cloister garth. In the S range of farm buildings, four blocked straight-headed windows, facing the yard. Two blocked pointed windows, apparently C14, on the W side of the W range. Others further S are post-Suppression. Much remained of the C13 E range when depicted by Buck in 1742. Built into the farmhouse garden wall a fragment of tracery. Several fragments of SEPULCHRAL SLABS, set into the buildings: e.g., facing the yard in the W range, the upper half of an early C14 four-circle cross slab, with inscription on the stem and a running leaf pattern. Of similar date a mutilated EFFIGY, set in a niche facing the yard in the E range.

RHYDYDDAUDDWR, ¾m. SSE. Vernacular C18 work, of brick. Symmetrical, of three bays, with a central arched window below a low-pitched gable. The other windows are broad casements.*

CRICCEN CROSS, 1¼m. SE. On a mound. Base and fragment of the shaft of a medieval cross.

PENGWERN, ¾m. SSW. The main block is of two and a half storeys and five bays, and there is a three-bay pediment on a giant order of Ionic pilasters which embrace the upper storeys. Detached two-storey wings face each other across a forecourt. In short, a Palladian conception, but it survives only in mutilated form. The wings, of brick with stone dressings, remain complete. Five bays, with cupolas and one-bay pediments. Quoins, pedimented doorcases, moulded surrounds etc. A rainwater head of 1770. The main block probably came later, as the rebuilding of an earlier house. It is of more delicate character, and Neale's *Seats* refers to work of 1778. In the pediment is a figure within a plaque, and the slenderness of the pilasters speaks of the Adam revolution. There were first-floor Venetian windows in the outer bays, and attached two-storey wings with canted fronts, but, following a fire in 1864, all that remains to the r. of the three-bay centre is the ground storey. At a later date the brickwork was stuccoed, and many features, including urns and finials from the pediment and blocking course, were removed or obscured. Venetian windows with Gothic glazing at the rear of the left-hand attached wing, and inside is a room with Adamesque ceiling. Staircase with cast-iron balustrading, probably post-1864 and rearranged.

STABLES adjoin the left-hand detached wing at an angle. Near the opposite end of the house, a two-storey COTTAGE,

* PEN-Y-BRYN, 1¼m. NNW, which seems to have been of similar character, though larger, was dated 1784. Now mutilated.

pedimented, and with over-large Venetian windows, one above the other. Single-storey wings, with Gibbs surrounds to arched windows.

RHYDYMWYN

ST JOHN EVANGELIST. By *J. L. Pearson*, and built 1860–3 under Davies-Cooke patronage (*see* Gwysaney, p. 399). Early Pearson in that it pre-dates the refined and rational churches of his final maturity. In no other sense is it immature, for it came well on in his career (that he was Pugin's junior by only five years is easily forgotten) and is a strong and disciplined High Victorian work of great confidence and dignity. Not large – it is aisleless – but generously scaled. French in character, but not slavishly so. Plate tracery and, in the E window, bar tracery. There is restrained polychromy in the form of horizontal banding. Shafts with foliated caps enrich the N porch, W bellcote, and W and E windows. Inside, the nave has stone bands and dressings. Banding of darker stone in the ashlar-lined chancel, and also carved caps and a foliated cornice. Similar cornice over the sgraffito REREDOS.

Unexecuted designs for a parsonage and school were made by *Pearson*, 1866.* As built, *c.*1868–9, the SCHOOL, near the church, and the VICARAGE, ⅛ m. NW, are by *T. H. Wyatt*.

Y BERLLAN, next to the vicarage. 1972–3 by *John Humphreys* for himself. A split-level plan exploits the sloping site. Timber cladding and grey brick, with monopitch roofs.

To the SW, in the valley of the Alun, were the Penyfron and Llynypandy Lead Mines, the latter worked in the late C18 and early C19 by John Wilkinson (*see* Bersham, p. 103). Both were served by THE LEETE, a watercourse extending some 3 m. along the E side of the valley from Loggerheads. It was probably built by the Cornish engineer *John Taylor*, following the taking over of these and other mines in the neighbourhood by his Mold Mines Company in 1823. A footpath now follows its course.

BETHEL, Penyfron, 1 m. SW. A small vernacular chapel of 1825, dating from the leadmining days.

COED DU, ¾ m. WSW. Entrance front of five bays, with an extension to the r. Nicholas refers to enlargements of 1813 and 1867. The former date would suit the earlier part of the front, and the latter a broad Italianate tower and a timber-framed oriel on the left-hand return. John Taylor rented the house, when managing the mines, and was visited by Mendelssohn.

PLAS WILKIN. A Victorian model farm, N of Coed Du.

---

* As discovered by Dr Quiney.

RHYL

CHURCHES

HOLY TRINITY, Russell Road. Small and cruciform, originally with a w gallery. By *Thomas Jones*, 1835. Neo-Perp windows, some with their mullions and tracery of cast iron. The rapid growth of Rhyl led to the extending of the s transept in 1850 and the N in 1852, and then to the building of St Thomas's nearby. Holy Trinity, overshadowed by its new neighbour, continued in use for Welsh services and is still the parish church. – Marble baluster FONT with gadrooned bowl. – STAINED GLASS. By *Ward & Hughes*: E window, 1879, signed by *H. Hughes*, and the chancel N, 1881.

ST THOMAS, Russell Road. A major church by *Sir Gilbert Scott*, designed c. 1860 and built in more than one stage, 1861-9. Lancets and plate tracery, and a clerestory of foiled circles. NE steeple providing, in the coastal plain, a landmark for miles around. Its tower has a vice turret and pairs of large lancet bell openings. A conventional and very lofty stone spire was intended but never materialized. Instead, *Scott* added in 1874 a highly effective recessed shingled superstructure consisting of a square clock stage and short broach spire. Crocketed gables over the clock-faces rise into the spire. Elsewhere, particularly internally, much use is made of attached shafts and foliated caps, as favoured by Scott: e.g. in the arcades and in arcading at clerestory level. Chancel with lofty arch and, on the s, twin arches and a central quatrefoil pier of polished granite. Shafts to the E window and the organ arch, and in the sanctuary there is diapering in arcading. ENCAUSTIC TILE flooring. – *Scott* FURNISHINGS include the REREDOS, STALLS and gorgeously sumptuous PULPIT. – STAINED GLASS. Much by *Ward & Hughes*, from 1867 onwards, including the s aisle westernmost by *T. F. Curtis* of *Ward & Hughes*, 1905.

A SE chapel was formed and new vestries were added in 1910 by *J. Oldrid Scott & Son*.

A parochial precinct includes Holy Trinity, St Thomas's, the CHURCH HALL, 1891, with cusped lancets, and the VICARAGE. On the site of HOLY TRINITY SCHOOL* is TRINITY COURT, fronting on to Paradise Street. By *Bowen Dann Davies Partnership*, 1977-8, for a housing trust.

ST JOHN BAPTIST, Wellington Road. 1885-7 by *David Walker*. A large octagon with tall E and W arches opening respectively into a chancel (with its own appendage of vestries etc.) and a one-bay aisled and clerestoried nave, or rather ante-nave. N and s gables and, on the diagonals, clerestory windows over arches. Two polished granite columns carry the resulting cluster of arches at the W end. Though the

---

*This was by *T. M. Penson*, 1842, enlarged by *R. Lloyd Williams*, 1855-7. *Lloyd Williams & Underwood* designed the former VICARAGE, 1860, on a different site, now also demolished.

interior is wonderfully spacious, the plan is not fully resolved,
with the E diagonal arches giving into residual corners. Bellcote over the chancel arch, and the octagon originally had a
spirelet. Consistent joinery and FURNISHINGS with unmitred
mouldings. – A Douglas-like PULPIT of 1891. – STAINED
GLASS. E window by *Goddard & Gibbs*, 1970. Though the
subject-matter is concentrated in a small area, the all too
frequent C20 misuse of clear glass is avoided, for the background is coloured. – Nave easternmost on S by *Alfred O.
Hemming*, 1906. – Nave easternmost on N by *Christopher
Charles Powell*. In the style of the late C19, but, incredible
though it seems, of 1932.

ST MARY (R.C.), Ffynnongroew Road. 1974–5 by *Weightman
& Bullen*. Three chambers in all, separated by movable partitions. Low brick walls, clerestory window strips, and tall
and slated pyramid roofs arranged with vertical windows at
their apexes.*

BAPTIST CHURCH, Sussex Street. 1862–3. Brick and stone
front, Italianate, with a two-column porch of giant Corinthian
order. *F. D. Johnson*, the architect, was presented with a gold
watch by the committee to mark their approval. (VH)

TABERNACL BAPTIST CHAPEL, Water Street. 1866–7 by
Richard Owens. Rock-faced front. Low-pitched gable, round
arches and Gothic detail.

CHRIST CHURCH CONGREGATIONAL CHURCH, Water Street.
1885 by *Owen Edwards*. (CW) Gothic. Asymmetrical façade,
with a short saddlebacked tower between the chapel and
lecture-hall fronts.

CARMEL INDEPENDENT CHAPEL, Queen Street, 1850. Asymmetrical front. Round-arched, with circles in the tracery.
Small tower with concave-pyramid roof.

METHODIST CHURCH, Bath Street. 1867–8 by *C. O. Ellison*.
Polygonal masonry. Lancets and a spiky timber porch.

BRUNSWICK METHODIST CHAPEL, Brighton Road. Round-
arched. Front with tall pedimented centre and lower
hipped-roofed bays either side. Schoolroom at rear dated
1873.

WELSH PRESBYTERIAN (CALVINISTIC METHODIST)
CHAPEL, Clwyd Street. 1855 by *W. Owen* of Llanrwst. Thin
and simple Gothic, in a hard brick with stone dressings.

WELSH PRESBYTERIAN (CALVINISTIC METHODIST)
CHAPEL, Warren Road. 1895 by *Thomas Parry* of Colwyn
Bay. Flat façade of bright red brick and terra-cotta.

PRESBYTERIAN CHURCH OF WALES, Princes Street. 1884–5
by *Richard Davies*. Red brick, stone dressings. Lancets and
plate tracery, and an octagonal corner turret with spirelet.

---

*The predecessor church, OUR LADY OF THE ASSUMPTION, 1863–4, was
designed by *Hungerford Pollen* for Father Wynne of the Voelas family (*see* p. 259).
Romanesque, originally polychromatic and with notable painted decoration, it had
been sadly mutilated, but its loss remains regrettable. Craftsmen involved included
O'Shea (VH) of Oxford Museum fame.

PUBLIC BUILDINGS

TOWN HALL, Wellington Road. Gothic, with polygonal masonry. 1874–6 by *Wood & Turner* of Barrow-in-Furness. Dull, except for a characterful clock tower, which rises straight from the pavement and has an octagonal slated spire. Symmetrical end to Water Street. The main front was also symmetrical, or nearly so, before the addition of a CARNEGIE LIBRARY, in similar style and materials, 1906–7. Previous town halls included a building of 1849 in High Street, and another in Wellington Road, 1854–6 by *T. M. Penson*.

ROYAL ALEXANDRA HOSPITAL, East Parade. Built as a children's hospital and convalescent home, the first stage in 1898–1902 (with foundation stone of 1894 transferred from another site) and continued *c*.1910 and later. It was designed by *Waterhouse*, and is recognizable as a late work. Brick. Stone dressings, and tending to Tudor, with mullions and transoms, and brick diapering in the gables. Frontage with administrative section in the middle and ward blocks either side. These have balconies (now filled in) between corner towers with steep pavilion roofs. The hospital had previously occupied converted premises which some time after 1873 acquired a CHAPEL by *Douglas*; with slight enlargement, this was re-erected and incorporated by *Waterhouse*. Much timberwork, including arcades enriched with tracery and with octagonal posts turning square. REREDOS, probably by *Douglas*, with Crucifixion and painted panels, and five two-light STAINED GLASS windows by *Kempe*, latest commemoration date 1900.

PRINCE EDWARD WAR MEMORIAL HOSPITAL, Grange Road. 1922–3 by *F. A. Roberts*. Shaped gables. Also Georgian features, including a Venetian window and a pedimented doorcase in the central gabled pavilion.

CEFNDY HOSTEL, Cefndy Road. For the mentally handicapped. By *Bowen Dann Davies Partnership* 1973–5, in association with the County Architect. Scandinavian-looking, and intentionally of domestic, non-institutional character. Low, spreading and irregular in layout and massing. Gently pitched concrete-tiled roofs, and a pleasing feel of organic materials in the use of timber and buff-coloured brick. Pitched roofs are exploited in section inside, and the main corridor, with exposed brick and festooned with planting, suggests an internal street, giving access to the main rooms and the residential units. The latter are arranged informally in their relation to each other and to the whole, though each in itself is to a standard repetitive plan.

A separate workshop block, CEFNDY ENTERPRISES, groups with the hostel.

MANWEB (Merseyside and North Wales Electricity Board), Cefndy Road. An extensive two-storey building, on an angled plan, providing offices, workshops, storage etc. By the *Biggins Sargent Partnership* of Chester, 1973–5. Solid-looking and rational. Concrete stanchions are exposed below, and the upper storey, with pre-cast fascias top and bottom, has windows between brick infill panels.

At the end of West Parade is VORYD HARBOUR, at the mouth of the River Clwyd. VORYD FRIDGE, completed 1932, comprises two steel spans, each of 150ft. By *R. G. Whitley*, County Surveyor.

SUN CENTRE. *See* Perambulation.

PERAMBULATION

What follows is not arranged as a perambulation. Of the buildings in the town centre to be mentioned, several are on East and West Parades (i.e. the promenade), and the remainder may be seen by following High Street inland, from the junction of these two, with a short diversion round Sussex Street, Queen Street and Wellington Road, followed by one to the E for Clwyd Street.

Rhyl, the earliest of the North Wales coast resorts, has developed as an unashamedly popular one, and its zestfulness and the accoutrements of amusement are in obvious contrast to the charm and greater decorum of Llandudno. The station platforms are enormous; the promenade extends for nearly two miles, and the town feels very much larger than in fact it is (the population in 1981 was little more than 22,000). It may also be sensed that there is a hard edge to it, as well as the fun. Rhyl may never have had its Pinkie Brown, but it is hard to imagine Llandudno figuring as the scene of an alibi in the A6 murder case, or Baron Corvo repairing to it from Holywell in search of youthful male company. Not a parochial place, and it was in Rhyl that the firm of Garnett, Cloughley, Blakemore & Associates began as *Garnett & Cloughley*, before moving on to design the psychedelic Chelsea Drug Store in the London of the Swinging Sixties, to establish an international practice, and to become house architects to the R.I.B.A.

Growth began in the late 1820s; a terrace and the first part of the promenade were built in 1846, the railway came two years later, and an Improvement Act was obtained in 1852. At one stage *Owen Williams* of Liverpool was responsible for some town-planning work. Among the earliest houses must be the stone-faced ones in CLWYD STREET, existing 1852. Evidence of systematic town planning may be seen at the intersection of QUEEN STREET and SUSSEX STREET, also existing 1852, with four splayed and slightly concave corners. In the early streets, and forming a really distinctive feature, are numerous canted bays, many with fluted corner columns, and many surviving as oriels in stuccoed façades above inserted shop-fronts. Bay-windows were the *sine qua non* of later streets and promenade terraces of boarding houses (lots of them now holiday flatlets) built in red and yellow brick.

The PROMENADE extends as EAST PARADE and WEST PAR-
ADE. Redevelopment has taken place at its initial nucleus (e.g.
QUEEN'S HOTEL, 1892), and the terrace of 1846 may remain
only in mutilated form, between Queen and Water Streets.
Immediately E of High Street, and probably pre-dating the
promenade, are REGENCY COURT and, with later Victorian
embellishment, DOLAWEN. Further along, a castellated
TOWER, one of a pair existing by 1852, and THE GABLES
(No. 42 East Parade), a Gothic villa of 1855.

As for the ARCHITECTURE OF RECREATION AND ENTERTAIN-
MENT, much has been lost, including the PIER, by *James
Brunlees*, 1866–7, which was demolished in 1972, and
had earlier been curtailed. The WINTER GARDENS by
Owen Edwards, 1876, occupied 35 acres between Wellington
Road and the Promenade. Promoted by the Rhyl Winter
Gardens, Aquarium, Land and Building Company with the
intention of providing assembly rooms, skating rink and an
art gallery, but few of these attractions, and perhaps not
even the aquarium, were completed. A theatre did materialize,
and continued in use until 1897, even though the ven-
ture as a whole was not a success and much of the rest of the
site had been sold off for building in 1894. The late C20
version of winter gardens presents itself at the SUN CENTRE,
East Parade, by *Gillinson, Barnett & Partners* of Leeds, built
1976–80. A steel portal frame of lattice girders encloses a
ground area of *c.*57,500 sq. ft. Full-height glazing on three
sides meets the roof, which is clad with bronze-tinted PVC.
Facilities offered include bathing pools (one a surfing pool;
the main one also has a wave machine) and an overhead
monorail. Tropical vegetation. The scheme was designed also
to have a theatre, which is intended as a second stage.

In HIGH STREET, the PLAZA CINEMA, by *S. Colwyn
Foulkes*, 1930–1, should first be noted. Brick, with the entrance in a canted bay at one end, its upper stage a recessed
loggia roofed with Roman tiles. Much small-scale Adamesque
ornament, extending to the fascia of the canopy and the adjoining pub. Deserving close study, the detailing is really too
good, or at any rate too delicate, for a busy street-corner site.
Bolder side elevation, anticipating the architect's strongly 119
rectangular subsequent cinemas. Panels with ornamented
brick surrounds, and stone masks atop brick fluting, articulate
the wall of the auditorium. Classical interiors, with a rich
frieze in the lower foyer, and Corinthian pilasters grouped
either side of the screen, though the auditorium (which
marked Colwyn Foulkes's first collaboration with *Holophane
Ltd* in a scheme for coloured lighting) has, alas, been divided
up.

The REGAL, 1935–7, demolished following closure in 1962, 118
represented the peak of *Colwyn Foulkes*'s achievement as a
cinema architect, and except perhaps for St Thomas's Church
it was the best building in Rhyl. The brick pub which adjoined it, now the KESTREL, is all that remains. The frontage

of the cinema proper was also of brick, with travertine facing framing the entrance below the canopies; elegant ornament adorned the canopy fascias and there was much excellent decorative brickwork. As well as a *Holophane* lighting scheme in the auditorium, the façade was, as Mr Vernon Hughes points out, designed with special regard for nocturnal appearance and lighting effects. Bright light was concentrated below the canopies; higher up, metal grilles in panels showed in silhouette, and slits in the frieze and in the brickwork of Corinthianesque pilasters contained subtly coloured neon tubes.

The ODEON (now ASTRA) was also opened in 1937. Brick (with channelling), faience, rounded corners, and, of course, by *Harry Weedon*. A semicircular projection containing the entrance, and set against a corner tower, may be compared to the less bombastic embayed feature at the Plaza. Here, too, the auditorium has been divided.

Of other town-centre buildings, only the MIDLAND BANK in WELLINGTON ROAD calls for mention. By *J. Francis Doyle* of Liverpool, 1899–1901, for the North and South Wales Bank. Brick and stone, three storeys, quadrant corner with a huge shell hood and Ionic columns above.

Finally, some suburban houses by *Garnett & Cloughley*, designed after Patrick Garnett had been working in America, and in each of which the newly formed partnership experimented with ideas and materials.* In MAES-Y-DON AVENUE is NEW HOUSE, 1961, blocky, of yellow brick, and with low-pitched hipped roofs and far-projecting eaves recalling Frank Lloyd Wright. Monumentally symmetrical entrance in a wide, deeply recessed porch. In THE BOULEVARD, a noncommittal face is presented by No. 7, 1960, with a screen of open-patterned concrete blocks at the entrance. They were designed by the architects and cast locally, and mark the first use in Britain of a device soon seized upon by spec builders and DIY enthusiasts. The house was built for Mr Garnett's mother; No. 1, of 1962, was for himself. With large areas of glazing, this has a flat-roofed and timber-framed superstructure (containing the living room), oversailing a base of grey brick. In contrast to this differentiation of the storeys by both massing and materials is No. 150 RHUDDLAN ROAD nearby. Its walls form a series of smooth-rendered and inward-curving screens, with the vertical voids between them continuing through both storeys. All is contained beneath a low-pitched hipped roof and wide-spreading eaves. Like a house in Clayton Drive, Prestatyn (q.v.), it was for a Garnett brother. By *Garnett, Cloughley & Blakemore*, 1965–6, after the practice had transferred to London.

---

* Mr Garnett kindly supplied information on these houses.

ST ASAPH / LLANELWY

CATHEDRAL

INTRODUCTION. It is believed that a monastery (*clas*) and episcopal see were founded *c*.560 by St Kentigern (St Mungo) after he had been forced to leave his see at Glasgow, and that on his return to Scotland, *c*.573, he was succeeded as bishop by St Asaph. Although the *clas* doubtless continued, the bishopric fell into abeyance until refounded in 1143 as part of the Norman reorganization of the Welsh Church – the last of the four episcopal sees to be thus established. The present cathedral is cruciform, with central tower and aisled and clerestoried nave. With a length of only 182ft it is the smallest of the cathedrals of Wales and England, and if viewed in any spirit of comparison with the medieval greater churches of England, it is inevitably a disappointment. Equally it should not be thought of merely as a large and orderly parish church. Dr Johnson noted that it 'has something of dignity and grandeur', and it is as a strong and grave Welsh cathedral church that it may be appreciated and enjoyed.

Some building is known to have been in hand in 1239, and this may have included the choir, which retained E.E. character until the C18. The remainder was largely rebuilt after the cathedral had been burnt by Edward I's troops in 1282, an attack made in revenge for the suspected complicity of Bishop Anian II in the uprising of that year. Although then expelled from the see, two years later he was permitted to return, and £100 was granted towards compensation for the damage to the building. A scheme on the part of King and Bishop to transfer the see to Rhuddlan came to nothing, and the reconstruction at St Asaph has been supposed to have begun in 1284 and to have continued until 1381. Breaks in the masonry and irregularities in the setting out would be consistent with prolonged execution, but some of these puzzles more probably result from the survival of earlier fragments, and the features of the Dec nave, transepts and crossing belong to a unified scheme and are datable to the early C14. Dr John Maddison ascribes the work to *c*.1310-20, and draws attention to significant affinities with the details of Caernarfon Castle.*

If this is the correct dating, St Asaph provides a notable early instance of extensive and consistent use of the wave and sunk chamfer – mouldings which, though highly characteristic of the C14, remained uncommon until *c*.1320. Their development in favour may be seen to have emanated from the example and impetus provided by Caernarfon; it was there, in the initial building period of 1283-92, that they were first

* 'Decorated Architecture in the North-West Midlands: An Investigation of the Work of Provincial Masons and their Sources', unpublished thesis, University of Manchester, 1978. I am indebted to Dr Maddison for many helpful comments and suggestions, and I wish also to acknowledge the assistance and observations of the Dean, the Very Rev. Raymond Renowden.

applied impressively and profusely, and they continued to be employed in the lengthy early C14 campaign. Master *Henry of Ellerton* was engaged upon the latter, first under Walter of Hereford, and in full control following the death of Master Walter in 1309, and the rebuilding of St Asaph may tentatively be attributed to him.

With the addition of the tower, 1391–2, by *Robert Fagan*, the cathedral was completed, only to be burnt by Owain Glyndŵr in 1402. The reroofing of the nave after this further calamity was probably undertaken by Bishop Robert de Lancaster (1411–33), though restoration was not completed until the time of Bishop Redman (1471–95). Repair after desecration in the Commonwealth was carried out by Bishop Griffith (1660–9) and his successor. In 1778–80 the choir was remodelled by one of the Turners. This was almost certainly *Joseph Turner*, though a 'Mr Turner' who carried out early C19 repairs and who furnished the choir, 1809–10, was probably *John Turner*. Some work was done by *Benjamin Gummow*, *c.*1810–11, and *Lewis Wyatt* inserted plaster vaulting in the nave, obscuring the clerestory, *c.*1822. Much of what was done in the C18 and early C19 was undone in the major restoration of 1867–75 by *Sir Gilbert Scott*. A restoration of 1929–32 was by *C. M. Oldrid Scott*, a grandson of Sir Gilbert.

23 EXTERIOR. The E.E. choir, the walls of which survived the fires of 1282 and 1402, was of three bays with a two-storeyed chapter house projecting from the middle bay on the N. A Perp seven-light E window belonged to Bishop Redman's work, though the arch and outer moulding of a C14 window had been reused. In the 1778–80 remodelling, the chapter house was demolished, and of the N and S windows some were walled up and others renewed to a new Gothic design. At the same time the Perp tracery of the E window was replaced with Geometrical, supposedly inspired by Tintern, and plaster vaulting was provided inside. The present appearance is due to *Scott*. Before the commencement of his general restoration, he renewed again the tracery of the E window, still retaining the C14 opening. His Dec design was executed under the local architect *H. John Fairclough*, 1864. (VH) Then in 1867–8 *Scott* gave back an E.E. appearance to the N and S sides, authentic in the elements, if not completely so in detail. A corbel table was reinstated (a castellated parapet had been introduced on the N), but there is no known authority for the shafts to the gabled buttresses. The original arrangement of windows was restored, with a three-lancet group for the westernmost bay and pairs elsewhere. Fenestration was introduced into the N bay against which the chapter house had abutted, and the recessed round-headed chapter-house doorway revealed. All windows have ringed shafts, but there are stiff leaf caps in the westernmost bay only, and the paired lancets have larger and detached shafts and dogtooth in the arches. This stems from the Dean and Chapter not having permitted a full investigation before the commencement of the work, which began at

the E end; only when the far bay was reached was evidence found to permit what was claimed to be a more correct restoration.

Further W, the only features which can definitely be said to pre-date the C14 Dec rebuilding are the gabled and chamfered buttresses of the W front, which are C13 survivals. The SW corner buttresses have a chamfered plinth, which previously extended across the façade, where now there are, as around the rest of the building, mouldings of the mid-C14 type. At no point can these moulded plinths be relied upon as authentic. Two W pinnacles are of c.1840 in their present form, and the N and S windows of the aisles are of 1830 and 1844 respectively, as are, no doubt, the N and S doorways. (The N entrance had been blocked, and replaced by a now vanished Perp doorway further E.) All other windows (including the two-light aisle W windows, which those on the N and S sides previously resembled) belong to the C14 work and display sunk chamfer. W portal with six orders of continuous sunk chamfers and no intervening caps. Good six-light W window, emphatically divided into three two-light sub-arches and with early Curvilinear tracery of daggers and mouchettes. Three-light reticulated E windows in the transepts, two in the S transept and one in the N. More interesting are the five-light transept N and S windows, with tracery of intersecting ogees and a two-tier reticulated pattern of vesicas (or daggers) and concave lozenges. The design is not far removed from the early Perp work in the Hereford chapter house of c.1364 (destroyed) and the E cloister at Gloucester of approximately similar date. Yet it may be assigned to the early C14 building campaign, albeit late within it. Nave clerestory of square multifoil windows, which, despite a change of masonry above the arcades inside, are likely to belong to this period rather than to the C15 restoration. *Scott* reopened those on the S and reinstated the N ones, which had been done away with in the 1822 alterations. The windows coincide with the spacing of the aisle bays on the N but not on the S. In fact the clerestories and the N aisle windows to a large extent correspond internally with the arcades, to which the S aisle bays do not relate. Though nave and transepts have probably always had corbel tables, parapets seem to have been introduced only in the late C18. Those of the nave were converted to battlements, almost certainly by *Lewis Wyatt*, and still remain as such on the N. Flat-roofed SE vestries of 1956.

Finally, the tower, which in 1391 *Robert Fagan* of Chester, mason, undertook to build, and to complete the following year. Three-light bell openings, each with a transom and tracery of intersecting ogees tending towards Perp. This is almost certainly authentic in design, though the upper part of the tower was rebuilt after storm damage in 1715, and the battlemented parapet was renewed, in simplified form, in 1806. NE vice turret.

INTERIOR. The choir presents itself as entirely the work of

Scott, who lined it with ashlar and replaced the C18 plaster vault with a panelled wagon ceiling. As externally, the reportedly more authentic windows of the westernmost bay differ from the others. They have clustered shafts and some stiff-leaf, in contrast to the dogtooth and detached polished shafts of the rest. Triple SEDILIA (Scott found fragments of a predecessor) and ENCAUSTIC TILE flooring.

Nave arcades of five bays, the westernmost shorter than the others. Arcades and crossing arches simple and uniform and, like the W doorway, with continuous mouldings and no capitals. The effect is consistent, harmonious and austere – the austerity being, as Dr Maddison has written, 'the architecture of men whose aesthetic was conditioned by their employment in a massive and continuing programme of military architecture'. The inner sides of the crossing arches are of three orders. Two prevail elsewhere, and the arcade piers are, in other words, four semi-octagons with their diagonals moulded. The ubiquitous C14 curve appears also on the bases, which consist of two double ogees – one for the plinth and one for the base proper. Different – with double rolls – are the bases of the SE crossing pier and of the outer responds of the arches between aisles and transepts. They are likely to be earlier than the rest, though only slightly so, and, like the others, they incorporate the wave plan of the shaft above.* Different again are the large unwrought plinths of the arcade W responds, and these must belong with the earlier buttresses of the W front. The southern one is not exactly in line with the arcade, and greater disparity exists between the axes of the choir and nave. On the N the arcade and crossing arch align with the wall of the choir, whereas on the S they are set some 2ft inwards. It may, incidentally, be noted that the narrow westernmost bay of the arcade would be the right dimension for six of equal size. The setting out of the S aisle (already mentioned as being out of step) would be partially, though not entirely, consistent with five equal bays.

In the nave and crossing *Scott* replaced Wyatt's plasterwork with timber vaulting, though that in the nave (where original carved corbels were utilized) is little more than a handsome ribbed and boarded ceiling, not of true vaulted form. Trussed rafter roofs in the transepts, possibly intended for timber wagon ceilings, were stripped of plaster in *C. M. O. Scott*'s restoration. Selective and misguided colouring and gilding of Sir Gilbert's roofs, including that of the choir, is of 1968.

FURNISHINGS. FONT. Perp in style and incorporating four quatrefoil panels from a predecessor destroyed during the Commonwealth. Said to be of the 1660s, but it looks C19. – Thoroughly good fittings belonging to *Sir Gilbert Scott*'s res-

---

* The E return of the SE crossing pier base, now hidden, is set at an angle. See *Archaeologia Cambrensis*, 7th ser., vol. I, 1921, p. 215. The suggestion is there made that a shafted pier with diagonal base was first intended, and that the line of this was extended, after the change of plan.

toration include the RAILS, the eagle LECTERN, the PULPIT, with some incised patterning and busts looking out from panels, and the REREDOS which, with the arcading either side, was completed in 1871. Its alabaster relief of the Procession to Calvary was executed by *Earp*. (VH)

STALLS. Late C15, dating from the time of Bishop Redman, 35 and the only remaining medieval canopied stalls in Wales. Mr Harvey considers they may have been designed by *William Frankelyn*. Ten either side. The canopies, splayed forward and vaulted, each have corner pinnacles and three crocketed gables. Miscricords, each with a semi-cone bracket and fleuron supporters. Restored by *Scott*, who replaced the traceried backs, apparently correctly, and also added a diagonally placed return stall either side. Although detached shafts probably existed originally, the present ones, of unsuitably early Gothic stamp, date only from 1906, when also the backs were interfered with. Before 1832, the stalls had occupied their present position in the choir, but in that year *Thomas Jones* moved them W into the crossing, adding SCREENWORK in the N and S crossing arches behind. He also inserted a stone ORGAN SCREEN in the W arch.* This was done away with by *Scott*, who moved the organ to the N transept and, as well as adding the return stalls, designed CHOIR BENCHES and DESK FRONTS and a canopied BISHOP'S THRONE. In 1932 *C. M. O. Scott* moved the stalls back into the choir, together with the throne, and only some of Sir Gilbert's desk fronts etc. and Jones's S screen remain at the crossing. – The ORGAN CASE, in its present form, is of 1966, and so is its inappropriate colouring.

STAINED GLASS. An E window of *c.*1800 by *Francis Eginton* was removed when the tracery was renewed by *Scott* in 1864. The pictorial lights went to Llandegla (*see* p. 192) and some of the heraldry is in the S transept northernmost window. – The present E window, 1864, is by *Ward & Hughes*. – Also by them the choir N and S windows. Of these the westernmost on the N and S have commemoration dates of 1889 and 1886 respectively, and the rest are a set of *c.*1870. – By the same, the S aisle easternmost, 1895. – N aisle easternmost by *Whitefriars*, commemoration date 1925. – The W window was by *Gibbs*, 1855–6; its tracery lights remain, but the rest was, regrettably, replaced with glass by *C. C. Powell*, 1940.

MONUMENTS. In the N transept: Richard Price Thelwall. By *Benjamin Bromfield*, 1775. Drapery below the tablet, urn against an obelisk above. – In the S aisle: effigy of a bishop. Probably Anian II †1293. Very well carved, and not Welsh in style or workmanship. Somewhat mutilated. The head rests on a diagonally set cushion. Canopy of a sub-cusped trefoil, with foliations, pinnacles and angels. Lion at his feet. The pedestal, on which it was set in 1932, was part of a monument

---

* It was probably in the alterations of 1778–80 that Bishop Redman's stone pulpitum, in the E crossing arch, was destroyed.

in the N transept to Bishop Luxmoore †1830, designed by *Thomas Jones*, which had been dismantled. – Dean Shipley. By *John Ternouth*, 1829. Free-standing seated effigy, life-size, holding a pen and scroll. – Sir John Williams †1830 and wife Margaret †1835. By *Sir Richard Westmacott*, with his device of symmetrical embracing angels, here full-length figures. – Sir John Hay Williams. Signed in Greek by *L. Droses*, Athens, 1873. Woman with infant and an older child. – Some C19 BRASSES, e.g. Dean Bonnor †1889. – Sarah Hay Williams †1876. A brass and enamel tablet. – Also a SEPULCHRAL SLAB of c.1330. Sword and heraldic shield and a hound and hare.

Iron-clad CHEST dated 1738. – (PASTORAL STAFF. Designed by *Sedding* and made by *Barkentin & Krall*, 1890.)
In the churchyard the TRANSLATORS' MEMORIAL, commemorating the tercentenary of Bishop William Morgan's Welsh Bible of 1588. By *Middleton & Prothero* of Cheltenham, 1892. Neo-Perp, octagonal. In niches, statues (executed by *Boulton*) of the Bishop and his precursors and collaborators in the translating of the scriptures into Welsh.

There is no precinct as such, but the following may be mentioned here.
DIOCESAN REGISTRY, at the NW corner of the churchyard. 1810. (DOE) Low-pitched battlemented gable ends. Gothic windows, two with iron glazing bars and tracery.
KENTIGERN HALL, N of the cathedral, built as CANONRY. Mid-Victorian Neo-Elizabethan with a scholastic whiff. Three-gable front, generously scaled.
DEAN WILLIAMS LIBRARY, SE of the cathedral. 1894 by *John Kendall*. Castellated. Reconstructed internally 1972–4.
72 Former BISHOP'S PALACE (Plas yr Esgob), W of the cathedral. Ashlar E front, dated 1791. Attributable to *Samuel Wyatt*, but the masonry is less smooth and crisp in execution than is usual in the Wyatt style. One and a half storeys, with panels between. Three bays either side of a three-window curved bow carrying a shallow dome. No window surrounds, but the doorcase has consoles and an entablature. The W front forms a striking contrast, being in Elizabethan, by *Edward Blore*, 1830–1. Tall, near-symmetrical, and rock-faced with sandstone dressings. Tall windows either side of the doorway light the entrance hall, which has stairs immediately inside. The building was converted into flats for elderly people, 1977–8, by *Brian Vaughan* for a housing trust. Large brick extensions involved the demolition of a S wing, and the interior was subdivided, but a room with a good marble chimneypiece remains in the C18 part. Also the upper room of the bow, with a heavy cornice.
ESGOBTY, the replacement bishop's house, immediately W of the cathedral. 1975 by *The Anthony Clark Partnership*.
ESGOPTY FARM, SW of the cathedral. Brick. According to DOE it is of c.1795, but with gable ends coped in stone and door-

way with semicircular hood the date must be much earlier in the c18. (Staircase still with a string, but fairly slender turned balusters also. Small gabled DOVECOTE. NMR) In the 1930s some panelling was transferred to the National Museum.

TOWN

ST KENTIGERN AND ST ASAPH, High Street. A double-naved church showing at the w end a change in masonry between the earlier s part and the Perp N extension. A single lancet remains on the s. All other windows, with cusping and four-centred heads, are Perp, as is the w doorway.* s nave E window of five lights with panel tracery. That of the N nave, of four lights, has two sub-arches and panel tracery above a transom. s porch, w bellcote and N vestry belong to *Sir Gilbert Scott*'s restoration of 1872. s door dated 1687. Five-bay arcade, its slender piers with keeled shafts and hollowed concave corners. Hammerbeam N roof with curved struts, slightly cusped, above the collars. The s roof has much moulding, fully cusped struts and bosses at the intersections of purlins and alternate rafters. It too has hammerbeams, but so slight as not to function as such. On the s a DOUBLE PISCINA. STAINED GLASS. Easternmost on s by *Kempe & Tower*. Commemoration date 1912. – MONUMENT. Thomas Humphreys †1698. Drapery, held by four winged cherubs, around the tablet. Heraldry and a garland above. – Painted ROYAL ARMS. Hanoverian, pre-1801.

EBENEZER WELSH PRESBYTERIAN CHAPEL (former), Gemig Street. 1843. Two-storey longitudinal front, of five bays. Domestic-looking doorway with fanlight and recessed columns. Another entrance at higher level, in the gable end.

CEMETERY CHAPEL, Mount Road. *c.*1848–9. Lancets and a w bellcote.

SCHOOL, Upper Denbigh Road, E of the cathedral. 1857 by *H. John Fairclough*. School house at one end and a gable containing a Gothic window at the other.

H. M. STANLEY HOSPITAL, ½ m. SE. The former workhouse, renamed after the explorer who, as John Rowlands, spent his childhood here. The younger *Thomas Penson* made designs, 1837, but *John Welch* seems to have been responsible for the building as executed, 1838. Two-storeyed limestone frontage, the ground-floor windows arched. Three-bay centre flanked by pedimented two-bay projections and two widely spaced bays at either end, i.e. eleven in all. Axial cruciform layout behind, now partially obscured, with a higher block inserted at the crossing.

BRIDGE. Across the Elwy. The road rises gently over five shallow arches. They are of unequal span, but arranged sym-

* An inscription of 1524 is recorded.

metrically with the widest in the middle. 1770 by *Joseph Tur-*
ner.* The upstream side now partially hidden by a separate
footbridge.

PONT DAFYDD, ½m. NE, beyond the by-pass. The bridge
which once carried the Holywell road across the Clwyd has
been deserted by both highway and river. Said to be of 1630.
Cobbled roadway.

The little town is sited on a spur of hill between the Clwyd and
the Elwy. The HIGH STREET slopes down to the bridge,
westwards from the cathedral, and offers pleasantly varied, if
unremarkable, architectural fare; e.g. below the Diocesan Registry (*see* above), BARBER SHOP, mid-C18, with quoins and
a moulded and hooded doorcase. Also the stone gable end of
the former CHURCH HOUSE (i.e. church hall) by *Douglas &*
Minshull, 1908–9. Opposite, the fronts are set back forming
a small square. The former MOSTYN ARMS has a Doric
porch, interfered with. Further down is the single-
storey MIDLAND BANK by *Woolfall & Eccles*, 1909–10. Mannerist. It eschews the cliché of a diagonal corner entrance.
Below, SHOPS etc. on both sides of the street are mostly C18
and mostly rendered, and include a range with two lunette
windows. ALMSHOUSES, of brick, single-storeyed and very
humble, were rebuilt in 1795. Now a restaurant. Across the
bridge and facing it THE OLD DEANERY, reached past suburban bungalows (DEAN'S WALK). By *Thomas Jones* for
Dean Luxmoore, probably *c.*1830. Simple Tudor, rendered,
with fancy bargeboards, labels, margin panes etc. Symmetrical on the main (garden) front and on one return (entrance
front) and originally so on both. Divided into flats, but retaining plaster vaulting in the hallway and over the staircase.

CHESTER STREET leads E from the cathedral. A single-storey
Italianate building with narrow arched windows and the
Royal Arms in the pediment may have been a POST OFFICE
but is similar to the former County Court at Holywell of
1855. Beyond the former railway the town is left behind, and
on the r. is THE BRYN, with a fine view of the Vale of Clwyd.
1912–13 by *Gronwy Robert Griffith* of Denbigh. Gabled, with
sash windows. Irregular entrance front, but the opposite side
of the main block is symmetrical. Influence of Philip Webb
may be discerned, though the brickwork is of the gently textured rustic sort, characteristic of the early C20. Opposite,
BRONWYLFA retains the ground-floor walls of a *Douglas*
house of *c.*1884, burnt in the late 1930s. A predecessor house
was the home of Mrs Felicia Hemans of *Casabianca* fame.
She lived also at RHYLLON, ½m. further NE, an C18 brick
farmhouse. This has a staircase, rising through two storeys,
with swept rail and columnar balusters.

In MOUNT ROAD, N from the cathedral, MOUNT HEY, 1960,
is the first house which *Garnett & Cloughley* designed after
setting up practice in Rhyl. Single-storeyed, with flat roof.

* According to Mr Howell.

BODEUGAN, Waen, 1¼ m. ENE. Central chimney and lobby entry plan. C17 staircase with moulded string, heavy turned balusters and small square newels. Chamfered beams and joists, the chamfer-stops moulded. Gabled brick DOVECOTE.

BRYN ASAPH, ⅝ m. SSE. A house by *Thomas Jones* similar in style to his Deanery (*see* above). The entrance and garden fronts and one end elevation were symmetrical. Traces of his work may be seen on the two latter, but refaced, for the house was remodelled, almost certainly by *Douglas*, 1879.* He used pebbledash and brick dressings and gave the entrance front a square turret with steep pyramid roof attached to a broader tower-like block with a pyramid roof and dormer. *Jones*'s glazed entrance screen remains, and there are original features inside. A simple *Douglas* chimneypiece in the dining room. His STABLES have a small but eventful gatehouse. Pyramid roof with dormer and crowning dovecote. Attached is a conical-roofed staircase turret of free sculptural form in its lower stage.

In Glascoed Road, 1¼ m. E, the factory of Chance Pilkington Ltd, and opposite it (across the Denbighshire border) that of PILKINGTON P.E. LTD, where electro-optical systems are made. A building of quality and elegance by *Ormrod & Partners* of Liverpool, 1966–7. Three-storey office block with tinted glazing and brick infill panels between exposed aggregate bands. A glazed link to the neatly clad factory proper on one side is continued as a reception unit on the other. In the entrance hall a fibreglass sculptural panel by *William Mitchell*.

SALTNEY

3060

A Chester suburb which extends into Wales.

ST MARK, High Street. *See The Buildings of England: Cheshire*.

ST MATTHEW, Saltney Ferry. 1910–11 by *Douglas*, though possibly to a *Douglas & Minshull* design of 1905. Brick outside and in, with lancets. A longer nave and a NW tower were intended. Broad nave and chancel and a S passage aisle. The arcade has arches of two chamfered orders dying into octagonal piers. Not impressive externally, even allowing for its being incomplete. The interior is more rewarding.

SANDYCROFT see QUEENSFERRY

SEALAND see QUEENSFERRY

* Some alterations seem to have been made at an intermediate date, and an iron veranda with cusped Gothic arches was not part of Jones's design.

SHOTTON *see* QUEENSFERRY

SOUGHTON HALL *see* NORTHOP

SYCHDEN HALL *see* NORTHOP

TALACRE

1080

TALACRE ABBEY. Talacre was the seat of a Roman Catholic branch of the Mostyns. Since 1920 it has housed an enclosed community of Benedictine nuns. By *Thomas Jones*, replacing a Jacobean house. It was begun 1824, burnt while under construction 1827, and completed 1829. Neat and symmetrical Tudor Gothic, of ashlar, with labels, miniature octagonal corner turrets, and battlemented parapets which continue over low-pitched gables. The main, NE, front, cannot be fully seen from outside the enclosure, and has been encroached upon by the later church. It had a gable either end, a projecting loggia of three four-centred arches, and a central oriel. Returns of three bays to the l. and five to the r., where there is an oriel and, thanks to the fall of the ground, a terrace on arcades. The rear elevation was probably always rendered asymmetrical by a service wing, where a large later extension now stands. It is this which is now mainly seen by visitors approaching from the SW and skirting the house on the SE. The CHURCH is of 1931-2, with a pyramid-roofed campanile of 1952. Peeping above the wall of the enclosure is a stone octagon, rising from the roof of a much larger one. This is said to have been a RIDING SCHOOL, and is similar in style to the house, and obviously contemporary. Also obviously by *Jones* the attractive STABLES, round three sides of a court, with central gable and clock cupola.

Former R.C. SCHOOL, ½m. S. 1857 by *J. Spencer* of Liverpool, at the expense of Sir Pyers Mostyn. Scholastic Gothic, rock-faced. Symmetrical arrangement of two L-shaped blocks (boys' and girls'), each consisting of a schoolroom and teacher's house.

Almost opposite the road to the Abbey is the C19 pumping engine house of the GRONANT LEAD MINE, now converted to offices. PENTRE, ⅛m. SW of it, has mullioned windows, including a couple in gabled dormers. Lintel, with label, dated 1574.

OLD COURTLANDS, Gwespyr, behind the farm of Brynllystyn, ¾m. SE of the Abbey. Another house whose mullioned windows include two in dormers. Lateral chimney, with gabled breast, and an inside cross passage. Of two units only, if a separate room linked to the main house is discounted. (Arched-braced roof. DOE)

LIGHTHOUSE, Point of Ayr, at the northernmost tip of the

Welsh mainland, beyond shacks, caravans and sandhills. A
tapering tower of 1777 by *Joseph Turner*. Altered *c*.1824; the
lantern stage is of this date. A further lighthouse, a piled
structure of iron, does not survive. It was by *Walker &
Burges*, 1844.

TALLARN GREEN*

4040

ST MARY MAGDALENE. 1872–3 by *John Edge*. Rock-faced.
Small, with nave and polygonal apse under one tall roof.
Lancets. A clock turret against the N porch, with square tiled
spire, was added in 1888.

The church was built at the expense of members of the
Kenyon family (*see* Gredington, p. 361, and Llannerch Panna,
p. 416). The Honourables Georgina and Henrietta Kenyon,
daughters of the third Baron, were also largely responsible
for the VICARAGE. With half-timbering above a brick ground
storey, this is by *Douglas*, 1882. It was built as a curate's
house in what was then part of the parish of Malpas, and,
although small, it is like a Douglas country house in miniature, with a well-fitted-up interior, still largely complete.
Built with an oratory, now used as a study.

KENYON COTTAGES, a short way SE of the church. 1892 by
Douglas & Fordham, for Henrietta Kenyon. Two single-storey dwellings for widows, and a labourer's house between.
Bright red roofs and chimneys, but otherwise an unusually
literal piece of vernacular revivalism, brick-nogged, with the
brickwork whitened in the local tradition.

SARN BRIDGE, ½m. WSW. Two segmental arches, a cutwater
(not full height) on the downstream side, and slab parapets.
Abundance of inscriptions, including the dates 1627, 1819
(with the name of *John Turner*, County Surveyor), and 1925,
to which latter time an upstream widening may belong.

THE GELLI, 1⅛m. E. The Misses Kenyon's own house, by
Douglas, 1877. Freely spreading, with three ranges at right
angles to each other, domino-fashion, along the edge of a
hilltop. Brick, with lozenge patterning, and some stone and
half-timber. There is a tower-like block, with pyramid roof
and bellcote. One range, single-storeyed, consists largely of
stabling, and has a dovecote turret. The main rooms face a
view to the N, but the drawing room has a S window as well.
Typical Douglas fittings and details, though in pine rather
than oak. Staircase landing with an arcade on turned posts.

On a nearby hill GELLI FARM is of genuine timber-framing. THE LODGE, an asymmetrical block of two cottages at the
entrance to the long drive, is, however, of 1892, and another
convincing piece of *Douglas & Fordham* brick-nogging.

Genuine half-timber at THE FIELDS, ¾m. SSW, and THE BUCK,
1¼m. SSW on the A road.

---

* In Maelor Saesneg.

WILLINGTON CROSS, Willington, $\frac{7}{8}$ m. SSE. Early or mid-C17. H-plan, but one of the front gables is smaller than its rear counterpart. Originally there was a true cross wing alongside, and the elevations were thus three-gabled. The front, including shaped gables, is now rendered, but brick, and brick mullions, remain exposed at the rear. Dog-leg staircase through two storeys. It has pierced and moulded flat balusters, newels with pierced finials, carved string and, unusually, ornament on the risers also.

CAE-LI-CAE, $\frac{5}{8}$ m. w, belonged to the Gredington estate, and the farmhouse is almost certainly another Kenyon job by *Douglas*.

MULSFORD HALL, I m. WSW. Dated 1746. Of brick. Five bays, with stone quoins and fluted keystones. The centre bay has brick giant pilasters and a brick pedimented doorcase.

(THE) TOWER *see* MOLD, p. 397

TRELAWNYD

An alternative name is Newmarket. This dates from the early C18, when John Wynne, a local landowner, enlarged the village and established a weekly market and annual fair, both later discontinued.

ST MICHAEL. A single chamber, with big, strongly rectangular w bellcote. Remodelled 1724, but late medieval roof trusses remain, arched-braced, with cusped struts above the collars. Whatever C18 character there was was eliminated by *Douglas & Fordham*, 1895–7. They inserted a Neo-Perp E window, put mullions and tracery into the round-headed S windows, removed internal plaster to expose rubble walling, and added a NW vestry. – STAINED GLASS by *Hemming*, in the E window, dates from this time. – FONT. Octagonal, diminishing to a square. – SEPULCHRAL SLAB, set upside down, in the vestry. Upper part of an early C14 shield and sword heraldic slab. – C14 CHURCHYARD CROSS. Chamfered shaft, and stop-chamfering at the projecting base of the head. Cusped panels in the head, cinquefoil on the w and E, containing respectively the Crucifixion, and the Crucifixion with Virgin and (missing) St John. – Outside the E end of the church a set of early C18 Wynne TOMBSTONES. Table type, and one of them a late example of the Welsh hooded tomb. Semicircular hood, formerly with a finial, enclosing a solid panel. Unscholarly ornament on the panels and the table sides.

VICARAGE, E of the church. Of 1842. Three by two bays. Pedimented storeyed porch, and a doorcase with a hood on consoles.

SCHOOL. On the main road. Thorough-going High Victorian of 1860. Cusped lancets and some plate tracery. The chief feature is a gable crowned by a bellcote, and with two closely spaced windows separated by a buttress. The integrated house is given less separate expression than was usual.

CHURCH HALL. On the main road, further E. Built 1909, and with the battered chimneystacks and buttresses of the period. Also a battered and battlemented corner tower.

GOP FARM, ⅜ m. WNW. A high C17 stone DOVECOTE, with stepped gables, now roofless.

The main road follows OFFA'S DYKE from Gop Farm for c. 1¾ m. towards Gorsedd.

The enormous stone CAIRN – the largest in Wales – on the summit of Gop Hill, ¼ m. NNW (SJ 087 802), can be seen dominating the plateau for many miles around. In spite of its fame and prominence it is not possible to give a date or explanation for its construction. At the end of the last century it was investigated by Professor Boyd Dawkins, who sunk a shaft down through the centre and then drove two 30ft-long tunnels along the surface of the bedrock at right angles to each other. However, he failed to find any burial or burial chamber. It is possible that the huge cairn, only slightly smaller than the mound at Newgrange, Ireland, might cover a similar cruciform passage grave, a Neolithic tomb type which has been found in Britain (at Barclodiad y Gawres, Anglesey, and the Calderstones, Liverpool). On the other hand it might be an exceptionally big Bronze Age burial cairn, for this plateau abounds in such monuments. However, most of the local barrows are built of earth, like the BARROW at SJ 096 804, which stands just N of the road beside a modern reservoir mound.

On the southern side of Gop Hill there is a ROCK SHELTER (SJ 087 801), which was also examined by Professor Boyd Dawkins. In this case he did find burials, more than fourteen individuals who had been buried all together in a rough enclosure or chamber built against the back wall of the cave. With these bodies there was a sherd of Peterborough pottery, a jet 'belt slider' and a polished flint knife, all indicative of a Late Neolithic date for the burials. The burial 'chamber' was built upon a thick layer of occupation debris with which were mixed the bones of much older, Pleistocene animals. The subsequent discovery of another narrow cave running off this open shelter revealed a more typical burial deposit of human bones pushed into narrow crevices in the rock and sealed by rough walling. In this cave there were several flint and chert implements, some perhaps Mesolithic in date, together with a Neolithic axe, a Graig Lwyd rough-out.

TREMEIRCHION

A hillside village. A group beside the steep and curving street includes the SCHOOL, 1865, in hard Elizabethan. The coped and finialed gables of the VICARAGE look earlier. The OLD SCHOOL, 1835, is at the opposite end of the churchyard.

CORPUS CHRISTI, formerly Holy Trinity. A single chamber, to which a N transept was added in 1864. W bellcote. The S and a blocked W doorway could be C14. A S window is Perp, and on the N is a domestic-looking one (C17?) encroached on by one of a set of large buttresses. Other windows were replaced by grouped lancets, seemingly in 1859. Late medieval arched-braced roof with, at the E end, the trussed rafters of a former wagon ceiling. Large S porch, also with old roof members, and a timber arch and open framing (renewed 1970) in the gable end. – FONT. Perp. Cusped panels on the stem and coving between stem and bowl. – STAINED GLASS. C15 fragments in the westernmost S window, including tabernacle work, a nimbed cleric, and the head of St Anne. – Third from E on S. A few early quarries, and interesting early C17 portrait panels of James I, John Williams (Keeper of the

Great Seal, Bishop of Lincoln and Archbishop of York) and
Charles I. – With commemoration dates of 1858 are, by *Oliphant*, the E window and, by *Ballantine & Son*, the N and S
easternmost and the transept window. – SEPULCHRAL SLABS.
Fragments of C13 and C14 slabs, e.g. set in the jamb of the
easternmost S window, and in the outside W wall of the porch.
Another loose in the porch, and part of a late C13 interlaced
cross slab in the porch W bench. – MONUMENTS. Late C13
effigy of a knight, thought to be Sir Robert Pounderling.
Cross-legged, grasping a sword, and with his head on a
cushion. – Dafydd ap Hywel ap Madog (Dafydd Ddu Hiraddug). A notable late C14 canopied tomb. Sub-cusped
cinquefoil canopy within a heavily moulded arch. Tonsured
and vested effigy of a priest, his head on a cushion and his
feet on a lion. He lies on a tomb-chest, its front divided into
seven compartments, each containing a shield, below crocketed gables. Both canopy and tomb-chest are dotted with a
small floral motif. For another C14 priestly effigy *see* St
Beuno's College (below). – Two Salusbury HATCHMENTS. –
The CHURCHYARD is circular. – Opposite the porch a
SUNDIAL, formed 1748 from the shaft of the CHURCHYARD
CROSS. The head is at St Beuno's College (*see* below).

(*Opposite*) Tremeirchion,
monument to Dafydd ap Hywel ap Madog
(Dafydd Ddu Hiraddug) and
(*right*) detail of effigy
late fourteenth century
(Colin Gresham, *Medieval Stone
Carving in North Wales*)

BENNAR, W of the church, but much lower, at the edge of the village. By *R. A. Briggs*, *c.* 1908. Roughcast and red-tiled. Between two gables is a semi-octagonal bow with its own pitched roof, a feature of which 'Bungalow Briggs' was fond.

ST BEUNO'S COLLEGE, ¾m. N. A Jesuit foundation. The buildings are on the hillside, overlooking the Vale of Clwyd. Gerard Manley Hopkins wrote much of his poetry while a student here (1874–7) and was greatly moved by the beauty of the Vale. The original parts, by *J. A. Hansom*, are of 1846–9,* and belong to the first generation of the Pugin-inspired collegiate and conventual genre. The verdict of Hopkins, who is known to have admired Butterfield's work, was 'decent outside, skimpin within, like Lancing College done worse.' The early part of the main (W) front has at its N end a four-storey tower with oriel, and to the r. of this the former library, with high roof and traceried windows, and on the S gable-end a canted bay. Panelled wagon roof inside. L. of the tower an extension by *Hansom & Son*, 1873–4. Impressively tall S front to the earlier build, climbing the hill. Internal courtyard, separated by the dining hall (no open roof, just a beamed ceiling) from a N entrance court. The 1873–4 addition, forming the W range of the latter, has five gables and, on either side of the entrance, segmental arches on columns rising out of buttresses.

Extending E from the collegiate buildings is the church, HOLY NAME, part of *Hansom*'s original work of the 1840s. Nave and S aisle, two-light Dec windows and a rib-vaulted polygonal apse. Complicated roof with hammerbeams, enriched with angels.

In the entrance court the head of the C14 CHURCHYARD CROSS (*see* above), on a new shaft. Ogee canopies on all four faces. Cinquefoil panels back and front containing respectively the Crucifixion, with Virgin and St John, and the Virgin and Child. Ecclesiastics with croziers in both the trefoiled side panels. (Also at the college and brought from the parish church are fragments of a late C14 effigy of an unknown priest, in low relief, worn and mutilated.)

OUR LADY OF SORROWS (Rock Chapel), ⅜m. SSE of the college. On a rocky eminence, but now partly hidden by trees. Semicircular apse and diminishing W tower with slender spire, all of miniature scale. Built 1866, and designed by *Father Ignatius Scoles*, while a student at the college. (DOE)

BRYNBELLA, ⅜m. S of the village. Dr Johnson's friend Mrs Thrale was born Hester Lynch Salusbury of the Lleweni family (*see* p. 249). Some years after their marriage, she and her second husband, the Italian music teacher Gabriel Piozzi, decided to settle in Flintshire, and their delectable new house, with its Welsh-Italian name, was built in 1792–5. It is by *C. Mead*, and although *Piozzi* himself is said to have had a hand

---

* Information on the buildings was kindly supplied by Mr Denis Evinson.

in the design, this is open to doubt.* Stuccoed E (entrance) front of two storeys and five bays plus a wing to the l. Delicate fanlight above a Doric stone doorcase, the entablature of which, with paterae in its frieze, has no architrave. The same sense of Neo-Classical freedom combined with refinement of detail characterizes the ashlar W front. Owing to the fall of 74 the ground, there is a basement storey. Two three-window segmental bows and, between them, a four-column Doric porch carrying a balcony. Paterae in the main frieze, and some use of shallow rustication. Five-bay side wings, with niches and three-bay pediments. Though always pedimented, the wings were originally lower, and their upper storey is a mid-C19 interpolation. Interiors of great elegance, said to be by *Michelangelo Pergolesi*. There is, however, no documentary evidence for this, and Adamesque elements, with which Pergolesi is associated, are absent. Indeed, much of the plasterwork is notably bold and substantial, and the fine marble chimneypieces were made by *Bromfield* of Liverpool to *Mead*'s own designs. Cornices and doorcases differ from room to room. Mahogany doors, and a stone staircase with delicate iron balustrade of circle and lozenge patterns. The original disposition included the drawing and dining rooms in the main block with breakfast room between. Beyond the drawing room (present dining room) was a bedroom suite in the S wing. Service quarters were in the basement and N wing. Upstairs is a room with a recess for Piozzi's chamber organ, and with musical instruments depicted on the chimney piece.

Mead was also involved with the layout of the GROUNDS, though his scheme for an ornamental canal was vetoed by Piozzi.

Brick STABLES by *Mead*, *c*.1795–6. Seven bays with three-bay pediment. Arched ground-floor openings and a cupola.

Contributing to the whole gracious ensemble are two sets of LODGE GATES. Single-storey three-bay lodges, of ashlar, with round-headed windows. Rusticated gatepiers.

BACH-Y-GRAIG, 1¼m. SSW. Built for Sir Richard Clough, who was Sir Thomas Gresham's agent in Antwerp, and was associated with him in building the Royal Exchange. Founded by Gresham in 1566 and opened by Queen Elizabeth I in 1571, the Exchange was not only Early Flemish Renaissance in style but made use of materials imported from Antwerp under Clough's supervision. Bach-y-graig was dated 1567–9, and it was in all probability in 1567 also that Sir Richard built Plas Clough (*see* p. 154). The two houses are believed to represent the earliest use of brick in Wales. Plas Clough marks the introduction of stepped gables, and Bach-y-graig was

---

*I am indebted to Mr Charles Glazebrook for much information relating to Brynbella. Letters from Mead to Mr and Mrs Piozzi are in the John Rylands Library, Manchester (English Manuscripts 607). The correspondence reflects a deterioration in relations between the two men as the work progressed, and makes sad reading.

of such strong Netherlandish character, and so alien both to
Welsh tradition and to English Renaissance development, as
to be unique in Elizabethan domestic architecture. *Hendrik
van Passe* of Antwerp, who supervised the building of the
Royal Exchange, may have been involved and the brick possibly imported from the Low Countries.

The house stood round three sides of a court, the N side of
which was open. A gatehouse was in the W range, and on
the E was a square main block which, according to Pennant,
rose 'into six wonderful storeys'. In fact it had but one main
storey, containing hall and parlour with basement below.
Above was a pyramid roof with two tiers of hipped dormers,
and then a high superstructure crowned by a cupola. All this
has vanished, but the two other ranges survive, albeit altered
and mutilated. Bands of plaster as decoration. Over the gateway
was a pyramid-roofed tower, now gone. The arches remain,
though blocked. The outer has a rusticated stone surround.
The extrados of the inner one is of brick, except for a keystone and two voussoirs bearing Clough's initials. A doorway
has a pediment containing crude scrolly strapwork and the
date 1567.* s range with, towards the court, a blocked Tuscan
colonnade and brick-arched windows above. The range may
have been planned as a warehouse, in connection with commercial purposes (utilizing the navigable Clwyd) which
Clough is reputed to have been contemplating. Suggesting a
simplified version of the arcades and niches of the Royal Exchange, this treatment originally extended for at least seven
bays, and returned towards the gatehouse in two. Blocked
mullioned windows to the s.

Bach-y-graig descended through the Salusburys, and thus
to Mrs Thrale. It was in decline when shown to Dr Johnson,
and, although repaired by Piozzi for a tenant, it seems that
the main block had been demolished by 1817.

FARM BUILDINGS. Stone and brick. One has mullioned
windows, a round-headed doorway, and some timber framing.

HENBLAS, ¾m. S. Gabled, with mullioned and transomed windows, some of stone, some of timber, some with labels. It
seems to be a small C17 H-plan house, altered or enlarged in
early C20 Arts and Crafts manner. s front advancing in three
planes from r. to l. On the W a canted bay and a garden porch.
Fanciful weathervane. TOPIARY GARDEN.

NANTLYS, 1½m. S. A mansion of brick with stone dressings. By
T. H. Wyatt, 1872–5, for a branch of the Pennant family. The
elements are mainly Elizabethan, though all three fronts are
asymmetrical, and there are Gothic details, e.g. foliated capitals to the columns of the porch. Steep hipped roofs at the
service end. Central staircase hall with rusticated arches at

---

* The date and initials occurred also in the form of iron ties, which, as Mr
Peter Smith has pointed out, represent Flemish usage. A door believed to be from
Bach-y-graig, dated 1568, is at Pentre Coch Manor, Llanfair Dyffryn Clwyd (*see*
p. 208). Mr Howell refers to other fittings being at Glasfryn, Gwynedd.

the upper level. It is lit, not from above, but by a stained-glass window giving on to an internal light well. The building provides a very complete example of Victorian country-house planning and its complexities. Unusually, there is no clear articulation between the main and service portions, and there is variation of storey heights within the one mass. In the library, doors in Flemish Renaissance style, communicating with the drawing room, beyond a Doric screen. Pine joinery throughout the house. GARDEN planting by *James Dickson & Sons* of Chester.

The little ravine behind Ffynnon Beuno (SJ 085 724) is notable for its limestone CAVES, excavated in the 1880s and the subject of a good deal of geological and archaeological controversy. The two most important ones are on the N side – Ffynnon Beuno and Cae Gwyn, where evidence of human as well as animal occupation was found. The former is easy to enter, but the latter, on the top of the cliff, is now virtually inaccessible. The caves were primarily hyena dens and contained many bones of these animals and their victims, as well as of the woolly rhinoceros and mammoth. In addition to the animal bones, Ffynnon Beuno produced six flint implements and Cae Gwyn one, of Aurignacian type, indicating that man had also used the cave for a time, *c*.30,000 bc. The occupation will have taken place during a warmer interval before the last glaciation when this area was once more covered with ice and the ravine and its caves would have become filled with clay and stone carried by the glaciers. Post-glacial erosion has again revealed the cliffs and cave mouths.

Near BRYNGWYN HALL (St Beuno's College), $1\frac{3}{8}$ m. ENE, there was a group of five BARROWS which were investigated by the Jesuits at the beginning of the century. Four of them covered single cremation burials as the centre, and only one had had other burials dug into the top. Two of these barrows can be seen just to the W of the road (SJ 102 736), and another survives within a wood inside the college grounds.

TREUDDYN

2050

ST MARY. 1874–5. Not large. Tall, however, with clerestory and apsidal chancel, and abysmally dull and pretentious. That *T.H. Wyatt* should have replaced thus a little whitewashed double-naved church inspired a stream of invective from Goodhart-Rendel. – ALTAR TABLE, S aisle. Adapted from a raised chest or hutch. – STAINED GLASS. In the N and S windows of the apse are fragments ascribed by Dr Mostyn Lewis to three separate C14 dates, and some C16 pieces. Arranged in roundels on the S, with some canopy work. On the N, under gabled canopies, are two early C14 monks, the head of the right-hand one not original. – A roundel of fragments in the W window. – Dugout CHEST with iron bands. – In the churchyard a quaintly shaped baluster SUNDIAL, its plate dated 1803. – LYCHGATE. Brought in 1975 from *Oldrid Scott*'s church at Llanddewi (*see* p. 190).

The VICARAGE, ½m. NW, of 1862, is far more decent architecturally than the church.

EBENEZER METHODIST CHAPEL, ⅜m. W. Gothic, of 1873, with polychromatic brick. Next to it a humbler predecessor (1823, enlarged 1833 according to the inscription) with longitudinal elevation and a cottage under the same roof.

An intermediate stage in chapel planning is seen at JERUSALEM, ¼m. SW of Ebenezer. Gable-end façade, but still with two doors and the pulpit backing on to the wall behind them. Built 1820 and enlarged, i.e. given its present form, in 1867.

PLAS-Y-BRAIN, 1m. WNW. Among the FARM BUILDINGS a small late medieval house. The hall, now divided, has remains of a lateral chimney (and of a central arched-braced·cruck with a cusped quatrefoil above the collar. Lower-end partition with central doorway). Diagonally set timber mullions in the gable end of a service portion. Upper-end cross wing, probably later (with an arched-braced truss, not of cruck type, and wind-braces).

A line of BARROWS stand on the ridge of high ground at Treuddyn. There were originally at least four, with a large STANDING STONE at the eastern end of the cemetery. The barrow at the western end behind Pentre (SJ 240 574) is still a fine mound, and that behind Lyndhurst (SJ 245 580) is easily recognizable, but the others have been almost flattened. The standing stone – Carreg y Llech (SJ 249 583) – is very broad, a rather unusual shape for a Bronze Age stone, but undoubtedly it belongs with the barrows, and the cemetery as a whole may be compared to that at Llandyfnan, Anglesey, which also has a stone at one end.

WEPRE *see* CONNAH'S QUAY

WHITEWELL *see* ISCOED

1070

WHITFORD / CHWITFFORDD

ST MARY. W tower, nave, gabled aisles, and no structurally separate chancel. Largely by *Ambrose Poynter*, Perp in style, with traceried windows, and very crisp in its detailing. Before his reconstruction it was double-naved, with no S aisle. The tower was built in 1842–3, and was at joint Mostyn and Pennant expense, as was the Poynter church at Mostyn (q.v.). The rest of the work is of 1845–6, paid for by Lady Emma Pennant. N aisle partly old, including the arched-braced roof and a three-light Perp and three two-light Dec windows. Also old the six-bay Perp arcade, with four-centred arches and

octagonal piers, copied by *Poynter* on the s. The church floor
slopes up to the w. Restoration of 1888 by *Ewan Christian*,
and by him the PEWS. - RAILS and sanctuary FLOORING by
Lingen Barker, 1876. (VH) - FONT Bowl with quatrefoils,
dated 1649. - Jacobean ALTAR TABLE with melon-bulb legs.
- STAINED GLASS. E window by *C. A. Gibbs*, *c*.1876. - N aisle
E by *Lavers & Westlake*, 1898. - N aisle easternmost by *Heaton, Butler & Bayne*, 1917, and a sorry come-down on their
part, though the next window shows that C20 glass could get
a good deal worse. - CHANDELIERS. One with two six-branch
tiers, given 1755. - A small one, given 1756, with elaborate
iron suspension which does not seem to belong. - Dugout
CHEST. - C14 or early C15 stone COFFIN, with eight trefoils
under crocketed gables. Found at Faenol Fawr, Bodelwyddan. - SEPULCHRAL SLABS. Fragments include those of two
late C13 slabs with interlacing. - Also the upper halves of two
cross slabs, one floriated and the other interlaced, and the
lower part of a slab commemorating Gruffydd ap Dafydd, all
early C14. - PILLAR STONES. One from Plas-yn-Rhos, Caerwys, C6, with Latin inscription commemorating Bona, wife
of Nobilis. - Another, with cross potent, C7-11, found in the
churchyard. - MONUMENTS. In the N aisle: Ellis Wynn
†1619 and Richard Coytmore †1683. Armorial tablets under
one cornice. Jacobean motifs. - Elizabeth Mostyn †1647. Incised slab, in crude framing, with representation of herself
and her family. - In the s aisle: Thomas Pennant, the antiquary and topographer, †1798. By *Sir Richard Westmacott*.
Portrait medallion against the base of an urn. Draped harp
and a mourning muse in front. - Three Pennant tablets, Grecian, two of them (with commemoration dates 1834 and 1835
respectively) signed by *Westmacott*. - Lady Caroline Pennant
†1824. Designed by *Rickman & Hutchinson* and thus Gothic.
- On the w wall: Thomas Thomas †1823 and Henry Thomas
†1824. By *W. Spence*. Pedimented. Medallion portrait against
an urn, seated mourning figure, and emblems of mortality. -
Against the N wall of the churchyard the TOMB-CHEST of
Moses Griffith, Pennant's illustrator, †1819. - The approach
to the church from the s is by way of flights of steps and a
stone LYCHGATE, which has a room above. An inscription,
recording a bequest of 1749, refers also to a bequest of 1624
towards its building. C19 window.

Pleasant village centre, but not improved by the tarting up of
the pub. Either side of the lychgate a rubble-walled C18
house. On the w, JESSAMINE HOUSE has segment-headed
casements. IVY HOUSE, later, turns its front, with one-bay
pediment and flush sashes, eastwards.

For the PENNSYLVANIA LODGE of Mostyn Hall, *see* p. 401.

E of the village are the grounds of DOWNING. The one-time
seat of the Pennants was burnt in 1922, and the ruins were
demolished in 1953. The house, built 1627, was altered by
Thomas Pennant *c*.1766 and by his successors, especially in
1814 by his son David, who built on the library wing, and

c. 1858 by *T. H. Wyatt* for Lord and Lady Feilding, later Earl and Countess of Denbigh. (*See* also Pantasaph.) She was Thomas Pennant's great-grand-daughter. Thomas Pennant's STABLE RANGE, dated 1766, remains. UPPER DOWNING, C18 but earlier in origin, also remains. At the NE corner of the park a castellated rectangular TOWER, with staircase turret. Built 1810, but domestic appendages are probably later.

MERTYN ABBOT, ¾m. SE. Formerly dated 1572. At the rear a stepped-gabled projection with a chimney. External stairs to a door in the side of the projection. Two further upper-level doorways, now without access and one of them blocked, in a gable end. BARN with two truncated crucks.

ISGLAN, Isglan Road, 2¼m. E. (Not to be confused with Mertyn Isglan.) Now rendered. Symmetrical, with two bays of windows and a central door. The doorcase, dated 1633, has a steep pediment, but is otherwise still of Tudor character. Three cruck trusses in the BARN.

MERTYN HALL, 1⅝m. ESE. C18 Gothic. Some ogee windows.

TYDDYN UCHA, ½m. SSE. Some mullioned windows with labels. C18 doorway hood. (Post-and-panel partition.)

A hilltop TOWER, ¾m. W, was built in the early C17 as a beacon watchtower to give warning of pirate raids. Circular and tapering, and with some castellation to the parapet. Now roofless. An inscription, recording restoration in 1897, perpetuates the error of its being a Roman pharos. A tower near Abergele and the church at Llandrillo-yn-Rhos (*see* pp. 100 and 193), together with a beacon at Deganwy, formed part of the chain.

GELLI, 1⅛m. W. Three-light mullioned windows with labels. There are also earlier features, for this was a grange of Basingwerk Abbey, and a pair of lancets and the four-centred doorway with hoodmould are pre-Reformation. So too probably are two windows with arched lights, at the rear. A three-light window in the gable end is a C20 alteration. Lateral chimney.

8 MAEN ACHWYFAN, 1m. WNW. A monolithic slab cross of the late C10 or early C11. T-fret pattern, ring knot and interlaced chain pattern exemplify Scandinavian influence, and there are Celtic motifs also. The disc head has a central boss back and front, and a ring cross with triqueta knots in its splayed arms. Looped knotwork in one. Further enrichment on the front (E) face, and four-cord plait at the sides. The shaft has three panels on the front, containing respectively plaitwork, key pattern with diagonals, and double-beaded knotwork framing the figure of a man. Panel on the back with double-beaded knotwork, including a double ring knot. Double-bead plait in a panel below. On the N side: T-fret, double-bead rings, ring knot, looped knotwork, key pattern etc. Also an animal. On the S side: interlaced chain. Also plaitwork etc. and figures and an animal. All figures and animals now barely discernible.

PLAS UCHAF, ¾m. NNW. (Stone overmantel dated 1603, with heraldry in a roundel between obelisk-like pilasters. NMR)

PLAS CAPTAIN, 2¼m. W. Double pile, with two stepped gables either end and another to a lateral chimney.

A group of four very large MOUNDS may be seen on either side of the road near Maen Achwyfan. Two of them are prominent mounds in rough ground at SJ 127 790 standing close together. The other two are to the S of the road. One is a sharp-sided, unploughed mound in a small wood. It is damaged on one side by a cottage. The other is an extremely large, smooth mound in an arable field. Such large mounds are characteristic of this region, and sometimes they seem so large and so smooth-profiled that their artificial origin might be doubted. However, the unploughed mound in the wood does look artificial and is very probably a Bronze Age BARROW.

A very large, smooth-profiled BARROW stands just opposite the farmhouse of Groesffordd (SJ 132 776).

For a BARROW at Berthangam, *see* Llanasa.

WILLINGTON *see* TALLARN GREEN

WORTHENBURY*

1040

ST DEINIOL. Rebuilt 1736–9, and there is no better or more 77 complete Georgian church anywhere in Wales. By *Richard Trubshaw*. Brick and stone. Semicircular apse and a three-storey W tower, both with balustraded parapets. Urn finials on the tower. There are corner pilaster strips, and round-headed windows and N and S doorways have stone surrounds with keystones. Some circular windows also, each with four radiating keystone motifs. Mouldings are used only sparingly. The interior has a coved ceiling, and at the E end a chancel is defined by rococo plasterwork and enrichment of the cornice. In the apse are Ionic and Corinthian pilasters, and a ceiling with dove, sunburst, and little patches of cloud, all in plaster. W gallery of 1830, on cast-iron columns. Excellent set of BOX PEWS, including a squirearchical pair in the chancel, with fireplaces. Heraldry and other devices on doors. But are the pews all original? Some have small-scale balustrading, a feature which appears also on the gallery front. – FONT with baluster stem. – PULPIT with backdrop and a heavy tester. Panels tending to Gothic. – STAINED GLASS. E window by *Betton & Evans*, but largely made up of medieval fragments. Most came from the Jesse window of 1393 at Winchester College, which Betton & Evans replaced with a copy in 1822–3. – CHANDELIERS. One given in 1816, of two tiers. – Another of 1898. – MONUMENTS. Broughton Whitehall †1734. Fluted pilasters and an urn in a broken pediment. – Sir Richard Puleston †1840. By *John Carline III*. Drapery

* In Maelor Saesneg.

arranged over a segmental entablature. Volutes and foliation at the base. – Tablet to Ellen Matthie † 1836, and one to W. Whitehall Davies and others, latest commemoration date 1841, both by *J. Blayney*. – ROYAL ARMS on canvas. – Three HATCHMENTS.

At the opposite end of the (largely unspoilt) village is the OLD RECTORY. Rebuilt *c.* 1833, stuccoed, with Tudor and Gothic elements, and incorporating part of the house which Judge Puleston of Emral Hall built in 1657 for the Rev. Philip Henry, father of the Nonconformist scholar Matthew Henry. Beyond the bridge, THE MANOR, of brick, with large shaped gables. Probably a remodelling of *c.* 1900 with later enlargement. The BRIDGE was rebuilt in vernacular manner, though with yellow brick intrados, by *H.J. Fairclough*, County Surveyor, 1872–3.

BROUGHTON HALL, 1m. E, was demolished in 1961. It was a large timber-framed house, much altered in the C19.

EMRAL HALL, which stood 1¼m. S, was restored in the 1890s and again after a fire in 1904, only to be demolished in 1936. It was seemingly a house of strangely haunting beauty, and even today there is some sense of atmosphere, and more than usual poignancy, about the secluded tree-shaded site. The three-storey front, with five-bay centre recessed between broad and deep wings, was by *Richard Trubshaw* and *Joseph Evans*, 1724–7. It was of brick with stone dressings, and had segmental-headed windows, Baroque doorcases, volutes to the middle first-floor window, and rusticated quoins of even length. The staircase was of this period, but much of the house was early or mid-C17, including the curved ceiling of the first-floor drawing room, depicting the Labours of Hercules, amid strapwork. The room, with its panelling probably of the 1720s, was rescued by Sir Clough Williams-Ellis and is at Portmeirion.

The site was an ancient, moated one; the Emral Brook formed one side of the moat on the E. The approach from this direction was axial, through a courtyard with STABLES either side and across a BRIDGE, all still remaining. The two stable ranges, built *c.* 1730–5, are pedimented. Doorways with entablatures and lugged architraves, and the central ones with segmental pediments. At the E end of the court were GATES attributed to *Robert Davies* and which, with their rusticated piers, are now at the church at Eccleston in Cheshire. Small gates at the bridge went to Ely Lodge, County Fermanagh. (Behind the N stable range a domed brick ICEHOUSE. DOE) Neo-Jacobean ENTRANCE LODGE.

HOLLYBUSH FARM, 1½m. SSW, across the main road, has a partly preserved MOAT.

SARN BRIDGE. *See* Tallarn Green.

MULSFORD HALL. *See* Tallarn Green.

YR WYDDGRUG *see* MOLD

ST MARY. Rebuilt 1836–7 by *John Welch* according to Goodhart-Rendel, though other sources say *Edward Welch*. Low-pitched roof, shallow altar recess, lancets, and a flat ceiling. w tower, with the modelling of buttresses and pinnacles stronger than usual for a church of this type. – FONT. Perp bowl, with quatrefoils. – STAINED GLASS. E window by *Hardman*. – MONUMENT. In the w porch, set upright, the C14 effigy of a vested priest. Canopy at the head. – CHURCHYARD CROSS. Octagonal base and part of the shaft.

BRYN SION, 1m. WNW. One of the series of small C17 houses with symmetrical fronts. Three bays. Mullioned windows. One room with panelling.

GELLILYFDY, Babell, 1½m. NNW. Probably built as a C17 storeyed house, with its first-floor room open to the roof, rather than being a remodelling of an earlier hall house. Three arched-braced trusses, and a lateral chimney with gabled breast. This, or a predecessor house, was the birthplace of John Jones (†*c*. 1658), scholar and collector of manuscripts. To the SE is a BARN. Four queen-post trusses, with raking struts. One carries a beautifully cut inscription of 1586 on a tie-beam, with the initials of William Jones, father of John. The completion of the barn was celebrated by the poet Y Gwisgl Gwyn.*

PANTGWYN MAWR, ½m. NNE. Three-unit plan. Irregularly disposed three-light mullioned windows, and a rusticated doorway with keystone. Gabled rear projections, including a lateral chimney.

LLWYN ERDDYN, 1⅝m. ENE. This was a house with lateral chimney, traces of which remain, and inside cross passage. Two cyclopean doorways. A later chimney encroaches on to the hall and backs on to the passage. Parlour at the upper end, and a later byre built beyond the service room at the lower.

GLEDLOM, ½m. SE. Much altered, but retaining the gabled breast of a lateral chimney and, over the porch, heraldry and the date 1645. A wing at right angles overlaps the main block only slightly, and represents the unit system.

COLOMENDY, 1¾m. SW, among the cultivated lower slopes of the Clwydians. Central chimney, datestone of 1663 (probably *ex situ*), and rear service wing. (Stone overmantel with five cusped ogee panels, each containing a shield. Also a much cruder overmantel, dated 1660. NMR)

PLAS-YN-CRWMP, Ddol, ⅛m. from the A541, at the foot of the road to Colomendy. Single-storeyed. (Two timber-framed cruck partition walls. DOE)

* Information from Mr Kyrke-Smith.

ARCHITECTURAL GLOSSARY

Particular types of an architectural element are often defined under the name of the element itself; e.g. for 'dog-leg stair' see STAIRS. Literal meanings, where specially relevant, are indicated by the abbreviation *lit*.

For further reference (especially for style terms) the following are a selection of books that can be consulted: *A Dictionary of Architecture* (N. Pevsner, J. Fleming, H. Honour, 1975); *The Illustrated Glossary of Architecture* (J. Harris and J. Lever, 1966); *Recording a Church: An Illustrated Glossary* (T. Cocke, D. Findlay, R. Halsey, E. Williamson, Council of British Archaeology, 1982); *Encyclopedia of Modern Architecture* (edited by Wolfgang Pehnt, 1963); *The Classical Language of Architecture* (J. Summerson, 1964); *The Dictionary of Ornament* (M. Stafford and D. Ware, 1974); *Illustrated Handbook of Vernacular Architecture* (R. W. Brunskill, 1976); *English Brickwork* (A. Clifton Taylor and R. W. Brunskill, 1977); *The Pattern of English Building* (A. Clifton Taylor, 1972).

ABACUS (*lit*. tablet): flat slab forming the top of a capital; *see* Orders (Fig. 18).

ABUTMENT: the meeting of an arch or vault with its solid lateral support, or the support itself.

ACANTHUS: formalized leaf ornament with thick veins and frilled edge, e.g. on a Corinthian capital.

ACHIEVEMENT OF ARMS: in heraldry, a complete display of armorial bearings.

ACROTERION (*lit*. peak): plinth for a statue or ornament placed at the apex or ends of a pediment; also, loosely and more usually, both the plinths and what stands on them.

ADDORSED: description of two figures placed symmetrically back to back. cf. Affronted.

AEDICULE (*lit*. little building): architectural surround, consisting usually of two columns or pilasters supporting a pediment, framing a niche or opening. *See also* Tabernacle.

AESTHETIC MOVEMENT: a Late Victorian confluence of the Arts and Crafts Movement (q.v.) with Pre-Raphaelite influence (particularly that of D. G. Rossetti) on decorative art. In architecture the detailing and ornament of W. E. Nesfield are characteristic expressions of aestheticism. The movement had wide popular appeal, and its supposed eccentricities and affectations were parodied by Gilbert and Sullivan in *Patience*.

AFFRONTED: description of two figures placed symmetrically face to face. cf. Addorsed.

AGGREGATE: small stones added to a binding material, e.g. in concrete. In modern architecture used alone to describe concrete with an aggregate of stone chippings, e.g. granite, quartz etc.

AISLE (*lit.* wing): subsidiary space alongside the nave, choir, or transept of a church, or the main body of some other building, separated from it by columns, piers, or posts.

AISLE TRUSS: roof truss supported mainly on aisle-posts within the walls of a building.

ALIGNMENT: Bronze Age (?) ritual monument with several upright stones set in a row.

ALTAR: elevated slab consecrated for the celebration of the Eucharist; cf. Communion table.

ALTARPIECE: *see* Retable.

AMBULATORY (*lit.* walkway): aisle around the sanctuary, sometimes surrounding an apse and therefore semicircular or polygonal in plan.

AMORINO: *see* Putto.

ANGLE ROLL: roll moulding in the angle between two planes, e.g. between the orders of an arch.

ANNULET (*lit.* ring): shaft-ring (*see* Shaft).

ANSE DE PANIER (*lit.* basket handle): basket arch (*see* Arch).

ANTAE: flat pilasters with capitals different from the order they accompany, placed at the ends of the short projecting walls of a portico or of a colonnade which is then called *in antis*.

ANTEFIXAE: ornaments projecting at regular intervals above a classical cornice, originally to conceal the ends of roof tiles.

ANTEPENDIUM: *see* Frontal.

ANTHEMION (*lit.* honeysuckle): classical ornament like a honeysuckle flower (*see* Fig. 1).

Fig. 1. Anthemion and palmette frieze

APRON: raised panel below a window or at the base of a wall monument or tablet, sometimes shaped and decorated.

A.P.S.D.: Architectural Publications Society Dictionary.

APSE: semicircular (i.e. apsidal) extension of an apartment: *see also* Exedra. A term first used of the magistrate's end of a Roman basilica, and thence especially of the vaulted semicircular or polygonal end of a chancel or a chapel.

ARABESQUE: type of painted or carved surface decoration consisting of flowing lines and intertwined foliage scrolls etc., generally based on geometrical patterns. cf. Grotesque.

ARCADE: (1) series of arches supported by piers or columns. *Blind arcade* or *arcading*: the same applied to the surface of a wall. *Wall arcade*: in medieval churches, a blind arcade forming a dado below windows. (2) a covered shopping street.

ARCH: for the various forms *see* Fig. 2. The term *basket arch* refers to a basket handle and is sometimes applied to a three-centred or depressed arch as well as to the type with a flat middle. A *transverse arch* runs across the main axis of an interior space. The term is used especially for the arches between the compartments of tunnel- or groin-vaulting. *Diaphragm arch*: transverse arch with solid spandrels spanning an otherwise wooden-roofed interior. *Chancel arch*: w opening from the chancel into the nave. *Nodding arch*: an ogee arch curving forward from the plane of the wall. *Relieving* (or *discharging) arch*: incorporated in a wall, to carry some of its weight, some way above an opening. *Skew arch*: spanning responds not diametrically opposed to one another. *Strainer arch*: inserted across an opening to resist any inward pressure of the side members. *See also* Jack arch; Triumphal arch.

ARCHED BRACES: *see* Roofs (3).

ARCHITRAVE: (1) formalized lintel, the lowest member of the classical entablature (*see* Orders, Fig. 18); (2) moulded

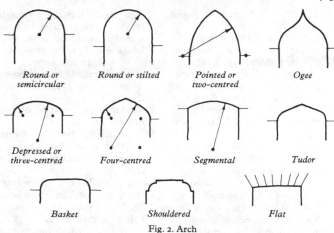

Round or semicircular   Round or stilted   Pointed or two-centred   Ogee

Depressed or three-centred   Four-centred   Segmental   Tudor

Basket   Shouldered   Flat

Fig. 2. Arch

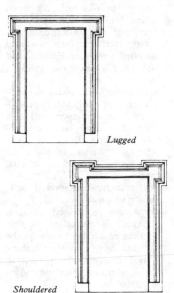

Lugged

Shouldered

Fig. 3. Architrave

frame of a door or window (often borrowing the profile of an architrave in the strict sense). Also *lugged architrave*, where the top is prolonged into lugs (*lit.* ears) at the sides; *shouldered*, where the frame rises vertically at the top angles and returns horizontally at the sides forming shoulders (*see* Fig. 3).

ARCHIVOLT: architrave moulding when it follows the line of an arch.

ARCUATED: dependent structurally on the use of arches or the arch principle; cf. Trabeated.

ARRIS (*lit.* stop): sharp edge where two surfaces meet at an angle.

ARTS AND CRAFTS: a movement in the later nineteenth century which took inspiration from the theories of John Ruskin and William Morris relating to craftsmanship. It gave birth to several societies and guilds and permeated progressive design in architecture, crafts and the decorative arts around the turn of the century.

ASHLAR: masonry of large blocks wrought to even faces and square edges.

ASHLAR PIECE: *see* Roofs (3).

ASTRAGAL: colloquially, a glazing bar (q.v.); moulding of semicircular section.

ASTYLAR: term used for an elevation that has no columns or similar vertical features.

ATLANTES (*lit.* Atlas figures, from the god Atlas carrying the globe): male counterparts of caryatids (q.v.), often in a more demonstrative attitude of support.

ATRIUM: inner court of a Roman house; also open court in front of a church.

ATTACHED COLUMN: *see* Engaged column.

ATTACHED PORTICO: a non-projecting portico or a blind portico; *see* Portico.

ATTIC: (1) small top storey, especially within a sloping roof; (2) in classical architecture, a storey above the main entablature of the façade, as in a triumphal arch (q.v.).

AUDITORY: type of Protestant church or chapel built for worship in which preaching is more important than the Eucharist, and hence with the pulpit rather than the altar as focal point. Such a building is usually a single chamber of simple rectangular plan.

AUMBRY: recess or cupboard to hold sacred vessels for the Mass.

AXE HAMMER: shafted stone tool of Bronze Age date with blade at one end and hammer at the other.

BAILEY: area around the motte or keep (qq.v.) of a castle, defended by a wall and ditch.

BALDACCHINO: free-standing canopy, properly of or representing fabric, over an altar supported by columns. cf. Ciborium.

BALLFLOWER: globular flower of three petals enclosing a small ball. Typical of the Decorated style.

BALUSTER (*lit.* pomegranate): a pillar or pedestal of bellied form. *Balusters:* vertical supports of this or any other form, for a handrail or coping, the whole being called a *balustrade*. *Blind balustrade:* the same applied to the surface of a wall.

BARBICAN: outwork defending the entrance to a castle.

BARGEBOARDS: corruption of vergeboards. Boards, often carved or fretted, fixed beneath the eaves of a gable to cover and protect the purlins.

BARROW: round barrow, a circular mound of earth covering a burial, normally of Early Bronze Age date. Circular arrangements of stakes or stones may also be found beneath them (stake circles, cairn rings, etc.).

BARTIZAN (*lit.* battlement): corbelled turret, square or round, frequently at a corner, hence *corner bartizan*.

BASCULE: hinged part of a lifting bridge.

BASE: moulded foot of a column or other order. For its use in classical architecture *see* Orders (Fig. 18).

BASEMENT: lowest, subordinate storey of a building, and hence the lowest part of an elevation, below the main floor.

BASILICA (*lit.* royal building): a Roman public hall; hence an aisled building with a clerestory, most often a church.

BASTIDE: term for the medieval fortified towns of France, laid out on a rectangular gridiron plan.

BASTION: one of a series of semi-circular or polygonal projections from the main wall of a fortress or city, placed at intervals in such a manner as to enable the garrison to cover the intervening stretches of the wall.

BATTER: intentional inward inclination of a wall face.

BATTLEMENT: fortified parapet, indented or crenellated so that archers could shoot through the indentations (crenels or embrasures) between the projecting solid portions (merlons). Also used decoratively.

BAY LEAF: classical ornament of formalized overlapping bay leaves; *see* Fig. 4.

Fig. 4. Bay leaf

BAYS: divisions of an elevation or interior space as defined by any regular vertical features such as arches, columns, windows etc.

BAY-WINDOW: window of one or more storeys projecting from

the face of a building at ground level, and either rectangular or polygonal on plan. A *canted bay-window* has a straight front and angled sides. A *bow-window* is curved. An *oriel window* rests on corbels or brackets and does not start from the ground.

bc: *see* p. 18 *n.*

BEAD-AND-REEL: *see* Enrichments.

BEAKER PEOPLE: group distinguished by the use of a pottery appearing at the end of the Neolithic period (*c.* 2000 bc) and originating in the Netherlands. They seem to have been the catalyst in many social and technological changes, notably the introduction of metallurgy.

BEAKHEAD: Norman ornamental motif consisting of a row of bird or beast heads with beaks, usually biting into a roll moulding.

BELFRY: structure to hang bells in. A *bellcote* (q.v.) stands on a gable; a *bell-stage* is a room on top of a tower; a *bell turret* is built on a roof.

BELGAE: Iron Age tribes living in north-eastern Gaul, from which settlers came into Britain between 100 and 55 bc and later. These immigrants may not have been numerous, but their impact on material culture in southern Britain was marked.

BELL CAPITAL: *see* Fig. 8.

BELLCOTE: belfry, usually in the form of a small gabled or roofed housing for the bell(s).

BERM: level area separating ditch from bank on a hillfort or barrow.

BILLET (*lit.* log or block) FRIEZE: Norman ornament consisting of small half-cylindrical or rectangular blocks placed at regular intervals (*see* Fig. 5).

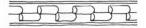

Fig. 5. Billet frieze

BIVALLATE: (of a hillfort) defended by two concentric banks and ditches.

BLIND: *see* Arcade, Balustrade, Portico.

BLOCK CAPITAL: *see* Fig. 8.

BLOCKED: term applied to columns etc. that are interrupted by regular projecting blocks, e.g. the sides of a Gibbs surround (*see* Fig. 13).

BLOCKING COURSE: plain course of stones, or equivalent, on top of a cornice and crowning the wall.

BOLECTION: *see* Mouldings.

BOND: in brickwork, the pattern of long sides (stretchers) and short ends (headers) produced on the face of a wall by laying bricks in a particular way. For the two most common bonds *see* Fig. 6.

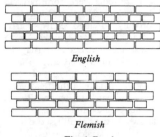

English

Flemish

Fig. 6. Bond

BOSS: knob or projection usually placed at the intersection of ribs in a vault.

BOWSTRING BRIDGE: with arch ribs rising above the roadway, which is suspended from them.

BOWTELL: *see* Mouldings.

BOW-WINDOW: *see* Bay-window.

BOX-FRAME: (1) timber-framed construction in which vertical and horizontal wall members support the roof. (2) in modern architecture, a box-like form of concrete construction where the loads are taken on cross walls, suitable only for buildings consisting of repetitive small cells. Also called *cross-wall construction.*

BOX PEW: *see* Pew.

BRACE: subsidiary timber set diagonally to strengthen a timber frame. It can be curved or straight. *See also* Roofs (3) and Figs. 23–7.

BRACKET. small supporting piece of stone, etc., to carry a projecting horizontal member. *See also* Console.

BRATTISHING: ornamental cresting on a wall, usually formed of leaves or Tudor flowers or miniature battlements.

BRESSUMER (*lit.* breast-beam): big horizontal beam, usually set forward from the lower part of a building, supporting the wall above.

BRICK: *see* Bond.

BRICK-NOGGING: timber framing (q.v.) in which the spaces between the structural timbers are filled with brickwork.

BROACH: *see* Spire.

BRONZE AGE: the period when bronze tools were dominant; in Britain *c.* 1800 to 600 bc. It is broadly divided into Early, Middle and Late Bronze Age at 1400 and 900 bc, and may be further subdivided into phases according to the type of tools made, usually called after a typical hoard, as Penard Phase, Wilburton Complex etc.

BUCRANIUM: ox skull used decoratively in classical friezes.

BULLSEYE WINDOW: small oval window, set horizontally; cf. Oculus. Also called *œil de bœuf*.

BUTTRESS: vertical member projecting from a wall to stabilize it or to resist the lateral thrust of an arch, roof, or vault. For different types used at the corners of a building, especially a tower, *see* Fig. 7. A *flying buttress* transmits the thrust to a heavy abutment by means of an arch or half-arch.

CABLE MOULDING: originally a Norman moulding, imitating the twisted strands of a rope. Also called *rope moulding*.

CAIRN: heap of stones, in prehistory normally covering a burial. *Long cairns* cover Neolithic burial chambers; *round cairns* (like barrows, q.v.) cover Early Bronze Age burials. There are several variations of design among round cairns, e.g. *kerb cairns, platform cairns* and *ring cairns*. Some of these variant monuments are for ceremonial rather than burial and may be akin to stone circles (q.v.).

CALEFACTORY: room in a monastery where a fire burned for the comfort of the monks. Also called *warming room*.

CAMBER: slight rise or upward curve in place of a horizontal line or plane.

CAMBERBEAM: *see* Roofs (3).

CAMES: *see* Quarries.

CAMP: Roman military site. *Auxiliary:* camp for the auxilia (non-legionary troops). *Marching:* earthworks dug each night by the army on campaign. *Practice:* earthworks dug during training.

CAMPANILE: free-standing bell-tower.

CANOPY: projection or hood usually over an altar, pulpit, niche, statue etc.

CANTED: tilted, generally on a vertical axis to produce an obtuse angle on plan, e.g. of a canted bay-window.

CANTILEVER: horizontal projection (e.g. step, canopy) supported by a downward force behind the fulcrum. It is without external bracing and thus appears to be self-supporting.

CAPITAL: head or crowning feature of a column or pilaster; for classical types *see* Orders (Fig. 18); for medieval types *see* Fig. 8.

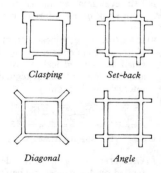

Clasping   *Set-back*

Diagonal   *Angle*

Fig. 7. Buttresses

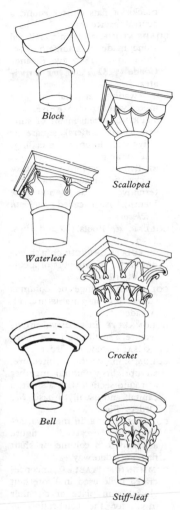

Block

Scalloped

Waterleaf

Crocket

Bell

Stiff-leaf

Fig. 8. Capitals

CARREL: (1) niche in a cloister where a monk could sit to work or read; (2) similar feature in open-plan offices and libraries.

CARTOUCHE: tablet with ornate frame, usually of elliptical shape and bearing a coat of arms or inscription.

CARYATIDS (*lit*. daughters of the village of Caryae): female figures supporting an entablature, counterparts of Atlantes (q.v.).

CASEMATE: in military architecture, a vaulted chamber, with embrasures for defence, built into the thickness of the wall of a castle or fortress or projecting from it.

CASEMENT: window hinged at the side. *See also* Mouldings.

CASTELLATED: battlemented.

CAST IRON: hard and brittle, cast in a mould to the required shape. *Wrought iron* is ductile, strong in tension, forged into decorative patterns or forged and rolled into e.g. bars, joists, boiler plates. *Mild steel* is a modern equivalent, similar but stronger.

CAVETTO: *see* Mouldings.

CELURE OR CEILURE: enriched area of a roof above the rood or the altar.

CENOTAPH (*lit*. empty tomb): funerary monument which is not a burying place.

CENTERING: wooden support for the building of an arch or vault, removed after completion.

CHAMBERED TOMB: *see* Megalithic tomb.

CHAMFER (*lit*. corner-break): surface formed by cutting off a square edge, usually at an angle of forty-five degrees. When the plane is concave it is termed a *hollow chamfer. Double-chamfer*: applied to each of two recessed arches. *Stop chamfer*: when a chamfer is not continued for the full length of a member.

CHANCEL (*lit*. enclosure): E arm or that part of the E end of a church set apart for the use of the officiating clergy, except in cathedrals or monastic churches; cf. Choir.

CHANCEL ARCH: arch separating the chancel from the nave or crossing.

CHANTRY CHAPEL: chapel, often attached to or inside a church, endowed for the celebration of masses principally for the soul of the founder.

CHEVET (*lit*. head): French term for the E end of a church (chancel and ambulatory with radiating chapels).

CHEVRON: V-shaped motif used in series to decorate a moulding: also (especially when on a single plane) called *zigzag*.

CHIMNEYPIECE: frame surrounding a fireplace, also called *mantelpiece* and sometimes surmounted by an overmantel (q.v.). A shelf, if incorporated, is termed *mantelshelf*.

CHOIR: the part of a church where services are sung. In monastic churches this can occupy the crossing and/or the easternmost bays of the nave. Also used to describe, more loosely, the E arm of a cruciform church.

CIBORIUM: (1) a fixed canopy of stone or wood over an altar, usually vaulted and supported on four columns; cf. Baldacchino. (2) canopied shrine for the reserved sacrament.

CINQUEFOIL: *see* Foil.

CIST: stone-lined or slab-built grave. *Short cists* are normally Early Bronze Age in date; *long cists* belong to the Early Christian period.

CLADDING: external covering or skin applied to a structure, especially framed buildings (q.v.), for aesthetic or protective purposes.

CLAPPER BRIDGE: bridge made of large slabs of stone, some making rough piers, with longer ones laid on top to make the roadway.

CLASP: *see* Industrialized building.

CLASSIC: term for the moment of highest achievement of a style.

CLASSICAL: term for Greek and Roman architecture and any subsequent styles derived from it.

CLERESTORY: fenestration at a high level, usually above adjacent roofs; particularly the uppermost storey of the nave walls of a church pierced by windows above the aisle roofs.

CLOSE STUD: method of constructing a wall by using closely spaced upright timbers.

CLUSTER BLOCK: multi-storey building in which individual blocks of flats cluster round a central service core.

COADE STONE: a ceramic artificial stone made in Lambeth from 1769 to *c.* 1840 by Eleanor Coade (†1821) and her associates.

COB: walling material of clay mixed with straw. *See* Pisé.

COFFERING: arrangement of sunken panels (coffers), square or polygonal, decorating a ceiling, vault or arch.

COGGING: a decorative course of bricks laid diagonally as an alternative to dentilation (*see* Dentil). Also called *dogtooth brickwork*.

COLLAR: *see* Roofs (3) and Figs. 24–7.

COLLEGIATE CHURCH: church endowed for the support of a college of priests.

COLONNADE: range of columns supporting an entablature; cf. Arcade.

COLONNETTE: in medieval architecture, a small column or shaft.

COLOSSAL ORDER: *see* Order.

COLUMN: in classical architecture, an upright structural member of round section with a shaft, a capital, and usually a base. *See* Orders (Fig. 18).

COLUMN FIGURE: in medieval architecture, carved figure attached to a column or shaft flanking a doorway.

COMMUNION TABLE: unconsecrated table used in Protestant churches in place of an altar (q.v.) for the celebration of Holy Communion.

COMPOSITE: *see* Orders.

COMPOUND PIER: grouped shafts (q.v.), or a solid core surrounded by attached or detached shafts.

CONSOLE: ornamented bracket of compound curved outline (*see* Fig. 9).

COPING (*lit.* capping): protective capping course of masonry or brickwork on top of a wall.

CORBEL: projecting block of stone or timber supporting something above. *Corbel course:* continuous course of projecting stones or bricks fulfilling the same function. *Corbel table:* series of corbels to carry a parapet or a wall-plate; for the latter *see* Roofs (3) and Figs. 23–6. *Corbelling:* brick or masonry courses built out beyond one another like a series of corbels to support a chimneystack, window etc.

CORINTHIAN: *see* Orders (Fig. 18).

CORNICE: (1) moulded ledge, projecting along the top of a building or feature, especially as the highest member of the classical entablature (*see* Orders, Fig. 18); (2) decorative moulding in the angle between wall and ceiling.

CORONA (*lit.* crown): used of spires and chandeliers; usually the latter are termed a corona when circular and of iron.

CORPS-DE-LOGIS: French term for the main building(s) as distinct from the wings or pavilions.

COTTAGE ORNÉ: an artfully rustic building usually of asymmetrical plan. A product of the late C 18/early C 19 Picturesque.

COUNTERCHANGING: of joists in a ceiling divided by beams into several compartments, when they are placed in opposite directions in alternate squares.

COUNTERSCARP BANK: small bank on the downhill or outer side of a hillfort ditch.

COUR D'HONNEUR: entrance court before a house in the French manner, usually with wings enclosing the sides and a screen wall or low range of buildings across the front.

COURSE: continuous layer of stones etc. in a wall.

COVE: a concave moulding on a large scale, e.g. to mask the eaves of a roof or in a *coved ceiling*, which has a pronounced cove joining the walls to a flat central panel smaller than the area of the whole ceiling.

CRADLE ROOF: *see* Wagon roof.

CREDENCE: in a church or chapel, a shelf within or beside a piscina, or for the sacramental elements and vessels.

CRENELLATION: *see* Battlement.

CREST, CRESTING: ornamental finish along the top of a screen etc.

CRINKLE-CRANKLE WALL: wall undulating in a series of serpentine curves.

CROCKETS (*lit.* hooks), CROCKETING: in Gothic architecture, leafy knobs on the edges of any sloping feature. *Crocket capital: see* Capital (Fig. 8).

CROMLECH: word of Celtic origin used of single free-standing stone chambers of Neolithic date.

CROSS DYKE: bank and ditch cutting off a promontory or dividing a ridge.

CROSSING: in a church, central space at the junction of the nave, chancel and transepts. *Crossing tower:* tower above a crossing.

CROSS-PASSAGE: space between opposed doorways at the end of medieval halls and later storeyed houses.

CROSS-WINDOWS: windows with one mullion and one transom (qq.v.).

CROWSTEPS: squared stones set like steps e.g. on a gable (which may also be called a stepped gable) or gateway; *see* Gable (Fig. 12).

CRUCK: cruck construction is a method of timber framing in which the ridge beam is supported by pairs of curved or inclined timbers extending from floor to apex. *Base cruck:* one terminating at the collar. *Scarfed cruck:* of two pieces mortised together. *Upper cruck:* one springing from the wall-plate.

Fig. 9. Consoles

CRYPT: underground or half-underground room usually below the E end of a church. *Ring crypt:* early medieval semi-circular or polygonal corridor crypt surrounding the apse of a church, often associated with chambers for relics.

CUP MARK: small artificial hollow cut in stone, Early Bronze Age in date and of unknown, but assumed religious, purpose.

CUPOLA (*lit.* dome): especially a small dome on a circular or polygonal base crowning a larger dome, roof, or turret.

CURTAIN WALL: (1) connecting wall between the towers of a castle; (2) in modern building, a non-load-bearing external wall composed of repeating modular elements applied to a framed structure.

CURVILINEAR: *see* Tracery.

CUSP: projecting point defining the foils in Gothic tracery, also used as a decorative edging to the soffits of the Gothic arches of tomb recesses, sedilia etc. When used decoratively within tracery patterns called *subcusps*.

CUTWATER: the pointed form of a bridge's piers; if built up to road level, the triangular platform forms a *refuge*.

CYCLOPEAN MASONRY: built with large irregular polygonal stones, but smooth and finely jointed.

CYMA RECTA and CYMA REVERSA: *see* Ogee.

DADO: the finishing of the lower part of an interior wall (sometimes used to support an applied order, i.e. a formalized continuous pedestal). *Dado rail:* the moulding along the top of the dado.

DAGGER: *see* Tracery and Fig. 31.

DAIS: raised platform at one end of a room, occupied by the high table of the head of the household and his family, usually in the great hall or principal living place.

DEC (DECORATED): historical division of English Gothic architecture covering the period from *c.* 1290 to *c.* 1350. The name is derived from the type of window tracery used during the period (*see also* Tracery).

DEMI-COLUMNS: engaged columns (q.v.) only half of whose circumference projects from the wall. Also called *half-columns*.

DENTIL: small square block used in series in classical cornices, rarely in Doric. In brickwork *dentilation* is produced by the projection of alternating headers or blocks along cornices or string courses.

DIAPER (*lit.* figured cloth): repetitive surface decoration of lozenges or squares either flat or in relief. Achieved in brickwork with bricks of two colours.

DIOCLETIAN WINDOW: semicircular window with two mullions, so-called because of its use in the Baths of Diocletian in Rome. Also called a *thermae window*.

DISTYLE: having two columns.

DOGTOOTH: typical E.E. decoration of a moulding, consisting of a series of small pyramids formed by four leaves meeting at a point (*see* Fig. 10). See also Cogging.

Fig. 10. Dogtooth

DOME: vault of even curvature erected on a circular base. The section can be segmental (e.g. saucer dome), semicircular, pointed, or bulbous (onion dome).

DONJON: *see* Keep.

DORIC: *see* Orders (Fig. 18).

DORMER WINDOW: window projecting from the slope of a roof, having a roof of its own and lighting a room within it. *Dormer head:* gable above this window, often formed as a pediment.

DORTER: dormitory; sleeping quarters of a monastery.

DOUBLE CHAMFER: *see* Chamfer.

DOUBLE PILE: *see* Pile.

DRAGON BEAM: *see* Jetty.

DRESSINGS: the stone or brickwork used about an angle, opening, or other feature worked to a finished face.

DRIPSTONE: moulded stone projecting from a wall to protect the lower parts from water; *see also* Hoodmould.

DRUM: (1) circular or polygonal stage supporting a dome or cupola; (2) one of the stones forming the shaft of a column.

DRYSTONE: stone construction without mortar.

DUTCH GABLE: *see* Gable (Fig. 12).

EASTER SEPULCHRE: recess, usually in the N wall of a chancel, with a tomb-chest thought to have been for an effigy of Christ for Easter celebrations.

EAVES: overhanging edge of a roof; hence *eaves cornice* in this position.

ECHINUS (*lit.* sea-urchin): ovolo moulding (q.v.) below the abacus of a Greek Doric capital; *see* Orders (Fig. 18).

E.E. (EARLY ENGLISH): historical division of English Gothic architecture covering the period *c.* 1190-1250.

EGG-AND-DART: *see* Enrichments.

ELEVATION: (1) any side of a building: (2) in a drawing, the same or any part of it, accurately represented in two dimensions.

EMBATTLED: furnished with battlements.

EMBRASURE (*lit.* splay): small splayed opening in the wall or battlement of a fortified building.

ENCAUSTIC TILES: glazed and decorated earthenware tiles used mainly for paving.

EN DÉLIT (*lit.* in error): term used in Gothic architecture to describe stone shafts whose grain runs vertically instead of horizontally, against normal building practice.

ENGAGED COLUMN: one that is partly merged into a wall or pier. Also called *attached column*.

ENGINEERING BRICKS: dense bricks of uniform size, high crushing strength, and low porosity, usually dark purple in colour. Originally used mostly for railway viaducts etc.

ENRICHMENTS: in classical architecture, the carved decoration of certain mouldings, e.g. the ovolo (*see* Mouldings) with *egg-and-dart*, the cyma reversa (*see* Ogee) with *waterleaf*, the astragal (q.v.) with *bead-and-reel*; *see* Fig. 11.

Egg-and-dart

Waterleaf

Bead-and-reel

Fig. 11. Enrichments

ENTABLATURE: in classical architecture, collective name for the three horizontal members (architrave, frieze, and cornice) carried by a wall or a column; *see* Orders (Fig. 18).

ENTASIS: very slight convex deviation from a straight line; used on classical columns and sometimes on spires to prevent an optical illusion of concavity.

ENTRESOL: mezzanine storey within or above the ground storey.

EPITAPH (*lit.* on a tomb): inscription in that position.

ESCUTCHEON: shield for armorial bearings.

EXEDRA: apsidal end of an apartment; *see* Apse.

EXTRADOS: outer curved face of an arch or vault.

EXTRUDED CORNER: right-angled (or circular) projection from the inner angle of a building with advancing wings, usually in C 16 or C 17 plans.

EYECATCHER: decorative building (often a sham ruin) usually on an eminence to terminate a vista in a park or garden layout.

FANLIGHT: window in the tympanum of a doorway, originally with fan-like glazing bars.

FASCIA: plain horizontal band, e.g. in an architrave (q.v.) or on a shopfront.

FENESTRATION: the arrangement of windows in a building.

FERETORY: place behind the high altar where the chief shrine of a church is kept.

FESTOON: ornament, usually in relief, in the form of a garland of flowers and/or fruit, suspended from both ends; *see also* Swag.

FIBREGLASS (or glass-reinforced polyester (GRP)): synthetic resin reinforced with glass fibre, formed in moulds, often simulating the appearance of traditional materials. GRC (glass-reinforced concrete) is also formed in moulds and used for components (cladding etc.) in industrialized building.

FIELDED: *see* Raised and fielded.

FILLET: in medieval architecture, a narrow flat band running down a shaft or along a roll moulding. In classical architecture it separates larger curved mouldings in cornices or bases.

FINIAL: decorative topmost feature, e.g. above a gable, spire or cupola.

FLAMBOYANT: properly the latest phase of French Gothic architecture where the window tracery takes on undulating lines, based on the use of flowing curves.

FLÈCHE (*lit*. arrow): slender spire on the centre of a roof. Also called *spirelet*.

FLEUR-DE-LYS: in heraldry, a formalized lily, as in the royal arms of France.

FLEURON: decorative carved flower or leaf, often rectilinear.

FLOWING: *see* Tracery (curvilinear).

FLUSHWORK: flint used decoratively in conjunction with dressed stone so as to form patterns: tracery, initials etc.

FLUTING: series of concave grooves, their common edges sharp (arris) or blunt (fillet).

FOIL (*lit*. leaf): lobe formed by the cusping of a circular or other shape in tracery. *Trefoil* (three), *quatrefoil* (four), *cinquefoil* (five), and *multifoil* express the number of lobes in a shape. *See also* Tracery.

FOLIATE: decorated, especially carved, with leaves.

FOLLY: amusing or fantastic structure, so named since presumed more costly than useful.

FORMWORK: commonly called shuttering; the temporary frame of braced timber or metal into which wet concrete is poured. The texture of the framework material depends on the imprint required.

FOSSE: ditch.

FRAMED BUILDING: where the structure is carried by the framework – e.g. of steel, reinforced concrete, timber – instead of by load-bearing walls.

FRATER: *see* Refectory.

FREESTONE: stone that is cut, or can be cut, in all directions, usually fine-grained sandstone or limestone.

FRESCO: *al fresco*: painting executed on wet plaster. *Fresco secco*: painting executed on dry plaster, more common in Britain.

FRET: a key pattern (q.v.).

FRIEZE: (1) the middle member of the classical entablature, sometimes ornamented; *see* Orders (Fig. 18). *Pulvinated frieze* (*lit*. cushioned): frieze of bold convex profile. (2) horizontal band of ornament.

FRONTAL: covering for the front of an altar. When solid called *antependium*.

FRONTISPIECE: in C16 and C17 buildings the central feature of doorway and windows above it linked in one composition.

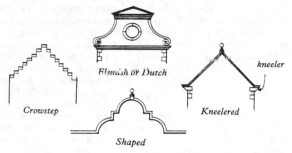

Fig. 12. Gables

GABLE: (1) area of wall, often triangular, at the end of a double-pitch roof. *Dutch gable*, characteristic of *c.* 1580–1680. *Shaped gable*, characteristic of *c.* 1620–80 (see Fig. 12). *Gablet:* small gable. *See also* Roofs.

GADROONING: ribbed ornament, e.g. on the lid or base of an urn, flowing into a lobed edge.

GALILEE: chapel or vestibule usually at the W end of a church enclosing the main portal(s).

GALLERY: balcony or passage, but with certain special meanings, e.g. (1) upper storey above the aisle of a church, looking through arches to the nave; also called tribune and often erroneously triforium (q.v.); (2) balcony or mezzanine, often with seats, overlooking the main interior space of a building; (3) external walkway, often projecting from a wall.

GALLETING: decorative use of small stones in a mortar course.

GARDEROBE (*lit.* wardrobe): medieval privy.

GARGOYLE: water spout projecting from the parapet of a wall or tower, often carved into human or animal shape.

GAUGED BRICKWORK: soft brick sawn roughly, then rubbed to a smooth, precise (gauged) surface with a stone or another brick. Mostly used for door or window openings. Also called *rubbed brickwork*.

GAZEBO (jocular Latin, 'I shall gaze'): lookout tower or raised summer house usually in a park or garden.

GEOMETRIC: historical division of English Gothic architecture covering the period *c.* 1250–90. *See also* Tracery. For another meaning, *see* Stairs.

GIANT ORDER: *see* Order.

GIBBS SURROUND: C18 treatment of a door or window surround, seen particularly in the work of James Gibbs (1682–1754) (*see* Fig. 13).

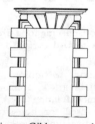

Fig. 13. Gibbs surround

GIRDER: a large beam. *Box girder:* of hollow-box section. *Bowed girder:* with its top rising in a curve. *Plate girder:* of I-section, made from iron or steel plates. *Lattice girder:* with braced framework.

GLAZING BARS: wooden or sometimes metal bars separating and supporting window panes.

GORSEDD CIRCLE: a modern stone circle; one is erected in Wales at a different site every year in connection with the National Eisteddfod.

GOTHIC: the period of medieval architecture characterized by the use of the pointed arch. For its subdivisions *see* E.E., Geometric, Dec, Perp, Flamboyant.

GRANGE (monastic): farm owned and run by members of a religious order.

GRC and GRP: *see* Fibreglass.

GRISAILLE: monochrome painting on walls or glass.

GROIN: sharp edge at the meeting of two cells of a cross-vault; *see* Vault (Fig. 34).

GROTESQUE (*lit.* grotto-esque): classical wall decoration in paint or stucco adopted from Roman examples, particularly by Raphael. Its foliage scrolls, unlike arabesque, incorporate ornaments and human figures.

GROTTO: artificial cavern usually decorated with rock- or shell-work, especially popular in the late C 17 and C 18.

GUILLOCHE: running classical ornament of interlaced bands forming a plait (*see* Fig. 14).

Fig. 14. Guilloche

GUNLOOP: opening for a firearm.

GUTTAE: *see* Orders (Fig. 18).

HAGIOSCOPE: *see* Squint.

HALF-TIMBERING: archaic term for timber framing (q.v.). Sometimes used for non-structural decorative timberwork, e.g. in gables etc. of the late C 19.

HALL CHURCH: medieval or Gothic Revival church whose nave and aisles are of equal height or approximately so.

HALL HOUSE: house in which the main room occupies the full height of the building.

HAMMERBEAM: *see* Roofs (3) and Fig. 27.

HEADER: *see* Bond.

HELM: *see* Roofs (1).

HENGE: ritual earthwork with a surrounding bank and ditch, the bank being on the outer side.

HERM (*lit.* the god Hermes): male head or bust on a pedestal.

HERRINGBONE WORK: masonry or brickwork in zigzag courses.

HEXASTYLE: *see* Portico.

HILLFORT: later Bronze Age and Iron Age earthwork enclosed by a ditch and bank system; in the later part of the period the defences multiplied in size and complexity. They vary from about an acre to over thirty acres in area, and are usually built with careful regard to natural elevations or promontories.

HIPPED ROOF: *see* Roofs (1) and Fig. 22.

HOODMOULD: projecting moulding shown above an arch or lintel to throw off water. When the moulding is horizontal it is often called a *label*. *See also* Label stop.

HUSK GARLAND: festoon of nutshells diminishing towards the ends.

HYPOCAUST (*lit.* under-burning): Roman underfloor heating system. The floor is supported on pillars and the space thus formed is connected to a flue.

ICONOGRAPHY: interpretation of the subject matter of works of the visual arts.

IMPOST (*lit.* imposition): horizontal moulding at the springing of an arch.

IMPOST BLOCK: block with splayed sides between abacus and capital.

IN ANTIS: *see* Antae.

INDENT: shape chiselled out of a stone to match and receive a brass.

INDUSTRIALIZED BUILDING (system building): the use of a system of manufactured units assembled on site. One of the most popular is the CLASP (Consortium Local Authorities Special Programme) system of light steel framing suitable for schools etc.

INGLENOOK (*lit.* fire-corner): recess for a hearth with provision for seating.

INTARSIA: *see* Marquetry.

INTERCOLUMNIATION: interval between columns.

INTERLACE: decoration in relief simulating woven or entwined stems or bands.

INTRADOS: see Soffit.

IONIC: see Orders (Fig. 18).

IRON AGE: the period after the introduction of iron to the coming of the Romans (c. 600 bc to A.D. 50).

JACK ARCH: shallow segmental vault springing from beams, used for fireproof floors, bridge decks etc.

JAMB (lit. leg): one of the vertical sides of an opening.

JETTY: in a timber-framed building, the projection of an upper storey beyond the storey below, made by the beams and joists of the lower storey oversailing the external wall. On their outer ends is placed the sill of the walling for the storey above. Buildings can be jettied on several sides, in which case a dragon beam is set diagonally at the corner to carry the joists to either side.

JOGGLE: mason's term for joining two stones to prevent them slipping or sliding by means of a notch in one and a corresponding projection in the other.

JOIST: one of the smaller timbers in a ceiling, supporting the floorboards, and itself often carried on larger members (beams).

KEEL: see Mouldings.

KEEP: principal and strongest tower of a castle. Also called donjon.

KENTISH CUSP: see Tracery.

KERB CAIRN: see Cairn.

KERB CIRCLE: low cairn with prominent kerb of contiguous stones, of Bronze Age date and probably a burial monument.

KEY PATTERN: continuous fret ornament, like a Vitruvian scroll, but drawn with straight lines at right angles (see Fig. 15).

Fig. 15. Key pattern

KEYSTONE: central stone in an arch or vault.

KING-POST: see Roofs (3) and Fig. 23.

KNEELER: horizontal projecting stone at the base of each side of a gable on which the inclined coping stones rest. See Gable (Fig. 12).

KNOTWORK: ornament of interlacing bands on Early Christian monuments.

LABEL: see Hoodmould.

LABEL STOP: ornamental stop at the end of a hoodmould.

LACED WINDOWS: windows pulled visually together by strips of brickwork, usually of a different colour, which continue vertically the lines of the vertical parts of the window surround. Typical of c. 1720.

LACING COURSE: one or more bricks serving as horizontal reinforcement to walls of flint, cobble etc.

LADY CHAPEL: chapel dedicated to the Virgin Mary (Our Lady).

LANCET WINDOW: slender single-light pointed-arched window.

LANTERN: (1) circular or polygonal turret with windows all round crowning a roof or a dome. (2) windowed stage of a crossing tower lighting the interior of a church.

LANTERN CROSS: churchyard cross with lantern-shaped top usually with sculptured representations on the sides of the top.

LAVATORIUM: in a monastery, a washing place adjacent to the refectory.

LEAN-TO: see Roofs (1).

LESENE (lit. a mean thing): pilaster without base or capital. Also called pilaster strip.

LIERNE: see Vault (Fig. 35).

LIGHT: compartment of a window defined by the mullions.

LINENFOLD: Tudor panelling where each panel is ornamented with a conventional representation of a piece of linen laid in vertical folds.

LINTEL: horizontal beam or stone bridging an opening.

LOGGIA: gallery open along one side of a building, usually arcaded or colonnaded. It may be a separate structure, usually in a garden.

LONG-AND-SHORT WORK: quoins consisting of stones placed with the long side alternately upright and horizontal, especially in Saxon building.

LONG HOUSE: house and byre in the same range, with internal access between them.

LOUVRE: (1) opening, often with lantern over, in the roof of a building to let the smoke from a central hearth escape; (2) one of a series of overlapping boards or panes of glass placed in an opening to allow ventilation but keep the rain out.

LOWER PALAEOLITHIC: see Palaeolithic.

LOWSIDE WINDOW: window set lower than the others in a chancel side wall, usually towards its w end.

LOZENGE: diamond shape.

LUCARNE (lit. dormer): small gabled opening in a roof or spire.

LUGGED: see Architrave.

LUNETTE (lit. half or crescent moon): (1) semicircular window; (2) semicircular or crescent-shaped area of wall.

LYCHGATE (lit. corpse-gate): roofed wooden gateway at the entrance to a churchyard for the reception of a coffin.

LYNCHET: long terraced strip of soil accumulating on the downward side of prehistoric and medieval fields due to soil creep from continuous ploughing along the contours.

MACHICOLATIONS (lit. mashing devices): in medieval military architecture, a series of openings under a projecting parapet between the corbels that support it, through which missiles can be dropped.

MAJOLICA: ornamented glazed earthenware.

MANSARD: see Roofs (1) and Fig. 22.

MANTELPIECE: see Chimneypiece.

MARQUETRY: inlay in various woods. Also called intarsia.

MATHEMATICAL TILES: facing tiles with one face moulded to look like a header or stretcher, most often hung on laths applied to timber-framed walls to make them appear brick-built.

MAUSOLEUM: monumental building or chamber usually intended for the burial of members of one family.

MEDALLION: round or oval decorated plaque.

MEGALITHIC TOMB: burial chamber built of large slabs and originally covered by a cairn, normally long. Built in many parts of Britain and Europe during the Neolithic for the communal burial of the dead. Also known as chambered tombs.

MERLON: see Battlement.

MESOLITHIC: 'Middle Stone Age'; the post-glacial period of hunting and fishing communities dating in Britain from c. 8000 bc to c. 4000 bc, when the farming communities arrived.

METOPES: spaces between the triglyphs in a Doric frieze; see Orders (Fig. 18).

MEZZANINE: (1) low storey between two higher ones; (2) low upper storey within the height of a high one, not extending over its whole area. See also Entresol.

MILD STEEL: see Cast iron.

MISERERE: see Misericord.

MISERICORD (lit. mercy): shelf placed on the underside of a hinged choir stall seat which, when turned up, supported the occupant during long periods of standing. Also called Miserere.

MITRE: the turning of a moulding at right angles at the junction of two members. The form and method differ according to the material, being either a joiner's or a mason's mitre.

MODILLIONS: small consoles (q.v.) at regular intervals along the underside of the cornice of the Corinthian or Composite orders.

MODULE: in industrialized building (q.v.), a predetermined standard size for co-ordinating the dimensions of components of a building with the spaces into which they have to fit.

MOTTE: steep mound forming the main feature of C11 and C12 castles.

MOTTE-AND-BAILEY: post-Roman and Norman defence system consisting of an earthen mound (motte) topped with a wooden tower within a bailey (q.v.), with enclosure ditch and palisade, and with the rare addition of an internal bank.

MOUCHETTE: *see* Tracery and Fig. 32.

MOULDINGS: enrichments of a member of a building, of uniform profile whether concave or convex or both. *Ovolo:* of quarter-round convex section, as in C17 window mullions. *Cavetto:* of quarter-round concave section. *Bolection:* projecting moulding joining two surfaces, as used round doorways and panels c. 1700. *Keel:* moulding whose outline is pointed in section like that of the keel of a ship. *Casement:* deep hollow in the outer reveals of Perp window frames. *Roll:* rounded moulding with its curve semicircular or more than semicircular. *Bowtell:* Gothic moulding similar to, but smaller than, a roll. *See also* Chamfer.

MULLION: vertical member between the lights in a window opening.

MULTI-STOREY: modern term denoting five or more storeys. *See* Cluster, Slab, and Point Blocks.

MULTIVALLATE: (of a hillfort) defended by three or more concentric banks and ditches.

MUNTIN: vertical part in the framing of a door, screen, panelling etc., butting into or stopped by the horizontal rails.

Fig. 16. Nailhead moulding

NAILHEAD MOULDING: E.E. ornamental motif consisting of small pyramids regularly repeated (*see* Fig. 16).

NARTHEX: enclosed vestibule or covered porch at the main entrance to a church.

NAVE: the body of a church w of the crossing or chancel which may be flanked by aisles (q.v.).

NECESSARIUM: *see* Reredorter.

NEOLITHIC: 'New Stone Age', dating in Britain from c. 4000 bc to c. 1800 bc, when metal became prevalent. The period of the first settled farming communities.

NEWEL: central post in a circular or winding staircase; also the principal post where a flight of stairs meets a floor or a landing. *See* Stairs (Fig. 29).

NICHE (*lit.* shell): vertical recess in a wall, sometimes for a statue.

NIGHT STAIR: stair by which monks entered the transept of their church from their dormitory to celebrate night services.

NIMBED: having a halo, as in representations of saints or angels.

NOGGING: *see* Brick-nogging.

NOOK-SHAFT: shaft set in the angle or a pier or respond or wall, or the angle of the jamb of a window or doorway.

NORMAN: *see* Romanesque.

NOSING: projection of the tread of a step. A *bottle nosing* is half-round in section.

NUTMEG MOULDING: consisting of a chain of tiny triangles placed obliquely.

OBELISK: tapering pillar of square plan and ending pyramidally.

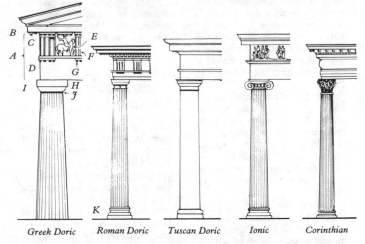

Greek Doric   Roman Doric   Tuscan Doric   Ionic   Corinthian

Fig. 18. Orders: A Entablature; B Cornice; C Frieze; D Architrave; E Metope;
F Triglyph; G Guttae; H Abacus; I Capital; J Echinus; K Base

OCULUS: circular opening or window in a wall or vault; cf. Bullseye window.

ŒIL DE BŒUF: *see* Bullseye window.

OGEE: double curve, bending first one way and then the other. Applied to mouldings, also called *cyma recta*. A reverse ogee moulding with a double curve also called *cyma reversa* (*see* Fig. 17). *Ogee* or *ogival arch*: *see* Fig. 2.

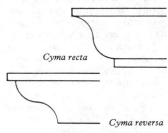

Cyma recta

Cyma reversa

Fig. 17. Ogee mouldings

ORATORY: (1) small private chapel in a church or a house; (2) church of the Oratorian Order.

ORDER: (1) upright structural member formally related to others, e.g. in classical architecture a column, pilaster or anta; (2) especially in medieval architecture, one of a series of recessed arches and jambs forming a splayed opening. *Giant* or *colossal order*: classical order whose height is that of two or more storeys of a building.

ORDERS: in classical architecture, the differently formalized versions of the basic post-and-lintel (column and entablature) structure, each having its own rules for design and proportion. For examples of the main types *see* Fig. 18. In the *composite*, the capital combines Ionic volutes with Corinthian foliage. *Superimposed orders*: term for the use of orders on successive levels, usually in the upward sequence of Tuscan, Doric, Ionic, Corinthian.

ORIEL: *see* Bay-window.

OVERDOOR: *see* Sopraporta.

OVERHANG: *see* Jetty.

OVERMANTEL: decorative panel above a fireplace. *See also* Chimneypiece.

OVERSAILING COURSES: series of stone or brick courses, each projecting beyond the one below it.

OVERTHROW: decorative fixed arch between two gatepiers or above a wrought-iron gate.

OVOLO: *see* Mouldings.

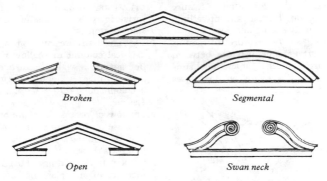

Broken

Segmental

Open

Swan neck

Fig. 19. Pediments

PALAEOLITHIC: 'Old Stone Age'; the first period of human culture, commencing in the Ice Age and immediately prior to the Mesolithic. The Lower Palaeolithic is the earlier phase, the Upper Palaeolithic the later.

PALIMPSEST (*lit*. erased work): re-use of a surface. (1) of a brass: where a metal plate has been reused by turning over and engraving on the back; (2) of a wall painting: where one overlaps and partly obscures an earlier one.

PALLADIAN: architecture following the examples and principles of Andrea Palladio (1508–80).

PALMETTE: classical ornament like a symmetrical palm shoot; for illustration *see* Fig. 1.

PANELLING: (1) wooden lining to interior walls, made up of vertical members (muntins, q.v.) and horizontals (rails) framing panels (*see* Linenfolds; Raised and fielded). Also called *wainscot*. (2) subdivision of a surface, e.g. between stone ribs.

PANTILE: roof tile of curved S-shaped section.

PARAPET: wall for protection at any sudden drop, e.g. on a bridge or at the wall-head of a castle; in the latter case it protects the *parapet walk* or wall walk. Also used to conceal a roof.

PARCHEMIN PANEL: in Tudor and Late Gothic woodwork, a panel with central vertical rib or moulding which branches top and bottom in ogee curves to meet the four corners of the panel. Sometimes combined with linenfold (q.v.).

PARCLOSE: *see* Screen.

PARGETTING (*lit*. plastering): plasterwork with patterns and ornaments either moulded in relief or incised on it, usually in timber-framed buildings.

PARLOUR: the small 'best' room in vernacular houses.

PARTERRE: level space in a garden laid out with low, formal beds of plants.

PATERA (*lit*. plate): round or oval ornament in shallow relief, especially in classical architecture.

PAVILION: (1) ornamental building for occasional use in a garden, park, sports ground etc.; (2) projecting subdivision of some larger building, often at an angle or terminating wings.

PEBBLEDASHING: *see* Rendering.

PEDESTAL: in classical architecture, a tall block carrying an order, statue, vase etc.

PEDIMENT: in classical architecture, a formalized gable derived from that of a temple, also used over doors, windows etc. For variations of type *see* Fig. 19.

PEEL or PELE (*lit*. palisade): stone tower, e.g. near the Scottish–English border.

PELE: *see* Peel.

PENDANT: decorative feature hanging from a vault or ceiling, usually ending in a boss.

PENDENTIVE: spandrel formed as part of a hemisphere between arches meeting at an angle, supporting a drum or dome (*see* Fig. 20).

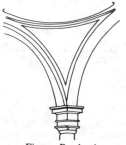

Fig. 20. Pendentive

PENTHOUSE: subsidiary structure with a lean-to roof; in modern architecture, a separately roofed structure on top of a multi-storey block.

PERISTYLE: in classical architecture, a range of columns all round a building, e.g. a temple, or an interior space, e.g. a courtyard.

PERP (PERPENDICULAR): historical division of English Gothic architecture covering the period from *c.* 1335–50 to *c.* 1530. The name is derived from the upright tracery panels then used (*see* Tracery).

PERRON: *see* Stairs.

PEW: loosely, seating for the laity outside the chancel. Strictly an enclosed seat. *Box pew:* with equal high sides, entered by a door.

PIANO NOBILE: principal floor, usually with a ground floor or basement underneath and a lesser storey overhead.

PIAZZA: open space surrounded by buildings; in the C 17 and C 18 used erroneously to mean an arcaded ground floor, especially adjoining or around an open space.

PIER: large masonry or brick support, usually for an arch. *See also* Compound pier.

PIETRA DURA: ornamental or pictorial inlay by means of thin slabs of stone.

PILASTER: flat representation of a classical column in shallow relief against a wall. *Pilastrade:* series of pilasters, equivalent to a colonnade. *Pilaster strip:* see Lesene.

PILE: row of rooms. The important use of the term is in *double pile*, describing a house that is two rows thick.

PILLAR: free-standing upright member of any plan, not conforming to one of the Orders.

PILLAR PISCINA: free-standing piscina on a pillar.

PILOTIS: French term used in modern architecture for pillars or stilts that carry a building to first-floor level leaving the ground floor open.

PINNACLE: tapering finial, e.g. on a buttress or the corner of a tower, sometimes decorated with crockets, especially in Gothic architecture.

PISCINA: basin for washing the Communion or Mass vessels, provided with a drain; generally set in or against the wall to the s of an altar.

PISÉ: structural walling of compacted earth mixed with straw, raised in successive stages between formwork (q.v.) and given a protective finish. Also known as *cob*.

PLAISANCE: summer house, pleasure house near a mansion.

PLAN: (1) the arrangement of accommodation within a building and the relation of one room or area to another; (2) two-dimensional representation on a horizontal plane of the shape of a moulding or member, or of the parts of any one storey or floor of a building. cf. Section.

PLATFORM CAIRN: *see* Cairn.

PLINTH: projecting courses at the foot of a wall or column, generally chamfered or moulded at the top.

PODIUM: continuous raised platform supporting a building. In modern architecture often a large block of two or three storeys beneath a multi-storey block covering a smaller area.

POINT BLOCK: high block of housing in which the flats fan out from a central core of lifts, staircases etc.

POINTING: exposed mortar jointing of masonry or brickwork. The finished form is of various types, e.g. *flush pointing, recessed pointing.*

POPPYHEAD: carved ornament of leaves and flowers, generally in the form of a fleur-de-lys, as a finial for the end of a bench or stall.

PORCH: covered projecting entrance to a building.

PORTAL FRAME: in modern architecture a basic form of construction in which a series of precast beams, placed in pairs to form 'portals', support the walls and roof. The upper part of each beam is angled up to where they meet at the roof ridge.

PORTCULLIS: gate constructed to rise and fall in vertical grooves at the entry to a castle.

PORTE COCHÈRE: porch large enough to admit wheeled vehicles.

PORTICO: a porch, open on one side at least, and enclosed by a row of columns which also support the roof and frequently a pediment. When the front of it is on the same plane as the front of the building it is described as a *portico in antis* (*see* Antae). Porticoes are described by the number of the front columns, e.g. tetrastyle (four), hexastyle (six). *Blind portico:* the front features of a portico applied to a wall; cf. Prostyle.

PORTICUS (plural porticūs): in pre-Conquest architecture, a subsidiary cell opening from the main body of a church.

POST-AND-PANEL: method of constructing a wooden partition with boards slotted upright into thicker posts.

POSTERN: small gateway at the back of a building.

PRECAST CONCRETE: concrete components cast before being placed in position.

PREDELLA: (1) step or platform on which an altar stands; hence (2) in an altarpiece or stained-glass window, the row of subsidiary scenes beneath the main representation.

PREFABRICATION: manufacture of buildings or components off-site for assembly on-site. *See also* Industrialized building.

PRESBYTERY: (1) part of a church lying E of the choir where the main altar is placed; (2) a priest's residence.

PRESTRESSED CONCRETE: *see* Reinforced Concrete.

PRINCIPAL: *see* Roofs (3) and Figs. 23 and 26.

PRIORY: religious house whose head is a prior or prioress, not an abbot or abbess.

PROSCENIUM ARCH: visual division or frame in front of a stage, state chamber etc.

PROSTYLE: with a free-standing row of columns in front.

PULPIT: raised and enclosed platform used for the preaching of sermons. *Three-decker pulpit:* with reading desk below and clerk's desk below the reading desk. *Two-decker pulpit:* as above, but without the clerk's stall.

PULPITUM: stone screen in a major church provided to shut off the choir from the nave and also as a backing for the return choir stalls.

PULVINATED: *see* Frieze.

PURLIN: *see* Roofs (3) and Figs. 23-6.

PUTHOLES or PUTLOG HOLES: holes in a wall to receive putlocks, the horizontal timbers on which scaffolding boards rest. They are often not filled in after construction is complete.

PUTTO (plural putti): small naked boy. Also called *amorino.*

QUADRANGLE: rectangular inner courtyard in a large building.

QUARRIES (*lit.* squares): (1) square (or diamond-shaped) panes of glass supported by lead strips which are called *cames*; (2) square floor-slabs or tiles.

QUATREFOIL: *see* Foil.

QUEEN-POSTS: *see* Roofs (3) and Fig. 25.

QUIRK: sharp groove to one side of a convex moulding, e.g. beside a roll moulding, which is then said to be quirked.

QUOINS: dressed stones at the angles of a building. They may be alternately long and short, especially when rusticated.

RADIATING CHAPELS: chapels projecting radially from an ambulatory or an apse; *see* Chevet.

RADIOCARBON DATING: method of dating organic material, normally charcoal, from archaeological sites by measuring the amount of surviving radioactive carbon 14. This isotope begins to decay at a known rate at the moment of 'death'. However it has been shown recently that these dates are younger than the true date by a factor of some 100–300 years.

RAFTER: *see* Roofs (3) and Figs. 23–7.

RAGGLE: groove cut in masonry, especially to receive the edge of glass or roof-covering.

RAGULY: ragged (in heraldry); or the term may apply to medieval funerary sculpture, e.g. a *cross raguly*, represented with its members notched in outline.

RAIL: *see* Muntin.

RAISED AND FIELDED: of a wooden panel with a raised square of rectangular central area (field) surrounded by a narrow moulding.

RAKE: slope or pitch.

RAMPART: stone or earth wall surrounding a castle, fortress or fortified town. *Rampart walk:* path along the inner face of a rampart.

REBATE: rectangular section cut out of a masonry or timber edge to receive a shutter, door, window etc.

REBUS: a heraldic pun, e.g. a fiery cock as a badge for Cockburn.

REEDING: series of convex mouldings; the reverse of fluting.

REFECTORY: dining hall of a monastery or similar establishment. Also called *frater*.

REINFORCED CONCRETE: concrete reinforced with steel rods to take the tensile stress. A later development is *prestressed concrete*, which incorporates artificially-tensioned steel tendons.

RENDERING: the process of covering outside walls with a uniform surface or skin for protection from the weather. *Stucco*, originally a fine lime plaster worked to a smooth surface, is the finest rendered external finish, characteristic of many late C 18 and C 19 classical buildings. It is usually painted. *Cement rendering* is a cheaper and more recent substitute for stucco, usually with a grainy texture and often left unpainted. In more simple buildings the wall surface may be roughly *lime-plastered* (and then whitewashed), or covered with plaster mixed with a coarse aggregate such as gravel. This latter is known as *roughcast*. A variant, fashionable in the early C 20, is *pebbledashing:* here the stones of the aggregate are kept separate and are thrown at the wet plastered wall to create a textured effect. Rendering may also refer to the *plastering* of internal walls.

REPOUSSÉ: decoration of metalwork by relief designs, formed by beating the metal from the back.

REREDORTER (*lit.* behind the dormitory): medieval euphemism for latrines in a monastery. Also called *necessarium*.

REREDOS: painted and/or sculptured screen behind and above an altar.

RESPOND: half-pier or half-column bonded into a wall and carrying one end of an arch. It usually terminates an arcade.

RETABLE: a picture or piece of

carving standing at the back of an altar, usually attached to it. Also called an *altarpiece*.

RETROCHOIR: in a major church, the space between the high altar and an E chapel, like a square ambulatory.

REVEAL: the inward plane of a jamb, between the edge of an external wall and the frame of a door or window that is set in it.

RIB VAULT: *see* Vault.

RIDDEL POST: post to carry riddel curtains, which hang behind or beside an altar.

RINCEAU (*lit.* little branch) or ANTIQUE FOLIAGE: classical ornament, usually on a frieze, of leafy scrolls branching alternately to left and right (*see* Fig. 21).

Fig. 21. Rinceau

RING CAIRN: *see* Cairn.

RINGWORK: early earthwork defence in the form of a circular bank.

RISER: vertical face of a step.

ROCK-FACED: term used to describe masonry which is cleft to produce a natural rugged appearance.

ROCOCO (*lit.* rocky): latest phase of the Baroque style, current in most Continental countries between *c.* 1720 and *c.* 1760, and showing itself in Britain mainly in playful, scrolled decoration, especially plasterwork.

ROLL: *see* Mouldings.

ROMANESQUE: that style in architecture (in England often called Norman) which was current in the C11 and C12 and preceded the Gothic style. (Some scholars extend the use of the term Romanesque back to the C10 or C9.) *See also* Saxo-Norman.

ROMANO-BRITISH: term applied to the period and cultural features of Britain affected by the Roman occupation of the C1–5 A.D.

ROOD: cross or crucifix flanked by the Virgin and St John, usually over the entry into the chancel, on a beam (*rood beam*) or painted. The *rood screen* beneath it may have a *rood loft* along the top, reached by a *rood stair*.

ROOFS: (1) *Shape:* for the external shapes and terms used to describe them *see* Fig. 22. *Helm:* roof with four inclined faces joined at the top, with a gable at the foot of each. *Hipped* (Fig. 22): roof with sloped instead of vertical ends. *Lean-to:* roof with one slope only, built against a vertical wall: term also applied to the part of the building such a roof covers. *Mansard* (Fig. 22): roof with a double slope, the lower one larger and steeper than the upper. *Saddleback:* the name given to a normal pitched roof when used over a tower. *See also* Wagon roof.

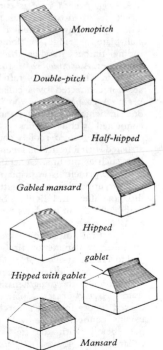

Fig. 22. Roofs: external forms

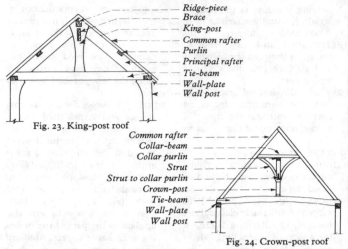

Fig. 23. King-post roof

Fig. 24. Crown-post roof

(2) *Construction:* Roofs are generally called after the principal structural component, e.g. *crown-post, hammerbeam, king-post* etc. See below under *Elements* and Figs. 23–7.

A *single-framed* roof is constructed with no main trusses. The rafters may be fixed to a wall-plate or ridge, or longitudinal timbers may be absent altogether. A *common rafter* roof is one in which pairs of rafters are not connected by a collar-beam. A *coupled rafter* roof is one in which the rafters are connected by collar-beams.

A *double-framed* roof is constructed with longitudinal members such as purlins. Generally there are principals or principal rafters supporting the longitudinal members and dividing the length of the roof into bays.

(3) *Elements: Ashlar piece.* A short vertical timber connecting an inner wall-plate or timber pad to a rafter above.

Braces. Subsidiary timbers set diagonally to strengthen the frame. *Arched braces:* a pair of curved braces forming an arch, usually connecting the wall or post below with the tie- or collar-beam above. *Passing braces*: straight braces of considerable length, passing across

other members of the truss. *Scissor braces:* a pair of braces which cross diagonally between pairs of rafters or principals. *Wind-braces:* short, usually curved braces connecting side purlins with principals. Sometimes decorated with cusping.

Camberbeam. A horizontal member rising in a low pitch to a point at mid span and on which purlins are laid direct, instead of on to a framed truss.

Collar-beam. A horizontal transverse timber connecting a pair of rafters or principals at a height between the apex and the wall-plate.

Crown-post. A vertical timber standing centrally on a tie-beam and supporting a collar purlin. Longitudinal braces usually rise from the crown-post to the collar purlin. When the truss is open lateral braces generally rise to the collar-beam, and when the truss is closed they go down to the tie-beam.

Hammerbeams. Horizontal brackets projecting at wall-plate level on opposite sides of the wall like a tie-beam with the centre cut away. The inner ends carry vertical timbers called hammerposts and braces to a collar-beam.

Hammerpost. A vertical tim-

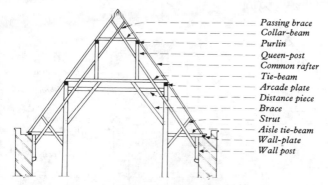

Passing brace
Collar-beam
Purlin
Queen-post
Common rafter
Tie-beam
Arcade plate
Distance piece
Brace
Strut
Aisle tie-beam
Wall-plate
Wall post

Fig. 25. Queen-post roof

ber set on the inner end of a hammerbeam to support a purlin; it is braced to a collar-beam above.

King-post. A vertical timber standing centrally on a tie- or collar-beam and rising to the apex of the roof where it supports a ridge.

Principals. The pair of inclined lateral timbers of a truss which carry common rafters. Usua' hey support side purlins anu their position corresponds to the main bay division of the space below.

Purlin. A horizontal longitudinal timber. *Collar purlin:* a single central timber which carries collar-beams and is itself supported by crown-posts. *Side purlins:* pairs of timbers occurring some way up the slope of the roof. They carry the common rafters and are supported in a number of ways: *butt purlins* are tenoned into either side of the principals; *clasped purlins* rest on queen-posts or are carried in the angles between the principals and the collar; *laid-on purlins* lie on the backs of the principals; *trenched purlins* are trenched into the backs of the principals.

Queen-posts. A pair of vertical, or near-vertical, timbers placed symmetrically on a tie-beam and supporting side purlins.

Rafters. Inclined lateral timbers sloping from wall-top to apex and supporting the roof covering. *Common rafters:* rafters of equal size found along the length of a roof or sometimes interrupted by main trusses containing principal rafters. *Principal rafters:* rafters which act as principals but also serve as common rafters.

Ridge, ridge-piece. A horizontal, longitudinal timber at the apex of a roof supporting the ends of the rafters.

Sprocket. A short timber placed on the back and at the foot of a rafter to form projecting eaves.

Strut. A vertical or oblique timber which runs between two members of a roof truss but does not directly support longitudinal timbers.

Tie-beam. The main horizontal, transverse timber which carries the feet of the principals at wall-plate level.

Truss. A rigid framework of timbers which is placed laterally across the building to carry the longitudinal roof timbers which support the common rafters.

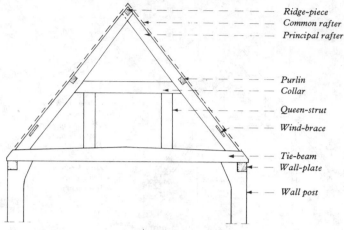

Fig. 26. Queen-strut roof

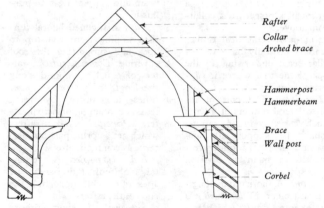

Fig. 27. Hammerbeam roof

Wall-plate. A timber laid longitudinally on the top of a wall to receive the ends of the rafters. In a timber-framed building the posts and studs of the wall below are tenoned into it.

ROPE MOULDING: *see* Cable moulding.

ROSE WINDOW: circular window with tracery radiating from the centre; cf. Wheel window.

ROTUNDA: building circular in plan.

ROUGHCAST: *see* Rendering.

RUBBLE: masonry whose stones are wholly or partly in a rough state. *Coursed rubble:* of coursed stones with rough faces. *Random rubble:* of uncoursed stones in a random pattern. *Snecked rubble* has courses frequently broken by smaller stones (snecks).

RUNNING DOG: *see* Vitruvian scroll.

RUSTICATION: exaggerated treatment of masonry to give an effect of strength. In the most usual kind the joints are recessed by V-section chamfering or square-section channelling. *Banded rustication* has only the horizontal joints emphasized in this way. The faces may be flat, but there are many other forms, e.g. *diamond-faced*, like shallow pyramids, *vermiculated*, with a stylized texture like worm-casts, and *glacial* (frostwork) like icicles or stalactites. *Rusticated columns* may have their joints and drums treated in any of these ways.

SACRISTY: room in a church for sacred vessels and vestments.

SADDLEBACK: *see* Roofs (1).

SALTIRE CROSS: with diagonal limbs.

SANCTUARY: (1) area around the main altar of a church (*see* Presbytery); (2) sacred site consisting of wood or stone uprights enclosed by a circular bank and ditch. Beginning in the Neolithic, they were elaborated in the succeeding Bronze Age. The best-known examples are Stonehenge and Avebury.

SARCOPHAGUS (*lit.* flesh-consuming): coffin of stone or other durable material.

SASH: glazed window frame; specifically one hung on cords in vertical tracks.

SAUCER DOME: *see* Dome.

SAXO-NORMAN: transitional Romanesque style combining Anglo-Saxon and Norman features, current *c.* 1060–1100.

SCAGLIOLA: composition imitating marble.

SCALLOPED CAPITAL: *see* Fig. 8.

SCARP: artificial cutting away of the ground to form a steep slope.

SCOTIA: a hollow moulding, especially between tori (q.v.) on a column base.

SCREEN: in a church, structure usually at the entry to the chancel; *see* Rood (screen) *and* Pulpitum. A *parclose screen* separates a chapel from the rest of the church.

SCREENS or SCREENS PASSAGE: screened-off entrance passage between the hall and the service rooms of a medieval, C16, or early C17 house.

SECTION: two-dimensional representation of the shape or profile of a moulding or member, or of the interior of a building on a vertical plane; cf. **Plan.**

SEDILIA (singular *sedile*): seats for the priests (usually three) on the S side of the chancel of a church.

SERLIAN WINDOW: *see* Venetian window.

SÊT-FAWR (Welsh): deacons' pew beneath the pulpit of a Nonconformist chapel.

SET-OFF: *see* Weathering.

SEVERN-COTSWOLD TOMB: Variety of megalithic tomb (q.v.) having a very complex ground plan and found in the Cotswolds and to the W of the Severn in Gwent, Glamorgan, Breconshire, and occasionally in N Wales.

SGRAFFITO: scratched pattern, often in plaster, with portions of a top coat removed to reveal a surface of different colour beneath.

SHAFT: vertical member of round or polygonal section, especially the main part of a classical column. *Shaft-ring:* ring like a belt round a circular pier or a circular shaft attached to a pier, characteristic of the C12 and C13.

SHARAWAGGI: a term, first used *c.* 1685 in Sir William Temple's *Essay on Gardening*, which describes an irregular or asymmetrical composition.

SHEILA-NA-GIG: female fertility figure, usually with legs wide open.

SHOULDERED: *see* Arch (Fig. 2), Architrave (Fig. 3).

SHUTTERED CONCRETE: *see* Formwork.

SILL: (1) horizontal member at the bottom of a window- or doorframe; (2) the horizontal member at the base of a timber-framed wall into which the posts and studs (q.v.) are tenoned.

SLAB BLOCK: rectangular multistorey block of housing or offices.

SLATE-HANGING: covering of overlapping slates on a wall, which is then said to be *slate-hung*. *Tile-hanging* is similar.

SLYPE: covered way or passage, especially in a cathedral or monastic church, leading E from the cloisters between transept and chapter house.

SNECKED: *see* Rubble.

SOFFIT (*lit.* ceiling): underside of an arch (also called *intrados*), lintel etc. *Soffit roll:* roll moulding on a soffit.

SOLAR (*lit.* sun-room): upper living room or withdrawing room of a medieval house, accessible from the high table end of the hall.

SOPRAPORTA (*lit.* over door): painting or relief above the door of a room, usual in the C17 and C18.

SOUNDING-BOARD: horizontal board or canopy over a pulpit; also called *tester*.

SOUTERRAIN: underground stone-lined passage and chamber.

SPAB: Society for the Protection of Ancient Buildings, founded in 1877 by William Morris, seeking to promote conservative principles of restoration, in opposition to destructively sweeping methods then prevalent.

SPANDRELS: roughly triangular spaces between an arch and its containing rectangle, or between adjacent arches. In modern architecture the non-structural panels under the windows in a framed building.

SPERE: a fixed structure which serves as a screen at the lower end of an open medieval hall between the hall proper and the screens passage. It has a wide central opening, often with a movable screen, between posts and short screen walls. The top member is often the tie-beam of the roof truss above; screen and truss are then called a *spere-truss*.

SPERE-TRUSS: *see* Spere.

SPIRE: tall pyramidal or conical feature built on a tower or turret. *Broach spire:* starting from a square base, then carried into an octagonal section by means of triangular faces. The *Splayed-foot spire* is a variation of the broach form, found principally in the south-eastern counties of England, in which the four cardinal faces are splayed out near their base, to cover the corners, while oblique (or intermediate) faces taper away to a point. *Needle spire:* thin spire rising from the centre of a tower roof, well inside the parapet: when of timber and lead often called a *spike*.

SPIRELET: *see* Flèche.

SPLAY: chamfer, usually of a reveal.

SPRING or SPRINGING: level at which an arch or vault rises from its supports. *Springers:* the first stones of an arch or vaulting-rib above the spring.

SQUINCH: arch or series of arches thrown across an angle between two walls to support a superstructure of polygonal or round plan over a rectangular space, e.g. a dome, a spire (*see* Fig. 28).

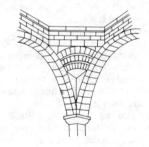

Fig. 28. Squinch

SQUINT: an aperture in a wall or through a pier usually to allow a view of an altar of a church otherwise obscured. Also called *hagioscope*.

STAIRS: *see* Fig. 29. A *dog-leg stair* has parallel flights rising alternately in opposite directions, without an open well. *Newel stair:* ascending round a central supporting newel (q.v.), called a *spiral stair* or *vice* when in a circular shaft. *Well stair:* term

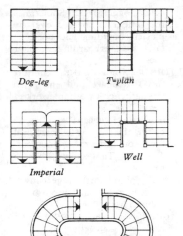

Dog-leg *T-plan*

Imperial *Well*

Perron

Fig. 29. Stairs

applied to any stair contained in an open well, but generally to one that climbs up three sides of a well with corner landings, e.g. the *timber-framed newel stair*, common from the C17 on. *Flying stair:* cantilevered from the wall of a stairwell, without newels. *Geometric stair:* flying stair whose inner edge describes a curve. *Perron* (*lit.* of stone): external stair leading to a doorway, usually of double-curved plan.

STAKE CIRCLE: *see* Barrow.

STALL: fixed seat in the choir or chancel for the clergy or choir (cf. Pew). Usually with arm rests. Often framed together like a bench.

STANCHION: upright structural member, of iron or steel or reinforced concrete.

STANDING STONE: large monolith, traditionally dated to the Bronze Age. They may have been erected for a number of reasons: some may be markers of routes, territories etc.; others stand near graves.

STEEPLE: tower together with a spire, lantern or belfry.

STEPPED GABLE: *see* Crowsteps.

STIFF-LEAF: type of E.E. foliage decoration. *Stiff-leaf capital: see* Fig. 8.

STONE CIRCLE: ceremonial site of Bronze Age date. Excavation has provided little evidence for the precise use of stone circles and, from their upland siting, it has often been suggested that they played some role in the worship or study of the stars.

STOP: plain or decorated blocks terminating mouldings or chamfers in stone or wood, or at the end of labels, hoodmoulds or string courses. *See* Chamfer.

STOREY-POSTS: the principal posts of a timber-framed wall.

STOUP: vessel for the reception of holy water, usually placed near a door.

STRAINER: *see* Arch.

STRAPWORK: late C16 and C17 decoration, resembling straplike interlaced bands of leather.

STRETCHER: *see* Bond.

STRING COURSE: horizontal stone course or moulding projecting from the surface of a wall.

STRINGS: two sloping members which carry the ends of the treads and risers of a staircase. Closed strings enclose the treads and risers; in the later open string staircase the steps project above the strings.

STUCCO (*lit.* plaster): *see* Rendering.

STUDS: subsidiary vertical timbers of a timber-framed wall or partition.

STYLOBATE: solid platform on which a colonnade stands.

SUSPENSION BRIDGE: bridge suspended from cables or chains draped from towers. *Stay-suspension* or *stayed-cantilever bridge:* supported by diagonal stays from towers or pylons.

SWAG (*lit.* bundle): ornament suspended like a festoon (q.v.), but usually representing cloth.

SYSTEM BUILDING: *see* Industrialized Building.

TABERNACLE (*lit.* tent): (1) canopied structure, especially on a small scale, to contain the reserved sacrament or a relic; (2) architectural frame, e.g. of a statue on a wall or free-standing, with flanking orders. In classical architecture also called an *aedicule*.

TABLET FLOWER: medieval ornament of a four-leaved flower with a raised or sunk centre.

TABLE TOMB: a memorial slab raised on free-standing legs.

TAS-DE-CHARGE: the lower courses of a vault or arch laid horizontally.

TERMINAL FIGURE: pedestal or pilaster which tapers towards the bottom, usually with the upper part of a human figure growing out of it. Also called *term*.

TERRA-COTTA: moulded and fired clay ornament or cladding, usually unglazed.

TESSELLATED PAVEMENT: mosaic flooring, particularly Roman.

TESTER (*lit.* head): flat canopy over a tomb and especially over a pulpit, where it is also called a *sounding-board*.

TESTER TOMB: C16 or C17 type with effigies on a tomb-chest beneath a tester, either free-standing (tester with four or more columns), or attached to a wall (half tester) with columns on one side only.

TETRASTYLE: *see* Portico.

THERMAE WINDOW (*lit.* of a Roman bath): *see* Diocletian window.

THREE-DECKER PULPIT: *see* Pulpit.

TIE-BEAM: *see* Roofs (3) and Figs. 23–6.

TIERCERON: *see* Vault and Fig. 35.

TILE-HANGING: *see* Slate-hanging.

TIMBER FRAMING: method of construction where walls are built of interlocking vertical and horizontal timbers. The spaces are filled with non-structural walling of wattle and daub, lath and plaster, brickwork (known as nogging or brick-nogging) etc. Sometimes the timber is covered over by plaster, boarding laid horizontally (weatherboarding, q.v.), or tiles.

TIMBER-LACED BANK: hillfort (q.v.) rampart built of earth strengthened by a framework of heavy logs.

TOMB-CHEST: chest-shaped stone coffin, the most usual medieval form of funerary monument. *See also* Table tomb; Tester tomb.

TORUS (plural tori): large convex moulding, usually used on a column base.

TOUCH: soft black marble quarried near Tournai.

TOURELLE: turret corbelled out from the wall.

TOWER HOUSE: compact medieval fortified house with the main hall raised above the ground and at least one more storey above it. The type survives in odd examples into the C16 and C17.

TRABEATED: depends structurally on the use of the post and lintel; cf. Arcuated.

TRACERY: intersecting ribwork in the upper part of a window, or used decoratively in blank arches, on vaults, etc. (1) *Plate tracery: see* Fig. 30(*a*). Early form of tracery where decoratively shaped openings are cut through the solid stone infilling in a window head. (2) *Bar tracery:* a form introduced into England *c.* 1250. Intersecting ribwork made up of slender shafts, continuing the lines of the mullions of windows up to a decorative mesh in the head of the window. The types of bar tracery are: *Geometrical tracery: see* Fig. 30(*b*). Tracery characteristic of *c.* 1250–1310 consisting chiefly of circles or foiled circles. *Y-tracery: see* Fig. 30(*c*). Tracery consisting of a mullion which branches into two forming a Y shape; typical of *c.* 1300. *Intersecting tracery: see* Fig. 30(*d*). Tracery in which each mullion of a window

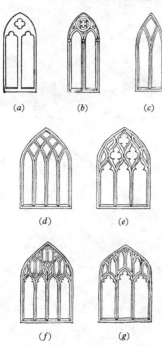

(a) (b) (c)

(d) (e)

(f) (g)

Fig. 30. Tracery

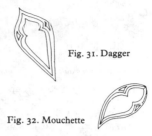

the dagger form, especially popular in the early C 14; *see* Fig. 32.

Fig. 31. Dagger

Fig. 32. Mouchette

TRANSEPT (*lit.* cross-enclosure): transverse portion of a cross-shaped church.

TRANSITIONAL: transitional phase between two styles, used most often for the phase between Romanesque and Early English (*c.* 1175–*c.* 1200).

TRANSOM: horizontal member between the lights in a window opening.

TREAD: horizontal part of the step of a staircase. The *tread end* may be carved.

TREFOIL: *see* Foil.

TRIBUNE: *see* Gallery (1).

TRIFORIUM (*lit.* three openings): middle storey of a church treated as an arcaded wall passage or blind arcade, its height corresponding to that of the aisle roof.

TRIGLYPHS (*lit.* three-grooved tablets): stylized beam-ends in the Doric frieze, with metopes between; *see* Orders (Fig. 18).

TRIUMPHAL ARCH: type of Imperial Roman monument whose elevation supplied a motif for many later classical compositions (*see* Fig. 33).

branches out into two curved bars in such a way that every one of them is drawn with the same radius from a different centre. The result is that every light of the window is a lancet and every two, three, four etc., lights together form a pointed arch. This also is typical of *c.* 1300. *Reticulated tracery: see* Fig. 30(*e*). Tracery typical of the early C 14 consisting entirely of circles drawn at top and bottom into ogee shapes so that a net-like appearance results. *Curvilinear* or *flowing tracery:* complex forms of flowing lines, ogees and geometrical forms woven together; typical of the Dec of the first half of the C 14. *Panel tracery: see* Fig. 30(*f*) and (*g*). Perp tracery, which is formed of upright straight-sided panels above lights of a window. *Dagger:* Dec tracery motif; *see* Fig. 31. *Kentish* or *split cusp:* cusp split into a fork. *Mouchette:* curved version of

Fig. 33. Triumphal arch

Cross- or groin-vault

Tunnel- or barrel-vault

Pointed barrel-vault

TROPHY: sculptured group of arms or armour as a memorial of victory.

TRUMEAU: central stone mullion supporting the tympanum of a wide doorway. *Trumeau figure:* carved figure attached to a trumeau (cf. Column figure).

TRUSS: braced framework, spanning between supports. *See also* Roofs.

TUDOR FLOWER: late Gothic ornament of a flower with square flat petals or foliage.

TUMBLING or TUMBLING-IN: term used to describe courses of brickwork laid at right angles to the slope of a gable and forming triangles by tapering into horizontal courses.

TUMULUS (*lit.* mound): *see* Barrow.

TURRET: small tower, usually attached to a building.

TUSCAN: *see* Orders (Fig. 18).

TWO-DECKER PULPIT: *see* Pulpit.

TYMPANUM (*lit.* drum): as of a drum-skin, the surface between a lintel and the arch above it or within a pediment.

UNDERCROFT: vaulted room, sometimes underground, below the main upper room.

UNIVALLATE: (of a hillfort) defended by a single bank and ditch.

UPPER PALAEOLITHIC: *see* Palaeolithic.

VAULT: ceiling of stone formed like arches (sometimes imitated in timber or plaster); *see* Fig. 34. *Tunnel-* or *barrel-vault:* the simplest kind of vault, in effect a continuous semicircular arch.

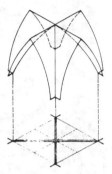

Quadripartite rib vault

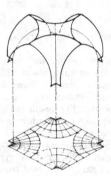

Fan vault

Fig. 34. Vaults

Groin-vaults (which are usually called *cross-vaults* in classical architecture) have four curving triangular surfaces produced by the intersection of two tunnel-vaults at right angles. The curved lines at the intersections are called groins. In *quadripartite rib vaults* the four sections are divided by their arches or ribs springing from the corners of the bay. *Sexpartite rib vaults,* most often used over paired bays, have an extra pair of ribs

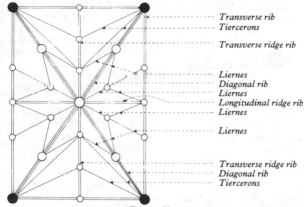

Transverse rib
Tiercerons

Transverse ridge rib

Liernes
Diagonal rib
Liernes
Longitudinal ridge rib
Liernes

Liernes

Transverse ridge rib
Diagonal rib
Tiercerons

Fig. 35. Vaulting ribs

which spring from between the bays and meet the other four ribs at the crown of the vault. The main types of rib are shown in Fig. 35: *transverse ribs*, *wall ribs*, *diagonal ribs*, and *ridge ribs*. *Tiercerons* are extra, decorative ribs springing from the corners of a bay. *Liernes* are decorative ribs in the crown of a vault which are not linked to any of the springing points. In a *stellar vault* the liernes are arranged in a star formation as in Fig. 35. *Fan-vaults* are peculiar to English Perpendicular architecture in consisting not of ribs and infilling but of halved concave cones with decorative blind tracery carved on their surfaces.

VAULTING SHAFT: shaft leading up to the springer of a vault.

VENETIAN WINDOW: a form derived from an invention by Ser-

Fig. 36. Venetian window

lio, also called a Serlian or Palladian window. The same motif is used for other openings (*see* Fig. 36).

VERANDA(H): shelter or gallery against a building, its roof supported by thin vertical members.

VERMICULATION: *see* Rustication.

VERNACULAR ARCHITECTURE: design by one without any training in design, guided by a series of conventions built up in a locality (Brunskill).

VESICA: oval with pointed head and foot, usually of a window or tracery.

VESTIBULE: anteroom or entrance hall.

VICE: *see* Stairs.

VILLA: (1) Roman country-house-cum-farm; (2) the type built by Palladio in the Veneto, with a portico and wings; its popularity in C 18 Britain led to (3), in Gwilt's definition (1842), 'a country house for the residence of opulent persons'; whence it came to mean (4) a slightly pretentious suburban house.

VITRIFIED: bricks or tiles fired to produce a darkened glassy surface.

VITRUVIAN OPENING: door or window which diminishes towards the top, as advocated by Vitruvius, book IV, chapter VI.

VITRUVIAN SCROLL: classical running ornament of curly waves (*see* Fig. 37). Also called Running dog.

VOLUTES: spiral scrolls on the front and back of a Greek Ionic capital, also on the sides of a Roman one. *Angle volute:* pair of volutes turned outwards to meet at the corner of a capital. Volutes were also used individually as decoration in C 17 and C 18 architecture.

VOUSSOIRS: wedge-shaped stones forming an arch.

WAGON ROOF: roof in which closely set rafters with arched braces give the appearance of the inside of a canvas tilt over a wagon. Wagon roofs can be panelled, boarded or plastered (ceiled) or left uncovered. Also called *cradle roof*.

WAINSCOT: *see* Panelling.

WALL MONUMENT: substantial monument attached to the wall and often standing on the floor. *Wall tablets* are smaller in scale with the inscription as the major element.

WALL-PLATE: *see* Roofs (3) and Figs. 23–6.

WARMING ROOM: *see* Calefactory.

WATERHOLDING BASE: type of early Gothic base in which the upper and lower mouldings are separated by a hollow so deep as to be capable of retaining water.

WATERLEAF CAPITAL: *see* Fig. 8.

WEALDEN HOUSE: medieval timber-framed house of distinctive form. It has a central open hall flanked by bays of two storeys. The end bays are jettied to the front, but a single roof covers the whole building, thus producing an exceptionally wide overhang to the eaves in front of the hall.

WEATHERBOARDING: overlapping horizontal boards, covering a timber-framed wall, most common after the mid C 18.

WEATHERING: inclined, projecting surface to keep water away from wall and joints below. Also called *set-off*.

WEEPERS: small figures placed in niches along the sides of some medieval tombs. Also called *mourners*.

WHEEL WINDOW: circular window with radiating shafts like the spokes of a wheel. *See also* Rose window.

WROUGHT IRON: *see* Cast iron.

Fig. 37. Vitruvian scroll

LANGUAGE GLOSSARY

Adapted, with omissions and a few augmentations, with the permission of the Director General of the Ordnance Survey, from the OS publication *Place Names on Maps of Scotland and Wales*. Crown copyright reserved.

a = adjective
ad = adverb
f = feminine
n = noun masculine

nf = noun feminine
np = noun plural
pl = plural
pr = preposition

abad, *n* abbot
abaty, *n* abbey
aber, *n & nf* estuary, confluence, stream
adeiladu, *verb* to build
aderyn, *pl* adar, *n* bird
ael, *nf* brow, edge
aelwyd, *nf* hearth
aethnen, *nf* aspen, poplar
afallen, *nf* apple-tree
afon, *nf* river
ailadeiladu, *verb* to rebuild
allt, *pl* elltydd, alltau, *nf* hillside, cliff, wood
Annibynnol, *a* Independent
ar, *pr* on, upon, over
ardd, *n* hill, height
argoed, *nf* wood, grove

bach, *a* small, little, lesser
bach, *pl* bachau, *nf* nook, corner
bala, *n* outlet of a lake
banc, *pl* bencydd, *n* bank, slope
bangor, *nf* monastery originally constructed of wattle rods
banhadlog, *nf* broom patch
banw, *n* young pig
bar, *n* top, summit
bechan, *a see* bychan
bedd, *pl* beddau, *n* grave
Bedyddwyr, *a* Baptist
beidr, *nf* lane, path
beili, *pl* beiliau, *n* bailey, court before a house bailiff
bellaf, *a* far
bendigaid, *a* blessed
betws, *n* oratory, chapel

beudy, *n* cow-house
blaen, *pl* blaenau, *n* end, edge; source of river or stream; highland
bod, *n & nf* abode, dwelling
bôn, *n* stock, stump
bont, *nf see* pont
braich, *n & nf* ridge, arm
brân, *pl* brain, *nf* crow
bre, *nf* hill
brith, *f* braith, *a* speckled; coarse
bro, *nf* region; vale, lowland
bron, *pl* bronnydd, *nf* hillbreast (breast)
bryn, *pl* bryniau, *n* hill
bugail, *pl* bugelydd, bugeiliaid, *n* shepherd
bwla, *n* bull
bwlch, *pl* bylchau, *n* gap, pass
bwth, bwthyn, *n* cottage, booth
bychan, *f* bechan, *pl* bychain, *a* little, tiny

caban, *n* cottage, cabin
cader, cadair, *nf* seat, stronghold
cadlas, *nf* close, court of a house
cae, *pl* caeau, *n* field, enclosure
caer, *pl* caerau, *nf* stronghold, fort
cafn, *n* ferry-boat, trough
canol, *n* middle
cantref, *n* hundred (territorial division)
capel, *n* meeting house, chapel

carn, *pl* carnau, *nf* heap of
    stones, tumulus

carnedd, *pl* carneddau, carneddi,
    nf heap of stones, tumulus

carreg, *pl* cerrig, *nf* stone, rock

carrog, *nf* brook

carw, *n* stag

cas (in Casnewydd etc.),
    n castle

castell, *pl* cestyll, *n* castle; small
    stronghold; fortified residence;
    imposing natural position

cath, *nf* cat. (In some names it
    may be the Irish word cath
    meaning 'battle'.)

cau, *a* hollow; enclosed

cawr, *pl* ceiri, cewri, *n* giant

cefn, *pl* cefnydd, *n* ridge

cegin, *nf* kitchen

ceiliog, *n* cock

ceiri, *np* *see* cawr

celli, *nf* grove

celynen, *pl* celyn, *nf* holly tree

celynog, clynnog, *nf* holly
    grove

cemais, *n from np* shallow bend
    in river, or coastline

cennin, *np* leeks

cerrig, *np* *see* carreg

cesail, *nf* hollow (arm-pit)

ceunant, *n* ravine, gorge

cewri, *np* *see* cawr

chwilog, *nf* land infested with
    beetles

cil, *pl* ciliau, *n* retreat, recess,
    corner

cilfach, *nf* nook

clas, *n* quasi-monastic system of
    the Celtic Church, existing in
    Wales, Cornwall and Ireland
    from the Dark Ages to *c.* 1200.
    Clasau comprised a body of
    secular canons

clawdd, *pl* cloddiau, *n* ditch
    hedge

cloch, *nf* bell

clochydd, *n* sexton, parish clerk

cloddiau, *np* *see* clawdd

clog, *nf* crag, precipice

clogwyn, *n* precipice, steep rock
    hanging on one side

clwyd, *pl* clwydydd,
    nf hurdle, gate

clynnog, *nf* *see* celynog

coch, *a* red

coeden, *pl* coed, *nf* tree

collen, *pl* cyll, coll, *nf* hazel

colwyn, *n* whelp

comin, *pl* comins,
    n common

congl, *nf* corner

cornel, *nf* corner

cors, *pl* corsydd, *nf* bog

craf, *n* garlic

craig, *pl* creigiau, *nf* rock

crib, *n* crest, ridge, summit

crochan, *n* cauldron

croes, *nf* cross

croesffordd, croesheol, croeslon,
    nf cross-roads

crofft, *pl* crofftau, *nf* croft

croglofft, *nf* garret, low cottage
    with loft under the roof

crug, *pl* crugiau, *n* heap, tump

cwm, *pl* cymau, cymoedd,
    n valley, dale

cwmwd, *n* commote
    (territorial division)

cwrt, *n* court, yard

cyffin, *n* boundary, frontier

cyll, *np* *see* collen

cymer, *pl* cymerau,
    n confluence

Cynulleidfaol,
    a Congregational

cywarch, *n* hemp

dan, *pr* under, below

derwen, *pl* derw, *nf* oak

diffwys, *n* precipice, abyss

dinas, *n & nf* hill-fortress (city)

diserth, *n* hermitage

disgwylfa, *nf* place of
    observation, look-out point

dôl, *pl* dolau, dolydd,
    nf meadow

draw, *ad* yonder

du, *a* black, dark

dwfr, dŵr, *n* water

dyffryn, *n* valley

eglwys, *nf* church

(ei)singrug, *n* heap of bran or
    corn husks

eisteddfa, *nf* seat, resting place

eithinog, *nf* furze patch

elltyd, *np* *see* allt

ellyll, *n* elf, goblin

eos, *nf* nightingale

erw, *pl* erwau, *nf* acre

esgair, *nf* long ridge (leg)

esgob, *n* bishop

ewig, *nf* hind

-fa, *nf* *see* ma-

fach, *a* *see* bach

faenor, *nf* Vaynor. cf. maenor

fawr, *a* *see* mawr

felin, *nf* *see* melin

ffald, *pl* ffaldau, *nf* sheep-fold, pound, pen, run

ffawydden, *pl* ffawydd, *nf* beech tree

fferm, *nf* farm

ffin, *nf* boundary

ffordd, *nf* way, road

fforest, *nf* forest, park

ffridd, ffrith, *pl* ffriddoedd, *nf* wood; mountain enclosure, sheep walk

ffrwd, *nf* stream, torrent

ffynnon, *pl* ffynhonnau, *nf* spring, well

fron, *nf* *see* bron

fry, *ad* above

gaer, *nf* *see* caer

ganol, *n* *see* canol

gardd, *pl* gerddi, garddau, *nf* garden; enclosure or fold into which calves were turned for first time

garreg, *nf* *see* carreg

garth, *n* promontory, hill enclosure

garw, *a* coarse, rough

gefail, *nf* smithy

(g)eirw, *np* rush of waters

gelli, *nf* *see* celli

glan, *nf* river-bank, hillock

glas, *a* green

glas, glais (as in dulas, dulais), *n* & *nf* brook

glo, *n* charcoal, coal

glyn, *n* deep valley, glen

gof, *n* smith

gogof, *pl* gogofau, *nf* cave

gorffwysfa, *nf* resting place

gris, *pl* grisiau, *n* step

grug, *n* heath, heather

gwaelod, *n* foot of hill (bottom)

gwastad, *n* plain

gwaun, *pl* gweunydd, *nf* moor, mountain meadow, moor-land field

gwely, *n* bed, resting-place, family land

gwen, *a* *see* gwyn

gwerdd, *a* *see* gwyrdd

gwernen, *pl* gwern, *nf* alder tree

gwersyll, *n* encampment

gwrych, *n* hedge, quickset hedge

gwryd, *n* fathom

gwyddel, *pl* gwyddyl, gwyddelod, *n* Irishman

gwyddrug, *nf* mound, wooded knoll

gwyn, *f* gwen, *a* white

gwynt, *n* wind

gwyrdd, *f* gwerdd, *a* green

hafn, *nf* gorge, ravine

hafod, *nf* shieling, upland summer dwelling

hafoty, *n* summer dwelling

helygen, *pl* helyg, *nf* willow

hen, *a* old

hendref, *nf* winter dwelling, old home, permanent abode

heol, hewl, *nf* street, road

hir, *a* long

is, *pr* below, under

isaf, *a* lower (lowest)

isel, *a* low

iwrch, *pl* iyrchod, *n* roebuck

lawnd, lawnt, *nf* open space in woodland, glade

llaethdy, *n* milkhouse, dairy

llan, *nf* church, monastery; enclosure

Llanbedr St Peter's church

Llanddewi St David's church

Llanfair St Mary's church

Llanfihangel St Michael's church

llannerch, *nf* clearing, glade

lle, *n* place, position

llech, *pl* llechau, *nf* slab, stone, rock

llechwedd, *nf* hillside

llethr, *nf* slope

llety, *n* small abode, quarters

llidiard, llidiart, *pl* llidiardau, llidiartau, *n* gate

llom, *a* *see* llwm

lluest, *n* shieling, cottage, hut

llumon, *n* stack (chimney)

llwch, *n* dust

llwch, *pl* llychau, *n* lake

llwm, *f* llom, *a* bare, exposed

llwyd, *a* grey, brown

llwyn, *pl* llwyni, llwynau, *n* grove, bush

llyn, *n* & *nf* lake

llys, *n* & *nf* court, hall

lôn, *nf* lane, road

ma-, -fa, *nf* plain, place

maen, *pl* meini, main, *n* stone

maenol, maenor, *nf* stone-built residence of chieftain of district, rich low-lying land surrounding same, vale

maerdref, *nf* hamlet attached to chieftain's court, lord's demesne (maer, steward + tref, hamlet)

maerdy, *n* steward's house, dairy

maes, *pl* meysydd, *n* open field, plain

march, *pl* meirch, *n* horse, stallion

marchog, *n* knight, horseman

marian, *n* holm, gravel, gravelly ground, rock debris

mawnog, *nf* peat-bog

mawr, *a* great, big

meillionen, *pl* meillion, *nf* clover

meini, *np* see maen

meirch, *np* see march

melin, *nf* mill

melyn, *f* melen, *a* yellow

menych, *np* see mynach

merthyr, *n* burial place, church

Methodistaidd, *a* Methodist

meysydd, *np* see maes

mochyn, *pl* moch, *n* pig

moel, *nf* bare hill

moel, *a* bare, bald

môr, *n* sea

morfa, *n* marsh, fen

mur, *pl* muriau, *n* wall

mwyalch, mwyalchen, *nf* blackbird

mynach, *pl* mynych, menych, myneich, *n* monk

mynachdy, *n* monastic grange

mynwent, *nf* churchyard

mynydd, *n* mountain, moorland

nant, *pl* nentydd, naint, nannau, *nf* brook

nant, *pl* nentydd, naint, nannau, *n* dingle, glen, ravine

neuadd, *nf* hall

newydd, *a* new

noddfa, *nf* hospice

nyth, *n & nf* nest, inaccessible position

oen, *pl* ŵyn, *n* lamb

offeiriad, *n* priest

onnen, *pl* onn, ynn, *nf* ash-tree

pandy, *n* fulling-mill

pant, *n* hollow, valley

parc, *pl* parciau, parcau, *n* park, field, enclosure

pen, *pl* pennau, *n* head, top; end, edge

penrhyn, *n* promontory

pensaer, *n* architect

pentref, *n* homestead, appendix to the real 'tref', village

person, *n* parson

pistyll, *n* spout, waterfall

plas, *n* gentleman's seat, hall, mansion

plwyf, *n* parish

poeth, *a* burnt (hot)

pont, *nf* bridge

porth, *n* gate, gateway

porth, *nf* ferry, harbour

pwll, *pl* pyllau, *n* pit, pool

rhaeadr, *nf* waterfall

rhandir, *n* allotment, fixed measure of land

rhiw, *nf & n* hill, slope

rhos, *pl* rhosydd, *nf* moor, promontory

rhyd, *nf & n* ford

saeth, *pl* saethau, *nf* arrow

sant, san, *pl* saint, *n* saint, monk

sarn, *pl* sarnau, *nf* causeway

sêt fawr, *nf* see Architectural Glossary

simnai, simdde, *nf* chimney

siop, *nf* shop

sticil, sticill, *nf* stile

swydd, *nf* seat, lordship, office

sych, *a* dry

tafarn, *pl* tafarnau, *n & nf* tavern

tai, *np* see tŷ

tâl, *n* end (forehead)

talwrn, *pl* talyrni, tylyrni, *n* bare exposed hill-side, open space, threshing floor, cockpit

tan, dan, *nf* under, beneath

teg, *a* fair

tir, *n* land, territory

tom, tomen, *nf* mound

ton, *pl* tonnau, *nf* wave

ton, tonnen, *pl* tonnau, *n & nf* grassland, lea

torglwyd, *nf* door-hurdle, gate

towyn, *n* see tywyn

traean, traen, *n* third part

traeth, *n* strand, shore

trallwng, trallwm, *n* wet bottom land

traws, *a & n* cross, transverse

tref, *nf* homestead, hamlet, town

tros, *pr* over

trwyn, *n* point, cape (nose)

twr, *n* tower

twyn, *pl* twyni, *n* hillock, knoll

tŷ, *pl* tai, *n* house

tyddyn, ty'n, *n* small farm, holding

tylyrni, *np* *see* talwrn

tywyn, towyn, *n* sea-shore, strand

uchaf, *a* higher, highest

uchel, *a* high

uwch, *pr* above, over

wŷn, *np* *see* oen

y, yr, 'r (definite article) the

yn, *pr* in

ynn, *np* *see* onnen

ynys, *pl* ynysoedd, *nf* island; holm, river-meadow

ysbyty, *n* hospital, hospice

ysgol, *pl* ysgolion, *nf* school

ysgubor, *pl* ysguboriau, *nf* barn

ystafell, *nf* chamber, hiding-place

ystrad, *n* valley, holm, river-meadow

ystum, *nf & n* bend shape

INDEX OF PLATES

INDEX OF ARTISTS

INDEX OF PLACES

Besides distinguishing Denbighshire (D) and Flintshire (F) locations, indication is given of places which were in Caernarfonshire before 1974, and of those transferred to Gwynedd in that year.

ADDENDA

p. 252 [Marchwiel]. The condition of Pickhill Hall deteriorated further when a fire occurred in the autumn of 1985. Early in December, however, proposals for restoration were under consideration.

p. 308 [Wrexham]. In MAESYDRE ROAD, off Penymaes Avenue, No. 4 (LANGLANDS) was designed for himself by *J. H. Swainson* (information from Mr Ian Allan), who began practice in Wrexham in 1889.

p. 316 [Wynnstay]. A section is devoted to the Wynnstay lodges in *Trumpet at a Distant Gate* by Tim Mowl and Brian Earnshaw (1985), and the following addenda are derived from this source.

p. 316 [Wynnstay]. RHOS Y MADOC LODGE, opposite the gatepiers, with canted apsidal front, may be by *James Wyatt*.

p. 317 [Wynnstay]. The Waterloo Tower is possibly by *Benjamin Gummow*. Though its gateway is blocked, it was built as a lodge, giving access to a drive cut in the rock.

p. 317 [Wynnstay]. Park Eyton Lodge is also known as Kennels Lodge and is attributable to *James Wyatt*.

p. 413 [Overton]. The major Italianate remodelling was *c.* 1850–2. Some minor work was done by *W. M. Fenton*, 1855. An unexecuted remodelling scheme was drawn up by *Douglas*, 1880–1, less dull than that carried out by Waterhouse.

p. 413 [Overton]. Documentary evidence confirms that these LODGES are indeed by *Douglas*, 1874–5.

p. 420 [Queensferry]. (ST ETHELWOLD'S SCHOOL, Shotton. By *Douglas* (information from Mr N. H. Davies). Built 1875 and later enlarged, possibly *c.* 1900. In photographs it looks very good. Now disused.)